THE BEST OF
JENNINGS

This edition first published in 2009 by
Prion
An imprint of the Carlton Publishing Group
20 Mortimer Street
London W1T 3JW

1 3 5 7 9 10 8 6 4 2

Jennings Goes to School, first published 1950
Jennings Follows a Clue, first published 1951
Jennings' Little Hut, first published 1951
Jennings and Darbishire, first published 1952

A CIP catalogue record for this book is available from the British Library.

ISBN 978 1 85375 724 2

Cover illustration by Ruth Palmer
Inside illustrations by John Ridgeway

Printed in Thailand

THE BEST OF
JENNINGS

Jennings Goes to School

Jennings Follows a Clue

Jennings' Little Hut

Jennings and Darbishire

ANTHONY BUCKERIDGE

PRION

Contents

INTRODUCTION

Physical age has never seemed of overriding importance in our family; being alive *now* was the mantra. Therefore, when Anthony died, although on one level I was very aware that he was 92, frail in body but still the same humorously ironic person in mind, it nevertheless came as a jolt that the year 2012 would mark his centenary. I was delighted and proud when Prion approached me with their plan to issue a *Best of Jennings* edition to mark the event and the first four books are included in this volume.

Anthony's writing was, of course, drawn from his life's experiences but it was undoubtedly *Children's Hour* that launched the Jennings stories so successfully. After the war he was teaching at St Lawrence College in Ramsgate and in his spare time he was both acting with the Palace Theatre, a local Rep company, and submitting one-off plays to the BBC for such programmes as the Wednesday and Saturday Matinees. Acting had always been part of his life style.

In 1948 he sent the first Jennings play to the BBC Drama Department but the script was sent to the wonderful David Davis – he of the most mellifluous voice! – and the play became the forerunner of a series that continued until 1964 when Children's Hour ceased to be. The instant commissioning of this series by a discerning director, caused Anthony to reflect in later years, and after various good-natured battles with commissioning editors, that he was sure that Shakespeare would never have got the outline of say, *The Comedy of Errors*, past the pilot stage of acceptance in today's world!

With the Jennings at School series firmly established on radio, Anthony decided to re-tell the stories in narrative form. The first title, *Jennings at School*, was published in 1950 and the series continued until 1994 when the 25th and last title was published.

I think that I can best summarise Anthony's writing in his own words:

Normally, my plan was to take a genuine situation that the readers could identify with, something quite ordinary and unremarkable that was happening as part of the normal routine of school. Having done that, I would allow the situation to develop one step further than it would have been allowed to develop in real life. Boys are imaginative and are continually planning wonderful schemes and adventures, which sound brilliant in theory but come to nothing when they are nipped in the bud by a master who sees that things threaten to get out of hand. But if the zeal of the masters can be logically delayed or diverted in some way for just long enough to enable the wonderful scheme to proceed a little further than it would have been allowed to go in real life, you are creating a situation which can lead to an entertaining climax.

Much of the comedy in Jennings goes to School and its successors depends upon the contrasting way in which the situation can be interpreted by the adult as opposed to the youthful point of view. Boys will say things and do things which to them are perfectly logical but appear incomprehensible to an adult who lacks the facility of looking into the developing mind and interpreting what is going on there. There is enough comic material to be found in this aspect of the youthful/adult character to fill more books than I shall ever write. *

The geography lesson in *Just Like Jennings* epitomises this: Mr Wilkins has prepared what he hopes to be an engrossing lesson on the ascent of Everest, only to be contradicted when he quotes the height of the mountain to be twenty nine thousand feet above sea level. That, according to Jennings's diary is wrong as his diary says that the height is twenty nine thousand and *two* feet. The ensuing fracas can well be imagined; Jennings tries to explain that the diary doesn't actually *say* that Mr Wilkins is wrong, the master is exasperated at the arguments that break out in class; the boys become fed up with Jennings and Jennings himself feels injured because it is only his interest that caused the interruption! Thus the harmony of the class is shattered. And Mr Wilkins himself is troubled as he feels that he has perhaps mishandled the situation.

The incident, especially the dialogue, is very funny; all teachers and classes could not fail to appreciate such misunderstandings and the result is a tribute, I feel, to the writing as the incident is explored from every angle.

Anthony quickly realised that current slang is ephemeral and concentrated on inventing his own and such epithets as *cloth-eared clodpoll, shrimp-witted*

8

besooka and *fossillised fishhooks*, seem to have survived among the people who read the books at the time.

Because Anthony was such a humorist, the early popularity of his work tended to focus on the farcical aspect of his plots, but this view often excluded appreciation of the quality of his literary style. He was a most reflective man and as his style developed his writing was pared down to essentials so that every word had to earn its keep; nothing superfluous was allowed to mask what he intended to say and what he had to say always reflected its innate morality.

He was fortunate, I think, that the later years led to a re-assessment of his literary style that brought recognition in the following ways.

First, he was represented in the exhibition at the National Portrait Gallery together with the accompanying book** which itemised the hundred writers for children who had made a seminal contribution to the oeuvre in the twentieth century.

Secondly, the Jennings books were then re-published in the nineties which resulted in the renewal of critical attention. Thirdly, in 2001, he was asked to speak at the Edinburgh Festival and this was a great success.

Incidentally, this event illustrated many things. He had a captive audience as his readers spread over three generations. They were each represented starting with grandparents from the era of Children's Hour in the late forties, parents and their children. Of course, it also naturally illustrated the fact that the books have survived only where readers are introduced to them - either by teachers or adults who themselves have remained readers. As parents ourselves it was heart warming to see that families who truly communicate, especially where there is a shared interest in literature, represent family life at its most nurturing - an optimistic view of the future.

And then in 2003 he was awarded the OBE for services to literature; it seemed to me to be a sort of crown to his life's work.

* *While I Remember*, Anthony Buckeridge, 1999
** *Beatrix Potter to Harry Potter*, Julia Eccleshare, 2002

JENNINGS GOES TO SCHOOL

INTRODUCTION

It would be a waste of time to describe Linbury Court Preparatory School in great detail,because, if you are going to follow Jennings through his school career, you will be certain to alter the shape of the building so that it becomes, in imagination, your own school. Jennings' classroom will be your classroom; his desk, your desk; his text books—well, those who want to know where Jennings was at school, have only to glance at his text books to find out. If you will open his *A Shorter Latin Primer*, carefully altered to read *A Shorter Way of Eating Prime Beef*, you will find the inscription:

> "If this book should dare to roam,
> Box its ears and send it home,
> to J. C. T. Jennings,
> Linbury Court School,
> Dunhambury,
> Sussex,
> England,
> Europe,
> Eastern Hemisphere,
> Earth,
> near Moon,
> Solar System,
> Space,
> near More Space."

This should satisfy the most inquisitive. But our search for geographical detail has led us too far ahead. Jennings has not yet arrived at Linbury; the Latin Primer is still unsullied, and J. C. T. Jennings is only a name on Mr. Carter's list of new boys.

So let's start at the beginning.

CHAPTER 1

JENNINGS LEARNS THE ROPES

IT was the first afternoon of the Christmas term and Mr. Carter was enjoying the peace and stillness, so soon to be shattered by the arrival of sixty-seven boys on the school train. A few had already arrived by car, and were importantly memorising the contents of the notice board in order to be first with the news when the main body arrived. To know who was who in such matters as prefects, dormitory captains and school librarians was important in itself, but to be able to broadcast this information to the masses before anyone else could get a word in edgeways, was more important still.

Mr. Carter was greeted enthusiastically by the group at the notice board.

"Oh, sir, how are you, sir? Have you had a decent holiday, sir?" came from ten voices simultaneously.

"We had a supersonic time, sir," said an eleventh voice. "We went to Scotland, sir, and we had gluey porridge every day and we got stuck in a bog, sir, and my father said that was where they got the porridge from, but it was only a joke really, sir."

The twelfth voice added its quota.

"Sir, we went to France, sir, and we had a spivish ozard crossing, but I wasn't sea-sick, honestly, sir. It's a jolly wizard job I'm not a chap I know at home's uncle, because he's always ill on boats, isn't it, sir?"

"Isn't it what?" said Mr. Carter.

"Isn't it a good job I'm not him, sir."

"Who?" asked Mr. Carter.

"The chap I know at home's uncle, sir."

"Yes, very probably," replied Mr. Carter.

Twelve times Mr. Carter shook hands; twelve times he was pleased to say that his health was excellent, and twelve times he informed the earnest inquirer that he had spent a pleasant holiday. He moved on, his right hand somewhat stickier than before.

In the dining hall, where he stopped to pin up the plan of the boys' places at table, the Headmaster was showing a clergyman round the school. The latter, whose look of anxious inquiry clearly labelled him "New Parent," was accompanied by a small-scale model of himself, labelled with equal clarity, "New Boy."

The likeness between father and son was remarkable; both had fair, curly hair, Father's being thinner on top, but tidier; both had pale-blue eyes and spectacles and, when they spoke, both the large and the small edition expressed themselves in a welter of glistening consonants, and managed to convey the impression that they were speaking in capital letters.

"Now one attractive feature of this dining-hall, Mr. Darbishire," the Headmaster was saying, "is that the air is kept at an even temperature by heated panels let into the walls."

"Really! Most interesting, most interesting!" said Mr. Darbishire, in block capitals.

"And these windows are all fitted with vita glass, which means that they allow the ultra-violet rays to pass through."

The Reverend Percival Darbishire peered closely at the vita glass windows, screwing up his eyes as though uncertain of the effect that the ultra-violet rays might be having upon his eyesight. It looked like ordinary glass to him, but one could never tell, and he was determined to be impressed by all he saw.

"Most remarkable, most remarkable!" he said.

"You will observe our system of overhead ventilation," the Headmaster went on, "which allows every boy a minimum of three thousand, five hundred cubic yards of air."

Mr. Darbishire, still blinded by science, was unable to see anything overhead, except the electric light fittings, but he obediently looked upwards, wondering vaguely whether a tea-urn at the far end of the hall might have something to do with the ventilation.

"Most interesting! Very remarkable and—ah—interesting," he said, now convinced that the tea-urn must have something to do with it.

The Headmaster was wondering whether he really did mean three thousand, five hundred cubic yards of air. Perhaps it was three hundred and fifty thousand cubic feet. He would have to work it out. There were twenty-seven cubic feet in a cubic yard, so that meant ... He gave it up; after all, you couldn't expect a classical scholar to be a genius at mathematics as well.

"Good gracious, it's four o'clock!" he said, changing the subject. "Now you must come along to my study for a cup of tea."

Mr. Carter returned to his room just as the patter of little feet announced that the main body had arrived by the school train. The little feet pattered up the stairs like a cavalry regiment thundering across the plain, and Mr. Carter was once more the centre of vociferous greeting.

"Have you had a wizard holiday, sir?"

"Yes, thank you, Temple."

"So did we, sir," said Temple. "We went to Guernsey by air; it was super-delectable. Actually it was a rotten swizzle, sir, because we flew through low cloud and we couldn't see a thing, but if it hadn't been for that, and if we'd flown about a hundred miles farther east, I could have wiped this school right off the map, sir, honestly."

"Really!" marvelled Mr. Carter.

"If I'd had a machine gun that is," Temple explained.

"We seem to have had a narrow escape."

Mr. Carter turned to the next boy.

"Well, Atkinson, what have you been doing with yourself?"

"I went to Lords, sir, to see Middlesex play Lancashire, and I took my autograph book to get all their signatures, sir."

"And did you?" inquired Mr. Carter.

"I got one, sir," said Atkinson proudly.

"And whose was that?"

"I'm not sure, sir, 'cos the chap's writing's a bit wobbly, and he just did a couple of squiggles and a flourish, and I didn't like to ask him what his name was," Atkinson confessed. "But if you look at it one way up it looks like B. K. Inman, and upside down it might be E. J. O'Reilly."

"And which do you think it really is?"

"Well, it's most probably Smith, sir, 'cos there wasn't an Inman or an O'Reilly in either of the teams, but there was a Smith on both sides," he explained, "so that makes it a two to one chance on its being one of them rather than anybody else, sir. But it's a pity his signature's so illiterate."

"Illegible," corrected Mr. Carter.

"Oh, he must have been that, sir, 'cos even if he's not eligible for Middlesex, he would be for Lancashire, wouldn't he, sir, or he wouldn't be playing?"

Mr. Carter was at a loss for the right answer to this one, so he proceeded to shake hands all round, and furtively wiped the damp stickiness from his palm on his handkerchief. "Line up," he said, "I want your identity cards, health certificates, money for the bank and trunk keys."

Order was restored and Mr. Carter started to check each boy's belongings. There were always snags in this. Temple had handed his identity card, as well as his ticket, to the collector at Victoria, and a hole had been punched in it before the error was discovered. Atkinson's father had departed to the city with his son's trunk key in his pocket; Venables' mother had lost his health certificate, but she sent a message to say that "it was all right, wasn't it?"—obviously trusting in Mr. Carter's shrewd glance to detect any germs that might be lurking about her offspring.

"Right," said Mr. Carter, "next boy."

"Me, sir, please, sir," said a voice.

Mr. Carter's first meeting with Jennings was the routine affair of a busy master, who saw in front of him a small boy not unlike the dozens of other small boys who were lined up outside his room. His suit, socks and tie conformed exactly to the regulation pattern. His dark brown hair, which still bore the faintest trace of a parting, was no different from that of his fellows, and his face was the average sort of face worn by boys of his generation. So Mr. Carter learned little from this first meeting. Later on, he was to learn a lot.

"A new boy, eh?" said Mr. Carter. "And what's your name?"

"Jennings, sir."

"Oh, yes, here you are on the list. J. C. T. Jennings; ten years, two months. Right?"

"No, sir, not quite right, sir; ten years, two months and three days last Tuesday, sir."

"We won't worry about that," said Mr. Carter. He had placed the new boy by now. Only that morning the Headmaster had shown him a letter from a Mr. Jennings, expressing doubts lest his son, who had never been away from home before, should not settle down at boarding school. Mr. Carter gave him another look; he seemed the sort of boy who knew how to look after himself.

"We shall have to show you the ropes, shan't we?" said Mr. Carter, sorting out the small pile of documents that Jennings placed before him.

"Identity card, yes; bank money, yes. Where's your health certificate?"

"I don't think I've got one of those, sir," said Jennings, not knowing what a health certificate looked like.

"You must have," returned Mr. Carter with mock gravity. "How do we know you're not suffering from mumps, measles, chicken-pox, whooping cough, scarlet fever and bubonic plague?"

A look of alarm passed over Jennings' face. "I'm sure I'm not, sir," he said. "I haven't even got any spots, honestly, sir. Look, sir!"

"Isn't this it?" asked Mr. Carter, extracting the certificate from Jennings' pocket and studying it. "Yes, I thought so. You're quite all right."

"Not even any bucolic plague?" asked Jennings, rather disappointed now that all was well.

"Not even a mump or a measle. That was just my little joke. Now we must get someone to show you round." His eyes searched the group clustered round the door.

"Come here, Venables," he said to an untidy looking boy of twelve.

"Yes, sir," said the untidy one.

"Come and be introduced. I want you to show Jennings the ropes. On my left," he proclaimed, in the manner of the best boxing referees, "on my left, Venables, easily distinguished by his trailing bootlaces."

"Oh, sir," protested Venables.

"On my right, Jennings, who's got to be looked after. Venables—Jennings: Jennings—Venables." As though to heighten this sporting comparison, a bell rang in the distance.

"There's the tea bell," said the self-styled referee. "Take Jennings to the dining-hall and treat him as you would your brother."

"Yes, sir," replied the trailer of bootlaces.

"On second thoughts, don't," added Mr. Carter. "I've seen how you treat your brother. Look after him as you do yourself and he certainly won't starve."

"Oh, sir!" said Venables in aggrieved tones. One had to sound aggrieved at the heavy-handed pleasantries of the staff, but actually it was rather flattering to be picked out for such a distinction. He led Jennings away to wash his hands for tea.

Old Pyjams, the general factotum, was putting up clean towels in the wash-room. His name was Robinson and he was in his early twenties, but he had to be called Old Pyjams because his opposite number, Hawkins, the night watchman, was known as Old Nightie.

"You'll 'ave to do without soap," Old Pyjams told them, "I ain't got around to getting it out yet."

This was all to the good because, by trailing their fingers under the cold tap and pressing hard on the clean towels, the boys were able to make impressions which would have delighted the fingerprint department of Scotland Yard.

Another bell rang and Venables led Jennings to the dining-hall where Mr. Carter was waiting to say grace. The buzz of conversation ceased.

"*Benedictus, benedicat,*" said Mr. Carter.

There was a scraping of chairs and the buzz broke out again.

"You'd better sit here, Jennings, next to this other new chap," said Venables. "Here, you, what's your name?"

"Charles Edwin Jeremy Darbishire," said the small edition of his father, in capital letters.

"You can keep the Charles Edwin Jeremy, you won't be needing it," said Venables. "And you'd better talk to Jennings as you're both new." And with the air of one who has already been over-generous to small new fry, he turned to the sublime heights of conversation with his equals.

Jennings and Darbishire looked at each other without interest. Having been bidden to talk, neither could think of anything to say. Finally, Darbishire cleared his throat.

"Magnificent weather for September, isn't it?" he said in his best rectory drawing-room manner.

"Uh?" said Jennings, out of his depth in polite conversation. "Oh, yes. Super .... I say," he went on, "how much cash have you got in the school bank? I've got a pound."

"I did have a pound," said Darbishire, "but I spent fourpence halfpenny on the way here this afternoon, so I've got—er—nineteen and—er—I've got a pound less fourpence halfpenny. I gave it to that master who said grace just now. What's his name?"

"I think he's Mr.—er—I say Venables, what's that master's name?"

With an effort, Venables descended from the sublime to the ridiculous. "Were you talking to me?"

"Yes. That master. What did you say his name was?"

"That's Benedick," replied Venables. "We all call him that, anyway. Actually, his name's Mr. Carter."

"Why call him something else?" demanded Jennings.

"Well, you heard him say grace just now. *Benedictus* and all that. And after meals he says, '*benedicto, benedicata*.'"

Jennings waited in case more explanation was forthcoming, but it wasn't.

"Go on," he said.

"I've just told you," said Venables with the patience reserved for imbeciles. "*Benedicata*—Benedick Carter."

"Oh," said Jennings. "Is that a joke?"

"You're a bit wet, aren't you?" replied Venables.

"It's Latin, Jennings," broke in the erudite Darbishire. "My father knows a lot of Latin. He's a clergyman, and he says—"

"Yes, but what does all that benedict—whatever it is, mean?" demanded Jennings.

"Don't ask me," said Venables. "I was thirteenth in Latin last term. I'll ask Bod; he's a brain." And calling to Temple on the opposite side of the table, he asked, "I say, Bod, there's a new chap here who wants to know what the grace means in English. You were first in Latin last term; you ought to know."

Temple, alias Bod, considered. When one is first in Latin, it doesn't do to confess ignorance. "Well," he said with an authoritative air, "when they say it before meals it means something like 'come and get it,' and after meals it means 'you've had it.'" And having given the ignorant newcomers the benefit of his learning, he returned to his shepherd's pie.

"But if what Bod said is right—" Jennings began.

"You mustn't call him Bod," said Venables, shocked. "New chaps aren't allowed to call fairly senior chaps by their nicknames until their second term."

"Then his name isn't really Bod, any more than Mr. Carter's name is Benedick," persisted Jennings, who liked to get things straight.

"'Course not," said Venables. "His name's Temple, and his initials are C.A.T., so naturally we call him Dog."

"But you didn't call him Dog, you called him Bod," argued Jennings.

"Give a chap a chance to get a word in," said Venables. "I haven't finished yet. It's a bit of a sweat calling him Dog, so we call him Dogsbody for short."

"But it isn't short," protested Jennings. "Dogsbody's much longer than Dog."

"Okay, then," replied Venables logically, "it needs shortening. Bod short for Body, and Dogsbody short for Dog. Really!" And he shook his head, sadly. "You new oiks are dim at picking things up."

"It's a nickname, Jennings," said Darbishire. "My father says that the word 'nickname' is derived from the Anglo-Saxon word 'eke-name' which means 'also named,' and it's true, 'cos if you say 'an eke-name,' very quickly, it sort of turns itself into 'a nickname,' doesn't it?"

They practised turning eke-name into nickname until Jennings received a peremptory demand from Atkinson to "pass the ozard and stop hiccuping."

Jennings looked up and down the table, but could see nothing that answered to this description.

"What did you say you wanted?" he asked, helplessly.

21

"The ozard," repeated Atkinson, marvelling that new boys could be so stupid.

"I don't know what—oh, d'you mean the jam?" asked Jennings.

"Of course I do," said Atkinson, cutting his bread and butter into minute cubes. "What else could I mean?"

"Yes, I can see there's nothing else," said Jennings, "but why is it ozard?"

Atkinson, as a new boy, had asked exactly the same question less than a year before, but his manner implied that he had been born with preparatory school jargon on his lips.

"School jam's rotten muck," he explained. "It tastes like hair cream. Of course, all school food's muck, but usually it's pretty decent, so that makes it wizard muck, if you follow me."

Jennings followed him.

"Okay then," proceeded Atkinson. "You've heard of the Wizard of Oz, of course. Well, obviously, the opposite of wizard is ozard, isn't it?"

Jennings conceded the point.

"That shepherd's pie we've just had was supersonic muck so it's wizard, but this school jam's ghastly so it's ozard. Everything ghastly is ozard; being a new chap's pretty ozard for a bit, but you'll get used to it when you've been here as long as I have."

"And how long have you been here?" Jennings wanted to know.

"Me? Oh, I've been here donkeys' years. Ages and ages," said Atkinson, and his voice came from the mists of antiquity. "Well, two terms, anyway," he compromised.

After tea Venables escorted Jennings and Darbishire to a classroom, where some dozen boys were laboriously engaged in writing postcards to let their parents know of their safe arrival.

"You wait here," said Venables. "If you haven't got a postcard, Old Wilkie'll give you one." With that he disappeared, leaving Jennings and Darbishire wondering which of the occupants of the room might be Old Wilkie.

Jennings approached the largest of the boys, who had finished writing his postcard and was dabbing the wet ink with his handkerchief in lieu of blotting paper.

"I say," said Jennings. "Are you Old Wilkie?"

The handkerchief paused in mid-blot.

"Am I Old Wilkie?" he said surprised. "Am I Old Wilkie?" And he went off into peals of laughter. "I say, you blokes," he gasped to the rest of the room when his laughter had subsided slightly, "there's a character here who wants to know if I'm Old—ha-ha-ha-ha; he wants to know if I'm Old—hee-hee-hee-hee." And turning again to Jennings, he said, "No, I'm not," and resumed Operation Blotting with his handkerchief.

Neither Jennings nor Darbishire could see anything to laugh at, so they smiled politely and waited. A moment later the door handle rattled noisily, and the door hurtled open as though a small charge of dynamite had been placed behind it, and Old Wilkie burst in. Mr. Wilkins was young and vigorous, the "Old" being merely a courtesy title. He was junior to Mr. Carter and offered a complete contrast to him in every way; for Mr. Carter remained quietly calm in the midst of the most frantic hurly-burly which occurs occasionally, even in the best regulated preparatory schools. But Mr. Wilkins had none of his colleague's placidity. He hurtled and exploded his way through life like a radio-controlled projectile.

"I want everybody's postcards, immediately," he boomed in a voice like a loud-hailer. "If you haven't finished, then you ought to have done. I can't wait all night. Lots to do."

"Please, sir, Darbishire and I haven't got any postcards, sir," said Jennings.

"New boys, eh! Yes, of course you are; must be. Thought I hadn't seen your faces about the place before. Here you are," he went on; "two postcards, two pens. Go and write them."

"Who do I have to write to, sir?" asked Darbishire.

"Not 'who', 'whom'," corrected Mr. Wilkins. "To your mother and father, of course, who else?" He paused, considering whether he should have said "whom else."

Darbishire still looked puzzled.

"Well, go on," said Mr. Wilkins. "Mother and father. No point in writing to the Archbishop of Canterbury; he won't be interested. Tell them you've arrived safely."

"But they know that, sir," said Darbishire. "My father came down with me."

"Can't help that," said Mr. Wilkins. "School rules say 'write postcard home.' All right then, write postcard home. Won't do any harm, will it?"

Jennings and Darbishire sat down at a desk. Darbishire sucked his pen while Jennings discovered, to his delight, that the ink-well was three-quarters full of ink-soaked blotting paper. With infinite care, he proceeded to fish for little bits with his nib and proudly displayed the results of his toil on the top of the desk, where the ink trickled down in little streams.

Darbishire decided to assure his parents that he was concerned about the state of their health. He headed his card, "*Linbury Court Preparatory School, Dunhambury, Sussex,*" in huge, sprawling writing that covered more than half the postcard. "*My dearest Mother and Father,*" he went on in letters half an inch high and nearly twice as broad, and discovered that there was only enough space left for one more line. "*I hope you are quite—*" He stopped, having completely filled up the available space. There was just room for a full stop, so he put that in and took his effort up for Mr. Wilkins' approval.

Mr. Wilkins adjusted his eyes to the outsize script and blinked.

"I hope you are quite—?" he read out, bewildered. "I hope you are quite, what?"

"No, not quite what, sir," corrected Darbishire gently. "Quite well."

"So one might gather," expostulated Mr. Wilkins. "But you haven't said that. You can't say 'I hope you are quite, full stop.' It's nonsense!"

"I hadn't got room for any more, sir," explained Darbishire. "And it's all right, really, 'cos my father'll know by the full stop at the end that I'd finished and wasn't called away unexpectedly in the middle or anything, sir."

"But don't you see, you silly little boy, it doesn't make sense? How's your father going to know what it is "quite" that you hope he is? For all he knows, you might be going to say you hope he's quite—" Mr. Wilkins was unable to think of a suitable comparison.

"But it's bound to mean quite '*well*,' sir," reasoned Darbishire. "After all, you guessed it, and if you can, sir, I'm sure my father could, and I wouldn't be likely to mean I hope you're quite '*ill*,' would I, sir?"

Mr. Carter would probably have sighed. Mr. Wilkins made a noise like an inner tube exploding under pressure. The back of his neck turned pink and he closed his eyes and breathed deeply. After a short period of convalescence, he opened his eyes and gave Darbishire another post-card.

Jennings had finished Operation Salvage in the ink-pot and was gnawing the end of his pen. It would take a week or so to chew his way down to the nib, he decided, but already the pen showed signs of giving way as the end was beginning to spray out like a paint brush. The noise of Mr. Wilkins' mental anguish recalled him to the realms of scholarship, and he set about collecting material for his literary masterpiece.

A postcard home was something new in his experience. What should he say? His mother had told him to be sure to pay his pound into the school bank as soon as he arrived. He could say he had done that, for a start. He was richer than Darbishire because he had only got a pound less fourpence halfpenny. What else? Well, there was that frightfully funny joke Mr. Carter had made about his having bubonic plague. What was it they called Mr. Carter? Benny something? And it had something to do with the grace that Bod could translate, because he was a brain at Latin. Oh, yes, and that shepherd's pie for tea had been lovely. Surely he had enough material now for his postcard. He wrote:

"*Dear Mother,*

"*I gave mine in to Mr. cater Darbsher has spend 4½ of his my healthser ticket was in my pocket he said I had got bubnick plag it was a jok he is called Benny Dick toe I think it is. We had ozard of wiz for tea Atkion says wiz is good and oz is garstly so do I. Love John.*

"*P.S. Temple is a brain, he is short for dogs boody.*"

Pleased with his effort, he trotted up to Mr. Wilkins and awaited his approval.

Mr. Wilkins did his best to decipher the message. As a solver of crossword puzzles, he felt that if only he had a clue, he might be able to read what appeared to be an ingenious code. But Mr. Wilkins hadn't a clue and, this time, his period of convalescence was longer.

The dormitory bell was ringing an hour later when Mr. Wilkins reluctantly accepted Jennings' postcard. It was his seventh attempt and Mr. Wilkins knew what it meant because Jennings, with infinite patience, had explained it. But to Mr. and Mrs. Jennings, who had no interpreter to help them, the postcard's message remained for ever a mystery.

CHAPTER 2

TROUBLE LOOMS AHEAD

"You sleep in this bed, Jennings," said Venables, "and you're next to him here, Darbishire. Go on, you've only got ten minutes to get into bed."

The dormitory was a small one. There were five beds, with a chair beside each; three wash basins by the window and a large mirror in a dark corner of the room.

Jennings was still enthralled by the novelty of this new method of living one's life, but to Darbishire, the sparse furnishing of the dormitory compared unfavourably with the comfort of his bedroom at home, and the sight of his pyjamas, sponge bag and Bible lying on his hard iron bed in this unfamiliar room was too much. He gulped twice and swallowed hard.

"What on earth's the matter with you, Darbishire?" asked Temple.

"Nothing," said Darbishire through misty spectacles. "Well, nothing much, except I don't like this place. When I'm at home my father always comes and talks to me when I'm in bed and—well, it's all so different here, isn't it?"

"Oh, I don't know," said Jennings philosophically, "we'll probably get used to it in three or four years."

"You'll have a smash-on lot to get used to," said Venables. "Wait till you get into the Head's Latin class; it's spivish ozard, isn't it, Atki?"

"Yes, rather," said Atkinson ghoulishly. "He made me write out the passive of 'Audio' twenty-five times once; it nearly killed me."

"And if you stop," added Temple, determined to make the worst of it, "if you take a breath even, when you're going through a verb, you get a stripe. I got fifty-seven stripes for Latin last term and I'm the best in the form."

Darbishire paled slightly, but Jennings was undaunted.

"What are the other masters like?" he demanded.

Venables, Temple, and Atkinson considered. They were all very happy at Linbury; they all liked the masters, and they knew that the rules of the school were made for their own good and for their own enjoyment. But one couldn't possibly admit all this, and only by making out that the school was one degree

26

removed from a concentration camp, and that the school rules would have been condemned by the Spanish Inquisition on compassionate grounds—only by such colouring of the truth could one hope to avoid cramping one's style, and hold the attention of an audience.

"Old Wilkie's pretty ozard," said Temple, twirling a sock round his head autogyrically. "Sometimes he's double that—that's ozard squared. And when he's in a rare bate, he's been known to touch ozard cubed, in five-second bursts." And standing on his bed, he proceeded to give an impersonation of Mr. Wilkins in the grip of ozardry, raised to the power of three.

"I—I—I—you—you—you—corwumph!" he spluttered. In point of fact, it was nothing like Mr. Wilkins, but the audience were not fussy about minor details of characterisation and applauded vigorously. "Come here, Temple—you miserable specimen!" continued the impersonator. "You—you—crawling earthworm! You pestilential buffoon! You—you—don't you know that the angles at the base of an isosceles triangle are jolly nearly equal? Write it out a hundred and fifty million times before tea." And, flushed with pride at the appreciative way in which his act was received, he hurled his pullover into space and attacked Venables with a few friendly straight lefts and short jabs to the body.

Darbishire disentangled himself from Temple's pullover, which had descended upon him, and felt even worse than he had done before.

"Do you mean he gets angry?" he asked with growing concern.

"We call it breezy," replied Atkinson. "And sometimes there's such a super-duper breeze that the windows rattle. It's wizard—well, it is if it's somebody else he's in a bate with and not you," he added as an afterthought.

"What's Mr. Carter like?" demanded Jennings.

"Oh, Benedick's all right," said Venables. "He's a bit crackers at times, but all masters are, anyway. It's probably a law of their union."

The boxing bout had ended as suddenly as it had begun and Venables felt it was time he took a hand in describing the joys of school life.

"Now what else have you got to know?" he went on. "First, you mustn't put your hands in your pockets, unless you're a prefect."

"Why?" asked Jennings.

"I don't know! It's just a rule."

"Supposing I want my handkerchief?" asked Darbishire. "It'll be years before I'm a prefect, if ever, and I can't sniff all that time, and my father said that if my catarrh gets—"

"You know what I mean," said Venables. "You mustn't strut about with

27

your hands in your pockets as though you owned the place. And you mustn't run in the corridors; you mustn't use fountain pens; you mustn't play conkers in the Assembly Hall; you mustn't read comics; you mustn't eat tuck before lunch; you mustn't wear your vest for football and you mustn't wear your cap like a spiv."

"You are allowed to breathe without special permission, though," added Temple, graciously putting in a good word for the authorities.

Venables had stopped, unable to think of any more "mustn'ts." But he was not defeated for long.

"Oh, yes," he added, making up a new rule on the spur of the moment. "If you make a duck in a house match or let a goal through, your name'll be Mud for the rest of the term."

"But I always do make a duck," lamented Darbishire. "I'm no good at games."

"That's all right, Darbishire," said Jennings. "I'll give you some coaching. I've seen the Australians play, so there's not much about how to play cricket that I don't know."

"Don't swank, Jennings," said Temple. "I don't suppose you know anything, really, and it'd be much easier to call Darbishire 'Mud,' anyway; it's shorter."

The discussion was interrupted by a bell ringing in the distance.

"Gosh!" said Atkinson. "That's the five minutes bell. Come on, let's get washed."

There was a frantic scurry of undressing; small clusters of clothes blossomed on the floor in untidy heaps. Later on, the topmost garment would be picked up and folded tidily to shroud the multitude of unsightly sins that lay beneath. But now Operation Ablution claimed their attention. Five boys into three wash basins works out at an impractical fraction, so tradition required that the old hands should wash first, while the recruits swelled the ranks of the great unwashed until their turn came.

Atkinson dashed wildly to his basin, turned on the tap and rushed madly back to his bed for his sponge-bag. His speed was largely wasted, because he had forgotten to put the plug in and, on his return, the basin was as empty as when he had left it.

Venables gave the impression of haste by a series of horizontal and vertical leaps over and across the beds, but he kept missing his footing and wasted time returning to the airfield for a fresh take off. But soon a few damp patches behind the ears denoted that he, too, was washing.

Temple hastened to retrieve his pyjama jacket from the top of the electric light shade, whence he had hurled it in his attempts to make his impersonation of Mr. Wilkins seem more life-like.

But Darbishire, who was not yet used to having his bedtime regulated by bells, sat on his bed and tugged forlornly at a knot in his shoe-laces.

"Oh, and there's another thing, Jennings," said Venables amidst splashes, "you have to wash your feet every night unless it's your bath night."

He grabbed his tooth paste and squeezed hard. "Oh, golly!" he said. "This is ozard muck. Look, I've squeezed out about a yard and a half. What'll I do with it? I can't put it back."

"You could write your name round the basin like they do with icing sugar," said Jennings, who had arrived to occupy the remaining basin. "Have you got enough to write 'many happy returns of the day?'"

"Haven't got time," replied Venables, "though it'd be quite a prang if we'd thought of it earlier." He took a mouthful from his tooth glass and gargled.

"I say, Atki," he said, "can you change gear when you gargle? Like this, look—I mean, listen."

He gargled again, starting on a low note and rising up the scale with forcible vocal contortions to show where the gears changed from low to second, from second to top. The car gathered speed and, as an artistic finale, faded into the distance.

"Super duper!" said Jennings.

"Smash-on prang!" agreed Atkinson.

"Yes, it's not bad, is it?" admitted Venables. "I've been practising quite a lot in the hols."

"All the same, I can do it just as well," said Jennings.

"So can I," said Atkinson.

The dormitory hummed with cars changing gear; light sports cars with super-charged engines and heavy lorries stalling on steep hills. Atkinson swallowed his gargle while changing down to take a hairpin bend, at eighty miles per hour, and had to be slapped on the back by his fellow motorists.

"I know something better than that," said Jennings. "I can be a super-jet fighter; listen …. Eee-ow-ow; eee-ow-ow; eee-ow-ow …. Dacka-dacka; dacka-dacka …" His machine gun spat venomously. "Eee-ow-ow; eee-ow-ow; eee-ow-ow …. Doyng!"

"What's the 'doyng'?" inquired Venables.

"That's the other plane crashing after I've hit him," said the aeronaut. "I'm going into a dive, now. Eee-ow-ow; eee-ow-ow …. Dacka-dacka; dacka-dacka …."

The Squadron's personnel was at once joined by Venables, Atkinson and Temple in Spitfires, and all four eee'd and ow'd and dacka-dacka'd and doynged with outstretched arms, wheeling, banking and diving, while Darbishire sat on his bed and put his fingers in his ears.

The door opened and the noise stopped abruptly.

"H'm," said Mr. Carter from the doorway. "If dorm No. 4 Fighter Squadron doesn't make a forced landing and get back to base, there'll be trouble; this light's going out in three minutes."

"Yes, sir," murmured the Fighter Squadron meekly.

The door closed on Mr. Carter.

"Come on, you chaps, get a move on," said Venables. "Benedick means it when he says—" He broke off, his eye affronted by a shocking disregard for tradition. "Here, Jennings," he thundered indignantly, "what are you doing at that basin?"

"Washing," said Jennings. "You said I'd got to wash my feet."

"But you can't have that basin first; it's Bod's. He bagged it last term; new chaps have to wash last."

"Well, I'm here now," said Jennings.

Temple came rushing across to defend his rights.

"That's my basin, Jennings. Get out," he ordered.

"Well, I didn't know," said Jennings.

"You jolly well ought to know. Go on; get out of the way."

Jennings refused to be cowed. "I was here first, so I'm going to wash first," he said.

"I wouldn't stand that from a new chap, Bod," said Venables. "It's just super-hairy cheek."

"'Course it is," put in Atkinson, "and spivish disloyal to the dorm rules."

"Don't worry," said Temple. "I'm not going to stand for any ozard oik of a new chap telling me what to do. I'm going to count three, Jennings, and if you don't get out, I'll squeeze this wet sponge down your pyjamas."

Jennings didn't like the situation much. Temple was easily the largest boy in the room and his allies stood on either hand, like Herminius and Spurius Lartius assisting Horatius in the brave days of old. Still, Jennings remembered, his father had told him to stick up for himself; he decided to try it.

"You can go and chase yourself, Temple," he said, as that worthy was mouthing "Three" in menacing tones.

"All right then," said Temple, and squeezed the sponge.

The water was cold and uncomfortable, and Jennings let out a piercing scream, which echoed all over the building, and dissolved into tears.

"You soaked me," wailed Jennings. "I'm all wringing wet!"

"Cave, Benedick!" said Atkinson with an eye on the opening door.

Mr. Carter sized up the situation.

"Who was responsible for that screaming noise?" he asked.

"I was, sir. It was Bod's fault, sir; Temple, I mean," gulped Jennings between sobs. "He squeezed a wet sponge down the back of my pyjama trousers and made me all wet."

"Sneak!" hissed Atkinson and Venables in tones which they mistakenly supposed were too soft for Mr. Carter's adult ear.

"Jennings, you don't quite understand," said Mr. Carter. "I didn't say who 'made' that noise, I asked who was 'responsible' for its being made; that gives the culprit a chance to own up without laying the victim open to the charge of telling tales; there's a difference you see."

"Yes, sir," said Jennings.

"Perhaps I'm still a trifle deaf from those aircraft noises you were making, and I didn't quite catch the answer to my question! Now, who was responsible for those screams?"

"I was, sir," admitted the defender of tradition.

"Thank you, Temple. We'll go into the merits of the case in the morning. Come and see me after breakfast."

"Yes, sir," said Temple.

"We'll have silence now while you get into bed—and get a move on," Mr. Carter said.

He waited while they washed.

Temple, seething with indignation at Jennings' treachery, hurtled into bed hoping that the ferocity of his manner would show Jennings what he felt about him.

Darbishire, unaccustomed to getting a move on, prepared for a lengthy getting-ready-for-bed ceremony which Mr. Carter had to cut short. He folded up Darbishire's clothes for him and waited while he read his prescribed ten verses from the New Testament; then he switched off the light.

"Good night, everybody," he said.

Temple waited long enough for Mr. Carter to reach the end of the passage; then he whispered, "You ruinous little sneak, Jennings. You wait! I'll bash you up tomorrow."

"Good Old Bod," said Atkinson in the same low tone. "Do it before tea, that's the best time."

"It wasn't my fault," protested Jennings loudly.

"Sh! Sh!" came from the three old-timers. "We're on silence. That means whisper."

"Benedick's got supersonic ear-sight," said Venables. "He can hear you even when he's downstairs."

"Well, it wasn't my fault," repeated Jennings in what was meant for a whisper.

"'Course it was," said Temple. "You needn't have yelled your head off like that, you great baby."

"Sorry, Temple," said Jennings.

"All right," said Temple ungraciously; "but don't do it again."

For a first-class bashing-up to peter out in apologies was not Venables' idea of a fitting climax. He decided to stir things up again.

"You're not going to let it go at that, Bod, are you?" he asked. "After all, even Benedick knew Jennings was in the wrong, 'cos he ticked him off for sneaking."

"Okay, then," said Temple. "We'll have the bashing-up, as arranged."

Darbishire felt himself constrained to speak.

"That's Not Fair," he protested in capital letters. "You've accepted Jennings' apology, so it's not a square deal if you bash him up now."

"I can if I feel like it," said Temple.

"My father says you should never go back on your word," persisted the champion of the square deal.

"Shut up, Darbishire, you hairy ruin; nobody asked you," put in Venables.

"Any more from you, Darbishire," said Temple, "and I'll bash you up tomorrow, when I've finished with Jennings. And you can tell your father so with my love."

Silence reigned for a few moments, until it occurred to Atkinson that the maximum enjoyment could be wrung from the situation only if Jennings was made to realise just what was in store for him.

"I say, Jennings," he said. "Temple won the school boxing championship last term. Oh, boy! Oh, boy! What a smash-on bashing-up it's going to be! Rare! Super-duper! And wizzo!"

"I don't care," said Jennings, caring very much.

"Well, I don't think it's fair—" began Darbishire.

"Shut up, Darbishire, nobody asked you," said the three old-timers in unison.

"You know, Jennings," proceeded Atkinson, warming to his task, "you're taking on a big job when you get on the wrong side of Bod; he's hefty daring. Why, d'you know what he did last term? He foxed into town on a bus, and there's a super-lethal punishment for foxing."

Atkinson went on to explain that this notorious feat, which had placed Temple on the dizziest pedestal of fame, had occurred one half-holiday. Quietly slipping away from Mr. Wilkins' cricket practice, Temple had taken a bus into the town and had gone to Valenti's, a sweet shop which specialised in the manufacture of Brighton rock.

"And he brought back sixpenny-worth of rock in a bag with the shop's name on to prove he'd been," ended the narrator in admiring tones.

"And I wasn't caught, either," put in the hero of the exploit. He glowed with pride at the mention of his heroism and determined to make a little more hay while the sun still shone. "That's the sort of chap I am, really," he said, with becoming modesty. "Of course, it's quite easy if you've got the nerve."

The audience murmured their appreciation.

"Still," he went on, reluctant to leave the topic, "no one else has ever done it. There's no one, except me, who'd dare to, I suppose. Well, good night, chaps," said the great one, condescendingly. "Oh, Atki, remind me to bash Jennings before tea tomorrow, just in case I forget."

Neither Jennings nor Darbishire realised that, ninety-nine times out of a hundred, these threats are never carried out. They have to be uttered, of course, to restore the shattered pride of anyone who imagines that he has been wronged, but before the penalty can be exacted, the insult has usually been forgotten and the protagonists have become close friends. In the present instance, the three old-stagers were not contemplating a gruesome outcome to their threat; they were merely administering a mild rebuke to Jennings, so that he might know his lowly station in life and not get above himself. Unaware that such face-saving procedure is merely a matter of form, Darbishire's feelings of fair play were outraged.

"It's not fair," he protested.

"And if Darbishire starts getting uppish I'll do him as well," said Temple.

"I wouldn't like to be you tomorrow, Jennings," shuddered Venables, with relish.

"I couldn't care less," replied Jennings. In point of fact, he couldn't have cared more, but he wasn't going to let anyone know. He tried to remember what his father had said about standing up for himself. Perhaps if he stood up for himself really well, he might even ... He fell asleep.

Darbishire lay awake with black despair in his soul. Whatever sort of a place was this that his father had so mistakenly sent him to? He had no idea that school was a place where life was governed by clanging bells and threats of being bashed up; where the rules were thwarting and masters made you write things out a hundred and fifty million times. Golly! However long would that take? Well, suppose it took you a minute to write it out once, that meant sixty times an hour and there were twenty-four hours in a day so that made ... Gosh! But you would have to stop to eat, wouldn't you? He tried again. After his third calculation, when the answer came to slightly more than forty-seven years, he fell asleep.

CHAPTER 3

JENNINGS GAINS A REPUTATION

JENNINGS had only the haziest recollection of the events of the following morning. It seemed as though he spent the time in getting into long lines which moved somewhere whenever a bell sounded. Where the line went he wasn't sure, but the manœuvre always ended up by a master asking him his name and how old he was. After that, the master would give him some exercise books, or a pair of football socks or some other suitable memento of the occasion.

As a party game it had its points, but as the presents were rather dull, he was glad when lunch time came. But this proved to be only a short respite for, after the meal was over, bells clanged again and everybody started to line up for another bout of to-ing and fro-ing.

Jennings had had enough, so he slipped unobtrusively out of the line as it rounded a corner and wandered off by himself. Remembering Temple's threat, he had a vague idea of keeping out of the way until tea-time when, perhaps, the danger would be passed. At the far end of the quad he discovered Darbishire all by himself.

"What are you doing here, Darbishire?" he demanded. "You ought to be marching about somewhere in a long line."

"I know," replied Darbishire, gulping visibly. Jennings could not see his eyes because of his spectacles, but streaks of grime down his cheeks told their own story.

"I say, Darbishire, you haven't been crying, have you?" asked Jennings.

"N-no, not really. I've just been wishing I was at home, and it's made my glasses go all misty."

"You've got nothing to worry about," Jennings consoled him. "How about me? I'm due for a bashing-up before tea."

"Well, so am I, if I get uppish," Darbishire replied.

"And have you been getting uppish?"

"No, I've been feeling downish all morning." And in a burst of confidence,

35

he added: "I don't like boarding school; everything sounds so awful, and—oh, I wish I'd never come!"

"Well, I'm not feeling too good, either," said Jennings. "I do wish I could see my father for a few minutes, so's he could tell me the best thing to do during bashing-ups; there's probably something you can do, if you know what."

"Oh, dear, I'm so miserable," lamented Darbishire. "My father says we should always strive to—"

"I say," said Jennings, as a brilliant thought struck him. "I say, Darbishire, I've got an idea! Shall we run away?"

"Run away?" gasped Darbishire, stunned by the boldness of the idea.

"Yes; go home. Then you can tell your father you don't like it here, and my father can tell me how to stand up for myself against the school boxing champion."

"But how can we run away?" objected the law-abiding Darbishire. "We're not allowed out!"

Jennings dismissed the trifling objection with a shrug of the shoulders.

"We could just walk down the drive and get a bus to the station and go home. And we could ask Mr. Carter for our pounds out of the bank, so's we could buy our tickets."

"But I've only got nineteen and something."

"That'll be masses to buy a ticket with," Jennings assured him. "I say, it'll be super exciting, won't it?"

Darbishire wasn't at all sure that he was cut out for that sort of excitement. "S'pose we get caught?" he asked anxiously.

Jennings considered. It was, of course, quite a point. Perhaps there was some way of reducing the risk.

"I know," he said after deep thought; "we could disguise ourselves. Then, perhaps, even if they saw us, we wouldn't be recognised."

"What, beards and false noses and things?" gasped Darbishire.

"Yes," said Jennings, as though the donning of disguise was an everyday occurrence with him.

"But I haven't got a beard," objected the practical Darbishire. "And, anyway, I'd look silly wearing a beard with short trousers."

Jennings wasn't going to let minor objections interfere with what promised to be a first-rate scheme.

"Well, p'r'aps not beards, then," he conceded; "but I could wear your glasses, that'd be something, and you could—er—"

What could Darbishire have?

"You could—you could walk with a limp!" he decided in a flash of genius.

For the first time since he had arrived at school, Darbishire began to enjoy himself. The idea of walking with a limp cheered him up enormously.

"Coo! Yes! Wizzo!" he said, all sorrows forgotten. "Like this, look!" And with staggering gait he hobbled round in small circles.

"You look more like a crab with chilblains," said Jennings. He began to feel he had been over-generous in giving Darbishire a rôle so rich in theatrical possibilities. "No, bags I walk with the limp," he amended; "I can do it better than you."

"That's not fair," protested Darbishire. "You said I could have it; besides, you're going to have my glasses, so there won't be anything for me."

"Well, you won't be wearing your glasses," Jennings argued.

"But it isn't a disguise just to be not wearing something."

"Well," conceded Jennings, "you can carry a stick and turn your collar up."

"Coo! Yes! And wear my sun hat with a dent in the top like a trilby," said Darbishire happily. "We must remember not to wear our school caps, mustn't we, 'cos that'd spoil the disguise."

"Come on, let's go and find Mr. Carter and ask for our money," said Jennings, and, full of excited optimism, they dashed wildly-into the building and up the stairs to Mr. Carter's study.

As they were about to knock on his door, Darbishire thought of a brilliant amendment to the plan.

"I say, Jennings," he said, "couldn't we both walk with a limp?"

Mr. Carter looked up from his desk. "Hallo," he said. "What do you two want?"

"We want some money from the bank, please, sir."

"How much?" inquired Mr. Carter.

"I want a pound, and Darbishire wants nineteen and whatever it is he's got."

"That's rather a lot, isn't it? What do you want it for?"

This was a difficult question.

"Do we have to say what it's for, sir?" asked Jennings.

"Well, a large sum of money like that's a bit unusual. I'm afraid I can't let you have it unless you tell me why."

Darbishire decided that the game was up, but Jennings was made of sterner stuff.

"Please, sir," he asked, "how much could we have without having to tell you what it's for, sir?"

"I shouldn't be curious up to about sixpence," said Mr. Carter generously.

"Oh …. Well, if that's all, can we have sixpence each, then, sir?"

Mr. Carter gave it to them. "You won't spend it on anything foolish, will you?" he remarked.

Mr. Carter smiled as the door closed on the two conspirators. He already had an idea that something was afoot and decided to hold a watching brief. In Mr. Carter's experience it did not pay to nip enterprises in the bud too early, as they had a habit of bursting out again in other directions. He opened the door and followed at a discreet distance.

On the far side of the quad Jennings and Darbishire held another council of war.

"Well, I s'pose that's that," said Darbishire philosophically. "And I was feeling quite excited about walking with a limp with my collar turned up; I was going to try and look like 'Dick Barton.' Of course, I know I wouldn't look like him really, in school socks—but that sort of chap. Still," he ended lugubriously, "it's all a wash-out, now."

"No, it isn't," said the irrepressible Jennings. "We've got sixpence each; that's enough to get to the station on the bus."

"But what about train fares?"

"We'll go by taxi," said Jennings in a lordly manner. "We'll get one at the station and my father'll pay when we get there. I live at Haywards Heath. It's only about fifteen miles away."

But Darbishire lived in Hertfordshire and thought it would cost at least a hundred pounds to get there by taxi. Jennings had the answer. They would go to Haywards Heath where Mr. Jennings, having paid for the taxi, would lend Darbishire enough money to get home by train. With Mr. Jennings' co-operation taken for granted, the scheme appeared flawless.

The coast was clear. Sounds of activity from the Assembly Hall indicated that the main body of the school was busily engaged in some communal pursuit.

"Come on, then," said Jennings, "give me your glasses and turn your collar up."

"Gosh, Darbishire," he continued when the spectacles were in position, "your eyesight must be rotten—I mean ozard. I can't see a thing with them."

"Well, I can't see a thing without them," complained Darbishire, peering shortsightedly in all directions.

The transfer of the spectacles had reduced visibility to ten-tenths fog for both of them and they were unaware that Mr. Carter was an interested spectator of their departure. Groping blindly and limping heavily, their sun hats pulled low over their brows, they proceeded down the drive in a series of furtive staggers. Though disguised to the hilt, Mr. Carter had no difficulty in recognising them, though he was slightly puzzled as to why they found it necessary to walk as though they were in the last stages of intoxication.

In this manner they passed through the school gates and on to the road. Fortunately, there was no one about, as their antics would have invited investigation by any kindly soul whose heart is wrung by the sight of small boys in physical agony.

"We turn right to get into the town," whispered Jennings in conspiratorial accents; "I remember it from yesterday. And I think there's a bus stop somewhere along here."

For fifty yards they stumbled uncertainly; then Jennings bumped into an obstruction which loomed up suddenly before his hazy gaze.

"I beg your pardon," he apologised to a post marked "Bus Stop," and again they moved on.

After a while Jennings stopped. "I can't go on wearing your glasses any longer, Darbishire," he said, "they're giving me a headache, and we must be nearly at the bus stop by now."

Darbishire put on his glasses.

"Yes, there it is," he exclaimed, "about twenty yards back; we've walked right past it. I can see it quite plainly now."

"So can I," said Jennings. It would be humiliating to confess that he had just apologised to it by mistake. "Come on, let's go back and wait for a bus. And if anyone comes along, we can nip behind the hedge."

"D'you think we need go on limping?" said Darbishire as they neared the bus stop. "It's smash-on tiring and there's no one about, anyway."

"Okay," said Jennings. "And we needn't talk in whispers either, as there's no one coming. Oh, golly! There is!" he gasped. "It's a man; he's coming out of the school gates. Quick! Get down behind the hedge!"

They hurled themselves behind the inadequate cover of the hedge and waited breathlessly.

"Who is it?" whispered Darbishire, and then spoilt the secrecy of the whisper with a loud yell. "Ow!" he wailed.

"Shut up, you fool!" hissed Jennings.

"But I'm kneeling on a nettle," groaned Darbishire.

"Keep your head down, you goof, or he'll see us!" He peered cautiously through a gap in the hedge. "Oh, heavens!" he gasped. "It's Mr. Carter and he's coming this way. Lie down and don't move."

Mr. Carter strolled slowly along towards the bus stop. Portions of small boy were visible through gaps in the hedge, but he affected not to notice. He was more than curious to know what the plan was, but he knew that if he were to discover the boys so early in the proceedings, he probably never would know. They would merely stand uncomfortably on one foot and remain silent in the face of questions. No, he decided, the only way to find out how those minds were really working was to play the comedy out a bit longer. He walked passed the bus stop and disappeared round a bend in the road.

As the footsteps receded in the distance, Jennings cautiously raised his head.

"He's gone," he whispered triumphantly. "Jolly wizard job he didn't see us, wasn't it?"

"Are you sure he didn't?" inquired Darbishire anxiously.

"'Course not; we crouched down, didn't we? Well, then, he couldn't have, possibly."

"Good," said Darbishire; "I think I'll get off my nettle now if you don't mind."

In the distance they heard a bus approaching.

The bus was a single-decker Southdown and it stopped in response to the frantic signals of the two boys. It was fairly full, but two seats in the front were vacant, and a man seated near the entrance alighted as Jennings and Darbishire, with anxious glances down the road, hopped quickly on to the platform and made for the front seats.

"You needn't go on limping, now," said Jennings, as Darbishire lurched forward with the sudden starting of the bus. "We'll be passing Mr. Carter in a minute," he continued, "so we'll have to crouch down very low in our seats; then he won't see us. Isn't this fun?"

But the fun ceased some five seconds later when the bus slowed down.

"What are we stopping for?" asked Darbishire, "we've only just started."

"I'll have a recce," said Jennings, raising his eyes cautiously to the level of the window.

The sight that met his gaze chilled the blood in his veins; Mr. Carter was standing in the road with hand upraised to stop the bus.

Mr. Carter took the seat next to the entrance and carefully avoided looking at the front seats. Indeed, they appeared to be empty, for Jennings and Darbishire were crouching so low that nothing was visible. From a vantage point, some two feet from the ground, Jennings essayed a furtive reconnaissance.

"He's sitting right at the back," he reported in a whisper, "and he hasn't seen us."

"Oh, golly, we shouldn't have done this," groaned Darbishire. "There'll be an awful row. My father says, 'Oh, what a tangled web we weave—'"

"He's looking out of the window. If those two fat ladies don't get off, he won't know we're here. What were you saying?"

"I was saying, 'Oh, what a tangled web we weave, when first we practise to deceive.'"

"Oh, shut up," retorted Jennings. "Here we are, in the middle of the most frantic jam and you start spouting proverbs!"

"Sorry, Jen," said Darbishire humbly. "It's only what my father—"

"Listen," whispered Jennings, "we'll go on crouching like this, and keep our heads down till Mr. Carter gets off; then, we'll be all right."

"Yes, but s'posing he—" objected Darbishire.

"Fares, please!" said the conductor.

This was going to be a ticklish manœuvre. Doubled up as they were, they had difficulty in getting their sixpences out of their trouser pockets, and the conductor was tapping his foot on the floor impatiently by the time they had succeeded.

"Two halves to the station," whispered Jennings inaudibly.

"Eh?" said the conductor. "Speak up, I can't 'ear yer."

"Two halves to the station, please," said Jennings, not daring to raise his voice.

"What's the matter, chum, laryngitis?" asked the conductor.

"Yes," croaked Jennings hoarsely.

"Can't yer pal talk neither? Where you going, son?" he boomed at Darbishire in a voice of thunder, as though the question might supply enough volume for the answer.

Darbishire's lips framed the word "Station," but no sound came. At the third attempt the conductor's lip-reading improved, and light dawned.

"Oh, station!" he said. "Well, why didn't yer say so? Two sore throats to the station—tanner each. I thenkyow." He punched their tickets and returned to the rear platform.

Several times the bus stopped. Passengers came and went, but Mr. Carter remained; the combined wishful thinking of Jennings and Darbishire was quite unable to budge him. Three times new passengers advanced to the front seat, believing it to be empty, and were startled by the crouching figures who mimed at them to go away.

At every stop Jennings made a cautious survey. Surely he would get off soon, but by now, they had reached the town and Mr. Carter was still sitting next to the exit. No amount of limping and trying to look like "Dick Barton" could deceive him at so close a range.

The bus stopped again.

"Station! Station!" called the conductor. "Hurry along, please!"

"Oh, golly! What shall we do?" moaned Darbishire.

"We'll just have to go a bit farther," said Jennings.

The conductor was anxious to be helpful. "Station!" he yelled down the bus. "Hey, chum, didn't yer want the station? Oi!" And he whistled shrilly at the seemingly empty front seats.

"Don't take any notice," whispered Jennings. "Pretend you haven't heard."

But the conductor was not to be put off.

"You lads deaf as well as dumb?" he inquired, approaching.

"We—we're going a bit farther," murmured Jennings.

"Okay," said the conductor, ringing the bell. "How far are yer going?"

"I—I don't know yet. I hope to know soon."

The conductor scratched his head. The Company's Regulations did not say how one should deal with passengers who folded themselves up and mouthed at you and hoped to know their destination in the near future.

"Better drop yer at the 'ospital," he decided, "and get them sore throats looked at; that'll be a tuppenny."

"Oh, goodness," said Darbishire, "we haven't got any more money."

"Oh!" said the conductor. "You'll 'ave to get orf then, won't yer?"

"But we can't get off," urged Jennings desperately. "You don't understand. Look, couldn't you give me your address and I'll send the fare on to you."

"I've 'eard that one before," said the conductor. "Well, come on. Are yer going to 'ave another ticket or ain't yer?"

Darbishire was on the verge of tears and even Jennings' resource was not equal to the situation.

"No, no. Wait a minute," he implored.

"I ain't got all day," replied the conductor, "either yer—"

"Can I be of any assistance?" inquired Mr. Carter politely.

"Oh, gosh!" said Jennings.

"Oh, golly!" said Darbishire.

Mr. Carter gave them a friendly smile.

"It's these lads, sir; acting a bit queer. They're either ill or barmy or trying to get a free ride. I want another tuppence from both of them."

Mr. Carter handed over the money.

"Would you mind stopping?" he said to the conductor. "I think we've all gone quite far enough."

They alighted in a silence that could be felt, and the two boys stood dejectedly on the pavement as the bus proceeded on its way.

"And now we'll have to catch a bus going the other way," said Mr. Carter. "I'm glad you've got your glasses back again, Darbishire; you looked quite lost without them."

"Oh, sir. D'you mean you saw us?" asked Jennings incredulously.

"I'm afraid I couldn't help it," said Mr. Carter. "And next time you hide behind a hedge, remember it's useless to put your head down if you leave your other end sticking up."

"Will there be an awful row, sir?" inquired Darbishire.

"Oh! I don't know," was the reply, "we all make mistakes. The best thing to do is to try and profit by them."

"But shan't we be expelled, sir?" persisted Darbishire.

"Why, would you mind very much?"

"I—I'd rather like it, sir," he confessed.

"I thought that was the trouble," said Mr. Carter. "We all start off by feeling homesick; it's just one of those things which has to be mastered."

He assured Darbishire that there would not be a row. But this didn't help Jennings, as the return to school meant that the bashing-up would have to be faced after all.

Mr. Carter sensed that all was not well.

"Well, Jennings?" he asked. "Is there anything else wrong?"

"Yes, sir," said Jennings. "If I go back now, I'm —oh—"

"Yes?"

"I can't tell you, sir. It'd be sneaking and you said last night we oughtn't to do that, sir."

"I think Jennings ought to tell you, sir," said Darbishire. "My father says that—"

"No. I can't," said Jennings, "and you can't make me, sir, 'cos of what you said about never listening to people who tell tales."

It is sometimes difficult for a master to draw the line between sneaking and genuine complaints, so Mr. Carter suggested that perhaps Jennings could find his own salvation. Jennings was doubtful, but refused to reveal the cause of his troubles, and decided to go back to school and face them.

Mr. Carter went down the road to inquire the time of the next bus back.

"I say, Darbishire," said Jennings when the master was out of earshot, "he's jolly decent, really, isn't he?"

"Yes," agreed Darbishire. "I thought he'd kick up no end of a fuss; jolly lucky for us he isn't the one who gets ozard squared."

"Lucky!" echoed Jennings. "What about my bashing-up?"

"Are you frightened?" asked Darbishire.

"Well, just a bit. So'd you be; but I'm jolly well not going to tell Mr. Carter."

Across the road was a sweet shop, and something about it rang a bell in Jennings' brain. Why should it appear vaguely familiar when he had never seen it before? "*S. Valenti & Son*" was inscribed in red letters above the shop front, and a sign in the window informed the world that father and son specialised in the manufacture of genuine Brighton rock.

Jennings remembered. That must be the shop which Temple had visited when he foxed out last term. An idea buzzed in his brain, ticked over gently for a few seconds, then roared into action in top gear.

"I say, Darbi," he said, with growing excitement. "That sweet shop over there—"

"I don't feel much like sweets at the moment, thanks," said Darbishire.

"But that's the shop Temple went to when he foxed out."

"Well, you don't expect me to get excited over that, do you?"

"No, but I am," returned Jennings, as the idea assumed a practical shape. "Bang-on! I can see how to ... Oh, blow! We haven't got any money; I wonder if Mr. Carter'll let me have some more bank?"

When Mr. Carter returned to say that the bus did not leave for an hour, he was a little puzzled about Jennings' insistence on buying Brighton rock; surely Jennings had plenty of sweets in his tuck box, hadn't he?

"Yes, sir," replied Jennings earnestly; "but that won't do; it's got to be Brighton rock, and it's got to be in one of Valenti's bags with the name on."

Mr. Carter looked searchingly at Jennings' anxious countenance.

"Is this rock very important?" he asked.

"Yes, sir. It's vital," Jennings assured him. "You know you said I'll have to settle this trouble by myself, sir? Well, I could do it if only I had some of that rock."

For a moment Mr. Carter considered, and then he decided not to ask any questions. His instinct told him that if he were to wield the probe of official inquiry, he would agitate the molehill of friction into a mountain of trouble. This, he decided, was one of those cases which heal more quickly without interference.

He made further inroads on Jennings' bank and handed him a shilling.

"Coo, thank you, sir, thank you ever so!" Jennings hopped on one leg in excited gratitude, and dashed across the road paying only the minimum of attention to his kerb drill.

Darbishire watched him, wondering what all the excitement was about. Then he looked at Mr. Carter doubtfully.

"Are you going to take us back to school, sir?" he asked.

"That was the general idea," Mr. Carter informed him.

"Oh," Darbishire said philosophically, "p'raps it won't be so bad, though. They say the first five years are the worst, don't they, sir?"

After Jennings' visit to Valenti's, Mr. Carter took them to a restaurant, explaining that it would be bedtime before they got back to school.

Baked beans on toast restored their spirits and loosened their tongues, and Mr. Carter was able to convince them that the rigours of school life were not nearly so bad as they had imagined.

"Venables, you dirty slacker, you haven't washed your feet!" said Atkinson.

The dormitory bell had rung some ten minutes before, and Temple, Atkinson and Venables had reached the gargling-gear-change stage of getting into bed.

They were rather puzzled at the absence of Jennings and Darbishire who had not appeared at tea, and seemed to have vanished from the face of the earth.

"Where on earth can those new characters have got to?" said Temple. "I haven't seen them since lunch."

"P'r'aps they're in the sick room," suggested Venables. "I say, Bod," he went on, as a thought struck him. "Weren't you going to bash one of them up before tea?"

"Gosh, yes! I forgot all about it," confessed the boxing champion. "Never mind, I'll do it tomorrow. No flowers by request; here lies Jennings; R.I.P."

"Who's talking about me?" demanded Jennings, sailing into the dormitory as though he had just bought the place. He was followed by a smiling Darbishire.

"Golly! Where have you two been?" asked Atkinson. "The dorm bell went hours ago."

"And where were you at tea?" inquired Venables. "You missed some super-wizard muck. I had four helpings!"

Temple didn't like the self-satisfied expression on Jennings' face and said so.

"I know where they were," he said. "They've been hiding from me 'cos they funked getting bashed up."

"Good heavens, no!" said Jennings. "I never gave you a thought. I've had other things to think about. As a matter of fact, you chaps"—and he tried to make his voice sound casual— "as a matter of fact, Darbishire and I foxed out; we went into town on a bus."

A stunned silence followed this incredible statement. Temple was the first to recover.

"You—you never did!" he said in a hushed voice.

"Yes, didn't we, Darbi?" Jennings turned to his fellow conspirator for confirmation.

"That's right," said the conspirator. "We went out disguised like 'Dick Barton'—well, something like, anyway. It was super."

"And you cut tea as well!" breathed Atkinson admiringly. "Gosh! There'd have been the most frantic hoo-hah if you'd been caught."

"I couldn't have cared less," said Jennings nonchalantly. "I'm that sort, really, and Darbishire's a bit of a desperado in his way, too."

"Oh, you shouldn't say that," simpered the desperado modestly.

"'Course he is," agreed Venables. "I think you're both wizard plucky and Bod isn't the only one after all. Good old Jen! You're smashing rare."

But Temple was not going to relinquish the victor's crown as easily as all that. "Don't you believe them," he broke in. "They're just making it up; I bet they can't prove it. Go on!" he jeered. "Just you prove it! I defy you to!"

Jennings produced the bag of rock with a flourish.

"Certainly," he said in the friendliest of voices. "Have a bit of Brighton rock, Bod; I got it at Valenti's."

Temple was so surprised that he couldn't speak, and Jennings passed the bag round with a lordly gesture that would have done credit to Mr. Toad of Toad Hall.

"Sorry to pinch your idea, Bod," he went on, "but we improved on it rather, with our disguises. And it was just as well we had them, too"—he paused just long enough to produce the required effect— "'cos Benedick got on the bus."

Again the remark was received in stupefied silence. Here, obviously, was some super-man!

"What?" gasped Venables when he had recovered from the shock.

"Oh, yes," said Jennings, as though evading the authorities was child's play. "But it was all right; we kept our heads, you see."

"Down," corrected Darbishire firmly.

"What's that, Darbishire?" asked Jennings.

"We kept our heads down," said Darbishire.

"And here we are to tell the tale," added Jennings, prudently leaving out quite a lot of the tale. "Have another bit of rock, Atki. It's genuine all right. See the name on the bag."

"Coo! Thanks, Jennings."

"Hand it round, Darbishire," Jennings went on. "Want another bit, Venables?"

"Coo! Thanks, Jennings," said Venables, his voice hushed with respectful awe. "I say, Jennings," he continued between mouthfuls, "look, you can share my basin if you like; you and Darbishire."

"No, have mine, Jennings," came from Atkinson, equally anxious to do homage to the famous. "Go on. And you and Darbishire can go first."

"Well, that's awfully decent of Atki," said Darbishire, basking in glory. "My father says that a generous impulse—"

"Don't be so modest, Darbishire," cut in Jennings. "No, I think we'll have Bod's basin."

Temple's throne tottered and fell.

"Well, yes; all right, Jennings," he heard himself say.

"I'll wash first, then Darbishire, then you."

"Well, okay, then, Jennings."

"And no rot about bashing-up, eh, Bod."

Temple assured him that any mention of bashing-up had been in the nature of a friendly joke.

Jennings washed in a leisurely fashion and turned again to Temple.

"Oh, Bod," he said. "By the way, you don't mind my calling you Bod, do you, Bod?"

"No, that's all right, Jennings," returned Bod with an effort.

"Good. Well, I'm feeling a bit fagged out after foxing into town. You might clean this basin out for Darbishire, now I've finished washing my feet in it, will you?"

This was the crowning humiliation, but Temple's defences were shattered.

"Yes, Jennings .... Okay, Jennings," he said.

CHAPTER 4

JENNINGS ARRIVES LATE

THE crowd round the notice board parted to allow Mr. Carter to pass through and pin the football teams on the board. The first practice of the term was due to start when afternoon preparation was over, and most of the new boys had been picked to play in "B" game; how they shaped in this would determine their football status for the next few weeks; the promising players would be promoted to "A" game, while the rabbits would find themselves relegated to the kick-and-rush contingent.

"Have you played much football, Jennings?" inquired Mr. Carter.

"Yes, quite a lot, sir," Jennings replied. "I'm not at all bad, really."

"That's for us to decide," said Mr. Carter, silencing the cry of "Swank" that went up on all sides. "And what about you, Darbishire?"

Darbishire had a profound distrust of ball games. His experience was somewhat limited as he had played football only once in his life, and what he chiefly remembered was that the ball travelled very fast and hurt when it hit you in the face and knocked your glasses off. This had happened early in the game, and he had removed his glasses for safety, with the result that his only other recollection was of being continually knocked off his feet by a seething mob who rushed around in pursuit of some apparently invisible object.

"I'm trying Jennings at centre-half," Mr. Carter was saying. "Where would you like to play, Darbishire?"

Positions on the field meant nothing in Darbishire's life and this seemed a silly question. Surely there was only one place?

"I'd like to play on that field behind the chapel, please, sir," he replied, "'cos it's next to the road, and I might be able to get some car numbers if they come close enough."

"What I mean is," explained Mr. Carter, "which position do you want to play in? Forward? Halfback or where?"

Darbishire understood at last. "I think I'd like to be wicket-keeper, sir," he said, surprising himself by his ready command of sporting terms. There was a howl of laughter from the rest of the group who echoed the remark at the tops of their voices for the benefit of those out of earshot on the fringe of the circle. But Mr. Carter kept a straight face.

"You'd better try outside-left, Darbishire," he said.

The bell rang for afternoon prep. It seemed a pity to have to waste the next forty minutes doing arithmetic, but the prospect of the game to follow gave Jennings sufficient strength to cope with the ordeal. He trooped off to his classroom and opened his books.

"Has anyone got my Arith. textbook?" demanded a certain Bromwich major, who occupied a place in the front row next to the master's desk. Nobody had, and Bromwich major bemoaned his fate.

"Oh, ozard egg!" he groaned. "Old Wilkie's taking prep and he'll blow up if I haven't got a book. Some ruinous oik's pinched it, I bet."

"You can have mine if you like, Bromo," said Jennings, "and I'll share with Darbishire."

"Coo, thanks," said Bromwich. "He'll never notice you two sharing at the back, but you must have a book if you sit where I do."

"Coming over by jet-propulsion," said Jennings. "Catch!"

Climbing steeply from a vertical take off, the airborne volume sped on its way to the front row. But the Bromwich control tower was late with the landing-signal, and the book sailed through his clutching fingers and crash-landed on top of an uncorked bottle of ink that was reposing on the master's desk.

The master's desk was close to the classroom door. One entered the room; one turned sharp left; and there one was. And there, now, the overturned ink-bottle was, with the ink flowing north and south over the desk, and gushing soddenly into tributaries and estuaries towards all the other points of the compass. Small lakes appeared at the lower contour levels, and shallow creeks to the north-west filled up as the work of irrigation spread.

"You clumsy goof," Bromwich shouted at his would-be benefactor, "you've spilt it all over the shop, and it's all down my exercise book, too. Gosh! There'll be a row about this; probably a number one priority hoo-hah; you see. Just you wait till Old Wilkie ..."

He stopped abruptly for the time of waiting had already passed. As though attacked from without by a battering ram, the door hurtled open and Mr. Wilkins was amongst those present. The door swung back on its hinges and crashed noisily into the corner of the master's desk, causing the overturned ink-bottle to roll gently over the top and come to rest in the middle of Bromwich major's exercise book.

Mr. Wilkins' rapid glance took in the situation; the pirouetting ink-bottle, and the door still vibrating under the force of the impact. All the evidence pointed to his meteoric entrance as being the cause of the deluge.

"Good Lord!" he said appalled. "Did I do that? Heavens, yes! I must have done. Very clumsy! Sorry; sorry. Get some blotting paper someone, quick, and wipe it up. Tut-tut, tut-tut. Stupid of me!" He tut-tutted like a typewriter rattling off a line of print. "All over your book too, eh, Bromwich?" he went on. "Oh, well, can't be helped; no good crying over spilt milk."

Darbishire's hand went up at once.

"And you can put your hand down, Darbishire," said Mr. Wilkins warmly. "I know just what you're going to say. Spilt 'ink,' not spilt 'milk.' Well, you needn't say it; I don't want to hear it. If I want to say milk I'll say milk, and I don't want anything about spilt ink from you, thanks very much."

"No, sir," said Darbishire humbly. "I was only going to say that there's a splodge of—er—milk on Bromwich major's nose, sir."

Mr. Wilkins emitted a sound like a mediæval fowling-piece being discharged at the Battle of Agincourt. "Cor-wumph," he barked.

The mess was mopped with blotting-paper and blackboard duster, Mr. Wilkins banning the use of off-white handkerchiefs that were freely offered and, in a highly explosive state of mind, he ordered work to begin.

Jennings was unable to concentrate on his arithmetic, as he was wondering whether he ought to confess that he was responsible for the spilt ink. He had not been asked to own up, of course, but that was merely due to Mr. Wilkins jumping so hastily to the wrong conclusion. Would it be kind to disillusion him? It was easy for masters when they did something frightful, such as upsetting ink; they said they were sorry and everyone rushed to mop up. No one called them "clumsy goofs," and prophesied frantic "hoo-hahs" to follow.

The most peaceful solution was obviously to let sleeping dogs lie, but Jennings' conscience kept throwing out a hint that it wasn't quite fair to let Mr. Wilkins reproach himself for imaginary bottle-tilting. On the other hand, if there was going to be a hoo-hah, Jennings decided that he would make a few guarded inquiries about the consequences. He put up his hand.

"Sir," he said, as Mr. Wilkins' raised eyebrow invited him to speak. "Sir, you know when you spilt the ink just now?"

"I do," said Mr. Wilkins coldly.

"Well, sir, s'posing you hadn't."

Mr. Wilkins raised the other eyebrow.

"No sense in supposing anything of the sort," he returned shortly. "If I spilt it, I spilt it; no point in making any bones about it. Get on with your prep."

"But, sir," persisted Jennings, "it's rather important. I know you thought you'd spilt it, and I know it looked as though you'd spilt it, but supposing you hadn't really spilt it after all, sir? What if it was just an optical illusion?"

Mr. Wilkins began to look explosive. Nothing ignited his fuses so quickly as the idea that a boy was trying to rag him, and he interpreted Jennings' quest for knowledge as a deliberate attempt to be funny.

"Are you trying to be facetious, boy?" he demanded.

"No, honestly, sir," Jennings answered, shocked that his motive was being questioned.

"Well, don't talk nonsense, then. I'm not blind; I've got eyes in my head. I can see ink when it spills; I don't see things that aren't there."

"Not as a rule, no, sir, but what if you were led astray by appearances, sir? What if it were someone else who'd spilt it and not you; would it be all right for the someone else to say 'sorry' like you did, or as he wasn't you, would there be a row, sir?"

Mr. Wilkins was sure by this time that the innocent Jennings was trying to be funny. The boys knew how easily Mr. Wilkins came to the boil and they frequently put this chemical experiment to the test in order to relieve the tedium of a dull prep. And Mr. Wilkins could not stand being ragged.

"I—I—I—you—you— That's quite enough from you, Jennings," he spluttered, the pinkish hue above his collar flashing a danger signal.

"No, but honestly, sir," Jennings persisted rashly; and then somebody laughed. It was this laugh, this open indication that a rag was on the schedule of operations, that touched off the fuse.

"Cor-wumph," he exploded, and this time it was as though Dumas' trio of musketeers had let fly with a fusillade of grapeshot from their blunderbusses.

"You can stay in during football," Jennings heard him say as the reverberations died away and the dust settled. "And now get on with your work; I don't want another sound out of you."

Jennings could hardly believe his ears; he had had no intention of being funny and he was not being punished for spilling the ink, for indeed he had not been given a chance to own up. Was it fair that truth should be muzzled, and his honest attempts to shed light on this ink-stained episode should meet with such a frightful fate? And he had been looking forward to playing football more than he could say. He returned to his sums with a rankling grievance against an unfriendly world.

"Books away, quietly," boomed Mr. Wilkins half an hour later. "Quietly!" he yelled in a voice of thunder as some unfortunate specimen in the front row let his desk lid fall with a bang. "Right. Down to the changing-room and get ready for football. All except Jennings, he stays here. Hurry up. No running in the corridors. Anyone not changed in five minutes doesn't play."

The form trooped out, scuffling sedately in their efforts to hurry without running. Jennings watched them unhappily; the thought of everyone, except him, enjoying themselves was too much; and the first game of the term, too! He had been going to show them how well he could play. He felt the tears welling up into his eyes as he turned his face away from the excited stream pouring out through the door.

Mr. Wilkins advanced to Jennings' desk and glared balefully at the top of Jennings' bowed head. He would show new boys what happened if they tried to take a rise out of him. If the little beast was feeling pleased with himself he could stay there until he was laughing on the other side of his face. And then the faint plop of a tear dropping in the ink-well suggested that the little beast was feeling anything but pleased with himself. Mr. Wilkins stared in surprise; perhaps he had been a bit harsh; perhaps … The truth was that Mr. Wilkins' fiery manner concealed a kind heart. He was aware of this, and deliberately tried to stifle it by assuming righteous indignation and sending his temperature up to boiling point to ward off attacks on the kindliness of his nature. Only by this means, he felt, could he assert his authority and prevent the boys from taking advantage of him; but the old stagers knew that though Mr. Wilkins' bark was brusque, his bite was largely bluff.

"What are you making that silly weeping noise for?" he demanded, steeling himself against the appeal for mercy that shone blearily through Jennings' tears.

"I don't know, sir," said Jennings damply.

"Suppose you want to be out playing football, eh?" Jennings nodded.

"Well, you've only got yourself to blame for that," said Mr. Wilkins. "You should have thought of that before you tried to be funny."

"But I wasn't trying to be funny," urged Jennings. "I was only trying to tell you that you didn't spill the ink."

"Oh! I didn't spill the ink, didn't I?" said Mr. Wilkins, switching on the current for his dangerous mood to warm up again. "I see; very funny. I didn't spill the ink, eh? Then since you know so much more about my actions than I do, do you mind telling me what I did do?"

"You didn't do anything, sir. You just came in and swung the door back."

"And I suppose the ink removed the cork from the bottle all by itself and then jumped out all over the desk?"

"No, sir."

"You surprise me. Who did spill it, then?"

"I did, sir."

Mr. Wilkins stared at Jennings searchingly; the boy didn't look as though he was trying to be funny; perhaps this was some subtle trick designed for Mr. Wilkins' humiliation and, if so, Mr. Wilkins wanted some more data before he struck. "Go on," he said dangerously.

Jennings told all; the loan of the book; its near miss in the target area and its unhappy forced landing some two feet farther on; Mr. Wilkins' cyclonic arrival and his error at jumping to hasty conclusions.

"And I was only going to tell you what really happened, sir, and you wouldn't let me and made me stay in," he finished, watching Mr. Wilkins covertly to see how he took this fresh interpretation of the facts.

Mr. Wilkins had been simmering gently during Jennings' recital; it was obvious that he was working up for something rather special. At last it came: with a bellow that could be heard by the boys in the changing-room below, he yelled aloud. Jennings shrank back in his desk to avoid damage by the blast, and then opened his eyes wide in amazement, for the bellow was not one of wrath, but one of mirth.

"Ha-ha-ha-ha!" roared Mr. Wilkins, and the vibration set the pen rattling on Jennings' desk. "Ho-ho-ho-ho! That's the funniest thing I ever ... Haw-haw-haw-haw!"

When Mr. Wilkins laughed the matter could never be hushed up; his sense of humour was simple and he let it rip. Indeed, a crack in the staff room ceiling was attributed, by Mr. Carter, to Mr. Wilkins' finding an unconsciously humorous sentence in a history essay that he had marked the previous term.

"Ha-ha-ha-ha!" The volume swelled like the diapason of an organ as Mr. Wilkins, his countenance now a deep purple, saw the funny side. At last he recovered.

"Well," he boomed, wiping tears of mirth from his cheeks. "And there I was calling myself everything for being clumsy, and you wanting to own up and I wouldn't let you. Go on," he continued, "get downstairs and get changed; you'll still have time if you hurry."

"But what about the punishment, sir?" asked Jennings. He was still feeling a trifle cowed, for Mr. Wilkins' humour was nearly as overpowering as Mr. Wilkins' anger.

"What d'you mean—punishment?" returned Mr. Wilkins. "There's no question of it, now I know you weren't trying to be funny on purpose."

"But for spilling the ink, sir."

"Oh!" said Mr. Wilkins. "I see. Well, supposing it really had been me who spilt it, what sort of a punishment do you think I ought to have had?"

Jennings considered.

"I should say you ought to be let off with a caution," he volunteered.

"All right," said Mr. Wilkins, "that suits me if it suits you; consider yourself cautioned; and now whip down to the changing-room before it's too late."

Jennings didn't need to be told twice. He shot out of the classroom and, unmindful of school rules, scampered along the corridors to the changing-room. As he ran, he practised imaginary shots at goal. Wham! A beautiful corner kick, he decided, as the imaginary ball swerved in mid-air and, eluding the imaginary goalkeeper's frenzied fingers, crashed with a resounding thud into the net. How the imaginary crowd cheered! "Good old Jennings!" they yelled, clapping him on the back. "One-nil." He smiled with becoming modesty at a fire-extinguisher on the wall and prepared for the next phase. He decided on a penalty kick and, increasing his speed to the maximum as he rounded the corner to the changing-room, he let fly with his foot, making perfect contact with the ball. The imaginary aspect of the kick ended with sudden abruptness as his foot made perfect contact with an object that was certainly not a football. It was the Headmaster, and he received the full force of the penalty kick just below the knee-cap.

"Ough!" said the Headmaster in unacademic tones.

Martin Winthrop Barlow Pemberton-Oakes, Esq., M.A. (Oxon), Headmaster, was not normally a devotee of the ballet but, on this occasion, he executed a number of *pas de chats* and *grands jetés* that would have done credit to a prima ballerina. When the pain had abated somewhat, he placed his injured leg gently back on the ground and looked down to ascertain the cause of the trouble.

"I'm terribly sorry, sir," said Jennings. "I didn't know you were coming round the corner."

"This is a school," began the Headmaster, "and not a bear garden. It has

56

rules for the benefit of people who wish to turn corners without being kicked on the knee-cap. If, therefore, I make a rule that no boy shall run in the corridors, I am at a loss to understand why my instructions are disregarded, and I find you running to the public danger and committing crimes of assault and battery."

"No, sir," said Jennings.

The Headmaster was not used to having odd remarks interpolated into his speeches.

"No, sir? What do you mean, 'No, sir?' Are you disagreeing with what I said?" he demanded in the iciest of head-magisterial tones.

"No, sir. I mean, no, I didn't suppose you could understand—er—what you said, sir. I was agreeing with you, really, sir."

"Kindly note, Jennings, that when I make a remark that is not a question, neither comment nor answer is required."

"Yes, sir—er—I mean—no comment," said Jennings hastily.

"You will return to your classroom, Jennings, and meditate upon the fate that awaits small boys who run in corridors. Why on earth you can't behave like a civilised human being is beyond me!"

Jennings was not sure whether this one required an answer, or was another of those "no comments." The Headmaster had certainly asked why, but Jennings decided that it might be rash to embark upon a lengthy explanation.

The teams had finished changing for games and were streaming out on to the field as Jennings returned to his classroom. He watched them gloomily from the window. This was the end; no football today and, if he went on like this, there probably wouldn't be any, ever.

He was still thinking bitter thoughts three minutes later when he saw the Headmaster standing in the doorway.

"Well, Jennings, have you meditated upon your misdeeds?" His knee-cap was hurting less now and he felt more inclined to be lenient to a new boy, who perhaps had not had enough time to become used to school life.

"Yes, sir," replied Jennings.

"In that case you may once more proceed to the changing-room, this time at a walking pace."

Jennings' first impulse was to say, "Coo, thanks, sir," but decided that it might be interpreted as a comment upon the Headmaster's judgment, so he said nothing.

"Well," said the Headmaster, "haven't you anything to say?"

"Yes, sir. Thanks very much, sir."

Masters were funny, Jennings thought, as he walked sedately to the changing-room. One minute they ticked you off for answering and the next they ticked you off because you didn't. Golly, but he would have to hurry if he wanted to play football; the game had started hours ago, and, if he wasn't there soon, he wouldn't be allowed to play.

There wasn't time to change properly and take everything off, so he removed his jacket and put his white sweater on instead. He wasted precious seconds trying to pull his football shorts over the trousers he was already wearing, but they were too tight, so he rolled up his trouser legs a couple of inches and pulled his voluminous white sweater down till it reached nearly to his knees and gave no sign of what he was wearing underneath. Socks were easier; the second pair went over the top of the first without much difficulty and he had only to put his football boots on and he would be ready. Gosh, it must be nearly half-time; everyone else had gone out ages ago!

Not quite everyone, though, for as he made a dive for his football boots, he saw Darbishire sitting on the floor in front of the boot-lockers.

"What on earth are you doing here, Darbi?" he demanded.

"It's these stupid boots," replied Darbishire. "My mother tied them together by the laces when she packed them, so's I wouldn't lose one without the other— not that I wanted to lose both"—he went on in case his meaning should not be quite clear— "but she thought there'd be more chance of neither getting lost if—"

Jennings cut short the explanation.

"Well, you haven't lost them, so why don't you put them on?"

"I can't undo the knot," said Darbishire sadly. "I've been tugging at it for about twenty minutes, and the harder I tug, the tighter the knot gets."

"Gosh! Yes, you have got it into a mess," agreed Jennings, inspecting the four lace ends tied inextricably together. "I shouldn't think anyone could undo that, now, but you'll just have to put them on and put up with it. There'll be an awful how-d'you-do if you don't turn up, and you don't want that, do you?"

"No, I don't want a 'how-d'you-do,'" said Darbishire, solemnly eyeing the laces. "What I really want is a 'how-d'you-undo.'"

Darbishire thought that his prowess as a footballer would be severely handicapped if he had to play with both feet tied together, but as this seemed preferable to the official wrath that his absenteeism would incur, he put on his boots and shuffled to the door. The tied laces permitted him to take a step of about ten inches and, assisted by Jennings, he proceeded in an ungainly shamble to the football field. They looked a queer pair, as Jennings' bulk was increased by his day clothes beneath his sweater, and as this capacious garment was pulled down almost to his knees, it appeared as though he had absentmindedly forgotten to wear any trousers.

Mr. Carter was taking the game and decided not to waste any more time in demanding explanations of their late arrival.

"I've put Brown at centre-half as you weren't here, Jennings," he said. "You'd better play—let me see—what are we short of?"

They were standing near the goal and the goalkeeper, one Paterson, immediately chipped in.

"Can I come out of goal, sir? I'm getting super cold standing about and Jennings has got a sweater and goalkeepers always wear sweaters, sir, it says so in the Laws of the game, honestly, sir, and as I haven't got a sweater, sir," he went on without pausing for breath, "I'm really breaking the rules, and Jennings ought to be jolly good in goal with a super sweater like that, oughtn't he, sir?"

As Paterson looked chilly, Mr. Carter despatched him to the forward line and sent Jennings to keep goal.

"And where did I say you were to play, Darbishire?" he asked.

"You said I was to be left out, sir," replied Darbishire.

"Left out of what?"

"I don't know out of what, sir; just left outside somewhere."

"Yes, I remember," said Mr. Carter, as light dawned. "Outside-left, not left outside."

The game was fast and furious and Mr. Carter was too busy to notice Darbishire's crippling progress to the left wing. It took him some time and much inquiry to get there, but finally he reached a spot near the touchline where he was out of the hurly-burly and there he stood, somewhat awkwardly, at ease.

Jennings' goal was hard pressed by the opposing forwards and after saving eight shots in four minutes—three good saves and five lucky ones—he began to feel uncomfortably warm, but to remedy his over-dressed condition would have been asking for trouble. He mopped his brow and saw that the opposing forwards were launching yet another attack. The ball came lolloping towards him—an easy shot to save—and he gathered it into his hands without difficulty, but before he could clear it to his forwards he was hemmed in on three sides by his determined opponents. What could he do?

Washbrooke major was winding up the whole of his six stone seven pounds for a tremendous barge which would have knocked Jennings and the ball far over the goal line. The goal-posts were not fitted with nets, so Jennings decided to retreat and, still clasping the ball, he stepped back over his own goal line, skipped nimbly round the post and punted the ball up the field. The whistle blew.

"Goal," said Mr. Carter.

"But, sir, it can't be," argued Jennings, "'cos I saved it; I caught it before it crossed the line."

"But you took it over the line when you dodged round the post," Mr. Carter explained.

"Oh, but that was just to get away from Washbrooke; I'd saved it hours before that."

Mr. Carter looked more closely at the perspiring goalkeeper.

"What are you wearing?" he demanded, and proceeded to investigate. "Vest, shirt, pullover, tie, underpants, braces, day trousers—with bulging pockets—boots, two pairs of socks and an outsize sweater," he reeled off. "Are you sure you wouldn't like your overcoat as well?"

Jennings' explanation was unavailing, and for the third time that afternoon he headed towards the changing-room as Mr. Carter restarted the game.

Darbishire rather liked playing outside-left. It was peaceful, he decided; the frantic battles of the midfield seemed remote, and it was unlikely that anyone would disturb the serene stillness by kicking the ball to this quiet backwater near the touch line.

There were some wild flowers growing on the bank a few yards away and he would have liked to wander off and pick them, but for the distressing handicap around his ankles. Never mind, he would pretend that he was a prisoner in a chain gang and was condemned to spend ten years with his feet securely ... The train of thought jolted to a sudden halt. The worst was about to happen; some ill-advised athlete had sent a pass out to the left wing and the ball was coming straight at Darbishire. Now what was it that one was supposed to do? Oh, yes, kick the ball; the direction didn't matter, the main thing being to boot the beastly thing as far away as possible and hope that it didn't come back.

"Go on, Darbishire," called his captain. "Kick!"

It would be stretching the facts to say that Darbishire kicked the ball, but the spirit was willing even though the flesh was weak and held together at the

60

ankles by boot-laces. He drew his right foot back the full ten inches that the latitude of his laces allowed and swung his boot forward as hard as he could. The impetus of the forward swing dragged the other foot with it; up into the air went both feet, and Darbishire fell flat on his back while the ball rolled harmlessly over the touchline.

The boys who assisted Darbishire to his feet were almost helpless with laughter.

"What happened, Darbishire?" they asked. "Did you have a stroke?"

"Oh, no, nothing so serious," Darbishire assured them. "It's merely a sort of temporary disability that I'm suffering from."

Mr. Carter took one look at the inextricable knots, and cut the temporary disability with his penknife. Two minutes later, as he blew his whistle to end the game, Jennings arrived, correctly changed and anxious for the fray.

CHAPTER 5

THE BELLS GO DOWN

"I DON'T think I shall ever get into the First Eleven," said Darbishire some days later; "not even if I tried ever so."

"Well, I'm jolly well going to try and get in," said Jennings. "I'm going to practise like anything, and I dare say if I go on getting better and better I shall play for England one day. Not for a few years yet, of course," he amended.

Jennings was certainly a promising player, though too erratic to be sure of a place in the Eleven, and he had felt a tinge of disappointment the previous Saturday when the team to play Bracebridge School had been posted and his name was not included. It was an "away" match, too, which was much more exciting as it involved a journey by motor coach, and the prospects of a large tea.

"You ought to take some interest in football, Darbishire, 'cos everyone'll think you're the most radio-active sissy if you don't."

"I know what, then," said Darbishire. "I'll be a sports reporter like they have in the newspapers, and I'll report the matches for the school magazine. Then everybody'll read my column and see what I've got to say, and I might even write some hints on how to improve your play like the Internationals do, and that'd make me spivish important in football circles, wouldn't it?"

"M'yes, so long as you only told people what to do and didn't try to give a demonstration."

The two boys were waiting for choir practice to begin. This consisted chiefly of practising sea-shanties for the end of term concert, and was a popular after-lunch event because Mr. Wilkins was in charge.

Mr. Wilkins did not teach music, as he was not considered sufficiently accomplished for so important an undertaking, but he could batter his way through "Shenandoah" and "A Drunken Sailor" on the piano, and the Headmaster considered that if Mr. Wilkins' voice was good for anything at all, it was good enough for sea-shanties.

Mr. Wilkins entered the Assembly Hall and marched towards the piano.

"Page forty-four, *Fire Down Below*," he announced in a voice which suggested that he was trying to broadcast to the nation without using a microphone. He struck a few chords tentatively.

"Ooh, sir!" winced Nuttall, who had a keen ear for harmony.

"What's the matter?" demanded Mr. Wilkins, pausing in mid-discord.

"Wrong note, sir. Right out of the target area, sir."

"Oh, I don't know," replied Mr. Wilkins. "It wasn't too bad for a near miss."

He pressed on. He did not claim to be a good pianist, and if at times he let not his right hand know what his left hand did, he got over this by drowning the piano altogether with his stentorian baritone.

The words and something vaguely resembling the tune of *Fire Down Below* were wafted by the breeze to the ears of Mr. Carter and the Headmaster as they crossed the quad.

"I've had another letter from Mr. Jennings," the Headmaster was saying. "Apparently he can't make much sense of the boy's weekly letter home, and he's still rather concerned to know how he's fitting in with school life."

The Headmaster prided himself on knowing everything about the boys in his care, and regretted that so far he had not had time to make a close examination of Jennings and his characteristics. All he knew was that the boy displayed a tendency to kick people on the knee-cap, and that was hardly sufficient evidence on which to form a judgment. Mr. Jennings' obvious concern seemed to indicate that his son was one of those delicate, highly-strung boys.

Mr. Carter did not agree; he thought Jennings was about as highly strung as a shrimping net and as delicate as a bulldozer.

"He's like a cork in the water," he explained, "you can push him under, but the next moment he's bobbing about on the top again."

The Headmaster decided to watch Jennings closely.

"What on earth is that extraordinary noise coming from the Assembly Hall, Carter?" he asked, as *Fire Down Below* started up again after a short break for resting the lungs.

They were just outside the windows by this time and they had to raise their voices to make themselves heard.

"It's Wilkins, sir. He's holding a choir practice."

"Speak up; I can't hear," said the Headmaster.

"Wilkins—choir practice," repeated Mr. Carter.

"Fire practice?" said the Headmaster in surprise. "But surely he doesn't imagine that singing *Fire Down Below* would be the slightest use in extinguishing a conflagration?"

"No, not 'fire' practice; 'choir' practice."

"Ah yes, of course. That reminds me," the Headmaster went on, his mind jumping from one topic to the other with the agility of a mountain goat, "we ought to have one this afternoon; we haven't had one for a long time."

Mr. Carter was a few moves behind in these mental gymnastics.

"But they're having one now, sir," he insisted. "I just told you; the choir are practising for the concert."

"No, no, no, Carter; I'm talking about 'fire' practice, not 'choir' practice; you mentioned it yourself. Now, when Wilkins has finished tuning the piano and making those extraordinary vocal contortions, we'll send the boys up to their dormitories and let them come down on the 'Pennetra' fire-escape."

The rules governing an outbreak of fire were prominently displayed in all dormitories, and practices were held at intervals. All boys stood quietly by their beds; a gong was sounded and when various formalities had been attended to, they would proceed down the main staircase in an orderly file.

The alternative was descent by the Escape. This consisted of a steel box screwed to the window frame and containing a roll of cable with a sling on the end. Placing the sling under the armpits, one lowered oneself into space from the window-sill, and descended gently to the ground as the life-line was automatically paid out from above. It was a very popular undertaking, but as a rule it was only used under the supervision of the masters.

"No," continued the Headmaster. "We'll go one better than that; we won't tell them to use the Escape. We'll just say that the staircase is impassable and let them use their initiative."

It was the Headmaster's custom to test the boys' intelligence and powers of leadership by making one of them responsible for discovering an imaginary fire and seeing how he reacted to the ensuing emergencies.

As soon as Mr. Wilkins had finished, the Headmaster strode into the Assembly Hall and addressed the school.

"Now that we've finished with *Fire Down Below*," he began, "we're going to start on 'fire up above.' Ha-ha-ha! Oh!"

Vacant expressions on seventy-nine faces indicated that his little joke had fallen flat, so he proceeded to explain.

"We are going to assume an outbreak of fire on the top landing outside Dormitory Four; now what is the first thing to do?"

Seventy-eight hands went up and the Headmaster noted that the absentee hand belonged to Jennings.

"Well Darbishire? Perhaps you can tell me."

"You use your intelligence, sir," said Darbishire, paraphrasing Fire Rule No. 1. "And if you can't think of anything intelligent, you call one of the masters and do what he says instead."

"M'yes," said the Headmaster, not knowing how to take this remark. "But supposing that no master is available?"

Again seventy-eight hands shot up, but Jennings was at Lord's, where he had just scored a century against the Australians in the most exciting Test match that had been seen for years.

The Headmaster decided that now would be the time to test the boy's initiative; he would put him in charge of the fire drill and see what happened.

"Let us assume," he continued, "that instead of being half-past two in the afternoon it is half-past two in the morning, and a boy in Dormitory Four—let us say Jennings, for example—awakens from sleep."

The mention of his name recalled Jennings from Lord's, where he had just put himself on to bowl at the pavilion end. He came to with a start.

"I beg your pardon, sir?" he said.

"I said, Jennings awakens from sleep," repeated the Headmaster; "but judging from your appearance while I have been speaking, I was beginning to think you had gone into a state of hibernation for the winter. I trust that is not so?"

"I don't know, sir," replied Jennings. "I don't know what hiber—what you said—means, sir."

"It applies to such creatures as toads, moles, bats and, apparently, to some small boys," explained the Headmaster; "derived from the Latin word *hiberna* meaning winter quarters, it means—well, think, boy, think."

Jennnings thought hard, but the atmosphere of Lords still hung about him.

"Well, Jennings, what does a bat do in the winter?"

"It—er—it splits if you don't oil it, sir," he said.

The Headmaster took the blow without flinching and explained the rules of the drill. Jennings, waking from slumber in the middle of the night, was to find a hypothetical fire; he was to assume that no master was at hand and, if his imagination stretched so far, that the stairs had fallen in. Could he cope with such a situation?

Jennings thought he could, but suggested that, if they had to assume the fire, and the fallen staircase was but a figment of the imagination, surely logic demanded that they could pretend to put on imaginary asbestos suits, or jump into a supposed sheet that they could pretend was being held below.

"Certainly not," said the Headmaster. "Having imagined the circumstances, everything else will be done exactly as though a conflagration had actually occurred. Exactly—do you understand? The rules for fire drill will be obeyed to the letter."

"Yes, sir, but supposing—"

"There will be no supposing. This is a test of your initiative, Jennings. I shall give you a few minutes to look over the rules and think out your plan of action; after that, you will sound the gong and I shall await the result with interest."

As soon as they were in the dormitory, Jennings took charge.

"Now, all put your pyjamas on," he said; "we're supposed to be hibernating to start with, and when you wake up the room's full of smoke."

"Coo, yes," agreed Darbishire. "And I vote we soak our towels in the wash basins and tie them over our noses and crawl round and round the floor where the air's purer."

"Coo, yes, spiv on," said Atkinson. "We could pretend we're looking for the way out, but the smoke's so thick, we keep crawling past the door without seeing it."

The list of fire drill instructions was discovered rammed in the keyhole of the door. Venables explained that a "super-hairy" breeze whistled through the keyhole and, sleeping where he did, a bung was necessary to exclude the draught.

"Get it out, then," said Jennings. "We'll have to see what to do."

"I know one thing it says," put in Temple, as Venables attacked the keyhole with his penknife, "we have to close all doors and windows; something to do with the draught."

"That's crackers," returned Jennings. "How can we get out if all the doors are closed, and who's going to worry about being in a draught, anyway, if the place is on fire?"

This led to a brief argument. One school of thought contended that doors and windows should be opened, while the rival philosophy held that doors should be opened to allow the exit of all personnel, while windows should be closed to prevent the fire from going out.

"But we want the fire to go out, don't we?" said Darbishire.

"Not out of the windows, we don't," replied Jennings. "No, I think it's open doors to make the flames burn up nice and bright, so's the firemen can see where the fire is."

The argument was ended by Venables producing the screwed-up copy of the rules from the keyhole.

"It says here," he announced, "that first of all we've got to use our initiative."

"I'd much rather use the staircase," said Jennings. "Here, let's have a look." And, taking the paper from Venables, he read out: "*Any boy discovering an outbreak of fire at night will sound the alarm gong and inform Mr. Carter, who will telephone for the fire brigade.*"

"Yes, but the Head said we were to do it without Mr. Carter?" objected Darbishire. "What's it say about that?"

"*If no master is available,*" continued Jennings, "*boys must use* ... Something. I can't read it."

"Staircase?" suggested Darbishire.

"No, 'initiative,' that's it. *Boys will keep calm and*— Blah, blah, blah." He skipped the next few paragraphs as they looked dull. "And there's a bit at the end that says the boy finding the fire will be Wally."

"Wally?" echoed Temple. "But that's crazy; we haven't got anyone called Wally."

"That's what it says, anyway."

Temple snatched the paper from Jennings and read: "*The boy who discovers the fire will be* ... Oh, you are a fool, Jennings, that's not 'Wally,' that's 'wholly.' You're to be wholly concerned with seeing that everyone—"

"Well, let's get cracking, anyway," said Jennings. "You chaps put your pyjamas on and start opening and closing all the doors and windows."

Darbishire was allowed to go out on to the landing with Jennings as "*assistant gong-biffer,*" and there he proceeded to warn his friend how careful one had to be with fire, as witness the minor calamity that had befallen the Darbishire household last holidays.

"My father was making a piece of toast on the gas stove in the kitchen," he recounted in dramatic tones, "and suddenly it caught alight, and before he knew where he was, there was a mighty 'swoosh' and—"

"Why didn't he know where he was?" demanded Jennings.

"He did. He was making a piece of toast in the kitchen."

"But you said it went 'swoosh' before he knew where he was," objected Jennings. "And if he was in the kitchen all the time, he must have known, unless he was suffering from loss of memory."

"Oh, don't be such a hairy ruin," said Darbishire. "Hadn't we better get this fire started?"

Jennings gave the matter some thought. Everything had to be done as though the fire were real, and not merely a Headmaster's whimsical notion of the best way to spend a half-holiday.

In an actual outbreak, Mr. Carter would telephone for the fire brigade, but one of the hazards of the exercise was that Jennings' own initiative must take the place of help from a grown-up source. Surely, then, the Headmaster expected him to summon the necessary assistance; that was what he must have meant when he had demolished the staircase with a wave of his hand; obviously a turntable ladder alone could save them from an inflammable fate. Probably the Headmaster had already warned the fire brigade and they were even now standing by with engines ticking over, waiting for the call to action. He must not fail in this test of initiative.

But Darbishire was appalled at so bold a plan.

"Couldn't you just pretend?" he suggested.

"Huh! You heard what he said when I suggested pretending to wear asbestos suits," Jennings scathed back at him. "I bet the first thing he says is, 'Have you given the jolly old hose squirters a tinkle on the blower?'"

"He doesn't talk like that," objected Darbishire. "And s'posing he hasn't—the firemen'll be ever so cross; s'posing they're just going to have their tea and s'posing it's something wizard—like baked beans on toast—it'd be all spoilt by the time they got back."

"How d'you know they have baked beans for tea at fire stations?"

"I don't, only—"

"Well, then, that proves it," said Jennings conclusively. "The trouble with you, Darbishire, is you've got no inish. Besides, how else can we get out if we can't go down the stairs?"

The logic of this argument swayed Darbishire. Neither he nor Jennings thought of the Escape. Never having used it, they vaguely imagined that the metal contraption on the window-sill was for ornamental purposes, or at best, some labour-saving device connected with polishing the linoleum. The other members of the dormitory had been instructed in the correct use of the apparatus in the past and might have guessed the Headmaster's intention, but they, alas, remained in ignorance of Jennings' plan of campaign.

Darbishire held the gong steady and Jennings beat it with gusto. While the echoes were still resounding throughout the building, windows opened in the dormitories; life lines whirred into action and an orderly evacuation began in all dormitories except one; for in No. 4 on the top storey, the boys, swathed

in damp towels, were crawling round and round the floor on their hands and knees according to instructions.

Jennings sped along to Mr. Carter's room. Fortunately this was on the top floor, so the difficulty of bridging the gulf left by the disappearing staircase did not arise. He tapped on the door; no answer. The room, as expected, was empty.

Jennings made for the telephone on the desk. What should he say? Well, he'd just ask them if they'd mind sending the turntable ladder as the stairs had fallen in and there were some people to be rescued on the top floor.

The clock on Mr. Carter's desk stood at ten minutes to three as Jennings lifted the receiver from its rest.

"Fire station, please," he said importantly.

Dunhambury Fire Station was situated in the centre of the town some five miles from Linbury Court. It was normally a smart and efficient station, particularly when Leading Fireman Cuppling was on duty. To him it was a matter of pride that branch-pipes glistened and stand-pipes shone; that hose was rolled with geometrical neatness, and that mechanical equipment went like clockwork.

Judge then, of the leading fireman's horror and dismay when at half-past two he went to inspect the appliance to which he had been assigned for the rest of the day. The board on which the crews and available appliances were marked had given no hint of the rude shock that awaited him. "Turntable ladder," read the board. "In charge: Leading Fireman Cuppling. Crew: Fireman Long and Fireman Short."

And the turntable, when the leading fireman reached it, was not upholding the traditions for spick-and-span smartness on which the station prided itself.

"Well, darn my socks!" he murmured, recoiling in distaste from the monstrosity before him. Tarnished brass, dirty wet hose, green slime on the suction-basket and mud on wings and windscreen met his astonished gaze. Never had he seen such an untidy vehicle. The crew's helmets and boots lay inextricably tangled amongst a welter of hose ramps, breeching-pieces and petrol cans, and the casual observer might have thought that the turntable had just finished coping with an outbreak of fire in a rubbish dump.

But this was not so. Life in the neighbourhood of Dunhambury was so devoid of excitement, that nothing but the spontaneous combustion of a haystack, or the accidental firing of a soot-filled chimney, ever disturbed the orderly routine of the fire station. And haystacks and chimneys were beneath the dignity of the turntable ladder. It was a magnificent appliance and, in the expert hands of Leading Fireman Cuppling, the hundred-foot ladder would rear up towards the sky, shooting forward and sideways, with the controlled ease of a sea-serpent stretching its flexible neck.

The pity of it was that such an intricate piece of machinery should be used only for rescuing stray cats from the church roof and cleaning the top storey windows at the fire station; but the type of fire needed to show off its paces was rare in that rural Sussex countryside.

Leading Fireman Cuppling blinked in dismay at the unkempt appearance of his pride and joy, and his expression was grim as he went in search of his crew.

Fireman Long and Fireman Short were admirable and intrepid fire-fighters, but they had a habit of retiring to some out of the way spot when the more unpleasant routine jobs had to be attended to.

Cuppling ran them to earth in the fire-tower where, comfortably seated on a pile of hose, they were mechanically stroking a stand-pipe with a polishing cloth in the intervals of filling in their football coupons.

"Oh, hallo, Archie. Come to give us a hand?"

Fireman Long, better known as Lofty, greeted his superior with a heartiness that was meant to disarm suspicion, while Fireman Short tactfully concealed the coupons in his cap.

"Not so much of the 'Archie,'" returned the Leading Fireman in official tones. "It's Leading Fireman Cuppling to you when I'm on duty, and don't you forget it. And what do you two think you're doing, hiding yourselves away like this?"

"Hiding?" echoed Fireman Long in pained accents. "Tut-tut, as though we would! Shorty and me are doing a bit of brass polishing. Got this stand-pipe up nice and bright, haven't we?"

"It doesn't take two of you to clean one stand-pipe."

"Oh, yes, it does," Lofty assured him. "You see, Shorty breathes on it while I give it the old howd'you-do with the cloth. Go on, Shorty," he added to his friend. "Get breathing."

Fireman Short obeyed by exhaling stertorously.

"Hurr-hurr-hurr." He emptied his lungs and paused for breath.

"Saves wasting brass polish, see?" explained Lofty.

"That's not funny," said Archie Cuppling. "And I seem to remember that's the same stand-pipe you were cleaning yesterday."

"That's right, Archie—er—Leading Fireman Cuppling, I mean," replied

Lofty. "Yesterday it was my turn to breathe while Shorty polished, see? So now it's only fair to ..."

The Leading Fireman cut short this plausible explanation and demanded to know why the turntable ladder was so dirty and untidy. He had been out all morning testing hydrants, but Long and Short had been posted to the turntable all day and could be held responsible for its condition.

The story was soon told. Early that morning they had been instructed to take the appliance to the river to test the pump and the hose. The river was tidal at Dunhambury, and as the tide was low, they had had to drive on to the mud flats in order to get near the water. There the worst had happened; the wheels had stuck in the mud, and in their efforts to release them, they had plastered themselves, and everything with which they had come in contact, with the fertile silt of the river Dun. A heavy shower of rain had not improved matters, but eventually the machine was freed; the pump was tested, the hose was found to withstand the required pressure per square inch, and Lofty and Shorty had returned to restore their jaded tissues with cups of tea and cheese sandwiches.

"But darn my socks!" expostulated the Leading Fireman when the recital was finished. "All this happened this morning. It's twenty to three and you haven't done a thing about cleaning it. You'd no business to have knocked off for dinner till you'd squared everything up. Come on, we're going to start work."

"Work?" echoed Fireman Short faintly. "What, only us three? You ought to have four men on a turntable, you know."

"Well, you can do the work of two," was all the sympathy he got from his Leading Fireman, who then proceeded to outline his plans for a pleasant Wednesday afternoon. "We'll have every piece of equipment stripped off and cleaned, and all that wet hose scrubbed and replaced." He glowed with enthusiasm for the job on hand and, bursting with vitality, led the way to the appliance with his fingers itching to get to work.

Lofty and Shorty followed at a more dignified pace.

"Pity he's rumbled us," said Lofty. "Nice and warm in the tower it was, too."

"Ah! What about our football pools?" put in Shorty. "If we lose fifty thousand quid whose fault will it be? Leading Fireman Cuppling's, that's whose, if Bolton Wanderers beat Charlton, which they've got a good chance of, and we miss the post on account of changing the hose an' all."

"Come on," shouted the Leading Fireman. "You don't get paid good money to hang about nattering all day. Everything off, now," he ordered; "branches, nozzles, stand-pipes, suction, breeching-pieces, wrenches—all of it."

Metallic clangs and dull thuds, accompanied by gruntings and blowings, announced that the crew were battling with the equipment.

Archie Cuppling set the pace and worked like a dynamo, which reminded Lofty that it was time he had a look at the carburettor. He was a good mechanic and felt that, when the work on fire stations became more than usually unpleasant, it was the privilege of all good mechanics to retire from the hurly-burly and devote themselves to some quiet and contemplative task such as inspecting plugs and testing leads. It was a fool-proof way of avoiding the miseries of hose scrubbing, for no one could deny the importance of a well-tuned engine. But today the ruse was unsuccessful.

"Come on out of it," called Cuppling, prodding him ever so gently from behind with a ceiling hook. "You can mess about under the bonnet when we've got all this hose scrubbed."

The good mechanic's feelings were outraged.

"Now, look here, Archie," he said, "be reasonable. If I've got to drive this perishing bus, I've got a right to check the engine."

"I've heard that one before," replied his superior, struggling to carry a thirty-foot ladder unaided. "As soon as there's any heavy work going you lie flat on your back and make out you've got to polish the exhaust pipe." With a super-human effort he heaved the ladder on to the *Self-Propelled*, and sped back to the turntable.

"But the jet's choked in the carburettor," Lofty complained. "We kept stalling all the way up from the river. If I don't get it cleaned, we'll be up a gum tree if we have to turn out to a job."

This was true; the carburettor had given trouble that morning, but Fireman Long had cried "Wolf" so often that Archie Cuppling took no notice and, in spite of his protests, Lofty was ordered to assist with the work of unloading.

By now the floor in the vicinity of the turntable was piled high with equipment, and Archie ordered all the dirty hose to be taken out into the yard.

"Cor! Blow me!" grumbled Shorty. "We aren't 'arf 'aving a spring clean! What'll I do with our boots; there's no room for 'em here?"

"Take them over there by the *Self-Propelled*," came the answer. "We'll have them washed before we put them back."

Shorty ambled across the room and dumped his load next to some dozen pairs of wellington boots which belonged to the other crews. A thought struck him.

"Here," he said, "hadn't you better tell the control-room as this turntable ladder isn't available? S'pose we got a fire call?"

It was then that Leading Fireman Cuppling made his big mistake.

"Don't you worry about that," he said. "The turntable hasn't been sent to a fire for three years, so I don't think that having the kit off for a quarter of an hour is going to be much of a risk." And with demoniacal energy that made Fireman Short feel quite faint, he picked up three lengths of wet hose and trotted briskly into the yard.

Soon the appliance had been stripped of all its equipment. Leading Fireman Cuppling, bubbling over with zest and vitality, made short work of the fertile silt of the river Dun, while sounds of splashings from the yard outside announced that Firemen Long and Short, having run out the dirty hose, were busily engaged in scrubbing it. *Busily engaged?* That, perhaps, is an exaggeration; but they were sluicing water in all directions, in the time-honoured belief that what was wet, was clean.

At nine minutes to three precisely, the bells "went down." With a clanging that woke the echoes for acres around, the alarm bells shrilled out their urgent message in tones to rouse the dead.

Fireman Long paused in the act of rolling a cigarette.

"Fire-call," he said, stating the obvious.

"We shan't be wanted, anyway," said Fireman Short, resting heavily on the handle of his broom.

It was taken for granted at Dunhambury that the turntable ladder would never be needed at local fires, and that the crew enjoyed a holiday from fire-fighting so long as they were posted to this particular vehicle; therefore, they did not hurry, but watched with a leisurely interest as firemen came running from all quarters at the summons of the alarm. Bodies slid down poles, heads popped up through trap-doors, and everywhere legs were running, feet were jumping into boots, and arms waved themselves into tunics.

The other appliances were manned and had their engines running when Lofty and Shorty sauntered into the appliance room. A second later an agonised figure shot out of the control room. It was Leading Fireman Archie Cuppling, and his face was contorted by every emotion from alarm to despondency.

"Turntable ladder!" he shouted, as he raced down the station. "Quick! Quick! It's a turn-out!"

The news was incredible, but the message he bore in his hand confirmed these strange tidings. "*Linbury Court School,*" it said. "*Persons believed trapped third floor. T.L. required for rescue.*"

"We can't turn out to no fire with our kit all over the shop like a blinking jumble sale," gasped Shorty. "What are we going to do?"

"Bung it all back again, quick," yelled his Leading Fireman. "Hurry up! Hurry up! Come on, you fellows, give us a hand," he called to the other crews who were now emerging from their appliances and de-booting themselves. "And get the engine started Lofty, quick. Oh, darn my socks!" he groaned to himself as the alarm bell ceased ringing. "We've wasted a minute already!"

A slow turn-out to a fire call is the most serious of crimes, and Archie Cuppling alternately boiled with rage and froze with shame at his own lack of foresight, as he led the work of piling on the equipment.

"Faster! Faster!" he encouraged them. "Chuck it on anywhere for now; we'll sort it out when we get there. But, for goodness' sake, get a move on!"

The entire station personnel hurried as they had never hurried before. They ran pell-mell with stand-pipes; they ran helter-skelter with branch holders; they ran full tilt with petrol cans, and they ran posthaste with the suction hose. But Leading Fireman Cuppling eclipsed them all in the ferocity of his attack upon the job in hand. He pell-melled; he helter-skeltered; he full-tilted, and he post-hastened until, some two minutes later, most of the apparatus was aboard.

Lofty was in the driver's seat with his hand on the self-starter, but the engine refused to co-operate.

"She won't have it," he shouted to no one in particular. "It's that there choked carburettor."

"What's that?" shouted Archie above the clatter of tinkling brass.

"She won't start."

"Of course she will. Here, you fellows, give us a push!"

The other crews rallied round to push the heavy vehicle on to the slope in front of the fire station.

"'Ere, wait for me," gasped Shorty. "I'm supposed to be riding on this 'ere bus."

"Have you got everything now?" a fireman called out, as Shorty's flying leap landed him on the running board.

"Hope so," returned Archie. "We'll have to risk it, anyway; we're about four minutes late getting away. Oh, darn my socks; there'll be a row about this! Okay, boys, give her a shove!"

"'Ere, 'arf a mo," put in Shorty.

"We can't wait any 'arf mo's," replied Archie.

"But we ain't got no boots."

"What?"

"You told me to take them all orf and we—"

"All right. Here, stop!" he yelled, as the volunteers began the launching ceremony. "Nip off quick, Shorty; you know where you put them."

Panting hard, Fireman Short reached the wellington boots stacked by the *Self-Propelled*. The neat line had been upset by someone in his efforts to hasten the loading, and the boots were all jumbled up.

"Never mind sorting them out," called Cuppling. "Take the first three pairs and sling them up. Oh, get a move on for Pete's sake!" he cried in agony, "it's five minutes since the bells went down."

Shorty seized an armful of boots and climbed aboard. On the slope outside the engine started, somewhat uncertainly, and with the bell ringing furiously, they back-fired their way down the High Street at a jerky 15 m.p.h. with the accelerator pressed hard down.

It had taken them six minutes to get out. What would the Column Officer say? Archie blushed beneath his perspiration at the thought of it. And then the more serious side occurred to him. "*Persons believed trapped on top floor.*" Heavens! And with the engine misbehaving itself like this they could only make a shaky fifteen miles an hour and there were five miles to be covered!

For three years Leading Fireman Cuppling had looked forward to a job of this kind. He had visualised a perfect turn out in less than thirty seconds; a 75 m.p.h. dash through the streets; the rescue effected in less time than it takes to tell, with the turntable responding perfectly to his expert touch. And now what a ghastly mess-up it all was! He would probably lose his stripe over it at least, and what if ... Cold beads of sweat broke out on his forehead at the thought of the trapped persons anxiously awaiting his arrival.

"Oh, heavens!" he groaned as they rattled past the church and he noted that the clock pointed to one minute past three. "Can't you step on it a bit more, Lofty?"

But Lofty was doing his best, and Archie could only fume and rage, and curse his own misplaced zeal. It was a good thing for his blood pressure that he didn't know that the fire call was a false alarm.

CHAPTER 6

THE INDIAN ROPE TRICK

THE HEADMASTER surveyed the rows of boys lined up before him on the quad.

"Mr. Carter," he said, "haven't you finished taking that roll call yet?"

"They're all present, sir, except Dormitory Four," replied Mr. Carter. "I can't think what's happened to them."

The Headmaster glanced at his watch.

"Tut-tut! Three o'clock. It must be ten minutes since the gong sounded. What on earth can they be doing?"

Accompanied by Mr. Carter and Mr. Wilkins, he had watched the other dormitories descending on their escapes in an orderly manner. Everything had gone according to plan, except for the unexplained absence of Dormitory Four.

"You'd better go and see what the matter is, Carter," he said.

Quickly Mr. Carter ran up the stairs and found Jennings standing alone at the top.

"Oh, sir, you can't come up these stairs, sir," Jennings began, "'cos they've fallen in and there's a big hole where you're standing and—"

Mr. Carter cut him short.

"What have you been doing all this time?" he demanded. "You ought all to be outside."

"Well, sir, I went to your room like the Instructions said and as you weren't there I did what you would have done if you had been there; only you weren't, 'cos the Head said you wouldn't be, sir."

"And what would I have done had I been there?"

"'Phoned for the fire brigade, sir."

It took a few seconds for the full meaning of this to register on Mr. Carter's brain.

"In the case of an actual outbreak, of course I should," he began, and then broke off as a horrible thought flashed into his mind. "What!" he gasped.

"Jennings, you don't mean you—what exactly have you done, Jennings?"

"Only what the Head said, sir, about using our imagination and all that."

"Oh, imagination!" repeated Mr. Carter in relieved tones. "Phew! Thank goodness for that! You gave me quite a turn, Jennings." He felt better now that the horrible thought had turned out to be Jennings' make-believe.

"For the moment I really thought you had 'phoned for the fire brigade. I was just thinking if you really had—ha-ha-ha!" Mr. Carter laughed at the fantastic absurdity of such a situation.

"I really have 'phoned them, sir. They ought to be here any minute now."

"Ha-ha-h—! Whirp!" The laugh was strangled in Mr. Carter's throat. A prickly feeling of dismay attacked him in every pore of his skin as the terrible truth spread through his mind.

"Jennings," he said, "you—you silly little boy! Tell me exactly what's happened—quickly."

Jennings told him. With infinite pride he described how he had deduced the Headmaster's intentions; the fallen staircase, the missing master, the smoke-filled building; all had added up neatly and pointed to the turntable ladder as being the only satisfactory solution.

"Oh, my goodness!" said Mr. Carter. "Well that has put the cat among the pigeons."

"Haven't I done right, sir?"

"Right? We shall all be prosecuted. False alarm with malicious intent!"

Jennings stopped feeling pleased as Mr. Carter delivered himself of a few well-chosen words on the subject of summoning fire brigades when there was nothing for them to do. The fact that Jennings had acted in good faith would not carry much weight when the facts came to light. Jennings felt worse when Mr. Carter explained what the Headmaster had really meant. Of course, how silly of him, he had never thought of using the Escape!

Mr. Carter groaned in spirit. There was nothing he could do now. It was ten minutes since the silly little boy had sent his message for help and any minute now the clanging of bells would announce the arrival of a crew bursting with eagerness to combat the non-existent flames. Mr. Carter could imagine their comments when they were informed that the solid oak staircase on which they were standing didn't exist any more! The Headmaster, too, would take the most serious view of the way in which his orders had been interpreted. The only ray of hope lay in the fact that it was seven minutes past three and there was no sign of the brigade's arrival. Was it possible that they had decided to take no action on the instructions of so youthful a voice on the telephone? It was doubtful, but like a drowning man Mr. Carter clutched at this straw of hope—a straw so slender that it would not have broken the back of the weariest of camels.

Jennings by now realised the enormity of his offence.

"Oh, gosh!" he said miserably. "And I was only trying to use my initiative. How was I to know the Head didn't mean what he said? Will there be an awful row, sir?"

"If they come there'll be a row," said Mr. Carter. "A most unholy one."

This was too awful to think about so, like Mr. Carter, he seized upon his ray of hope.

"Perhaps they won't come, sir," he said, "'cos Darbishire says they have baked beans on toast at fire stations, and it has to be a super-important fire before they'll let it get cold—the baked beans I mean, not the fire; and Darbishire ought to know sir, 'cos his father's had a lot of experience with fires, when he's been making toast and that sort of thing, sir."

"If they're not here in a minute or two," said Mr. Carter, "there's a chance they won't come." But there was no conviction in his tone.

The Headmaster was a patient man, but he could not wait all day. It was some minutes now since Mr. Carter had gone to investigate the mystery of the missing dormitory, and still nothing had happened. At the expense of a slightly ruffled dignity, the Headmaster ran up the stairs and almost collided with Mr. Carter on the first landing.

"Oh, there you are, sir," said Mr. Carter. "I'm afraid there's been a rather unfortunate misunderstanding, and briefly what's happened is—"

"We haven't time for explanations now, Carter," broke in the Headmaster. "I'm determined to put that dormitory through its escape drill, and it'll be dark before we've finished, at this rate. Go down and take charge on the quad and send Wilkins to me, will you?"

"Yes, but the circumstances are rather exceptional," Mr. Carter began again, but found he was addressing the empty air, for the Headmaster had pursued his upward flight towards the top storey, and his expression implied that he was in no mood to stand any nonsense.

Mr. Carter shrugged his shoulders. At any moment the blow might fall, but there was nothing anyone could do about it—not even the Headmaster; whereas if the summoned assistance failed to arrive, there was no point in making a song and dance about the telephone message. Not, at any rate, while the Head was in such a testy mood. Later on, all could be explained, if not forgiven and forgotten.

Martin Winthrop Barlow Pemberton-Oakes, M.A., Headmaster, flung wide the door of Dormitory No. 4 and stood rooted to the threshold by the sight that met his eyes. Instead of preparing for an orderly evacuation, Temple, Venables, Atkinson and Darbishire, wearing pyjamas over their suits, were crawling round the floor on their stomachs. Their faces were swathed in dripping towels, which left a damp snail's trail behind them as they crawled. Jennings was staring anxiously out of the window with the expression of a prophet foretelling the future, and not liking the look of it.

The Headmaster's face fell like a barometer. Dark rain clouds appeared on the horizon of his countenance, accompanied by a drop in the temperature. A deep depression was approaching; thunderstorms seemed imminent, and the future outlook was anything but settled.

"What on earth are you boys crawling about like that for?"

Like veiled women of the East, the four crawlers arose. Darbishire removed his yashmak.

"Please, sir," he said, "the smoke's not so thick if you keep your nose on the floor, and you can breathe."

"Breathe? Smoke? What are you talking about, and why are you wearing your pyjamas?"

"You said it was the middle of the night, sir," replied Venables.

"It was my fault, sir," said Jennings. "You said pretend it was a real fire and I thought you meant do everything properly, sir, like sending a message to—well, you see, sir, I'm most terribly sorry, but what actually happened was—"

How on earth could he soften the blow? The expression on the Headmaster's face made it almost impossible for him to proceed at all.

"Well, sir, it's like this, if you see what I mean," he stumbled on, "or rather the point is—"

"The point is, Jennings, that you've behaved in a muddle-headed and irresponsible manner," the Headmaster broke in, giving Jennings no opportunity to confess to the crime which he had unwittingly committed. "When I sent you up here, Jennings, what do you suppose I meant you to use?"

"Our initiatives, sir," replied Jennings.

"Yes, yes, of course; but what else?"

"The 'Pennetra' Fire Escape, sir; Mr. Carter just told me."

"Exactly," said the Headmaster. "The whole lot of you are completely unreliable, and I think an extra hour's preparation this evening may help you to think a little more clearly in future."

The burning topic of the fire brigade was still uppermost in Jennings' mind and he made another attempt to explain matters.

"I'm terribly sorry, sir," he said, "and if they do turn up, sir, it won't really be mal-malpractice with intent like Mr. Carter said, 'cos I really thought you meant me to; and as they haven't come already, perhaps they won't now, will they, sir?"

As a lucid explanation, there was something lacking in this statement, and having lost so much time already, the Headmaster was in no mood to listen to what he imagined was a rambling apology. Jennings was silenced.

The door burst open with hurricane force and Mr. Wilkins approached noisily.

"Mr. Carter said you wanted me, sir?"

"Ah, yes, Mr. Wilkins. These boys have no idea how to behave at fire drill. Will you kindly explain the working of the Escape to them." And the Headmaster swept out to inspect the other dormitories and to satisfy himself that the great evacuation had left no untidiness in its wake.

For two and a half miles the turntable ladder crawled fitfully along at an uneasy 15 m.p.h., while Archie Cuppling relieved his feelings by ringing the bell continuously and with a savage ferocity. But once out of the town, Lofty put in a complaint.

"You don't have to go on clanging like that on an empty road," he said. "Won't make the old bus go any faster."

"I wish something would," groaned Cuppling. "It's quarter of an hour now since we got the 'phone call; ought to have been there ages ago, and got the ladder up by this time. Darn my socks, there won't half be a row about it!" he moaned for the twentieth time.

They were going uphill now, and the speedometer needle dropped back to eight miles per hour.

"She won't take it," said Lofty. "She's conking."

"She's got to take it," Cuppling growled between clenched teeth. He rocked backwards and forwards in his seat in the hope, presumably, that the momentum of his body would give the wheels that extra bit of impetus needed to reach the top of the slope; but it takes an infinite amount of wishful thinking to urge several tons of machinery up a hill when every one of its fifty-seven horse-power is protesting. The speed dropped to a crawl; the engine gasped, coughed apologetically, and was silent.

Lofty jumped down, hurled open the bonnet and got to work on the carburettor while Archie wrung his hands in despair.

"It'll take me a few minutes," said Lofty, busily wielding a spanner.

"Cor! And another two and a half miles to go yet," groaned his Leading Fireman. "Hurry up for heaven's sake!"

Shorty piped up from behind.

"Let this be a lesson to you," he said. "It don't do to be too efficient. You stick to brass cleaning another time."

"That's enough from you, Fireman Short." Archie had no wish to listen to a lecture on his misdirected enthusiasm. "There's no point in us sitting here like a couple of spare puddings. Come on, we'll be getting our boots on; that'll save a bit of time when we get there."

Fireman Short rummaged amongst the heap of wellingtons and made a suitable selection for his left foot. Then he rummaged again and an air of bewilderment spread across his features.

"That's funny," he said. "I can't find any right boots nowhere; this here boot's a left-footed 'un; so's this 'un; so's this. Well, blow me, if I haven't brought six left boots and no right 'uns!"

Leading Fireman Cuppling groaned inwardly. What had he done to deserve this? What would become of his reputation? He who prided himself on the slickness of his turn-outs and the unruffled efficiency of his firemanship!

"It was you rushing me like that at the last minute," Shorty was saying. "There was about twenty boots, see, all mixed up and you said grab the first six and—"

"All right! All right! You don't have to make a speech about it," the Leading Fireman snapped irritably. "We'll just have to put up with it and wear two left boots. Oh, heavens, it's twelve minutes past three already! We shan't be there before half-past at this rate. Get a move on, Lofty, for Pete's sake; you don't have to take the whole engine to bits, do you?"

"All very well for you to start moaning now, Leading Fireman Archibald Cuppling," said Lofty bitterly. "If you'd let me get on with cleaning the engine instead of mucking about with wet hose, we shouldn't be stuck where we are now." And Lofty attacked the carburettor ferociously with a screwdriver.

Heaving and straining, Shorty forced an unwilling left boot on to his right foot. It was a size too small and it pinched painfully.

"Cor!" he grumbled. "It don't 'arf give me chilblains the works! I don't want

82

to be what you'd call critical, Leading Fireman," he went on, "but shan't we look a bit daft turning up at a fire all wearing left-'anded gum boots?"

"It'll be something if we get there at all," replied Archie miserably. "When I think of that burning building and those people shouting for help"—Archie's voice throbbed with bitter emotion— "and us still stuck here when we ought to have had the ladder up and the hose run out hours ago ...."

"Well, blow me!" interjaculated Shorty. "I just thought of something."

"What is it?"

"We ain't brought no 'ose."

"What???"

"S'right; we got all the dirty 'ose out in the yard, see, and what with all that carry on of loading the bus up, I clean forgot to get some more out of the store."

The Leading Fireman shuddered like a shock-absorber under the impact of this new blow, and the faint hope that perhaps someone else had remembered the clean hose was shattered when, with trembling fingers, he flung open the hose lockers. They were as empty as the vessels which make the most sound.

What, Archie asked himself, was the use of having a dozen men to pile on equipment if everyone left the most important item to his neighbour? The delightful proverb of many hands making light work had given place to its terrible sequel of the broth-spoiling cooks. Archie Cuppling was not given to melodrama; he did not tear his hair or beat his breast; neither did he rend his garments. It is doubtful whether he even gave his teeth more than a half-hearted gnash, but he felt justified in asking Fate a question as he stood dejected and left-booted on the roadside.

"Why should this have to happen to me?" he wanted to know.

When Dormitory Four had shed their slumber-wear, Mr. Wilkins began to expound.

"Now the way this—ah—the way this thing works is extremely simple," he began. "This round metal thing is a container. It contains a coil of cable. And protruding through this aperture here—"

"What, sir?" asked Temple.

"Sticking out of this hole," amended the lecturer, "is a strap, or sling, which goes underneath your armpits. And this—er—gadget here is an adjustable—er—adjuster which you move up and down if you want to adjust it. In other words ..." He sought in vain for the correct technical term. "In other words, it's adjustable."

"What's it just able to do, sir?" inquired Venables innocently.

"I didn't say it was just able to do anything."

"Well, what's the good of it, then, sir, if it doesn't do anything?"

"It does do something," said Mr. Wilkins irritably. "You sling it along the slide, or rather you slide it along the sling to tighten the strap across your chest so that you don't—er—slide out of the sling."

Mr. Wilkins felt he wasn't explaining it very well. However, he pressed on to stage two.

"Now this second sling and coil of cable," he said, "must be slung out of the window before you start, so while you're going down, this other one is coming up ready for the next person, and while he's coming down your sling's going up again." He paused again. It was more than obvious from the blank expressions on all faces that his audience was not with him.

"Is that quite clear?" he asked, knowing it wasn't, but hoping they wouldn't say so.

Venables, Atkinson and Temple knew perfectly well what Mr. Wilkins meant as they had been through it all before, but they held their peace.

"But where are you, sir?" asked Darbishire.

"Me? I'm here," replied Mr. Wilkins. "I'm going to watch you do it."

"No, not you, sir; me, sir, or whoever it is who gets slung out on the first sling. I mean, when the sling comes up again, doesn't he come up with it?"

"Of course not," said Mr. Wilkins. He tried hard to remember the official instructions in the handbook.

"When the—er—the escapee has completed his descent," he quoted, "he disengages the clasp governing the fastenings of the harness and remains on terra firma."

"You mean he slides out of the sling," said Darbishire, summing it up neatly.

Mr. Wilkins decided to cancel the remainder of his lecture in favour of a demonstration, so the harness was put round Darbishire's chest and made fast with the adjuster. Mr. Wilkins opened the window and threw out the second cable while Darbishire climbed uncertainly on to the window-sill. It looked an uncomfortably long way down to the ground, but if everyone else could do it, he was sure he could. There was just one point, however, on which he wanted reassurance.

"Sir," he said, "what happens if the rope breaks?"

"That's all right, Darbishire," said Temple unfeelingly; "we can easily get another rope."

"It can't break," said Mr. Wilkins; "it's a metal cable."

The rest of the dormitory crowded round to speed his departure with words of comfort.

"I say, Darbishire," said Venables cheerfully, "just supposing we don't see you again, could I have your four-bladed penknife?" And he smiled like an undertaker who scents a likely client.

"Don't be such a ruin," said Darbishire. "I shall be all right. My father says—"

"Off you go, then, Darbishire," said Mr. Wilkins. "You go down quite slowly. Get into a kneeling position with your feet behind you and push yourself gently away from the wall as you go down."

"Why, sir?" asked Darbishire, suspecting some new trap for the unwary.

"You've got to keep clear of the ivy that's growing up the wall; you don't want to get caught up on that, do you?"

"Hadn't I better just make a famous last speech, sir, like John of Gaunt and Sidney Carton, and all that lot?" said Darbishire, savouring the dramatic possibilities of the situation.

"Are you going to get out of that window or aren't you?" demanded Mr. Wilkins impatiently.

"Oh, yes, sir. I was only going to—well, goodbye, chaps," said Darbishire hurriedly, catching sight of Mr. Wilkins' expression. "This is a far, far better thing I do than I have ever done." Kneeling on thin air he launched out into space and disappeared slowly from sight as the Escape whirred into action.

"It is a far, far better place I go to than I have ever known." His famous last speech became fainter and finally faded out altogether.

Unfortunately, Darbishire forgot to push himself gently from the wall and keep his legs in a kneeling position, with the result that some five seconds later his feet touched down unexpectedly on the window-sill of the room immediately below his dormitory. He was wondering whether the sill would make a suitable runway for a fresh take off, when a thought flashed into his mind and, releasing the clasp that secured him to the sling, he climbed in through the open window of Dormitory Two.

"It was lucky I thought of it in time," he told himself. If this drill was to be a dress rehearsal for the real thing, no detail should be left incomplete, and, in the excitement of the moment, he had left his four-bladed penknife, with cork-screw, behind in his dormitory. He would never have left that to be lost in the flames, so it was jolly lucky he had remembered it while there was still time to go back. Leaving the cable hanging outside the window, he climbed into the empty dormitory and started to make his way back to his own room.

Mr. Wilkins was somewhat surprised when the whirr of the Escape stopped abruptly some five seconds after Darbishire's departure. He had just been saying how easy it all was, and was prophesying a happy landing for Darbishire some quarter of a minute after being airborne. Something had gone wrong with the estimated time of arrival and, distinctly puzzled, Mr. Wilkins put his head out of the window for a quick reconnaissance. A strangled cry of amazement rattled its way through his vocal cords.

"Glip!" he gulped. There, swinging gently in the breeze some fifteen feet below, was the sling which should have contained a boy, but the boy had vanished.

Mr. Wilkins looked down, but Darbishire was not on the ground below; Mr. Wilkins looked sideways and even upwards, though this was hardly necessary.

"I—I—I— What—what—what— I don't understand .... It's not possible .... It just can't be."

The rest of the boys gathered round the window with suitable queries on their faces, but none could explain the mystery.

"Perhaps it's a new version of the Indian rope trick," vouchsafed Jennings; "only instead of going up a rope, Darbishire's invented a way of doing it backwards."

The door opened and the Headmaster appeared. He had finished inspecting the other dormitories, and had missed Darbishire's dramatic entry through the window below, by a few seconds.

"What's the matter, Mr. Wilkins?" he asked. "Is anything wrong?"

"I'm glad you've come, sir," replied Mr. Wilkins. "I'm seeing things, or rather I'm not seeing things; not the things I ought to be seeing, if you see what I mean."

The Headmaster didn't, and Mr. Wilkins endeavoured to explain, but so much was wholly inexplicable, and his manner was so agitated, that the Headmaster refused to believe him.

"Disappeared, Mr. Wilkins?" he said. "Nonsense; he can't have." And striding to the window he, too, looked down upon an empty sling.

"Good heavens!" he said. "Are you quite sure you put him in the sling to start with?"

Mr. Wilkins called upon the remainder of the dormitory as witnesses.

"But it's unheard of," said the Headmaster. "The cable's all right; the sling's all right; it's uncanny; it's ..."

The dormitory door opened and Darbishire walked in.

It is difficult to describe the emotions aroused by his dramatic entrance. Shakespeare might have done it with a flourish of trumpets, and hautboys without, but the printed word can hardly do justice to the stupefied reaction of Messrs. Pemberton-Oakes, Wilkins and party.

The Headmaster was the first to recover the power of speech.

"Where have you been, Darbishire?" he demanded.

Darbishire couldn't think why everyone was staring at him in so marked a fashion.

"Nowhere, sir," he said.

His audience were almost ready to believe that nowhere was the right answer, and that Darbishire had been spirited away by fairy hands to some non-existent locality, but the Headmaster prosaically demanded details.

"Nowhere special, I mean, sir," said Darbishire. "You see, I was coming down on the Escape and approaching Dorm Two window, sir, and suddenly, before I knew where I was, I'd ..." He stopped. What a good job he had remembered the penknife in time; the Headmaster would be ever so pleased with this conscientious regard for detail.

"Go on," prompted the Headmaster. "Before you knew where you were—?"

"Oh, I did know where I was, really, sir, like my father did when he was making toast in the kitchen that time."

The Headmaster failed to understand why Darbishire's father making toast in the kitchen should have any bearing on his son's mysterious disappearance. Darbishire explained, but he was doomed to disappointment if he thought that salvage operations for four-bladed penknives would be accepted as a good reason for returning to a burning building.

"You came back?" said the Headmaster incredulously.

"Yes, sir."

The Headmaster turned on his irony.

"What an intellect!" he murmured. "What a masterly grasp of the correct procedure to be followed when evacuating a burning building. You came back! I congratulate you!"

Darbishire smiled modestly and was about to express his thanks in a few well-chosen words, but a glance at the Headmaster's expression showed him that the time was not ripe. He made a hurried alteration in the programme and cancelled the vote of thanks.

"Would it be placing too great a strain on your intelligence, Darbishire," the Headmaster continued, "to ask you to consider why returning to this dormitory after you had already left it, was a stupid mistake?"

Darbishire thought. Surely you weren't expected to leave four-bladed pen-knives behind to be consumed by the nearest flame? It must be something else he had done.

"Oh, yes, I know, sir," he said brightly. "I came back up the stairs that weren't there. Yes, that was rather silly of me. Oh, but, sir, you must have come up those stairs, too, sir, so either I did right or we both made stu—er—we both committed errors of judgment, sir."

"You can be exasperatingly stupid at times, Darbishire. The cardinal error you committed was to come back to a supposedly burning building. 'Life before property' is the motto of all good firemen."

"Oh, gosh!" said Jennings suddenly. "I'd forgotten the firemen." By twisting his head until it was nearly upside down, he could see the time by Mr. Wilkins' wrist-watch. It was twenty-one minutes past three.

"Well, that settles it," he said to himself. "They won't be coming now."

Jennings spoke too soon. On a lonely stretch of road some two and a half miles away, Fireman Long was putting the finishing touches to his handiwork. The carburettor had not been in a co-operative mood, and it had taken him longer than he had anticipated. This delay had done nothing to improve Leading Fireman Cuppling's frame of mind. He stared up and down the road in the hope of seeing a car whose aid he could summon. By this means he, at least, could get to the scene of the fire and see what was happening, and leave the turntable ladder to follow when it was ready. Unfortunately, it was a lonely stretch of road and no traffic had passed during the anxious minutes of the breakdown. Archie knew, too, that there was no telephone for two miles in either direction, so he was unable to send a message for assistance to the fire station. They were stranded; the situation was hopeless. All they could do was to wait until Lofty's skill had changed the engine from an inert mass of metal to a high-powered machine.

Archie had decided not to go back for the hose; after all, the rescue was the most important job to be tackled, and the ladder at any rate, was in working order.

It was twenty-two minutes past three when Lofty leaped back into the driver's seat and pressed the starter.

"She's okay now," he said. The engine leaped to life and, in his skilful hands, the speedometer needle crept up, fifty, sixty, seventy miles per hour. Archie rang the bell as though his life depended on it; as it happened other lives did, for farm hands and stray cows had only just time to hurl themselves to safety in the hedge as the turntable ladder flashed past. But whatever their speed now, nothing could make up for earlier delays. It would be three twenty-five before they got to Linbury; thirty-four minutes to answer a five-mile call. Horrors!

Fireman Long's eye was glued to the road and his hands were glued to the steering-wheel, but his tongue was by no means glued to his mouth.

"You haven't half done it this time, Leading Fireman Cuppling, Esq.," he yelled, and his voice was scarcely audible above the clanging of the bell. "You haven't half boxed it all up nicely. Getting to a fire half an hour late, at fifteen blinking miles an hour, with no hose and all wearing left-footed boots. I wouldn't be in your shoes when we get back."

"I wouldn't mind whose shoes I was in," said Shorty, clinging to the ladder for dear life, "so long as they wasn't these 'ere left 'anded gum boots. Cor! They 'aren't 'arf letting me chilblains know about it."

On they thundered, ready and eager to get to grips with the fire which, after all this time, must be a raging inferno, and worthy of the attention of the most intrepid of fire-fighters. How one got to grips with such a situation when one had no hose was, of course, a debatable point, but Archie's determination was such that he felt ready to beat out the flames with his bare hands, if such a course could restore his lost prestige. Seventy-three, seventy-four, seventy-five miles per hour read the speedometer, as they streaked through the countryside on their life-saving pilgrimage.

CHAPTER 7

SUSPENSE AND SUSPENSION

"MR. WILKINS," said the Headmaster when he had finished rebuking Darbishire, "these boys seem to have no idea of what is expected of them in an emergency. Will you kindly demonstrate the correct method of descending by the Escape."

"Certainly, sir," said Mr. Wilkins. Rapidly he hauled in the cable, fastened himself into the sling, and leapt on to the window-sill.

"Now watch me carefully, you boys," boomed the demonstrator, "and you'll see how easy it is." They crowded round the window and Mr. Wilkins disappeared from view with his commentary still running.

"Now I want you to observe how I push myself ..." The running commentary suddenly ceased. So did the whirr of the Escape as, for the second time, an unrehearsed incident enlivened the proceedings.

"Gosh, it's stopped again!" said Temple.

"What's happened?" asked Darbishire, from the rear of the group.

"Stand back, you boys," said the Headmaster, thrusting them aside and leaning out of the window.

An unfortunate occurrence had marred what would otherwise have been a perfect demonstration. Mr. Wilkins, directing the stream of his commentary to the window above his head, had omitted to push himself gently away from the wall, and the strap across his chest had caught on a thick branch of ivy. To his chagrin, he found himself suspended in midair. Mr. Wilkins struggled to free himself, but his efforts bore no fruit. The weight of his body kept the cable taut and, without a foothold, he was unable to slacken the tension and unhook himself; the branch of ivy was strong and showed no tendency to break. It was an uncomfortable, though not a dangerous, situation, and certainly not one to assist the dignity of the expert demonstrator.

"What's happened, Mr. Wilkins?" inquired the Headmaster, somewhat unnecessarily.

Snatches of semi-audible comment and a muffled "Cor-wumph" drifted up to the group in the dormitory above.

"It's no good," called Mr. Wilkins, after further battle with the ivy. "The sling's caught tight, and I can't get any leverage on the branch to break it."

Headmasters are admirable in crises. Action, prompt and immediate, was the watch-word of M. W. B. Pemberton-Oakes, Esq. He seized on the nearest boy, who happened to be Jennings, and gave his orders in a crisp and concise manner.

"Quick," he said. "Run and find Robinson and tell him to bring a ladder. Explain that Mr. Wilkins is suspended, like the sword of Damocles, on an obstinate tendril of ivy."

"Suspended on a what, like whose sword, sir?" inquired Jennings.

"Never mind what," said the Headmaster. "Just tell him to bring his longest ladder, and be quick about it. Explain that Mr. Wilkins is caught up sixty feet above ground level."

Jennings rushed off in quest of old Pyjams, while the Headmaster satisfied himself that Mr. Wilkins was in no immediate danger.

"You're sure you can't release yourself?" he called.

A disgruntled "Cor-wumph" from below implied that, if Mr. Wilkins had been able to release himself, he would have done so, and that he was not dangling sixty feet above the ground purely for his own selfish pleasure.

"Rotten luck, isn't it, sir?" said Atkinson.

"Most unfortunate," agreed the Headmaster. "I shall certainly get Robinson to cut all this ivy down, first thing tomorrow."

"What's that you said?" called Mr. Wilkins from below.

The Headmaster raised his voice.

"I was saying I shall have the ivy cut down tomorrow."

"Tomorrow?" echoed Mr. Wilkins. "But, bless me, I can't stay here all night!"

The Headmaster leaned further out of the window and issued a communiqué to the effect that Operation Rescue would receive priority treatment, and steps were even now being taken to ensure a satisfactory solution to the problem. After that, they tried to pull Mr. Wilkins up; they heaved and gasped and strained, but the odds were against them, for not only did Mr. Wilkins weigh thirteen stone, but also the branch of ivy was holding the sling in such a way that pulling on the cable merely tightened its grip.

Soon Jennings returned with the disquieting news that old Pyjams—he begged sir's pardon, he meant Robinson—could not help. The longest ladder on the premises was only thirty feet and would not reach anywhere near the top floor. Furthermore, Robinson begged to state that he had never heard of the sword of whoever it was, and doubted whether it would be much use, anyway.

"Most annoying," exclaimed the Headmaster. "We ought to have a sixty-foot ladder on the premises. I shall certainly order one the next time I go to London."

From below, Mr. Wilkins demanded to be kept abreast of the latest developments.

"What did you say, then?" he called.

"I said I'm going to order a ladder the next time I go to London."

"Yes, but good heavens—I mean, dash it, sir—I can't go on hanging here all that time!"

"This is an intolerable situation," said the Headmaster. He could not leave Mr. Wilkins to cool his heels indefinitely. Ah, he had it!

"I shall telephone the fire station immediately," he said, "and request them to send a long ladder, without delay."

It is said that opportunity knocks once at the door of every man. Jennings heard the knock and answered it.

"Please, sir," he said; "I've done that already."

"You've telephoned for the fire brigade?" said the Headmaster, in surprise.

"Yes, sir; you see, I was trying to use my initiative and I thought—"

"Thank you, Jennings. I congratulate you. Your action was perhaps a little unorthodox, but with Mr. Wilkins in his precarious position I'm inclined to agree that there was no time to be lost."

The Headmaster looked at Jennings with a new interest. He had misjudged him. How many other boys, he wondered, on hearing that Robinson's ladder was too short, would have had the initiative to rush forthwith to the telephone and call for assistance.

Jennings felt he ought to explain that the telephone call was due to his stupidity; that he had made it half an hour before, and that the fire brigade weren't coming, anyway. But, basking in the glory of the Headmaster's congratulations, he decided that this was not the moment to start shattering anyone's illusions.

"Let me see," said the Headmaster, consulting his watch. "H'm. Let us say that it is three, or perhaps four, minutes since you telephoned; they have roughly five miles to come, so that even if they started at once, we can hardly expect them to be here for another ..." He broke off abruptly as the distant clanging of a fire bell caught his ear. It was not often that Martin Winthrop Barlow

Pemberton-Oakes, Headmaster, betrayed his feelings, but now his eyes opened wide in bewilderment. There could be no doubt of it, the clanging was louder now. In two strides the Headmaster reached the window and was just in time to see a fire engine swing round the corner and come tearing up the drive.

"Well, I—bless my—words fail me," he said, and hurried out to direct operations from below.

What an amazingly efficient brigade, he thought, as he took the non-existent stairs two at a time. They must have left the fire station a split second after receiving the call, and streaked along the roads like a flash of lightning.

The turntable ladder skidded round the bend of the drive on two wheels and pulled up outside the main entrance with a screeching of brakes.

"Can't see any fire," said Lofty. "I reckon it's got tired of waiting for us and burnt itself out. What do you think, Shorty?"

"I don't think," replied Fireman Short. "I'm that uncomfortable with me right foot stuck in this left-'anded boot, it's made me so numb I can't think."

The Headmaster was approaching at a brisk pace. Archie leapt smartly to meet him.

"Turntable ladder; Leading Fireman Cuppling in charge," he said.

He was surprised at the warm welcome expressed in the Headmaster's answering smile. He had been expecting a fusillade of complaints; a volley of criticism; a broadside of angry protestation at the unforgivable delay: in short, anything but a smile.

"Excellent, excellent," beamed the Headmaster. "You have been quick! We sent for you because one of our assistant masters is in a state of suspension just round here." And he led him round the corner and pointed upwards to where Mr. Wilkins appeared to be flowering amongst the ivy.

"Is that all, sir?" inquired the Leading Fireman.

"It's enough, isn't it?" replied the Headmaster.

"I mean, no fire or anything like that?" persisted Archie.

"No, no fire; nothing like that."

It seemed too good to be true; surely there was a catch in it somewhere. But there was no catch, and in a matter of seconds the turntable was in position.

"Get to work!" shouted Archie. In his skilful hands the ladder responded like some prehistoric monster roused from sleep. Strong legs unwound themselves and planted feet of steel firmly on the ground to take the strain of the monster's weight; the ladder rose from the gantry as though the beast were lifting its head and stretching its serpentine neck.

Lofty was on the tiny platform at the head of the ladder, and he shot rapidly skywards as Archie accelerated, and the creature's growl became a whine. By this time the entire school had congregated on the quad. With bated breath and eyes agog, they watched the monstrous neck spanning the space between the ground and Mr. Wilkins' rapidly cooling heels, as Archie's deft fingers on the controls worked miracles of extension and elevation. Gently, the neck craned forward and came to rest alongside Mr. Wilkins.

With his feet solidly on the ladder, it was the work of a moment for Mr. Wilkins, assisted by Lofty, to free himself from the sling, and a minute later both men were safely on the ground.

A buzz of excited chatter broke the tension as soon as the rescue was completed. Breath was 'unbated' and eyes were 'ungogged' as everywhere the conversation turned upon the topic of the moment.

"Super-duper, smashing priority prang, wasn't it?" said Brown major.

"Yes, hefty spivish," agreed Thompson minor.

"Hairy famous, too," added Rumbelow. "And wizard decent of old Wilkie to get stuck specially so's we could see him rescued."

"I wish I'd thought of it when I was coming down," put in Darbishire. "It'd be prangish rare to come down on the turntable. Why do masters have all the luck?"

Mr. Wilkins felt that he had received enough notoriety for one afternoon and would have preferred to have made an unobtrusive exit, but he was unable to evade the admiring throng that crowded round him.

"You are lucky, sir! Was it nice up there, sir?"

"Sir, did you mean to get stuck so's we could see how the fire brigade worked, sir?"

"Sir, are you going to do it again, because you didn't really finish coming down on the sling, sir."

"Perhaps you didn't bend your knees and push the wall hard enough, sir."

"Sir, if you push the wall too hard you might get into a tail spin, mightn't you, sir?"

"All right, all right. Be quiet," said Mr. Wilkins, and turning to Leading Fireman Cuppling, he rendered suitable thanks for his deliverance.

"That's all right, sir," said Archie. "I'm sorry you had to stay up there so long."

Mr. Wilkins assured him that the inconvenience had been trifling, and that he was none the worse for it.

They must be tough, these schoolmasters, Archie decided. Stranded for over half an hour on the end of the cable was certainly no joke, and this chap seemed as fit and hearty as though he'd been up there only a few minutes.

Now that the rescue was over, Archie had time to think. So far they had had a lucky escape; as there was no fire to extinguish, the question of the forgotten hose did not arise, but the unheard of delay of thirty-five minutes in answering the call could not be so easily forgotten. He decided to find out how serious a view the Headmaster was taking.

"Excuse me, sir," he said hesitantly. "I suppose there's no chance of your overlooking what time we arrived, is there?"

"There certainly isn't," replied the Headmaster genially.

"You mean you're going to report it to the fire station?"

"Most definitely," replied the Headmaster.

Archie's spirits dropped. Of course, no one could be expected to overlook such an interminable delay. There would be an official inquiry. He would have to write endless reports and he would be certain to find himself charged with neglect of duty …. He forced his attention back to the Headmaster and listened with growing amazement to his words. What on earth was the chap talking about?

"… and I shall certainly write to your Commanding Officer," he was saying, "and tell him how impressed I was by the speed of your arrival. Why, you must have left the fire station in a flash and swept through the town like a rocket."

Archie rocked slightly on his heels and gripped the turntable for support.

"Well, darn my socks!" he muttered.

"And your gallant crew as well," proceeded the Headmaster, indicating Firemen Long and Short with a sweep of the hand. "I shall certainly mention the verve and aplomb with which they carried out the rescue."

"What's that he's saying?" whispered Shorty.

"He says we rescued the bloke with verve and aplomb."

"No, we never," said Shorty. "We used the turntable. I reckon we must have left the verve and what he said, behind with the 'ose."

A look of concern passed over the Headmaster's features as his eye rested on Fireman Short.

"You appear to be limping," he said. "I do trust you haven't injured yourself in effecting the rescue."

"That's all right, guv'nor," replied Shorty. "It's only these 'ere left gum boots."

Leading Fireman Cuppling felt it was time to go before more questions were asked. He did not understand why their unfortunate chapter of accidents should be regarded as a triumphant achievement, but if ever there was a time for letting sleeping dogs lie, this was it. He muttered something about his chief's concern at their being away so long.

The Headmaster laughed heartily at this pleasantry and delivered an apt quotation from the classics to prove that their phenomenal speed must surely be due to their borrowing the winged shoes of Mercury.

"If these 'ere left-'anded gum boots belong to Mercury," grumbled Shorty, "he can keep 'em." And he climbed aboard and massaged his right foot.

Just as they were about to start, Jennings asked the Headmaster whether he might put a question to the Leading Fireman.

"Certainly," smiled the Headmaster. "What is it? Some mechanical intricacy of the turntable which has set your mind wondering?"

"No, sir," replied Jennings. "I want to ask him why all firemen have to have two left feet. Of course, it must be super for playing outside left, but how would you keep in step when you were doing P.T.?"

"Don't be frivolous, Jennings," replied the Headmaster as Archie blushed a delicate pink and looked uncomfortable. "Now, if you had some sensible question to ask, about the 'Pennetra' Escape, for instance, I'm sure the Leading Fireman knows a lot about Escapes, isn't that so, Leading Fireman?"

"Yes, sir," replied Archie meaningly. "And I think I've just had a very lucky one."

Lofty let in the clutch and the appliance disappeared round the bend of the drive.

The school was despatched from the quad and the boys dispersed to busy themselves with various occupations designed, in the words of the Headmaster, to develop their creative faculties. Some tinkered with bits of wire and cats' whiskers, as home-made wireless sets took shape; others strove with chisels and balsa wood to produce models of Spanish galleons, and others again hacked with blunt knives at odd strips of leather and produced shapeless objects that defied description. The last were usually designed as Christmas presents for fond aunts, who used them to wedge windows in draughty Tudor cottages.

The thrilling rescue of Mr. Wilkins was still the main topic of conversation and would be for days, but Darbishire was worried about a matter of pressing importance and went in search of Jennings to ask his advice. He found Jennings kneading an unwilling piece of damp clay. The finished product was going to be either an ashtray for his father or a china nest egg for a poultry-keeping godmother—depending on which article his handiwork most resembled when it was finished.

"What are you looking so worried about, Darbishire?" he asked.

"It's about my Cake List," said Darbishire. "I've been making a Cake List ever since the beginning of term, of all the people I've promised a bit of cake to when my grandmother's parcel came." He produced, for Jennings' inspection, a large and crumpled sheet of paper headed Cake List in block capitals. There were some forty names, nearly all of which had been crossed out and filled in again two or three times.

"It's like this," he explained. "When a chap's been smashing decent to me, I put his name on my Cake List, and then, if he incurs my serious displeasure after that, I cross him off again."

It had sounded simple enough when Darbishire had worked it out, but in practice snags arose which he had not foreseen. For instance, Temple had been placed on the List for lending Darbishire a piece of blotting paper, but when on the following day he had called Darbishire a "radio-active suet pudding," he was informed that his name had been expunged from the roll. Temple's answer to this was that unless he was re-admitted to the ranks of the chosen, Darbishire would be bashed up forthwith. Might conquered right, and Temple was reinstated, and his policy was immediately adopted by everyone else. Those who were on the List threatened reprisals if they were crossed off, and those who were not included in the first place, hinted darkly at what would happen if their names were not added.

"So you see the mess up it all is," ended Darbishire sadly. "I started off thinking it was a wizard wheeze to reward virtue and keep everyone friendly, but now I've had to put all sorts of bogus oiks on the List, just to protect myself."

Jennings agreed that this was unfortunate, but could not see why Darbishire regarded the matter with such anxiety.

"Well," said Darbishire, "my grandmother's cake came this morning, and I'm going to take it in to tea today, and if you come and have a look at it, you'll jolly well see how urgent it is."

Jennings left his masterpiece of clay, and together they went down to the tuck-box room.

"There," said Darbishire, throwing back the lid of his tuck box. "You see what I mean, don't you?"

Jennings saw. Possibly, Darbishire's grandmother had intended the small sponge cake for her grandson alone. Certainly, she had not reckoned on sup-plying forty clamouring Cake List claimants. The cake measured barely six inches in diameter and was about an inch thick.

"How on earth is that going round forty people?" demanded Darbishire. "Mind you, I'm very grateful, but you would think grandmothers had more sense, wouldn't you?"

"Why not cross some of the names off the List, then," suggested Jennings.

Darbishire sighed. Most of the boys were bigger than he was, and to cross names off at random was asking for trouble. He frowned hard at the List.

"You can cross off Perry and Alsop and Binns minor, and Plackett," said Jennings. "They won't kick up much of a fuss because they're smaller than you are."

"Yes, I know," replied Darbishire; "but I put those four on because they were decent, and not because of what they said they'd do if I didn't."

Darbishire battled hard with his conscience; it seemed unfair to cross chaps off just because they were mild and inoffensive and leave others on for fear of offending them.

"No," he said resolutely, "those four are going to stay and four others can come off." He closed his eyes and made four random strokes across the List with a pencil. It was not a success the first time, for the words he crossed out included Jennings, Cake List, Venables, and the date. But at last he had reduced the roll to a round three dozen.

"Now what?" he demanded.

Jennings had an idea. Both the boys had started to learn geometry, and here was a chance to put their knowledge to the test.

"There are three hundred and sixty degrees in a circle," he announced. He knew this because he had had to write it out twenty-five times for Mr. Wilkins.

"All right, then, if there are thirty-six people on the Cake List, they can have ten degrees each."

"Gosh! Yes, of course," said Darbishire, impressed.

They rushed off to their classroom and returned with protractor, ruler and compass. The discovery had shattered the popular belief that mathematics was of no practical value. With the protractor laid centrally across the cake, they pricked tiny holes with the point of the compass at ten-degree intervals round the circumference.

Ten-degree portions of cake looked somewhat inadequate when the meas-uring up process was finished, and seemed to bear little resemblance to the theoretical calculations.

"Well, anyway," said Jennings as the tea bell sounded, "there'll be a titchy hunk all round, so no one'll have any reason to grumble."

Darbishire bore his cake proudly to the dining hall, while Jennings carried the geometrical instruments in case of dispute.

"Of course, it's all very well to work it out on paper," said Darbishire, when the first course was finished, "but somehow I don't think those ten-degree hunks are going to work." As he wielded the knife, he was conscious of the eyes of thirty-six shareholders awaiting their dividend.

"You see, we didn't allow for the thickness of the knife, and all these crumbs."

"It just proves what I've always said," remarked Jennings. "Geom. and Maths. and stuff, only works out in exercise books. It goes to pieces completely the moment you try to make it do something sensible."

"It couldn't go to pieces any more than this cake is," said Darbishire. "Look, Jen, these hunks are coming out all wrong. It strikes me we've either got to cut the beastly cake into four decent sized pieces or thirty-six large crumbs." He sliced it into four quarters and sighed at the impossible task which lay ahead. It would take a precision instrument of the utmost delicacy to cut each of the resulting slices into nine wafers.

"I tell you what," said Jennings. "I'll take it up to Matron and see if she can cut it up small like you want it."

He seized the plate with the four slices and trotted up to the top table where Matron was standing in earnest conversation with Mr. Carter. But before Jennings got there, the door opened and the Headmaster entered and joined the two adults by the top table. Thereupon, all three embarked upon a lengthy discussion on the uninteresting subject of whether Parslow major should be punished for losing his football socks, or whether Mrs. Parslow was the real criminal for sending her son to school without having sewn his name on the offending articles.

Jennings hung about diffidently on the edge of the discussion group hoping to catch Matron's eye, but he was unsuccessful. Eventually, the Headmaster turned round and saw Jennings at his elbow, holding a plate containing four slices of sponge cake of medium size.

"Oh," he said. "Is this for me? How very nice!"

It was impossible for Jennings to say no, so he smiled a sickly smile as the Headmaster innocently helped himself to the rations of nine hopeful shareholders.

"Very kind of you," smiled the Headmaster. He had not the slightest desire to eat any cake, but he felt that it would be churlish to refuse and might hurt the boy's feelings, so he forced himself to do his duty.

"Excellent cake, don't you think so, Matron?" he inquired.

Matron could not say, not having sampled it, so Jennings took the only course left to him and offered a piece to her and a third one to Mr. Carter. He caught Darbishire's eye and felt he wasn't handling the situation very well, but what else could he do? The thirty-six interested parties watched with horror as the cake was demolished, with some effort, by the three grown-ups. None of the three realised the havoc that they were causing; they didn't even know that the plate contained the total sum of grandmother Darbishire's generosity, but supposed them to be slices cut from a larger cake.

Darbishire goggled in wide-eyed amazement. What on earth did Jennings think he was doing? There was still one slice left, but by this time, Darbishire's mistrust was so pronounced that he would not have been surprised had the traitorous Jennings presented the remaining portion to the housekeeper's cat.

The Headmaster swallowed the last of his cake.

"Ah, Jennings, yes," he said, "that reminds me." He called for silence, and those whose appetites had not been destroyed by the horrifying spectacle they had just witnessed, stopped eating and gave ear.

"This afternoon," he began, "our fire practice was enlivened by an unusual incident which was beyond our control. However, the prompt action of Jennings in telephoning for the fire brigade meant that Mr. Wilkins suffered only slight inconvenience. Now, there is an excellent example of using one's initiative, and I congratulate you, Jennings, on your resource and intelligence. That doesn't mean," he went on hurriedly, "that boys may normally use the telephone without permission, but this was an exceptional occasion, and Jennings rose to it with exceptional verve and aplomb." He paused, remembering the scene in the dormitory before Mr. Wilkins' mishap.

"Earlier on," he proceeded, "I had had occasion to be dissatisfied with the boys of Dormitory Four, and I awarded an extra hour's prep in consequence, but I have now decided to cancel this imposition, as I feel that such outstanding initiative should be rewarded. Don't you agree, Mr. Carter?" he asked, turning to his assistant for confirmation.

Mr. Carter's conscience told him that he didn't agree at all. On the other hand it seemed a pity to be a wet blanket when everyone was so pleased with the way things had turned out. Carter versus Conscience was a keen contest, and Conscience won on points.

"Well, sir," he began, "there is another aspect of the matter which seems to have escaped your notice—"

"No, no, no, Mr. Carter," broke in the Headmaster. "Let us not be niggardly. Honour where honour is due. In fact," he went on in a sudden burst of generosity, "I think it would be fitting to excuse the whole school from evening preparation as a token that I am not slow to recognise meritorious conduct."

Seventy-eight pairs of hands clapped loudly, while Jennings clutched the cake plate and cast his eyes downwards, with becoming modesty.

It was not until the following day that Mr. Carter discovered the true facts about the Cake List calamity. Darbishire had managed to salvage the fourth piece of cake for himself, but he had had a difficult time in explaining the facts to those who had hoped for a share. Mr. Carter felt a little guilty, so he went into the town and bought Darbishire a cake, and this time the diameter was twelve inches and the depth was five.

Darbishire thanked Mr. Carter in a dozen different positions and ambled happily out of Mr. Carter's room hugging the gift tightly. But a moment later he was back.

"Please, sir," he said, "have you got such a thing as a large piece of paper I could have."

"I think so. How about this sheet of exam. paper?"

"Thank you very much, sir," said Darbishire.

He deposited the cake in his tuck box and took the sheet of paper to his classroom and sat down at his desk.

"Revised Cake List," he wrote in block capitals.

"The following persons on the list here below can get one bit per head but not if they do not be decent:

1. Mr. Carter
2. Jennings
3. Venables
4. ——"

The tea bell rang just as he finished the List, and Jennings appeared.

"I say, Darbi," he said, "would you like me to help you cut your cake up and hand it round?"

"No jolly fear," said Darbishire.

CHAPTER 8

THE LITERARY MASTERPIECE

HALF-TERM came, and with it a break in the routine of going into class, and changing for football; of being called by one's surname, and saying "Yes, sir." For one weekend this could be forgotten, and yet it was impossible to forget. One weekend wasn't long enough to change anyone from a unit in a boarding school to a member of a family; and new parents who arrived expecting to find their sons the same as they were at home, were puzzled and sometimes disappointed.

When half-term Saturday dawned, the boys rose eager and excited, and put on their best suits. Heads were sleeked with unaccustomed smears of hair cream, and Matron gave ear crevices a critical survey before she passed any boy as fit to go out with his parents. Matron's inspection was thorough; she examined them tooth and nail, and woe betide any miserable specimen who tried to slip past with a missing shirt button, or high-tide marks at wrist or neck.

The Reverend and Mrs. Darbishire arrived from the wilds of Hertfordshire, forearmed with questions about academic progress and winter-weight underwear.

Mr. and Mrs. Jennings motored over from Haywards Heath, eager for every detail of their son's new way of life.

"I'm so excited about seeing him again," Mrs. Jennings said to her husband as the car passed through Dunhambury. "I'm just dying to hear all about it; we'll let him talk while we just sit back and listen; won't it be fun!"

"I expect he'll be full of it," replied her husband. "I'm looking forward to hearing how he's getting on with his work. I'll get him to let me know if he's having difficulty with any of his lessons."

"Do you think I ought to see Matron about his going to bed early if he feels tired?"

"Well, let's see what he has to say first."

But they were doomed to disappointment. Jennings had plenty to say, and didn't propose to waste time talking about such dull subjects as Algebra and cough-mixture; and all their efforts to probe what they considered to be the more important side of school life, were promptly side-tracked. They had to listen, instead, to a long account of why Venables had had to come down to breakfast wearing his pyjama jacket because his shirt fell in the wash basin.

"Yes, dear, I'm sure that must have been very awkward for him," said Mrs. Jennings; "but what we want to know is whether you're settling down all right; how do you like being at a boarding school?"

"Oh, it's all right, thanks."

"And have you made lots of nice friends?"

"Oh, yes; they're all right, thanks."

"How about your appetite? Are you eating well?"

"Oh, yes, all right. I say, Atkinson's got a super blister on his ankle." Jennings felt it was time to turn the conversation to more interesting topics.

"How are you getting on in school; top of the form yet?" inquired his father.

"No, not yet. He's going to have it lanced on Tuesday, and Matron says Atkinson's blister is the—"

"How do you like learning French?"

"Oh, all right. Bod's got a super wizzo frog; it's got sort of yellow spot things all down its back."

"And is Mr. Carter giving you your pocket money every week?"

"Yes .... He keeps it behind the boot lockers."

"Behind the boot lockers?" echoed his father. "It doesn't sound a very safe place to me."

"Oh, it can't get away," Jennings explained. "It's in a cardboard box with moss and wet leaves."

"Are you talking about your pocket money?" asked his father.

"No, the frog; it's spivish rare. Bod was told to get rid of it 'cos he took it into the common room. The Head made an ozard hoo-hah about it." Jennings laughed at the recollection, and his mind rushed off at a tangent.

"It was wizard," he said. "When he laughs he's got a gold tooth."

Mr. Jennings was left to speculate whether the gold tooth belonged to the Headmaster, Bod or the frog, and where it went when the owner was not laughing, for Jennings had already launched out on the story of how Brown minor had filled an ink-well with stale cake crumbs. But of himself, of the things they had come to hear, there was scarcely a word. Questions about his welfare were answered briefly with, "All right, thanks," or "Pretty ozard," or "Supersonic."

They all enjoyed the weekend with its lunches in hotels, and teas in cafés, and drives in the car, but, when it was all over, Mr. and Mrs. Jennings returned home baffled. They had no more knowledge of the things that really mattered than when they had started.

"What are we going to tell Grandma?" said Mrs. Jennings on the way home. "She'll be dying to know all the details."

Mr. Jennings accelerated to pass a lorry.

"We'll just have to pass on the information as we got it," he said helplessly, "and see if she can make anything of it."

Grandma greeted them excitedly when they stepped out of the car.

"Well," she beamed, "and how is the dear boy?"

"Oh, all right, thanks," said Mr. Jennings.

"Only all right?" queried Grandma, suspecting the worst.

"Not too ozard," put in Mrs. Jennings, struggling to appear at home in a foreign tongue.

"Yes, but I want to hear all about everything," Grandma persisted. "Does he like school? Is he keeping well? Has he grown? What did the dear boy have to say?"

"He said a lot of things," replied Mr. Jennings. "I didn't follow it all, but I gathered that the most important event of the term was when some ozard oik's frog came down to breakfast in his pyjama jacket."

"No, dear, that's wrong," corrected his wife. "The frog was the property of a bogus ruin and it ate stale cake crumbs out of an ink-well behind the boot lockers."

Grandma's face wore question marks.

"Is that so very important?" she asked.

"Important?" echoed Mr. Jennings in tones of mock incredulity. "My dear Grandma, it's more than that. It's—it's super-wizzo-sonic!"

Half-term passed, and Jennings and Darbishire settled more comfortably into the pattern of school life. Jennings was no genius, but he did his best and managed to hold his own about half-way down the form. Darbishire was a few places higher; his knowledge was slightly better, but it wavered erratically like an aircraft off the beam, and led him to make wild statements with an air of such profound wisdom that the ignorant accepted them as true.

They worked hard for Mr. Carter because they liked his lessons. They worked hard for the Headmaster because they dared not do otherwise, and they worked hard for Mr. Wilkins when his manner told them that they had gone quite far enough in the opposite direction. There were other masters on the staff and mistresses too, but they only taught Form Three for occasional lessons, for which they were thankful.

Jennings tried hard to get into the First Eleven. He was hovering on the brink of a place in the side, and when the team was posted on the notice board before each match, he would rush to be the first at the board and scan the list hopefully. But, so far, he had always been disappointed. He knew that if he failed to make the grade this term, he would have to wait a whole year for another chance, for in the Easter Term they played rugger.

Darbishire played football in "D" game, the lowest and the most rabbity of all, and though his boots were no longer tied together, it made no difference to the standard of his play.

In the classroom one evening, some four weeks after half-term, Jennings tackled his friend about it.

"You know, Darbi, your football's pathetic," Jennings told him. "A chap your age shouldn't be playing with Binns minor and all that crush; can't you do something about it?"

"Well, I'm writing an article called *Practical Hints on Positional Play and Advanced Tactics*," was the proud reply. "I asked Mr. Carter if he'd put it in the school magazine, and he said he might think about it."

"And who d'you think's going to read it, when they know it's written by a chap who can't even see the ball coming, let alone kick it?"

"That's what Mr. Carter said," Darbishire admitted, "so I think it might be better if I used a pen-name, like 'Old Pro,' or 'Wembley Wizard,' or something, don't you think so?"

"H'm," said Jennings, not impressed.

"As a matter of fact," Darbishire went on, "Benedick said he'd rather I wrote something I knew more about for the mag., so I'm thinking of doing a detective story."

"What do you know about detectives?" Jennings asked him.

"Well, anyone can write a detective story," replied Darbishire. "You've only got to think of some characters and a plot, and there you are."

"Yes, I s'pose so," said Jennings, struck by the simplicity of the formula. "But do you think they'd print it? After all, we're not even supposed to read blood and thunders, so I bet they wouldn't print one."

"It needn't be all thud and blunder," replied Darbishire. "We could put some bits of poetry in to make it more highbrow; you know, the hero could quote Shakespeare and stuff, like 'To be or not to be, that is the question.'"

"What is the question?"

"To be or not to be."

"That isn't a question; besides it doesn't make sense. What is to be or not to be?"

"That is the question; I just told you."

"Well, what's the answer?"

"I don't know. It might be anything. It might even be the mystery that the detective's got to solve."

"Oh!"

Detective stories sounded fairly easy, especially if you could put poetry and difficult questions in when you were unable to think of anything else to write.

"How'd it be if I helped you?" said Jennings. "We could write one together. You write Chapter I and I'll do Chapter II, and so on."

"Okay," said Darbishire. "Let's go and start now."

Evening preparation was over and there was half an hour before bedtime, so they took their literary zeal and a notebook down to the tuck-box room and got to work. Darbishire suggested that the library might be a better place in which to woo the muse, but Jennings rejected this on the grounds that it was too quiet and might cramp their style.

"First of all," said Darbishire, licking his pencil, "we've got to think of a name for the detective."

They thought hard for a few moments.

"It ought to be something out of the ordinary," said Jennings.

"Yes, what about Mr. Nehemiah Bultitude?"

"Why?"

"Out of the ordinary; or Mr. Theophilus Goodbody if you like."

"Oh, don't be daft," said Jennings. "You can't have detectives called things like that. Anybody called Theophilus Goodbody would have to be a clergyman; they always are. And if a chap's a farmer, his name's always Hayseed or Barleycorn, or if he's a schoolmaster he's Dr. Whackem or something like that."

They discussed this at length and decided it was obviously a rule to be obeyed.

"You've only got to look in the library," argued Jennings, "and you'll see all Dickens' bods have got names that suit them, like Pecksniff and Cheeryble and Cruncher, and they live at places called Eatanswill."

"But what I can't see," objected Darbishire, "is how anyone knows what they're going to be like before they're born. According to that, if you've got a name like Fuzziwig you could never be as bald as a coot however hard you tried, and if your name's Marlinspike Mainbrace, f'rinstance, you've just got to be a sailor, even if you don't want to be."

"Well, what sort of a name do you have to be born with so's you can be a great detective?"

The work of research went on and yielded the information that, unless your surname consisted of a single syllable and your parents had been generous enough to give you a two-syllabled first name, you could never hope to succeed in the world of crime-detection. Sherlock Holmes, Sexton Blake, Nelson Lee, Dixon Hawke, Falcon Swift, Ferrers Locke—all the best detectives were most careful to have the correct number of syllables to their names.

"Well, what about Egbert Snope?" suggested Darbishire. "That sticks to the rules all right."

"Yes, but it doesn't sound right," objected Jennings. "Pity we don't know any real detectives. We've got a policeman at home," he continued after more thought, "he's not a detective, of course, but he may be one day, and his name's Bill Smithson."

"He can't hope to be much of a detective with a name like that," said Darbishire scornfully, "unless he turns it round and calls himself Billson Smith."

"We want something with more zip, like—I know, what about Flixton Slick?"

"Wizard prang! That'll be super."

"Don't be so wet, Darbi. If a chap was called Wizard Prang he'd be a conjurer, not a detective."

"No, I mean Flixton Slick is wizard prang. I don't mean he is really …. I mean, yes, it's a jolly good name."

"All right, then, we'll call the story 'Flixton Slick—Private Investigator.'"

Darbishire moved an amendment that Private Investigator was too cumbersome, and after further debate they decided that Super Sleuth was a more fitting description.

"'Flixton Slick—Super Sleuth,'" Jennings rolled the syllables round his tongue. "H'm, okay; it's a bit tricky to say, of course; you keep getting 'sloops' in it if you say it too fast."

They decided not to work out the plot before they started. Darbishire was to write Chapter I, leaving the hero in a difficult situation which Jennings would have to cope with in Chapter II. Thus the story would provide thrills and surprises for authors as well as readers right up to the final gripping climax; and the time to start worrying about the gripping climax would not come until the page before was completed.

The dormitory bell rang and the super sleuth was temporarily banished to his Baker Street flat, his dressing gown and his pipe dreams.

The following day was Friday, and the team to play Bretherton House School the next day appeared on the board at morning break.

Jennings rushed out of class and crashed through the queue. He no longer expected to see his name on the board, but there was always a chance and—yes, there it was! He could hardly believe his good fortune. Right-half! Oh, prang! Oh, jolly g! Oh, hefty ziggety door knobs!

"Budge out of the way, Jennings, you're not the only one who wants to see the team."

But Jennings was unable to move. He was held by the magic of his name up there on the board in typewritten capital letters. He walked away in a dream some five minutes later, and then realised that he had been staring at his own name so intently, that he had not the slightest idea of who else had been picked to play, so he had to return to the board and start all over again.

He spent twenty minutes after lunch in cleaning his football boots. He scraped them with a penknife and applied boot polish to soles and uppers, and also to his jacket and trousers, but one could not worry about minor details like that at a time like this.

"There," he said, displaying his handiwork proudly, "how about those, Bod? I ought to be able to play jolly well tomorrow with my boots as clean as that."

"Well, you are screwy," Temple replied. "You'll get them all muddied up practising this afternoon."

"Gosh, yes!" said Jennings. "I never thought of that. Never mind, I'll do them again this evening."

But, by the evening, he wasn't feeling too well. He had surpassed himself during the practice game and he felt slightly sick at the end of it. He sat quietly through afternoon school, and at tea-time he was unable to eat a thing. This was unheard of, as shepherd's pie was on the menu, and usually Jennings sent his plate up three times; for though custom demanded that one called it muck, yet this was muck with a difference.

"Gosh!" said Venables. "Jennings hasn't had any shepherd's pie. What's the matter, Jen, are you going into training for the match tomorrow?"

"No," he replied, surveying the bread and butter with a jaundiced eye. "No, I just don't feel I want anything to eat; I feel sick."

"Why don't you go to Matron, then?"

"I can't. She'd pack me off to bed, or say I couldn't play or something. I'll be all right in the morning."

Morning dawned, and his inside still felt as though he were descending a sky-scraper in an express lift.

"I'll go and fetch Matron," said Atkinson.

Matron was brisk and hearty, and stood no nonsense. She radiated energy and vigour, and the more ill one felt, the brisker and heartier was Matron. She bounced into the room with a gay snatch of song on her lips, and came to rest before the unwilling invalid.

"Well, well, well," she said. "What's gone wrong here?"

"Well, Matron, I—I feel a bit—umph!"

With lightning speed she whipped a thermometer from its case, like a dagger from its sheath, and plunged it between her patient's teeth before he could finish his sentence.

"Right as rain yesterday," Matron carolled blithely. "Can't have you being a deathshead at the feast like this."

"Well, Matron, I—"

"Quiet, quiet. Never talk with a thermom in your mouth. Now, then, you others"—she turned to the rest of the dormitory who were clustered round the bed like flies round a honey-pot— "off you go. The breakfast bell will be going in two shakes of a lamb's tail."

She hummed contentedly for a minute, took the thermometer from Jennings' mouth, and narrowed her eyes to see the fine column of mercury.

"We'll soon have you up and about again," she said brightly. "No, no, no, not yet awhile," she continued, as Jennings started to get out of bed. She diagnosed a bilious attack and sentenced him to stay where he was for the morning.

"But I'll be all right for the match this afternoon, won't I, Matron?"

"Match this afternoon? Good gracious, no! Quite out of the question."

"Oh, but, Matron, please, I must—"

"I may let you up for a bit this afternoon; you can sit on the couch in my sitting room, but no football; rigidly taboo."

This was a catastrophe; this was the end of everything. After weeks of effort, he had worked and played and willed his way into the team only to spend the day of the match in bed. It was a morning darkened by the fog of despair.

After a light lunch, Matron allowed him to come to her sitting room.

"Rise and shine," she sang as she bustled into the dormitory. "We'll have you as right as a trivet by tomorrow."

"But it's no good being all right tomorrow," Jennings lamented. "It doesn't matter how ill I am then; it's today. And they'll go and play Johnson in my place; I bet they do."

"Very nice for Johnson," said Matron. "It's an ill wind that blows nobody any good. And after the match, I've promised Darbishire he can come up to my sitting room and talk to you. That will be nice and cheery, won't it?"

Darbishire's conversation sounded a poor substitute for playing in the match, and Jennings spent a nerve-racked afternoon. He could hear the cheering on the football pitch, but he could see nothing, and it was infuriating to listen to cheers and not to know what they portended.

Darbishire arrived after the match, and Jennings demanded details.

"We won," said Darbishire. "One nil, and Johnson scored the goal; he played a super game. Everyone said how good he was, and he'll probably stay in the team now."

He chatted on, unconsciously rubbing salt into the wound.

"It's just as well for the school that you were ill, 'cos Johnson wouldn't have been playing otherwise, and then we shouldn't have scored."

It does nothing to soothe the nerves of a convalescent to tell him that his suffering is a blessing to the community, and Jennings was anything but pleased with the heavy-handed attempts to cheer him up. So when Darbishire proudly announced that he had brought Chapter I of "Flixton Slick—Super Sleuth" with him, Jennings' mood of criticism was hostile.

"All right, chuck it over," he said. "I don't suppose it's much good, but I might as well read it."

Darbishire handed over the notebook reverently and sat back with the smile of the author who knows that praise is on its way.

Jennings read aloud: "'*Chapter I. A vast crowd had gathered at the airfield to*

111

see Flixton Slick—Super Sleuth—take off the wings of his aeroplane ...' What's he want to take the wings off for?" he demanded.

"It doesn't say that," said Darbishire. "There should be a full stop after take off. They'd come to see him take off. Full stop."

"Oh, I see," said Jennings. "'*The wings of his aeroplane glistened in the sun. How the vast crowd did cheer as the aeroplane was airborne and waved handkerchiefs...*'" He broke off. "That's daft," he said. "How can an aeroplane wave handkerchiefs? You might as well make it flap its wings."

"No, you goof," said the author. "I mean the crowd waved handkerchiefs."

"Well, why don't you say what you mean?"

He was certainly not going to be kind to the masterpiece after listening to Darbishire's praise of Johnson.

"Oh, go on," said Darbishire. "You know perfectly well what it means."

"'*It was not a very exiting journey ...*'" He stopped again. "Well, of course it wasn't," he said. "You don't keep making exits from an aeroplane like you do when you're playing 'Henry V' and things."

"I don't know what you're talking about," said Darbishire.

Jennings showed him the passage.

"That's supposed to be *exciting* not exit-ing," the author explained. "I don't think you're trying. Read properly."

Jennings clicked his tongue reproachfully.

"'*Soon Flixton Slick arrived at Scotland Yard ...*'" he read. "'*He had been sent for to investigate a mysterious spy who was working for a foreign power. His nickname was the Silent Shadow and his real name was only whispered ....*' Was he a Red Indian, then?" Jennings demanded, breaking off.

"No, why?"

"They have names like *Sitting Bull* and *Laughing Mountain*, so I thought *Only Whispered* might be a name like that."

"Oh, you are a ruin," exclaimed the author in some distress. "Go on. His real name was only whispered *because* ... and then it goes on."

"Oh, yes '... *because it might cause embarrassment to a member of the cabinet called Sir James, who was a Minister without Portfolio.*'"

"That means he hadn't got one of those despatch case things," the author explained.

"Why hadn't he?"

"Well, if you read on, you'll see. He'd had his portfolio stolen by the Silent Shadow with the secret plans in."

"Oh, I see. '*Sir James was at Scotland Yard telling the Chief of Police about this when Flixton Slick arrived, and while the Chief of Police told him all about it, Sir James remained without.*' Does that mean he remained outside, or remained without portfolio?" the critic inquired.

"Well, both, really. It doesn't matter which way you take it. Go on! It's good, isn't it?"

"'*The Chief of Police told Flixton Slick that the Silent Shadow's headquarters were in this warehouse that I shall tell you about later, so Flixton Slick left Scotland Yard with three uninformed constables. ....*'" Jennings stopped again to inquire what it was they had not been informed about.

"You can't read properly," objected Darbishire, "you're spoiling it. It doesn't say anything about their not being informed."

"Well, what's this, then?" demanded Jennings, passing the exercise book back to the author.

"Oh, sorry, yes, I made a slip. It's meant to be *uniformed*. Look, would you like me to read it to you; you don't seem to be doing it very well."

"It doesn't make sense whoever reads it, as far as I can see," Jennings grumbled.

Darbishire's pride was shattered by this time, but he made a last attempt to silence the hostile criticism.

"Well, this bit that's coming's ever so exciting," he said. "Listen; I'll read it this time. '*So Flixton Slick left Scotland Yard with three uniformed constables and went to the warehouse. He burst in. The Silent Shadow was hiding in a corner with the portfolio belonging to the Minister without Portfolio on a table in front of him. When he saw Flixton Slick he whipped out a revolver. Crack! Crack! Crack! Three shots rang out. Two policemen fell dead and the third whistled through his hat—*'"

"Wait a minute," Jennings interrupted. "The third did what?"

"Whistled through his hat."

"He must have been crazy."

"Who? The Silent Shadow? Yes, he was really, you see—"

"No, the other policeman. If two of your friends got shot dead you might take off your hat as a mark of respect, but you wouldn't whistle through it. Besides, they wear helmets, not hats."

"It doesn't mean the policeman whistled through his hat, you ozard oik." Darbishire became red in the face with anger at this further attempt to deride his masterpiece. "It means the third bullet whistled through Slixton Flick's hat."

"You can't even get the name right now. Slixton Flick—Slooper-Sooth," Jennings jeered.

Darbishire hurled the book at him, but missed by several feet.

"Rotten shot!" said Jennings. "It wasn't even near enough to whistle through my hat, even if I'd had one."

"You're being ozard squared beastly on purpose," Darbishire shouted. "I've a jolly good mind not to be friends with you any more. My father says—"

"Go on then, don't be," Jennings called back, just as loudly. "And I don't care what your father says either. You come in here to cheer me up, and tell me what a marvellous player Johnson is, and what a good thing it is that I'm too ill to play."

"Well, there was no need for you to be all stupid about Flixton Slick when you knew all the time, really .... And I'm jolly well going to cross you off my Revised Cake List, so that'll show you."

They were both shouting; Darbishire nearly in tears, and Jennings angry and miserable.

The door opened and Matron bounced in to find out the cause of the uproar.

"Now, now, now," she said. "Come, come, come. What's this? What's this? I leave you as thick as thieves and, hey presto, I come back to find you going for each other hammer and tongs."

Jennings wondered why on earth Matron always had to talk like that. Normally, he enjoyed her conversation but, in his present mood, her hearty banter annoyed him.

"Off you go then, Darbishire," she said.

Darbishire departed, muttering darkly about severed friendships.

"And I shan't let you invite friends into my sitting room," Matron went on, "if you're going to start a rough and tumble as soon as my back's turned."

"No, Matron," said Jennings.

"And you'd better go down into school after tea; you seem hale and hearty enough."

"Yes, Matron."

She went out, leaving Jennings alone with the bitterness of his thoughts. He'd had a bad day, and a small wave of self-pity splashed over him. What a rotter Darbishire was! What an out-and-out cad! He was glad he had seen through him. Fancy bursting in on an invalid, in a delicate state of health, and shattering his nerves to pieces with blood and thunder stories of missing portfolios. It was enough to have given him a relapse. And more important still—but, no, he couldn't bring himself to think about the match.

He was still trying hard not to think about the match when Mr. Carter looked in.

"Hallo, Jennings," he said. "Pity you had to miss the match. Very good game it was, too. Johnson played well," he added, unnecessarily.

"Yes, I know, sir. I was awfully fed up about it. I don't s'pose I'll get another chance now."

"But of course you will," said Mr. Carter; "next Saturday."

"Oh, is there a match next Saturday? Coo, wizard prang!"

"We're playing Bracebridge School," Mr. Carter told him.

"Mm, yes, but now Johnson's turned out to be so jolly good, I don't s'pose I'll get a look in."

"Yes, you will. I'm going to play you and Johnson next time, and drop somebody else from the forward line."

The grey mist of gloom which had lain heavily over Jennings' spirits suddenly cleared.

"Oh, super-duper-sonic, sir," he said. "Thanks most awfully, sir. Gosh, I'm looking forward to next Saturday!"

He was feeling fine when he went downstairs, and the first person he saw was a dejected and miserable Darbishire. He was standing by a basket in the common room, tearing his deathless prose manuscript into little strips. And, as each scrap of paper fell into the basket, it was as though another link had been severed in the chain of their friendship.

"Poor Darbi," thought Jennings, eyeing him through the rose-coloured spectacles that his place in the team had lent him; he had misjudged Darbishire. What a wizard decent cove he was really! His mood of happiness was so strong, that it wiped out the resentment that he had felt earlier on.

"Hallo, Darbi, old fellow," he called from the doorway.

Darbishire looked up disgustedly.

"Oh, it's you, is it?" he said. "Well, jolly well go away; I've finished with you." And he tore the last page into sixteen small pieces.

"Now, look here, Darbi," said Jennings. "I'm terribly sorry I was so ozard about your story; I thought it was jolly g., really."

Darbishire looked up suspiciously, hoping, but not expecting, to find an olive branch within reach.

"Are you pulling my leg?" he asked.

116

"No, honestly. But I wasn't feeling quite myself after the match. I was something—what d'you call it—like effervescent?"

"Convalescent?"

"Yes, but I'm all right now."

"Well, of course, if it comes to that," Darbishire said, "I s'pose I can be said to have ridden roughshod over your feelings about not playing."

"Oh, forget it," said Jennings. "Tell you what, let's write 'Flixton Slick' out again. I'll do it if you like."

"Okay," said Darbishire, thawing visibly. You—you ..." He was proud of Chapter I, and there lingered in his mind the nagging thought that Jennings was seeking a further opportunity to mock his literary efforts.

"What?" said Jennings.

"You do really like Chapter I, don't you; as far as you got, anyway?"

"Of course I do. It's first rate. Nearly as good as *Treasure Island*. Come on, you dictate and I'll write."

Armed with a new notebook they went to the tuck-box room.

Darbishire felt important now that he was about to dictate. He had never had a secretary before. He cleared his throat.

"'A vast crowd had gathered at the airfield to see Flixton Slick take off. Full stop.'"

The rift had been healed.

CHAPTER 9

MR. WILKINS HAS AN IDEA

ON Monday Jennings wrote in his diary, "*Only five days to the match or four if you do not count today or Saturday morning.*"

On Tuesday he wrote, "*Only four days more or three not counting today and Sat.*" And those with a bent for mathematics can work out the diarist's entries for the remainder of the week. By Friday morning, when only one day remained—or none, if you counted the other way—Jennings' excitement was beginning to interfere with his work.

Mr. Wilkins didn't like Fridays. He had to take Form Three for two lessons before the break and again immediately afterwards. Half-way through the second lesson Mr. Wilkins began to send out tremors indicating that an earthquake might be expected at short notice. Form Three regarded this as a promising sign; it meant that the rest of the morning would teem with interest, always provided, of course, that someone else received the brunt of the attack.

Mr. Wilkins strode between the desks, peering critically at the geometrical figures that the boys were copying from the board. When he arrived at Jennings' desk, he stopped and a look of anguish clouded his features.

"My goodness," he said, "what d'you call those?"

"Those are incongruous triangles, sir," Jennings explained.

"They certainly are," said Mr. Wilkins; "but they're not meant to be. You can't draw congruent triangles with sprawling lines like that. Look at them; they ought to be thin, and these lines are as thick as—well, I don't know what!"

"As thick as thieves, sir?" prompted Darbishire.

"It's my pencil, sir," explained Jennings; "it hasn't got much of a point."

"Neither has your compass," complained Mr. Wilkins, examining the contents of the geometry box. "What have you been doing; playing darts with it? Just look at this ruler, and this protractor!"

They were, indeed, a sorry-looking collection of instruments. The ruler was warped and chipped, for one cannot fight rapier duels without damaging one's weapon. There were intricate carvings, too, which suggested that the ruler had been used as an Indian totem pole; and though it might have passed muster as a bread knife, it was no longer a reliable instrument for drawing straight lines. There was a piece missing from the protractor—a neat rectangle of celluloid which Jennings had removed in order to make a windscreen for his miniature motor car; and the point of his compass had done duty for so many tasks requiring a sharp point, that it was bent like a fish-hook.

"How on earth do you expect to draw straight lines and accurate angles with this junk?" fumed Mr. Wilkins. "Look at this figure you've drawn here; what's it meant to be?"

"Two parallel lines with a thingummy going across, sir."

"Yes, but look at the shape; look at this angle; what sort of an angle is it?"

Jennings regarded it dubiously.

"Well, sir, it's a little difficult to say, but I think it's meant to be an alternate angle, sir."

"You *think*!" boomed Mr. Wilkins. "You *think* it's meant to be alternate! Well, don't think; you're not meant to think; you're meant to know."

"Yes, sir," said Jennings.

"And if it is an alternate angle," continued Mr. Wilkins, giving the wavering lines the benefit of the doubt, "it must be alternate to another one. Now, then, which angle is it alternate to?"

Jennings surveyed the maze of thick lines helplessly.

"I don't know, sir," he confessed.

"You don't know!" echoed Mr. Wilkins. "Well, think, you silly little boy, think!"

"But you just told me not to think, sir. You said I wasn't meant to think."

The class rocked with laughter. They went on laughing long after the joke had ceased to be funny. They forced themselves to go on laughing because a joke, even though it is a bad one, is a signal for a laugh, and the longer it can be kept up the better.

But Mr. Wilkins did not laugh. They were laughing at him, and not with him, and nobody enjoys that.

"Quiet," he ordered.

The laughter died away slowly and then the comments started.

"Sir, Jennings was quite right, sir, you did tell him he wasn't meant to think; didn't you, sir?"

"Sir, you meant he should think and then, when he's thought, he shouldn't have to think any more; didn't you, sir?"

"But, sir, if you tell him to think one minute, and then the next minute you tell him not to—"

"Silence," thundered Mr. Wilkins. "Sit up and fold your arms, all of you."

By the loudness of his voice and the fury in his eye, the class was silenced. But it was the shallow silence of necessity and not the deep silence of respect. They stopped talking but took delight in pretending to be frightened by the violence of Mr. Wilkins' anger. They sought shelter behind exercise books, and quaked with exaggerated grimaces of terror. They raised their coat collars about their ears and crouched low in their seats as the imaginary blast whistled fearfully above their heads.

"The next boy who makes a sound will be ..." threatened Mr. Wilkins; he could think of no punishment drastic enough. "... Well, he'd better look out," he finished lamely.

The class could distinguish between bark and bite. They were silent, but they smiled and they looked at one another with the sort of expression that Mr. Wilkins found far more infuriating than speech. Everything had been all right, he told himself, until that fatal burst of laughter. Now they were out of hand, and the angrier he became, the funnier they thought it was. True, they were quiet, but if Mr. Carter or the Headmaster were in charge, it would be a different sort of quietness. What should he do? He could keep them in, of course, but they didn't seem to mind that. What he needed was a punishment that would really make them sit up. Something so drastic that it would command instant respect for evermore. He was still trying to think of a suitable punishment when the bell rang for break, and he dismissed the class.

Jennings raced downstairs to the notice board. Yes, there it was. "First Eleven versus Bracebridge School"; and there was his name in the forward line. Johnson, as befitted the star discovery of the previous week, was playing right-half, but Bromwich major had been dropped and Jennings was playing inside-right. He feasted his eyes on the typewritten inscription and checked his name twice for spelling mistakes. All was in order, and he rushed off to find Darbishire.

Darbishire was still in the classroom with his exercise book open on the desk before him. He was studying a gaily-coloured booklet issued by a shipping company, which set out, in extravagant terms, the delights in store for anyone who booked a passage to Australia in one of their liners.

"Come and look at the board, Darbi," called Jennings. "The team's up; I'm playing inside-right."

"Good," said Darbishire, and went on studying the booklet.

"But don't you want to see it?" asked Jennings, unable to believe that anyone could resist the temptation of seeing it with their own eyes.

"I believe you," said Darbishire. "No point in going down and reading what you've already told me."

"Oh," said Jennings. "I'm glad I'm playing, aren't you?"

"Yes," replied Darbishire, intent on his ocean-going research.

"Inside-right, I'm playing," said Jennings.

"I know, you've just told me."

"Bromo has been dropped, and I'm playing inside-right."

"That's the fifty millionth time you've told me that in two seconds," said Darbishire. "You're playing inside-right. Okay, I know now. If anyone asks me if I know where you're playing, I'll say, 'Yes, inside-right.' I don't s'pose anyone will, but if they do, I'll have the answer off pat. 'Inside-right,' I'll say." There was meant to be subtle irony and reproach against swanking in Darbishire's remark, but it was wasted on Jennings.

"Yes, inside-right," Jennings said. "Don't forget. If anyone asks you, just say I'm playing inside-right."

"I'll put it up on the blackboard if you like," Darbishire replied, and his tone was heavy with sarcasm.

"I shouldn't bother," said Jennings, "you'll remember anyway."

Darbishire returned to his study of the Antipodes.

"What are you doing?" asked Jennings.

"Well, I haven't done my geog. prep, and Wilkie's taking us next lesson."

"Gosh, neither have I," said Jennings. "What is it, anyway?"

"Wheat farming in Australia," replied Darbishire. "Mind you, I'm not going to make a habit of working during break," he went on. "I mean, that sort of thing leads to nervous breakdowns and brainstorms and things, but judging from what old Wilkie was like last lesson, I think it would be as well if we got our prep. done."

"Think there'll be a hoo-hah if we haven't?"

"Yes, I do. A supersonic hoo-hah cubed."

Reluctantly Jennings went to his desk and took out his geography book.

"What goes on in Australia?" he asked.

"Rabbits," replied Darbishire. "Millions and millions of them; they're a pest,

121

and they eat all the wheat that the farmers spend their time trying to grow."

"Well, that'll do for a start, anyway," Jennings said. "Now shut up talking, I'm going to write my essay." He retired to the mental realms of scholarship and wrote. His crossed nib splayed widely apart on his down-strokes and clicked scratchily, sending out thin showers of inky vapour on every up-stroke of the pen.

Darbishire wore a puzzled frown as he studied his travel booklet. It described the splendour of Australia in glowing terms; the sunsets, the climate, the grandeur of the scenery were painted in the richest colours, for the author's intention was to put his readers in holiday mood, and not to worry about the mundane tasks of making a living by toil and soil. Darbishire sighed; still the chap ought to know what he was writing about, so he started to copy the opening paragraph into his exercise book. "It ought to please old Wilkie, anyhow," he thought.

Unaware of this treat in store, Mr. Wilkins paced his sitting room like a caged lion; he had got to do something to show those boys that he was a force to be reckoned with. But what? He had already dismissed the commonplace punishments as being ineffective and, in twenty minutes, he would have to face the form again. He ceased his pacing and went upstairs to consult Mr. Carter.

The door of Mr. Carter's study quivered under the assault of Mr. Wilkins' knock; the handle rattled like a burst of machine gun fire, and the papers on the desk fluttered in the breeze as the door was flung wide.

"Really, Wilkins," Mr. Carter protested. "Must you always come into my room like a herd of buffalo stampeding across the prairie?"

"You'd be feeling a bit frantic if you'd just had Form Three for two lessons running," came the answer. "I tell you, Carter, that form's turning my hair grey. Can't behave; will talk; won't work; must fidget. I've been shouting myself hoarse in there all morning."

"That's probably the trouble," Mr. Carter replied. "Have you ever tried talking quietly? You see, Wilkins, if you rampage round a classroom like a bull in a china shop, they just think it's most frightfully funny."

"Nonsense," barked Mr. Wilkins. "I've got to make myself felt. The trouble is, I'm too easy with them. I tell you, Carter, I haven't got enough authority in this school. I wish I were the Headmaster; I'd soon see things were done properly."

"I doubt it," replied Mr. Carter. "It's not so easy being a Headmaster as you might think."

"Nonsense," Mr. Wilkins dismissed the difficulties with a wave of his hand which knocked a brass ashtray off the mantelpiece. "Sorry, old man," he said, retrieving it. "What was I saying?"

"You were saying that a Headmaster's job was a bed of roses."

"So it is," said Mr. Wilkins. "There's nothing in it. Why, if I were in charge, I could run this school with my eyes shut."

"Yes," agreed Mr. Carter, "that's just about how you would run it; both eyes so tightly shut, that you wouldn't know what was going on."

"I—I—well, you know what I mean." Mr. Wilkins felt he wasn't getting the sympathy he deserved. "It's all very well for you," he went on, "they do as you tell them without any funny answers. You don't even have to shout at them; you just give them a look and they eat out of your hand. I wish I could do it."

"Well, for a start, try talking quietly and don't move around like a bulldozer dancing the Highland fling."

"You're not much help, are you?" Mr. Wilkins said. "I thought you might be able to suggest a suitable punishment for the next time they try to be funny."

"You could give them a detention," suggested Mr. Carter.

"That's not enough by itself," Mr. Wilkins vetoed the idea. "I've done that before. No, I want something that'll make them see they can't play fast and loose in my lessons and, by jove, when I've thought of something, that form's going to get it in the neck."

The telephone on Mr. Carter's desk rang.

"Excuse me," he said, and picked up the receiver. "Hallo! Linbury Court School .... Yes, Carter speaking .... Oh, hallo, Parkinson, how are you? ... Are you bringing a strong team over tomorrow?"

The voice at the other end of the wire said that it was sorry, but that it wouldn't be bringing a team over at all. German measles had claimed a victim at Bracebridge School some time earlier, and though the patient had now recovered, the school's month of quarantine would not expire until the following week. Mr. Parkinson apologised profusely for forgetting to let Mr. Carter know earlier, but there it was. It was too near the end of the term to arrange another game, so they would have to regard the fixture as cancelled.

Mr. Carter replaced the receiver and relayed the news.

"Oh, pity," said Mr. Wilkins. "I was looking forward to seeing that match tomorrow; should have been a good game. The boys will be disappointed."

Already his old enemy, the kind heart, had switched his feelings from wrath at the boys' misdeeds to sympathy at their being deprived of a match.

"Jennings will be upset," he went on. "Keen as mustard, and a jolly good little player he is, too. Still, if the game's scratched ..." He broke off, as the Idea flashed into his mind. The Idea took root and grew, spreading its branches and flowering profusely in every corner of his mind until he was almost dazzled with its brilliance.

"Good heavens, yes," he murmured ecstatically. "Why not? It's just what I've been waiting for."

"What is?" inquired Mr. Carter.

"Now I've got Form Three where I want them! Any more nonsense from them and I'll cancel the match against Bracebridge tomorrow."

Mr. Carter sighed, and he spoke with the patience normally reserved for explaining the nicer points of English grammar to lower forms.

"But it's cancelled already," he said gently. "I've just told you. They're in quarantine for German measles."

"Yes, yes, yes," Mr. Wilkins broke in impatiently. "I know that; you know that. But the boys don't know it. It's the very weapon I wanted. The first bit of trouble I get, I can say, 'Right. The whole lot of you can stay in tomorrow, and there'll be no match.' Just like that, see?"

Mr. Wilkins was delighted with his Idea. If they thought he had the power to cancel football matches, they would eye him with a new respect; and when they saw that he actually put this terrible threat into execution, there wouldn't be any more funny answers during his lessons.

Mr. Carter was shocked.

"You can't do that!" he protested. "It's making out that you've got the authority to do things which you can't do. Why, even the Head would think twice before cancelling a match as a punishment."

"But I'm not really cancelling it; that's done already. I'm just pretending to."

Mr. Wilkins stuck to his Idea. He argued that his mild deception would be a good thing for his discipline, and would make no difference whatever to the existing state of affairs. If the match had to be cancelled, why shouldn't he use it to his advantage?

"But it's not cricket," objected Mr. Carter.

"Yes, but don't you see, Carter, that I'm being most frightfully lenient; why, I shan't be punishing them at all, really, if they can't play tomorrow, anyway."

"I don't like the idea," Mr. Carter muttered. "It's—it's—unscrupulous. Besides, they might all behave so well that you don't want to punish them."

Mr. Wilkins thought this remark was very funny. He laughed long and loud at such a fantastic idea, and he was still laughing some minutes later when the bell rang.

"Ah," he said. "Now I'm going on the warpath with a vengeance, and I'm going into Form Three looking for trouble."

"I don't like it," repeated Mr. Carter, as Mr. Wilkins stalked towards the door with a determined look in his eye.

Mr. Carter clutched the papers on his desk. He said: "Don't slam the—"

The door slammed loudly behind Mr. Wilkins.

In the classroom, Form Three opened their books for the next lesson.

"It's geog. with Wilkie," said Venables. "He'll probably be in a super bate. I did a rotten essay."

"Never mind," said Jennings. "Bracebridge match tomorrow; I'm playing inside-right." He practised some imaginary shots at goal with vocal accompaniment. "Wham! ... Pheeew! ... Doyng! ... Goal! ..." He shook hands with himself and bowed left and right.

"Don't swank," said Temple.

"Well, I'm better than you, Bod," Jennings replied. "I must be 'cos I've seen Manchester United play in a cup tie; I stick up for Manchester; I shall probably play for them when I grow up."

"I bet!" jeered Atkinson.

"Only every other Saturday, of course," Jennings amended, "'cos I'll be playing rugger for the Harlequins the other times."

"Why do you stick up for Manchester?" inquired Temple. "I bet you've never even been there."

"Well—no," Jennings agreed; "but I've got a good reason to stick up for them, 'cos my godmother lives in Liverpool and they're joined by a canal, so that almost makes me a Manchesterian, doesn't it?"

"If it comes to that," Darbishire put in, "my mother's got a carpet sweeper called the Northampton cleaner, so that means I'm entitled to stick up for Northampton Town."

"Shut up, Darbishire," said Temple, "nobody asked you."

Heavy footsteps could be heard approaching along the corridor; there was never any need for a lookout when Mr. Wilkins was due to take a lesson.

"Get our your geography prep.," he called, while still some five yards from the classroom door. There was a note of confidence in his voice, but it passed unheeded in Form Three.

Venables put up his hand as Mr. Wilkins took his seat.

"Did we have to write our prep. in our books, sir?" he asked.

"Where else would you expect to write it; on the ceiling?"

"No, sir. I mean, I wondered whether we just had to learn about Australia and not write an essay."

Mr. Wilkins glared.

"So you haven't written an essay, eh? Very well, then, if you're looking for trouble—"

"Oh, but, sir, I have written one."

"You said you hadn't."

"No, sir. I just wondered, that was all."

"Don't talk nonsense," said Mr. Wilkins. He called Jennings up to the master's desk and inspected his efforts. "'*In Austeralia*,'" he read aloud, "'*there is wheat but the rabits are a pest like rats so the farmers get very cross because the rabits eat the wheat in England rabits are not a pest you can have chinchla and angora mine was white with some brown fur on and his name was Bobtail and so I got a tea chest and put straw down and made a hutch ….*'" Mr. Wilkins stopped reading. "Of all the muddle-headed bone-heads—!" Words failed him for a moment. "What d'you mean by serving me up with nonsense like this?"

"But, sir, it's not nonsense," Jennings protested. "It's true. My rabbit was brown and white; my uncle gave him to me for my birthday."

"But I set an essay on Australian wheat growing; not the life story of some wretched rodent!"

"Bobtail his name was," Jennings corrected.

"I don't care if his name was Moses," Mr. Wilkins expostulated. "It's not the point; it's not geography; it's—it's not—"

"My father would say it was 'not germane to the issue,' sir," Darbishire put in helpfully.

"That's enough, Darbishire." Mr. Wilkins turned back to the rabbit fancier. "You illiterate nitwit, Jennings, can't you see that your essay's miles away from the subject? It's a perfect example of—er—of—"

"Juvenile delinquency, sir?" suggested Darbishire.

"Be quiet, Darbishire." Mr. Wilkins turned on him angrily.

"Sorry, sir," Darbishire said meekly.

"The trouble with you, Jennings, is that you're half-asleep. You need waking up. Go and put your head under the tap in the washroom and see if that'll clear your brain at all."

"What, now, sir?" Jennings asked.

"Yes, now, and perhaps you'll come back a bit brighter. Go along."

Jennings departed to the washroom, and Mr. Wilkins called Darbishire up to his desk and began to read his essay. He read, "'*The grandiose splendours of the Australian countryside unfold a never-to-be-forgotten scenic pageant that remains a priceless jewel in the memory for all time. Fair and fragrant is the vast undulation of the plains stretching relentlessly to the horizon, where in the declining rays of the setting sun, the eye of the observer is entranced to behold* …'" Mr. Wilkins looked up, but, unlike the observer, his eye was not entranced with what it beheld. "I suppose you're going to tell me that this is all your own work?" he said.

"Well, no, not entirely," Darbishire confessed; "but I went to a lot of trouble and did research and stuff, sir."

"And what about the wheat growing?"

"Oh, that comes later," Darbishire explained. "Much later actually; in fact, I haven't quite got up to writing it yet. All this early part is just to put the reader in the right mood, sir."

"It's putting me in a mood, Darbishire," Mr. Wilkins admitted; "but it's not by any means the sort of mood you're aiming at."

The door opened and Jennings appeared. His visit to the washroom had made him brighter of eye, but his head bore no signs of immersion. Mr. Wilkins looked at him narrowly. This was deliberate disobedience. Very well, he was ready to meet it.

"You've been very quick, Jennings," he said, with studied calmness. "Come here."

Jennings came.

"Did you put your head under the tap as I told you?"

"Yes, sir."

Mr. Wilkins produced his ace.

"Then do you mind telling me," he inquired patiently, "do you mind explaining why your hair is quite dry?"

"Well, sir, you never told me to turn the tap on."

For the second time that morning the class rocked with laughter. Natural hearty laughter to start with, but, after a while, this was exhausted and they had to fall back on pantomime. The genuine laughter of schoolboys doesn't take the form of knee-smiting and thigh-slapping, but in their efforts to give the impression that their mirth was uncontrollable, they rolled about in their seats and smote their knees and slapped their thighs; then they smote their neighbours' knees and slapped their neighbours' thighs, and gave each other coy and playful pushes—anything to focus the spotlight of attention upon their counterfeit glee. Speech came through tears of merriment.

"Oh, sir, isn't Jennings smashing! Jolly g. answer, wasn't it, sir?"

"You asked for that one, sir. A real priority prang!"

"He was more awake than you thought, wasn't he, sir?"

"Sir, you should have told him to turn the tap on, sir."

"Sir, did you forget to tell him to turn the tap on, sir, because if you didn't actually tell him to turn the tap on, sir, he wouldn't know he had to, would he, sir?"

Mr. Wilkins waited—grimly, quietly patient. He could afford to wait, for very soon the tables would be turned. Silence came at last, and Mr. Wilkins spoke in tones unusually quiet for a person of his forceful nature.

"I've never in all my life," he began, "heard such a deplorable exhibition of hooliganism. If that is your idea of being clever, Jennings—"

"But it was only what you told him to do, sir," put in Venables.

"... and as the rest of the form obviously appreciates this cheap type of humour, they will have to suffer for it. The whole class will come in for two hours detention tomorrow afternoon."

"Oh, sir!" said the whole class.

Temple put up his hand.

"Sir, you can't keep us in tomorrow, sir," he said, "because of the match, and even if we're not in the team, we have to watch it, sir; the Head said so."

"Yes, sir, the Bracebridge match, sir," echoed three other boys anxious to share in the propagation of the news.

The class exchanged superior smiles; knowing glances that plainly said that that had cooked Mr. Wilkins' goose for him. They waited for him to retract his rash statement; but Mr. Wilkins paused just long enough to secure the right effect, and then he pounced.

"You will not be playing Bracebridge School tomorrow," he announced. "You can consider the match cancelled."

The form was incredulous. Had Mr. Wilkins some new powers that they had not been informed of? That was hardly playing the game.

"Oh, but, sir," they expostulated, "you can't do that, sir; really, you can't, sir."

"You heard what I said," Mr. Wilkins repeated gravely. "I warned you and you took no notice. Very well, then—no match."

"Oh, sir," said the class, stunned and resentful, but forced now to believe the terrible news.

Darbishire intervened with a policy of appeasement.

"Supposing we behave most frightfully decently from now on, sir, won't you let us off?"

"I'm not prepared to argue; the match is cancelled," repeated Mr. Wilkins in tones of finality. He had been careful not to state, in so many words, that he, personally, was responsible for the cancellation; but if they had formed that impression, he was certainly not going to disillusion them.

As the awful consequence of their behaviour spread through the minds of the class, their resentment was switched from Mr. Wilkins to the cause of the trouble and, in a matter of seconds, Jennings ceased to be the hero and became the villain of the piece.

"Jen-nings!" they jeered derisively, united in venom against the new foe.

"You are a fool, Jennings!"

"Yes, you pestilent oik. You did it on purpose. Why couldn't you behave decently and do what Mr. Wilkins told you?" Venables, whose hearty laughter had been a feature of the uproar barely a minute before, now sounded shocked that anyone could have been guilty of a joke in such bad taste.

"Well, you thought it was funny, anyway," Jennings said.

"I never thought it was funny," Venables replied in tones of outraged innocence. "I thought it was just too putrid for words."

"So did I," put in Temple. "It *would* be Jennings to get the match cancelled!"

Jennings tried to defend himself, but the odds were against him. The form wanted a scapegoat, and he was the obvious choice.

Mr. Wilkins allowed the criticism to run its course. He was above it now; an aloof figure who made decrees of world-shattering importance. "Well, they asked for it," he told his protesting conscience. Aloud he said, "And now, perhaps, we can resume the lesson."

"Sir," said Jennings, "it was all my fault, sir. Can I do the detention and you let the others off so they can have the match, sir?"

"No, Jennings."

"But, sir, it's not fair to them," he protested miserably. "Please let them have the match, sir, and I'll stay in even though"—he could hardly bring himself to utter the dread words— "even though it means I can't play. And—and I'll go back and get my head wet, too, sir," he added generously.

Mr. Wilkins cast a disdainful glance at the author of the funny answer and, for a moment, the sight of the pathetic, troubled expression, made him relent. But only for a moment. He steeled himself and spoke in tones of simple dignity.

"I'm not in the habit of having my decisions questioned by insignificant little boys," he said. "And now, Darbishire, we will continue to read your essay."

Form Three sat in dejected silence, stunned and numb, and there was a song in Mr. Wilkins' heart as he picked up Darbishire's exercise book and turned his attention to the scenic splendours of the Antipodes.

CHAPTER 10

THE POISONOUS SPIDER

THE news travelled fast, and by lunch time it had spread all over the school. "Old Wilkie's cancelled the match tomorrow, and all because of Jennings." The grim tidings passed from mouth to mouth and little pieces were added on and facts were twisted round.

"I say, have you heard? Old Wilkie's cancelled the Bracebridge match."

"He can't do that!"

"Can't he? He's done it, and all because of Jennings; he told him to put his head under the tap."

"Gosh, did you hear that? Jennings told Wilkie to go and stick his head under a tap. No wonder Wilkie got mad."

Jennings' name was Mud throughout lunch, and he had little appetite for the meal. He knew he was largely to blame for Mr. Wilkins' decision, but it seemed unfair to him that those who laughed the loudest when all was well, should now be the loudest in their condemnation. Only Darbishire remained faithful, and after lunch he slipped away from the anti-Jennings protest meeting which was going on in the common room, and went in search of his friend. He found him brooding darkly behind the boot-lockers.

"Never mind, Jennings," said Darbishire. "Can't be helped; and I don't think it was your fault, really, 'cos if they hadn't laughed like that, old Wilkie wouldn't have got in such a bate. My father says that—"

"Wilkie's a mean cad," said Jennings. "He's as ozard as a coot."

"You can't say that," objected the knowledgeable Darbishire. "You can only be as bald as a coot."

"Who can?"

"Anyone; it's a simile," the pedant explained. "What you meant was, either Wilkie is as bald as a coot—"

"I never said he was bald," Jennings objected.

"No, but if you wanted to."

"Why should I want to say he was bald if he isn't? I said he was ozard, that's all."

"Of course," mused Darbishire, "I s'pose you could make up a simile and say he was as ozard as a buzzard. My father says that the history of the English language—"

Jennings was in no mood to listen to a lecture on the origins of language.

"Come on," he said. "Let's go."

"Where?"

"Anywhere; I couldn't care less."

Aimlessly they slouched across the main hall, where their gaze was affronted by the team list for Saturday's match, hanging limply by its drawing pin, and across the sheet of paper was the word "Cancelled" in bold block capitals of red ink. Vaguely they wandered across the quad, and round the corner to the yard behind the kitchen where tradesmen's vans unloaded laundry and meat and groceries. Old Pyjams was there, opening a crate with hammer and pliers.

"I bet you I know what's for tea," Jennings said. "I bet you a million pounds I do."

"I bet you a million pounds you don't," replied Darbishire.

"Take me on, then?"

"Okay."

The fate of a fortune hung in the balance as the first millionaire led his colleague towards old Pyjams.

"I say it's bananas," said Jennings. "Don't forget, you said a million, if I'm right."

They inspected the crate; it was full of bananas.

"All right," said Darbishire, resigning himself to his loss with admirable fortitude. "It serves me right, I s'pose; my father says we shouldn't gamble."

Old Pyjams was wrenching the side off the crate which was marked "*Jamaican Produce*" in large stencilled letters.

"Like to bet me another million I don't know where that crate's come from?" asked Jennings, scenting further money-making possibilities.

"No, thanks. I've lost quite enough for one afternoon; I'm broke."

The ex-millionaire watched old Pyjams with interest. What was he going to do with all that wood? Perhaps he could spare a little for the model of Columbus' ship, the *Santa Maria*, that Darbishire was going to make for the end of term history modelling display. What did Jennings think?

"Prang idea!" said Jennings. "I want some wood too; I'm making a model of one of those things they used in the French Revolution that Louis XV got gelatined with."

"Don't you mean guillotined?" suggested Darbishire.

"Probably. Anyway, I've got a razor blade for the knife part," Jennings went on, "and half a bottle of red ink for the blood, but I haven't found any wood yet."

"You ask him, then," urged Darbishire.

Old Pyjams, when approached, replied that the wood was needed for his kindling. In a whispered undertone, the model-makers debated this point. Darbishire maintained that old Pyjams required the wood for his nephews and nieces.

"You know, kith and kin," he explained; "but as they're young ones they're '-ling,' like duckling, and gosling, and—er—"

"Starling?" suggested Jennings.

He approached old Pyjams again.

"I say, Robinson," he said, "d'you think your kindling wants all that wood? Would you mind asking him—er—her?"

"Them," corrected Darbishire.

"Look out!" shouted old Pyjams suddenly. Both boys jumped slightly and looked out. There, sidling furtively out between the bars of the crate, was an enormous and evil-looking spider.

"Golly," said Jennings, enchanted; "you've got a stowaway! Isn't he a beauty! He's nearly as big as my hand. I vote we capture him and—"

"Come away off on it; don't you touch 'un," warned old Pyjams. "Poison most like. Come from Jamaica it has," he went on. "Snakes and spiders, and all them foreign reptiles is poison."

He aimed a blow in its direction with a piece of wood, but the spider, with all its six eyes focused upon him, saw it coming and ran as fast as its eight legs could carry it. It took refuge beneath a bunch of bananas and waited for the all-clear.

"Don't kill it, Pyjams—er—Robinson," urged Jennings. "It might be worth a lot of money; you know, a defunct species."

"I'll bash it one and be done with it," retorted Old Pyjams. "I don't like 'em. Catch the rabies most like if it bit yer."

"Yes, but what if it's rare? I vote we catch it and take it to Mr. Carter; he knows all about insects; he's a—a taximeter."

"Don't be so wet, Jen," corrected Darbishire. "A taximeter only stuffs them. Benedicks an—an entomologist. Anyway, let's catch it, and bags it be mine."

Robinson was still anxious to leap into action with his piece of wood, but the boys persuaded him that it would be an injustice if the insect were killed before Mr. Carter had identified it. The next problem was how to effect the capture without being bitten—or stung, whichever it was that a spider did. Darbishire's pencil box was voted the best way. Approaching cautiously with box and ruler at the ready, Jennings was to propel the insect into the box and Darbishire would clap down the lid. In practice it was more difficult, as both boys were extremely nervous, and the spider obstinately refused to co-operate.

"Ready?" said Jennings at the third attempt.

"Okay," said Darbishire.

"Golly, it can't half shift!" Jennings said, as the result of the manœuvre was to send the spider scuttling in the opposite direction; but at last it was cornered and, with a twitch of the ruler, Jennings jerked it into the box and Darbishire shut the lid.

Old Pyjams was sceptical.

"Ah, eat its way through the box and all most like. I knew a chap got bit once; arm swole right up; 'ad to cut 'is sleeve to get 'is jacket orf of 'im."

"What, just from a spider's bite?"

"No; snake this was. But they're all the same, them foreign reptiles; deadly, that's what."

Clasping the box gingerly, they made their way to Mr. Carter's room, but repeated knocks on the door produced no answer. The identification would have to be postponed. The dormitory was out of bounds in the daytime, but no one was about, so they decided to go there. Cautiously, they moved along the passage and opened the door; the coast was clear. The next stage of the operation was to transfer the spider from the cramped quarters of the pencil box to the more spacious surroundings of a tooth glass. This, they decided, would make an admirable observation turret where the spider could be examined more closely. It should also have the effect of putting it in a sunnier temper, when it realised how its comfort was being studied. A slight difference of opinion arose on the question of whose tooth glass should be used. Darbishire argued that Jennings' glass was the obvious choice, because Jennings had been the first to see the spider. Jennings, for the opposition, contended that the spider was the legal property of Darbishire as he had *bagsed* it, and it was the first duty of animal lovers to provide fodder and shelter for their own dumb chums. But as Darbishire was afraid that the spider's footprints might leave poisonous traces in his tooth glass, they compromised and used Temple's glass instead. This was not because they wished any harm to befall him, but because his tumbler contained smears of tooth paste which, the tube advertised, was guaranteed to kill germs, and might therefore be relied upon to remove traces of poison.

With infinite caution, Jennings opened the lid of the pencil box half an inch and peered in. The spider was sitting moodily in the middle of the box with its legs tucked in, and the dejected droop of its body seemed to suggest that it was not happy.

"He's got a sort of worried look, hasn't he?" Darbishire whispered softly, as though afraid that his normal voice would be too much for the insect to bear in its present state of woe.

"He's suffocating, that's why," Jennings explained, "or maybe he's got cramp." Quickly he opened the lid wide and clamped the inverted glass over the captive. Then he turned the glass the right way up so that the pencil box stopped doing duty as a floor and became a ceiling. The spider righted itself and stood up. With its legs extended, it stretched the width of the tumbler, and its attitude was fierce and hostile. It stood on seven legs and waved the eighth in a manner that boded evil.

"Golly, isn't he a beauty!" gasped Jennings, wonderingly. "Massive hairy legs. I say, he's in a super bate; look, he's gnashing his fangs. He looks hefty poisonous, doesn't he? Oughtn't we to get him something to eat?"

"Bananas?" suggested Darbishire.

"No, you goof. They don't live on bananas, they only live in them. Where can we get some insects from?"

"There's a fly-paper hanging up in the tuck shop," suggested Darbishire. "P'raps we could scrape some off. Bags you do it, though."

"He looks lethal poisonous now," said Jennings, as the spider stopped waving its legs and started on a tour of exploration. It made one or two attempts to walk up the side of the glass, but its efforts would hardly have inspired Robert Bruce with the determination to go out and win battles, for very soon it gave up.

"I wonder if he's a—a something like ta-ranta-ra?" said Jennings.

"Tarantelle," corrected Darbishire. "No, that's a dance, but it's something like that. It's bang-on dangerous if it is. I read a story once about some man-eating spiders; you don't think it's one of those, do you?" He was breathless with horrified hope.

"Might be," returned Jennings. "He seems to be drawing the line at Bod's tooth paste, though."

"I knew a joke, too, it was putridly funny." Darbishire giggled with nervous excitement. "There's some chaps talking, and somebody says to somebody else, 'Have you heard of the man-eating spiders?' And then somebody else says to another chap, or it could be the first chap; you know, the one that somebody had said to him about the man-eating spiders. Anyway, it doesn't matter which one it is, but the other chap says, 'No, but I've heard of the man-eating sandwiches.'" Darbishire became convulsed with mirth, but Jennings looked at him stonily.

"Good, isn't it?" gurgled Darbishire. "Have you heard it before?"

"No, what is it?"

"I've just told you. Somebody says to somebody else—"

"Oh, that—what's funny in that?" Jennings said, in a tone which would have spread a wet blanket over the funniest of stories. "There's no such thing as a man-eating sandwich. Anyone knows that."

"Oh, you're crackers," Darbishire objected. "You can't even see a joke."

"Oh, was it a joke? Very funny, I'm sure," he said in a dull, flat voice. "Loud titters and hearty grins!"

"Oh, shut up!" said Darbishire. "I shan't tell you any more."

The spider seemed safe enough with the pencil box acting as a roof, so they slipped a piece of chocolate into the glass in case the prisoner should feel hungry. Then they went downstairs to the library to consult the encyclopædia. The work of identification was not easy, for there were four closely printed pages describing the anatomy and habits of dozens of spiders—several of which fitted the Jamaican stowaway perfectly. Darbishire maintained that it was either a poisonous tarantula or a bird-eating spider from South America. When Jennings pointed out that the banana crate had come from the West Indies, Darbishire contended that, as the spider was known to have made one ocean journey, it could easily have made two. His friend poured scorn on this idea of a hitch-hiking globetrotter.

"I bet it's not," he said. "I don't s'pose it's even a—a tarradiddle."

"Tarantula," Darbishire corrected, after a furtive glance at the book.

"Well, I bet it isn't. I bet you a million pounds it isn't."

"Well, I bet you two million pounds it is. Take me on?"

"You haven't got two million pounds," Jennings scoffed.

"Well, I bet you a penny then," replied Darbishire, prudently descending to brass tacks. "It's either that or a bird-eater, and if it's not that, it's so rare it's defunct, and I vote we write to the British Museum and say we've got a thing that's so defunct it isn't in the encyclopædia, and will they please send an expert down at once to say what it is."

He paused for breath.

"Yes, rather," said Jennings. "Prang idea!"

They stood silent for a moment, for in the minds of both the boys there formed a mental picture of the arrival of the expert. Darbishire's expert was a short-sighted professor, with a long white beard and an old-fashioned frock coat, who peered intently at the spider through a magnifying glass, while making exclamations of wonder and delight. Jennings' gentleman was a tall thin man with aquiline features. He wore a uniform with brass buttons and, above the shiny black peak of his regulation cap, the words "British Museum" were inscribed in letters of silver wire.

"I vote we don't tell Benedick till the Museum's been, or he'll want a share of the reward," Darbishire said.

"What reward?"

Darbishire insisted that some recognition of their services was almost inevitable, for if the spider was rare, the cream of the insect-studying world would hurry from all parts to write books about it; on the other hand, if it was a crop-destroying pest, a grateful government would not be slow to reward public benefactors. Jennings was sceptical; it seemed unlikely to him that the captive was anything but a large and hairy-legged insect with no instinct to harm anyone, and he was all in favour of consulting Mr. Carter before calling in the British Museum. Still, it was Darbishire's spider, so he did not pursue the matter.

The bell rang for afternoon preparation before Darbishire's letter was begun, and he went into the classroom bursting to tell everyone the news. After preparation and during football practice the news spread with lightning rapidity, and the school buzzed with excitement and shuddered with horror as they heard that Darbishire's death-dealing monster was imprisoned in the dormitory.

"I say, have you heard the latest? Darbi's got a hefty smash-on spider. It's as hairy as a ruin and super lethal."

"Stale buns! I knew that a hundred years ago; Jennings told me; and he said Darbishire was trying to make out that it eats sandwiches."

"No, it doesn't then, 'cos he looked it up in the encyclopædia; it's something Latin; tarantula or something."

"I bet that's not Latin."

"'Course it is. It goes like *mensa*. Tarantula—tarantula—tarantulam—tarantulæ—tarantulæ—tarantula. So that proves it."

"Shut up, we've got Latin this afternoon; we don't want any more now."

The group in the classroom ceased their speculation as Darbishire entered, wearing a dignified look suitable to one who has heavy entomologic responsibilities.

"Hallo, you chaps," announced the entomologist. "Anyone like to do me a favour? It's spivish important."

"I will," said Atkinson.

"Well, I've been doing some research, and my latest theory is that my spider's definitely a bird-eating one, so will you go and find old Pyjams and tell him to be sure not to let the hens out till the British Museum's been." There were still five minutes before afternoon school at four o'clock, and Atkinson sped on his errand of mercy while Darbishire continued his scientific discourse.

"Old Pyjams said that if it bites you, your arm swells up and they have to cut your coat sleeve to get it off—your coat, I mean, not your arm. He just took one look at the spider and he knew. It happened to a friend of his, you see, so we know it must be true."

The younger members of the group felt a little uneasy, but Darbishire, with his expert knowledge, was able to assure them that the spider was quite safe in its observation turret, and they need have nothing to fear.

The necessity of writing at once to the British Museum was uppermost in his mind during afternoon school, and several times he was in trouble for not attending to the lesson, but the bell rang at last and, surrounded by an awe-struck throng, he produced his writing pad.

"I think I'll write direct to the manager," he said, "and tell him I've got a gargantuan tarantula—if I can spell it."

"I thought you said it came from Jamaica?" queried Venables.

"So it does; gargantuan means the size, not the place. The Museum'll be wizard interested, I should think; they might even make me a Fellow."

"Jolly good!"

"No, just an ordinary one," said Darbishire. "I'm a bit worried about what to feed him on, though. We tried him with chocolate, but I think he was off his food a bit, 'cos he wouldn't look at it."

"Coo, super daring!" breathed Atkinson admiringly. "I wouldn't like to feed him. Ugh!" He shuddered, and ran spidery fingers down the neck of the boy standing beside him.

"Oh, it's quite easy," Darbishire said modestly. "Of course you've got to know something about taxid—er—ornith—er—it's easy if you know anything about insects. Jennings hypnotised him, while I popped the chocolate in."

The group pressed him for details of how to put spiders under hypnotic spells.

"Well," he said, "you have to fix it with a glittering eye, like the old codger in the poem who shot an albatross—Paul Revere or whatever his name was. You just do to the spider what he did to the wedding guests, and it stands still and doesn't move."

It was always shepherd's pie for tea on Fridays, and Jennings made as poor a meal as he had done the previous week. The injustice of fate spoiled his appetite and made him miserable. Last week he had been unable to play in the match because he was ill, and now that he was fit, Mr. Wilkins had spoiled everything. He knew that he himself was partly to blame, and he knew, because everyone made it abundantly clear, that his guilt would long be remembered in the minds of his fellows. He decided to go and see Mr. Wilkins, and plead with him to alter his decision. He would say he was willing to take the punishment, if only the others might be allowed to play the match, as arranged.

After evening preparation he went to Mr. Wilkins' room, but there was no reply to his knock, so he decided to call back later and to pass the time in watching Darbishire's spider. No one was about, so he slipped into the dormitory. There it was, still standing in its observation turret. Like Jennings, it had lost its appetite, and had made no attempt to eat its piece of chocolate. He gazed at it long and earnestly. It was certainly a beautiful specimen, but Jennings could not share Darbishire's belief that it was either so poisonous or so rare that the work of the British Museum must be interrupted. How stupid they would look if it turned out to be harmless after all! In his imagination, he could see innumerable experts chafing and complaining at the way their time had been wasted, while the Headmaster stood by ready to take action when the experts had departed. Surely Mr. Carter would know; he was an expert of sorts, even though he didn't wear a uniform with brass buttons.

Jennings picked up his soap dish from the wash basin, washed it out, and turned his attention once more to the spider. He removed the pencil box from the tumbler and replaced it with the soap dish. A quick movement and the spider somersaulted from the upturned glass into the dish, and the top was placed firmly into position. Carefully, Jennings left the tooth glass and pencil box as he had found them, and departed to Mr. Carter's room.

Mr. Carter looked up from his desk.

"Come in, Jennings," he said. "What can I do for you?"

"Please, sir, do you know anything about taximeters?"

"No, practically nothing," Mr. Carter replied. "Why?"

"But I thought insects were your hobby, sir?"

Mr. Carter explained the difference between a taxidermist, who stuffs animals, and an entomologist, who studies insects, and Jennings gingerly removed the cover from his soap dish.

"My word, he's a fine fellow," said Mr. Carter. "Where did you come across him?"

"In Temple's tooth glass, sir."

"Uh!" Mr. Carter looked puzzled. It seemed an odd place for such a discovery.

"And before that he was in a crate of bananas, sir," Jennings explained. "Robinson says your arm swells up if it bites you, and Darbishire's going to get the British Museum to call, but I didn't think it was a tarran something, so I borrowed it to ask you, sir."

Mr. Carter looked at the spider and then, to Jennings' horror, he picked it up and held it in the palm of his hand.

"Sorry to disappoint Darbishire," he said; "but this chap's quite harmless."

"Isn't he even poisonous of any kind?"

"Not even of any kind." He turned his hand over as the spider, savouring its newly-found liberty, stretched its legs and ran on to the back of Mr. Carter's hand and made for his sleeve. "No, you can't go up there," said Mr. Carter, gently removing the insect. He put it on his blotting pad where, after running a few steps, it stood still as though deep in thought.

"I'm afraid he looks rather startling," Mr. Carter said, as though apologising for the spider's appearance, "but he's quite gentle, really. He wouldn't hurt a fly! Or rather, he would hurt a fly, but he wouldn't hurt anything else," he amended.

As there seemed no prospect of Mr. Carter's coat sleeve having to be cut off, Jennings took courage and picked the insect from the blotter and replaced it in the soap dish. The dormitory bell sounded, and Jennings prepared to leave.

"I'd better put it back in the tooth glass, then, sir," he said, "'cos Darbishire doesn't know I've got it, and he'll be rather worried if he thinks it's escaped." The telephone rang as Jennings was making for the door, and Mr. Carter picked up the receiver.

"Hallo, Linbury Court here .... Who? ... Bracebridge School? ... Oh, yes."

Jennings started guiltily at the mention of Bracebridge, and the soap dish slipped from his hand and fell open on the carpet. The spider made a dash for liberty and took cover behind a bookcase. Quickly, Jennings cut off its retreat by blocking the bookcase at one end, and then set about the difficult task of poking behind the books with a pencil, in order to drive the spider back into the open.

It was not that he meant to listen to Mr. Carter's conversation on the telephone, but he could not go while the spider was still at large, and he found it impossible to help overhearing what Mr. Carter was saying.

"What's that? You're coming over tomorrow after all?" Mr. Carter said into the telephone. "But Mr. Parkinson rang me up at break this morning and cancelled it; he said you'd had German measles."

Jennings pricked up his ears and completely forgot the spider as he focused his mind on this unexpected development. He waited, hardly daring to breathe, while Mr. Carter listened to what was obviously a long and involved explanation from the other end of the line.

Then Mr. Carter said, "Oh, I see. Yes, I believe you're right. It is only three weeks for German measles, and if you started on the fourteenth, you'd be out of quarantine yesterday."

The unseen voice buzzed again.

"Yes," said Mr. Carter. "When Parkinson said a month, I took his word for it. Well, I'm very glad anyway, and we'll expect you tomorrow at two-thirty as we arranged .... Right. Goodbye." He replaced the receiver and turned to see Jennings kneeling by the bookcase.

"What are you doing here, Jennings?" he asked.

"I thought you had gone."

Jennings explained how the spider's bid for freedom had delayed him, and Mr. Carter got down on his knees and together they tried to entice the insect from its retreat. And all the time Jennings was thinking furiously. If Bracebridge had cancelled the match because of its German measles, the uproar in the classroom couldn't have been the genuine reason. Furthermore, if Bracebridge had 'phoned during morning break, Mr. Wilkins must have known that the game was cancelled before he imposed the punishment. And now there was some further complication, and they were coming after all. It was all very confusing.

"Well, you haven't helped much," said Mr. Carter. He rose to his feet and placed the spider back in the soap dish. "You'd better tell Darbishire to let it go; outside somewhere, not in the building."

"Sir," said Jennings. "Mr. Wilkins said the match was scratched because I didn't turn the tap on, and everyone made a row; and you said on the 'phone—"

"That 'phone call, Jennings, was a private conversation between Bracebridge School and me."

"Yes, but Mr. Wilkins can't do that, can he, sir? It's not fair; and what'll happen tomorrow when they turn up?"

Mr. Carter said, "Go to bed, Jennings, and don't ask so many questions. You remember what happened to the Elephant's Child with his 'satiable curiosity?"

"Yes, sir," said Jennings. When he got to the door he paused. "Yes, but, sir—"

"It's entirely a matter between you and Mr. Wilkins," Mr. Carter informed him. "And if he says that your form has to be in detention tomorrow afternoon, that's that, as far as I'm concerned."

"Yes, sir," said Jennings. "I wasn't going to argue, sir; I was only going to say that the Elephant's Child may have been nosey, but he did pretty well for himself in the end, didn't he, sir?"

On the landing outside, Jennings met Mr. Wilkins and delivered his carefully thought out speech.

"Sir," he began, "I must see you, sir. It's urgent." Mr. Wilkins was not pleased to see him.

"Well?" he said.

"Sir, will you keep me in tomorrow and not the others? Honestly, sir, it wasn't their fault, and they're down on me like anything."

"I'm not surprised," said Mr. Wilkins, not without satisfaction. "And what's more, I'm not altering my punishment. When I say something, it goes." He'd let them see he was someone to be reckoned with.

Jennings was about to explain that there was some mystery about the cancellation of the match, but Mr. Wilkins cut him short.

"You're late for dormitory, and you haven't changed into your house shoes. Go downstairs and do it at once."

Still clasping the soap dish, with the spider inside, Jennings descended to the basement, while Mr. Wilkins went to call upon Mr. Carter. He found him filling his pipe and wearing an amused smile which he was doing his best to conceal.

"Oh, Wilkins," he said. "Bracebridge have just been through on the 'phone. Apparently Parkinson thought that the quarantine period for German measles was one month."

"Well?" demanded Mr. Wilkins, suspiciously.

"It isn't; it's only twenty-one days; and as they've not had any more cases in the last three weeks, we can play them tomorrow without fear of catching anything."

Mr. Wilkins appeared stunned by the news.

"What?" he gasped.

This new development would make a hollow mockery of his drastic punishment. True, he could keep Form Three in detention during the match, if he insisted, but he grew hot and cold when he thought of the triumphant smiles that would greet the news when it was announced.

It was a delicate situation, in all conscience, and if he insisted on his detention now that the match was going to be played, his action would merely weaken the First Eleven, and it would be his fault if the school lost the game.

"What am I going to do?" he asked. "When I cancelled the game this morning, they got a nasty jolt they hadn't bargained for. They'll laugh their heads off if I climb down now."

"Well, I did warn you," Mr. Carter said. "I think you'll have to find a reason to let them off."

"Yes," said Mr. Wilkins. "But how? Needs thinking out, doesn't it?"

His blustering manner had departed; he left Mr. Carter's study deep in thought, and wandered off to take duty in the dormitories.

CHAPTER 11

BEWARE OF THE THING!

AT the first sound of the dormitory bell, Darbishire led the way upstairs, with the excited spectators at his heels. Only Dormitory Four would be privileged to see the spider in all its glory, for the boys were not allowed into any room except their own. But in order to alleviate the disappointment of the rest of the school, Darbishire had agreed to take the observation turret for a short walk along the corridor, so that the eager throng might enjoy a brief glimpse of the pride of the species *Araneœ*. With Temple, Venables and Atkinson pressing close behind, he flung wide the dormitory door and made a bee-line for the tumbler on the shelf.

"We must be careful not to frighten it," he said, "'cos it's probably super sensitive and—"

He stopped dead some three feet from the shelf. The expression of self-satisfied importance slid from his features like a landslide, and was replaced by a look of amazed horror. He stared wide-eyed and open-mouthed at the empty tumbler. "Oh, golly!" he gasped. "Oh, gosh! It's—it's escaped!"

"What!" Aghast, the spectators pressed nearer and, as the evidence of the empty glass confirmed the tidings, they stepped gingerly away out of range.

"It must have crawled up the glass and squeezed its way out," Darbishire continued excitedly. "Yes, look, the pencil box has been moved; it's got edged over a bit since Jen and I left it. Oh, golly, what are we going to do? It's lethal dangerous, don't forget."

The little group stood awkwardly, nervously silent. A cautious survey of the shelf revealed no trace of the spider and, with some misgivings, they decided that a thorough search was the only solution to the difficulty.

"It must be somewhere in the dorm," said Temple, glancing nervously over his shoulder. "We're bound to find it if we look. Mind out if anyone sees it, though. We mustn't touch it because of its deadly venom."

"Supposing it rushes at us?" Atkinson inquired timidly. "What'll we do?"

Darbishire replied, without conviction. "We'll have to try hypnotising it. Pity

145

Jennings is late coming up; he's rare at doing that."

Treading with the utmost delicacy, they started the hunt; all except Atkinson, who was scared to move from the centre of the floor for fear he should accidentally tread on the object of their search. The thought that the spider might be ensconced in someone's bed, or nestling snugly in the folds of someone's pyjamas, did nothing to lessen their uneasiness, and in the intervals of their cautious peering, Darbishire's entomological exploits came in for some harsh criticism.

"You are a dangerous maniac, Darbi," Temple said. "Just because you want to be made a jolly good fellow of the British Museum, we have to suffer, and now we can't even get into bed."

"Well, how was I to know it could get out?" Darbishire defended himself. "Must have got hairy strength."

"Anyone knows a great hefty spider like that could have pushed a box off the top," Temple went on. "I expect it made a great leap as soon as your back was turned, and now it's sitting in a corner laughing at us and waiting to spring."

"Oh, shut up," said Darbishire, thoroughly rattled. "Let's go on looking." With infinite caution, he lifted a piece of soap and searched beneath, and in his agitation he swept a tooth brush off a basin with his elbow. The brush fell to the floor with the faintest of clatters, but the four boys started violently and spun round in the direction of the sound.

Darbishire gulped and said, "All right, chaps; false alarm. We must go on looking, but for goodness' sake don't let it bite you!"

"No fear," added Venables, "'cos your arm swells up like a balloon, don't forget, and they have to cut your jacket off."

"I vote we all take our jackets off first, then," suggested Atkinson.

"Fat lot of good that'd be if it bit you in the foot," Temple retorted. "It'd be more sense to put our gum boots on in case it nips us on the ankle."

Darbishire thought that the boys in the other dormitories should be warned, in case the spider had gone on a voyage of exploration. He was not keen to make the announcement personally, as experience in his own dormitory had taught him that the news would not be sympathetically received. He decided, therefore, to compromise and display a warning notice on the door, so that passers-by in the corridor might be put on their guard. He had a small piece of white chalk in his pocket, so he tiptoed into the corridor and paused to consider the wording of his notice. He would like to have written, "*Beware of the dangerous gargantuan tarantula which is not now in captivity*," but he had not enough chalk for so lengthy a warning. He shortened the notice and started off, "*Beware of the—*" but without the encyclopaedia to refer to, he was uncertain how to spell tarantula, and there was also the doubt that the spider might belong to some other species, anyway.

Finally, he wrote, "*Beware of the Thing!*" in large capitals and left the rest of the school to puzzle over this cryptic warning for the remainder of the evening.

He returned to his dormitory, where the search was still going on in a timid and half-hearted fashion, for no one dared to make a thorough investigation under or behind articles of furniture which might conceal the lurking foe.

Temple said, with a sigh of relief: "Well, it's not in my pyjamas, anyway, thank goodness. Have you looked in your bedroom slippers, Venables?"

"Yes," Venables said uncertainly; "but I can't see right up to the end of them."

"Put your hand in, then, and feel," suggested Atkinson.

"Oh, yes, and get my fingers bitten. No, thanks!" Darbishire lowered himself gingerly on to his hands and knees, and peered under the beds. Suddenly, a strangled cry broke from his lips and the other boys leapt like startled deer.

"What's the matter, Darbi?"

"Did it get you, Darbi? Are you all right?"

"Shall I go and get Matron?"

The whole dormitory was alert and attentive, and Atkinson had already produced his nail scissors in order to cut the victim's coat sleeve, when Darbishire announced that his discovery was only a piece of fluff.

"It looked just like it, though," he explained.

But this fresh shock had unnerved them. The thought that the deadly enemy might be lurking in sponge bag, dressing gown or towel, was a terrifying one.

"We might even have to get the floor boards up to find it," Temple said helplessly. "It's not safe to get undressed, let alone get into bed."

"And if we did get into bed," added Atkinson, "it might suddenly rush at us in the dark and we'd all wake up like swollen balloons .... Swollen balloons!" he repeated in awe-struck tones, as a covey of elephantine barrage balloons drifted across his imagination. He shuddered, and then rose quickly from the bed on which he had thoughtlessly seated himself.

Something had to be done, and as none of them felt safe standing by their beds within reach of the spider's fangs, Darbishire suggested that they should put their bedside chairs in the middle of the room and stand on them. This would keep their feet clear of the floor and enable them to see the approach of the foe. Walking as delicately as Agag, the boys assembled their chairs and climbed up to commence their vigil.

After a strained and miserable silence which lasted for nearly a minute, Atkinson spoke the question which was uppermost in all their minds.

"Have we got to stand like this all night?" he said.

"Jolly well hope not," Venables muttered. "Gosh, you are a maniacal lunatic, Darbishire."

"I'm going to find Wilkie," announced Temple. "He's on duty, so he ought to know how to deal with venomous spiders, or if he can't, p'raps he could get the British Museum to hurry up a bit, otherwise"—he shrugged his shoulders helplessly— "otherwise we'll have to evacuate."

Temple departed on his errand, but it took him some time to locate the master on duty. This was unusual, for normally Mr. Wilkins spent the bedtime half-hour in bursting into each dormitory, every few minutes with injunctions to "Get a move on and take a brush to those knees." But this evening he had retired to Matron's sitting room, where although officially on duty, he could find the peace and quiet necessary for one who had a problem to resolve.

The school clock struck eight, and down in the boot-room Jennings suddenly realised that he had wasted ten minutes in changing his house shoes. True, he had spent most of the time in giving the spider an airing, and admiring its style as it sidled majestically round the boot-lockers, but the chimes of the clock reminded him that he would have to hurry if he was to be in bed before the bell. He picked the spider from the toe of a football boot where it had been marking time gracefully, and replaced it in the soap dish. Golly, he'd have to hurry, and Darbishire would be getting worried about what had become of his rare specimen. How small he would feel when told that his spider was quite harmless!

Clasping the soap dish, he made his way upstairs, unaware just how worried Darbishire actually was.

At the door, he paused to read the notice: "*Beware of the Thing!*" What on earth did that mean? They must be crazy! When he opened the door and saw Darbishire, Atkinson and Venables standing forlornly on their chairs as though in fear of some rising tide, he was quite sure of it. They certainly were crazy!

148

"What are you all doing up there?" he asked.

"It's the spider," Darbishire replied in a nervous voice. "It's got loose. Get your chair and bring it over here if you want to be safe."

"Yes, don't stand there like that," urged Atkinson.

"It might charge at you suddenly and then you'd be liquidated."

A slow smile spread across Jennings' features as he realised what had happened.

"Well, you are a lot of funks," he said scornfully, as he placed the soap dish on the shelf above his bed. "Fancy being scared of a little tin-pot spider!" And he laughed contemptuously as he took off his jacket and shoes.

"You—you're not going to get into bed, are you?" gasped Venables.

"Of course I am; I'm not scared." Jennings hummed gaily to prove it.

"Coo, super daring," breathed Atkinson. "I wouldn't. You know what'll happen if it nips you, don't you? Balloons!" And with one finger he sketched the uncomfortable outline in the air above his head.

Jennings dismissed the danger with a laugh and proceeded to get undressed. He was aware of the sensation he was causing, and his movements were casual and slow as befitted one who cares nought for danger. He sang snatches of song in the intervals of telling the others how cowardly they were. They were awestruck and envious, but they did not dare to follow his example. Jennings was enjoying every minute of it. From time to time he stole a glance at the soap dish, but all was well; it gave no sign of its guilty secret.

Presently Darbishire said: "Mind how you turn your bed down, Jennings." And a second later he yelled aloud: "Look out!"

Even Jennings jumped, although he knew there was no danger, while Atkinson and Venables nearly fell off their chairs in their agitation.

With a dramatic sweep of the hand, Darbishire pointed to Jennings' pillow.

"There," he croaked. "Look! The poisonous spider's venomous footprints."

Jennings inspected his pillow.

"Oh, rats!" he replied. "Those are cake crumbs. I foxed a hunk up to eat in bed last night, but it went all crumbly and got all over the sheet. Massive tickly." A mischievous expression came into his eyes. "Not so tickly as the fangs of a dangerous spider, though," he went on, his voice shaking in mock horror. Then he burst out laughing. "You do look funny up there," he gurgled. "You are a lot of funks! Who's frightened of a titchy little incey-wincey spider?

149

"Incey-wincey spider, climbed the waterspout,
Down came the rain and washed the spider out,"
he recited gleefully.

"You're just a swank," said Venables, but he was unable to conceal a trace of admiration in his voice.

"Jennings may be very brave," commented Darbishire; "but he's behaving most recklessly. My father says that discretion is the better part of valour, so I'm staying up here till Wilkie comes to tell us what to do."

"Oh, goodness!" said Jennings, his wave of enjoyment ebbing visibly. "Does Wilkie know about this?"

"Bod's gone to fetch him," said Atkinson.

Jennings thought for a moment. He had decided to make a last appeal to Mr. Wilkins to reconsider his decision to punish the form, and it would not improve matters if Mr. Wilkins thought that Jennings was responsible for this new interference with the smooth running of the school routine.

"I say, Darbi," he said. "Come outside on the landing a mo'; I want to talk to you privately."

"I daren't get down," said Darbishire, unhappily.

"But it's urgent. Look, you can see it's clear as far as the door. I'll convoy you and hypnotise the spider if it jumps out of an ambush and attacks us."

With some misgiving, Darbishire left his perch and followed Jennings on to the landing.

"Well?" he demanded.

"Look, it's quite all right about the spider," Jennings assured him in a conspiratorial whisper. "It's in the soap dish on the shelf over my bed. I borrowed it to show Benedick, and he says it's quite harmless, unless you're a fly."

"Honest injun?"

"Yes."

"Coo! What a swizzle!"

Relief at their safe deliverance was mingled with disappointment that the spider was not a rare specimen after all. "Good job I haven't posted my letter to the Museum yet," Darbishire said, and then another aspect struck him which was almost as unpleasant to think about as the ordeal through which they had just passed.

"Golly!" he said. "What'll the other chaps say when they find out? They'll think I've been fooling them; they'll never believe me after all this hoo-hah if

I just walk in with a light laugh and say it isn't poisonous after all. They're bound to say I knew all the time and then I'll get bashed up for pulling their legs."

"You'd better keep quiet about it, then," Jennings advised.

"Yes, but I can't let them go on thinking it's dangerous and leave them standing on chairs all night. Oh, gosh, I wish I'd never found the beastly thing, and I was counting on that reward from the British Museum to buy a meccano set with, too."

Jennings pointed out that this was not the only difficulty. If they were to produce the spider forthwith and announce it to be harmless, Mr. Wilkins would think that Jennings had borrowed it specially to spread alarm and despondency throughout the dormitory. And though this was not the case, Mr. Wilkins would be only too ready to believe the worst and would be in no mood to cancel the detention.

"Wilkie'll get into a hefty bate if he knows I had anything to do with it," he went on. "You see, there's just a chance there may be a match tomorrow after all, so I've got to get him in a good mood."

"What had we better do, then?" Darbishire wanted to know.

"Well, the less either of us has to do with finding the wretched thing, the better. You, 'cos you'll get bashed up, and me, 'cos Wilkie'll think I pinched it to put the wind up everyone."

They decided that the best thing to do was to remove the lid of the soap dish without being seen, and allow someone else to make the discovery. The spider could then be caught and disposed of without anyone suspecting its non-poisonous qualities. They returned to the dormitory again and Darbishire mounted his chair to allay suspicion. A moment later he shouted "Look!" and pointed to the far end of the room. Atkinson and Venables turned horrified eyes in the required direction, and while their attention was diverted, Jennings reached up and took the lid off the soap dish.

"Oh, sorry," said Darbishire, "another false alarm; it must have been that splodge on the wall I was looking at."

Atkinson and Venables turned shakily away from the false alarm, and their eyes continued to rove round the room in their ceaseless quest. But, although their gaze passed frequently over the shelf above Jennings' bed, neither of them noticed the spider. It was so obviously visible that Jennings and Darbishire had difficulty in keeping their eyes away from it, and the spider seemed to be doing its best to attract attention by making little darting sallies along the shelf.

Jennings became anxious at the delay; he wanted the spider safely imprisoned before Mr. Wilkins arrived, so that his innocence would be unquestioned, and he would be free to open up the vexed question of the detention.

Heavy footsteps on the landing outside indicated that Mr. Wilkins was approaching. He had not been feeling in the best of tempers when Temple had run him to earth in Matron's sitting room, and the news that he was required to round up a dangerous insect was not well received. Heedless of the warning on the dormitory door, Mr. Wilkins strode in, followed by Temple, who appeared relieved to see that all present were still fit and well.

"Now, what's all this tomfoolery about?" Mr. Wilkins barked. "What are you boys doing on those chairs? Get down at once."

"But, sir, it's poisonous," protested Venables, "we daren't get down. It isn't tomfoolery, really, sir."

The serious note in his voice made Mr. Wilkins pause.

"Let's get this straight," he said. "Temple comes to me burbling like a half-wit with some cock-and-bull story about a spider. Well, how d'you know it's poisonous for a start?"

"But we proved it, sir," Temple assured him. "Darbishire looked it up in the encyclopædia; it's either a tarantula or something like a blank window."

"What?" said Mr. Wilkins, at sea.

"Black widow, sir," corrected Darbishire.

"And it came out of a crate of bananas," Temple went on. "And Robinson said it was just like one that bit a friend of his."

"And he 'swoled' up like a balloon," added Atkinson.

Mr. Wilkins knew nothing of insects. It might be true or it might not, but it would be better not to take risks in a case of this kind.

"All right," he said, seizing a hairbrush; "we'll take precautions and have a thorough search."

"Shall I go and fetch you a cricket bat, sir?" asked Temple, eager to assist. "You can have mine willingly. It's locked up for the winter, but I can easily get the key and—"

"No, sir, have mine," urged Venables, "it's full size; Temple's is only a size four."

"Sir, mine's got a rubber handle on, sir," Atkinson put in. "Unfortunately I left it at home last hols, but if I'd thought, I could have brought it back and it'd be super, wouldn't it, sir?"

"Be quiet, all of you," Mr. Wilkins ordered.

"I've got some batting gloves at home, too, sir," added Atkinson. "They'd be a bit small for you, even if I'd got them here, but they've got rubber fingers, and—"

"Will you stop this chattering!" Mr. Wilkins sounded annoyed, and Jennings decided to broach the question of the punishment before the situation became any worse.

"Please, sir," he said. "I wanted to talk to you about the detention. I'm quite willing to stay in if you'll let the others off."

Mr. Wilkins was exasperated beyond measure.

"For goodness' sake, Jennings, can't you see I've got something more important to do than talk about detention. This is a serious business. If this spider's really poisonous it—it—well, it might bite someone."

"Yes, sir, but this detention—"

"Go away. Go and stand on a chair with the others."

Jennings gave it up for the time being; he took his chair and joined the group in the middle of the room.

Mr. Wilkins glared round the dormitory defiantly; he brandished the hairbrush as though challenging the spider to come out and fight.

"Well, I can't see any sign of it," he said. He moved towards Jennings' bed and prodded a dressing gown with the hairbrush. By now he was standing immediately below the shelf, while the spider performed a ceremonial war-dance just above his head.

Jennings and Darbishire watched entranced, and it was with the greatest difficulty that they held their peace. From their vantage point on the chairs, it was clearly visible. If only the others would stop looking at Mr. Wilkins and raise their eyes to the shelf above. Then Temple saw it …!

"Ooh!" he gasped.

Mr. Wilkins turned.

"What's the matter, boy?"

"I can see it, sir."

"You can? Where? Let me get at it."

"No, sir, don't move, sir," Temple warned him. "Don't even bat an eyelid, sir."

"But where is it, you silly little boy?" demanded Mr. Wilkins, looking in every direction except the right one.

They had all seen it now.

"Keep still, sir, don't move," called Atkinson. He gripped his nail scissors firmly, ready to deal with any sleeve-cutting crisis that might arise.

"I'll throw a slipper at it," Venables suggested.

"No, don't do that," Jennings reproved him. "You might miss and hit Mr. Wilkins. Sir, about this detention, sir ..." he began again.

Mr. Wilkins was rattled; he knew the foe was close at hand, and this was no time to talk about detention.

"I can't see the beastly thing," he said. "Where is it?"

"It's about an inch above your head," answered Temple shrilly. "It's coming nearer—it's on the edge now; it's taking off—oh, sir, keep still; it's touched down on your shoulder."

Mr. Wilkins aimed a sharp blow at his left shoulder, and out of the corner of his eye, he caught his first glimpse of the spider. It was on his right shoulder and walking determinedly towards his collar. Mr. Wilkins froze; rigid and motionless he stood, and the spider did the same. Mr. Wilkins made a movement with his left hand and immediately the spider resumed his walk. Mr. Wilkins stopped, and the spider stopped. It was clear to Mr. Wilkins that if he made any further movement, the spider would continue along its dangerous course. The only way to postpone an encounter at unpleasantly close quarters, was to remain perfectly still. Unfortunately, the insect was so close to his collar by this time, that he could not see it without twisting his head, and every movement made an attack more imminent. For five seconds both Mr. Wilkins and the spider might have been statues; then the larger of the two opponents spoke out of the corner of his mouth.

"What's it doing now?" he asked.

"It's giving you a sort of look, sir," Temple said.

"Stand still, you boys," Mr. Wilkins ordered; "I'm going to knock it off with a sharp blow."

"It might bite your hand, sir," objected Atkinson.

For half a second Mr. Wilkins considered.

"Here, Darbishire," he said, "you looked this thing up in the book; which end bites—the back or the front?"

"All over, I think, sir," replied Darbishire. "And, anyway, I don't know one end from the other."

A strangled gasp from Temple indicated that the spider had become tired of this waiting game and was about to make a practice run over the target area. The situation was desperate, and Mr. Wilkins did not like it at all.

Suddenly Jennings stepped down from his chair and approached the master with hand outstretched.

"It's all right, sir," he said. "Keep still and I'll get it off."

"Don't touch it, boy; don't touch it," warned Mr. Wilkins.

"But I know how to handle it, sir. I can hypnotise it, sir, honestly." Jennings stared hard and the spider returned his gaze. Then he gently picked the insect from Mr. Wilkins' collar and placed it safely in a tooth glass.

For some seconds the spectators were dumbfounded; then slowly they recovered the power of speech.

"Coo!" they murmured reverently. "Coo! ... Gosh! ... You have got a nerve, Jennings."

Jennings smiled modestly.

The tension was eased now that the danger had passed; everyone breathed sighs of relief and, slightly disappointed, Atkinson put his nail scissors back in their case.

"Jolly daring, wasn't it, sir?" said Temple. "Why, p'raps Jennings has even saved your life, sir."

"Well done, Jennings! Super prang nerve!" The dormitory was unanimous in its praise.

"Er—yes, thank you very much, Jennings, I'm grateful," said Mr. Wilkins. "Of course, I could have coped with it quite easily, myself, in the normal way, but it had me—er—it had me at a disadvantage. Very plucky of you; it does you credit."

"That's all right, sir," Jennings replied. "I didn't want you to suffer, sir. And sir—sir, about this detention; it was all my fault, really, and I was wondering whether—that is—"

He stopped, as though reluctant to ask a favour of one who was so much in his debt that he could hardly refuse. Here was the answer to Mr. Wilkins' dilemma; it was his cue and he took it.

"Ah, yes, the detention," he said. "Well, now, we've just witnessed a—er—an extremely commendable action on Jennings' part."

"Hear, hear," said Darbishire.

"So in recognition of this—er—"

"Meritorious conduct," prompted Darbishire.

"Be quiet, Darbishire. In recognition of this—er—of this, I shall cancel the detention for tomorrow afternoon."

"Coo, thank you, sir!" The dormitory waved their sponge bags round their heads in appreciation.

"And I'll go further," Mr. Wilkins added generously, "the match against Bracebridge will take place, as arranged. The cancellation is—er—cancelled."

"Hooray! Super-wizzo-duper! Smash-on!" Dormitory Four cheered the good news to the echo, while Mr. Wilkins stood smiling and satisfied.

"And now if you'll hand me that tooth glass, Jennings," he said, "I'll take the beastly thing downstairs and kill it."

"Oh, no, please don't do that, sir," Darbishire pleaded.

"But it's dangerous!"

"Oh, but, sir, it's only—"

Jennings trod on Darbishire's toes warningly.

"… Ow! Shut up, Jennings. I—I mean it's only poisonous if you don't know how to handle it."

Mr. Wilkins refused to allow the insect to remain a danger to all and sundry, so Jennings suggested that Mr. Carter should be asked to despatch it humanely in his butterfly killing bottle.

"Then he can give it back to us and we can stuff it," he suggested.

"Stuff it?" repeated Mr. Wilkins, surprised.

"Yes, sir," Jennings answered. "Like a taxi—er—a taxi—what d'you call it?"

"Entomologist," corrected Darbishire.

"That's right. I know where we can get some straw to stuff it with," he went on excitedly.

"Straw wouldn't do for this," said Darbishire. "It'd need sawdust or feathers, and p'r'aps we ought to get some buttons for the eyes, like they have for stags and things."

"H'm," said Mr. Wilkins. "It's going to look an odd sort of specimen by the time you've finished with it. Hurry up and get into bed; this light should have been out ten minutes ago."

He left them making arrangements to exhibit the spider in the school museum.

"We could make a glass case," Jennings was saying, "and have an inscription engraved—it'd have to be in Latin, though, if it's a tarantula, 'cos it goes like *mensa*, and that's first declension."

Mr. Carter looked up from his desk as Mr. Wilkins entered with a tumbler containing a familiar occupant.

"I say, Carter," he said, "will you put this ghastly insect in your killing bottle.

The wretched thing nearly bit me just now; if it hadn't been for some pretty prompt action by Jennings, I might be in a rather bad state by this time."

Mr. Carter smiled and reached for the tooth glass. "It's no laughing matter," said Mr. Wilkins. "It's poisonous. Here, don't touch it," he shouted, as Mr. Carter tipped the spider into the palm of his hand.

"Oh, no, it's not," Mr. Carter assured him. "It's quite harmless. I told Jennings it was when he brought it in earlier this evening."

Mr. Wilkins' jaw dropped slightly at this new revelation.

"What?" he gasped. "You told—? You mean Jennings knew that the thing was harmless all the time? And he let me ... Cor-wumph!" he exploded. "So that was the game, was it?"

Mr. Carter didn't follow.

"But, dash it, he—he picked it off my collar and I congratulated him on his bravery!"

"Did Jennings tell you it was poisonous?"

"Well, no, he didn't," Mr. Wilkins admitted; "but everybody else seemed to think it was, and I said they could play the match tomorrow because of his conduct."

Mr. Carter pointed out that Mr. Wilkins would have had to have done that, anyway. "It gave you a very good excuse," he said.

"Yes, I know, but ..." Mr. Wilkins sawed the air in his effort to find the right words to describe his feelings. "... Dash it, Carter, the wretched little boy must have been ... Right! I'll see he doesn't get away with it .... It's—cor-wumph— it's—dash it, it's deceitful."

Mr. Carter filled his pipe while the storm blew itself out. Then he said:

"I don't think I'd take the matter any further, Wilkins; you see, Jennings, was here when the 'phone message came through from Bracebridge, and quite by accident he found out that your scratching the match this morning was— well, not cricket."

"Oh!" Mr. Wilkins stopped fuming, and became quietly thoughtful.

"So all things considered," Mr. Carter went on, "I think it'd be better to let sleeping dogs lie, don't you?"

Mr. Wilkins stood silently for a moment, tracing a pattern on the carpet with the toe of his shoe. At last he spoke.

"H'm .... Yes, perhaps you're right, Carter," he said slowly. "... Perhaps you're right."

CHAPTER 12

JENNINGS USES HIS HEAD

JENNINGS spent most of Saturday morning with his fingers crossed. So many obstacles had arisen to block his path to the First Eleven, that he could hardly believe that they had been successfully overcome. Now, however, with bilious attacks and detentions safely behind him, there was nothing to stop him from realising his ambition. All the same, he was on his guard lest fate should intervene with another cruel blow.

His usual method of going down to breakfast was to take the stairs two at a time, and the last three in one enormous leap, but today he walked sedately, grasping the banisters firmly in case a chance slip should result in a sprained ankle. Carefully he scanned the faces at the breakfast table, fearful lest some wretched creature had come out in spots during the night and it would be Linbury's turn to telephone messages of cancellation. However, everyone's complexion seemed as flawless as could be expected, and Jennings breathed again.

At two-thirty, two taxis turned into the school drive, and the Bracebridge team arrived, accompanied by an apologetic Mr. Parkinson.

"I'm most terribly sorry for that stupid mistake about the quarantine," he said, as Mr. Carter greeted him. "It must have put you to considerable inconvenience."

"That's quite all right," Mr. Carter assured him. "It didn't cause us any trouble, did it, Wilkins?" He turned to his colleague for confirmation.

"Eh? Oh, no, no, no; not at all; not at all," Mr. Wilkins replied hastily, avoiding Mr. Carter's eye.

The home team was already on the pitch, resplendent in quartered shirts of magenta and white. In honour of the occasion, Jennings had washed the back of his knees as well as the front, and had obtained some new white laces which he had twisted under and over and round his boots in a cat's cradle of complex design. He then tied two knots on top of the bow for safety, and a third one for luck. The youngest member of the team was ready for the fray!

As soon as the visitors had changed, they streamed out on to the field and Mr. Carter, in shorts and blazer, blew his whistle and the game began.

It was soon obvious that the teams were evenly matched, but to start with both sides were keyed up, with their nerves on edge and sharpened by the importance of the occasion. As a result, the standard of play suffered, for an excited atmosphere breeds dashing and wasteful energy rather than careful and scientific play. During the first ten minutes both goals were bombarded with shots, some lucky, some wildly impossible. Gradually, however, their nerves were steadied and their play improved; tactics and skill replaced brute force and ignorance. In fifteen minutes, they had settled down to concentrate on control of the ball, fleetness of foot, and combination of movement.

The teams played in dogged silence, while the spectators on the touchline shouted encouragement.

"Linbury!" they yelled, in rolling waves of sound, and held on to the last note of their cry until their breath gave out. "Linbury! Play up, Linbury!"

Loudest of all the school supporters was Mr. Wilkins. It was as though he kept an amplifier in his throat for these important occasions, and as he swept up and down the touchline, his thunderous encouragement surged out across the pitch so that the players had difficulty in hearing the referee's whistle. In contrast to this, Bracebridge had only the thin and reedy tones of Mr. Parkinson to urge them on, and his voice was as the soft sighing of the west wind compared with Mr. Wilkins' stentorian north-easterly gale. The only other supporter for Bracebridge was their linesman who, owing to his rôle, should really have been impartial, but he was an opportunist, and he carefully waited for the lulls between the shouts for Linbury to squeak, "Play up, Bracebridge!" at the top of his voice.

The play swept from one goalmouth to the other. Now, the Bracebridge forwards had the ball and were attacking strongly. A long, low, swerving shot came in from the left wing and Parslow in goal for Linbury, dived to make a brilliant save. The school clapped and cheered and smacked each other on the back, and Mr. Wilkins switched on his loud-hailer at full volume.

"Good save," he boomed. "Jolly well done!"

The ball was cleared and away went the Linbury forwards, Temple, at outside-left, streaking down the field with the ball at his toes. A moment later he, too, had made a long, low, swerving shot and it was the Bracebridge goalkeeper's turn to dive and gather the ball safely to his chest before kicking it clear. Linbury clapped the goalkeeper dutifully while their faces registered disappointment, and Mr. Wilkins reduced the volume-control to half-way for his congratulations to the opposing custodian.

The Headmaster, perched precariously on his shooting-stick, looked down the line of spectators to make sure that none had committed the ungentlemanly fault of failing to applaud his opponents.

All through the first half the battle raged evenly and neither side scored. Jennings was playing a hard game, but he knew that he was not playing his best. As it was his first match and he was so much younger than the rest of the side, his sense of nervousness would not wear off. Desperately he sought to make up in dynamic energy what he felt was lacking in cool control.

His first chance came in the second half—and he missed it! Linbury were attacking, and a pass came to him from the left wing. The goalkeeper was out of position and Jennings, with the ball coming straight towards him, was unmarked, less than ten yards from the goal. Even Darbishire could not have missed such an easy shot, and had Jennings been content to direct the ball gently into the net, he would have scored. But the sight of the open goal filled him with a desire to drive the ball with irresistible, net-severing force. He drew back his right foot and swung it forward with all his might—and missed the ball completely! Johnson was just behind him, cool-headed and capable, and avoiding the floundering Jennings, he trapped the ball dead and casually propelled it into the net.

The whistle blew: one-nil.

The crowd on the touchline went wild with delight while Mr. Wilkins, as excited as the youngest of them, shouted, "Goal! Jolly good shot," with such volume that Mr. Parkinson, who was standing nearby, decided to watch the rest of the match from the other side of the pitch. He departed, gently massaging his ear to relieve the air-pressure on his eardrum.

Jennings walked up the field feeling very small. It was satisfying to be one goal up, but it was maddening that he, who could have scored so easily, should have thrown away his chance and left the capable Johnson to put the damage right. He tried hard to make up for his lapse and for the next few minutes he played an inspired game.

"Well, I'm doing all right now, anyway," he told himself, and then he proceeded to make his second unforgivable blunder. The Bracebridge forwards were pressing hard now, eager to level the score, and Jennings dropped back to his own penalty area.

"Get up the field," Johnson told him. "You're miles out of position."

Jennings took no notice; he would show them how well he could save a desperate situation, and no one could blame him for being slightly out of his place if he stopped the other side from scoring. He was standing by the side of the goalkeeper when the Bracebridge centre-half kicked the ball towards the goal. It was never meant to be a shot, and it was not even a good pass, for the ball bounced slowly towards the goalkeeper, and Parslow would have had no difficulty in catching it waist high, and clearing to the wing. He was already cupping his arms to take the ball when Jennings leaped in front of him and attempted a prodigious clearance kick. He was not quite quick enough, however, for instead of taking the ball fairly on his instep, it glanced off the side of his boot and was deflected in a wide parabolic curve into the corner of the net.

The whistle blew: one all.

The groan that rose to the lips of the spectators was silenced by the Headmaster's reproving stare, and, as in duty bound, a tepid clapping of gloved hands was just audible above the delighted squeaks of the Bracebridge linesman.

"Why do we have to clap when we're sorry, sir?" Atkinson asked Mr. Wilkins.

"You're applauding your opponents' good play," was the reply.

"But it wasn't good play, sir. Their chap didn't even mean to shoot, did he, sir? It was Jennings who scored, wasn't it, sir?"

"Yes, I suppose it was, really."

"Well, why do we have to clap then, sir?"

"Because ... Oh, watch the game," said Mr. Wilkins.

Jennings had never felt so unhappy in his life. It was an accident certainly, but a stupid, clumsy sort of accident that would never have happened if he had kept his place and not tried to interfere. Nobody said anything, but their silence was so eloquent that he squirmed with embarrassment as he took his place for the restart of the game. Both sides were playing grimly now; there were only a few minutes to go and the level score urged them to play as though their lives depended on it.

On the touchline, Darbishire, with notebook in hand, was wondering what to write next. As self-appointed sports reporter, he wanted to give his friend a good press notice, but it was straining the bonds of friendship to have to lavish praise on one who was so obviously responsible for this disaster. He consulted Atkinson and showed him what he had written:

"*On the last Saturday of term,*" Atkinson read, "*a massive crowd of indivigils gathered on the touchline to witness a gargantuan struggle when we played Bracebridge School in the Royal and Ancient sport of Kings as it is called known as Assosiasion football better known as soccer. They won the toss and chose to play down the inkline although it is not much of a one and you can hardly call it a slope."*

"It's all right up to there," said the press correspondent, "but in the next para. I call Jennings the doughty pivot of the team. Here, look, just after this bit about the ball being literally glued to his flashing feet."

"What's a doughty pivot?" demanded Atkinson.

"I'm not sure," Darbishire replied; "but I got it out of a newspaper, so it's bound to be a pretty stylish way of saying he's spivish rare, and now he's gone and made that frantic bish and scored a goal against us."

"Well, why not leave out all that about the glue on his feet and say that Jennings would have been a pivot if he hadn't made a bish. Benedick's looking at his watch, it must be nearly time."

"Yes, I suppose I … Gosh, what's happening?" Darbishire looked up as the cheers of the spectators rose to a full-throated roar, for in the last minute of the game, Jennings had found his form. Intercepting an opponent's pass, he was off down the field in a flash, dribbling the ball so brilliantly that Darbishire's reference to his flashing feet seemed almost credible. He swerved right and left through the Bracebridge forward line and left the attacking half-backs standing helpless and defeated. The Linbury forwards sprinted down the field in his wake, but they had been hanging back, and Jennings was now a good twenty yards ahead of his colleagues. With a deft flick, he pushed the ball round the Bracebridge full back and was away again with only the goalkeeper to beat. For a moment the goalkeeper hesitated, started to rush out, changed his mind and retreated between the posts.

Jennings bore down upon him, every line of his body expressing confident determination. He could not fail now. In the fifty-ninth minute of the eleventh hour his chance had come; alone he had swept through the ranks of the opponents and now victory was in sight. One sure, swift shot and he would have made a glorious atonement for his disastrous mistake.

The touchline seethed with hysterical excitement, but Jennings was oblivious to everything except the ball at his feet, and the agitated goalkeeper ahead. He steadied himself, and drew back his foot for the shot of a lifetime. He could not miss!

He could!

The goal was seven feet high by twenty-one feet wide; the goalkeeper was four and a half feet high and one foot wide. It was the deepest of tragedies that, with nearly one hundred and fifty square feet of goalmouth yawning like a cavern before him, Jennings had to direct his shot straight at the diminutive figure hopping nervously in the middle of the goal. The goalkeeper cannot be said to have saved the shot, for he was too agitated to be capable of skilful movement, but his presence on the goal-line was sufficient. The ball hit him fairly on the right knee and soared upwards and over the bar.

Jennings did not hear the disappointed groans of the spectators; he stood stock-still, unable to believe his eyes, but the damage was done, and the whistle had sounded for a corner kick. Why, oh, why, did he have to go and throw away the chance of a lifetime? he asked himself, and after that inspired run down the field too! He could have kicked himself. Now, of course, there would be no time to make good the damage, for Mr. Carter was looking at his watch and would blow the final whistle immediately after the corner kick had been taken. There was nothing more to be done; he had had every chance to justify his place in the team, and he had failed.

A despairing silence gripped the spectators as Nuttall, on the right wing, prepared to take the corner kick.

Darbishire was busy with his notebook; he had been trying to decide whether Jennings could still be described as a doughty pivot; that last run down the field would certainly have qualified him for the highest honours, but for that final, fatal bish. He compromised by altering the description to "doubtful," pivot, as it had a similar sort of sound without being too lavish in its praise. Then he looked up to watch the last kick being taken. He caught sight of Jennings, and his heart was wrung by his friend's expression of woe. Unmindful of the fact that one does not cheer when the ball is out of play, he suddenly broke the deathly silence by shouting:

"Never mind, Jennings. Better luck next time!"

Nuttall was just running up to take the kick when Darbishire shouted, and, at the sound of his name, Jennings turned his head for a split second towards the spectators on the left touchline. Thus it was that he did not see the ball hurtling towards his head until it was too late. Out of the corner of his eye, he saw an object about to hit him and, without stopping to think, he jumped to avoid it. his instinct, however, betrayed him, and instead of flinching away from the missile, he jumped right into the trajectory of its flight. With a slight thud, the ball hit him squarely in the middle of his forehead and knocked him off his feet.

He lay on the ground for a moment with his eyes shut, while he recovered from the shock. Thus he did not see the Bracebridge goalkeeper picking the ball from the back of the net; he did not hear Mr. Carter blow his whistle to indicate a goal, and immediately afterwards, blow a long, final blast as a signal that the game was over; he was unconscious of the stampede of hysterical delight which swept along the touchline, as sixty-eight pairs of gum boots executed an ungainly war-dance, while an equal number of vocal chords vied with one another in building up a roaring cataract of cheers.

The first thing Jennings knew was that the entire First Eleven were helping him to his feet and patting him on the back.

"Jolly well done, Jennings," said Nuttall, pounding him heavily between the shoulder blades. "A rare priority smasher!"

"Rather," echoed Temple. "Hefty skilful! Just like a professional!"

Jennings blinked uncertainly at the ring of smiling faces around him. What on earth were they feeling so pleased about?

"Finest header I've ever seen," said Brown major. "The way you leaped at it and then, wham!—right into the top corner of the net."

"And the force of it, too!" added Johnson. "You must have put all your weight behind it or you wouldn't have gone down flat like that, after you'd whammed it in."

It took Jennings a few seconds to grasp the significance of these remarks. So they had won the match after all, and it was all due to his alleged header in the final second! Well, it was very gratifying, of course, to be acclaimed as the hero of the hour, but what would they say if they knew that his wonder goal was the accidental result of the most frightful bish in the history of soccer?

"Well," he said hesitantly, "it's jolly super of you chaps to be so decent about it, but ..." The temptation to bask in unearned glory was strong, but virtuously he decided to tell the truth. "As a matter of fact, the whole thing was just a fluke."

Cries of protest greeted this statement.

"Go and boil yourself," they said affectionately. "You can't fool us like that."

It was all very well to be modest and self-effacing, but Jennings was surely entitled to take the credit for his spectacular shot.

"It was a goal in a thousand," said Temple, admiringly.

"Rats!" said Jennings.

"Well, a goal in a hundred, then."

"Rot!" said Jennings.

"Well, anyway, it was a goal," Temple amended. "Oh, well," said Jennings. If they wouldn't believe it was an accident, what more could he say?

Happily, the team escorted their visitors off the pitch.

"There's one thing about old Jennings," Brown major said to Johnson, as he splashed in the knee-bath some ten minutes later. "He doesn't swank as much as he used to. The way he back-pedalled about that super header of his; anyone who didn't know, might really think it had been a fluke after all."

"Yes," agreed Johnson, "he certainly knows how to use his head."

CHAPTER 13

MR. CARTER MAKES A SUGGESTION

DARBISHIRE sat at his desk, busily blacking out squares on a home-made calendar, and as he worked, he sang:

"This time next week where shall I be?
Not in this Academy."

He licked the worn stub of pencil and bent to his task with far more concentration than he was accustomed to display in class.

"We're tired of maths and we're tired of French,
Leaving Latin will be no wrench,
No more of Wilkie's super bates,
When once I'm out of these prison gates,"

he warbled.

"What are you doing, Darbi?" Jennings asked, strolling about the room with the restless curiosity that the last day of term always brings with it.

"I'm just doing my mammoth how-many-more-to-the-end-of-term calendar," replied the vocalist, ceasing the song abruptly.

Jennings came over to have a look.

"H'm, it's a bit complicated," he remarked, looking, without comprehension, at the maze of squares and figures.

"Yes, but it's superer than the ordinary sort;" Darbishire replied proudly. "All the other chaps just have so many more days to the end of term, and just cross out a square every day, but mine's got meals and hours and lessons and things, too. Look, I started it last week and this is how much more there is to go."

Jennings cast his eye over the work of reference.

"Famous Mammoth
How-Many-More-To-The-End-Of-Term Calender
by
C. E. J. Darbishire, O.C.C."

"What's O.C.C.?" he inquired.
"Official Calendar Compiler," replied the author with pride.
Beneath these credentials was written:

"No. of days more.	*7, 6, 5, 4, 3, 2, 1, 0.*
No. of hours more.	*See page 2. Not enough room here.*
No. of Latin lessons.	*5, 4, 3, 2, 1, 0.*
No. of times for suet pud.	*3, 2, 1, 0.*
No. of times for clean sox.	*2, 1, 0."*

Jennings raised an objection.
"s-o-x doesn't spell socks."
"Well, what does it spell?" demanded Darbishire, logically.
"s-o-x spells—well, of course it does, really," Jennings conceded.
"There you are, then," replied the O.C.C. "I know how to spell socks as well as anyone, but that's another of my inventions. Shorthand, you see; it saves wearing your wrist out when everyone knows what you mean anyway."
Over the page, the number of hours remaining filled seventeen lines. Starting at the imposing total of one hundred and sixty-eight, the figures had been crossed out until only twenty-one remained.
"It's a bit of a hairy fag, of course, crossing out the hours," Darbishire explained, "'cos sometimes when it's time to cross one off, you're doing something else, but it's wizard to come downstairs in the morning and swoosh off about ten all in one go."
Jennings was impressed. His own calendar consisted of a drawing of a wall with ten green bottles hanging from it. Every day he had rubbed out one bottle and had drawn what was meant to represent the mounting débris of broken glass at the bottom of the wall. Darbishire had obviously tackled his task more thoroughly. Perhaps next term, Jennings decided, he would go one better and

keep a tally of the passing time in minutes. He took pencil and paper to work out the details, and only abandoned his scheme when he discovered that there were some ten thousand minutes in a week, and it would be more than a full-time job trying to keep the record up to date.

The school was in the grip of that mounting excitement which always accompanies the last days of term. Tuck boxes had been packed days before it was necessary; and desks were tidied, untidied and re-tidied daily, in order to nourish the feeling of impending departure which these preparations always brought, with them. Completely useless articles which were discovered in the murkier recesses of tuck boxes and lockers were bartered freely, and the announcement, "Quis for a piece of junk!" would be answered by a deafening, "Ego!" which shattered the fast-crumbling nerves of the less placid members of the staff.

With an artistic flourish, Darbishire completed the current entries on his mammoth calendar.

"What shall we do now?" he demanded.

"Let's go and pack our tuck boxes again," Jennings suggested.

"But I've only just done mine," said Darbishire.

"Never mind," Jennings replied. "It's our last chance, 'cos they'll be taking them to the station this afternoon. Oh, wiz! I can hardly believe we're going home tomorrow. Come on, let's be bombers."

With outstretched arms, they wheeled and circled round the room.

"Eee-ow-ow .... Eee-ow-ow—!" The bombers banked steeply to get through the door, and only the pilots' skill and their patent retractable wingtips saved the planes from serious damage.

"Eee-ow-ow .... Eee-ow-ow—! Dacka-dacka-dacka-dacka!"

The tail gunner of "J for Jennings" squeezed the trigger for a five-second burst that went through the passage window and shot up a tradesman's van which was just turning into the drive. Unaware that he had been liquidated, the vanman drove steadily on—a spirit driver in a phantom chariot.

The pilots flew towards the tuck box room by dead reckoning, alert to notice every new sign that portended the passing of the term. Timetables, notices and regulations, had all been taken down. The library shelves were full, and the boot-lockers were empty. Masters clutching files of reports, and lists of travelling arrangements, moved purposefully along corridors, and their expressions were harassed or happy, according to how much of their work still remained to be done.

Old Pyjams, assisted by the gardener, was lowering trunks out of the dormitory windows on the end of a rope. They were watched by an enthralled crowd of boys, filled with the secret hope that the rope might break when someone else's trunk had started its journey. They climbed on the luggage as it was piled up on the quad, and as each trunk appeared on the window-sill, it was greeted by rousing cheers from the watchers below.

"Come up here," called Venables; "it makes a super grandstand!"

Old Pyjams shouted from above: "Come on off of it, some of you," as the trunk lids sagged beneath their load.

"We can't possibly come on off till we've seen our own trunks come down," Jennings reasoned. "Supposing they got left behind?"

At last they were rewarded by seeing their luggage dangling on the end of the rope, and completely satisfied, they set course once more for the tuck box room.

At the bottom of Darbishire's tuck box they found a notebook. The covers were slightly smeared with marmalade and chocolate spread, and an occasional date stone dropped from between the dog-eared pages as Darbishire turned them over.

"'*Flixton Slick—Super Sleuth*,'" he announced reverently. "And we never got beyond the first chapter!"

"We can still take it to Mr. Carter," said Jennings. "Tell him it's the first instalment of a serial and we'll get chapter two written next term—p'r'aps."

"Yes, but would he put it in the mag.?" mused Darbishire. "He turned down my special sports reporter account of the Bracebridge match."

"He never did!" Jennings exclaimed. "Why, it was jolly good; especially those four pages about me."

"He said the style was too ex—something."

"Exciting?"

"No, execrable, I think. And, anyway, he said thirteen pages was too long; he made me cut out all those super descriptions and all the atmosphere I'd carefully worked up, and by the time I'd got it short enough for him, all that was left was, '*The First Eleven beat Bracebridge by two goals to one on the last Saturday of term*,' and it didn't seem worth calling it a special report with my signature underneath, just for that!"

"Well, never mind," Jennings consoled him. "If he's turned down your football account, he can't very well refuse Flixton Slick, 'cos that'd probably discourage us, and he keeps on about how we ought to send stuff in to be printed."

"Okay, then," agreed Darbishire, "let's take it up to him when we go to bed, because there's the ping-pong tournament this afternoon, and films this evening."

Mr. Carter was always busy on the last evening of term. After a hurried cup of tea, he returned to his room and set to work. The boys' train tickets and travelling arrangements were stacked in a neat pile ready to be given out at breakfast on the following morning. His empty cash box witnessed that the school bank had satisfied its last customer. So far so good. He took up a folder from his desk containing a sheaf of reports; he would finish these first, and then begin the more exacting task of editing the manuscripts intended for the school magazine.

For forty minutes he concentrated on the reports and then, with a sigh of relief, he noticed that only one more remained to be done. When he saw that the sheet was headed "J. C. T. Jennings" he was glad that he had left it till the last, for he was not sure how to express his opinion. On the one hand, Jennings was keen, alert, willing, truthful, polite and bubbling over with high-spirited enthusiasm for everything that was going on about him; yet, when Mr. Carter cast his mind back over the more hair-raising events of the term, he could not help thinking how these virtuous qualities belonged to one who repeatedly dropped metaphorical spanners into the smooth-running machine of school life. Attached to the report was a note from the Headmaster to the effect that Mr. Jennings still seemed uncertain whether his son was settling down as he should, and would Mr. Carter make some suitable comment on this in his house master's report.

He was considering what to write when he heard furtive whispers outside the door.

"Bags you knock, Darbishire," said the first whisperer.

"No, bags you; it's mostly my story, so I don't like to seem too eager," he heard the second voice reply.

"Well, I'll just do a soft biff then, in case he's busy and doesn't want to be disturbed."

Mr. Carter called, "Come in," quickly, to forestall the thunderous onslaught on the door panels that he knew would follow this announcement. "I'm terribly busy," he said.

"Shall we hoof off, then, sir?"

"Shall you what?"

"Oh, sorry, sir. I mean, shall we take our departure, sir?"

"You'd better wait outside for a moment; I'm writing reports."

"Have you done mine yet, sir?" Jennings asked. "Hope you're going to give me a super decent one, sir. What are you going to say about my football, sir?"

"Yes, sir," Darbishire put in. "You ought to say something spivish smashing after that goal he headed on Saturday, sir."

"I think the less said about that goal the better," said Mr. Carter, meaningly.

Jennings looked uncomfortable.

"Did you know it was a fluke, then, sir?" he asked.

"I'm afraid I did," Mr. Carter replied. "I was standing a lot nearer to you than the spectators were, and in my experience the best goals are never headed with the eyes tightly shut."

Jennings looked more uncomfortable.

"Well, I did tell them it was a fluke, sir, but they wouldn't believe me; and we've got something here for the magazine we want to show you, sir," he said, quickly changing the subject.

"Well, if you like to wait on the landing while I finish this report, I'll see you in a few minutes."

"Yes, sir." They retired, closing the door behind them.

Mr. Carter found it impossible to concentrate with Jennings and Darbishire standing outside in the corridor. The door was by no means soundproof, and every low-toned syllable was clearly audible. He tried vainly to sum up Jennings' character in a few well-chosen words as the Headmaster had requested, but all the time he found himself becoming more and more engrossed in the conversation that was going on, in reverberating whispers, outside his door.

"It'd be the wizardest of prangs," Jennings was saying, "'cos if we've got something to eat that's really cooked, we can pretend our carriage is a dining-car, and we shall be ever so hungry, 'cos we shan't have had any breakfast if we put them in our pockets to eat on the school train."

"But s'posing they're not hard-boiled?" the listener heard Darbishire object. "It's all very well to say let's put them in our pockets for a feast, but if they smash and run all over the linings, we shall be almost dead with hunger by the time the train gets there, because of not eating them at breakfast time."

"Don't be such a bazooka," Jennings replied. "We've had eggs for breakfast every Friday this term, haven't we? And have you ever known them to be anything but hard?"

"Well, no, I haven't," Darbishire was forced to admit.

"Well, then, that proves it. You know what they're like in school kitchens; they can't be bothered to boil them for long enough to make them really nice and soft."

Mr. Carter returned to his report. "*He enters very fully into all out-of-school activities, and takes a lively interest in the corporate life of the school,*" he wrote.

"Talk quietly, or else he'll hear us," Jennings went on, and Mr. Carter could imagine the finger pointed towards his door.

"Now, there'll be eight chaps in our carriage, and if we all put our eggs in our pockets and eat them when we get on the train, we can chuck the empty shells at the chaps farther down the train when they put their heads out of the windows. Wizard prang!"

Thumps in the corridor indicated that an informal dance was being held to celebrate this idea.

Mr. Carter turned to the report again, and wrote: "*He has a vivid imagination and definite qualities of leadership, but these traits must be carefully guided into the right channels.*" And he made a mental note to see that all the breakfast eggs were consumed on the premises.

"Okay, then, we'll do that," said Darbishire, as the dance ended. "It'll be super, won't it?"

"Witch prang!" exclaimed Jennings.

"What do you mean, which prang? There is only one."

"No, I don't mean which prang, I mean Witch Prang. W-I-T-C-H. You know, black cats, and flying on broomsticks."

"Who's flying on broomsticks?" Darbishire wanted to know.

"Witches do."

"Well, what if they do? What about it?"

"Nothing," explained Jennings, with some impatience. "Only when you agreed to my wheeze, I just said Witch Prang."

"Why?"

"It's the feminine of Wizard Prang. Witch Prang is Wizard Prang's wife."

"How d'you know?"

Mr. Carter felt that the conversation was getting beyond him.

"I made up a story about them in bed the other night," he heard Jennings say. "I shall probably ask Benedick to put it in the mag. when it's done, only he might turn it down, 'cos there aren't many murders and things in it."

Mr. Carter raised despairing eyes to the heavens.

"You see, the neighbours don't know they can work spells," Jennings went on, "and they just think they're Mr. and Mrs. W. Prang of 'Elm Villa,' and they've got a son called Goblin Prang, Esq., who works in a post office .... Oh, yes, and Mrs. Witch Prang doesn't have a broomstick, she flies in a super auto-gyro, and instead of a magic cauldron she's got a thermostic-controlled electric dishwasher and ..."

In despair, Mr. Carter stopped working and called them in.

"Now, then," he said. "What is it you want to see me about?"

Shyly, Darbishire produced his masterpiece.

"This is just the first instalment of a little thing we dashed off for the magazine, sir," he said.

Mr. Carter glanced through the pages of "*Flixton Slick—Super Sleuth.*" He sighed. It seemed a poor reward for a term spent in teaching them to write English. Why couldn't they write something that didn't depend upon impossible hairbreadth escapes? Why this untidy pile of corpses that littered every other page?

"I wish you wouldn't model your style on 'blood and thunders,'" he said. "I don't encourage you to read them."

"Well, sir, you do sometimes," said Darbishire; "because you told us to read *Treasure Island*, and my father says Stevenson wrote it as weekly instalments for a penny dreadful, so if you print Flixton Slick in the mag. in little bits, it might turn out to be a classic just like *Treasure Island* did."

"Yes," said Mr. Carter; "but your style isn't as good as Robert Louis Stevenson's."

"Oh, but, sir, we went to an awful lot of trouble and looked up all the best authors, sir." Darbishire took up the notebook and scanned the pages in search of an example. "Look at this bit, sir, you can't say this isn't classical."

Mr. Carter read:

"*Flixton Slick was bound hand and foot and was wondering how to get free when he saw that the Silent Shadow had accidentally left a dagger on the table. That gave him an idea for he had been highly educated and was on nodding terms with the Bard. 'Ha!' he said. 'Is this a dagger that I see before me the handle toward my hand. Come let me clutch thee.' He stretched forward but he could not quite reach it. 'Oh dash it,' he exclaimed. 'I have thee not and yet I see thee still. If only I could get thee I could get free and then I could photograph the fingerprints before the filthy witness washes his hands.'*"

Mr. Carter laid down the book.

"You see what I mean, sir?" said Darbishire. "I borrowed quite a lot of that from *Macbeth*, and you can't say Shakespeare isn't good style, can you, sir?"

Mr. Carter groaned. "I'm sorry," he said; "but it's just too dreadful; I can't possibly put this sort of stuff in the magazine."

He rose from his desk and paced the room, while Jennings and Darbishire watched him reproachfully. They felt he ought to be looking pleased at having such gifted contributors to assist him to fill up his columns, but instead of that his expression conveyed that he, too, like Macbeth and Flixton Slick, was suffering from a surfeit of daggers of the mind. Mr. Carter was conscious of their unspoken reproach: Darbishire gazed beadily at him through his spectacles, and Jennings stood on one leg and massaged his right calf with his left foot. Their attitude plainly said that Mr. Carter was falling painfully short of the qualities demanded of a literary talent spotter.

Finally Mr. Carter spoke.

"Have you ever met any detectives or criminals, socially?"

"No, sir," answered Jennings, somewhat surprised.

"Then you can't expect anything you write about them to be convincing. If you're going to write a story for the magazine, choose a subject that you really know something about."

Jennings and Darbishire looked at each other, and their glances clearly indicated what they thought of Mr. Carter's suggestion.

"What could we write about then, sir?" Jennings asked.

Mr. Carter considered.

"Well, think of all that's happened since you came here, and try describing your first term at school."

"Oh, sir, that'd be silly," objected Jennings. "Nothing ever happens at school; no murders; no crooks; never anything exciting; and everybody here is so ordinary. We never get a chance to do anything worth writing about."

"Oh, I don't know," replied Mr. Carter. "You think it over. You might call it—er—something like, '*Jennings Goes to School*.'"

Jennings was sceptical; it was all very well for grown-ups to make absurd and impossible suggestions. He'd like to see them do it.

"Well, sir," he said at length, and his tone was most polite, "don't think I'm trying to be critical, sir, but if you think it's such a good idea, why don't you do it yourself?"

"I might," Mr. Carter replied unexpectedly. "It's certainly an idea."

Disappointed, the two authors took their leave. Outside in the corridor, where they mistakenly supposed that they were out of earshot, Jennings and Darbishire expressed their views on Mr. Carter's shortcomings as a literary critic.

"I think Benedick's crackers," said Darbishire.

"He's more than that," said Jennings, "he's super-screwy squared. Why, I bet you a million pounds nobody in their senses would ever want to read stories about chaps like us!"

On the other side of the door Mr. Carter smiled as he filled his pipe.

"Wouldn't they?" he murmured to himself. "I'm not so sure."

JENNINGS FOLLOWS
A CLUE

CHAPTER 1

MR. CARTER READS ALOUD

DURING THE first half of the Easter term the weather chose Wednesdays when it wanted to be unpleasant. This was because Wednesday was a half-holiday, and for two weeks in succession the grumbling February sky had decided that the half-holiday should be a wet one. Outside, the rain pattered down and the trees dripped, and big puddles on the rugger pitch grew into little lakes. Inside, the seventy-nine boys of Linbury Court Preparatory School refused to be depressed, and settled down for another afternoon of indoor activity.

In the common room, the noise made by a group of twenty boys suggested that to be active indoors meant creating enough sound to raise the roof and shake the foundations of the building. Odd pieces of wood were being hammered and chiselled into model yachts; biscuit tins were being beaten into gleaming aeroplane wings; the stage-manager of the puppet theatre, busily rehearsing the sound effects for the next production, was imitating rolls of thunder with a tea-tray and a gong stick; while his assistant smote an empty box with a riding crop, in the vain hope that it sounded like rifle fire. Near the rattling windows, members of the wireless club with home-made sets tuned to rival stations, relayed grand opera, military bands and talks in Norwegian all at the same time. Other boys were playing an improvised game of hockey, by knocking a boxing glove round the room with cricket stumps and making the floor vibrate with their perpetual commotion.

In the middle of the room where the uproar was most deafening, Jennings and Darbishire, with their fingers pressed to their ears, were enjoying a quiet game of chess.

Jennings was the taller of the two, a friendly-looking boy of ten with an untidy fringe of brown hair and a wide-awake look in his eyes. His opponent was fair and curly; he had a pink and white complexion and pale blue eyes that gazed beadily at the chessboard through large spectacles. Doubtfully he moved a pawn, hesitated, changed his mind and shifted his king to the next square. Jennings unplugged his ears and shaped his hands into a megaphone.

"You can't do that, Darbishire," he shouted at the top of his voice. "You've made a bish and put yourself in check."

A resounding crash of thunder from the puppet theatre drowned his words and Darbishire cupped one hand to his ear, while his raised eyebrows signalled for the message to be repeated.

"I said," Jennings began again, but at that moment the boxing glove landed in the middle of the chessboard, scattering the pieces over a wide area.

Darbishire grovelled about on his hands and knees to retrieve them, while Jennings relieved his feelings by hurling the boxing glove at Bromwich major who had come to claim it.

"You ozard oik, Bromo," Jennings shouted. "Can't you see Darbi and I are playing an important game? This is supposed to be the finals of the Form III chess championship."

The words had little effect on Bromwich major as he was unable to hear them, but the boxing glove, catching him squarely on the nose, made Jennings' meaning quite clear, and the hockey players retired to the far end of the room.

Darbishire replaced the chessmen, and Jennings tried again to explain that it was against the rules to move into check; but Binns minor was hammering a biscuit tin with his house-shoe and the words were carried away in the stream of sound.

"What did you say?" Darbishire mouthed back at him politely, though his voice was inaudible.

Jennings took a deep breath and replied with the full force of his lungs, but at that moment the door opened and the Headmaster appeared.

Instantly the noise of the room was stilled; loudspeakers were switched off, the thunder died away, hammers paused in mid-beat and the hockey players changed to statues wearing fixed, innocent smiles. The Headmaster looked round, satisfied at the sight of so much indoor activity. He had no objection to noise in the common room provided that it ceased whenever he entered.

But it had not ceased entirely; Jennings, with his back to the door and his fingers still pressed to his ears, was unaware of the Headmaster's arrival, and carried on at full volume.

"I said you can't move there, Darbi," he shouted. "And that's the second time you've bished up the rules. You've got no more idea how to play chess than a suet pudding ..."

He stopped abruptly, aware that his voice alone was shattering the unnatural silence and that Darbishire, round-eyed with apprehension, was blinking out an agonised signal of warning.

Jennings looked up; the Headmaster was standing just behind him.

"I am at a loss to understand, Jennings," the Headmaster began, "why you should find it necessary to make more noise than everyone else in the room put together. I should be the first to agree that the making of model aeroplanes and wireless sets cannot be done in complete silence; and yet, when I enter the room, these noises are hushed, and the only sound which affronts my ears is your voice, upraised in brawling discord at an opponent who is seated less than two feet away from you."

"Yes, sir," said Jennings.

"Darbishire is not deaf so far as I am aware, though undoubtedly he soon will be if you continue to bellow down his ear in that ungentlemanly fashion."

"Yes, sir," said Jennings. It was useless to explain that, until the Headmaster's entry, the chessboard had been an oasis of silence in a desert of tumult, for Mr. Pemberton-Oakes had passed on to the next stage of his lecture.

"Chess," he continued, "is a game that demands quiet, thoughtful concentration. And as you appear to be unable to play without disturbing everyone else in the room, you will cease to enjoy the amenities of the common room for the remainder of the day."

"I shall cease to enjoy what, sir?" asked Jennings, unable by this time to feel like enjoying anything.

"You will not be allowed to use the common room," translated the Headmaster.

"Yes, sir," said Jennings. It was rather unfair, he thought, that the first remark which he had been able to make Darbishire hear for twenty minutes should be followed by this unfortunate punishment. He'd like to see the Headmaster indulging in quiet, thoughtful concentration with Binns minor banging a biscuit tin half an inch from his ear. However, one does not argue with Headmasters. Jennings walked sadly from the room, leaving Darbishire still wondering what it was that his friend had been trying to tell him.

It was still raining hard and Jennings made for the tuck-box room, as he felt that only ginger biscuits and milk chocolate would cheer his drooping spirits. As he entered the door, he noticed with shocked surprise that two boys were trying to open his tuck-box.

181

"Hey, Venables," he called, as the elder of the two looked up on his approach. "Who gave you permish to go to my tuck-box?"

"It's all right, Jennings," replied Venables, a tall boy of eleven, "we shan't touch anything. You see, Atkinson and I are being cat burglars."

"Yes, it's super rare," explained Atkinson eagerly. "We're the terror of half the capitals of Europe, and we go about barking defiance at the police of every continent." He was a thin, rather nervous-looking boy of ten who looked incapable of defying anything for very long. "Your tuck-box is a fireproof safe with a super decent combination lock that we've got to pick, so that we can steal the secret plans."

"What secret plans?"

"Any ones'll do. All safes have secret plans. You can be the detective who's after us, if you like."

"Coo—yes," said Jennings, cheering up at once. "I'll be Chief Detective-Inspector Jennings. Look out, I've got a gun!" He levelled a broken pencil at them and hissed a series of sharp clicking noises through his back teeth.

The thieves abandoned the safe, leapt through an imaginary window and scaled an imaginary drainpipe with the detective in pursuit. An exciting rooftop chase followed, as the burglars scrambled over tuck-boxes and took cover behind boot-lockers. All three were heavily armed, and the tuck-box room rang with a fusillade of exploding shots as the three boys clicked and hissed their way from corner to corner.

"Dacka—dacka—dacka—dacka!" Jennings discarded his automatic and conjured up a machine-gun out of thin air. "Come on, Atkinson! I got you that time," he called.

"No you didn't then," objected the safe-breaker, "because my pullover is a bullet-proof waistcoat."

"Ah, but I got you in the leg," countered the chief detective-inspector.

"But it's not fair to shoot below the belt, is it, Venables?" Atkinson appealed to his partner, but Venables had gone to earth behind the farthest boot-lockers and was not going to betray his whereabouts.

"You're under arrest, Atkinson," Jennings announced.

"I don't think it's fair," protested the terror of half Europe. "I wasn't ready that last time, and below the belt doesn't count anyway."

"Well, I like that," retorted the detective. "I gave you five bursts of machine-gun fire at point-blank range, so you can't grumble. And in any case, you're standing on Paterson's tuck-box and that's an unexploded minefield, so that proves it."

Atkinson, still complaining bitterly about the injustice of the police, was led away and handcuffed to the door-knob by his tie, and Jennings went in search of the second arch-criminal. Again his machine-gun spluttered viciously.

"Come on, Venables," he called. "I can see you lying there. Get up and come out—you're dead!"

"No, I'm not," replied Venables. "I dodged."

"You couldn't have dodged all of them. I gave you a ten-second burst."

"Well, anyway," argued the corpse, logically, "if I'm dead I can't get up and come out."

Venables' protests were ignored and he, too, was led away and secured to the door-knob.

"Now," said Jennings, "you've got to stay there while I round up the rest of the gang. And if you try to run away I shall shoot you within an inch of your life."

The chief detective-inspector skipped nimbly into his autogyro and, waving his arms round his head like a propeller, raced off down the corridor with his engine roaring, and his ammunition spattering at stray foes lurking behind orderly rows of rugger vests.

"Eee-ow-ow! Eee-ow-ow! Dacka-dacka-dacka-dacka ... Whomp!"

It does not often happen that a schoolmaster in his early thirties turns a corner and collides with an autogyro. Mr. Carter winced, for Jennings head was hard and it caught him on the third button of his waistcoat.

Jennings recoiled and sat down; then, gabbling profuse apologies, he jumped up and retrieved Mr. Carter's pipe from behind a radiator, where the force of the collision had thrown it.

"Oh, sir, I'm terribly sorry, sir, honestly I am, sir. I didn't mean to bump into you, sir."

Mr. Carter breathed heavily while he regained his composure.

"Why on earth can't you go along a corridor like a civilised human being? Do you find it difficult to walk without waving your arms and legs like a wind-mill?"

"No, sir."

"This is the third time this week," said Mr. Carter, "that your flailing ten-tacles have nearly knocked me down. On Monday, you explained that you were practising imaginary leg-breaks. Yesterday, you were a paddle-steamer on the Congo. What are you this time—a revolving door or a Catherine wheel?"

"Neither, sir. I'm an autogyro."

"I see. And what are you doing down here?" Mr. Carter asked. "I thought that you and Darbishire were going to settle down quietly and play off the final of the Form III chess tournament?"

"Yes, we were, sir," Jennings explained, "but the Head came in and said that our chess was disturbing the people who were trying to hammer."

Mr. Carter glanced down the corridor to the open door of the tuck-box room.

"And why," he wanted to know, "are Venables and Atkinson wearing their ties round their wrists? Is it a new fashion?"

"No, sir, they're handcuffed," Jennings explained. "You see, they're a gang of international safe-breakers, and they're armed to the teeth with guns and bombs and things, and I'm a famous detective in an autogyro, and we keep shooting each other, sir."

Mr. Carter sighed. "And that, I suppose, is your idea of how a detective goes to work?"

"Well, perhaps not in real life, but that's how they do it in books, isn't it, sir?"

"No," said Mr. Carter, "not in the best books. Haven't you ever read *The Adventures of Sherlock Holmes*?"

"I'm afraid I haven't, sir."

"Well, Sherlock Holmes trained himself to observe clues that other people had overlooked, or dismissed as being unimportant," Mr. Carter said. "Then he'd fix his mind on the problem he was trying to solve until he had fitted all the clues together, like pieces of a jig-saw puzzle. No autogyros, no machine-guns, just intelligent deduction."

"Sounds rather a dull way of doing it, sir."

"Dull!" Mr. Carter was shocked. He looked out of the window at the falling rain. There was no chance of letting the boys out on to the playing field to work off their surplus energy; on the other hand, the tuck-box room was not the place for roof-top chases and hairbreadth escapes.

"Go and untie Venables and Atkinson," he said, "and then all three of you come along to my room, and I'll read to you."

"Coo, will you really, sir! Super thanks, sir! Something decent, sir?"

"I will read you *The Adventures of Sherlock Holmes*," said Mr. Carter, "and then, perhaps, you will see that using your brain is a better way of playing at detectives than stampeding about the corridor like a herd of wildebeeste crossing the veldt."

Five minutes later Jennings, Venables and Atkinson were seated on the rug in front of the fire in Mr. Carter's study. It was a pleasant, comfortable room. There were thick rugs and large armchairs, and the walls were lined with books wearing coloured dust-jackets. In one corner stood a radiogram with cases of gramophone records stacked beside it; and looking oddly out of place amongst the modern pictures on the walls, was a fifteen-year-old photograph of a university rugger team, in which a younger, thinner Mr. Carter stood self-consciously in the back row.

Mr. Carter settled himself comfortably in an armchair and read aloud; and as the plot unfolded, Jennings' lively imagination was soon at work, adapting the story so that it fitted in with his own surroundings. Gradually, the housemaster's study merged into Sherlock Holmes' flat in Baker Street. The rain beating on the windowpanes became a thick London fog; a gas mantle glimmered in the electric reading lamp, and the dust-jackets shrouded the great detective's casebooks.

Very soon, Jennings and Sherlock Holmes became, in imagination, the same person. The M.A. gown on the back of the door was his dressing gown, the raincoat and brown felt hat were his cape and deerstalker. Casually, Jennings took a broken pencil from his pocket and held it between his teeth; but it was no ordinary pencil—it was an old briar pipe with a stem which was curved like a saxophone.

Once or twice, Mr. Carter raised his eyes from the page and noted that the thoughts of the great detective were being faithfully mirrored in Jennings' features. When Sherlock Holmes was keen and alert, so was Jennings; when the detective sat back with his fingertips pressed together and surveyed his client through half-closed lids, Jennings leant against the coal scuttle and screwed up his eyes as though blinded by a beam of light. There was no doubt about it; half an hour of *The Adventures of Sherlock Holmes* had convinced Jennings that there was more in being a detective than blazing away with imaginary machine-guns.

"Coo—thank you, sir, that was supersonic!" said Venables, as Mr. Carter put the book down.

"Yes, thanks for reading. It was wizard decent of you, sir," added Atkinson. But Jennings' brain was buzzing too busily to allow him to utter more than a polite "Thank you, sir," as he walked out of the room.

"Come on, Jennings, let's go and do our stamp albums," suggested Venables, "and we can pretend Atkinson's a crook who's pinched a stamp that's so rare it's extinct, and we have to chase him to get it back."

Jennings shook his head. Chasing about was all very well as a game, but a real detective's world was made up of something more subtle—clues, theories, motives, observations and deduction.

Venables and Atkinson raced down the stairs from Mr. Carter's room, but Jennings followed slowly, deep in thought. It should not be too difficult to become a detective, once you knew how it was done. He sat down on the bottom stair, determined to see whether clear reasoning and minute observation would deduce any interesting facts from a wastepaper basket and a notice board, which were the only objects in sight. With his pencil gripped between his teeth and the tips of his fingers pressed together, he was surveying them through half-closed lids, when his mood was shattered by the sudden appearance of Darbishire.

"Golly," said Darbishire, "have you gone bats? You look like the ghost of Hamlet's father."

Jennings came out of his trance and got up.

"I've been looking for you everywhere," Darbishire went on. "I thought you'd go to the games room when the Head turfed you out for kicking up a hoo-hah, and I went and bagged the ping-pong table, and then you never turned up."

"I've been busy," Jennings replied. "Mr. Carter's been reading to us. It was super! He just sits back and looks at you through half-closed eyelids, and deduces things like, say, for instance, you bowl left-handed off-breaks, or you had measles when you were young."

"What!" exclaimed Darbishire in surprise. "Mr. Carter says that?"

"No, Sherlock Holmes does. You see," he went on hurriedly, "he said he'd read to us because I beetled round a corner in top gear and doynged into him."

"Who, Sherlock Holmes?"

"No, Mr. Carter. Why don't you listen? He's been reading to us about Sherlock Holmes. For instance, he can tell, just by looking at you, that your uncle's got a wooden leg. You'd be surprised."

"Yes, I would if he told me that," Darbishire. replied solemnly, "because my uncle hasn't got a wooden leg, and my father says that—"

"Don't be so dim, Darbishire; you don't *have* to have an uncle with a wooden leg."

"Well, why should Sherlock Holmes say that I had?"

"That's just an example of deduction," Jennings explained. "He can deduce things that you don't know about."

"Oh, I see!" Darbishire pondered this for a moment; then he went on: "Of course, I *have* got an uncle in Australia whom I've never seen. He might have got a wooden leg, mightn't he?"

"Well, there you are then!" said Jennings triumphantly. "That proves it. And when you gasp with astonishment he just says—'Elementary, my dear Watson! You know my methods.'"

An electric bell shrilled out its message, and together they went to the wash-room to get ready for tea.

"Gosh," said Jennings longingly, drying his hands on the legs of his trousers. "Gosh, I wish I was a famous detective."

"Fat lot of good it is wanting to be a detective at boarding school," retorted the practical Darbishire. "It's all very well for Sherlock Holmes and people—things happen to them, but nothing ever happens to us."

"I know, it's a swizz. You never get any decent murders and things at school. Still, we could have a bash at deducing things by looking at people, couldn't we?"

"Well, what can you tell by looking at me?" asked Darbishire, as he splashed his curly hair with water and combed vigorously.

Jennings narrowed his eyes and stared at his friend intently.

"H'm," he said at length. "I should say you'd had an egg for breakfast this morning."

"Gosh, yes, you're right," cried Darbishire. "Super decent deduction! How on earth did you know?"

"You've got traces of egg on your tie which are faintly invisible except to the trained eye," Jennings explained. "Of course, ordinary people might not be able to spot them, but it's quite easy if you're any good at observation."

Darbishire contorted the muscles of his jaw and squinted down his nose, trying to see the knot of his tie.

"You don't have to make a face like a bullfrog," his friend pointed out. "Look, there's a hunk of egg stain lower down—just between those two inks-pots."

"Golly, so there is. I think that's wizard!"

Darbishire was thrilled at the possibilities that lay open to the trained mind. "And even if, supposing, they weren't egg stains; supposing they were rare chemicals, say—of course they're not, but they might easily be—and just supposing they were, you'd be able to tell that I was a —" He broke off as his flight of fancy suddenly made a forced landing. "Ah, but we *all* had eggs for breakfast this morning," he went on, as light dawned, "so you knew anyhow. You want to try deducing clues on people you didn't have breakfast with."

"Well, anyway," said Jennings, "you know what I mean. How would it be if we practised being detectives? At least," he amended, "bags I be the detective and you can be my assistant."

"But there's nothing to detect," objected Darbishire, "and my father says—"

"Don't be such a saturated wet blanket," Jennings interrupted. "There may be all sorts of things that need detecting—only the eye of the untrained observer can't see them, even though they're staring him straight in it."

"Straight in what?"

"Straight in the eye. Besides, even if there are no murders and things, it'd be spivish useful to find things out about people. We could study chaps' footprints and fingerprints, to begin with.

"And see if they've got any egg stains on their ties. Yes, massive idea," agreed Darbishire, as the tea-bell rang. his eyes shone with enthusiasm as he followed the famous detective into the dining hall.

CHAPTER 2

LN. CT. DET. AG.

Jennings and Darbishire spent most of their spare time the next day in planning the details of their detective organisation, and collecting crime-solving equipment. During morning break they went to the tuck-box room, for Jennings had decided that the best place for their headquarters would be behind the boot-lockers at the far end of the rows of tuck-boxes.

"We must have a headquarters," he explained, "where we can meet and work out clues and things. We might even put up a notice so that chaps will know where to come when they want mysteries solved. Something like *Linbury Court Detective Agency—Chief Investigator, J. C. T. Jennings* .... And then in quite small letters underneath that," he added as an afterthought, "we might put *Assistant Chief Investigator, C. E. J. Darbishire.*"

"Well not *too* small letters," objected the Assistant Chief Investigator.

They argued for some minutes about the best way to word their notice. Darbishire was in favour of *Families waited upon daily—Distance no object,* but Jennings maintained that *Results guaranteed—Money back if not satisfied* was a more promising way of drawing attention to their services.

"But we aren't going to charge them money," objected Darbishire, "so it wouldn't really be true to say that they got it back, and my father says that truth in small matters—"

"Of course it would be true!" Jennings broke in indignantly. "If we don't charge people we shan't owe them anything if they're not satisfied, and that's what my suggestion means."

They left the text of the advertisement to be settled later on, and set about the more important task of assembling equipment which would be useful in the work of detection. This was easy as they had so little to assemble. From his tuck-box Jennings produced a small telescope, a Morse buzzer and a drooping moustache of ginger-coloured crêpe hair; Darbishire's contribution was a mouth organ and a pair of toy handcuffs. It was not an imposing collection of scientific aids.

189

"If only we had a magnifying glass," said Jennings. "Still, I suppose we can make do with the telescope, but it's going to be spivish awkward studying fingerprints through it—we shall have to stand about a hundred miles off."

His assistant picked up the instrument, put it to his eye and peered round in all directions. "It's bust," he announced. "I can only see a sort of inky blackness."

"You haven't taken the metal cap thing off the end, you goof."

"Oh, sorry," said Darbishire humbly.

The Morse buzzer actually buzzed, and would be useful in sending messages for any distance up to about five yards—or rather less as the battery became used up. The moustache was no use—not even as a disguise, for the eye of even the least-trained observer could spot traces of congealed marmalade and the work of moths. And with deep regret they dropped it into one of Venables' football boots, as there was no wastepaper basket at hand. The handcuffs were broken, and both agreed that the mouth organ served no useful purpose.

"Mind you, Sherlock Holmes was pretty decent at music," said Jennings, picking pieces of fluff from the instrument with his penknife, "so I suppose it might help if I had a bash on this." But Jennings' rendering of "Good King Wenceslas" seemed a poor substitute for Holmes' sensitive fingers coaxing inspiration from his priceless violin.

"For goodness' sake turn it up!" urged the assistant chief investigator as *Deep and crisp and even* went into a jarring discord for the third time. "Fat lot of crimes you'll solve making that row!"

Jennings broke off his musical search for inspiration and slipped the mouth organ back in his pocket.

"I tell you what," he said. "I vote we practise sending messages to each other in Morse. It's bound to come in useful, and later on, perhaps, we'll invent codes so we can talk to each other without the criminal knowing we suspect him."

Neither of them knew the Morse code by heart, but the alphabet, with the appropriate dots and dashes, was plainly marked underneath the wooden base of the Morse buzzer, and Darbishire found a similar chart printed in his diary. Jennings sat down on a tuck-box with the buzzer in front of him, and his assistant retired to a distance where the sound was just audible. There he stood, alert and ready to check each dot and dash with his chart.

"Get ready," said Jennings. "Message starting now."

A confused buzzing whirred across the intervening space as the chief investigator pressed the control knob of his transmitter. Progress was slow because he had to stop and turn the instrument upside down between each letter, so that he could consult the chart on the bottom. At the receiving end, Darbishire had difficulty in keeping track of anything at all, and complained that Jennings' dots were longer than his dashes. After five minutes' hard work, the buzzing stopped.

"End of message," Jennings announced. "Have you got it?"

"Was the last one but three, a dot or a dash?"

"It was neither really," Jennings confessed. "Actually, it was a space, but I accidentally kept my hand on the tapper while I turned it over. What do you make of the message anyway?"

"It's a bit difficult to say," admitted Darbishire, "but I make it *bip fog nip nop*, and then there's a bit I couldn't quite get, and it ends up *merx pritzh ump thopshozz*. Sounds like Swedish to me!"

"Oh, you're bats," said Jennings irritably. "How could it possibly be that?"

"I thought it might be in code."

"Yes, so it is."

"Well, how can you expect me to work it out if I don't know the code word?"

"Not that sort of code—Morse code," Jennings explained. "It was meant to be—*My name is Jennings. It's a lovely day today*—and the dot at the end was the full stop."

"Oh! Well, either we need more practice, or your Morse code chart is a different edition from mine."

The bell for the end of break put an end to further practice, and it was not until later in the day that the two detectives were able to carry on their preparations. Jennings disappeared after tea, so Darbishire retired to the library, and with his diary in front of him, practised transcribing a magazine article into Morse. It was tiresome work and he was growing weary of it, when the door opened and Jennings appeared.

"I knew I'd find you here, Darbi!" he announced triumphantly, as though he had trailed his friend's footsteps with magnifying glass and bloodhounds. "Look, what do you think about that!"

With a flick of his wrist he turned back the lapel of his jacket, and revealed a small cardboard disc marked *LN. CT. DET. AG.* in smudged capitals. "And I've made one for you, too," he went on, thrusting a similar disc before Darbishire's peering gaze. "Super decent, aren't they?"

191

"Coo, yes, spivish!" Darbishire agreed. "I think they're smashing—er—what are they?"

"They're our special secret badges."

"Oh, I see. And I suppose *LN. CT. DET. AG.* spells something in our special secret code."

"No," said Jennings impatiently. "It stands for Linbury Court Detective Agency, and we both pin our badges underneath the lapel of our jackets, so that no one can see them."

"But what's the good of them, if no one can see them?"

"Well, whenever we meet each other, we turn back our lapels and that proves you're a member of the organisation, and you can tell that I'm one too."

"But we know that already," objected Darbishire, "'cos there's only us two in it, anyway."

His objections were brushed aside and the badge was pinned into place. Then they practised the wrist-flicking drill, until both could prove their membership in a polished, professional manner.

"I thought of another wheeze during afternoon school," said Jennings. "We ought to have a camera, so's we can take photos of footprints and clues and things."

Darbishire nodded and sucked his thumb which he had pricked on the pin of his secret badge. "As a matter of fact," he said thickly, "there's some advertisements for rather decent cameras in this mag I've got here." He removed his thumb and flicked through the magazine, smearing each page with microscopic bloodstains.

"There you are, how about that one!" he said, pointing to the photograph of an expensive-looking model which, the manufacturers informed the world, was the *Grossman Ciné Camera de Luxe. Motion pictures in colour, 16 mm.*

"What's mm.?" Jennings wanted to know.

"It's a thing like centigrades and kilowatts. It means the depth or the height or something," Darbishire explained. "Of course, it's a movie-camera really, but that'd be all the better, because supposing we find a suspicious character and he tried to get away, we could follow him and make a film of it; and then perhaps the Head would show it with those educational flicks we have on Wednesdays. Gosh, wouldn't it be super!"

His eyes sparkled excitedly behind his spectacles as he pictured the sensation it would cause. First perhaps, they would have "Plant Life in the Andes" because that was one of his favourites; next say, "Rice Growing in China" because that always turned up in the programme several times a term; and then the epic, epoch-making film of the year, "The Chase and Capture of ..." He was hazy about the details, but he had no difficulty in imagining the enthusiastic applause of the audience. He could almost hear their comments in apt, film-trailer language. "It's terrific!" they cried. "It's colossal—it's stupendous—it's the picture of the century!" Darbishire came out of his trance to find that his chief was in full spate.

"... and it would be useful for other things too," he was saying. "We could make an educational slow motion picture of you doing your maths prep."

"Or a fast motion one of you eating your tea in gorgeous technicolour," added Darbishire.

"Yes, we mustn't forget the colour!" Jennings' enthusiasm was fired. "We could get Mr. Wilkins into a supersonic bate—that always makes him go red in the face, and then we could take a film of him, and the more he got the breeze up, the quicker the colour would change."

They bellowed with laughter at the absurdity of the idea, and then stopped abruptly, as the door hurtled open and Mr. Wilkins burst into the library to find out who was making all the noise.

Mr. Wilkins was a tall man with a short temper; he made a great deal of noise himself, but he was not particularly pleased when other people did the same.

"What on earth's all this row about?" he demanded loudly. "You know very well that the library is only to be used for silent reading."

"We were just laughing at something we thought of, sir," Jennings explained.

"Well, what was it?" barked Mr. Wilkins. "Come along, let's all share the joke, if there is one."

"Actually, sir, we were laughing at—" Jennings began, and then realised that this was an awkward question. Mr. Wilkins' countenance was already assuming a delicate shade of pink, and one could not explain that the joke depended upon its becoming pinker. "Well, perhaps it wasn't very funny after all," he amended, "and we didn't really mean to make a noise, sir."

"I can't help what you meant—you *were* making one. This library has got to be treated as a quiet room, and you won't be allowed to use it, if you can't learn to make a noise quietly, like anyone else. Er, I mean, if you can't make less noise."

"Yes, sir."

Mr. Wilkins departed, and the quiet of the library was again shattered as he slammed the door behind him with a deafening crash.

Jennings and Darbishire turned once more to the advertisement. It was a beautiful camera and just the thing for detective work, but as Darbishire pointed out, it would probably cost about a hundred pounds, and the two friends could only raise eleven and eightpence between them. There would be no harm, however, in writing for a catalogue as the advertisement suggested. Perhaps the firm made models which were rather less expensive than a hundred pounds—something in the region of eleven and eightpence, say. They took the magazine with them and dashed off to their classroom, where Jennings produced his writing pad.

"*Dear Sir*," he wrote, and then stopped, uncertain how to proceed. For some minutes they discussed the correct wording for a business letter of such importance.

"How would it be," Jennings pondered, "if I said— 'Hope you are having decent weather; we aren't.'"

"No," said Darbishire firmly, "Tell him to send a catalogue and ask him how much the cameras are, because we want to buy one."

"But we haven't got enough dosh—we've only got eleven and eightpence."

"Perhaps we'd better leave that bit out then."

"On the other hand, there's nothing to stop me saying I'd *like* to buy one," Jennings argued, "because I would, and anyway that doesn't mean I'm *going* to. And I can't write and say I'm *not* going to buy one, because then he won't send me the catty, and it'd be a super decent thing to have."

Jennings' pen scratched busily for three lines as he made his meaning clear on paper. Darbishire, meanwhile, discovered to his great joy that if he wedged his little finger into the inkpot, he could turn it upside down without the ink spilling. It was a satisfying achievement, until the time came to withdraw his finger. "Oh golly, I'm stuck!" he said.

"Yes, so am I," said Jennings, and laid down his pen.

"I can't just say this—it only takes up about an inch, and Mr. Carter says we should never write less than a page."

"But there's nothing else to put," argued Darbishire, forcing his finger out with a plop that sprayed globules of ink over Jennings' writing pad, "unless of course, you say what we usually do in our Sunday letter."

"That's an idea," agreed Jennings. "I could tell him we beat Bracebridge School at rugger, and we ought to be practising for the sports next month, only it always rains on half-holidays, so we can't."

"Fat lot he'll care about that!"

"Well, it fills up the page a bit, and then what about hoping he's quite all right. Yours truly, J. C. T. Jennings."

It was not an impressive letter, and certainly not worthy of the proprietor of a first-class detective agency wishing to increase his stock of scientific instruments. And when Jennings had finished blotting Darbishire's ink splashes with his handkerchief, they decided it would not do.

There were half a dozen boys in the classroom, and Jennings decided to enlist the help of someone who possessed greater literary talent. Temple, known as Bod, which was short for Dogsbody, because his initials were C. A. T., had the best handwriting in the form. He was seated at a desk on the far side of the room, sand papering the fuselage of a half-built model aeroplane, and he looked up as Jennings charged towards him waving an inky sheet of notepaper.

"I say, Bod, will you do me a favour?" Jennings began, "because you've got a twelve horse-power brain, and you can do supersonic grown-up writing; you know, all slopey and illiterate."

"You mean illegible," corrected Darbishire from the rear.

"Yes, just like grown-ups—that's what I said. You see, I want a catalogue, and I bet the chap won't send it if he thinks I'm just a chap at school, because he'll know I haven't got enough dosh; but if you write it, he'll never guess. Look, here it is in rough, and we want you to make it sound more grown-up."

Temple's twelve horse-power brain soon grasped what was expected of it, and he stared searchingly at the rough copy that Jennings had written.

"*Dear Sir*," he read aloud. "*I would like to buy one so how much are they and please send one at once but not if they are more than eleven and eight if so just a catalog. We beat Bracebridge School in the end. There was Sports practics last Wedednesday only there was not any owing to the wet it was scratched. Hopping you are quit all rit. Tours truly, J. C. T. Jennings.*"

Temple raised both eyebrows. "You're bats!" he said. "What on earth does it mean?"

Jennings showed him the advertisement for the *Grossman Ciné Camera de Luxe*.

"Oh, I see," said Temple, as light dawned. "But what's all this *quit hopping* stunt?"

"Well, it's only decent to hope he's quite all right," Jennings explained, "and if he isn't—if he's got chicken-pox, or something, he'll be wizard pleased to know that somebody cares about him."

Temple agreed to write the letter properly, and produced a sheet of his own very expensive notepaper. It had *Linbury Court, Sussex*, embossed in tasteful letters, and the school crest, with the Latin motto beneath, on the left-hand side of the paper. Jennings was glad that the heading made no mention of the fact that Linbury Court was a school. He knew from past experience that many firms were not anxious to send their catalogues to schoolboys who had no intention of buying their goods.

"Go away Atkinson and Venables, and all of you. It's private!" Jennings announced, as the remainder of the common room gathered round, eager to know what was happening and show a friendly interest. Temple started work, but he had to keep stopping to push back the crowd which surged round the desk.

"What's the address of this place?" the letter-writer asked. "You have to write it above *Dear Sir.*"

"Why, the chap knows where he lives, doesn't he?" asked Atkinson.

"It says the address in the advertisement," Darbishire pointed out. "Somewhere in Oxford Street."

"Good old Oxford!" shouted Parslow with enthusiasm.

"Rotten old Oxford—good old Cambridge!" countered Bromwich major.

"No, they're not then," Jennings joined the discussion group at full volume. "Oxford's miles better! *Cambridge on the tow-path, doing up their braces—Oxford on the river, winning all the races.*"

"No, it's not then," shouted Atkinson. "It's the other way about! It's *Oxford on the tow-path, doing up their braces …*"

"They don't wear braces in the boat race," Jennings argued back, "so that proves you're wrong!"

"Well, a moment ago you said they did! You said *Cambridge on the …*"

"Shut up all of you," yelled Temple, at the top of his voice. "I'm trying to write a letter!"

"Yes, shut up, chaps," urged Jennings, whose voice had contributed most noise to the uproar. He clicked his tongue at them reprovingly. "How can you expect Bod to concentrate with all this hoo-hah going on? Besides, everyone knows that Oxford is gallons better. Mr. Carter went to Oxford and Mr. Wilkins went to Cambridge, so that proves all oiks are Cambridge."

"And all ruins are Oxford," shouted Venables, and the noise swelled again. "I stick up for Cambridge, Arsenal and Lancashire!"

"And I'm Oxford, Charlton Athletic and Middlesex!" yelled Johnson.

"Shut up!" bawled Temple. In the silence that followed, Darbishire, who had not previously spoken, could be heard murmuring— "And I'm Oxford—"

"Shut up, Darbishire!" shouted the whole room in unison.

"Nobody asked you anyway," added Venables. "You only say you're Oxford because Jennings does."

"No, I don't then," Darbishire defended himself. "I've got a reason. My brother stuck up for Oxford till his last term at school, and then he had the ghastliest hunk of bad luck."

"Why, what happened?"

"He won a scholarship to Cambridge."

"What filthy, rotten luck!" the Oxford supporters consoled him. "I bet he was fed up."

"He seemed quite pleased actually. Spivish disloyal, I call it!"

"You ought to stick up for Cambridge then," said Bromwich major, scenting a new supporter.

"I know; it's made it jolly difficult for me," Darbishire replied, "but I get over it like this—in boat races and things, I like Oxford to be first and Cambridge second."

In due course the letter was finished and Temple read it out:

"*Dear Sir,*

I am thinking of buying one of your cameras ... You needn't actually buy one of course," he explained, "but nobody can stop you thinking about it ... *and I shall be glad if you will send me a catalogue ...*"

It was a beautiful letter and as Jennings dropped it in the post box, he reflected that it was one step, even though a small one, towards obtaining a first class collection of crime-solving equipment.

CHAPTER 3

THE GREEN BAIZE BAG

Sports day at Linbury was always held during the Easter term; for the Headmaster considered that strenuous athletics, in the heat of the summer, was bad for the boys' health, and worse for their cricket. Occasionally, on half-holidays, rugger was cancelled and sports practice was held instead; and it was towards the end of one of these practices, a week after the formation of Jennings' detective agency, that something sensational happened.

Jennings and Darbishire were studying, in a professional manner, the foot-prints made by the jumpers in the long-jump pit, when they saw a thin, elderly man walking slowly up the drive. There was nothing remarkable about his grey trilby hat and neat blue suit, but he was a stranger and therefore promising material on which to practise deduction.

Jennings saw him first and said: "Now's your chance, Darbi! What facts can you deduce from this chap coming up the drive?"

Darbishire thought hard: "Well," he said, after a pause, "he's not wearing an overcoat and he's carrying an umbrella, so I'd say it must be a warm day and it's not raining."

Jennings expression was scornful.

"But we know that already," he said contemptuously. "You don't have to have strangers walking up the drive to know what the weather's like."

"Well, you have a bash if you're so clever," Darbishire muttered.

"H'm!" Jennings summoned up his powers of keen observation. "I'd say he's a piano tuner, and that he's come to tune the piano."

"Well, of course that's what he's come for, if that's what he is," said Darbishire, with scant respect for his friend's keen observation. "You wouldn't send for a piano tuner to inspect the gas meter, would you? How can you tell, anyway?"

"You know my methods, my dear Darbishire," the keen observer replied coldly.

"No, what are they?"

Jennings felt that Sherlock Holmes had been fortunate in having a friend who always said the right thing at the right time. Darbishire was a poor substitute for Dr. Watson, and the detective's tone was crushing as he explained his reasons. He pointed out that the stranger's hat was just like the hat worn by the man who tuned the piano at Jennings' home in Haywards Heath. Also, the visitor was carrying a green baize bag, which, had it not been empty, might well have held a piano tuner's tools. Scientific deduction, therefore, proved that he must be a piano tuner who had forgotten to bring his equipment.

"But if he's forgotten his tools," argued Darbishire, "why does he cart the bag about with him?"

"He probably carries his lunch in it," came the reasoned reply.

"But he must have had his lunch by now; it's nearly three o'clock."

"Of course," Jennings explained patiently, "that's why the bag's empty."

It took his friend a few moments to grasp the flaw in this argument. When he had done so he said: "But a moment ago, you said it was empty because he'd forgotten his tools, and if he'd remembered to put his lunch in his tool-bag it would have reminded him of what he'd forgotten."

"Ah, but what I meant was—" Jennings stopped short, not quite sure what he did mean. Darbishire could be exasperating at times; Dr. Watson would never have embarrassed Sherlock Holmes with such awkward questions. He would have gasped with admiration and said: "Wonderful, my dear Holmes, I can hardly believe it!" The trouble with Darbishire was that he could hardly believe it either, only he said so with the wrong sort of expression in his voice.

The stranger had passed them by this time, and was heading for the front door.

"Come on," said Jennings, "let's follow him! Perhaps if we can get near enough, we'll hear him telling whoever opens the door who he is, and then we shall know if I'm right."

They hurried after their quarry, taking care not to draw attention to themselves. Twenty yards from the front door, they took cover behind a holly bush and Darbishire announced: "Look, he's ringing the bell! I wonder what he's come for?"

"Famous detective *you'll* make!" snorted Jennings. "Sherlock Holmes would go and *tell* him what he'd come for, just in case he'd forgotten, along with the tools."

The front door was opened by the housekeeper, Mrs. Caffey, known for obvious reasons as Mother Snackbar. After a murmur of explanation, the visitor was admitted and the door closed behind him.

Jennings and Darbishire turned and made for the changing room. The whistle had sounded, and boys were streaming off the field and dashing towards knee-baths and showers. They were followed, at a more dignified pace, by Mr. Hind and Mr. Topliss, who had been on duty on the playing field.

Darbishire pondered over the stranger's identity so deeply, as he stood underneath the shower bath, that he turned the cold tap full on by mistake. His shrieks were quickly silenced by Mr. Wilkins, who refused to see any difference between shouts of mirth and shouts of agony. Darbishire recovered his breath, stretched for the hot tap and splashed happily.

"You know, Jennings," he said, as his friend appeared, trailing wet footmarks along the duck-boards, "I bet you're wrong about that chap. My father says that appearances are deceptive, and for all we know, he's probably someone hefty decent who's come to ask for a half-holiday."

"It's a pity we couldn't see his boots," Jennings replied, looking around vaguely for his towel. "We could have told then. Sherlock Holmes always knew where a chap had come from, just by sitting with half-closed eyelids and seeing what sort of mud he'd got on them."

"But he wouldn't have any," Darbishire objected, "not unless he'd been playing rugger."

"Of course he would! You don't go about without boots."

"No, I mean he wouldn't have any mud on his eyelids."

"I didn't say that, you ancient relic," Jennings answered curtly. To add to his annoyance, he remembered that he had left his towel in the dormitory, and with one eye on Mr. Wilkins he started to dry himself on his sweater. A few minutes later, struggling damply into his shirt, he said: "Well, anyway, Darbi, I bet I'm right, and he *is* the piano tuner. I bet you a million pounds Mother Snackbar's taken him along to the music room."

Jennings was wrong. Mrs. Caffey had shown the stranger into the library, where he handed her a visiting card marked: *H. Higgins, Jeweller and Silversmith*. "The Headmaster's expecting me," Mr. Higgins explained.

Mrs. Caffey went off to find the Headmaster, and Mr. Higgins lowered himself carefully into the depths of a large armchair, and looked around him. The library was a comfortable room, with books shelved all along the oak-panelled walls; not calf-bound volumes with their solemn air of gloomy dignity, but hundreds of carefully chosen books whose authors ranged from Stevenson to Buchan and from Bunyan to Ransome.

Above the oak panelling hung dozens of brightly coloured shields, bearing the crests of public schools to which the boys of Linbury had won scholarships, and on the mantelpiece over the large brick fireplace stood a row of silver cups. Cricket, soccer, rugger, swimming, boxing, gymnastics—each cup had a ribbon of magenta or white tied round its base, to show which of the two houses had won the trophy at the last contest. In the middle, and overtopping its neighbours by six inches, stood a large, two-handled chalice on which was engraved *Linbury Court Inter-House Sports Cup. Presented by Lieut-General Sir Melville Merridew, Bart., D.S.O., M.C.*

Mr. Higgins knew the cups well. Every year he engraved "Raleigh" or "Drake" on each, when the winning house had smilingly accepted its trophy from the hand of some distinguished Speech Day visitor.

The door opened and M. W. B. Pemberton-Oakes, Esq., M.A.(Oxon.), Headmaster, walked in.

"Ah, good afternoon, Mr. Higgins."

The jeweller rose to his feet. "Good afternoon, sir," he replied. "I've called for the sports cup."

"Ah, yes," said the Headmaster, taking it down from the mantelpiece. "The cup was won by Raleigh House last year. I meant to ask you to engrave it before, but it slipped my memory. However, there's three weeks yet before our Annual Sports."

"Half an hour will be enough for me, sir," replied Mr. Higgins, scribbling "Raleigh" in his notebook. "I'll do it straight away, as soon as I get back to the shop."

"Excellent! And if there's anyone going to the village this afternoon, I'll ask them to call for it."

"Very good, Mr. Pemberton-Oakes." The engraver placed the challenge cup reverently in his green baize bag. "Handsome piece of silver, isn't it, sir?"

"Very. It was presented by General Sir Melville Merridew, you know—one of our most distinguished old boys."

"Really, fancy that now!" said Mr. Higgins, hushing his voice to a respectful whisper. The Headmaster had made the same remark to him every year for the past ten years, but the jeweller could not have shown more suprise and delight if he had been told that the cup had been presented by William the Conqueror.

Mr. Higgins walked back down the drive. He carried the sports cup carefully in his green baize bag, and was quite unaware that his progress was being watched from the changing-room window.

"Look, there's the piano tuner going back!" said Jennings. He had dressed, and was passing the time, while waiting for Darbishire, by stretching a garter over his head, so that it sat on his scalp like a tight, elastic crown.

"We didn't deduce much from him, did we?" replied Darbishire, searching vainly on the floor for the missing garter.

"No, I suppose not, but ... Gosh!" Jennings stopped suddenly and raised his eyebrows in astonishment. The action caused the garter to shoot off his head with a faint *phut*. It described a circle in the air and came to rest at Darbishire's feet. The surprised owner put it on and said: "What's the matter?"

"Gosh!" repeated Jennings. "I say, Darbi, I've just detected a brand new supersonic clue."

"What?"

"That empty bag the piano tuner's carrying is full!"

"Oh, don't be crazy!" Darbishire hastened to the window. "An empty bag can't be ... Oh, yes, I see what you mean."

"I wonder what he's got in it?" said Jennings, his suspicions aroused.

"Perhaps it's his lunch, because you said ..."

But Jennings was not listening. His keen mind was at work reconstructing the stranger's movements. Mother Snackbar could not have taken him to the music room, for not more than fifteen minutes had elapsed—certainly not enough time to tune two pianos. Well, supposing she had shown him into the library, and had then gone off to tell the Head that a stranger had called. He would have had plenty of time to put one of the challenge cups in his bag, and then walk out of the building before the housekeeper returned. And there was something about the shape of the green baize bag—some hint in the outline made by whatever object was shrouded within; the contours, for instance, of a large silver cup with two handles.

Jennings hesitated no longer. Observation and deduction had pointed the way; the time for action had arrived.

"Quick, Darbishire!" he shouted, his eyes sparkling with excitement. "We must dash up to the library. There's not a second to lose."

Darbishire knew nothing of his friend's train of thought and looked up, surprised. "But I don't want to go to the library," he objected. "I haven't finished reading the book I got out last Sunday. There's 268 pages, and I've only got to page 97, and anyway, it's no good going now because—"

"I'm not talking about changing your book, you twittering nitwit!" Jennings' tone was a mixture of excitement and exasperation. "That chap's a thief, don't you see? He's beetling off with one of our cups in his bag. At least, I think he is, but we'll breeze upstairs and make sure. Come on!"

Together they ran out of the changing room and up the stairs. As they rounded a blind corner, Jennings collided heavily with Venables, who was walking carefully down the stairs, balancing a board and a box of chessmen on his head. Castles, knights and bishops flew in all directions, but Jennings' errand was too pressing to allow him to stop.

"Sorry, Venables," he called back over his shoulder. "Can't stop now. I'm on an urgent, top priority, hush-hush job."

Venables glowered after the disappearing figures. "You just wait till I catch you!" he cried, and the expression on his face suggested that there would be no hush-hush when it came to telling Jennings what he thought of him.

Up the stairs and along the corridors; Jennings raced ahead and Darbishire panted after him. Soon they reached the library. Jennings flung open the door and rushed in, followed by Darbishire, chattering with nervous excitement.

"It's a good job we didn't waste any time," he was saying, "because my father says that procrastination is the thief of ... Jumping jellyfish!" He stopped dead in his tracks and stared at the empty space on the mantelpiece.

"Gosh!" said Jennings. "I was right. He *was* a burglar!"

His friend gazed at him in round-eyed wonder. "It was super smart of you to spot that bag, Jennings," he said in respectful tones.

"Elementary, my dear Darbishire. You know my methods."

Jennings did his best to look calm and unruffled, but his voice trembled slightly with excitement. "We mustn't stand here nattering," he said. "Let's go after him quick."

"Hadn't we better tell Mr. Carter, or someone?"

"We haven't got time. We shall lose him if we don't follow while the scent's still warm."

"Scent!" Darbishire had a fleeting vision of Jennings and himself sniffing their way across open country, like bloodhounds with their snouts to the trail. He giggled, and his friend at once detected his line of thought.

"Oh, don't be so bats, Darbishire," he said. "You know what I mean. We mustn't let the chap get out of sight."

"All right," Darbishire agreed, "but it may be dangerous, don't forget. How do we know this chap isn't a member of an international gang of crooked piano tuners?"

It was an exciting thought, and Jennings could easily picture the inoffensive Mr. Higgins skulking evilly in an ill-lit thieves' kitchen, surrounded by characters from the pages of *Oliver Twist*. As a precaution, they decided to tell someone of their intentions, and as the next person they saw was Venables, they told him.

He marched into the library, smouldering with fury. He had recovered his chess set, and was hotfoot on Jennings' trail. But all thoughts of revenge were forgotten when he heard what had happened.

"And you say the thief's hoofing off down the drive with it," he gasped. "What cheek! Raleigh had to run like mad to win that cup."

"Yes, and if we don't run like mad, they'll lose it." Jennings' tone was urgent as he explained. "It's all right, Venables, all you've got to do is to tell Mr. Carter that Darbishire and I are going to do some detective work, and track the thief to his kitchen."

"How d'you know he's going to the kitchen?" Venables wanted to know.

"He must be. If you'd read any good books lately, you'd know that burglars always live in thieves' kitchens."

"Don't the thieves mind, then?"

"Oh, don't be such a crumbling ruin!" Jennings snorted. "They're the same people."

Venables was left with a vague impression of evildoers swarming round a communal gas oven, as Jennings and Darbishire rushed headlong out of the room.

There was no afternoon school on Wednesdays, and the boys were free to follow their own pursuits until the tea-bell sounded at six o'clock. The detectives had more than two clear hours ahead of them, which should be enough time to bring even the most wily criminal to justice.

Darbishire was worried about leaving the premises without permission but, as Jennings pointed out, they would lose their quarry if they did not start at once, and their disregard for the rules would be forgiven when they returned in triumph. Jennings could picture the scene—the whole school lined up on the quadrangle and cheering wildly as a police car swept up the drive. The two members of the Linbury Court Detective Agency were seated in the back holding the sports cup. As they stepped out of the car they would be greeted by the

Headmaster's smile of gratitude. Oddly out of place in the background of the picture, a snarling Mr. Higgins was beating his manacled hands vainly against prison bars.

Jennings forced his mind back to the job on hand.

"We shall have to get a move on," he said, as they scampered across the quadrangle. "He'll be nearly at the end of the drive by now."

Darbishire was not a good runner. "Phew," he gasped, "not so fast! I've just thought of something."

"What?"

"Suppose he's got a car waiting for him at the end of the drive. What do we do then?"

Jennings had a ready answer. "We stop the very next car that comes along and say to the driver: 'Quick, follow that car!' That's what 'Dick Barton' does anyway, and it always works."

Darbishire carried his objections a stage further.

"Well, supposing he catches a bus?"

"Then we stop the next one, and tell the conductor to follow the one in front."

This did not satisfy Darbishire. He pointed out that the bus service was limited to one bus every hour, and that as they all went to the same place anyway, there was little point in barking terse instructions at the conductor.

They had rounded a bend half-way down the long drive, when Jennings suddenly gripped his friend's arm, and the next moment pulled him into the thick yew hedge.

"Ssh!" he whispered. "Don't make a noise! I can see him!"

Darbishire glanced nervously over his shoulder. "Where?" he breathed voice-lessly.

"He's just turned the corner at the end of the drive."

Darbishire came out of the hedge and removed traces of yew from his collar. "Well, what do we have to whisper for?" he demanded. "The chap's at least two hundred yards away and if he's gone round the corner, he can't see us, anyway."

"We've got to be careful." Jennings' tone was official. Detective-inspector was written all over his features. "It's taking care of little things like that that proves you're a decent detective. Now, we mustn't let him hear us or see us, so I vote we walk on tiptoe and be ready to jump into the hedge if he looks round."

In this fashion they reached the end of the drive, and after Jennings, on hands and knees, had peered furtively round the gatepost, they followed the innocent Mr. Higgins along the road to the village.

The only other person in sight was an old farm labourer, flat-footedly trundling a wheelbarrow of leaf mould up the hill, and Darbishire pointed out the significance of this. "Jolly wizard job he hadn't got a fast car waiting for him," he whispered, "because the only next thing that's coming along is that old codger with a barrow, and we'd look silly trying to chase him in that."

They kept close to the hedge, walking in single file. Once Mr. Higgins turned to admire the view and the two followers dived, as one man, into the ditch. Although still very muddy, the ditch was not the rushing torrent it had been a week earlier, and when Mr. Higgins continued his journey, two bespattered figures climbed out and again took up the trail.

For a hundred yards they tiptoed in silence, their eyes and thoughts fixed on the slim figure in the neat blue suit. Then Darbishire said: "What a rotter the chap must be—pretending to be a piano tuner and being a burglar all the time!"

"Oh, I soon saw through him," Jennings answered. "Mind you, that story about coming to tune the piano was good enough to take old Mother Snackbar in, but it didn't work with me." He had convinced himself by this time that Mr. Higgins' visit had followed, in every detail, the lines which his imagination suggested.

"You know, I had a feeling he was up to no good the moment I saw him," Darbishire remarked confidentially. "In fact, I think I told you so."

"You told me—" Jennings stopped so abruptly that his friend bumped into him. "You told me you thought he was a super decent cove who'd come to ask for a half-holiday."

"Oh," Darbishire smiled wanly. "Anyway, I was right when I told you what my father said about not judging by appearances."

The profound sayings of the Reverend Percival Darbishire were relayed by his son at every opportunity; Jennings, in common with the rest of the school, was beginning to tire of them.

"And I don't think your father's such a frantic brain as you make out," he retorted, "because when we were dashing into the libe you told me your father said that procrastination was the thief of jumping jellyfish. I thought it sounded a bit queer at the time, but I wasn't going to argue, because it was the thief of silver sports cups that I was after."

"I didn't say that," Darbishire protested. "What I said was, my father says that—"

"Well, never mind now," Jennings interrupted. "Come on, we mustn't lose sight of the burglar."

It was half a mile to the village of Linbury, but after they had trailed stealthily for a further hundred yards, Darbishire made a suggestion.

"I say," he said, "must we go on walking on tiptoe? It's super tiring, and I'm beginning to feel like a ballerina."

"All right!" Jennings came down on his heels with a sigh of relief. "I suppose he can't hear us at this distance."

Mr. Higgins, being rather deaf, would not have heard them if they had danced behind him in hobnailed boots. He strolled on towards the village, enjoying the peace of the afternoon and blissfully unaware that bloodhounds in human shape were dogging his innocent footsteps.

CHAPTER 4

DARBISHIRE KEEPS WATCH

THE VILLAGE of Linbury, according to the guidebook, lies four and a half miles east of the market town of Dunhambury. Its main architectural features are an early Norman church and a late Victorian horse trough: the population is three hundred and ninety-eight.

The guide book says nothing of Linbury as a shopping centre, which is not surprising, for most of the three hundred and ninety-eight inhabitants catch the hourly bus to Dunhambury to make their purchases. There are, however, three shops: *Chas. Lumley—Home-made Cakes and Bicycles Repaired; Linbury Stores and Post Office*, which offers a varied stock of goods ranging from caraway seeds to corn plasters; and *H. Higgins, Jeweller and Silversmith*. It may seem unusual that a shop with such an imposing description as Jeweller and Silversmith should be found in Linbury, but one glance at the shop window should dispel any idea that it is out of place in such rural surroundings.

When Mr. Higgins retired from his jeweller's business in Dunhambury more than ten years previously, he was not happy in idle retirement; so he turned the front room of his house into a small shop, and busied himself in repairing clocks and engraving dog collars. He sold screw-top pencils and butterfly brooches, and as he did not depend upon this for his living, it did not worry him that his customers were few. It was enough, he felt, to justify the sign over his front door. *Jeweller and Silversmith* gave him a comfortable, satisfied feeling whenever he looked at it.

Mr. Higgins entered his shop, laid his engraving tools on the counter and set to work on the Merridew Sports Cup. Outside in the village street, Jennings and Darbishire came to a stop, uncertain what to do.

"Golly, isn't this exciting!" Jennings breathed. "I bet Sherlock Holmes wishes he was here. Let's walk past that shop he went into and see if we can see anything. But don't stare at it—just pretend you're out for a stroll."

"Right-o!" Darbishire agreed.

"We ought to go past one at a time, as though we didn't know each other,"

Jennings continued. "Most detectives do that, so as not to give themselves away, in case anyone's watching. You walk past first and try to look natural, and wait for me by that horse trough in the middle of the road."

Darbishire was not good at looking natural to order. Normally, people would not have looked twice at this very ordinary ten-year-old boy in a grey suit, with curly hair and large spectacles: but Darbishire tried so hard to appear unconcerned that passers-by turned and stared. Some thought that he had eaten something which had upset him—others, that he must have got his braces uncomfortably twisted across his shoulder blades.

He started off down the street with huge, slow strides, as though he were measuring out a cricket pitch. He felt this to be wrong and changed to quick mincing steps, like a cat on spiked railings: he was conscious of his arms swinging like pendulums from his shoulders, and he had a feeling that his hands were swelling to the size of boxing gloves. He put his hands in his pockets, wondering why it was that they felt so clumsy; then his left ear started to itch—a thing that never happened as a rule. "Gosh, what a bish I'm making of it!" he thought. "I can't scratch it yet—it'd look funny." But his itching ear allowed him no peace, and he jerked his hands clear, scattering the contents of his trouser pockets all over the road.

After that, he tried marching with head erect, but people were beginning to cast suspicious glances, and he found himself lunging forward, left arm with left leg—right arm with right leg. What on earth was the matter with him? He never made bishes like this during P.T.! He changed step two or three times, but it was no use. After a very artificial journey he reached the horse trough, and suddenly remembered that he had been too flustered to notice the jeweller's shop at all.

Jennings joined him a few moments later. "What on earth's the matter, Darbi?" he demanded. "You went prancing down the street like a crab with chilblains. You couldn't have drawn more attention to yourself if you'd hopped like a kangaroo!"

"Sorry, Jen."

"Now," said Jennings, getting back to business. "I've discovered something that might be important."

"Yes?" Darbishire was eager again, now that his ordeal was over.

"The shop's called H. Higgins, Jeweller and Silversmith."

"That's a spivish feeble sort of clue," observed Darbishire, who had been expecting a revelation.

"Oh, is it? That just shows how much you know! Why does he call himself Jeweller and Silversmith, then? You answer me that, if you're so clever. Why not just—piano tuner?"

"Because he isn't a piano tuner," returned Darbishire logically.

"Exactly. I knew he wasn't all the time, and this proves it."

"No, you didn't. You said he *was* one at first." Jennings clicked his tongue with impatience. "I know I did, but that was because he was *pretending* to be a piano tuner, don't you see? But if he really *was* one, he wouldn't paint it up over his shop, in case Mother Snackbar saw it when she went to the village."

Jennings' clear reasoning was too deep for Darbishire, who by this time was floundering out of his depth.

"So you think he really is a piano tuner who's pretending he isn't?" he asked.

"Yes," said Jennings decisively.

"But a moment ago you said he wasn't. You said he was just pretending to be one."

"Oh, you're bats," said Jennings, and wisely decided to let the point drop. "Anyway, we know now that he's a jeweller."

"Real or pretending?"

"Pretending of course. Yes, that must be it! He pretends to be a jeweller so that he can trade in stolen watches and things."

They sat on the edge of the horse trough while they thought this out; then Jennings said: "Gosh, yes, it all fits in! I read a story once, where the police raided a jeweller's shop, but they heard them coming and hid all the booty in a trice."

"Hid it in a what?"

"A trice," Jennings repeated. "I suppose it's a secret cupboard, or some-thing—the book didn't say."

"And you think this Higgins chap has got a trice hidden away in his shop?"

"Bound to have."

They sat silent for a few seconds and then Jennings rose to his feet. "What I ought to do now," he announced, "is to try and find some evidence."

"Yes, good wheeze," Darbishire agreed. "How are you going to do it, though?"

"I haven't a clue."

This time it was Darbishire's turn to speak his mind. "Well, of course you haven't," he said, with surprising heat. "If you had, you wouldn't have to find any."

"I didn't mean that," returned Jennings, "and don't get in a flap—I'll think of something."

Jennings wondered what Sherlock Holmes would do. Probably he would keep watch, and note any suspicious comings or goings. He might even disguise himself as a roadsweeper or a pedlar, so that he could loiter without arousing any comment. A pedlar would be better, because then he could go inside the shop pretending to sell his wares. The scheme had obvious drawbacks, but as he could think of nothing else he suggested it to his assistant.

Darbishire thought it was an excellent idea. He knew that after his recent performance, he was not likely to be cast for a rôle that demanded much acting talent, and that the difficult part would have to be played by Jennings.

"Okay, then," he said with enthusiasm. "I vote we do that. Let's be pedlars— or rather, you be a pedlar."

"That's all very well," Jennings replied, "but what could we peddle?"

"Bicycles?" suggested Darbishire brightly.

"Oh, don't be such a crumbling ruin," snorted Jennings. "You don't peddle bicycles!" And after a pause he added: "Well, you *do*, of course, but not that sort of peddle. Anyway, I should look daft as a pedlar—they're usually ragged blokes in dirty clothes."

Darbishire looked at his superior shrewdly.

"That's just how you look," he said encouragingly. "What a good job that ditch we took cover in wasn't quite dry. And you tore your pocket on the hedge so—"

"No," said Jennings firmly. "Let's think of something else."

At length he produced a foolproof idea. He would walk boldly into the shop in the guise of a customer, and see if his trained eye could pick up any clues. Darbishire was to keep watch outside, in case the bogus jeweller became suspicious and tried to escape. As an excuse for loitering, he could pretend to be an artist busily painting the village street, with the ornamental horse trough in the foreground. Jennings produced a blue crayon and the back of a letter, as the artist's stock-in-trade.

Darbishire was appalled.

"But I can't draw horse troughs," he protested. "I can only draw aeroplanes."

"Well, draw aeroplanes then."

"But there aren't any, and anyway, you know how people come and look over artists' shoulders while they are working," he went on, bolstering up his objection. "They'd know I was a fraud then."

Jennings brushed this flimsy argument aside. "If they do that," he said, "you can say you've just done a lightning sketch of an aeroplane that's just flown over, and that now you're going to draw a horse trough underneath."

"Yes, but—"

"Oh, don't be so feeble, Darbishire! You've got miles the easiest job; and anyway, if the worst comes to the worst, turn the wretched aeroplane upside down and pretend it's a horse trough. They'll just think you're one of these super modern artists."

"Oh, all right." Darbishire resigned himself to his fate. "I suppose I might as well have a bash at it." After all, his was the easier task. He felt faint with nervousness when he thought of the risks that Jennings would have to undergo. "What are you going to do when you get in the shop?" he asked, in a voice which he was unable to keep steady.

Jennings had it all worked out. He would go in and look round the shop, jingling the fourpence in his trouser pockets to give the impression that he was a customer of some substance. He would examine any priceless jewels which happened to be lying around, and then he would casually lead the conversation to the subject of silver cups. "I shall try and frighten him," he decided.

He damped his handkerchief in the horse trough and sponged the mud from his knees. A wealthy customer mustn't look as if he had recently emerged from a ditch. "I shall say," he went on in official tones, "that a silver cup has been stolen and that certain clues have led me to form a tent—er, a tent—something."

"A tenterhook?" suggested Darbishire, feeling that this state of suspense summed up the situation neatly.

"No, a—a tentative theory, that's it."

"But that won't help," his assistant objected. "He won't give it back to you."

"I know, but I shall be watching him carefully. Perhaps through half-closed lids even, and if he goes pale and starts suddenly—"

"Starts what suddenly?"

"Not starts anything." The detective's voice grew edgy with exasperation. "I mean if he stops short in his tracks, and then starts guiltily."

Darbishire wondered how anyone could stop in their tracks before they had started, but he didn't like to say so, for Jennings' expression was forbidding. He explained that, if the outcome of the stopping and starting test was satisfactory, he would hasten out of the shop and try to find a policeman. If, meanwhile, the criminal tried to bolt, Darbishire must take up the chase and bring him crashing to the ground with a low rugger tackle.

Darbishire gulped hard and swallowed. He said he was not much good at rugger.

"Well, a moment ago you said you were feeble at art," Jennings replied. "You'll wizard well have to pull your socks up if you're going to help. We can't afford to make a bish of our first case."

He strode off towards the shop; his heart was thumping heavily and he had an uncomfortable feeling in the pit of his stomach, but he was not going to let his assistant know that he felt nervous.

Darbishire watched him go, and then turned his attention to art. It was half-past four and beginning to grow dark—not the best time of day for an artist to start work out of doors; but on the other hand, the failing light would conceal the worst defects of his drawing. He held his crayon at arm's length and shut one eye, measuring the proportions of the horse trough. Then he drew three jet-propelled fighters, with machine-guns blazing and aviators descending by parachute. Ack-ack fire was bursting all over the picture, with dotted lines indicating the paths of the exploding shells. It bore little resemblance to the village street of Linbury, even when turned upside down, but it was the best he could do. Fortunately, no one seemed to be taking much notice.

He worked on, colouring the aeroplane wings with thick blue shading, and wondering what was happening to his friend. Gosh! it was hairy daring, walking bang into a thieves' kitchen like that! Jennings must have supersonic, ice-cold nerves! What if the burglar attacked him? What if, at this very moment, he was in a perilous plight? Supposing … Darbishire's train of thought suddenly veered off the rails, as he looked up to discover that he, also, was in a perilous plight—or soon would be.

A herd of cows was lowing its way up the village street. A thirsty herd, too, for as soon as the animals sighted the horse trough, they made for it, as one cow. Unlike most artists who prefer to sit well away from their model, Darbishire was perched on the edge of the object which he was supposed to be drawing. He could not retreat without losing sight of H. Higgins' shop door, and he was hemmed in on the other three sides by the trough and the cows plodding thirstily towards it.

Darbishire was fond of most animals, but cattle did not appeal to him. Now, it seemed, he had suddenly become the hub of a large herd, all pushing and jostling and looking forward to a long, satisfying drink.

"It's all right," he told himself. "Cows don't hurt you—unless they're bulls."

Cautiously he tried to edge his way to safety, but his escape was cut off by two lively heifers who drank their fill from the trough, and spilt what they did not want over Darbishire's feet. At every moment he expected them to tread on his toes or lean on him, for these cows were not the bashful kind, who shy at the approach of a human being. Waving tails flickered before his eyes and put a stop to any pretence of going on with his drawing. "Oh, gosh, this is awful!" he thought. "How can anyone expect art to flourish in the middle of a frantic hoo-hah like this?"

A small boy in a torn jersey came up. He was brandishing a stick and was obviously in charge of the herd. He shouted, "Giddup, giddup, will you!" and obediently the cows started to move on. "It's all right, mate, they won't hurt you!"

Darbishire tried to look as though no such thought had entered his head; but he was secretly envious of one so young, whose orders were so promptly obeyed.

The last cow finished her drink and stared over Darbishire's shoulder at the picture which he was still clutching in his hand. She did not appear to think very highly of it as a work of art, for she lowed at it in a melancholy fashion, and wandered off to join the rest of the herd.

"Phew!" murmured Darbishire. "Why do these things always pick on me to happen to?" Then his thoughts returned once more to his colleague. "Golly! I'd clean forgotten about old Jen! I hope nothing dreadful's happened."

Nothing dreadful had. As Darbishire stared anxiously in the direction of the shop door, it opened, and Jennings appeared. He was carrying the Merridew Inter-House Sports Cup under his arm.

"Jumping jellyfish!" shouted Darbishire, in amazed delight. He was so surprised that he nearly toppled backwards into the horse trough.

CHAPTER 5

TRIUMPH AND DISMAY

JENNINGS had been feeling distinctly nervous when he had first entered Mr. Higgins' shop. An electric bell rang shrilly, and kept on ringing while he stood on the threshold, holding the door ajar. With some misgiving he shut it, and approached the counter.

"Have you any, er—?"

The shop was stocked so modestly that it would sound out of place to ask to be shown priceless jewels. his trained eye roamed round in search of some other object, and fell upon a pair of cheap earrings fastened to a card.

"Have you any earrings?" he mumbled, feeling rather silly.

Mr. Higgins, being slightly deaf, thought that he was being asked for key-rings. "Yes," he said, groping beneath the counter. "I've got some very nice ones here. Just the thing for a lad like you."

"Oh, they're not for me," said Jennings hastily, and felt his courage ebbing. "I want them for, er—well, it doesn't matter really. I think I'll leave it, if you don't mind."

H. Higgins, Esq., Jeweller and Silversmith, gave him an odd look and, for a moment, he panicked.

"What I mean is, I want them as a present for someone else," he went on wildly, hardly conscious of what he was saying. "Someone who isn't here, and I don't know what sized ears they take—I mean I don't even know whether they've got any already, so it doesn't matter, thanks all the same."

Mr. Higgins stared at Jennings over the top of his spectacles. "Speak up, laddie," he said. "I'm a bit hard of hearing—who is it who hasn't got any ears?"

Jennings clutched the counter and tried to control his emotions. "This won't do," he told himself, "you're making a most frantic bish of things! For goodness' sake pull yourself together! Sherlock Holmes wouldn't let himself get rattled like this." He took a deep breath, and began again.

"Well, I—er, the point is," he said, "I'm making some inquiries about a silver sports cup belonging to Linbury Court School."

He watched Mr. Higgins narrowly, but the jeweller did not blench; neither did he start violently nor stop dead in his tracks. Instead, a slow smile of understanding lit up his features.

"Linbury Court, why of course! Yes, I've just done it."

Jennings was surprised. "You—you admit it then?"

"It's quite ready," returned Mr. Higgins brightly. "You've come to take it away, I suppose?"

"Well, yes, but I—I hardly expected you'd give it up as easily as all that."

Mr. Higgins produced the newly-engraved cup and wrapped a layer of tissue paper round it. "Mind you," he said roguishly, "I wouldn't give this cup to anyone who just walked into the shop and asked for it. Might be a thief, see!" He shot his head forward to make his point clear and Jennings recoiled, fearing some trick. "But I know a bit about thieves, see, being a jeweller," he said, with a crafty wink.

"Yes," Jennings gulped, "I'm sure you do!"

The situation was getting out of hand. Mr. Higgins was not behaving at all in the way that any self-respecting criminal ought to behave. A horrible doubt came into Jennings' mind. Perhaps Mr. Higgins was not a thief after all! Perhaps there was some explanation for this extraordinary game that the jeweller was playing with school property! Jennings could not think what it could be, for it never entered his head that the man had any connection with the names "Drake" and "Raleigh" engraved on the cups. With an effort, he forced his attention back to what Mr. Higgins was saying.

"Oh, yes," the jeweller replied. "I know quite a bit about burglars and their little ways—and about detectives too. Take Sherlock Holmes for example!" He pointed to a shelf, high up on the wall behind the counter. Sandwiched between table napkin rings and cut-glass cruets he had found a place for his favourite books, and Jennings could see *A Study in Scarlet*, *The Memoirs of Sherlock Holmes*, and *His Last Bow* amongst a dozen or more detective novels.

"Now, Sherlock Holmes has taught me a few things; and as soon as you mentioned Linbury Court, I knew at once that you weren't an impostor. And how did I tell that?" he asked, with a cunning smile.

Jennings made a last, half-hearted attempt to frighten Mr. Higgins into a confession of guilt. "I suppose your conscience must have told you?"

Mr. Higgins laughed merrily.

"My conscience! Good gracious, no! Whatever makes you say that?" He dropped his voice to a low conspiratorial whisper. "I'll tell you. It was your school tie and your school socks. That proved you were genuine. That's deduction, see?"

Jennings took the cup from Mr. Higgins and walked out in a daze, trying to piece together the ruins of his shattered theories.

It was almost dark when they made their way back from the village. Jennings was strangely silent, searching for some reasonable explanation of Mr. Higgins' conduct. But Darbishire was bubbling over with excitement, and demanding details.

"But what happened?" he persisted, for the sixth time. "How did you manage to get it back? Did the chap put up much of a struggle?"

"Well, actually," Jennings replied slowly, "I think I've made rather a bish of the whole issue. You see, I'm not even sure that he is a burglar, now."

"You mean he used to be one, and now he's given it up?"

"No, I don't think now, that he ever was one."

"But he must be," Darbishire proclaimed with emphasis. He was not going to allow any feeble anti-climax to spoil the events of the afternoon. "Dash it all, Jen, he pinched the cup, didn't he?"

"Yes, I know," said Jennings, still very puzzled, "but he gave it back without any hoo-hah. He even seemed to expect that someone might come and ask for it."

This time it was Darbishire's powers of deduction that provided the explanation. As they trotted along, he pointed out that the whole business was a gigantic bluff. As soon as Mr. Higgins was aware that Jennings knew his guilty secret, he realised that the game was up. What else could he do, but hand the cup back, and pretend that the whole thing had been an unfortunate misunderstanding?

"You frightened him, you see," he explained. "He knew wizard well that if he hadn't given it back, you would have had the police on him like lightning. For all he knew, the building was surrounded already—perhaps he even saw me keeping watch and thought I was—" He left the sentence unfinished. Even in his state of flushed excitement, he knew that no one could have mistaken him for a plain-clothes policeman.

There was certainly something to be said for Darbishire's argument, and as it seemed to be the only solution, Jennings was forced to admit that he had been deceived by the jeweller's clever acting.

"Yes, of course," he said. "I never thought of that! Gosh, Darbishire, I've been swindled!"

Darbishire pressed home his advantage. "He must have taken you for a chump," he said with relish. "I bet he's laughing his head off now. I bet they all are!"

He drew a lively picture of the thieves' kitchen behind Mr. Higgins' shop. Crafty, low-browed desperadoes were slapping their knees and rolling about, helpless with mirth.

Apart from this, however, they both agreed that the expedition had been a success. The stolen cup had been recovered, and the detectives could return to school well satisfied with their work.

It was quite dark when they reached Linbury Court. They had hurried so that they should not be late for tea at six o'clock, and they arrived with half an hour to spare. The first person they met was Binns minor, the youngest boy in the school.

"Gosh," he squeaked in his shrill, Form I treble. "You two are going to cop it! Old Wilkie's on duty, and he's been searching the building for you. He guessed you'd hoofed out without permish, and he's in the most supersonic bate. I bet he sends you to the Head, and then—pheeew—doyng! pheeew—doyng!"

His sound-picture of a visit to the Headmaster was most life-like, and he skipped happily along the corridor, *pheeew-ing* and *doyng-ing*, and swishing the air with a bootlace.

Jennings was not worried. "It's all right, Darbishire. Wait till they know what we've done for them," he said, and together they made for the common room.

Here, their welcome was more satisfying; Venables, Temple, Atkinson, Bromwich major and a dozen more crowded round in enthusiastic greeting. Venables had told them of the burglary and the pursuit. He had sworn them to secrecy, so that small fry such as Binns minor, and similar persons of low estate, should not have the pleasure of knowing that something sensational was afoot.

"What happened, Jennings?" they all shouted at once. "Did you catch him?" and then, as they caught sight of the cup bursting through its layer of tissue paper, a long gasp of amazement ran round the room.

"Gosh, it's the sports cup!" breathed Venables.

"Golly, super daring!" Atkinson's eyes shone with admiration.

"What happened? However did you get it back?" Temple wanted to know.

Jennings could not resist the temptation to bask in well-earned glory. "Elementary, my dear Temple," he said, a smile playing round the corners of his mouth. "You know my methods. I tracked the burglar to his den. It's not too difficult, if you're any good at detective work."

"Yes, it was wizzo," added Darbishire, "and I disguised myself as an artist and drew aeroplanes, so that people wouldn't suspect."

"Wouldn't suspect what?"

"That the horse trough was really three jet-propelled fighters, upside down."

Nobody knew what Darbishire was talking about, and they pressed for details.

"Well," said Jennings, "I just walked into the thieves' kitchen, and spoke to the chap like Sherlock Holmes would have done. And he got the wind up and gave it back without a struggle."

"What's a thieves' kitchen like?" Venables had been trying all afternoon to picture domestic arrangements beyond the reach of the law.

"They vary quite a bit," Jennings informed him, from his superior knowledge. "This one had got earrings."

"Gosh, how spivish!" Venables promptly added seafarers and gipsies to the staff of his kitchen. He could almost hear the jangling of the gold circlets hanging from their lobes, as his criminals bent over their pastry-boards and frying pans.

"Did you tell Mr. Carter what had happened?" Jennings asked him.

"No," said Venables. "I couldn't find him. I think he must have gone out. I did try and tell Mr. Wilkins, but he got in a bate and wouldn't listen properly. I told him about the crook and all that and he said: 'Cor-wumph! Don't come bothering me with cups and cooks and kitchens. Can't you see I'm busy?'"

There was no doubt that Jennings' first exploit as a detective had been a great success. The group of boys stood round the smiling sleuths and showered congratulations on them. Fantastic prices were mentioned as the reward that the Headmaster would certainly feel called upon to make, when the bogus jeweller was behind prison bars.

The common room rang with shouts of lavish praise.

"Good old Jennings! Good old Darbishire! Three cheers for the Linbury Court Detective Agency!"

Jennings and Darbishire, bursting with pride and trying to look modest, enjoyed their moment of glory. But it was over all too soon, for half a minute later Mr. Carter walked into the common room, and tried his hand at deduction.

He had just come back from Dunhambury in his car, and was on his way to his room, when the excited hubbub told him that something unusual had taken place. In two seconds he was surrounded by a throng of boys, each one raising his voice in an effort to drown his colleagues and be first with the news.

"Sir, please sir, something super exciting has happened, sir," shrilled Atkinson.

"Yes, sir—there's been a rather decent burglary, sir," called Bromwich major.

"But it's all right, sir," added Temple, "because we've got it back, thanks to Jennings. He's super at sleuthing sir, isn't he, sir?"

"Be quiet!" said Mr. Carter softly, and immediately the room became silent. "I haven't the slightest idea what you're talking about," he went on. "Twenty people jabbering away at once isn't the best way of sorting things out. Come along, Jennings, you tell me what it's all about."

Holding the sports cup lovingly in his arms, Jennings recounted the afternoon's adventures. When he had finished, Mr. Carter said: "Well, well, poor Mr. Higgins! He little knows the commotion he's caused."

"What do you mean, sir?" asked Venables.

Mr. Carter did not reply. Instead, he took the cup from Jennings and looked at the words engraved on the front.

"There you are, you see, sir," Darbishire chimed in, fearful lest he should be denied his share in the glory. "It's the sports cup all right, isn't it? Are you going to tell the police, sir?"

"I hardly think that will be necessary, Darbishire," Mr. Carter returned gravely.

"Oh, sir, you must!" pleaded a dozen voices. "Otherwise, sir, all Jennings' famous detective work will be wasted."

Jennings looked hard at Mr. Carter, and suddenly detected a look of amusement which the master was trying to suppress. All at once his doubts returned. He knew now that there was something suspicious about the whole affair. It had been too easy.

"I agree with Mr. Carter," he said, to the surprise of the crowd. "We've got the cup back—that's the main thing, and besides, the burglar wasn't such a bad old stick. I thought he was quite decent, all things considered."

Mr. Carter smiled and said: "I should go even further than that, Jennings. I should say that your burglar was the most obliging thief you could possibly hope to meet."

The crowd continued to gape. They, too, sensed by this time that all was not as it should be, and listened with breathless expectancy as Mr. Carter went on: "He's even taken the trouble to engrave last year's winner on the cup he stole." He pointed to *Raleigh* and the date, which everyone knew had not been on the cup when they had last seen it.

There was a painful silence, and then Jennings said slowly: "Oh ... I see ... So I did make a bish of being a famous detective after all!"

"I'm afraid so, Jennings."

The boy tried hard to hide his disappointment. "Well," he said, unhappily, "all I can say is, I'm jolly glad Sherlock Holmes won't get to hear about it!"

Then the tea-bell rang. The tension broke and roars of laughter swept from the lips of the crowd as the explanation became clear. But Jennings and Darbishire were not laughing. They followed the hilarious crowd to the dining hall, wondering what on earth they could say when confronted by an angry Mr. Wilkins.

CHAPTER 6

FURTHER OUTLOOK—UNSETTLED

THERE WAS, of course, trouble. Mr. Wilkins took a serious view of their leaving the school grounds without permission, and reported them to the Headmaster.

"Just like Old Wilkie," sighed Jennings, as they walked with dragging footsteps towards the study. "I bet Mr. Carter wouldn't have kicked up such a supersonic hoo-hah, if he'd been on duty."

Binns minor danced lightheartedly behind them: "Pheew ... doyng!" he prophesied with a gay smile, and then turned and ran to the shelter of his own form room.

Jennings said: "Don't take any notice of those Form I ruins. We'll deal with Binns later." They were both wearing an extra pair of underpants, but this precaution proved unnecessary; Mr. Pemberton-Oakes left his cane in his cupboard and talked ... and talked.

"I have noticed for some time," he was saying twenty minutes later, "that your interests are becoming lawless and unrestrained. Instead of going quietly about the building like members of civilised society, you charge like an armoured division, mouthing mechanical engine noises. The energy which you should be devoting to organised games is being wasted in worthless horseplay. It is little more than a week since I had occasion to speak to you about your unseemly conduct at the chessboard. Little did I think that my remarks would pass unheeded; little did I think that ..." And on ... and on.

Jennings and Darbishire listened dutifully for the first fifteen minutes. After that their faces paid attention, but their minds were unable to cope with the ceaseless flow of words. Jennings counted the flowers on the patterned wallpaper behind the Headmaster's head. There were twenty-five in each row and forty rows in all, so that made ... his eye was fixed steadily on the Headmaster, but his brain was busy with mental arithmetic. Darbishire picked out random words from the torrent swirling about his ears; with his finger he traced the outline of each letter on the seam of his trousers, but his gaze never shifted from the tortoiseshell spectacles on the Head-magisterial nose.

After thirty-five minutes they were allowed to go. Binns minor was lurking near the study door with his ears tuned to catch any sound of *pheew-ing* and *doyng-ing* that might come from within. It was not that he bore Jennings and Darbishire any ill-will, but if these unpleasant things were going to happen anyway, he wanted to be the first to know about it.

"Oh, well," said Darbishire, as they prepared for bed later that evening. "I suppose we've had it now. I didn't listen to all he said, but I had a sort of feeling that he might get into a bate if we did any more famous sleuthing."

"He never said that." Jennings put his spare underpants back in the drawer. "He said—well, I can't remember either, but I'm sure he didn't mean we've got to pack up the detective agency."

He was more determined than ever to carry on, because Venables and his friends had wasted no time in spreading the story of Jennings' "frantic bish" all over the school, and wherever he went he was greeted with shouts of derision. It was the joke of the term and Form III enjoyed it to the full.

During the next few days Jennings managed to rouse Darbishire's enthusiasm once again, and together they made up endless codes and copied them down in their diaries. Then they practised sending each other code messages while Mr. Wilkins was taking their form, but even this turned out disastrously.

Mr. Wilkins took Form III for geography. His methods were vigorous and his voice was loud. He strode about the room dictating notes at shorthand speed and demonstrating the rotation of the earth with a large, faded globe.

Jennings sat in the back row and stared out of the window. He was half a page behind with the dictated notes, so he gave up struggling and decided to copy them out afterwards. Surely, he thought, there must be some way of proving his detective skill! He brooded over this for some minutes and could spare only a small part of his brain for Mr. Wilkins' demonstration of how the earth goes round.

"Now, look at this globe carefully," boomed Mr. Wilkins, "and you'll see that these lines going round the earth, North and South of the Equator, are lines of latitude—or parallels as they are sometimes called. And these others are longitude lines and they go round from North to South and meet at the Poles. All clear?"

"Yes, sir," chorused the form.

"Good. Now for six months of the year as the earth spins round, the North Pole is pointing away from the sun—like this." Mr. Wilkins gave the earth a vigorous tilt and slapped it smartly in the Pacific Ocean, so that it creaked round protestingly on its rusty axis. "So, although it's turning round once in every twenty-four hours, it's always dark in the North Polar regions and light at the South Pole. And vice versa for the other six months."

"You mean it goes round as it's doing now, only it doesn't squeak?" asked Darbishire.

"Exactly. And if the earth were *not* tilted like this"—Mr. Wilkins defied the laws of Nature and made the earth upright—"then we should have twelve hours' day and twelve hours' night all through the year. Is that clear? ... Rumbelow?"

"Yes, sir."

"Do you understand, Temple?"

"Oh yes, sir."

"Jennings?"

Jennings was still looking out of the window. Hawkins, the night watchman, was crossing the quadrangle with a heavy tread. He was known as Old Nightie and the boys saw little of him, for his labours started when they were safely in bed. With his hunched shoulders and drooping head he looked an odd sort of character, and he had a habit of shooting stealthy glances in all directions whenever he spoke. Jennings had met him occasionally, emerging from the boiler-room, but had not paid much attention to him. Of course, it was possible that he was just an innocent old ...

"Jennings!" repeated Mr. Wilkins in a voice which would have shattered the deepest day-dream.

"Oh, er—I beg your pardon, sir."

"Corwumph! Wake up, boy. I asked you if that was clear."

"Oh, yes, perfectly, sir, thank you," replied Jennings politely.

"Then perhaps," said Mr. Wilkins, in persuasive tones, "you'll be good enough to explain it to me."

"But you know it already, sir."

"Of course I know it already," barked Mr. Wilkins, and the persuasive tone had vanished. "I wouldn't be asking you if I didn't know, would I?"

"You mean the other way round, sir," suggested Darbishire, helpfully. "You *would* ask him if you *did* want to know, wouldn't you, sir. But you don't really want to know, sir—you just want to know if he knows."

"I ... I ... Corwumph! Of course I don't really want to know—that's why I'm asking—I mean ... Well anyway, what did I say?"

Jennings thought hard. "You said that longitude and latitude are a lot of

lines which are parallel and they meet at the North and South Poles, sir."

Mr. Wilkins turned three shades pinker. "But, you silly little boy, if they're parallel, how on earth can they meet?"

"I thought, perhaps, that was one of the things you wanted to know, sir." And then, as Mr. Wilkins began to *Corwumph* again, Jennings hastened on: "Well sir, I think why these parallel lines meet is because the earth goes round all tilted."

"Corwumph! you haven't been listening to a word I've said."

"Oh, yes, sir, I heard it all, sir," Jennings assured him. "You said that the real reason that causes the earth to go round is the rotation of the earth, sir, and if it didn't it would be night and day both at the same time."

Mr. Wilkins clutched his head in his hands and Jennings hurried on, anxious to show how much he had understood: "And it would be versa-visa—er—viva voce, sir, for the rest of the year, because the earth takes six months to turn round every twelve hours, and the other six months it turns round the other way, sir."

"I ... I ... I ..." Mr. Wilkins swallowed hard, summoned up his reserves of patience and marched to the blackboard where, with brisk bold strokes of the chalk, he started his explanation all over again.

Jennings listened carefully for a few minutes, but the picture of Old Nightie, with his shambling flat-footed gait and furtive expression, floated back into his mind. Mr. Wilkins, now hoarse with explanation, was dashing off sketch maps on the board and Jennings took advantage of this lull to take his diary from his pocket. After consulting the key, he wrote a note in his secret code, rolled it into a small pellet and flicked it with his ruler towards Darbishire in the second row. Unfortunately his aim was poor; the pellet soared far beyond the target area and landed on the master's desk.

"Oh, gosh," he groaned in dismay. "It *would* have to go and pancake, bang on the top of the control tower."

Mr. Wilkins, busy at the blackboard, saw it too, but for the time being he affected not to notice it.

When he had finished his sketch map of the earth and the sun, he turned from the board and walked straight towards the master's desk.

Jennings froze, and then breathed again as the master turned away without seeming to see the pellet. Mr. Wilkins spent the next two minutes walking up and down past his desk, and Jennings' heart missed a beat every time the footsteps turned about. Would he see it, or wouldn't he? The suspense was unbearable. But Mr. Wilkins' volcanic manner concealed a kind heart; he hated to see boys suffer, so he put Jennings out of his misery by discovering the note the next time that he passed. He unfolded the paper and saw a collection of letters, figures and signs of the zodiac scrawled all over it.

"Who wrote this?" he demanded.

Jennings' hand went up. "Please, sir, I did."

"Oh, did you? And will you come up here and translate it, so that all may enjoy the benefit of your artistic efforts."

Jennings came with a heavy heart. He knew Darbishire wouldn't laugh, but he didn't want to give the rest of the form a chance to repeat their jeers at his expense. For a moment he was tempted to pretend that his message referred to the previous Saturday's rugger match, but he was a truthful boy so he took a deep breath and translated: "Do you think Old Nightie is an escaped convict? I do," he read aloud, feeling rather foolish.

Form III was delighted.

"Oh, sir, make Jennings give his reasons, sir," they pleaded.

"Well, go on, Jennings," barked Mr. Wilkins, determined to get to the bottom of it. "Why do you think Old—er—why do you think Hawkins is an escaped convict?"

"Oh, I don't, really, sir," Jennings said uncomfortably. "It was just an idea. You see, good detectives always make inquiries about suspicious-looking characters, sir, and Nightie's got a funny way of looking at you, so I thought he'd be a good chap to practise detective work on, sir. He ... well, that's all, really sir," he finished lamely.

"But ... Corwumph, you silly little boy, Hawkins has been night watchman here for nearly forty years."

"Yes, of course, sir, I'd forgotten that."

"Now, look here, Jennings," said Mr. Wilkins, "we've had quite enough of this detective nonsense. It's interfering with your work and causing a lot of trouble all round. Any more of this and you'll find yourself in serious trouble. Do you understand?"

"Yes, sir," said Jennings sadly.

He was given an hour's detention for flicking the pellet, but it was not this that distressed him—it was the continued sniggers of his colleagues, who seized on the instance as a further excuse to laugh at his efforts.

"It's no good, Darbishire," he said, as they sat in their headquarters in the tuck-box room after school. "There's just nothing here that needs detecting.

We might as well be living in a concentration camp for all the fun we get."

Someone had scrawled *Ha, ha, ha!* right across the notice advertising the *Linbury Court Detective Agency*, and Jennings snatched it down and threw it into the wastepaper basket. Their detective equipment, which they had collected with such pride, seemed to mock them. The glass had fallen out of the telescope, the battery of the Morse buzzer had run down and the mouth organ would make no sound, since it had been accidentally dropped in the wash basin. There was, of course, the illustrated catalogue of the *Grossman Ciné Camera Co., Ltd.*, which had arrived a few days after they had written for it. Jennings glanced through its pages. It was a beautiful catalogue, and they had spent hours poring over the illustrations of the cameras advertised between its glossy covers.

"Gosh, that's a super one," said Jennings, pausing once more to admire a ciné de luxe model priced at ninety-five guineas. "If only we'd got that!"

"But we haven't," Darbishire pointed out, "and if we had, I don't see that it'd be any good, if we've got no crimes to use it on."

"Well, it'd come in handy for other things," Jennings argued. "Sports Day, for instance. I could take a photo finish of you winning the half-mile."

He roared with laughter at his joke, and Darbishire gave him a bespectacled blink of reproach. "You needn't make a joke about it," he said.

Darbishire's entry for the half-mile open was considered to be the second funniest joke of the term.

He was no athlete; when he joined his fellows in a practice run, he would finish the lap panting and exhausted, a hundred yards behind the leaders. He clenched his fists and threw his legs high into the air behind him, but for all his efforts he moved at the pace of a penguin prancing amongst the Antarctic snows.

"It's jolly well not fair to laugh," he complained, as Jennings tossed the catalogue back into the tuck-box. "I can't help it if I'm a bit slow. Some chaps are good at one thing and some are good at others, and my father says—"

"And what are you good at?"

"I'm good at—well, I'm good at other things, and anyway, I don't like running. I'm only going in for the half-mile to help win the sports cup for Drake."

"Coming in last won't help much."

"There's always a chance," Darbishire defended himself. "Supposing, say, Bod gets measles the day before, and MacTaggart sprains his ankle in the high

229

jump, and then perhaps, for instance, if it was a hot day and Nuttall got a touch of sun-stroke, because he does sometimes—"

"You're bats!" Jennings interrupted. "The only way you could win would be if Mr. Carter accidentally shot everyone else in the foot with the starting pistol. Dash it all, Darbi, you couldn't beat a performing seal running on its flippers."

Darbishire sighed. If only he could run like Jennings, who was an easy favourite for the 440 yards and the long jump, under twelve.

"My father says—" he began, and then trailed off as he had forgotten which wise saying of his father's had occurred to him. Instead, he began replacing their useless equipment in the tuck-box. "Come on," he said, "let's put all this junk away and go for a practice run round the field. If Drake doesn't win the cup this year, no one can say it's because I didn't practice hard enough."

CHAPTER 7

JENNINGS SEES THE LIGHT

IT WAS a week later when Jennings first saw the light in the sanatorium. He awoke unexpectedly to hear the school clock striking eleven, and slipped out of bed to fetch a drink of water.

Tooth-glass in hand, he stood looking out of the dormitory window in the direction of the sanatorium on the far side of the quadrangle. It was a two-storeyed, detached building and a light was shining from a ground floor window. As he watched, a shadow passed across the blind; head and shoulders were clearly outlined, as the figure stood, for a moment, before the window.

"Someone must be ill," he decided. "Glad I'm not Matron—beetling about taking temperatures at this time of night." He finished his drink, tumbled back into bed and was soon asleep.

The next morning during class he suddenly had a thought. This was unusual in itself, for Mr. Hind's arithmetic period seldom provoked him to mental effort; but his idea had nothing to do with the problem which they were studying, of how long it would take to fill a tank with water flowing in through pipe A and pipe B, while at the same time it was pouring to waste through pipe C. Instead, it was an idea full of exciting possibilities. No one was ill; there had been no absentees at the morning roll-call. Why then, should Matron, or anyone else, be casting their shadows on the blind of the sanatorium late at night?

He urged his reasoning powers a step further. Surely, the figure at the window could not have been Matron, for she always wore a flowing nurse's headdress, and the shadow on the blind had been a clear-cut, bareheaded silhouette. The more he thought of it, the more convinced he became that the unknown profile was that of a man. It had not looked like the Head, or Mr. Carter, or any of the masters; perhaps it was a burglar, perhaps ...

Mr. Hind's soft, purring voice caught his ear. "Have you finished that sum yet, Jennings?" he cooed.

Jennings glanced at the page before him. "No, sir," he confessed. "I haven't actually quite *finished* it yet, sir."

231

"How much have you done?"

"I haven't actually quite started it yet, sir."

"Too bad, too bad," murmured Mr. Hind, but no one was deceived by his soothing manner; it was known that Mr. Hind could pounce like a hawk out of the clear blue sky, when he felt so inclined.

"And why," he inquired, "have we not actually quite finished it yet?"

Jennings thought rapidly. "Well, sir, it doesn't really make sense. You see, if you wanted to fill this tank and you turned on pipe *A* and pipe *B*, you'd put the plug in if you had any sense, so it wouldn't keep running out of pipe *C*, sir. I mean, you'd be crazy if you didn't, wouldn't you, sir?"

Mr. Hind remarked that he was not aware that there was anything wrong with his mental powers.

"Oh, I don't mean *you* would be crazy, sir—I mean anyone would. And even if they hadn't got a proper plug they could bung up pipe *C* with a handkerchief or a sponge, or something, and that'd make the sum come out ever so much easier, sir."

"Jennings," said Mr. Hind sadly, "you are an illiterate nit-wit, an uncouth youth, a sub-human relic; in short, my dear boy, you are a miserable specimen." And with that he passed on to Darbishire, who informed him that the answer came to approximately seven years, one week, four days and twenty-three seconds.

Mr. Hind did not blink. "The right answer," he purred, "is twelve and a half minutes."

"Oh!" Darbishire seemed surprised. "That puts me a bit outside the target area, sir. It's just as well I said my answer was only approximate. May I have a mark for scoring a near miss, sir?"

The lesson dragged on. Jennings tried hard to cope with the antics of imaginary plumbers turning taps on and off for no apparent reason, but the shadowy figure at the sanatorium window kept appearing in his mind's eye.

He made a bee-line for Darbishire the moment the lesson was over.

"Listen," he said, urgently, "I really think I'm on to something supersonic at last." The confident note was back in his voice again, and his eyes sparkled. "I woke up last night and had a dekko out of the window, and what do you think I saw?"

"Old Wilkie dancing in the moonlight," answered Darbishire facetiously.

"Oh, don't be so feeble! This is the real thing—at least, it might be. I'll tell you what I saw"—he paused dramatically. "I saw a light in the san."

"Well, what of it? I expect Matron forgot to turn it off."

"We'll soon see about that," said Jennings. "Come on, we'll go and ask her."

Mystified, Darbishire followed the confident footsteps of his chief up to the door of Matron's sitting room on the first floor.

"You wait here," Jennings whispered. "I'm going to make some inquiries."

He returned a few minutes later wearing a wide, satisfied smile, and said: "Matron didn't go into the san. at all last night, because I asked her. What's more, we haven't had a mump or a measle all the term, so no one's been over there except one of Mother Snackbar's sewing-maids. She counts the laundry, or something, but she's only there in the daytime—I found that out too."

"Yes, but what's all this leading up to?"

"Well, I shouldn't be surprised if the chap I saw was a—" He stopped. He'd been going to say "burglar" but his recent experience had taught him to be careful of using such a description lightly. "My theory is," he went on, "that tramps have been using the place to sleep in. They could easily find out that no one ever goes there at night, unless they've got the measles, so why shouldn't they do that."

"Why shouldn't the tramps catch the measles?"

"No, you bazooka. Why shouldn't they sleep there?"

"I can think of several reasons," objected Darbishire. "First, they'd be more comfortable under a hedge than they would be on hard school beds, and secondly—"

"Well, it needn't be tramps," urged Jennings. "It could be army deserters or—or escaped convicts even."

Darbishire giggled. "Like Old Nightie?"

"Oh, don't be bats! Anyway, if Old Nightie was any good at his job, he'd have seen the light himself. I bet he was snoring his head off down in the boiler-room."

"Did you tell Matron about your theory?" Darbishire asked.

"Of course not. This is a man's job. There's no point in frightening the women about it." He drew himself to his full height—a chivalrous guardian of the weaker sex. "I just sort of led the conversation round to it, and I found out that the masters never go over there either; they can't without her knowing, because they haven't got a key!"

This last argument swayed Darbishire. "Golly," he said, "sounds as though we're on to something, doesn't it?"

"Pity we can't get in and investigate," Jennings mused. "Never mind, let's go and have a look at the outside, and see if we can spot anything suspicious."

"Hadn't we better tell Mr. Carter? Remember what a frantic bish we made last time."

"All in good time," replied the chief of the detective agency. "It's no good telling Mr. Carter until we've got proof."

They ran down to their headquarters to collect their equipment, and then crossed the quadrangle and stood staring at the creeper-covered walls of the sanatorium. It had originally been a large cottage, but as it stood well away from the main building, it made a suitable place to isolate boys when they were ill. Two upstairs rooms were used as wards for the patients, and a bed-sitting room on the ground floor provided for the needs of a night nurse. In case of emergency, she could telephone to the main building by means of a private wire.

Only one room was in daily use, except in times of epidemic; this was on the ground floor next to the night nurse's quarters, and here Ivy, the sewing-maid, darned socks, sewed on buttons and sorted the laundry.

She was rather surprised, on looking out of the window, to see that her movements were being watched from the quad. Jennings, a battered telescope to his eye, was surveying the cottage walls searchingly. His work was hampered by the fact that the lens kept dropping out, but he persevered, screwing up his nose and baring his teeth in an effort to improve his vision.

"Well, I like their cheek," bristled Ivy and pulled down the blind. She could not afford to waste time on Tuesday mornings, for she worked to a strict routine. On Tuesdays she checked the soiled linen and packed it into the large laundry baskets; on Wednesdays she had only to add the boys' pyjamas to the top of the pile, and the baskets were ready for the laundry van's weekly visit.

When she pulled up the workroom blind, a few minutes later, she noticed that the two keen observers had gone. They were holding a council of war in the privacy of their headquarters; for although nothing had been learned from their close scrutiny of the cottage windows, Jennings was already planning the next move.

"I've got a cracking idea!" he said. "We'll keep watch, and if we see the light again we'll hoof over to the san. and spy on the tramps red-handed. Then we can beetle down to that telephone box at the end of the drive and dial 999."

"Coo, yes, spivish decent wheeze," agreed Darbishire.

"And we'll take cricket stumps, or hockey sticks, or something in case we're attacked, and we'll let ourselves out of the dormitory window on the fire escape lifeline."

"Wouldn't it be easier just to walk down the stairs?"

"I suppose it would, really. I never thought of that," Jennings confessed. The staircase as a means of descent seemed rather dull compared with the fire escape, but he didn't press the point. "Anyway," he said, "we can both see the san. windows from our beds, so we'll keep watch by turns. You stay awake tonight until it strikes ten, and then wake me up."

This plan was found to contain one serious flaw when they tried it out. With the best will in the world, Darbishire was unable to keep his eyes open until ten o'clock. It was warm between the blankets, and he felt sleep creeping over him when he had been on duty for half an hour.

"Gosh, this won't do," he told himself. "There's always the most frantic hoo-hah if sentries go to sleep at their posts." He strained his eyes towards the unlighted cottage. "Now whatever I do, I mustn't go to sleep," he murmured, and the next thing he knew, the rising bell was shrilling its morning message, and shafts of sunlight were playing on the dormitory wall above his head.

Jennings was furious.

"You great, crumbling ruin," he complained. "You've gone and bished things up again! If you were in the army, you could be shot at dawn for doing a thing like that."

"Sorry, Jen," said Darbishire humbly.

"Not this dawn, of course," Jennings corrected, "because that's been over for about a hundred years. It's too bad, Darbishire. There we were, fast asleep, and for all we know the san. was knee-deep in trespassers tramping all over the place."

"You mean tramps trespassing, not trespassers tramping."

"Don't quibble. You've made a frightful bish and you're about as much use as a radioactive suet pudding."

"Sorry, Jen," Darbishire said again, as he got out of bed and reached for his slippers.

"Now, tonight," Jennings decided as they stood at the wash basins, "there'll be no nonsense. We'll do it the other way round, and I'll take first watch."

When Jennings had been on watch for forty minutes he began to realise that his criticism of Darbishire had been rather harsh. It was more difficult to keep awake than he had thought. "It's because I'm too comfortable," he told himself. "If I got out of bed, I'd be too cold to fall asleep."

For five minutes he stood at the window and shivered; his bare feet on the linoleum grew so cold that they ached, so he put on his slippers and dressing gown. Three minutes later he added his top blanket, and shortly after that he decided that standing up was adding unnecessarily to his suffering. "After all," he persuaded himself, "horses go to sleep standing up, so I might, too, if I don't look out."

He compromised by kneeling on the foot of his bed with his elbows resting on the bed-rail, his chin cupped in his hands. And it was in this strange, doubled-up attitude that Mr. Carter found him, fast asleep, when he walked round the dormitories at ten o'clock.

A further meeting of the detective organisation was held the next after-noon.

"It's no good this trying to keep awake," the chief detective explained. "We'll have to think of something else."

The meeting was silent while the members thought. Then Jennings had an idea, and the wide-awake look came back into his eyes.

"I say, Darbi," he said, "I think I've got it. If we had an alarm clock, I could set it for eleven o'clock, and fix it on to my ear by tying my braces round my head." He waved his hands vaguely round his ears by way of explanation. "Then I could sleep on one side and put my pillow on top of it."

"Why do all that?"

"So's to soften the noise when it goes off. We don't want Venables and Co. getting out of bed, thinking it's a fire practice." He lowered his voice: "Besides, Mr. Carter might hear. He's got supersonic earsight."

"I see. Yes, quite a massive wheeze." Darbishire gazed at his friend admir-ingly. "But suppose you fell out of bed, or turned over in your sleep—you might bust the glass."

"No, I shan't," his chief explained, "because when I've tied it on, I shall lie on my side, and you can tie my hands to the bed-rail with my tie, so that I can't turn over." For some minutes they debated the point of how he was to switch the alarm off with his hands securely tied, and eventually it was decided that Jennings, wak-ened by the alarm, should call quietly to Darbishire in the next bed. his assistant would then leap nimbly from sleep, and report for switching-off duty.

"All right then," agreed Darbishire, rising from his tuck-box. "Let's do that—it'll be a cracking priority prang. Do it tonight, shall we?"

He made for the door with the air of one whose problem had been neatly solved. He could always trust his friend, when it came to thinking out a really first-class, foolproof plan.

Jennings called him back. "There's just one snag," he said slowly.

"Surely not," said Darbishire. "What is it?"

"*We haven't got an alarm clock*!"

The question of how they were to wake was shelved for the time being, as there seemed to be no obvious solution. Perhaps it would just happen, Jennings thought optimistically, and they passed on to the next stage of their preparations.

"What we ought to do," the senior detective decided, "is to write a note, in case things go wrong, and we have to be rescued."

"Oh, golly, is it going to be as dangerous as all that?" Darbishire enjoyed making plans; it made him feel important, and as there was a good chance that they would never be carried out, he could plot with ruthless daring. But suddenly he wondered what would happen if this scheme ever became a reality. He was secretly appalled at the idea of invading a sinister sanatorium, bristling with hostile trespassers.

"I think we ought to tell Mr. Carter at once," he demurred, "because my father says it's better to be safe than sorry, and I think he's right."

Jennings was scornful. The time to tell Mr. Carter would be when they had proved beyond doubt that their suspicions were justified.

"It'll be all right," he added confidently. "We shan't come to any harm if we leave a note, because that tells them where we've gone, and then they can surround the place with flying squads and things. I read a book once, all about a chap who was going to another chap's house, but he didn't trust this chap, the first chap didn't; so this first chap gave a note to his butler, and if he hadn't come back to his house by next morning, he was to take it to Scotland Yard."

"Who was to take what?"

"The butler was to take the note that the chap gave him. And when ..."

"Yes, but what's the point of telling me all this?" Darbishire interrupted. "Even if we wrote a note like this chap did, we haven't got a butler to give it to."

"But you don't *have* to have a butler," Jennings explained patiently.

"You said we did."

"No, I didn't. I said that's what the chap did. The first chap, I mean, not the chap whose house—"

"All right, all right, you needn't go through it all again," protested Darbishire. "I don't think much of this scheme anyway—we haven't got the right sort of gear. First, we haven't got an alarm clock, and now we haven't got a butler. I'd like to see how your first chap would have got on if he'd only had a busted telescope and a dumb mouth organ to help him."

"Okay then, we won't bother about the note," Jennings agreed. "We'll just tell someone we're going—someone we can trust, of course, because the whole thing's got to be kept super-spivish secret."

They decided that Venables could be trusted not to reveal their plan. Jennings had not really forgiven him for his gibes of the previous week, but, as he explained to Darbishire, someone had got to be in the know, in case the worst happened.

That evening, after tea, Venables sat in his classroom, making spectacles with twisted pipe-cleaners. He made one pair and put them on, and was busily engaged on the second when he heard his name being breathed in a hoarse whisper. He peered through the glassless rims which sat drunkenly on his nose, and saw that Jennings was beckoning to him to come into the corridor. Several times during the day, Jennings had been on the point of taking Venables into his confidence, but always someone had approached within earshot and the attempt had been abandoned. Jennings was taking no chances, and Venables was unable to discover the reason for the furtive stage-whispers, until they reached the tuck-box room. Then Jennings spoke:

"I say, Venables, will you do me a super cracking favour? Do say yes!"

Venables had been caught that way before. "If you mean will I swop you my ten-cent Liberian three-cornered stamp—"

"No, no, it's not that."

"And I'm not going to lend you my spiked running shoes either."

"Not that sort of favour," said Jennings. "It's the san. I've seen lights there and I think it's tramps, and Darbishire and I are planning to go over and investigate one night, only we don't know when, yet. If we don't come back, we want you to go and tell Mr. Carter."

"Gosh, how super!" breathed Venables. His eyes lit up behind his wobbling pipe-cleaners. One eyepiece was twice the size of the other, and the white fluffy rims gave him something of the appearance of a giant panda.

He absorbed such details as Jennings was able to give, and returned to his classroom, flushed with the joy of knowing an important secret.

CHAPTER 8

MR. WILKINS GROWS CURIOUS

VENABLES DID not really mean to give Jennings' secret away; but as the evening wore on, he found it more and more difficult to keep the news to himself.

"If only Atki knew what I know," he thought, as the dormitory bell rang, "I bet he'd be surprised!" For although Venables had only a minor part to play, he knew that he would come in for a certain amount of reflected glory if he told Atkinson. And after all, Atkinson was his best friend—he wouldn't let it go any further.

As he washed his knees, Venables had a short battle with his conscience; then he approached his friend and said in a hushed undertone: "I say, Atki, what d'you think?"

"Oh, buzz off, Venables," retorted Atkinson.

"You're always coming round asking me what I think. How do I know what I think if you don't tell me? If you think I can guess what I'm supposed to be thinking when I haven't even got a clue—"

"All right then, I won't tell you, but you'll be sorry. I shouldn't be surprised if you lived to regret it, even, especially as it's an urgent hush-hush job like invasion plans and things."

"What is?"

"I shan't tell you. You told me to buzz off."

"Okay, I take that back," Atkinson compromised.

"Tell me—go on, be decent."

"'Fraid I can't; it's lethal confidential."

"But a moment ago you said—" Atkinson began, and then changed his tactics. "Look, if you tell me, I'll put you on my cake list."

"But you haven't got any cake!"

"Maybe not. But that's no reason why I shouldn't make a list of chaps I'd like to give a hunk of cake to if I *had* got any."

"Well, promise you won't split?" And after Atkinson had solemnly agreed,

Venables dropped his voice to the right pitch for revealing secrets. "Well, what do you think?" he began.

Atkinson threw a wet sponge at him. "That's what you said before," he stormed.

"Oh, sorry," said Venables and started off again. It was a good secret as it stood, but Venables could not resist the temptation of adding a few details of his own.

"Jennings and Darbishire think they're tramps," he finished up, "but I shouldn't be surprised if they're spies who've landed on the beach, and are hiding in the san. because it's nice and quiet; but you won't tell anyone, will you?"

Atkinson sat next to Temple in the dining-hall. Next day at lunch he said: "I say, Bod, I've heard something—it's massive daring."

"I suppose you've been ear-wagging again," returned Temple shortly. He was bolting his suet pudding as fast as he could, and keeping one eye on Matron who was dealing with second helpings.

There were only a few portions left, and he would have to clear his plate like lightning, if he was going to achieve the second helping that he hoped for.

"No, I haven't honestly," protested Atkinson, "but Jennings has seen lights in the san. and Venables thinks it's spies, but I've got a better idea."

Atkinson's theory was that black marketeers were using the unoccupied wards as a warehouse; he drew a vivid picture of the rooms crammed with rare valuables. Boxes of four-bladed penknives were stacked on the floor; model yachts and batting-gloves lay piled on the beds; rare stamps and model locomotives were scattered in all corners of the room.

"Mind you, I don't know," he admitted. "It's just what I think. And you won't tell anyone will you, because it's a hefty rare secret?"

Temple had been so interested in the news that he had unconsciously slowed down the pace of his eating. He glanced at Matron and saw, to his horror, that the dish containing second helpings was empty.

"Oh, gosh," he groaned, "and I'd have given anything for a refill of that suet! It was the wizardest muck we've had this week."

His only consolation was that he knew a secret. It would be quite safe with him; he would never dream of telling a soul—except of course Parslow, because Parslow could be trusted not to spread it—beyond, perhaps, mentioning it to Martin-Jones, who was a close friend. Johnson received a garbled account from Martin-Jones, and Bromwich major heard the news from Johnson; then it spread via Nuttall, Brown major, Thomson minor, Rumbelow and Paterson, until the information was shared by three-quarters of the school.

Venables sat in his classroom that evening after tea; he was wearing his pipe-cleaner spectacles and making pipe-cleaner poodles. Binns minor, who usually chose to be a jet-propelled aircraft at that time of day, flew in at desk-top level. Spotting Venables through his bombsights, he banked sharply, throttled back his engine with a sharp snap of his teeth, and circled down to make a perfect landing on the runway between the desks.

"I say, Venables, have you heard about the light in the san?" he shrilled importantly.

"Of course I have—I was the first one to know. It's hairy stale buns by now. It's supposed to be a corking secret, but if it gets round like this we might as well have it broadcast on the six o'clock news." He was annoyed to think that such a closely guarded secret should be common property. How could it have leaked out?

"I think it's a bit thick, the way chaps can't keep their mouths shut," Venables grumbled on, eyeing the jet-propelled Binns minor with distaste. "I know all about it because Jennings told me himself. He said I was the only chap he could trust, and now even Form I knows."

Binns minor immediately put his finger on the flaw in the security measures.

"Who's told everyone? You have!" he squeaked in triumph.

"I only told Atkinson—he's not everybody," Venables answered reasonably. "Anyway, the damage is done now. The only people who don't know about it are the masters. Thank goodness they've got no way of finding out!"

Mr. Carter laid his newspaper down when he heard the heavy footsteps approaching his room. He knew from past experience that reading was out of the question, when Mr. Wilkins decided to pay him one of his tumultuous visits.

A sound like a naval twelve-gun salute signified that his visitor was knocking, and the next moment the door shuddered on its hinges, as Mr. Wilkins burst into the room.

"I say, Carter, I've discovered something you ought to know about," he began, as though he was addressing a vast, open-air meeting. "Jennings has seen lights in the sanatorium, late at night."

"Yes, I know," Mr. Carter murmured gently.

"You know?"

"Everybody knows by now, don't they? And if they didn't know before, they can probably hear you telling me all about it."

"Sorry, old man, was I speaking loudly?" Mr. Wilkins had a voice like a loud-hailer, but now he lowered his tone as though adjusting the knob of his volume-control. "I heard Thomson minor and Rumbelow whispering away in the changing room, at the tops of their voices. Sounded like a particularly confidential secret, from the row they made over it." He thudded heavily into an armchair, and the protesting springs twanged like a harp. "Who told you anyway?" he demanded, as the music died away.

"Nobody told me," replied Mr. Carter, hoping that his armchair would stand the strain. "I deduced it. I happened to be in dormitory four when someone mentioned the word 'sanatorium.' There was a sudden, deathly hush, and everyone looked at me and then looked away again quickly." Mr. Carter smiled. Because he had let the incident pass without comment, it was mistakenly supposed that he had not noticed anything unusual.

"Well, I'll tell you another thing," said Mr. Wilkins earnestly. "Jennings has seen tramps going in and out of the back door—or so Rumbelow says. Time something was done about it, don't you agree?"

"No, I don't think I do," replied Mr. Carter unexpectedly, as he filled his pipe. If only Wilkins would go, he could get on with his crossword puzzle.

"You—you mean to sit there and tell me that you don't propose to do anything about it?"

"Quite right."

Mr. Wilkins leapt to his feet to the accompaniment of a deep musical note from the springs of the armchair. "But good heavens, Carter," he expostulated, pacing up and down the room, "this is a serious matter—how serious, you don't seem to realise."

He emphasised his point with a sweeping gesture which brought a tobacco jar crashing down on top of a record that lay on the radiogram. "Oh, sorry, old man," he apologised, gathering up the broken pieces and dropping them on the fire. "Never mind, it was only an old record ... Now what was I saying? Oh, yes. This is a serious business. If tramps are using the sanatorium to sleep in, it's a matter for the police."

"I don't think we'll bother the police just yet," returned Mr. Carter. "There's quite a simple explan—" He broke off, sniffed the air keenly, and glanced towards the fireplace.

The gramophone record was giving off a stream of dense smoke, and fumes of burning wax were filling the room. Mr. Carter seized the coal tongs and shovel, grabbed the flaming fragments and threw them out of the window, on to a flowerbed below.

His expression had lost some of its usual calm, when he returned to his chair. "Now, look here, Wilkins," he said. "This sanatorium business is nothing to worry about, and anyway, I'm extremely busy. At least, I intend to be busy doing a crossword puzzle. Do you mind leaving this matter in my hands?"

"Yes, but dash it all, Carter," protested Mr. Wilkins. "You can't let tramps use the place as an hotel—think of the damage! They've probably been stealing the furniture. I shouldn't be surprised if the place has been practically emptied already!"

Mr. Carter picked up his newspaper and said: "You know, Wilkins, you jump to conclusions just as Jennings does. However, if it will give you any satisfaction, we'll take a stroll over there at eleven o'clock, and you can see for yourself."

"Yes, but—"

"Eleven o'clock," replied Mr. Carter firmly, and turned to his crossword puzzle.

A gust of wind like the slip-stream of an aircraft, followed by a thunderous crash, denoted that Mr. Wilkins had swept out of the room, and slammed the door behind him.

At eleven o'clock he was back, bursting with suppressed excitement. "They're there," he announced dramatically. "The light's on in one of the downstair rooms!"

Mr. Carter sighed. He had not quite finished his crossword puzzle.

Together they descended the stairs and crossed the quadrangle, Mr. Wilkins tense with expectation and Mr. Carter wearing an amused smile.

The front door was open and they went in. A light was shining from a crack beneath the sewing room door and Mr. Carter put his hand on the doorknob. "Don't be too violent with the tramps, will you, Wilkins?" he said in tones of mock gravity. He opened the door and Mr. Wilkins hurried into the room.

"Oh!" he said.

Old Nightie, armed with a mop, was polishing the linoleum with soft, gentle strokes, as though afraid of wearing out the pattern. He looked up, surprised, for he seldom had the pleasure of welcoming visitors.

"'Evening, Mr. Carter, sir, 'evening, Mr. Wilkins," he said, and leaned heavily on his mop handle. "Anything I can do for you, sir?"

"It's all right, thank you, Hawkins," returned Mr. Carter. "Mr. Wilkins wanted to assure himself that all was well. He thought you were—"

"I—I—well actually, as a matter of fact, Hawkins," Mr. Wilkins interposed quickly. "The point is, if you follow me—" He stopped, uncomfortably aware that Old Nightie did not follow him. The old man was giving him one of his queer looks, and Mr. Wilkins cast a despairing glance at Mr. Carter, who obligingly came to his rescue. He explained to Old Nightie that the sanatorium lights were the subject of strange rumours among the boys. "I thought I'd let you know," he continued, "because there's a remote chance that one or two of them might decide to investigate at first hand. If they do, I want you to let me know at once. You can phone through to my room from the night nurse's quarters next door, and I'll come over and deal with them."

"Yes, sir," replied the night watchman, his thin, wrinkled face creasing in a wide smile. "Well, fancy them thinking that! Why, I've been sweeping up over here regular as clockwork for thirty-nine years, and we haven't had a tramp or burglar in all that time. Ten forty-five on the dot, I finish down the boiler-room, pick up the key and over I come—bar when there's anyone ill in bed, of course."

He straightened his back and looked round the barely-furnished room. "I reckon as a burglar would have to be pretty hard up before he came to the san.," he grinned. "There's nothing here worth pinching."

He waved his mop towards a small table, on which were stacked a hot-water bottle, two packets of cottonwool, an ear syringe and several rolls of bandage. The laundry baskets, a chair and Ivy's sewing materials were the only other objects in the room. "Don't you worry, sir, we shan't get troubled with no burglars breaking in here."

"Satisfied, Mr. Wilkins?" his colleague asked.

But Mr. Wilkins was not entirely satisfied. As they crossed the quadrangle on their way back, he demanded that Mr. Carter should ban amateur detectives' games altogether. "Put your foot down firmly," he urged. "You're Jennings' housemaster. Tell him that all this nonsense about deducing clues has got to stop; and take those Sherlock Holmes books away from him, too."

"It was I who introduced him to Sherlock Holmes," Mr. Carter observed, "so I can't very well forbid it. Besides, so long as he's only *playing* at detectives it can do no harm, and if you stop them playing one sort of game, they'll only think up another one."

He knew from experience how true this was, and he decided that his best course was to keep a finger on the pulse of Jennings' activities, without drawing everyone's attention to them. "Don't worry, Wilkins," he advised, as they entered the main building. "While Jennings is puzzling over the lights in the cottage, he's not likely to turn his attention to anything worse."

"But supposing they go over there? They're always devising wild and impossible schemes, you know."

"They can scheme till they're black in the face," said Mr. Carter, "provided they don't actually carry them out; and I don't think they will—they can't keep awake long enough, for one thing."

Mr. Wilkins suddenly stopped, turned to his colleague and slapped him heartily on the back. "Carter," he said, "I think it would be a good thing if they *did* carry their plans out. Might curb their taste for adventure. If they go over there and find it's only old Hawkins after all, they'll feel a bit sick, won't they?"

"Just as you did," Mr. Carter interposed. He had not quite recovered from the slap on the back.

"Never mind about me," Mr. Wilkins put in hastily, "but these silly little boys have made such a fuss over this secret discovery nonsense, that if it turns out to be a damp squib it'll put paid to the whole business. And then, perhaps, Jennings will get his mind back to doing a little more work in class, and the whole school can look forward to a spot of peace."

Mr. Carter did not agree with this easy solution. "Oh, no," he said. "We can't actually let him go over there—that would never do. But you needn't worry, Wilkins, it won't come to that."

"It'd be a good thing for the whole school if it did," his colleague answered. And, as it happened, he was right. But Mr. Wilkins had no notion of just how accurately he had hit the nail on the head.

CHAPTER 9

JENNINGS MAKES AN ENTRANCE

THE GREEN of the playing field was sprinkled with the white shorts and running vests of seventy-nine boys practising for the sports. There was one week to go before Sports Day on the following Wednesday, and now that half-term had passed and the weather was kinder, the boys were determined to make the most of their opportunities to practise.

Sports Day was not, however, a formal occasion attended by a large crowd of parents, for March is never a good month for outdoor social gatherings. The custom was to regard the event solely as an athletic contest, which parents might attend if they wished, but only those who lived close at hand were expected to do so.

In the long jump pit, Binns minor was happily building tunnels in the sand, and leaping for his life every time a jumper hurtled past the take off board; Atkinson and Venables were practising starts on the hundred yards track, and the Raleigh and Drake relay teams were perfecting the difficult task of passing the baton without losing speed.

Jennings finished the last few yards of the "220" at top speed, and then went to look for Darbishire. He found him at the high jump standards. With gritted teeth and fingernails dug deeply into the palms of his hands, he was vainly trying to jump over the bar, which rested three feet from the ground.

Darbishire felt that he could clear this height easily, if only he could decide which leg to hurl into the air first. Whichever way he tried, he always arrived at the point of take off with the wrong foot foremost, and had to turn himself round in mid-air like a ballet dancer.

"Gosh," said Jennings, as he watched his friend's efforts to become airborne. "You're hopeless! You look like a pelican trying to take off on an ice rink."

Darbishire rubbed his bruised knees. "Well, it doesn't really matter," he replied, "because I'm not going in for the high jump—I'm just going to concentrate on the half-mile."

This was the longest track event in the programme and Darbishire had entered for it as he felt that any shorter race would be over before he was properly off the mark. There was also the advantage that, as only six boys had entered, it would not be necessary to run heats, and Darbishire knew that he could not be weeded out of the running before the great day dawned. "I'm going in for the egg-and-spoon race too, of course," he added, "because sometimes, the slower you are the better chance you've got, and as I'm miles the slowest I might win. Gosh, I wish I could run like you though, Jennings!"

Jennings sat on the high jump landing-mat and took his shoes off. Venables had a pair of proper spiked running-shoes, and as he was Jennings' closest rival in the 440 yards under twelve, this advantage gave Jennings much food for thought.

"How would it be," he pondered, "if I bunged some drawing pins through the soles of my gymshoes? Would that turn them into spiked running-shoes, d'you think?"

Darbishire agreed that it might be a good idea, provided that he remembered to stick the pins through the right way round. "You could lend them to me if it works," he said, "because you're not in the half-mile, and I shall need all the help I can get, if I'm not going to come in last."

"You'll need more than spikes," Jennings replied. "I can't see anything less than jet-propelled skates getting you twice round the track before it gets dark. I shouldn't be surprised if Mr. Carter puts his stopwatch back in his pocket, and times you with a calendar."

Darbishire ignored the insults. "As a matter of fact," he said importantly, "I've worked out a theory that I might win, after all. My father says that when the hare and the tortoise had a race—"

"Yes, I know," Jennings broke in, "the hare went to sleep and the tortoise won. I think that's a crazy story, and if you imagine that Nuttall and Bod and Binns major are going to lie down in the middle of the running track, and have a snooze with everybody yelling their heads off, you must be bats."

He put his gym shoes on and struggled into his blazer. "Come on," he said, "let's go and have another look at the san. If only we could get in and have a good snoop round upstairs, we might be able to spot imperceptible traces."

"You think the tramps are still there, then?"

"Not in the daytime, of course. But what's to stop them getting in when the place is empty? It's just the spot for a good night's rest, and the next morning Ivy would never, know they'd been there."

"She might if she went upstairs," Darbishire objected, "because if they've been sleeping there for as long as you make out, it's high time they had clean sheets, and you're not going to tell me—"

"Well, perhaps they don't bother about sheets, and if they tidy up a bit before they leave in the morning, how's the eye of the untrained observer going to find out?" It was obvious that only someone skilled in the art of deduction could detect the tell-tale traces, and Jennings was anxious to try his hand.

It was nearly a week since Venables had accidentally set the whole school talking about Jennings' discovery. As Mr. Carter had prophesied, interest had waned as nothing further had happened, and everyone had dismissed the sensational news as being another of Jennings' wild-goose chases. Everyone except Jennings; he was reluctant to give up hope, and still did his best to stay awake on the chance of seeing the light again. One night he had managed to keep his eyes open till eleven-thirty, but it so happened that it was Hawkins' night off duty, and the sanatorium had remained unlighted and unswept.

They trotted across to the sanatorium and stared once more at the creeper-covered walls. Ivy was busy darning socks in her room, but she left her chair, as a laundry van crossed the quadrangle and turned into the cottage garden. The driver got down as Ivy opened the door, and after chatting for a few moments, he started to drag the heavy laundry baskets along the hall and pile them into the back of the van.

"Wait here, Darbi," whispered Jennings, "I'm going to try and fox in through the back door, while Ivy's talking to that chap at the front."

Stealthily, he made his way across the small garden which surrounded the cottage. He knew that he would not be seen so long as the maid and the vanman were busy, but time was short and he would have to hurry. He tried the back door; it was locked. What should he do? Then he remembered the sewing room window. He had noticed that it was open when they had stood watching Ivy busy with her darning, and if the laundry man had now removed all the hampers, the room should be empty. He rounded the corner, and caught a glimpse of Darbishire standing on one leg, and twisting his fingers in an agony of guilty suspense.

The window was open at the top, and peering through he saw that the coast was clear; Ivy and the vanman must still be chatting at the front door. Carefully, Jennings raised the bottom sash, and as soon as it was wide enough to admit his slim figure, he started to crawl through, head first. Head and shoulders and the top half of his body were through the window when, suddenly, there was a jarring, shuddering noise, and the lower half of the window slid down and came gently to rest on the small of his back.

The sash cord at one side had broken months before, and the remaining cord refused to carry the extra weight. Jennings struggled, but he was unable to free himself, for the window, resting on his wriggling figure, pinned him to the sill like a botanical specimen to a drawing-board. His hands beat the empty air of the sewing room, while his feet danced lightly in space above the flower beds outside.

He was not hurt, but the position was extremely uncomfortable; he dared not shout to Darbishire for help, for his head was the wrong side of the window, and cries for assistance would sail down the hall and be heard by Ivy at the front door.

It seemed a long time before he felt small hands clutching at his legs. At last! Darbishire had raced to the rescue. Now all would be well. It would be the work of a moment for him to raise the ill-balanced sash and release his struggling friend, before the maid had noticed anything amiss.

Darbishire was not at his best in a crisis, and he was too flurried to give much thought to the best way of achieving his object. All he knew was that he must do something, and do it soon. He seized the waving ankles and tugged, in the mistaken hope that the rest of his friend would follow in the same direction.

Jennings felt the tug, and his opinion of Darbishire as a friend in need sank like a lift-shaft. "The bone-headed ruin!" he stormed to himself. "Why doesn't he lift the window up?" But though Darbishire was so close at hand, Jennings had no means of telling him what to do.

Darbishire heaved again, and Jennings lashed out wildly with his feet, as a signal that this was not the best way of effecting a rescue. "The stupid idiot," Darbishire muttered to himself, "why doesn't he keep his feet still, so's I can get a good grip!"

Battling against fearful odds, Darbishire succeeded in getting a fresh hold on the flailing legs. He tugged again. Jennings' gym shoes and ankle socks came away in his hands, and the rescuer sat down with a sudden thump amongst the delphiniums.

The door of the sewing room opened and Ivy walked in.

"Jennings! What on earth!" she began, and then started to shriek with laughter at the legless body wriggling on the window-sill. She was still laughing when she opened the window, and helped the victim into the room.

Jennings did not laugh; it was undignified for detective-inspectors to flap helplessly in mid-air, and he felt his position keenly. He'd tell Darbishire a thing or two when he found him again!

"What's the game?" demanded Ivy. She stopped laughing and looked sternly at the barefooted figure before her. "You know you're not allowed over here. I've a good mind to report you to Mr. Carter."

Jennings said nothing. There was nothing he could say.

"Playing hide-and-seek and all that carry on! And out of bounds too. You ought to be ashamed of yourself," grumbled Ivy.

Hide-and-seek! Did Sherlock Holmes ever suffer such indignities? He opened his mouth to protest and then closed it again. It was better to bear this disgrace than to embark on difficult explanations.

"You'd better make yourself useful, now you're here," said Ivy. "I've forgotten to bring Mr. Wilkins' laundry over and Les Perks is here with the van. Will you take him across and show him Mr. Wilkins' room for me?"

"Yes, all right," said Jennings, "and Ivy, you—er—you won't report this to Mr. Carter, will you?"

"Perhaps I will, perhaps I won't." But Jennings knew by the tone in which she said it that his breaking of bounds would go no further. "She's not a bad old stick," he thought, as he led the vanman across the quadrangle.

Darbishire had disappeared, and Jennings was conscious that Mr. Leslie Perks was looking at his freezing feet with some curiosity. He was a young man and he wore a chauffeur's cap; but there his attempt at a uniform stopped, for he was dressed in an old brown sports coat and dirty flannel trousers.

"Thinking of going for a paddle, son?" he inquired, as Jennings picked his way painfully over the gravel.

When they reached the main hall Jennings said: "If you go along to the end and turn left up the stairs, you'll see Mr. Wilkins' room opposite."

"Okay, son," replied the vanman.

He strolled down the hall looking about him with interest, while Jennings stood on one leg and searched his smarting feet for fragments of gravel and traces of frostbite. When he looked up again, he caught sight of the youthful Mr. Perks turning right, into the library, instead of left, to mount the stairs. He scampered after him to correct the mistake, and found him standing in the middle of the library floor, admiring the trophies on the mantelpiece.

"You've gone the wrong way. You should have turned left when you got to the end," Jennings explained. "This is the library."

"Okay, son, I heard you," the man returned pleasantly. "No harm in having a look round, is there?" He walked to the door and disappeared up the stairs.

Jennings found Darbishire in the tuck-box room. He was giving his spectacles their weekly polish with a football sock, and breathing hard on the lenses to remove the sticky smears which had blurred his vision for the previous seven days.

"Oh, hallo," he said, rather sheepishly. "What happened?"

Jennings scowled.

"Darbishire, you're the world's ozardest oik. You've got no more idea of how to be a detective than a cabbage!"

"D'you mean no more idea than a cabbage has of how to be a detective, or than I have of how to be a cabbage?" Darbishire inquired earnestly.

"There was I struggling like blinko and signalling with my feet, and all you do is try and pull me in half instead of getting me free."

"Oh, sorry," Darbishire apologised. "I thought that was the idea."

"What—to pull me in half?"

"No, to get you free. But what happened when Ivy hoofed in?"

"She thought I was playing hide-and-seek and ticked me off. She didn't kick up too much of a hoo-hah, though."

Jennings sat down on a tuck-box and massaged his numbed feet. "Still, if you hadn't bished it up like that, I might have found something super important, if I'd gone upstairs. It's all your fault."

Darbishire decided to change the subject. "You know," he said, "I've been looking at that ciné camera catalogue again, and I've had a rare wheeze. You know we've got eleven and eightpence between us?"

"We *had* eleven and eightpence," corrected Jennings. "We've only got three and sevenpence now."

"Well, three and sevenpence then. It's not much, but it's something. Now, suppose we both get a pound for our birthdays and another pound for Christmas, and save up all the dosh we're given to bring back to school—why, we'd have masses in no time."

He replaced his spectacles, and found to his surprise that he could see through them fairly well. All traces of dust, jam and ink had been carefully wiped away, and only his thumb and fingerprints in the centre of each lens clouded his vision. He took the catalogue from the tuck-box and glanced longingly at the illustrations of the super de luxe model. "What about it, Jen?"

"We'd be wasting our time," his friend decided. "It would take us about a hundred years to save up ninety-five guineas. We might just as well forget the whole thing. Come on, I'm going to get changed now; my feet will need de-icing apparatus and two gallons of anti-freeze, if I don't get my socks on soon."

Although Jennings had given up hope of securing the super de luxe model, the Grossman Ciné Camera Company had not given up hope of securing J. C. T. Jennings as a customer. In a small office, high above the steady rumble of London traffic, Mr. Catchpole, the sales manager, sat staring glumly at a chart on the wall. It was a graph showing the number of cameras that his firm had sold since the beginning of the year; and the more Mr. Catchpole stared, the more gloomy his expression became. The red line of the graph wobbled unsteadily through the space devoted to the sales for January and February, but when it came to the first week in March, it fell like a barometer in a thunderstorm. They had sold a mere handful of cameras since the beginning of the month, and Mr. Catchpole was determined that something had got to be done. He pressed the bell on his desk, and his secretary appeared.

"Oh, Miss Haskins, bring me all the inquiries about ciné cameras we've had in the last month." He drummed his fingers on the desk impatiently, and soon Miss Haskins returned with a folder containing a bundle of letters. She stood by while Mr. Catchpole thoughtfully frowned his way through the small pile. Finally, he looked up and said: "Send Mr. Russell to me, at once."

Mr. Russell was middle-aged, keen and alert. He was an excellent salesman and his colleagues claimed that he could sell sunshades to Eskimos and fur coats to Hottentots if he had a mind to do so.

"Sit down, Mr. Russell," said the manager. "I've sent for you because things are not going too well and something has got to be done. I repeat—got ... to ... be ... done." He emphasised each syllable with a bang on the desk.

"Quite," Mr. Russell agreed.

"I've been going through these inquiries we've had lately. We've sent out dozens of catalogues and hardly anyone has written back and ordered anything. The trouble is, we're getting slack. Every inquiry should lead to a sale, if you go the right way about it."

"Quite," Mr. Russell agreed. He had to sit and listen to the manager's tirade every time the sales graph took a step downwards, and he was quite used to it.

"Now, here is an example," Mr. Catchpole continued, taking a letter at random from the pile and quoting: "*I am thinking of buying one of your cameras and I shall be glad if you will send me a catalogue, as advertised. Yours truly, J. C. T. Jennings.*" He paused. "Now, Mr. Russell, what does Mr. Jennings' letter suggest to you?"

"That he wants a catalogue."

"No, no, no." Mr. Catchpole rose from his revolving chair and paced the office. "He's had a catalogue: we sent it weeks ago—and what's the result?"

"We hear no more," Mr. Russell deduced neatly.

"Exactly, because we're not going the right way about it. We've got to be more careful with our wealthy clients. They expect the personal touch."

"Does he say he's a wealthy client?" inquired Mr. Russell.

"Not in so many words, he doesn't; but reading between the lines it's obvious. Look at this." He thrust Temple's carefully written letter into Mr. Russell's hand. "Look at it," he repeated. "Finest quality notepaper with *Linbury Court, Sussex*, in embossed letters. You don't call your house a Court if you live in a prefabricated bungalow! And look at the crest! And the old family motto in Latin. Do *you* have crested notepaper? No ... Do *I* have crested notepaper?"

"No," said Mr. Russell, supplying the expected answer.

"And why not?" But Mr. Catchpole had no intention of letting his assistant work out the answer to this question for himself. "I'll tell you why not," he went on. "Because these coats-of-arms are the prorigrative—er—pogrogative—er—I should say the perigratov—"

"Prerogative," corrected Mr. Russell.

"That's what I said. They are the prerogative of wealthy aristocratic families with big houses and large country estates."

Mr. Catchpole warmed to his task. This Mr. Jennings, he explained—he might even be *Sir* J. C. T. Jennings for all they knew—was probably the squire of the village, rolling in money, and more than willing to buy expensive cameras, if he was approached in the right way.

Mr. Russell was impressed with the manager's keen powers of observation and his uncanny ability to read between the lines.

"Very well, sir," he said. "I think perhaps you're right. I'll go down to Sussex one day next week and try the personal touch." He rose from his seat and made for the door.

"One moment," Mr. Catchpole called him back. "I want you to understand just how important this is. If my deductions are correct, it may lead to bigger things. If this Mr. Jennings buys a camera, everybody who *is* anybody in his part of the county will be wanting one too."

"Don't worry, sir," replied Mr. Russell. "I know how to treat a man in his position. I'll find out his interests and get him talking; I dare say he'll be keen on hunting, shooting and fishing and all that. You leave it to me."

"Good," said Mr. Catchpole. "I suggest you go next Wednesday, and take our latest model and plenty of film to demonstrate with."

Mr. Russell's hand was on the door-knob, as the manager added good-humouredly: "And don't you dare to come back without selling a camera!"

"Trust me," grinned Mr. Russell, and the door closed behind him.

Mr. Catchpole smiled happily. He knew he could rely on his head salesman not to let him down.

CHAPTER 10

ALARMING EXCURSION

LIEUT.-GENERAL SIR MELVILLE MERRIDEW, Bart., D.S.O., M.C., had agreed to present the sports cup to the winning house. The news was announced at breakfast on the day before the sports, and it raised the enthusiasm of the rival houses to a simmering pitch of excitement.

They had not been expecting such an important visitor, for it was only on Speech Day, in the summer term, that the school usually welcomed distinguished Old Linburians.

Jennings spent the morning break in borrowing drawing pins to convert his plimsoles into spiked running shoes, and Darbishire retired to the library to try to pick up a few hints from a book on athletics.

"What's so cracking wizard about it," Temple observed in the dormitory that night, "is that as it's not Speech Day, the old geezer will only have to hand over the cup and ask for a half-holiday. And that means we shan't have to sit and listen for three and a half hours while he tells us that being at school is the happiest time of your life."

"My father was asked to say a few words to the infants' school in his parish last term," said Darbishire, looking round with an important air. "He had to present the plasticine modelling prize to the *under fives*, and he told them that education was derived from the Latin word *educare*, meaning to lead out and—"

"That's just the sort of thing your father *would* say," Atkinson broke in. He was sitting on his bed, trying to lasso his toes with his dressing gown cord, and he had no wish to listen to the wise words of the Reverend Percival Darbishire.

"This time tomorrow," he sang out gaily, "Raleigh will have won the cup for the third time running. Super-wizzo-sonic!"

"No, they won't, then," Jennings called out from the wash basin. "Drake will. Good old Drake. Yippee!"

Of the five boys who slept in Dormitory 4, he and Darbishire were the only members of Drake; and they were desperately keen on helping their house to wrest the challenge cup from last year's victors. "Up with Drake and down with Raleigh," he shouted, breaking off his washing operations to perform a restrained war dance round the beds. He still carried his sponge, which dripped soddenly on to the end of each bed as he passed by, while little streams of soapy water trickled down his spine and chest until they reached the top of his pyjama trousers.

"Raleigh for ever!" called Venables, waving his toothbrush like a tomahawk.

"Good old Raleigh!" sang out Temple and Atkinson in unison.

"Good old—" Darbishire began.

"Shut up, Darbishire," the Raleigh supporters turned on him threateningly.

"Nobody asked you to butt in," Temple added. "It's just super hairy cheek for an oik who can't run for little apples to start airing his opinions like that."

"I was only going to say— 'Good old General Sir Melville Merridew for asking for a half-holiday'—just supposing that he does," Darbishire explained.

The next moment Mr. Carter came in to see what all the noise was about.

"We'll win tomorrow, won't we, sir?" Jennings appealed to his house-master for support. "Raleigh won't have an earthly, will they, sir?"

"It won't be a walk-over for either side," Mr. Carter replied. "It's going to be the closest competition we've had for years."

The contest was so arranged that the winners of the different events scored points for their houses, and Jennings knew that Drake was relying on him to do well in the under twelve class. "Gosh!" he said, drying his neck vigorously, "I've simply got to win the long jump and the '440' tomorrow."

Mr. Carter waited until they were all in bed; then he switched off the light.

Jennings was soon asleep. He had given up his nightly vigil of the sanatorium, and had little time to worry about the mystery, now that the inter-house sports were filling his mind and claiming his energy. And he would have continued in his deep, dreamless sleep until the shrilling of the rising bell next morning, if Mr. Wilkins had not offered to help his colleague with his supervision duties.

Mr. Carter made a practice of walking round all the dormitories after the boys had gone to sleep.

He patrolled quietly, stopping here and there to tuck in a sliding blanket, or to straighten some fidgety sleeper who was in danger of falling out of bed. But on that Tuesday evening he was busy making final arrangements for the sports, and Mr. Wilkins volunteered to see that all was well in his stead.

He set off on his round, striving to soften his usual heavy footsteps by walking on tiptoe; but he was not accustomed to this nightly patrol in the dark, and when he reached Dormitory 4, he collided heavily with the foot of a bed. The sleeper stirred, uttered a mournful moan and turned over, and Mr. Wilkins passed on, satisfied that he had not disturbed anyone's rest.

The disturbed sleeper did not, however, fall asleep again. As the piercing squeak of Mr. Wilkins' tiptoeing shoes echoed down the dormitory, the drowsy figure sat up, vaguely wondering what had wakened him. There was a noisy click as Mr. Wilkins closed the door with extreme care, and a heavy thump as he accidentally kicked it with his departing heels.

Jennings lay down and was about to fall asleep again, when the school clock struck eleven. As he counted the strokes, he thought of the last time he had heard this nightly chime, and he suddenly sat upright. The next moment he was at the window, shivering with excitement and staring across the deserted quadrangle. The first floor of the sanatorium was, as usual, in darkness, but a dim light was shining through the sewing room blind.

He sped across the room to the sleeping Darbishire, and shook him.

"Darbi, wake up ... wake up!"

"Uh?" grunted the sleeping Darbishire.

"Wake up, man—it's urgent."

"Wasmarrer?" came from below the sheet.

"It's me—Jennings. Are you awake?"

"I'm not sure: I think I am."

"Well, listen," Jennings hissed in an unsteady whisper. "I've seen the light."

Darbishire raised his head and blinked at the shadowy figure before him.

"You've done what?"

"I've seen the light."

"Oh, well done," said Darbishire sleepily. "I'm so glad. My father knew a man in his parish who saw the light. He became quite a reformed character in the end, but up to that time he'd been a notorious evil-doer." He closed his eyes, and settled himself down comfortably on the pillow.

"Wake up, and don't natter," whispered Jennings. "Listen—it's the tramp."

"Oh, I don't think he was a tramp," murmured Darbishire, still vague with sleep. "My father said he was a brand plucked from the burning."

"Who was?"

"The notorious evil-doer who saw the light."

Jennings shook him again. "Pull yourself together, Darbishire. "There's someone in the san."

"How do you know?" Yawned the bundle beneath the bedclothes.

"I've just told you. I've just—well, there's a light burning. Come on, we're going over there. Don't you understand?"

Suddenly Darbishire was wide awake and wishing that he wasn't. He understood only too well; the moment that had been such fun to talk about had become a reality. If only he could cope with these situations like the children in the library book that he was reading. They were known as the *Fearless Four*, and they excelled in this sort of adventure. They rode ponies with the skill of Middle-West cowboys; they handled sailing dinghies in rough seas like experienced yachtsmen; much of their time was spent in searching for buried treasure, which they never failed to discover every time they went for a country holiday. Dealing with tramps in empty cottages would have been meat and drink to the *Fearless Four*, but Darbishire knew that he was not cut out for such desperate action. He brought his mind back to Jennings' hair-raising invitation and swallowed hard.

"When you say *we* are going over there," he inquired anxiously, "do you mean—er—*me*, too?"

"You said you would," Jennings reminded him.

"I know I did," Darbishire admitted. "And it did seem rather a good wheeze in the day-time, but I don't think I'll bother now, if you don't mind. You see, my father says that discretion is the better part of valour, and I don't want you to think I'm trying to back out of it, but—"

"Oh, don't be a funk! All the chaps said you'd be frightened," Jennings urged, "so here's your chance to prove them wrong."

"Oh, gosh!" said Darbishire unhappily. There was no sound in the dormitory, except the rhythmic breathing of the other occupants. How he envied them! "I can't prove them wrong," he said in a cracked, unnatural voice, "because I shall still be frightened, even if I do go."

"You'll be all right," his friend assured him. "It's quite safe, really. We'll just have a quick squint to make sure it really *is* tramps, and then we'll beetle back and tell Mr. Carter."

Darbishire pushed back the bedclothes and put one foot on the linoleum. "Well, no dacka-dacka stuff and pretending to take prisoners, like those gang games we used to play."

"Of course not: this isn't a game—this is the real thing."

"I know, that's the trouble," Darbishire complained as he got out of bed and fumbled for his dressing gown. "As it isn't a game, you can't say *pax* when you've had enough."

Jennings was unable to prevent his hands from trembling as he groped beneath his bed for his shoes. He could not find his bedroom slippers, but fortunately his newly-cleaned gym shoes were under his chair, ready for the next afternoon. Quickly he slipped the first shoe on, and a strangled shriek rang out as he pressed his foot on to a drawing pin. Then he remembered; he had converted them into spiked running-shoes, and one of the spikes must have worked its way back inside. What a good thing he'd discovered it in time; supposing they had all worked through during the "440!" He removed the drawing pins and left them on the floor, where Atkinson's bare feet discovered them the following morning.

Darbishire was looking anxious when Jennings rejoined him.

"Oughtn't we to have a weapon, or something?" he inquired. "We might be attacked."

Jennings assured him that this was most unlikely, for the purpose of their expedition was merely to spy out the lie of the land. Brave though he was, Jennings had no intention of tackling an unknown number of desperadoes. However, they decided that the feel of a weapon in their hands would be comforting, so they tiptoed out of the dormitory and made for the housemaid's cupboard on the landing. Jennings selected a long-handled mop and Darbishire, after some thought, armed himself with the suction-hose of a vacuum cleaner.

Stealthily, they crept along the landing and past Mr. Carter's room. A light shone from under the door and volcanic rumblings of conversation from within told them that Mr. Wilkins was paying the housemaster a visit. This was a good thing, for Mr. Wilkins' voice made a sufficient barrage of sound for the two boys to reach the head of the staircase without being heard. Cautiously they descended, crossed the main hall and slipped back the bolt of a side door which opened on to the quadrangle.

It was cold outside, but it was not only the temperature that caused Darbishire's teeth to chatter like a clicking turnstile; and after they had gone a few yards he halted uncertainly.

"Can't we go back?" he suggested.

"Gosh, no, don't be such a funk. It'll be all right," his chief assured him.

"Oh, please don't think I'm frightened: at least, not much. It's just that—er—I've got a sore place on my heel, and Matron said not to walk on it too much, if I want to be fit for the half-mile tomorrow."

"But if we go back now, we'll miss all the excitement," Jennings urged. He was not going to admit defeat now they had come so far; but Darbishire was feeling anything but eager, and said: "Well, we could still talk about it, and after all, these sort of things are miles wizarder fun to talk about than they are to do."

Jennings faced his assistant squarely. "We can't possibly go back now," he insisted. "Can't you just imagine the hoo-hah that Temple and Atkinson and everyone would kick up, if they found out that we'd seen the light, and then bished it all up because we didn't dare to follow it up? Gosh, our names would be mud with a capital M."

They walked on across the quadrangle. It was deathly quiet, save for the eerie hooting of an owl which brought Darbishire's heart into his mouth the first time he heard it. "They've seen us—they're signalling with owl noises," he gasped.

"Rats," said Jennings, "that's a proper owl. Come on, we're nearly there."

The light was clearly visible in the sewing room window, and every step they took, the more jumpy Darbishire became. He tried to think of some comforting advice from the wise sayings of his father, but the only words which he could call to mind were about the folly of rushing headlong into danger. Jennings walked in silence, but Darbishire's nervousness took the form of a continuous stream of prattle about improbable and impossible perils which might, or might not, lie ahead.

"I feel like that chap in a poem my father made me learn," he said. "It's all about a chap *who on a lonesome road doth walk in fear and dread ...*"

Jennings was not listening. "I think I can see his shadow moving on the blind," he whispered excitedly.

"*And having once looked back, walks on and turns no more his head,*" Darbishire quoted.

"Ssh! We mustn't let him see us. We'll have to creep like mice."

"*Because he knows a frightful fiend doth close behind him tread,*" he finished with a gulp.

Jennings' eyes were staring ahead, and his mind was but dimly aware that his friend was talking.

"What did you say, Darbi?"

"I said," Darbishire replied, "that a frightful fiend doth close behind him tread."

"Treads close behind who?"

"Anyone on a lonesome road who doth walk."

Jennings glanced back the way they had come. What was that strange white figure lurking on the rugger pitch? He breathed again, as he recognised it as a goal post.

"I can't see anyone treading behind us," he said uneasily.

"Of course you can't—there's no one there."

"You said there was."

"No, I didn't. I said the chap in the poem thought there was, so having once looked back, he walked on and turned no more his head."

Jennings was tempted to knock his assistant over the head with his mop.

"You ancient, prehistoric remains, Darbi!" he jerked out in a hoarse, voiceless whisper. "Here we are, bang up to the eyebrows in the most supersonic hoo-hah we've ever struck, and you have to start reciting poetry."

"Sorry, Jen," Darbishire whispered humbly.

They crept on, and a moment later they reached the small garden. Jennings had no clear idea of what he was going to do next. Had he been able to see his quarry through the window, he would have considered that to be sufficient evidence, and returned to school for help. Unfortunately the blind was down and he could see no one, and with some misgiving he decided that they would have to go in.

They made a circuit of the garden, and when they reached the back of the building, Jennings gripped his companion's arm.

"The back door's open. That means I shan't have to use my skeleton key, after all."

"I didn't know you'd got one."

"Well, it's my tuck-box key really," Jennings explained, "but it fits the stationery cupboard and the music room, so it would probably open anything in an emergency. Ssh! Come on."

"Just a minute."

"What is it now?"

"Well, we've neither of us got our special secret Linbury Detective Agency badges on. Don't you think we ought to go back for them?"

"No, I don't! And anyway, we're not going to get close enough for anyone to read them, if I can help it."

Holding their weapons poised, they tiptoed through the back door into the kitchen, where they stood for a moment, straining their ears to catch the tell-tale sound of an intruder. They could hear nothing except their own heavy breathing, though they were both conscious of the loud pounding of their hearts.

With mop upraised, Jennings took a step forward, and suddenly froze in his tracks. Thin rays of moonlight shining through the uncurtained window revealed an unnerving glimpse of a shadowy figure not two feet away. The figure held a stick and stood ready to strike.

"Oooh!" Jennings gasped, and sprang sideways to dodge the threatened blow. But the blow did not fall; and when he glanced quickly in the direction of his assailant, he understood the reason. He had been standing in front of a large mirror screwed to the kitchen wall, and the shadowy figure with upraised stick had been J. C. T. Jennings with his mop at the ready. He breathed again and looked round. Darbishire had disappeared.

"Darbi!" he whispered softly. "Where are you?"

A breathless squeak from beneath the kitchen table told that his assistant had taken cover at the first sound of his chief's startled gasp. Somewhat shaken, he emerged, and together they tiptoed to the door leading into the hall. All was quiet. Jennings said "Ssh!" and cautiously turned the knob and opened the door a few inches.

The hall was dark, but the light was still shining from beneath the sewing room door and, as they listened, they could hear faint sounds coming from within. They advanced a few paces, and then came to an uncertain halt.

"Ssh! There's someone there," Jennings whispered. "He's moving about. Ssh!"

"D-don't keep saying 'Ssh!'" Darbishire whispered back. "It m-makes more r-row than not sh-shushing at all."

"Sounds as though he's moving the furniture," Jennings observed in an undertone, as a low scraping noise became audible.

"Come on, let's g-go then. We've got to tell Mr. Carter."

"Okay. I wish you'd stop your teeth chattering. You sound like a tap dancer."

"I've got the w-wind up," Darbishire admitted. "My heart's beating like a s-sledge-hammer."

Jennings decided to retreat. They had not actually seen their man, but they knew beyond all doubt that he was there.

"Right then, we'll slip out the way we came in, and dash straight back and tell Mr. Carter."

He turned to lead the way back to the kitchen, and in the darkness he bumped into Darbishire who was standing close behind him. Darbishire dropped the vacuum cleaner suction-hose in his agitation and Jennings, slightly off his balance, tripped over it and crashed to the floor.

He lay where he fell, not daring to breathe, and it was as much as Darbishire could do to stop himself from shouting for help; for immediately the scraping noise in the sewing room ceased, and a second later the light clicked off. Then the door swung open, and footsteps were coming towards them along the darkened hall.

CHAPTER 11

MR. WILKINS ANSWERS THE PHONE

"Quick!" yelled Jennings, as all need for caution was now over. "Get back into the kitchen!"

But as he scrambled to his feet, he was blinded by a powerful beam of torch-light shining in his eyes, and before they could find the kitchen door, their unknown adversary had rushed up and seized Darbishire by the arm.

Jennings saw the torch waving wildly, as the man sought to hold Darbishire, and he brought his long-handled mop down with a crashing blow on what he hoped was the tramp's head: but the dazzling light in his eyes spoiled all chance of a straight aim, and his mop cut through empty air. The next moment the torch went out, and he felt a strong hand grabbing at his arm.

"Let me go," Jennings shouted; "take your hands off me!"

"You keep quiet," came a low, gruff voice, from just above his head. "We don't want no more of that shouting."

Darbishire emitted a voiceless "H-h-help!" which died at once, as their assailant clapped a hand over his mouth. Struggling and squirming, the two boys were dragged across the hall to the door which stood opposite the kitchen. It opened, under pressure of a kick from their captor's foot, and they were roughly bundled inside.

The gruff voice spoke again. "You get in 'ere, both of you, and stop that row. If you make a sound you'll cop it."

He shut the door and turned the key, and the boys could hear his footsteps crossing the hall, and retreating through the kitchen, and out of the back door.

Jennings was the first to find his voice. "Are you all right, Darbi?" he gasped.

"I ... I ... think so," came out of the empty blackness in the middle of the room. "But, oh, golly!"

Darbishire felt once again that he was not keeping up the standard of cool daring which the children in his library book would have expected of him. The *Fearless Four* often met sinister assailants in darkened passages, and had no difficulty in getting the better of them, and tying them up with lengths of strong twine, which, by chance they always had in their pockets.

But not Charles Edwin Jeremy Darbishire! He knew that he would never be capable of such feats, even if his pockets were bulging with strong twine. He stood breathing heavily in the middle of the room, while he fumbled to replace his spectacles. They had suffered during the encounter, and now hung from one ear with the lenses dangling below his chin.

Jennings leapt at once into action. He found the light switch by the door, and they stood blinking, as the room was flooded with light.

"Where are we?" asked Darbishire, peering round short-sightedly.

"We're in the room that the night nurse uses when there's somebody ill," Jennings explained, and his eyes shone with excitement. "And look, Darbi, I've got a valuable clue."

"What?"

Jennings opened his clenched fist and revealed a small, brown sleeve button. "I got hold of his arm and it came off," he exclaimed in triumph.

"You mean he'd got a false arm?"

"No, you goof. The button came off. Gosh, I bet the police will say it's a wizard clue. Come on, we've got to get out, quick."

"Oh, gosh! Have we got to chase him, and start that struggling business all over again?" asked Darbishire, appalled.

"We don't want him to make a getaway, do we?"

"I do. The farther the getaway the better. I'll shout for help if you like, though."

"Fat lot of good that would be. No one would ever hear you."

Jennings tried the door, and then rushed to the window; but it was blocked by a large mirror, forming part of a heavy dressing table. By the time they had moved it, their enemy would be far away. Quickly, he glanced round the room, seeking other methods of escape. Then suddenly, he shouted: "Look, Darbi, look over there!"

Darbishire looked round vaguely. "I can't see very well," he mumbled. "My teeth are still chattering."

"You don't see with your teeth, do you?"

"No, but I'm still suffering from tremble-itis, and I can't put my glasses on properly."

In two bounds Jennings crossed the room, and stopped before a small table in a far corner. On the table was a telephone.

"Super-duper-sonic," he cried. "We're saved, Darbi! We can phone the police and get them to send a flying squad. It'll be miles quicker than getting through the window, and going all the way back for Mr. Carter."

He grabbed the receiver and put it to his ear. "Oh, golly, I don't know what the number is."

"That doesn't matter," said Darbishire. "You just ask for Ambulance or Police. And when you get the police, it might be a good wheeze to ask for an ambulance as well, just in case we meet that chap again."

"The exchange are a jolly long time answering," Jennings complained. "Either that, or the line's dead. There's no buzzing, or clicking, or burring, or anything going on. Of course, if that chap was a burglar and not just a tramp, he might have cut the telephone wires, mightn't he?"

"Give them a bit longer," Darbishire urged. "After all, they're probably in bed, and they've got to get up and find their dressing gowns and slippers and things."

"But dash it all, this is urgent. All the time they're crawling about looking for their slippers, our burglar is getting farther and farther away."

He jogged the receiver-rest up and down and fidgeted with impatience. Opening his clenched fist he looked again at the intruder's sleeve button. He must be careful; there might be fingerprints on it, he decided. In point of fact there were, but the prints were those of J. C. T. Jennings.

He slipped the button into his dressing gown pocket, intending to hand this valuable clue to the police. What on earth was the matter with the telephone exchange? Surely they were not still looking for their slippers?

Then he noticed a small brown box with a handle, standing next to the telephone. It was a generator, and as the sanatorium was only an extension of the main telephone line, it was necessary to turn the handle before the instrument could be used.

It was Darbishire who discovered this first. "Look," he said, "I think I know what's wrong. My father once explained how the telephone works. Try putting the receiver back, and turning this handle thing first."

Jennings did so.

"That's right," said Darbishire. "You'll be through in no time now."

In one respect Darbishire was right. The wire hummed, and a few moments later a voice answered. But the line was not switched through to the exchange as the boys supposed: it was, instead, connected with the telephone in Mr. Carter's study.

Mr. Wilkins broke off in the middle of a sentence, when the telephone rang.

"That's odd!" he exclaimed. "Who on earth is ringing us up at this time of the night? Hope it's not General Merridew to say he can't come."

Mr. Carter looked up from the sports list he was checking. "It can't be," he replied. "That's not the exchange—it's one of the extension lines. Probably the Head to tell me—" He broke off, and narrowed his brows in a puzzled frown. "No, it can't be the Head either. This call is coming from the sanatorium."

Mr. Carter was usually at home in the evenings, and for this reason the small switchboard was situated in his room. He could switch incoming calls through to the Headmaster's study, or the sanatorium, and anyone wishing to speak from either of these places had to contact Mr. Carter before they could be put through to the exchange.

"The sanatorium!" echoed Mr. Wilkins in surprise. "But there's nobody there, except Old Nightie, propping himself up with a broom-handle. He's not likely to—"

"Wouldn't it be better to answer the phone and find out," his colleague broke in, as the bell sounded again. "Much more satisfactory than playing guessing games."

Mr. Wilkins snatched the receiver from its rest. "Hallo," he said.

A high-pitched, excited voice at the other end of the line said: "Is that the exchange? I want the police station, please—it's urgent. There's been a burglary at Linbury Court School with assault and battery, and another boy and I have been locked in, and we want the police to send a flying squad."

"Hold on a moment," said Mr. Wilkins, taking the receiver from his ear; he clapped his hand over the mouthpiece and his face turned a deep purple, as he struggled to stifle the laughter that was shaking his powerful frame like a pneumatic drill.

Mr. Carter raised his eyebrows. "What's the joke?"

For a moment Mr. Wilkins was unable to speak, and then with an effort he controlled himself, and sank his loud voice to a whisper. "It's Jennings," he croaked, voicelessly. "They've gone over to the san. and Old Nightie has collared them and locked them in. That ought to cool their hot heads for them!"

his shoulders heaved and his hands shook. When Mr. Wilkins thought that something was funny, the matter could never be kept quiet.

Mr. Carter threw down his pencil in annoyance. "Silly little idiots," he muttered. "I wish to goodness I'd had them up here and dispelled all this burglary nonsense at the start."

It was, he felt, largely his fault; but he had been so certain that the sanatorium expedition would never come to anything, that he had decided to let the excitement die a natural death. Nine times out of ten this would have been the right course to adopt—but this was the tenth time, and he had not reckoned with Jennings' single-tracked keenness for the job on hand.

"It's all right," Mr. Wilkins whispered. "Nothing to worry about. It'll do them far more good than a lecture from you. If Old Nightie has given them a bit of a scare, they won't be so eager to try these capers any more. He'll probably be up in a moment to tell us he's bagged a couple of very worried detectives."

A shrill voice could be heard buzzing indistinctly from the other end of the line. Mr. Wilkins removed his hand from the mouthpiece and listened. Then in an assumed voice he said: "One moment, please. I'm trying to connect you."

Mr. Carter stared at him in astonishment. He was preparing to start for the sanatorium at once, but Mr. Wilkins signalled to him to stop. Covering the mouthpiece once more, he said: "Wait till Old Nightie comes across; he won't be long."

"Why bother to wait? Those boys ought to be—"

"Yes, I know," Mr. Wilkins broke in. "But let's finish the joke first."

His face turned a deeper shade of purple as he savoured the humour of the situation to the full. "It's no good, Carter," he went on. "I can't resist the temptation. I've always wanted to be a policeman." And to Mr. Carter's shocked surprise, he spoke into the instrument in a heavily disguised voice. "Hallo," he said. "Police Station here. Sergeant Snodgrass speaking."

"Oh, thank goodness," came the voice from the other end of the wire. "You've been ages. I'm so afraid it'll be too late."

The voice launched into an involved stream of explanation, while the bogus Sergeant Snodgrass sat and rocked in silent mirth, and Mr. Carter wondered why fate had given him a colleague who enjoyed such a puerile sense of humour.

"'Ere, 'ere, 'ere, not so fast," rumbled the self-appointed sergeant. "So you've had a burglar, eh! Well, fancy that now. You're sure he was a burglar, I suppose, and not just a chap who'd come in out of the rain?"

"Of course I'm sure," replied Jennings. "Besides, it's not raining."

"Well, well, so it isn't; I never noticed. Smart of you to spot that. You'd make a good detective you would," said the sergeant admiringly, and Jennings was too agitated to detect anything unusual in Sergeant Snodgrass's methods of coping with urgent cases of housebreaking. Neither did he pause to wonder why a Sussex policeman should have a strong Lancashire accent.

"Oh, do hurry up," he said. "We're locked in the sanatorium, and we can't do anything until you send a flying squad."

"Locked you in, eh! Tut, tut, tut, that's bad! The larks these burglars get up to. Well, I never did!" Mr. Wilkins was enjoying himself. He was very pleased with his impersonation, and was unmindful of the fact that the East Sussex Constabulary would have been horrified had they known that such a travesty was being carried out in their name. "Yes, but if I come round to a sanatorium," the flat Lancashire accent dragged on, "I'd be more likely to catch measles than burglars."

Mr. Carter raised despairing eyes to the ceiling, and wondered how much longer his colleague intended to indulge in Third Form humour. He fidgeted impatiently as the conversation went on.

"Then what was he doing in a sanatorium if he wasn't ill?" Mr. Wilkins inquired heavily, and after a babble of explanation from the other end, he said: "Ah, maybe he wasn't when he first went in, but he's bound to have caught something by this time."

Jennings could hardly believe his ears. That a member of the police force, and a sergeant at that, should talk in such a ridiculous manner was more than he could understand. "Look here," he said, "are you going to send a flying squad, or aren't you? Because I've jolly well had enough of these questions."

Mr. Carter tapped his colleague on the shoulder as a sign that this nonsense had gone quite far enough, and Mr. Wilkins rang off, after promising to investigate the matter the next time he happened to be passing. Then he sat back in his chair and roared with laughter.

"They'll feel so silly when they find out it was Old Nightie who locked them in," he gasped.

"Come on," said Mr. Carter. "Hawkins doesn't seem to be coming over, so we'd better go and let them out."

Together they went down the stairs, and as they reached the hall they heard the sound of footsteps coming up the lower flight of steps from the basement.

Old Nightie, with mop and bucket, came into view and wished them "Good evening."

"Good evening, Hawkins," Mr. Carter replied. "I gather you've got two boys safely in your care."

Old Nightie looked surprised. "No, sir," he said. "I haven't got no boys, nowhere."

"In the sanatorium, I mean," Mr. Carter explained. "The two boys who came over while you were cleaning up."

The expression on the night watchman's face grew more mystified. "No, sir," he said. "I've not been over to the sanatorium yet; I'm just going now."

"What!" shouted Mr. Wilkins. "You—you—you mean you've not locked any boys in?"

"No, sir. I got held up, cleaning out the clinker down in the boiler-room. First time for years I've been late in sweeping out the san. Ten forty-five as regular as clockwork, bar tonight."

"But if you haven't been over there—" Mr. Wilkins began, and broke off, unable to make sense of it all.

"It's all right, Mr. Wilkins, I'm going now," Hawkins replied. "I've got me key and I'll get finished there by half-past twelve, if I get a move on." He was rather upset that, for once, his record for punctuality had been spoiled. "If it hadn't been for cleaning out the clinker in the boiler—"

"I don't understand this," Mr. Carter broke in, and turning to his colleague he asked: "Wilkins, didn't Jennings tell you he'd been locked in?"

"Yes, he said they'd met a burglar. I took it for granted it was Old Ni— I beg your pardon, Hawkins, I mean I thought it was you."

"Couldn't very well have been me, could it?" Hawkins answered, "seeing as I was down the stokehold cleaning out the clinker in the boiler. First time I've been late these—"

Mr. Carter spoke sternly. "Come along, we're going over there, at once. I don't like the sound of this, at all."

He led the way at a brisk pace and Mr. Wilkins sprinted behind him. Old Nightie, still muttering about cleaning clinker out of boilers, hobbled after them, as fast as his flat feet would permit.

CHAPTER 12

THE EMPTY MANTELPIECE

As THEY ran, Mr. Carter delivered himself of a few curt remarks. "Really, Wilkins, I think you might have found out what had been going on over there, instead of playing the goat on the telephone like that. Sergeant Snodgrass indeed—what nonsense you talk!"

"Sorry, old man," panted the ex-sergeant, "but if you'd put your foot down a week earlier, this would never have happened."

"I know all about that," Mr. Carter answered. He was distinctly worried, and blamed his own error of judgment for the unexpected turn that events had taken. "Can't you run any faster?" he asked irritably.

"I … I … Corwumph! Give me a chance, old man," said Mr. Wilkins. "I may be ten years younger than you, but I'm thirty-eight round the middle, don't forget."

Soon they reached the small garden that surrounded the cottage. There they paused, and Mr. Wilkins remarked that if there really was a burglar, he might still be lurking about in the bushes, and the best thing to do would be to have a good look round before going in.

"The boys' safety is the important thing," Mr. Carter reminded him.

"They'll be all right for a minute. They're shut up in the nurse's bedroom, so they won't come to much harm."

The next moment, he seized the housemaster's arm and dragged him into the cover of the hedge. "Ssh! I thought I saw someone," he whispered.

For some seconds the two men stood motionless; then Mr. Wilkins stiffened. Footsteps were approaching round the corner from the back of the building, and a moment later a shadowy figure appeared on the path in front of them. The figure paused uncertainly. Judging his distance, Mr. Wilkins hurled himself forward in a brilliant rugger tackle, which took his opponent just above the knees and felled him to the soft earth of the flower bed. A moment later as he was trying to pinion the flailing arms, a shaft of moonlight lit up the frightened features of his adversary. Mr. Wilkins' jaw dropped slightly.

"Oh, good heavens," he gasped. "I'm terribly sorry, Hawkins. I didn't know it was you."

He helped the night watchman to his feet, as Mr. Carter joined him.

"Well, really, Wilkins," he exclaimed, "what on earth are you playing at now?"

"It was just a mistake. I heard footsteps, so I jumped. I'd no idea Hawkins had followed us over. Sorry, Hawkins—I didn't hurt you, did I?"

Old Nightie gave Mr. Wilkins one of his queer looks. He was not hurt, but night watchmen as a class, are never very pleased at being brought down by low rugger tackles, when on duty.

"I came over as fast as I could. I couldn't see no sign of anybody, so I went round the other way, to see where you'd got to. Of course, if I'd known people was going to start jumping out of bushes—" He left the sentence unfinished, but Mr. Wilkins had the feeling that his name was now bracketed with the clinker in the boiler, as being the chief cause of Old Nightie's troubles.

Mr. Carter decided to waste no more time. If a burglar had been lurking about before, he certainly would not be there after all the noise of the last few minutes.

The night watchman's key was not needed, for the back door was still open and the three men hurried through.

Mr. Wilkins dashed into the hall and switched on the light. "That's where they are!" he cried, pointing to the night nurse's room.

Jennings and Darbishire recognised the voice.

"Gosh, it's Old Wilkie!" Jennings exclaimed in surprise. "He's got here before the police. Wonder how he knew we were over here." Raising his voice, he shouted: "We're in here, sir, and the door's locked."

"I'm coming," called Mr. Wilkins. "Stand back, Hawkins, I'm going to break the door down." He took a deep breath and prepared to hurl the whole of his thirteen stone six in a thunderous shoulder-charge on the door panels.

Mr. Carter stopped him.

"The fact that Jennings can't open the door from within," he said quietly, "is no reason why we should smash the place up." And he pointed to the key, which the intruder had left in the lock.

"Sorry, old man," apologised Mr. Wilkins. "I didn't bother to look."

He unlocked the door and the two masters hurried in, leaving Hawkins to make a tour of the building and estimate the extent of the burglary.

"Oh, sir, I'm ever so glad you've come, sir," a rather chastened Jennings confided to his housemaster. "There's been a burglary, sir."

"Yes, I know—he's got away, I'm afraid. Are both you boys all right?"

"We're all right, sir, honestly," Jennings answered, and Darbishire added: "I'm feeling just a bit shaken up, sir, but I'm very well, thank you, considering."

"Thank goodness," Mr. Carter sighed with relief. "I was very worried about you."

Jennings was touched; he had no idea that masters possessed such human feelings about the boys in their care. On the other hand, of course, awkward questions and unpleasant punishments were certain to be the next item on the evening's programme, when once the excitement of liberation was over, so perhaps it would be as well not to stress their fitness too strongly.

"When I say we're all right, sir," he amended, "I mean I shouldn't be surprised if we weren't both suffering from shock. So don't you think it might be a good idea if we were to take things quietly in class for the next few days, sir?"

"It'd be a change, anyway," said Mr. Wilkins. "It's not often you're quiet in my class."

"I didn't exactly mean that, sir. I meant it might be a good plan not to overdo things by working too hard and straining ourselves."

"That," said Mr. Carter, "would *not* be a change. Come along, if you're all right. You'd better be getting back to bed. It's too late now to discuss why you stupid little boys came over here—that'll keep until the morning."

"Oh, but sir, I know we're out of bounds, sir, but it was a good job we were, wasn't it? Otherwise, sir, you wouldn't have known about the burglar, would you?"

"Never mind about the burglar," said Mr. Carter sharply. "That's for me to worry about."

It was odd, he reflected, that for so many years Hawkins had arrived to clean the sanatorium punctually at ten forty-five, and in all that time nothing out of the ordinary had ever disturbed the routine of his work. "Isn't it just like Jennings," he murmured to Mr. Wilkins. "The one and only time we have a burglar, and the one and only time Hawkins is late—and Jennings has to choose this night, of all nights, to come gallivanting over here."

As they were making for the door, Old Nightie appeared and reported that the cottage showed no sign of having been burgled.

Mr. Carter stopped, and looked at Jennings inquiringly.

"Oh, yes, sir, there was a burglar here, all right," the boy insisted. "Wasn't there, Darbishire?"

"I think so," Darbishire replied. "Of course, it was dark and I've never actually met a burglar before, except the man my father knew who saw the light, and he was only a brand plucked from the burning—so he probably wouldn't count, would he, sir?"

"You come and see for yourself, sir," Old Nightie said. "The whole place is in apple-pie order. There's no sign of anyone breaking in—bar the back door being open." He cast one of his queer looks in the boys' direction and added meaningly: "And these two boys could have done that when they come in."

"I believe you're right, Hawkins," Mr. Wilkins exclaimed, and turning to Jennings, he boomed: "Now, look here, if this is all some practical joke, you're going to find yourselves in very serious trouble."

"Oh, but, sir, honestly," protested Jennings, almost tearful that his story was not being believed. "We did meet a burglar, really. Look, sir, I've got a clue," and he produced the sleeve button for their inspection.

Mr. Wilkins refused to accept this as evidence. He pointed out that lots of people lose sleeve buttons, and in any case they were next door to the sewing room where buttons were as plentiful as pebbles on the beach.

"There's one point you're overlooking," Mr. Carter broke in. "Did Jennings and Darbishire lock themselves in and leave the key on the outside?" He crossed to the window and ran his finger along the dusty ledge. "And they didn't come in this way, judging by the dust."

Old Nightie looked away uncomfortably—he did not like people examining his handiwork too closely.

Jennings slipped the button into the pocket of his pyjama jacket as Mr. Carter turned towards him with a reassuring smile. "It's all right, Jennings. I don't want you to imagine for one moment that I'm doubting your word. I make it a rule never to do that." His smile broadened: "I just wanted to show you that I've learnt a thing or two from Sherlock Holmes, as well."

They left Hawkins settling down to his labours, and set off across the quadrangle. Mr. Carter was anxious to get Jennings and Darbishire back to bed as soon as possible. He would have to report the matter to the Headmaster, of course, and then the police would have to be told; though it was doubtful whether they could track a criminal who had stolen nothing, and had left so little evidence of his visit. In fact, had it not been for Jennings' interference, they might never have known that a burglar had been on the premises at all. Mr. Carter wondered how the Headmaster would deal with the matter; breaking bounds was a serious business, even though it was done with the best of intentions.

They crossed the quadrangle in silence, and entered the hall of the main building. Then Mr. Carter said: "Go to bed, you two. I'm going upstairs to phone the police."

"Oh, but sir, I've done that already!" Jennings exclaimed. "They've promised to send a flying squad. I can't think why they're not here already."

For a moment, a smile flickered across Mr. Carter's worried features. "I can," he said; "can't you, Mr. Wilkins?"

Mr. Wilkins studied his fingernails with great interest, and said nothing.

"The sergeant said he'd see to it, but he sounded a very stupid sort of man, sir. He seemed to think it was funny."

Mr. Wilkins' interest in his fingernails became deeper, as Jennings went on: "Binns minor would have made a better policeman than the man I talked to, sir. He'd got no sense at all."

"Fancy!" said Mr. Carter. "What do you make of that, Mr. Wilkins?"

"All right, all right. I ... I ... I ... Corwumph!" Mr. Wilkins said hurriedly. "It's time these silly little boys were in bed."

Jennings and Darbishire went upstairs, and the two masters made for the Headmaster's private quarters at the other end of the building.

"I hope he deals with them pretty drastically," Mr. Wilkins remarked. "All that fuss and nonsense, and chasing about for nothing."

"Well, they *did* find a burglar," Mr. Carter reminded him. "I admit it was a thousand to one chance, but—"

"Burglar!" Mr. Wilkins snorted. "I don't believe there was a burglar at all. It was just Jennings' vivid imagination getting the better of him. Dash it all, if anyone had really broken in, he would have stolen something, and it's quite obvious that nothing's been touched."

As they passed the library, they felt a strong draught blowing through the open door. "Old Nightie has forgotten to close the windows," Mr. Carter remarked. "He must be having rather a tiresome night, what with cleaning out clinker and warding off rugger tackles."

He walked into the library and switched on the light. Fluttering curtains told of a wide-open window, but it was not this that halted Mr. Carter in his tracks. Instead, he stood staring at the mantelpiece which should have held a row of gleaming silver cups.

But the mantelpiece was empty.

M. W. B. Pemberton-Oakes, Esq., Headmaster, was not pleased when a loud banging on his bedroom door woke him from sleep. There was only one member of his staff who could make so much noise, and he had no difficulty in deducing that Mr. Wilkins wished to speak to him.

It was shortly after midnight, and the Headmaster was tight-lipped with exasperation, as he rose from his bed and prepared to deal with his volcanic assistant. If Wilkins had disturbed him because of some trifling matter that could well have waited until the morning, Mr. Pemberton-Oakes was prepared to be very terse indeed. He remembered an occasion, not long since, when his assistant had arrived, late at night, to report that the scullery had been struck by lightning; and investigation had shown that the trouble had been caused by the housekeeper's cat knocking down a nest of saucepans.

"Well, Wilkins, what is it?" the dressing gowned figure of the Headmaster inquired coldly.

"There's been a burglary, sir. The cups have been stolen from the library."

"What? ... And the Merridew Sports Cup as well?"

"Yes, that's gone, too. The thief got in through the window. I think you'd better come along, sir."

The Headmaster hastened down to investigate, and found Mr. Carter in charge. He had telephoned for the police, and soon the wheels of a police car scrunched on the gravel, and came to rest outside the front door.

Sergeant Hutchinson, of the East Sussex Constabulary, had little in common with the mythical Sergeant Snodgrass. He was alert and business-like, as he listened to Mr. Carter's summary of the events of the evening. Occasionally he asked a question, and Mr. Wilkins grew hot and cold with embarrassment at the thought of having to explain his impersonation of Sergeant Snodgrass to this cool and efficient representative of the police; he was repentant, now that the incident had ceased to be funny, and he hoped that Sergeant Hutchinson would not show too much interest in the actual words of the telephone conversation.

Hawkins was sent for and confirmed that, apart from the silver cups in the library, nothing else had been taken, and there was no sign of disorder.

The Headmaster rose from his chair at the library table and paced the long length of the room. "What I am at a loss to understand," he said, "is why this midnight intruder, having stolen the athletic trophies, should go to the sanatorium at all." He gazed pensively at the chandelier, as though expecting its bright beams to shed light upon the mystery.

"I think it happened the other way round," Mr. Carter suggested. "He found nothing worth taking at the cottage, so he came over here and found his luck was in."

Sergeant Hutchinson looked up from his notebook and said: "With your permission, I should like to have a word with the two boys you spoke about."

"I think it would be better if you were to interrogate them in the morning," the Headmaster replied, as he returned to his chair. "Don't you think so, Carter?"

"I certainly do," the housemaster agreed.

"Jennings and Darbishire have had more than enough excitement for one night."

It was nearly two o'clock in the morning when Mr. Carter made his final inspection of the dormitories. Sergeant Hutchinson had completed his first examination of the premises and had driven away, promising to return as soon as it was light. The Headmaster had gone back to bed, distressed beyond measure at the thought of General Merridew arriving to present a trophy that was no longer there to present.

Mr. Wilkins, also, had retired to his room; and Matron, on the floor below, had her slumbers disturbed as thuds from above announced that the former Sergeant Snodgrass was taking his shoes off, and preparing for bed. Old Nightie had gone to earth in the depths of the boiler-room, where he sat sipping a cup of cocoa, and casting reproachful glances at the heap of clinker that had contributed so much to the evening's disaster.

All was quiet in the dormitories, as Mr. Carter padded noiselessly along the rows of beds. In Dormitory 4, he stopped first before the curled-up bundle that was Darbishire, snuggling beneath the bedclothes. The only things visible were a strand of light curly hair straying across the pillow, and the tip of a nose which twitched like a rabbit's, whenever it felt the tickle of the fleecy blanket.

Mr. Carter crossed to Jennings' bed, missing the upturned drawing pins by inches. Jennings was asleep too, but as Mr. Carter watched, the boy's eyes opened for a moment, and he smiled as he recognised the housemaster at his bedside. "Oh, sir, wasn't it smashing!" he said, and promptly fell asleep again.

CHAPTER 13

ALIBI FOR OLD NIGHTIE

THIN STREAKS of sunshine smiled feebly through the gaps in the billowing March clouds. They filtered gingerly through the struts of the toothbrush rack, and danced like timid ballerinas on Venables' sleeping eyelids. He awoke, and lay still for a moment, collecting his thoughts. Then he yelled "Yippee!" with a blood-curdling howl that roused the sleepers of Dormitory 4 far more effectively than the rising bell, which sounded at the same moment.

"Sports today!" sang out Venables joyfully. "On your marks ...! Get set ... Wham!"

Sitting up in bed, he mimed the actions of a hundred-yard sprint as well as his restricted position would allow. His arms beat back and forth across his chest like the pistons of a reciprocating pump, as he hurtled along an imaginary race track at Olympic speed. Snorts, grunts and whistles through his clenched teeth showed the severe strain to which he was being subjected. He increased his speed for a final spurt, and the impetus sent his bed rolling gently on its castors across the linoleum.

"Gosh," exclaimed Atkinson, "how wizard! Come on, let's have a jet-propelled bedstead race."

He shook himself backwards and forwards with the energy of a small dynamo, and soon his bed was slithering across the dormitory floor in jerky pursuit. Inch by inch the intrepid drivers urged their vehicles towards the wash basins; and Venables was within a hand's-breadth of victory, when a violent backward swing of his elbow hit the bed-rail behind his hunched shoulders, and he retired from the race considerably shaken. Atkinson vibrated the protesting castors to the finishing post, and leapt to the floor with a triumphant bound.

It was then that he discovered the drawing pins, and the next few minutes were loud with the groans of both competitors.

"I say, you chaps," Jennings announced loudly, when the noise had died away. "Something spivish rare happened last night when you were all snoring.

Darbishire and I went over to the san. and caught a burglar."

Venables, Temple and Atkinson stared at him in amazement.

"You did what?" gasped Temple.

"We caught a burglar. Didn't we, Darbi?"

"Well, actually, the burglar caught us," Darbishire corrected, and shivered slightly at the memory.

"Yes, it was super-duper-sonic. I saw the light again, you see, so I woke Darbi and he nipped out of bed like lightning, and we ankled over to the san, hot-foot on the trail."

Jennings had the full attention of his gaping audience; he pressed on, carefully editing the story, and hurrying over the parts which he thought it wisest not to dwell upon in detail.

"We armed ourselves with vacuum cleaners and things, and crept in and spied on him, just like Sherlock Holmes. Gosh, it was exciting! Then Darbishire tripped me up, and there was a struggle and I caught hold of his sleeve button."

"What on earth did you want to start fighting Darbishire for?" Temple asked incredulously.

"I didn't. It was the burglar who started it."

"You said Darbishire did. You said he tripped you up."

"That was an accident. Anyway, after I got his sleeve button—"

"Whose—Darbishire's?"

"No, not Darbishire's. He was wearing his dressing gown—I meant the burglar's. Besides, his spectacles had come off—"

"Whose—the burglar's?"

"No—Darbishire's. Why don't you listen properly?" urged the exasperated storyteller. "Anyway, we were overpowered in the end, and he locked us in a room and I telephoned for the police."

"And did they come?"

"Well, no, as a matter of fact, they didn't. But Mr. Carter and Old Wilkie came instead."

Jennings was beginning to feel that he was not telling the story very well. The first gasp of astonishment had died away under Temple's cross-examination, and Jennings was aware that his audience was regarding him with suspicion.

"But if this chap locked you in," Temple persisted, "how did you get out to go and telephone?"

"There happened to be a telephone in the room."

Temple smiled meaningly, and looked at the others. "A likely story!" his raised eyebrows seemed to be saying.

"What happened to the burglar?" asked Venables. "Did you catch him?"

"No, he got away."

"What did he steal?" Atkinson demanded.

"Well, actually, he didn't steal anything, because Old Nightie came over and had a look."

Venables, Temple and Atkinson stared, hostile with disbelief, and Jennings pointed to his assistant. "You ask Darbi, then. He was there so he ought to know. And you all said he'd be frightened to go, and he wasn't, were you, Darbi?"

"Well," said Darbishire, "my father says that courage in adversity is a quality, which can only be—"

"Rats!" shouted Temple. "I don't believe a word of it. I bet you've made it all up."

"No, I haven't, I tell you."

"Prove it, then."

"Okay," said Jennings. "I'll show you the button I pulled off his cuff."

He plunged his hand into his dressing gown pocket; then, anxiously, into the other pocket. He fumbled and felt and nearly pulled the pockets off the dressing gown, but it was all to no purpose. The vital clue was missing.

"I know I put it in my dressing gown," he muttered worriedly. "I can remember doing it, when I was waiting for the telephone exchange to wake up. You saw me, didn't you, Darbi?"

"Yes, it was just before I told you to turn that handle thing."

"Oh, gosh! It must have dropped out, somehow."

Temple, Atkinson and Venables hooted with derision.

"I know what it is," Atkinson explained knowingly. "They made such a hoo-hah about the detective agency and seeing the light, that they reckon they've just *got* to pretend something happened, so's we'll be impressed." He turned away and carefully eased his socks on to his injured feet.

"It's just like last time," said Venables, "when they thought they'd got a burglar, and it turned out to be the chap who puts the names on the cups. I bet they didn't really meet anyone at all. I bet they didn't even go over there."

The door opened and Mr. Carter walked in; he could sense the heavy atmosphere of suspicion that lay over the room.

"Good morning, sir," came from five voices.

"Good morning."

"Sir, please sir," Temple announced. "Jennings said we had a burglar last night. He's quite mad, isn't he, sir?" And he smiled pityingly at his room-mate's mental decay.

"And he said the burglar didn't steal anything, sir," Venables added.

"I'm afraid Jennings is wrong," Mr. Carter said, and the three disbelievers smirked at the unfortunate detective with glances of satisfied triumph.

"He did steal something."

The smirks died away, and the astonished faces rounded again on Mr. Carter. "He stole all the cups from the library. The police are waiting there now to see Jennings and Darbishire. Get dressed quickly, and go and see them before breakfast."

Mr. Carter walked out, leaving a bubbling cauldron of excitement to boil over, as soon as the door shut behind him.

When the two boys reached the library, they found that the Headmaster and Mr. Wilkins were in the room. The Headmaster introduced them to Sergeant Hutchinson and then left, with a curt instruction that the boys were to report to him after breakfast.

Mr. Wilkins said nothing, but sat by the window staring moodily across the rugger pitch.

Sergeant Hutchinson soon put the boys at their ease. They told him what had happened the previous evening, and he made notes from time to time in his little book. Then Jennings said: "And it wasn't only last night, you know. I've seen lights there before, but I was just waiting to get some evidence and stuff before I pounced."

"You needn't worry about the other times," Sergeant Hutchinson smiled. "Mr. Carter's told me all about that."

"Mr. Carter! D'you mean to say he knew and never did a thing about catching them?" This was astounding. What deep game could his housemaster be playing?

"It's all quite simple, really," the sergeant explained; and he told them how last night had been an exception to Hawkins' rule of arriving with clockwork regularity.

"Gosh," Jennings gasped, as light dawned. "So if I'd gone over there any other night, I should have cooked up the most frantic bish you could think of!"

The boys' evidence did not amount to much. They had not seen their assailant

283

so they could give no description of him, but when Jennings told of how he had telephoned the police station, the sergeant looked puzzled.

"You say you actually spoke to the police station on the phone last night?" he queried, for he knew that the first news of the robbery had come from Mr. Carter.

"Yes. I spoke to Sergeant somebody or other. He said he didn't want to come to the san. in case he caught the measles, instead of the burglar."

A loud "Corwumph" came from the direction of the window, and Mr. Wilkins said hurriedly: "That's all right, Sergeant. I can explain all about that, afterwards."

The sergeant looked again at his notebook. "When this man locked you up, did you see whether he was carrying anything?"

"I'm sure he wasn't," Jennings answered, "because he used both hands to drag us across the hall."

"He'd got a torch though," Darbishire added, "but I think he put it in his pocket, and after he'd locked us in we could hear him running away, so he couldn't have had the cups with him then."

Sergeant Hutchinson had already reached this conclusion. The most likely explanation was that the burglar's first call had been at the sanatorium. It had yielded nothing, except a surprise visit from Jennings and Darbishire; and having dealt with them, the man must then have made his way over to the main building. He had probably broken into the library at the same time that Mr. Carter and the rescue party were releasing the boys from the locked room, and he had made his escape before their return.

One thing was certain. The burglar could not have known very much about the nightly routine of the school, or he would not have paid his illegal visit at a time when Hawkins was normally engaged in sweeping-up operations. The sergeant was inclined to think that the robbery was the work of some tramp chancing his luck—a tramp who had no idea of how slender the thread was on which his luck had held.

"I'd better have a look at this sleeve button," the sergeant said, and Jennings' face fell. He could not imagine Sherlock Holmes having to admit to the police that he had lost a vital clue.

"Well, never mind," the sergeant consoled him, when Jennings explained that it was missing, "perhaps we'll be able to find it later on."

There were tomatoes on fried bread for breakfast, but Jennings was unable to enjoy his favourite dish. He could have kicked himself for losing the only clue which might throw some light on the mystery. He took a far more serious view of his failure than Sergeant Hutchinson did, for Jennings did not realise the difficulties of tracing the unknown burglar, even if the missing button could be found.

Then, there was the interview with the Headmaster, scheduled to take place after breakfast. This, in itself, was enough to make the tomatoes on fried bread turn to dust and ashes; which was a pity, for Mrs. Caffey had been specially careful not to let this happen before the food left the kitchen.

The dining hall pulsed with excited comment. "I bet old General Merridew will be furious," said Venables. "I'd like to hear what he says to the Head." He drew an exciting, but inaccurate picture of an angry general thumping the study desk and waving his walking stick, while M. W. B. Pemberton-Oakes, Esq., stood shuffling uneasily from one foot to the other.

Atkinson was furious to think that a thief could be so heartless. "It's nothing short of hairy cheek," he protested, "pinching our cups on the very day we've simply *got* to have them. Gosh, I'd like to get hold of that burglar!"

"You wouldn't," said Darbishire, with feeling. "I've done it, so I know."

He was not enjoying the meal either. Like Jennings, he voted the Wednesday menu the best breakfast of the week; for their great delight was to eat the tomatoes first, and then spread their marmalade on the fried bread. But today, even this attraction palled before the thought of the visit to the Headmaster's study.

"Never mind, Darbi," Bromwich major comforted him. "If they catch him, there might even be a wizard reward—perhaps, say, a hundred pounds even, and you and Jennings ought to get some of it, by rights."

They argued fiercely about the reward, which ranged from a thousand pounds, at the highest estimate, to six of the best for breaking bounds, at the more pessimistic end of the scale.

"Well, what's going to happen after the sports?" Temple wanted to know. "The old geezer can't dish out a cup, if it's not there."

"Perhaps he'll give us an I.O.U.," suggested Martin-Jones. "But it'll be a bit thick, having to beef round the track all the afternoon for a piece of paper, and all the time the burglar's gloating over our cup, and perhaps, even, drinking his tea out of it."

There was plenty to talk about during breakfast, and much of the conversation was about the gallant efforts of the *Lin. Ct. Det. Ag.*; but somehow, Jennings and Darbishire were unable to enjoy the praise that was lavished upon them.

Mr. Pemberton-Oakes, when they went to see him, lavished no praise; instead, he spoke of "misdirected energy," "foolhardy stupidity," and "wanton disobedience."

"Normally," he said, "I am not in favour of corporal punishment. I do not consider it to be a good thing"—and though they did not say so, Jennings and Darbishire agreed wholeheartedly with this opinion.

"However," he continued, laying aside his good principles in a way that the boys thought was treacherous, "I think that in this case ... ah ... um ..." He left the sentence unfinished, and turned towards the cupboard, where he kept the cane that he professed to dislike.

They left the study smarting under the injustice of grown-ups, and the corporal punishment of which nobody was in favour. The latter was soon over, but Jennings was upset because the grown-up mind would not see that he had acted from the highest motives. School rules were all very well when life was running smoothly, but surely one must cut through red tape at times of crisis.

Nobody seemed able to concentrate on their work during the lessons before morning break. Wandering minds would wrench themselves away from the burglary, only to veer off out of the window to the running track, or the long jump pit; for the playing field was dotted with little flags and whitewashed lines, marking out running lanes and starting points.

From his desk near the window, Jennings could follow the course of the quarter-mile track, until it disappeared out of sight behind a clump of bushes at the end of the field, and once or twice, he caught sight of Sergeant Hutchinson and a constable moving briskly between the main buildings and the sanatorium.

During break, Darbishire led Jennings down to the tuck-box room.

"That book I was reading about athletics has got some super-spivish hints in it," he said. "It says athletes ought to eat a lot of fruit, so I vote we spend break tucking into my fruit parcel, that my father sent me." He opened his tuck-box and produced an assortment of bulging paper bags.

"It'll take more than that lot to make you win the half-mile," Jennings said, "and anyway, you should have started weeks ago—it's too late now."

"I don't see why," Darbishire argued. "We shall just have to make up for lost time. There's still about four hours before the sports, and if we eat, say, three or four pounds of apples and a box of dates and half a dozen oranges and all these bananas, it ought to make us run like blinko this afternoon."

"Yes, but it won't make us run the right way. We shall be running up to Matron to say we've got collywobbles, and can we go to bed."

As they sat on their tuck-boxes and munched apples, Jennings' mind was still on the burglary. Presently he said: "I wonder if Sherlock Holmes could have solved it?"

"Of course he could," his friend assured him. "He'd just say: 'Elementary, my dear Jennings—you know my methods.' You told me yourself that's how he did it."

"Well, if *he* could solve it, why can't *we*? Here we've been practising nearly all the term with Morse buzzers and telescopes and secret codes and things, and as soon as we get a real problem we don't know where to start." The chief detective glared at his assistant, as though holding him responsible.

"Well, don't look at me like that," Darbishire defended himself. "My nerves haven't quite gone back into shape after last night, and anyway, if anyone's made a bish, you have." He took a large bite of apple and added accusingly: "Who lost the button? I bet Sherlock Holmes wouldn't have done that."

"Perhaps he wouldn't," Jennings reasoned, "but that's because he's only a chap in a book. It's miles easier for them. Now, if we were chaps in a story, we could start off by suspecting the person who's least likely to have done it. The criminal always turns out to be someone you'd never dream of."

"Well, let's do that then," suggested Darbishire. "Go and tell the Head you suspect him of burgling his own school."

Jennings threw his apple core at his assistant. "Don't be so bats—you know what I mean. In a detective story, the thief would turn out to be someone like—" He broke off and stared into space with unseeing eyes. When he spoke again, his voice had taken on a new note.

"I say, Darbi, you don't think it could have been Old Nightie, do you?"

"What?"

Jennings jumped up and paced the tuck-box room with official strides. "Why not?" he demanded. "In the first place, no one would dream of suspecting him. Besides, he was supposed to be in the san., when he said he wasn't there. Golly, if only we could find out if he's got a coat without a button on it."

"He has," said Darbishire helpfully, "I've seen it."

"Have you? When?"

"Oh, last week sometime. There were no buttons on it at all, and it was done up with safety pins. I saw him coming out of the boiler-room."

Jennings clicked his tongue reproachfully. "Darbishire, you've got as much sense as that apple core. I don't care if Old Nightie had got fifty million coats without buttons last week. The one I want is a coat that *had* got a button last week, and hasn't got one now."

"Oh, I see," replied Darbishire humbly. "I'm sorry if I'm a bit feeble as a detective, but I did notice one thing which proves Old Nightie couldn't have done it."

"What?"

"Well, when he came over last night with Mr. Carter and Old Wilkie, he wasn't wearing his jacket; he was in his shirt sleeves."

Jennings considered this theory and rejected it.

"But, don't you see, that was part of his bluff? He had to take his coat off when he came back with Mr. Carter, in case I spotted the button."

"You couldn't have spotted it. It wasn't there to spot. It was in your dressing gown pocket."

"Oh, don't be such a pre-historic remains. You're muddling things up, and it's quite clear really. Now this is what I think happened. Old Nightie locked us up, so that everyone would think there was a burglar about, and then he beetled off to the libe and pinched the cups. After that, he met Mr. Carter and pretended he'd never even been over to the san.—we know that happened because Sergeant Hutchinson told us before breakfast—and that gave him an ali—ali—something."

"Alligator?"

"No, alibi, that's it!"

"But what does Sergeant Hutchinson want an alibi for?"

Jennings swung round on his assistant angrily. "Are you trying to be funny, Darbi? You may be as crazy as two coots, but I should have thought even Binns minor would have understood what I meant."

Darbishire removed his spectacles and polished them with his tie. "I know perfectly well what you meant," he said mildly, "and as a matter of fact, I *was* trying to be funny."

"But don't you realise how serious it is?"

"It'll be a wizard sight more serious for you, if you go and tell Old Nightie he's a crook—dash it all, Jen, he's been here since before Julius Cæsar's time. If he wanted to pinch anything, he'd have done it ages ago."

"I'm not so sure," Jennings argued. "How do we know he hasn't been plan- ning this burglary for years, but it wasn't till last night he had the chance to put the blame on somebody else. Anyway, I'm going to tell Sergeant Hutchinson my theory, when I see him again."

He did not see the sergeant again that morning, for the Headmaster had asked him to postpone his inquiries until late in the afternoon. Mr. Pemberton-Oakes disliked having policemen on the premises at all, and considered that to have them trapesing about the grounds while the sports were in progress, would ruin the keen athletic atmosphere that should prevail on these occasions.

Sergeant Hutchinson agreed to return to Dunhambury for the time being, for there was much to be done at the police station. A description of the missing property had been sent out, and inquiries were being made at places where the thief might try to dispose of his plunder. He was not expecting to make an early arrest, and the few matters which he had yet to attend to at the school could be left until the sports were over.

The police car was turning out of the drive as the bell rang to signal the end of break, and Jennings and Darbishire turned reluctant footsteps towards their classroom.

CHAPTER 14

THE HEADMASTER IS NOT AMUSED

"What's the next lesson, somebody?" Martin-Jones demanded, as Form III trooped into their classroom after morning break.

Several somebodies consulted their timetables.

"It's Latin with the Head," groaned Venables. "Oh, gosh, and I made an ozard bish of learning my prep."

"That's all right," Rumbelow consoled him. "There's quite a rare chance he won't be able to take us this lesson. He was talking to that police sergeant five minutes ago, so with any luck, he'll be too busy to come in."

"Don't you believe it; I've been caught that way before," Venables answered, and they all opened their Latin books for a last minute revision of the pronoun, *hic haec hoc.*

"I bet he tests us," said Bromwich major, fumbling to find the page. "I wrote it out last night, but I haven't the vaguest idea how it goes."

"It goes like a machine-gun, Jennings told him. Crouching in his desk, like a tail-gunner in his turret, he aimed his ruler at an imaginary enemy fighter. "*Hic hic hic … haec haec haec … hoc hoc hoc … hic haec hoc … hic haec hoc … hic haec hoc,*" the gun spattered raucously.

Form III was delighted with this foolproof method of learning Latin pronouns, and hastened to join up as Roman rear-gunners in Cæsar's fighter legion.

"Wizard wheeze!" sang out Temple, hastily making a patent bombsight out of a paper-fastener. "Here comes a jet-propelled Feminine Ablative blazing away in Latin, *hac hac hac … hac hac hac … hac hac hac.*"

"I'm an anti-aircraft Accusative Singular," Bromwich major announced; "*hunc hanc hoc … hunc hanc hoc … hunc hanc hoc.*"

"Take cover," warned Nuttall, "Genitive dive bomber zooming down to zero feet. Eee-ow-ow! *Horum harum horum … horum harum horum …* Eee-ow-ow!"

"Ancient Roman wireless operator, sending out Morse signals in Latin,"

Venables joined in, and jerked out in brisk, staccato fashion, "*Hi hae haec ... hos has haec ...* Go on, Atkinson, you answer me."

"Okay. *Huic huic huic ... huic huic huic ... huic huic huic,*" flashed back the transmitter from the Atkinson control tower.

The classroom throbbed with the activity of the Roman Air Force. Cæsar's Bomber Squadron, led by Wing-Imperator Rumbelow, set off on a mission to divide all Gaul into three parts with the aid of well-placed blockbusters; but they were intercepted by a strong force of enemy fighters, and had to return to base and take cover beneath their desk lids.

"*Hac hac hac ... hac hac hac ... hac hac hac ...*" the Feminine Ablatives blazed away from the back row.

"*Hunc hanc hoc ... hunc hanc hoc ...*" replied the heavy flak of the Accusative Singulars, from just below the master's desk.

"*Horum harum horum ... horum harum horum ... horum harum horum ...*" droned the Genitive Plural dive bombers.

"*Huic huic huic ... huic huic huic ...*" clicked the wireless operators, tapping their forefingers on rulers held firm by desk-lids.

Never had Form III shown such interest in their pronouns, and the aerial battle was at its height, when the Headmaster walked in.

Immediately, engines cut out and machine-guns jammed in mid-burst. But the unfortunate pilot of J for Jennings, who was suffering from combat fatigue, was slow to react to this new danger. His plane had been hit by Nominative Singular tracer bullets in the second row—his engines were stalling, and his machine was about to blow up.

"*Hic-haec-hoc ... hic-haec-hoc ... hic-haec-hoc ...* B-A-N-G!" were the words which greeted the Headmaster as he stood in the doorway. He walked to the master's desk in ominous silence.

"Which boy went on talking, after I came in?" he demanded.

Jennings raised his hand. "I wasn't really what you'd call talking, sir."

The Headmaster raised his eyebrows.

"Then what were you doing?"

"I—I spoke, sir."

"You were not talking, but you spoke. I regret that my simple mind is unable to detect any difference between the two things."

"I was learning my Latin pronouns out loud, sir."

"I see. And since when has the pronoun *Hie* ended with the word Bang?"

"It came out by accident, sir."

"Really!" The Headmaster turned and walked along the rows, inspecting the exercise books in which the boys had written out their preparation. The copies were neat, for Mr. Pemberton-Oakes had a horror of slovenly writing, and when he arrived at Jennings' desk, a shadow of annoyance passed over his features.

"You know perfectly well that I never allow pencil to be used in exercise books. Why didn't you use your pen?"

"It broke, sir," Jennings admitted unhappily, and produced the two halves for the Headmaster's inspection. At one time, the wooden penholder had been six inches long, but absent-minded chewing had reduced it to half this length; and the two fragments, which Jennings held out before the Headmaster's horrified gaze, consisted of a crossed nib in a metal socket, and an inch of ink-stained wood, splayed out like a shaving-brush.

Mr. Pemberton-Oakes averted his eyes from the miserable object.

"It broke!" he murmured softly. "Of its own accord, naturally. I notice, Jennings, you don't say '*I* was talking' and '*I* broke it,' but '*it* came out by accident' and '*it* broke.' Most unsatisfactory; bring your Latin book up to my desk. I shall test you orally."

Back to his desk strode the Headmaster. He perched himself on the high stool, and glanced at the cover of the book which Jennings laid before him. Again his face darkened.

"Jennings," he said, "when the author wrote this admirable book, he saw fit to call it *A New Latin Grammar*. Had he wished to call it *A New Eating Grammar*, I have no doubt he would have done so."

Jennings shuffled uncomfortably from one foot to the other. He had whiled away many a dull prep in making suitable alterations to his textbook, but he had not reckoned on having his handiwork inspected by the Headmaster.

"Of course, I cannot hold you reponsible." There was a note of irony in the Headmaster's voice. "Your pen obviously decided to alter the lettering, before it accidentally broke itself in half."

"No, sir; I did it, sir."

"Really! And do you know what happens to boys who scribble in textbooks?"

"Yes, sir."

The Headmaster opened the book and found that the author's work had been revised in some detail. Pencilled sketches of knights in armour and daffodils in bloom adorned the margin; racing cars swerved between columns of irregular verbs. On the title page was written:

> *"If this book should dare to roam,*
> *Box its ears and send it home."*

This was followed by the owner's address which took up eleven lines, and gave full details of the continent, hemisphere and solar system to which the straying volume should be returned.

"This," said the Headmaster severely, "has ruined a perfectly good book."

"Yes, sir. You did tell us to write our names in them though, sir."

"I am unaware that I instructed you to smear illiterate doggerel all over the covers."

With obvious distaste, he read aloud:

> *"Latin is a language, as dead as dead can be.*
> *It killed the ancient Romans, and now it's killing me."*

He glanced round the room, and the boys in the front row hastily turned the pages of their Latin books to cover up any poetic efforts of their own. His voice was heavy with irony as he turned back to Jennings and said, "What brilliant wit! What biting satire! What a masterly condemnation of the teaching profession!"

"Oh, I don't mean it's *really* killing me, sir," the poet explained. "You have to take the poem meteorologically, sir."

The Headmaster rose with a dignified look. He did not actually call for bell, book and candle, but by the time he had finished, Jennings looked as woebegone as the bedraggled Jackdaw of Rheims.

The first part of the punishment sounded fair enough—Jennings was to pay five shillings for a new copy of the Latin book out of his pocket money; but as the full meaning of the rest of the punishment became clear, the Drake House members of Form III stifled groans of despair.

"... and you will stay in this afternoon during the sports and write out your preparation twelve times with an unbroken pen. I am aware that your house is relying on you to compete in various races, and this will, perhaps, bring it home to all, that boys who spoil expensive textbooks punish not only themselves, but their friends and colleagues as well."

Jennings went white with misery as he heard his sentence passed, and his eyes were moist as he returned to his desk in the hushed classroom. He felt that the bottom had dropped out of his world. If he could not compete in the sports, those few vital points would be lost, and Drake would have no chance of winning the contest. He would willingly have written out his preparation fifty times and paid for a dozen books, if only the punishment could be postponed until later in the day. What would his house say? What would Mr. Carter think? To let the house down at a moment like this was the most serious crime that anyone could imagine.

Mr. Pemberton-Oakes knew that the boy was feeling the punishment keenly, but this was the second time in one morning that Jennings had crossed his path, and he was determined to stand no more nonsense.

"And now," he said, "we will have a test on *hic haec hoc*."

Jennings came out with top marks in the test. He tried as he had never tried before, hoping that the Headmaster might relent; but the hope was in vain.

Five minutes before the lesson ended, there was a knock at the door and Mary, one of the housemaids, came in.

"Excuse me, sir," she whispered in the Headmaster's ear. "There's a gentleman called to see Mr. Jennings."

The Headmaster looked surprised. "*Mister* Jennings?" he repeated.

"That's what he said, sir, but I expect he meant Master Jennings, really. The gentleman says his name's Mr. Russell, sir. I've shown him into the library."

"Mr. Russell?" The name meant nothing to the Headmaster and he inquired: "Do you know a Mr. Russell, Jennings? Is he a relation?"

"No, sir," Jennings replied blankly.

"H'm. A friend of the family, perhaps, who has come down to watch the sports?"

"I don't know, sir—he might be."

The Headmaster turned to the waiting housemaid. "Tell Mr. Russell that I will send Jennings to see him at the end of the lesson, and say that I shall be pleased to make his acquaintance as soon as I am free."

"Yes, sir."

Mary returned to the library, where Mr. Russell was wondering what type of man his prospective customer would turn out to be. So far the salesman was delighted, for his first impressions were that Mr. Jennings was a man of such obvious wealth that he would not quibble over the price of an expensive ciné camera.

Mr. Russell had arrived at Dunhambury by train, and had hired a taxi for the last part of the journey. Everything had confirmed his employer's theory that Linbury Court was the home of the squire of the manor. The taxi had turned in through ornate, wrought-iron gates, and had sped up a long drive, lined with thick yew hedges, which had prevented him from seeing the rugger pitches behind them.

When the taxi came to rest before the wide sweep of steps leading to the front door, Mr. Russell was sure that he had arrived at one of the stately homes of England. He was not far out in his judgment, for the house had originally been the country seat of the fourth Lord Linbury, and from the outside, it bore little trace of the changes which had taken place within its walls.

He was led across a large entrance hall and shown into a well-stocked library. Mr. Russell did not read the titles of the books, or he might have been surprised at the squire's strong liking for boys' stories. But he noted with approval the shields painted with public school crests; these, obviously, were the coats-of-arms of different branches of the extensive Jennings family.

When Mary returned and asked him if he would wait a few minutes, he was confident that the ciné camera was as good as sold already.

"Certainly," he smiled. "What a charming room this is. I think Linbury Court is one of the finest country houses I've ever visited."

"Yes, sir," said Mary and prepared to go, but the salesman was anxious to learn all he could of the squire's interests.

"I imagine it needs a large staff to look after a place this size," he said casually.

"Oh, yes, it does," the housemaid agreed. "There's me and three other maids and cook and Mrs. Caffey and two house-parlour men and Robinson for the odd jobs. Then there's the outdoor staff as well."

Mr. Russell smiled. If the squire employed so many servants, he must be a man who enjoyed spending money. "I take it that Mr. Jennings is a gentleman of some fortune?"

Mary stared at him for a moment, and then broke into an idiotic giggle. "*Mister* Jennings!" she tittered. "Hee! hee! hee!"

Wondering whether the girl was half-witted, Mr. Russell turned to the squire's interests in sport. He had borrowed a book about country life the previous day, and had spent the train journey to Dunhambury in learning all he could about the habits of rural gentlemen. No one could say that Mr. Russell was not thorough.

"I suppose there's plenty of hunting, shooting and fishing and all that sort of thing?"

Mary giggled again. "There's no hunting, sir. There's riding, though."

"Oh, yes, of course. And shooting?"

"Yes, sir," Mary replied, remembering Mr. Topliss' weekly class in the tiny shooting-range behind the gymnasium. She would have been surprised if she had known that her answer stirred Mr. Russell's mind to visions of nobility and gentry, in hairy tweeds, sitting on shooting-sticks, while keepers beat the surrounding foliage for pheasants.

Perhaps he's a military type, Mr. Russell thought, and aloud he asked: "Has Mr. Jennings any special rank or title?"

Waves of helpless giggles engulfed the housemaid. Either this chap with the camera was a lunatic, or he was trying to be funny. Fancy asking such questions about a ten-year-old boy in Form III!

"What I meant was," Mr. Russell explained, "is he a Colonel, for instance, or a Brigadier, or—"

"Hee! hee! hee! hee!" Mary tried hard to control herself, but even the thought of what Mrs. Caffey would say failed to stem the tittering flow of giggles. "No, he's not in the army," she managed to say— "at least, not yet, he isn't."

She felt the giggles coming on again, and turned and bolted for the door with a breathless: "Excuse me."

"Here, don't go," called Mr. Russell. "Wait—"

The door shut behind the helpless housemaid, and Mr. Russell was left wondering what on earth was the matter with the girl.

He unslung the Grossman Ciné Camera de Luxe from his shoulder and placed it on the table with the small suitcase, in which he carried a further supply of coloured film. Then he settled himself in an armchair.

CHAPTER 15

THE FRIEND OF THE FAMILY

MR. RUSSELL had not long to wait. After a few moments the door opened, and he sprang to his feet to greet his wealthy client.

"Good mor— Oh!"

A boy in a grey suit, with brown hair and a wideawake look in his eyes, came into the room.

"Please, sir," said the boy, "I'm Jennings."

"You're—? You mean, you're Mr. Jennings' son?"

This struck Jennings as being rather a silly question. "Yes, of course I am. I'd have to be, wouldn't I?"

"Yes, yes, of course. What I meant was, it's your father whom I've come to see."

Jennings looked at his visitor curiously. "Oh, but my father doesn't live here; he lives at Haywards Heath. He just comes down to see me for the weekend sometimes."

"But surely, this is his address isn't it?"

"Gosh, no," said Jennings. "You wouldn't expect to find him still at school at his age, would you?"

The room swam before Mr. Russell's eyes.

"What?" he gasped, as a ghastly suspicion flooded his mind. "Did you say *at school*? Do you—do you mean to tell me this is a school?"

"Yes, of course," Jennings answered, wondering why this strange man was behaving in such an odd manner. "Linbury Court Preparatory School."

"Good heavens!" the salesman murmured weakly. The ghastly suspicion had changed to a beacon which was shedding light on the explanation of the whole business. "Well, of all the— Then you must be J. C. T. Jennings!"

"Yes," said Jennings. He thought that had been clear from the start.

"And it was you who wrote to us about the ciné camera?"

Suddenly Jennings, too, was conscious of a light dawning. "Oh, golly!" he said aghast. "Is *that* who you are?"

"It certainly is," retorted Mr. Russell angrily. "And I've come all this way to sell you one."

Jennings was horrified.

"But I never meant you to *come*," he explained. "I never even asked you to. I only wanted a catalogue. The advertisement said I could have one, if I wanted one."

"You didn't tell me you were a schoolboy," Mr. Russell argued, leaning heavily against the table. "You said you wanted to buy a camera, and here I've come down from London—"

"Well, I still want to," Jennings assured him, "only I'm a bit short of dosh—er—money."

Mr. Russell seized the camera in its leather case, and waved it under Jennings' nose. "Do you know how much this camera costs?" he asked fiercely. "Ninety-five guineas! … Ninety-five guineas! And how much have you got?"

"Three and sevenpence," mumbled Jennings apologetically.

"Three and sevenpence. Cor!!!"

Mr. Russell paced up and down the library, swinging the camera savagely by its strap. When his feelings were again under control, he turned to the unhappy object before him and said: "Listen, my boy. You've got me here under false pretences. Smart notepaper, imposing address, embossed crest and all that carry-on. What were we to think?"

"I'm sorry," said Jennings.

"Sorry! So I should think. I've given up a whole day, cancelled important engagements, travelled sixty miles to get here, and all for what?" he demanded, waving his arms dramatically. "To be offered three and sevenpence for a ninety-five guinea movie camera!"

"But, Mr. Russell, I never meant—"

"For the first time in my life, I've been taken for a mug. It's absurd—it's ridiculous." Stooping until his face was on a level with Jennings' distressed features, he barked: "When I go back to London and tell the manager I've been wasting time and money like this, he'll—he'll foam at the mouth and explode!"

Jennings' eyes became round as saucers at this entrancing prospect. But Mr. Russell retired to an armchair, and thought hard.

First, he thought how furious he was, and how he would like to give J. C.

T. Jennings a good hiding. And then he thought of Mr. Catchpole foaming at the mouth and exploding, and the idea was so ludicrous that, in spite of his anger, he stopped scowling, and a slow grin spread over his face. He was a kind-hearted man, and there was something about the wide-awake look in the eyes of the boy standing before him that made it impossible for Mr. Russell to go on being angry for long. Besides, he reflected, the joke was on Mr. Catchpole—for it was he who had been so sure that J. C. T. Jennings was a wealthy aristocrat.

Mr. Russell had a keen sense of humour, and now that his first outburst of wrath was over, he began to see the funny side of things. Ten seconds later, he started to laugh.

Jennings gaped in surprise at the rapid change in the salesman's manner. Only a minute before, he had been pacing the room in towering anger, and now he was sitting in the armchair, shaking with silent mirth.

Mr. Russell had a peculiar laugh which sounded like a railway engine: he never let himself go wholeheartedly, but seemed, instead, to bottle it all up inside him, and only a curious *choof-chooof* sound was allowed to escape through the safety valve of his lips.

"I can just imagine what the manager will say when I tell him," Mr. Russell said, when his railway engine had *choof-choofed* to a stop. "'Your Mr. Jennings,' I'll tell him—and I can just picture his face when I say it— 'Your Mr. Jennings is a ... *Choof-choof-choof-choof!*'"

He started to shake again as he recalled Mr. Catchpole's words; "'Wealthy aristocrat,' I'll tell him ... 'Squire of the village ... Everybody who is anybody in his part of Sussex will be wanting a ...' *Choof-choof-choof-choof!* ... 'Careful how I handle important customers!' Oh dear, oh dear!"

He *choofed* quietly, but the tears trickling down his face showed how rich Mr. Russell considered the joke to be. "Three and sevenpence for our most expensive ... *Choof! choof! choof!* No wonder the maid thought I was up the pole. Hunting, shooting and fishing! She must have thought I was ... *Choof-choof-choof!* Well, thank goodness I can see the funny side of it."

He pulled himself together, and dabbed his eyes with his handkerchief, while Jennings stared at him with a mixture of amazement and despair.

"I wish I could see the funny side of it," he said.

"Well, can't you?"

"No. It hasn't got a funny side for me."

"Nonsense," said Mr. Russell gaily. "If I can take it as a joke, with all the business I'm losing, I'm sure you can."

"But you don't understand. The Headmaster's coming along in a minute, to find out why you've come to see me."

"Is he, by Jove! He'll laugh himself silly when I tell him what's happened."

"No, he won't." Jennings shook his head sadly. "You don't know Headmasters. They're not good at seeing things like other people, and there's a frantic hoo-hah going on already."

"There's a *what*?"

It was not often that Jennings confided his troubles to a complete stranger, but he did so now, because Mr. Russell seemed anxious to listen. He explained that twice already that morning he had fallen foul of the Headmaster, and was being kept in, when he should be helping his house in the sports.

"... and it's all because I put my name and address and a sort of poem thing in my Latin book, and everyone turns *Latin* into *Eating*, anyway."

"Come again?" queried the perplexed salesman.

"Oh, you wouldn't understand," Jennings told him, "but it's super-ozard squared, because Drake will all be as sick as mud, and Mr. Carter won't say anything at all; and that'll be worse, because I like him, and if you let him down it's awful. And I got full marks in the test, hoping he'd let me off for Drake's sake, but he never did."

There was much that Mr. Russell did not understand, but he gathered enough to realise that the future outlook was cloudy.

"And it'll be worse in a minute," Jennings continued, "because the Head will say I shouldn't have written to you, and he'll think I asked you to come down on purpose, and we're not allowed to have anyone to see us, except relations and friends, and there'll be another row about that."

Mr. Russell listened with a grave expression. He could not explain why, but his sympathy was aroused by this boy who had caused him so much trouble. The situation seemed serious, and Mr. Russell rose to the occasion like a hero.

"Well, that's all right," he said cheerfully. "If friends are allowed to visit you, there's nothing to worry about. I'm a friend of yours, now. We've known each other for nearly ten minutes."

"I'm not sure that you'd count," Jennings said, doubtfully. "You don't even know my family."

Mr. Russell thought for a moment; then he said, quite truthfully, "Well, as a matter of fact, I do happen to know a Mr. Jennings. He lives at er—um—"

"Haywards Heath?"

"I'm just trying to remember. It might have been."

"Of course, if you really know my father that would make all the difference. Gosh, wouldn't it be wizard if you did!"

The salesman frowned thoughtfully at the toe of his shoe. The only Mr. Jennings that he could recall was a vague business acquaintance whom he had not seen for years. He hardly remembered what he looked like, or whether he was young or old, tall or short. On the other hand, who could say whether it might not be the same man?

"Well," he said slowly, "it's just as likely to be him as any other Mr. Jennings, isn't it?"

Jennings had no time to reply, for at that moment the Headmaster arrived to inspect the visitor for himself.

"Good morning, Mr.—er—um—"

"Russell."

"Ah, yes—Mr. Russell."

The salesman felt the Headmaster's eye examining him, from his glossy black hair to his glossy black shoes; for Mr. Pemberton-Oakes was careful to protect the boys in his charge from unsuitable visitors. Then Jennings was sent to wait outside in the hall, and as soon as the door was shut the Headmaster said: "May I inquire, Mr. Russell, whether you are a relative of the Jennings' family?"

"No, no. I can't claim to be more than a casual friend—if that; but I used to do business with a Mr. Jennings of—of—"

"Haywards Heath?"

"That name does ring a bell certainly. However," he went on hastily, "as I was in the district I decided to call."

"Very kind of you. The boys are always pleased to welcome friends of the family."

The Headmaster thawed considerably, and Mr. Russell knew that he had passed his test as a suitable Sports Day visitor.

His first impulse was to chat politely for a few minutes, and then excuse himself on the grounds of urgent business, and make his way back to London. He had done all that could be expected of him, and had helped his young friend to avoid further trouble in the matter of unwelcome visitors; but as Mr. Russell sat listening to the Headmaster's lengthy opinion of the weather, he suddenly thought that, as a friend of the family, he should do more. A good friend, for

301

example, might bring up the question of Jennings' detention during the sports.

He was far too good a salesman, however, to make such a request outright. Instead he remarked: "I was hoping I might be allowed to watch the sports this afternoon. I'm sure Mr. Jennings would be interested to hear a first hand account of the 440 when I see him again—which may not be for a long time," he added to himself.

"I am afraid that Jennings will not be competing," the Headmaster replied. "A little matter of discipline, you understand."

Mr. Russell rose to his feet and casually picked up the ciné camera from the table. "That's a pity; you see, I've brought my camera. I was just thinking what excellent material the sports would make, for a colour film. Have you got a projector you could show it with?"

"Oh, yes, we have films every Wednesday evening. I hire them from a film library in London."

"But how much more satisfactory to show a film which you have actually made yourself," said Mr. Russell persuasively. This was the moment for a sales talk, and he made the most of it.

"I see it something like this ... Imagine a Wednesday evening—the school sitting tense with excitement, waiting for the film to start. The lights go down—a caption appears on the screen—*The Annual Sports*. Then, a long shot of the grounds with the school in the distance, the coloured flags fluttering gaily in the breeze, the sun streaming down and the boys streaming out, in bright technicolour blazers. Next, a medium shot of the runners lining up for the start ... Close-up of the starter's finger trembling on the trigger of the gun ... They're off!"

Mr. Russell's voice thrilled with excitement, as he pressed on with his running commentary. "Then we switch to a crowd scene ... Excited spectators shouting themselves hoarse ... The camera pans back to the runners ... Number 3 trips up, and Number 5 crashes down on top of him ... Number 4's in the lead, in the greatest race of the day ... Close-up of his determined expression!"

The commentator set his jaw and clenched his teeth in an all-out effort, and noted that Mr. Pemberton-Oakes was sitting forward on the edge of his chair, drinking in every detail of the scene.

"The camera tracks to the finishing tape," Mr. Russell hissed breathlessly, through still clenched teeth. "We see a medium shot of the judges trying to look calm beneath their mounting excitement—and what excitement! Oh dear, oh dear, there's never been anything like it!"

The salesman was now pacing the room and scattering handfuls of tense atmosphere in the direction of the fireplace. "Close-up of the stopwatch ticking remorselessly on ... Tick ... tick ... tick!"

The Headmaster stared; he seldom met human beings who carried on in this unusual way.

"Back to the running track ... We see a long shot of the runners ... They're in the straight ... Number 4 is in the lead ... Number 1 is coming up on the inside ... He's gaining ... he's ... he's done it! ... Number 1 wins! The camera shoots the smiling winner being slapped on the back by admiring friends ... Next a close-up of the winner shaking hands with the Headmaster. Hold it! ... The Headmaster turns full face to the camera, the sunlight picking out the colours of his old school tie. He smiles warmly ... Slowly, the picture fades."

Mr. Russell sank into an armchair and mopped his brow. "What an idea for a picture!" he murmured ecstatically. "It's an inspiration ... It's a masterpiece!"

Mr. Pemberton-Oakes would probably have dismissed the sales-talk as an undignified exhibition, but for the fact that the subject was dear to his heart. He had for some time been wanting to buy a ciné camera for just such an occasion as this.

"You're right, Mr. Russell, you're quite right," he said, rising to his feet with enthusiasm. "A film like that would be a permanent record to thrill future generations, and recapture the memories of old boys visiting their *alma mater* forty years on, when afar and asunder, parted are those who are—"

"Quite. What a pity it's just an idle dream!"

"Idle dream!" The Headmaster was astounded. "But, Mr. Russell, you yourself suggested—that is, if you've brought your camera specially, this is just the opportunity."

"On second thoughts, I'd better be getting back to town." He replaced his handkerchief, got up from his chair and began collecting his camera, his suitcase, his overcoat and his gloves.

"Oh, but, surely—" Mr. Pemberton-Oakes could not understand it. Had he offended his visitor in some way?

"Well, it's like this, Headmaster. The reason I came down with my camera was to see our friend Jennings. I had hoped to interest him in—" He broke off and smiled: "But that's another story. However, if he's being kept in this afternoon, he won't be able to appear in the film."

The Headmaster assured him that the other seventy-eight boys of Linbury Court would provide excellent material for the camera.

"I'd rather not, if you don't mind," said Mr. Russell. "If Jennings could be in it, it would be different, but I think the family would be disappointed if he wasn't in the picture. He usually is, I should imagine. Well, I'm glad to have met you. D'you mind if I telephone for a taxi to take me to the station?"

Mr. Pemberton-Oakes thought hard. He would dearly have liked a film of the sports, and it was just the thing that was needed to console the boys for the loss of their cup.

"Now, just a moment, Mr. Russell," he said. "Perhaps I was rather hasty, but defacing Latin textbooks is a serious matter. Excuse me a moment, will you?"

He opened the library door, and called to Jennings who was sitting forlornly on the staircase, on the opposite side of the hall. Jennings came in expecting more trouble, and could hardly believe his ears when the Headmaster solemnly announced: "I have decided, Jennings, that Drake House will be placed at a disadvantage if they are deprived of one of their entrants for this afternoon's contest. Partly for the sake of your house, therefore, but chiefly because Mr. Russell wishes to include the entire school in a cinematic record, I have decided to allow you to compete in the sports."

"Oh, thank you, sir! Thank you ever so much, sir!"

"You will, of course, do your imposition this evening."

"Yes, sir! Willingly, sir! Thank you, sir!"

"I think, perhaps, Mr. Russell deserves your thanks more than I do," said the Headmaster ruefully, and Jennings turned to his benefactor almost tearful with gratitude. Mr. Russell waved the thanks aside. Making people change their minds was all part of the day's work for an expert salesman.

"Now, Mr. Russell," smiled the Headmaster. "May we discuss the film which you are so kindly going to make for us? As a title I would suggest 'Sports Day at Linbury' and underneath that, some apt quotation from the classics such as—er—*Hic ... Hic ...* How does it go? It's on the tip of my tongue. *Hic ...*"

Mr. Russell could only think of hickory dickory dock, and Jennings' suggestion of *hie haec hoc* was rejected with a frown of annoyance.

"Ah, I have it. *Hic dies, vere mihi festus, atras eximet curas.*"

"Come again?" said Mr. Russell, out of his depth.

"This day, in truth a holiday to me, shall banish idle cares," the Headmaster translated. *"Horace, Book 3—Ode Number 14."*

"Ah, yes, of course. Good old Horace," nodded Mr. Russell, trying to look as though the quotation were familiar to him. Suddenly, he found himself wondering what Mr. Catchpole would say, when he discovered that a considerable length of expensive colour film had been used, with no thought of who was going to pay for it. He decided that he could best pacify his manager by giving the firm a free advertisement.

"Now, after this—*Hic*—er—what you said," the salesman went on, "we should have a credit title saying, '*This film appears by kind permission of the Grossman Ciné Camera Co., Ltd.*'"

"Quite," the Headmaster agreed.

"And there's one more we ought to have, too, Mr. Russell," Jennings suggested.

"And what is that?"

"*Jennings appears by kind permission of the Headmaster.*"

Mr. Russell's shoulders began to shake once more. "*Choof-choof-choof-choof*," he rippled helplessly.

CHAPTER 16

DARBISHIRE RUNS A RACE

MR. RUSSELL had lunch in the tuck-shop, where a light meal was served to any parents or friends who arrived early.

General Merridew, as the guest of honour, had been invited to sit at the high table in the school dining hall, but at the last moment, he telephoned to say that he had been delayed, and would not be able to arrive until four-thirty.

"Sorry, Headmaster," his voice crackled over the telephone. "I'm afraid I shall miss most of the sports. Still, I shall be there in time to award the cup, and that's the main thing, eh!"

Award the cup! Mr. Pemberton-Oakes had been hoping to break the news gently, when Mrs. Caffey's excellent cooking had put the General in a good humour. It was difficult to explain such an unfortunate incident over the telephone. General Merridew was a man of moods, and most people made sure that his mood was a good one, if their news was bad. The Headmaster sighed.

"I regret to say that we have been the victims of a most distressing occurrence," he began into the telephone.

"Speak up; can't hear you. The line's bad. What did you say about pressing currants?"

"You misheard me—I said a distressing occurrence ... We had a robbery late last night."

"You had to corroborate *what*, last night?"

"No, no. What I said was ..."

"Well, never mind," the line crackled. "Tell me when I get there."

Mr. Pemberton-Oakes sat down to luncheon envying the youngest boy in the school. His eye rested upon Binns minor. How delightful life must be for him! No cares, no responsibilities, no hasty-tempered generals to be pacified!

Binns minor stopped talking with his mouth full, when he saw the Headmaster looking at him. How wizard to be an arch-beak, he thought—no maths, no detentions, no one to tick you off when you put your elbows on the table!

The weather had made good its early promise, and the afternoon was as bright and warm as one could hope for in the last week of March. After lunch, Jennings showed Mr. Russell round the school, and introduced him to Darbishire, who goggled with embarrassment when he first heard who the visitor was.

Quite soon, however, they were talking like old friends. They told him about the burglary and he *tut-tutted* in sympathy; they told him about the Linbury Court Detective Agency and their hopes of obtaining a camera; they showed him the broken telescope, the mute mouth organ and the silent Morse buzzer, and the salesman agreed that any detective, famous or otherwise, was worthy of better equipment.

Then the boys went to change, and soon the playing field was speckled with magenta-and-white blazers. They clustered round Mr. Carter, like flies round a honey-pot, anxious to be picked for some duty.

"Sir, please, sir, can I do the tinkles on the blower for you, sir?"

"Can you do *what*, Venables?"

"Can I ring the handbell for you, sir, before you start the races?"

"All right, Venables. I hereby appoint you Official Director of Campanology."

"What's that, sir? Something to do with putting up the tea tent?"

"No. Campanology is the science of bell-ringing," Mr. Carter told him, for the boys always insisted on having high-sounding titles for their appointments.

"And what can I do, sir?"

Mr. Carter considered: "You, Binns minor, can be Chief Salvage Officer and Deputy Armourer."

"Coo, thank you, sir," came the delighted reply. "Thanks most awfully—er—what does all that mean, sir?"

"It means that when I fire the starting pistol, you gather up the used cartridge cases."

"I see, sir. Oh, wizzo! I've always wanted to be a picker-upper. Are you going to use the pistol to start all the races, sir?"

"Of course. What would you expect me to use—a bow and arrow?"

Binns minor thought for a moment and then shrilled delightedly: "Oh, but you don't use a gun for the high jump, sir. I caught you there, didn't I, sir?"

"You'll be for the 'high jump,' if you go on asking silly questions," the master smiled, and Binns minor rushed off, to boast to his Form I friends of how he had soundly beaten Mr. Carter in a battle of wits.

At two-thirty the bell rang; the starting pistol shattered the tense silence, and the 100 yards, under twelve, was under way.

Drake gathered half the points for this event, but Raleigh jumped into the lead by winning the "Open," for the senior race carried more marks. The Junior 220 was a victory for Raleigh, as their team sprinted round the track to finish first, second and fourth. Jennings was third, and so managed to score one point for his house. Next came the high jump, and Drake clapped and cheered as their score crept up, and drew level with their rival's.

Mr. Russell was enjoying himself. It was a novelty for him to spend an afternoon surrounded by an eager, milling throng of boys, and he dashed about shooting dozens of feet of colour film, heedless of what Mr. Catchpole would say when he found out; there were so many exciting shots to be made that the salesman had almost forgotten that the real object of his visit had been to sell the camera. The Headmaster was at his elbow most of the time, dragging him from starting-point to finishing-tape and back, so that nothing should be missed by the camera's recording eye. He, too, was enjoying the afternoon, and had banished all thoughts of burglaries and irate generals to the back of his mind.

"Excellent, Mr. Russell," he beamed. "Your shots of the high jump will be an inspiration for years to come. I shall tell Jennings to write to his father and say how pleased we all were that you were able to come down, today—or perhaps you will be seeing Mr. Jennings yourself. I suppose you meet him quite often in the course of business?"

"Well, er—as a matter of fact—oh look, they're lining up for the long jump," Mr. Russell said hastily. "I must get a shot of this. Excuse me," and he dashed across to the long jump pit, before he could be asked any more awkward questions.

The Headmaster followed at a more dignified pace. "Ah, Wilkins, this is going to be a Sports Day I shall long remember," he said pleasantly, little knowing how true this prophecy was to be. "I'm learning quite a lot about film photography, too. Did you notice how one should crouch low on the ground to take pictures of the high-jumpers? That's either called tracking—or is it panning? or—well, anyway, it's most interesting."

Together, they walked towards the long jump pit. Mr. Wilkins, because of his powerful voice, always announced the results of each event; and although he had a megaphone for this purpose, he seldom needed to use it.

The Official Announcer's Assistant was Bromwich major, who trotted along

behind Mr. Wilkins, wearing the megaphone on his head like a witch's hat. Whenever he passed a visitor, he raised it politely by the handle.

The long jump was in full swing when they arrived; Mr. Russell was crouching at one end of the pit, so that the oncoming jumpers seemed to be leaping right into the eye of the camera.

Jennings was jumping badly. At his first jump, his foot had passed the take off board at the end of his run, and Mr. Hind, who was judging, had signalled "No jump." Things were no better in the second round; Jennings was so determined not to overstep the mark, that he jumped from a foot behind it, and landed far in the rear of the other competitors.

Now he had one more jump to make. He started his run, reached top speed, arrived at the take off board with the right foot foremost, and hurled himself high and far—his arms beating the air like wings and his face twisted with effort.

It was the best jump he had ever made; he passed the marks of his rivals by a foot, and in the split second before he landed, he had a glimpse of the crouching Mr. Russell, desperately trying to back away out of range.

The photographer was too late, and Jennings landed heavily on top of him knocking him flat on his back. The camera whirred on, automatically recording a distorted close-up of Jennings' left foot, a patch of sky, tree tops and jumbled faces, as it shot round in a wide arc and finished up on the grass, whirring away at Binns minor's ankle socks.

It was lucky that neither Jennings nor Mr. Russell was hurt, for the spectators were far more concerned about the fate of the camera. Human beings soon recover from a few bruises, but expensive cameras are more sensitive. They stared spellbound, while Mr. Russell examined it, and cheered with relief when he smilingly told them that no damage had been done.

"Gosh, what a hairy bit of luck," gasped Temple. "The faces Jennings made when he was jumping were enough to bust it, and then he has to go and knock it for six with his great feet."

Mr. Wilkins broadcast the result, in a voice which was clearly audible above the drone of a passing aeroplane. "First, Jennings ... second, Martin-Jones ... third, Johnson."

Drake was now leading by one point. Jennings looked for Darbishire so that they could rejoice together, but his friend had wandered off by himself during the long jump, and was nowhere to be found.

"Have you seen Darbi anywhere, Bromo?"

"Can't hear a thing," complained Bromwich major. "I was standing next to Old Wilkie, using the megaphone as an ear-trumpet, when he gave out the long jump result. It went in one ear, and it hasn't come out of the other yet." He wandered off, wondering how long his deafness would last.

Venables rang the bell, and Mr. Carter announced: "Throwing the Cricket Ball—Open," and the crowd moved away to another part of the field.

"Ah, there you are, Mr. Russell. Not hurt, I hope," the Headmaster inquired.

"Do you mean me, or the camera?"

"I mean both, naturally," replied the Headmaster. "In fact, I was just thinking how very fortunate you are to own a camera like that. I wish I had one."

Mr. Russell felt that business was looking up. "This is getting interesting," he murmured to himself.

"It would be invaluable," continued the Headmaster, stepping back quickly to avoid a cricket ball that had veered badly off its course. "Think of the films we could take! Cricket, football, boxing, swimming, concerts, picnics, Scouts—yes, Mr. Russell, I'd give a lot to own a ciné camera like yours."

"Ninety-five guineas?"

"I beg your pardon?"

"I'll sell you this one, for that."

The Headmaster blinked in surprise. "Oh, but that's yours—you need it yourself. I wouldn't dream of depriving you. After all, it is your hobby."

"Hobby! If he thinks I trundle around with this gadget six days a week, just for the fun of the thing, he's mistaken," the salesman said to himself. Aloud he said: "Oh, that's all right—I can easily get another one, besides"—he might as well admit it— "selling movie cameras happens to be my business."

"Really! I'd no idea. What a happy coincidence that you should decide to visit Jennings today!"

"Er—yes, quite a coincidence. It must have been fate."

The sale was arranged, and soon Mr. Russell was following the Headmaster round the sports field, giving him a lesson in the correct way of using the Grossman Ciné Camera de Luxe.

Raleigh won "Throwing the Cricket Ball." This was unexpected, for Parslow of Drake had a strong arm and was the obvious favourite; but luck was against him, for the ball curved away on its flight, and crashed through the pavilion window.

Darbishire was in the pavilion, getting ready for the half-mile, and he was so startled by the shattering glass, that he shot out of the building at a speed that would not have disgraced a hundred-yards sprinter.

The half-mile was the next event. As it was the longest race, it was usually held last, but the order had been changed because two of the long-jumpers had entered for the 440 and Mr. Carter had decided to give them a longer rest between their events. The half-mile, the 440 and the relay were the only events now remaining for which house points could be scored; the rest of the pro-gramme consisted of odd items such as the egg-and-spoon and the obstacle races, which were not strictly athletic, and did not count towards winning the competition.

Outside the pavilion, Darbishire ran into Jennings, who took one look at him and said:

"Gosh, Darbi, whatever's the matter? Have you got pneumonia?"

The half-miler was wearing his raincoat on top of his overcoat, and his travelling rug was draped round him from shoulder to ankles.

"No, I haven't got pneumonia, but I'll probably get heat stroke any minute now. I've got two sweaters and my blazer on, under this."

"Whatever for?"

"It says you should, in that book on athletics I was reading. I copied a few notes down—I've got them somewhere."

The athlete's head disappeared beneath the travelling rug; he dug through the various layers of clothing until he reached his blazer pocket. Then his face emerged, warm but smiling, and he waved an envelope through a gap in the rug.

"It says here," he read out, "*The muscles are stimulated to greater degrees of activity by the maintenance of an optimum body heat*—so I'm maintaining the optimum."

"What's that mean?"

"It means it's spivish hot inside all this clutter. I shall take it off when the race starts, of course. I've eaten a lot more fruit, too," he went on. "Five apples and four bananas since lunch, but somehow, I think the book's wrong about that—it hasn't made me feel I could run much faster."

"Half-mile—Open," Mr. Carter's voice drifted across to them. "Nuttall, Temple, Clarke, MacTaggart, Binns major and Darbishire."

"Oh golly! This is it! Wish me luck, Jen—it's my big moment."

The two boys scampered across to the starting point, Darbishire's rug trailing from his shoulders, and tripping him up every few yards.

"You look like a Red Indian Chief," Jennings told him.

"Never mind what I look like. If it helps me to maintain the optimist, it may do the trick. My father says that—"

"Darbishire!" shouted the other half-milers, impatient to be away.

"All right, I'm coming." His voice was edgy with nervous excitement as he joined the little group gathered round the starter. There was a short interval while Darbishire shed the load of his garments, and Mr. Carter gave them a word of advice.

"You've got to go round the track twice, and it's quite a long way, so don't go too fast to start with. Remember to keep this side of the flags, especially when you're out of sight behind the bushes at the end of the field … On your marks … Get set …"

The crack of the pistol made Darbishire leap like a startled deer, but he soon recovered and settled down to a steady jog-trot.

"Go it, Bod," called Venables, as Temple ran by. "Gosh, I hope he wins. Who do you stick up for, Jennings?"

"Darbishire, of course, but he hasn't got an earthly. He runs like a lobster in elastic-sided boots. He's supersonic at the egg-and-spoon though," he finished loyally.

"We'd better be getting ready," Venables suggested. "It's the 440 yards next."

"Oh, there's bags of time yet—they've only just started."

MacTaggart, known as MacBonk, was in the lead, as the six runners rounded the first bend. Half-way round the course, the white line disappeared behind a small clump of bushes, and for a few seconds the runners were not visible. When they appeared again, Temple was leading and MacTaggart had dropped to second place. Darbishire, remembering Mr. Carter's advice, had not yet reached the bushes, and was plodding along sixty yards in the rear of the leaders.

"Come on, MacBonk … Good old Bonko!" yelled the Drake supporters, as the runners came down the straight on their first lap.

"Run up, Bod!" shouted the House of Raleigh, as Temple strove to increase his lead.

Jennings would have shouted, "Come on, Darbishire," but unfortunately, his friend was so far behind that he was out of earshot.

"Last lap," called Mr. Carter, as Temple and MacTaggart passed him, closely followed by Binns major, Nuttall and Clarke.

"Gosh, it's going to be close," exclaimed Venables, as the runners started on their second lap. "There's not more than ten yards between the lot of them."

"Except for Darbishire," corrected Jennings. "He's still about twenty miles behind."

Darbishire plodded on, doggedly refusing to give up hope. He was disappointed that the trouble he had taken in keeping warm and eating fruit was not *stimulating his muscles to greater degrees of activity* as the book had promised; but there was still a chance that something sensational might happen—a sudden thunderstorm, for instance; perhaps the group of runners two hundred yards ahead would get struck by lightning or attacked by cramp.

He had just completed the first circuit, when his rivals disappeared behind the bushes for the second time, and a moment later Binns major, running strongly, came into view, with Temple and MacTaggart straining to overtake this new rival for first place.

"Now's the time for my extra special burst of speed," Darbishire muttered, and quickened his pace by a good two miles an hour. But the strain began to tell. "Oh, gosh, I wish I hadn't had all those apples," he groaned, as he felt a painful stitch in his side. He struggled on, but the stitch became worse; he would have to take a short rest, or he would never finish the course. He panted to a halt behind the clump of bushes and doubled himself up, touching his toes and drawing in great lungfuls of air. Vaguely, he was aware of the excited tumult in the distance.

"Come on, Bod ... Good old Temple!"

"Go it, Binnski ... Stick to it!"

MacTaggart had dropped to third place, and Binns major and Temple were running neck and neck.

The Headmaster, under Mr. Russell's guidance, was filming every step of the desperate struggle. The white figures flashed past his lens and breasted the tape with inches between them. The cheers swelled, then died away as the result was announced—Binns major first, Temple second, MacTaggart third.

Raleigh roared again, for they had won first and second places and were now three points ahead. In the wave of excitement that billowed across the field, nobody noticed that Darbishire was missing.

"440 yards—under twelve," called Mr. Carter, and Jennings lined up with Venables, Atkinson, Martin-Jones and Rumbelow.

"You're lucky, Venables, having spiked shoes," said Martin-Jones enviously.

Jennings, busily digging footholds with a penknife, remarked: "I'm going to run in my bare feet, if they'll let me. My famous home-made spiked shoes fizzled out into spivish lethal torture, when I put them on."

"Get to your marks," said Mr. Carter. "Hurry up, Jennings—we're all waiting."

"I've got to dig holes to get a good start, sir."

"You needn't dig half-way down to Australia. You'll fall into it, if you dig a pit that size."

"Yes, sir. Please sir, may I run in my bare feet?"

"No. For goodness' sake get to your mark—I'm waiting to start the race."

"Yes, sir."

"It's one lap remember, but don't try to sprint the whole way. On your marks ... Get set ..."

There was a sharp report and the race had started.

Darbishire recovered his breath behind the clump of bushes. His stitch was better, and he felt ready to go on. Although he knew the race was over, wise words of his father's about *Never saying die*, and *Going on to the bitter end*, floated into his mind. No one should say that C. E. J. Darbishire gave up and failed to finish the course.

He ran on, leaving the cover of the bushes as Jennings, with Venables close on his heels, rounded the first bend, eighty yards behind him.

The going was fast and the spectators were cheering with mounting excitement, as the Headmaster seized the ciné camera from its case.

"Quick, Mr. Russell," he said, "am I holding it properly?"

"Have a look through the view-finder," replied his instructor. "What can you see?"

"They're just disappearing behind the bushes," said the Headmaster, holding the camera to his eye, and a moment later he exclaimed: "Here they come; they're out on the other side. Venables is running third, Jennings is second and ... Who is that boy in front?"

He narrowed his eyes, and then opened them wide in surprise. "Good heavens, it's Darbishire! ... Run up, Darbishire, faster, boy, faster."

"Jennings is gaining on him," shouted Mr. Russell, as excited as any Form I boy.

"He won't do it," cried the Headmaster. "Darbishire's lead is too great ... Run up, Darbishire, run up ... you'll win, if you stick to it!"

He hurried across to the finishing tape, and the camera whirred into action. Darbishire winning a race was an event not to be missed!

The runners raced down the final straight and surged past the tape—a breathless Darbishire was in the lead, while Jennings, wearing a puzzled look, finished a yard behind him.

"Darbishire first, Jennings second," exclaimed the Headmaster. "Well run, Darbishire! I didn't think you had it in you." But Darbishire had no breath left to reply.

"It's amazing, Carter," the Headmaster went on, as his assistant approached. "I never thought that boy would beat Jennings."

"He didn't," Mr. Carter corrected. "Darbishire wasn't in that race."

"But of course he was in it. He's just won it by a yard. I saw him."

"No, sir. That wasn't Darbishire winning the 440—that was Darbishire coming in last, in the race before!"

From behind him, the Headmaster heard a sound like a wheezy railway engine.

"*Choof-choof-choof-choof!*" Mr. Russell's sense of humour was troubling him again.

CHAPTER 17

THE VITAL CLUE

THERE WAS an interval for lemonade and buns, which were stacked on trestle tables in front of the pavilion. The boys made short work of this, while the visitors retired to the tea tent, where Mrs. Caffey waited upon them with tea and paste sandwiches. Mr. Russell politely refused a second cup of tea, and emerged from the tent to find Jennings waiting for him.

"Oh, please, Mr. Russell, will you try and take a photo of Darbishire in the egg-and-spoon? You can't count him as being in the last race because they made him a displaced person?"

"I'm afraid I can't, Jennings. Your Headmaster has bought the camera now. He went a bit higher than your bid of three and sevenpence, so I sold it to him."

"Oh, cracko!" Jennings flipped his fingers with delight. "That means we shall be able to have films about all sorts of things now. I wonder if he'll let us use it."

"Not if he wants to keep it in one piece," the salesman replied. He was feeling more light-hearted than he had done for years. He had spent a delightful afternoon in pleasant surroundings—it was all so different from his usual dull routine; and in his wallet was a cheque for ninety-five guineas, signed by M. W. B. Pemberton-Oakes. That ought to please Mr. Catchpole! In a sudden burst of generosity, Mr. Russell whipped the wallet from his pocket and took out a ten shilling note.

"By the way, that Latin book you've got to pay for—how much is it?"

"Five shillings, I think."

"Well, here's ten. Call it your commission on the sale of the camera; I shouldn't have sold it, if it hadn't been for you."

"Oh, no, really Mr. Russell. I couldn't possibly," Jennings protested. "It's awfully decent of you, but I'd rather not—you've done more than enough for me, already."

Nothing could persuade Jennings to accept the present, so Mr. Russell shook hands and prepared to leave. He had telephoned for the village taxi, which drove up as he was making a round of goodbyes.

"I'm so glad to have met you," the Headmaster smiled, "and I'm more than pleased with the camera. It's astonishing how many interesting things one sees, which would be lost for ever, were it not for the camera's all-seeing eye. For instance, I happened to be taking a shot of Mr. Wilkins drinking a cup of tea outside the tent, when Mr. Carter accidentally let the starting-pistol off just behind him; and I now have a permanent photographic record of Mr. Wilkins' facial expression as he spilt the cup of tea on his knees. Most diverting. Ha! ha! ha!"

The camera had done much to take the Headmaster's mind off the depressing subject of the burglary, and he was in a jovial mood as he shook hands with his guest.

"Goodbye, Mr. Russell," he said as the salesman stepped into the waiting taxi. "And you will remember me to the family next time you see them, won't you?"

"Family? Which family?"

"Mr. Jennings, of course. Mr. Jennings of Haywards Heath."

"Mr. Jennings of Haywards Heath! Suddenly something clicked in Mr. Russell's mind, and he remembered clearly where his old business acquaintance lived. It was a disturbing memory, and it worried his conscience.

"Oh, yes, Mr. Jennings, of course. By the way, Headmaster, I've just remembered something."

"Oh, and what's that?"

"I've just remembered that the Mr. Jennings that I know lives at Weston-super-Mare."

The taximan, anxious to be off, let in the clutch and Mr. Russell disappeared down the drive, leaving a puzzled M. W. B. Pemberton-Oakes, Esq., behind him.

"Now, whatever did he mean by that?" he asked himself, and sent Bromwich minor to find Jennings.

They were lining up for the egg-and-spoon race when the message was delivered. Jennings had not entered for this, and he was giving Darbishire some last minute coaching in the art of egg balancing.

"You're wanted by the Arch-beako," Bromwich minor announced cheerfully. "I don't know what's up, but I should say he's briefing himself for a roof-level attack."

Jennings sensed trouble looming up again and went in search of the Headmaster; he found him staring thoughtfully down the drive.

"Yes, sir?"

"Oh, yes, Jennings—didn't you tell me that Mr. Russell was a friend of your family."

"No, *he* said that, sir—I didn't," Jennings replied. "He told me he thought he might be, but he couldn't be sure."

The Headmaster was mystified. "But if he isn't a family friend, why on earth should he come down here to see you? The school rules are most particular on that point."

"Well, sir—you see, sir, it was like this, sir."

How could he explain? There seemed to be school rules about everything— perhaps about writing for catalogues, and certainly about encouraging salesmen to pay visits. Jennings was wondering where to begin, when Mr. Carter suddenly announced the start of the egg-and-spoon race.

"Sir, aren't you going to film the egg-and-spoon, sir?" Jennings said quickly. "It ought to be a jolly decent race for your camera, sir, with everybody dropping their eggs all over the place, sir."

"Don't prevaricate, Jennings. I want to get this business of Mr. Russell straightened out. I am at a loss to understand—"

He glanced towards the running-track as the starting-pistol fired, and was so amused by what he saw that he postponed his awkward questions, and reached for his camera.

The sudden shot had made Atkinson jump; his egg leapt up into the air, and he was making frantic efforts to catch it in his spoon, before it reached the ground.

"Oh, sir, do look at Atkinson, sir," implored Jennings, anxious to keep the Headmaster's attention as far away as possible from questions about unlawful visitors. "And Darbishire, too, sir. He's having an awful lot of trouble with his egg, sir."

Darbishire's expression was a study in earnest concentration, as he battled against overwhelming odds. His egg was wobbling on his spoon and his spectacles were wobbling on his nose. Before he had gone very far, his egg was bouncing about on his spoon like a ping-pong ball.

"By Jove, yes! I mustn't miss this," said Mr. Pemberton-Oakes. "Now, let me see: I think I'd better track forwards for a medium close-shot. Stand back, you boys, you're in the way."

The camera whirred and the cheers rose, as the competitors spooned their china eggs unsteadily through the air. Collisions were frequent, and the Headmaster laughed so much that he had difficulty in holding the camera steady.

"Look at Darbishire, sir," laughed Jennings. "He's dropped his egg and his glasses have come off, and now he can't find his glasses to look for his egg!"

The egg-and-spoon race, however, was over all too soon, and again the Headmaster started his investigations. With a heavy heart, Jennings told the story of the Grossman Ciné Camera advertisement; of the letter asking for the catalogue, and the unexpected arrival of the salesman.

Mr. Pemberton-Oakes looked stern when Jennings had finished. "This is most disturbing," he said. "It appears that I have been entertaining a false impression of the status of this Mr. Russell, and I feel that the matter is of sufficient importance for me to take certain steps."

"Oh, but please, sir, really sir—" Jennings urged desperately. It had been such a splendid afternoon that he could not bear to think of it ending in disaster—the third disaster since breakfast. But the Headmaster's face was forbidding as he continued.

"My considered opinion, therefore, is that if Mr. Russell is not a friend of your family—" he paused in thought while his eye travelled round the playing field, noting the happy, excited atmosphere created by seventy-eight boys enjoying themselves to the full. Now, thanks to this Mr. Russell and his camera, that happy atmosphere had been captured for ever. He turned to his seventy-ninth boy, who stood unhappily before him, and his stern expression relaxed.

"If Mr. Russell is not already a friend of your family," he said, "he most certainly deserves to be one in future."

Jennings mumbled his heartfelt thanks and made his escape, as the sound of a car was heard coming up the drive. Mr. Pemberton-Oakes stepped forward expecting the new arrival to be General Merridew; and a shadow of annoyance passed over his face as he saw that it was not the General, but Sergeant Hutchinson returning to continue his investigations.

This was the third false alarm in ten minutes. The first time it had been Mr. Russell's taxi, then the Dunhambury Float Iron Laundry van had rattled up the drive on its way to collect the hampers from the sanatorium. The Headmaster was becoming anxious; it was essential for him to have a few words with the General before the sports ended, so that he could prepare his important guest for the unpleasant shock which awaited him.

The police car stopped and Sergeant Hutchinson stepped out. "Good afternoon, sir. Will it be all right for us to carry on now, or are we too early?"

"You are rather early," replied the Headmaster. "You see, I'm expecting a distinguished Old Linburian to arrive any moment now. He happens to be the donor of the largest of the stolen cups, and I am afraid he will be most distressed—as indeed we all are—when he hears the sad news." He lowered his voice: "Quite frankly, Sergeant, I'm not at all sure how he'll take it, and I'm most anxious that his first impression will not be of—er—um—"

"You mean he won't like it if he finds the place knee-deep in policemen?"

"Well—I should hesitate to put it quite like that, but I think it might be better if you and your constable, were to—ah—um—"

"Make ourselves scarce. Very good, sir."

Sergeant Hutchinson got back into the car; he drove past the running track and stopped out of sight behind the clump of bushes at the end of the field.

"Coo, look Darbi, there's that policeman again," said Jennings, as the car passed them. "Gosh, I do feel mad about letting him down over that clue I lost."

"And you were going to tell him your suspicions about Old Nightie, too, don't forget."

"Yes, I know. I wonder if he'll think they're important. I don't want him to think I'm making something up, just because I bished up the vital clue."

"Perhaps he'll think you made that up too," suggested Darbishire. "After all, he's only got your word that there ever *was* a button."

"But you can prove that, can't you?"

"Well, I wouldn't like to swear to it, because I hadn't got my glasses on properly, and if you remember I was feeling a bit too much up a gum tree to take things in at the time. My father says that you should never—"

"Oh, you're crackers," Jennings retorted. "Anyway, Mr. Carter and Old Wilkie saw it, so that proves it."

"Well, why don't you ask them to go and tell him?"

"Okay, I will."

They trotted across to Mr. Carter, who was busy organising the start of the relay. It was the final event and confined to the older boys, and as the score between the houses stood level, the result would decide the whole contest.

Mr. Carter seldom allowed anything to disturb his usual calm, and in the middle of directing eight highly-tensed runners to their stations and listening to Mr. Wilkins complaining about the stopwatch, he still had part of one ear available for Jennings' inquiry.

"... and I thought that as I've lost it, sir, you might be willing to tell the policeman, because Darbishire says he might not really believe me, sir. And you know it's true, don't you, sir?—because I had it in my dressing gown pocket last night when I showed you and Mr. Wilkins, and this morning it wasn't there, sir."

Mr. Carter brought his mind to bear on the problem, and ignoring the impatience of Mr. Wilkins and the feverish excitement of the relay teams, he said: "I can remember your taking the button out of your dressing gown, but I can't remember your putting it back there. In fact, now I come to think of it, I believe you put it back in the pocket of your pyjama jacket."

"Gosh, yes," Jennings gasped. "Of course I did! I remember now, sir. Golly, what a bish not thinking that before. Thank you a million times, sir." And he dashed away in the direction of the school buildings.

"Here, wait for me," panted Darbishire. "Not so fast! You seem to forget that I've run one half-mile already this afternoon—well, more or less."

Jennings slackened speed. "I'm going to get the button, so's I can give it to the sergeant."

"Well, what's the hurry? Finding the button doesn't catch the thief, does it?"

"No, I know, but it's a clue; and besides, it'll show the sergeant I'm not such a bad detective as everyone makes out. After all, I'm the head of the Linbury Court Detective Agency and I've got my reputation to think about. If Sherlock Holmes lost a button, what would he do?"

"Use a safety-pin."

"Oh, you're bats!" said Jennings. "If he lost a valuable clue, and then someone gave him a clue about where this clue might be—like Mr. Carter has—he'd be after it in a flash."

"Well, we'd better get a move on, or we shall miss the relay."

"I was getting a move on, and you stopped me. Come on, let's hurry."

Into the building, up the stairs and along the empty corridors they raced at top speed, until they reached the dormitory. Jennings rushed to his bed and tore back the bedclothes and then, with growing concern, groped under his pillow and searched the floor beneath the bed.

It was all to no purpose—his pyjamas were nowhere to be found.

CHAPTER 18

PERILOUS JOURNEY

JENNINGS AND DARBISHIRE stood and stared at each other in bewilderment.

"This is crazy," Jennings burst out. "They *must* be about somewhere, and I know I didn't leave them in the bathroom, so where are they?"

"Perhaps there's been another burglary," suggested Darbishire.

"Oh, don't be so bats. Who'd want to pinch my pyjamas?"

"Old Nightie, of course, so's he could destroy the evidence."

"But he'd only take the button—he wouldn't beetle off with the whole jacket. I suppose I must have dumped it somewhere, when I was getting a move on to go and see Sergeant Hutchinson before breakfast."

Darbishire started searching, in the hope that Jennings had put his pyjamas in somebody else's bed, by mistake.

"That's funny," he exclaimed with a puzzled expression. "Atkinson's had his pyjamas pinched too!"

He rushed to his own bed, and then to Temple's and Venables', and his face was grave as he looked up and propounded his theory: "Somewhere," he announced, "there must be a vast, black-market network of second-hand, stolen pyjamas. There isn't a single pyjam left in the whole dorm!"

Then Jennings remembered. It was Wednesday—when they always had clean pyjamas, and the dirty ones were sent to the laundry.

He sank down on his bed, deep in gloom. If only he had remembered before! Now it was too late, and the clue had vanished for ever. His pyjamas would not be back from the laundry for a week, and it was most unlikely that the button would still be in the pocket.

"What super-rotten-sonic luck!" he muttered. Now that the vital clue had really vanished, it seemed even more important than it had done before. He had no notion of the almost impossible task that he had been expecting Sergeant Hutchinson to accomplish—a task which might have included the examination of every sports jacket in Sussex and beyond. To Jennings, a clue was a clue, and any detective worthy of the name should be able to put it to some useful purpose.

Outside on the running track, the starting pistol sounded for the last time.

"Oh, golly, and we've missed watching the relay," Darbishire said in dismay. They hurried to the window and were in time to see the first pair of runners tearing along the track. Raleigh carried a baton bound with magenta ribbon, and Drake had a similar one in white.

"There they go," shouted Jennings, forgetting his worries in the new excitement. "Old Hippo's beefing it like mad. Run up, Hippo!"

Together they yelled encouragement, though their words were lost in the general uproar that surged up from the field below. R. K. Stoddington, the Drake House captain, was living up to the zoological nickname, and charged along the course with all his might. He was the largest boy in the school, and although only thirteen and a half, he was already five-feet-nine, and growing rapidly.

The second pair of runners were hopping up and down, marking time at the double, as though they could hardly wait to seize the baton and dash off on the next stage of the race. The Raleigh runner was five yards in the rear, as R. K. (Hippo) Stoddington thrust the baton into the waiting hand of his colleague. Together they ran a few paces as the exchange was made, and then the Drake House captain sank exhausted on the grass, blowing and snorting like his namesake of the African rivers.

"Go it, Flybow!" yelled Jennings and Darbishire in unison, as Flittonborough major streaked round the field, now ten yards ahead of his Raleigh opponent.

Then came disaster. Flittonborough major dropped the baton in the act of passing it to Wyatt, the third Drake runner, and precious seconds were wasted. Raleigh shot ahead, and the watchers in the dormitory grandstand moaned aloud as their man got off to a bad start, twelve yards behind the vanishing heels of his rival.

The next section of the track was not visible from the dormitory, for a corner of the classroom block jutted out and obscured the view; and Jennings and Darbishire could only wait with growing impatience until the final pair should streak into sight, fifty yards from the finishing tape.

"It's no good," Darbishire muttered. "We shall never make up the distance after a bish like that." They strained their eyes ahead, and soon the last Raleigh runner flashed into the straight, pursued by Pringle of Drake, only six yards behind.

"Come on Drake!" Jennings yelled. "Go it Pringo!"

He was too far away to see the set expression on the runners' faces; too far, also, to judge whether Pringle was gaining fast enough to sway the result. They watched spellbound now, forgetting even to cheer, while Pringle cut down his rival's lead to inches, then drew level. As they shot past the tape, the cheering on the field rose to a thunderous roar, but the two boys could not make out which side was being acclaimed the winner.

"I think it's Raleigh," Jennings argued. "It looked like a dead-heat from here, but they wouldn't be kicking up all that hoo-hah if nobody had won, would they?"

"We should have stayed out on the field," complained Darbishire. "Now we'll have to wait until—"

"Ssh!" said Jennings.

The cheering died away to a rumble, and Mr. Wilkins' voice could be heard, soaring at full volume across the surrounding acres.

"Re-lay result," he boomed. "Drake House is the winner."

"Hooray!" Jennings hurled himself at Darbishire, and they wrestled happily on Temple's bed, until Darbishire's glasses fell off, and the match was abandoned.

"Good old Drake!" they shouted to the empty dormitory, and danced wildly round the room like a nightmare *corps de ballet*.

Again Mr. Wilkins' voice floated in through the window, adding stop-press news to his last announcement.

"Time for the relay—58.9 seconds ... Distance—six inches."

"Six inches," echoed Darbishire. "The man's mad! They had to run more than a hundred yards each, and you couldn't take fifty-eight seconds—"

"No, you ancient relic. He means there were only six inches between the runners, when they finished. If Pringo had been a bit thinner, we might even have lost."

"Well, we didn't anyway. And the next thing is the line-up for the old General—I haven't seen him anywhere, and it's time he got cracking on the—" Darbishire stopped short. That wretched burglary *would* keep cropping up to wither the bloom of everyone's enjoyment.

Jennings hung out of the window. He was overjoyed that Drake had won, but now that the cheering had died away, there was nothing to take his mind off his failure to retrieve the vital clue. Below him, on the playing field, Mr. Topliss, Mr. Hind and other members of the staff were shepherding the boys in the direction of the pavilion steps, where they were to stand to welcome the

General's arrival. The Headmaster was looking at his watch and peering down the drive; it was twenty minutes to five, and there was still no sign of the important visitor.

As Jennings watched the scene, his gaze travelled round and came to rest on the front door of the sanatorium. Suddenly, his eyes sparkled, and he yelled aloud.

"Quick, Darbi, quick. It hasn't gone yet!"

"What hasn't gone?"

"The laundry. The van's still there—come on, we may just do it, if we run."

Jennings pelted down the stairs two at a time, and took the last four in one enormous leap. Darbishire descended by banister rail, and together the two detectives raced out of the building and across the quadrangle. They took no notice of their friends streaming towards the pavilion, and lining up in straight, orderly files in front of the steps.

They arrived, panting and breathless, to find the van still standing outside the cottage. The baskets had all been loaded, and snatches of conversation from the hall suggested that Les Perks, the driver, was arguing with Ivy about a missing sheet.

"Come on," said Jennings. "Let's see if we can find my pyjamas," and he climbed in through the open doors at the back of the van.

"But what about the driver chap? Hadn't we better tell him?"

"Yes, we will when he comes out, but he won't want to hang about all day. We'll get cracking and see if we can find them first."

There were eight large hampers piled up inside the van, and fortunately, they all bore labels of what they contained. *Dormitory* 4 was marked on the basket at the far end nearest the driver's cab, and the boys scrambled over the other hampers to the object of their search. First, they had to lift another hamper, marked *Dormitory* 6 *and Dining Hall*, from the top of the pile. It was heavy, but they managed to bump it down and stack it behind them.

Jennings fumbled with the straps, and then threw open the lid of the *Dormitory* 4 hamper. On the top was a pile of night clothes. Atkinson's pyjama trousers were dragged out, and beneath them, Jennings could see the distinctive red and white stripe of his own jacket.

"Here it is, Darbi!" he whispered breathlessly, as his fingers fumbled for the pocket, and a moment later he was smiling in triumph and clutching a small brown button.

326

"Gosh, what a bit of luck, and only just in—"

There was a loud bang behind them and the van doors slammed shut. Footsteps scrunched on the gravel, and the next moment someone leapt into the driver's seat and pressed the starter.

"Hey, quick, open the doors!" yelled Jennings, and Darbishire groped his way past the hampers to the rear of the van. It was practically dark inside, now that the doors were shut, and only a gleam of light shone through the little window in the partition which separated them from the driver.

Darbishire reached the rear doors. "I don't know how to open them," he called back, in a worried tone, "and I can't see."

"Oh, gosh, this is awful," Jennings muttered. "The driver doesn't know we're here and he'll be starting off in a—"

It was unnecessary to finish the sentence, for at that moment Leslie Perks let in the clutch, and the van reversed slowly down the little garden path. He was unaware that he had passengers, and the ancient van creaked and rattled so loudly with the engine in low gear, that their shouts for help were inaudible.

They were still jolting in reverse, when the *Dormitory* 4 laundry basket toppled from the pile of hampers on which it was balancing and overturned. Jennings was knocked off his feet, and for a moment all was confusion in the darkened interior. Darbishire beat loudly on the rear doors, and Jennings found himself kneeling amongst a jumbled pile of socks, shirts, vests, handkerchiefs and pyjamas that gave little jumps with each jolt of the vehicle.

He put out his hand to steady himself, and in the dim light his fingers touched something unexpectedly solid.

He groped again, and felt rounded contours and jutting handles, and then, scarcely able to believe his senses, he pulled the Merridew Sports Cup from its protective pile of soiled linen.

"Gosh," he gasped. "Darbi—quick, quick!"

"I'm being as quick as I can," replied the dim form of Darbishire, "but I still can't find the handle thing."

Jennings didn't stop to explain. He was convinced now that Old Nightie was the thief—any casual burglar would have taken the cup away with him, but a nightwatchman who lived on the premises would find it safer to remove it under cover of the laundry van's weekly visit. He had no time to wonder how Old Nightie was going to reclaim his stolen property, for something had to be done at once to stop the van.

Jennings struggled to his feet and peered through the little window of the driver's cab. He could see the man's left hand resting on the steering wheel, and the next moment he saw something that checked his knuckles in the act of rapping on the glass. The driver's jacket was brown, and one of the buttons was missing from his cuff!

Jennings' mind worked at full speed. In two seconds, Old Nightie had left the court without a stain on his character, and his place in the dock was taken by Les Perks, in his brown jacket. In a flash, he recalled the scene some weeks earlier, when he had helped the driver in his quest for Mr. Wilkins' laundry, and the man had wandered off into the library.

"No harm in having a look round, is there?" The words came back to him, as he swayed in the semi-darkness of the rickety van. Many details were still obscure, but the main point was plain—the thief was making off with his booty right under the nose of the police. And if something didn't happen soon, the thief would be making off with the two amateur detectives as well.

Holding the cup in one hand, he scrambled along the van to Darbishire, who was still fumbling with the catch on the double doors.

"It's no good, Jen," he gasped. "It must be stuck or something. Whatever shall we do?"

"Here, let me have a go." And Jennings set to work, rattling the catch vigorously.

"The man will be ever so cross when he finds he's got us all mixed up with the dirty washing," said Darbishire, who had no idea of the sensational discovery which his friend had just made. "We shall have to apologise and everything. Oh, gosh, I wonder how far we've gone."

The sanatorium was far behind. The van crossed the quadrangle, passed the main buildings and turned to follow the long line of the drive to the school gates. Before it reached the yew-lined avenue, it skirted one end of the running track and passed in front of the pavilion steps. Here, Perks slowed down, as his path was blocked by lines of boys in bright blazers, patiently waiting for General Merridew to arrive.

The staff were gathered on the pavilion steps, and Mr. Hind marched forward and cleared a way through the throng of boys, and signalled the driver to come on. Slowly, the van edged its way through and began to pick up speed again. The next moment, masters, boys and visitors were gaping in stupefied amazement, unable to believe their eyes.

The double doors at the back of the van shot open and Jennings was revealed, clutching the Merridew Sports Cup in one hand, while the other waved wildly in his efforts to prevent himself from falling headlong out of the back. Beside him stood a dishevelled Darbishire, blinking in the sudden light and swaying dangerously as the van gathered speed.

For a moment no one moved. Then Mr. Carter seized the megaphone from Bromwich major and shouted to the police car at the far end of the track. Mr. Wilkins charged down the drive in the wake of the van, but soon realised that he was unable to run at thirty-five miles per hour, and retired "Corwumphing" with exasperation.

The school seethed with excitement and wonder.

"Gosh, what's happening?"

"Didn't you see?"

"Yes, of course I saw, but what's it all about?"

"Perhaps they're being kidnapped!"

"Don't be so crazy. More likely they took the cup themselves, just for a joke."

"They wouldn't do a thing like that!"

"Well, why are they hoofing off in the van, then?"

"I don't know."

Nobody knew what was happening, though there were plenty of wild guesses. Binns minor was so excited that he hopped up and down, flipping his fingers and barking like a sea-lion. Then he bit his tongue by accident, and became very quiet.

The Headmaster stood quite still and stared at the disappearing figures with an expression of horror and alarm. The next moment, the sleek, black police car was at his side—the constable at the wheel, and Sergeant Hutchinson standing on the off-side running-board. Mr. Carter flung open the door, pushed the Headmaster inside, and scrambled in after him, as the car streaked off in pursuit.

Round the first bend they overtook Mr. Wilkins, glaring down the drive in baffled fury. As they drew level, he leapt on the near-side running-board, and Mr. Carter shot his hand out of the rear window and steadied the floundering thirteen-stone-six, with a firm grasp.

"They went that way!" Mr. Wilkins shouted, waving his free hand wildly at the drive in front of them.

"Naturally," Mr. Carter replied calmly. "There's no other way they could have gone."

The constable accelerated, and round the next bend they sighted the laundry van in the distance, jolting along towards the gates. Jennings and Darbishire were still standing in the back, and as soon as they saw the police car, Jennings waved the Merridew Sports Cup above his head.

"Gosh, look, Darbi, they've got on our trail. Oh, wizzo!"

"Thank goodness," Darbishire sighed with relief. "I don't like this a bit. My father says that—"

What Darbishire's father said was never revealed, for at that moment Leslie Perks caught sight of the police car in his driving mirror. He had been feeling quite sure of himself until then, for he knew nothing of his passengers in the back, and even the shouts of Mr. Wilkins had failed to make themselves heard above the noisy engine.

At first, he decided to take no notice; if he were stopped he would plead ignorance of what the hampers contained; but he could not help feeling worried by the purposeful stance of Sergeant Hutchinson on the running-board. Then he glanced over his shoulder through the little window behind him, and caught a brief glimpse of the wide-open doors, and a figure brandishing a silver cup out of the back.

Leslie Perks was not an experienced thief, and this was the first time that he had tried his hand at housebreaking. Immediately, he became flustered, and without stopping to think, he plunged his foot down on the accelerator, in a desperate effort to shake off his pursuers. The old van swayed drunkenly on its creaking springs, and in the back, boys and baskets were tossed about as the vehicle lurched forward protestingly.

"Oh, this is dreadful!" Darbishire's teeth were rattling with the vibration, and he clung to a wobbling pile of baskets for dear life. "Why do these ghastly things always have to pick on me to happen to?" he wanted to know.

The police car was gaining rapidly, as they approached the wrought-iron gates standing open at the end of the drive, and the van plunged on towards the blind corner at reckless speed. Shaking in every nut and bolt and with its engine flat out, it had reached a point barely ten yards from the main road, when a grey Rolls Royce purred quietly in through the main gates and blocked its path.

With screeching brakes the van swerved crazily, mounted the bank, and shuddered to a halt in the hedge; and a moment later, as the police car reached the scene, two figures leapt from the running-boards and rushed up the bank in pursuit.

From the Rolls Royce stepped Lieut.-General Sir Melville Merridew Bart., D.S.O., M.C.—purple with rage.

"You—you wretched road hog!" he spluttered in the direction of the laundry van. "What on earth do you think you're doing—hey?"

He caught sight of the Headmaster amongst the figures dashing between drive and hedge, and barked: "Look here, Pemberton-Oakes, what's going on? What's the meaning of—?"

"One moment, General," the Headmaster broke in, "a state of emergency has arisen. We are trying to catch a burglar."

"Splendid, splendid," retorted the General, who always enjoyed states of emergency. "Anything I can do?"

"Yes, you can hold this for me." The Headmaster thrust a ciné camera into the astonished General's hands, and hurried off into the hedge, to make sure that Jennings and Darbishire had come to no harm.

General Merridew was a man of action. He had no notion of what was going on, but he found himself with a camera in his hands, and a scene of confusion before him. So he put the camera to his eye and pressed the switch.

CHAPTER 19

WEDNESDAY EVENING MASTERPIECE

So MANY things were happening at once that no one, except the General, had a very clear picture of the scene as a whole. Leslie Perks had leapt from his seat when the engine stalled, and dashed back on to the drive in an effort to escape through the main gates; but Mr. Wilkins saw him coming, and brought him crashing to the ground with a superb rugger tackle.

Jennings and Darbishire, both badly shaken, scrambled down from the back of the van and assured the anxious Mr. Pemberton-Oakes that they were unhurt.

"Yes, sir, thank you, sir, I'm quite all right, sir," gasped Jennings. "Oh, sir, isn't it corking! I mean, isn't it wonderful, sir? We shall be able to have the cup presented after all."

"Never mind about that," replied the Headmaster. "The main thing is that you two impetuous little boys have suffered no ill-effects."

"We haven't suffered very much yet, sir," said Darbishire, expecting to suffer far worse if the Headmaster should take a serious view of their activities. "We tried to get out before it started, sir, but—"

"Coo, look!" said Jennings, suddenly.

Two hampers had been tossed out of the van when it hit the hedge. One of them had scattered a pile of laundry over the drive, and through the broken wickerwork sides of the other could be seen the outlines of the cricket cup, carefully protected by table napkins.

Mr. Carter opened the other hampers. The soccer cup was nestling at the bottom of a basket marked *Dormitory* 2, the rugger and gymnastics cups were found amongst the staff laundry and roller-towels, and the swimming and boxing trophies came to light amongst the linen of *Dormitories 5 and 6*.

It was too late for the flustered thief to deny all knowledge of what the hampers contained. The fact that he had tried to run away when the van struck the hedge, was a clear indication of guilt, and he offered no further resistance when Mr. Wilkins removed his thirteen-stone-six and got to his feet.

Sergeant Hutchinson scribbled busily in his notebook, and a few minutes later Perks was escorted to the police car, which left soon afterwards for Dunhambury. After that, Mr. Carter drove the van out of the hedge and backed it farther up the drive, where it waited for Sergeant Hutchinson to arrange for its removal.

"Come along, get in," ordered the General, stepping into his Rolls Royce. "It's high time I presented that cup before anyone else tries to make off with it."

The Headmaster sat in front with his guest, and the two boys, with Mr. Carter and Mr. Wilkins, climbed in the back and nursed the seven trophies.

"I still don't quite see what happened," Jennings queried, as the General pressed the starter. "Why didn't he take the cups away with him, last night?"

"Because this way would have been much safer—if it had worked," Mr. Carter replied. "He could use the van only when he was on duty, and if the police had seen him walking through Dunhambury in the middle of the night with a large parcel, he'd certainly have been stopped. I'm afraid we were all a bit off the track in thinking he'd been to the sanatorium first, though."

"You mean he broke into the library to start with, and then took the cups across to the san. with him?" Mr. Wilkins asked.

"Yes. He'd obviously thought it all out, and when Jennings and Darbishire found him, he was hiding the cups in the baskets, ready to drive them away this afternoon. It's unlikely that anyone would have found them, because if you boys hadn't met him, no one would have known he'd ever been there."

"Wait a moment," put in Mr. Wilkins. "Hawkins would have known, wouldn't he?"

"Not last night," said Mr. Carter. "You forget the clinker in the boiler. That chap didn't know about Hawkins. It was just good luck for him that he chose the right night."

"And bad luck for him that we did, too," added Jennings.

But there was one point that still puzzled him. How was it that the cups were not discovered when his pyjamas were packed that morning? It puzzled Mr. Carter, too. But Leslie Perks could have answered it; for he had counted on Ivy's strict routine of adding the pyjamas to the top of the baskets, and not interfering with the carefully packed linen below.

"All the same," Darbishire argued as the pavilion came into sight, "I bet the police would have found them in time. They'd have searched through the baskets this evening, I expect."

"But by this evening, they wouldn't have been there," Mr. Carter reminded him. "I expect he was planning to drive to his house and take the cups out, before going on to the laundry."

The Rolls Royce purred quietly up the drive and stopped in front of the pavilion. The ranks of excited boys straightened as the car approached, and all eyes strained, in the failing light, to see the passengers seated inside. They saw Jennings, pale but triumphant, with Darbishire smiling self-consciously at his side; they saw Mr. Wilkins, grimed with dust and wearing his tie knotted beneath his left ear, in the style usually favoured by Binns minor; they saw the Headmaster, trying to look as though nothing out of the ordinary had happened, and General Merridew looking pleased—as a man of action should be—at the successful outcome of the skirmish by the main gates. Then they saw the Merridew Sports Cup in Mr. Carter's lap, and seventy-seven boyish throats cheered themselves hoarse.

The Headmaster stepped out of the car and raised his hand for silence. The noise ceased at once, and everyone craned forward eagerly. It was clear that Mr. Pemberton-Oakes was about to make an announcement, and the school stood with bated breath to hear the sensational news.

"As we are a few minutes behind schedule," the Headmaster said, "tea will be at six-fifteen this evening, instead of six o'clock."

Not a word about the climax of the most exciting event of the term! Seething with thwarted curiosity, the boys made their way into the lighted pavilion; in baffled silence they listened as General Merridew was introduced, and talked for twenty-five endless minutes about school days being the happiest time of his life.

Late that evening, Mr. Carter knocked out his pipe and glanced at the clock on his study mantelpiece. It was time he started off on his nightly tour of the dormitories. The General had gone, after asking for a half-holiday and presenting his cup, which once more occupied the place of honour in the library. This time, however, the white ribbon of Drake was tied round its stand instead of the magenta of Raleigh, and H. Higgins, Jeweller and Silversmith, would soon be engraving the name of the new winner on the trophy's side.

The fame of the Linbury Court Detective Agency had spread round the school during the evening; its health had been drunk in the dining hall at cocoa-time, and gargled in the dormitories at bedtime. The Headmaster, however, had drunk no healths. He was pleased that the burglar had been caught and the challenge cups returned, but he was distressed at the way in which it had happened.

"You see, Carter," he had explained to his assistant, after lights out, "they might easily have run into danger. However good their intentions were, they had no business to allow their zeal to outrun their discretion in this disturbing manner. Frankly, I am in a quandary. They assure me that their journey in the van was accidental, and was the result of being unable to alight before the vehicle started. Am I to punish them for breaking school rules, or congratulate them on restoring stolen property?"

"I'll have a word with them tomorrow if you like, sir," Mr. Carter had promised. "I think perhaps I can guide their interests away from detection, and give them something more suitable to do."

"I wish you would." The Headmaster had sounded relieved. "Perhaps it would be as well if you were to absorb their energies in another chess tournament. Admirable game, chess—there's nothing like it for developing the powers of quiet, thoughtful concentration."

When Mr. Carter reached Dormitory 4, he found that Jennings was still awake.

"Hallo, sir," he said, in a loud whisper.

"Aren't you asleep yet, Jennings?"

"No, sir—I'm much too excited. Darbishire is, though, sir. He was just telling me what his father always says about something, and he dropped off in the middle. But I don't feel like going to sleep yet, sir—I want to go on thinking about the burglary and whether Sherlock Holmes would have done what I did … And I've thought of a wizard game we could play next time it rains on a half-holiday, sir—all about detectives, sir."

Mr. Carter sighed as he sat down on the bed.

"Oh, Jennings, whatever am I going to make of you? The harder I try to turn you into a quiet and peaceable citizen, the worse you get."

"Sorry, sir."

"This business of playing at detectives has got to stop. I know I thrust Sherlock Holmes at you, but I had no idea it was going to lead to all this. So from now on, no more Linbury Court Detective Agency—understand?"

"Yes, sir."

There was a short pause, broken only by the heavy breathing of the sleepers around them; then Jennings said: "Sir, is Sergeant Hutchinson a detective, sir?"

"No, I don't think so. Not all policemen are detectives; why?"

"Well, I was thinking, sir, if we're not allowed to play detectives, would it be all right if we played ordinary policemen who *aren't* detectives? You see," he hurried on, "Venables, or someone, could be a burglar and Atkinson could be locked in a room like Darbishire and I were—only it'd have to be behind the boot-lockers really—and Darbishire could be the telephone exchange, if we can get a new battery for the Morse buzzer, and I could be a police sergeant, sir. And then, we could pretend that the tuck-boxes were police cars and laundry vans, and things—"

"And then you'd all rush round the corridors with your arms rotating like roundabouts, and bump into me whenever I turned a corner. Sorry, Jennings—it won't do. Why can't you play something quiet—chess, for instance?"

"Oh, but sir, the Head won't let me. He said it made too much noise the last time I played."

"I think he might stretch a point, if you were really keen."

"Well, all right then, sir," Jennings conceded. "We could bring that in too. We could give Venables, or whoever the burglar was, twenty years in prison, and then we could take it in turns to be warders and go and play chess with the lonely convict, to cheer him up a bit, in his cell—only it'd have to be behind the boot-lockers really, sir ..."

For several minutes the eager voice prattled on in the darkness, while Mr. Carter sat on the bed and listened to the imaginings of Jennings' mind. Then the prattle became slower, like a gramophone beginning to run down, and finally, it slurred off into sleepy fragments and stopped altogether.

Everything was quiet now; and so much had happened in the last twenty-four hours, that Mr. Carter was more than thankful that life was back to normal. From where he sat, the master could see the sanatorium and the silhouetted form of Old Nightie, as he moved, mop in hand, in front of the lighted windows.

When he looked down again, he saw that the principal of the former Linbury Court Detective Agency was fast asleep.

Mr. Carter crept quietly from the dormitory and returned to his room. It had been a tiring day and he was quite ready for bed; but one task yet remained to be done. He took a sheet of paper from his desk, and started to work out the details of a long and complicated chess tournament which would occupy Jennings' spare moments for the rest of the term.

"This won't leave much time for Sherlock Holmes," Mr. Carter murmured to himself, as he laid down his pen.

Every Wednesday evening, the boys hang up the screen in the common room and the Headmaster fixes the projector. Many of the films are old ones that they have seen before, but this in no way spoils their interest. The boys sit close up to the screen and watch "Rice Growing in China" and "Plant Life in the Andes" as though they were attending the première of the latest Hollywood production. After this, comes a two-minute newsreel of the house boxing finals, or the rugger match against Bracebridge School, and these are watched for the twentieth time with an enthusiasm that never grows stale.

Sometimes, the Headmaster includes the most popular film of all— "Sports Day at Linbury." Everyone has seen it over and over again, but it is such an epic of the screen that the room grows tense with excitement, when the title flickers into view.

"Oh, wizzo, it's the sports again! Super-duper-sonic!" exclaims the audience.

"Look, there's the start of the hundred-yards. Gosh, look at old Hippo, hoofing like a fire engine!"

"Watch out for the next bit—I'm in that. You can just see the back of my heel, if you look in the bottom corner."

Mr. Russell was a skilful cameraman. The common room gasps with wonder, as the high-jumpers soar up into the air; then it crouches in mock terror, as the long-jumpers seem to hurl themselves off the screen, right into the lap of the enthralled audience.

Darbishire enjoys the finish of the 440 yards better than anything else. He knows, and everyone knows, what really happened, but he can never suppress his excitement when he sees himself pounding towards the tape—a clear yard in front of Jennings. It is the nearest that Darbishire will ever get to appearing in an Olympic Games newsreel, and he enjoys it to the full.

"It's the egg-and-spoon, in a minute. Do watch Rumbelow—he's got his mouth wide open, as though he's trying to eat it!"

"Yes, I know, and Atkinson looks as though he's playing tennis with his!"

The biggest laugh of the evening is always reserved for Mr. Wilkins outside the tea tent. There is a puff of smoke from the starting pistol in the background, and the teacup jumps into the air and lands upside-down on his knee. The Headmaster had intended to cut this scene out, but his assistant would not hear of it; and no one laughs louder than Mr. Wilkins, as a coloured close-up of his enraged expression fills the screen, and his lips move in a soundless *"Corwumph!"*

There are glimpses of Mr. Carter starting the races; of Bromwich major wearing the megaphone on his head; of the dropped baton in the relay, and the neck-and-neck finish at the tape. But it is after all this has passed, that the film works up to its gripping climax.

The Headmaster always insists that he was photographing the boys lining up before the pavilion steps, and had no intention of including the Dunhambury Float Iron Laundry van in the picture. When the van doors were flung open, he was so surprised that he forgot to switch off the camera for some seconds, and the shot of Jennings and Darbishire's anxious faces as the van recedes, is always hailed with cheers by Binns minor and his colleagues in Form I.

"Ssh!" says the rest of the audience sternly, and leans forward to watch the last act of the drama.

It opens with some confused photography caused by General Merridew's lack of skill as a cameraman. Blurred figures and leaning backgrounds suggest that the General must have been looping the loop when he recorded the pictures, but these distorted fragments soon drop into an ordered pattern. There are brief shots of running feet—then legs, and finally the complete figure of Mr. Wilkins flying through the air to bring off the rugger tackle of a lifetime. This part of the film is often commended to the first XV as a perfect demonstration of tackling low.

Then the camera's eye rests on the laundry baskets, and low gasps of wonder fill the common room as Mr. Carter brings the sports cup to light.

"What a swizz we didn't know he was taking photos," Darbishire whispers to Jennings in the darkness. "We don't look a bit like detectives—I'm hopping about like a cat on hot bricks, and you look as though you'd just seen the ghost of Hamlet's father. Still, my father says that you can never judge people by appearances and—"

"I should wizard well hope not," Jennings whispers back. "Why, I bet even Sherlock Holmes would look a bit of a chronic ruin, if he'd just been through a frantic hoo-hah like that."

There is a shot of Mr. Carter with an armful of trophies and a close-up of Jennings, trying to look unconcerned as he hugs the Merridew Sports Cup to his chest. Then the picture fades into inky blackness; the projector whirrs to a stop, and the lights go on.

There is no doubt, in the mind of the audience, that the film is a master-piece.

JENNINGS' LITTLE HUT

CHAPTER 1

THE SQUATTERS

IT WAS only a little hut, but Jennings was very proud of it. He crouched in the low doorway and a glow of happiness warmed him as his gaze drifted round the draughty interior.

Of course, it was still rather muddy he thought, but they could use the planks of the front door for duckboards until they had finished digging the patent drain on the marshy side of the floor. The roof was rather thin on top and the walls were on the bald side, too, but they could easily stop the wind whistling through by collecting a few more reeds and branches. And until Darbishire had finished making his famous ventilating shaft out of that disused drainpipe, it was just as well that they *had* got air-conditioned walls.

All around him, Jennings could hear sounds of activity as neighbouring hut-builders cocooned themselves in their reedy igloos; they had been quick to copy his idea and claim squatters' rights, but it was he who had thought it all out in the first place.

The grounds of Linbury Court Preparatory School were spacious. The main buildings were grouped round the quadrangle; then came the cricket pitches, the Headmaster's garden, and stretches of rough grassland. Past these, and reaching to the limits of the forty-acre estate, was the wood; and in the wood was the pond. It was an obliging sort of pond that seemed to ask for exciting, tracking games to be played round it, and the shrubs and bulrushes growing about its banks almost implored people to build huts in them. Jennings and Darbishire were building a hut together, and they had made up their minds that it was going to be the finest residence in the whole colony, when it was finished.

It was Jennings' third term at Linbury and he was nearly eleven. He was an eager, rather impetuous boy with a wide-awake look in his eyes and a head of brown hair that no comb could keep parted for long. As he knelt on the soggy clay floor, loud metallic bangings came from an inner compartment at the far end of the hut.

"Don't kick up such a frantic hoo-hah, Darbishire," Jennings called. "Can't you hammer a bit more quietly?"

From the inner sanctum, a pink and white face, topped with fair curly hair, peered out. It was a serious face with spectacles.

"I'd like to see you do better!" it said. "It's pretty tricky making a famous prefabricated ventilating shaft, when you've only got your shoe to hammer with. I wouldn't be surprised if it's not dangerous, too, because I've got those sort of iron horseshoe things on my heel, and every time I wallop the drainpipe, it sparks like a welding machine." The craftsman crawled through into the larger room, dragging his drainpipe behind him. "There you are," he said. "It's finished now. I bet nobody else has got a patent, prefabricated ventilating shaft in their hut."

"Neither would we, if you hadn't sat on it and bent it in the middle," replied Jennings. "I was going to get a small hunk of mirror and make it into a periscope and bung it through the roof, so's we could see people coming."

"You don't need a periscope for that," Darbishire objected. "The walls are so thin you can see people coming through them, anyhow."

"If anyone wants to come in," said Jennings, "they can wizard well use the front door. If people start coming in through the walls ..."

"No, I didn't mean that. I meant—oh, well, never mind. Let's put the shaft up, shall we? It'll help to prop up the roof, and from outside it'll look as though we'd got a chimney. Gosh, Temple and Venables and all the other chaps will be as fed up as two coots when we show them all our labour-saving gadgets. They haven't got anything half as decent as this in their huts." Darbishire's eyes sparkled behind his spectacles; the junior partner was every bit as keen as his colleague on building a hut which would be the envy of all who were invited to admire its classic architecture.

There was a small puddle in the middle of the floor, for even in June the marshy ground near the pond retained its moisture; so they knelt on small, inadequate dock-leaves and set to work to erect the shaft.

The lower end gurgled its way into the mud and the top was pushed through the sparse foliage of the roof. They knew, of course, that the drainpipe had no air-conditioning properties to speak of, but it added tone to the place. One could say: "We've got a supersonic patent prefabricated ventilating shaft in our hut," in the same tone that one might say: "We've got a television set in the billiard room."

"Come on," said Jennings. "Let's go and get some more reeds to block up

344

the walls." They crawled through the low entrance and scampered down to the water's edge.

Huts of every shape and style were growing up near the bank. Some were merely leafy tents that only their owners or the ancient Picts and Scots would have described as desirable residences; others were more ambitious and had sun-parlours and twisty tunnels of bramble between one room and the next. Venables and Temple had built so low a structure that they had to crawl like snakes all the time they were inside, while Atkinson's shanty was tall enough to house a giraffe, but so narrow that the animal could never have wagged its tail.

Martin-Jones and Paterson were making a hut up a tree, and Bromwich major had decided upon a semi-basement type of dwelling which sank into the earth like an elephant-trap.

Venables and Temple emerged from their hut like burrowing moles, as Jennings and Darbishire staggered past with armfuls of reeds.

"Come and see what we're doing," Jennings invited. "Our hut's simply smashing—at least it will be when we've made the roof a bit thicker and drained the floor."

Venables, a tall thin boy of eleven, rose to his feet and brushed the mud from his knees. "I bet it's not so good as ours," he said. "Ours is so snug there isn't room to breathe, let alone turn round, and we have to beetle out in reverse gear, don't we, Bod?"

His friend nodded. Temple had answered to the name of Bod ever since his initials, which spelt CAT, had been altered to DOG and "shortened" to Dogsbody.

"Yes, but ours has got two rooms," argued Jennings. "A living room in front and a small back room where Darbishire goes and invents things."

Venables and Temple left their low-built apartment and followed the pioneer squatters to the little hut.

"Here we are," said Jennings, throwing down his bundle of reeds. "This is the front door."

"Where?" asked Temple.

"Well, this is the place where it goes when it's working. We've got it on the floor at the moment—that's one of Darbishire's inventions. When you don't want it as a door you can use it as duckboards."

"I don't know about duckboards," retorted Venables, picking his way between the puddles. "You'll need stilts if it gets any wetter."

"Ah, but I've got plans to dig a special irrigation drainage canal," Darbishire explained, as the sightseers crawled in. "And actually, it's super decent to have masses of water. Supposing we were besieged—we'd be able to hold out for months. Why, we could even wash, if we felt like it!"

"And we're going to use this tin can to store the water in—it's another of Darbi's supersonic wheezes," Jennings chimed in. He rolled an empty five-gallon oil drum to the middle of the hut. "I fished it out of the pond yesterday. We can have it either as an emergency drinking supply—only you mustn't really drink it, of course, because it's a bit tadpoley—or we can use it as a patent fire-extinguisher. Just at the moment we use it as a tribal tom-tom when we feel like a spot of drum music." He performed a short percussion solo, which rumbled round the little hut like gunfire.

The guests were deeply impressed. "Fancy Darbishire thinking all that up!" said Temple admiringly. "I'd always put you down as a bit of a wet dishcloth, Darbi—I'd no idea you were such a genius."

"Oh, I don't know," smiled the inventor, bursting with pride. "It's just a gift, I suppose." He gave a little self-conscious laugh, and blew his nose to hide his embarrassment.

The visiting squatters found that the conducted tour of the hut imposed a severe strain on the human form. Unlike their own hut, the roof was not so low that they had to crawl; but on the other hand, it was just not high enough for them to stand upright. Venables shambled about with bent knees, in a curious crouching attitude, and Temple bowed his shoulders and drooped his head so that he was unable to see anything higher than the floor, unless he stood a long way off. Darbishire was short enough to be able to prance about in an upright position, and Jennings had solved his head-room problems with cardboard kneepads, on which he shuffled around rapidly.

The hut was circular and the main room was about six feet in diameter; from outside, it looked like a rather thin beehive. The hosts displayed their furniture and fittings with some pride. There was a cane-seated rustic chair which Jennings had made from broken branches and bulrushes; it was perfectly safe, provided that no one actually sat on it. There was a pair of bicycle handlebars, salvaged from the pond and now in use as a hat stand; they were still searching hopefully for a hat to hang on it. There was a bookshelf, a bootscraper, and a brass curtain rod, and wedged tightly into the wall, Venables found a biscuit tin.

"What's this for?" he demanded.

"That's the refrigerator," Jennings explained. "At least, it will be. We're going to put a leaky tin of water on the roof, so it drips down the outside wall and keeps the fridge cool. We're saving up for a banquet, you see; we've got a pork pie already and we're keeping it till we get this month's sweet rations to go with it. It'll be supersonic, won't it?"

Venables opened the biscuit tin and then shut it again quickly. "It's supersonic already," he announced. "Your pork pie's going much faster than sound—it's growing cotton wool round the edges in spite of your air-conditioned walls."

"Never mind," said Jennings, "we can give it to the moorhens—they're not fussy. Perhaps we can get some potatoes and things later on and make a fire and actually cook them."

"We'll come and help you, if you like," Venables suggested. "I'm a pretty good cook. I made a cake at home, once. It was super! I got some flour and stuff and boiled it for three hours in a pudding cloth. Then we ate it."

"The cake, or the cloth?"

"The cake, of course. We threw the cloth away. Although actually," he admitted, for he was a truthful boy, "actually, it might have tasted better if we'd thrown away the cake and eaten the cloth."

They crawled through the hole into the small back room, and examined the half-finished arts and crafts with which Jennings and Darbishire were planning to improve their home comforts. Painted jam jars stood ready to serve as flower vases; curtains, hand-woven from bulrushes awaited a few finishing touches, and on the wall hung a sugar-sack with the words, *Welcome to Ye Oldë Worldë Huttë* picked out in a tasteful variety of colours.

"That's the door-mat," Jennings explained. "And we're doing the lettering by sticking the tops of fizzy-drink bottles through the sacking. It took us weeks to collect all those bottle tops. I had to haunt the tuck-shop like a leech."

"It's not bad," Venables admitted. "Except that you can't spell."

Jennings and Darbishire glanced at each other with superior, knowing smiles. "That just shows how much *you* know!" said Jennings. "This is an ancient rustic hut, I'd have you know, and we've been to a lot of trouble to get everything just right. And you have to put an 'e' on the ends of words because that's how they spelt it in the Stone Age. I expect we'll have finished it by next week, and it'll look spivish outside the front door. Of course, it's not for wiping your feet on—it's just a work of art."

Venables felt that open-mouthed admiration of a rival hut had gone quite far enough. "Of course, ours will look pretty super when we've finished it," he said. "We've got all sorts of plans in mind."

"What sort of plans?" demanded Jennings.

"Oh—er, just different sorts of plans. We've thought of lots. For instance ..." He paused, seeking desperately for just one face-saving improvement. "Well, like, say, for instance, such as a hunk of corrugated iron to make a porch with. We saw one in the pond yesterday and we're going to try and get it out."

"A corrugated iron porch!" Jennings' tone was disdainful. Corrugated iron struck a jarring, modern note amongst this old-world rusticity. There was something not quite old-English about corrugated iron.

A whistle sounded in the distance. "Come on!" said Temple. "There's Mr. Carter blowing the 'all-in.' Let's get back over the bridge before the rush hour starts."

On all sides bodies were emerging from huts as the four boys hurried towards the slope which led to higher ground. There was a quagmire at the foot of the slope where the pond had overflowed across the path, and here the pioneer hut-builders had erected the Darbishire Pontoon-Suspension Bridge.

It was an unusual feat of engineering which the inventor had conceived on the lines of the Forth Bridge, using branches and string in place of girders and rivets. But the first time it was used, it sagged so low that it floated on the water and the builders had been obliged to prop it up with pontoons made from petrol cans. By and large, it was still considered to be a suspension bridge; the only difference was that it was the traveller, and not the bridge, who was in a state of suspension as he swung himself across an awkward gap, with the aid of an overhanging branch.

Single-line traffic and no overtaking was the rule, and it was this bottleneck that slowed the hurrying tide of hut builders to a snail-paced crawl. Mr. Carter's whistle sounded again—impatiently this time, as the boys awaited their turn to cross.

"Oh, gosh, this is frantic!" bemoaned Darbishire. "If we're not back when the dorm bell goes, the Head will put the pond out of bounds again. I nearly fainted with shock when he let us come over here in the first place."

"Why shouldn't we come?" demanded Temple. "After all, it's wizard well educational. Think of all the nature craft and stuff you learn by watching moorhens and tadpoles and building suspension bridges and things."

"It was jolly decent of Mr. Carter to ask the Archbeako to let us," said Jennings. "It's not often you find grown-ups who are keen on huts. They seem to turn against things like that when they get old."

"Mr. Carter's not old," protested Temple. "Oh, he is. He's at least twenty-five or thirty. More than that, probably—say, forty-five or fifty, even. He must be pretty ancient because I happen to know he was alive in the olden days."

"He ought to be able to read your oldë worldë Stone Age huttë language, then."

"Well, not all that old, of course," Jennings amended. "But he can remember right back to the time before they'd invented jet-propelled aircraft and coupons for sweets. Why, when he was young, I don't suppose they'd ever heard of identity cards and railway engines and things."

In single file they picked their way across the pontoon-suspension bridge and ran full tilt past the cricket pitches. Mr. Carter was waiting for them on the quad.

Seen at close quarters, the master did not appear to be the sole surviving relic of a by-gone age that Jennings' description had suggested. He was in his early thirties—a friendly, unhurried sort of man who remained calm amidst all the excitements which ruffled the surface of boarding-school life. "How are the huts progressing?" he inquired.

"They're going fine, sir," Jennings told him. "And we're all learning masses of natural history and botany, sir."

"Really!" marvelled Mr. Carter. "Such as what?"

"Well, sir, I've learned you can cut your finger on bulrushes and you can't keep newts out of a hut, however many anti-reptile traps you dig round it, sir."

"I see. Well, there's one point you'd better bear in mind. If anyone gets his feet wet, or falls into the pond—or even if he gets stuck in an anti-reptile trap—it will mean the end of hut building. The Head's most particular about your not getting dirty and spoiling your clothes."

"Yes, sir," chorused the hut-builders, trying to edge behind one another in their efforts to conceal muddy socks and pond-slimed shoes.

"Don't shuffle about when I'm talking," said Mr. Carter. "I'm not blind; I'm just giving you a friendly warning. You'd better be getting upstairs now—the dormitory bell's just going."

In the bathroom that evening, they could talk of nothing but huts. It was a week since they had been given permission to start building operations, but as opportunities of going over to the pond were confined to the hour before bed-time, the venture was only just beginning to take shape. But now, walls were up and roofs were on—except in a few cases where the weight of the roof had collapsed the walls—and every squatter was eager to convert his makeshift cabin into a comfortable home-from-home.

"Our hut's easily the best," Jennings proclaimed through a film of soap bubbles. "Thanks to Darbi's famous inventions, it's just like an ideal home exhibition."

"Well, I bet you haven't got a knocker and a front door bell," retorted Atkinson, three baths away. "I've made a super bell out of a cocoa tin with pebbles in it. All I want now is a front door to hang it on, and it'll be just the job." He lay back in his bath turning the taps on and off with his toes, while his mind conjured up an endless stream of visitors queueing up to rattle pebbles in a cocoa tin.

The latest improvements were discussed in detail, above the trickle of running taps. Martin-Jones had written home for an air-cushion and a string hammock. Rumbelow had carved a name-plate with *Cosy Nook* in letters of bark, and Binns minor was making a similar one, inscribed *No Hawkers*. Nuttall's hut boasted two plastic mugs and a flagpole with a flag on it. Brown major had a first-aid outfit consisting of two bandages and a corn-plaster, and Johnson had found an inner tube which could be used as a life belt if anyone fell into the pond. Everyone was anxious to broadcast the merit of his scheme of interior decoration.

Everyone, except Bromwich major. He sat in his bath rubbing carbolic soap into his thick black hair, and said nothing.

"How are you getting on, Bromo?" Jennings inquired from the next bath. "I should think it must be a bit gloomy having a hut that sinks down like an air raid shelter."

"I'm getting on all right," said Bromwich major, "and I'm going to have something in my hut that none of the rest of you would think of, if you guessed for a million years."

"What?"

"Ah! You wait till you see it. It's a top priority secret. My mother's coming down to take me out after chapel tomorrow, and she's bringing it with her. And when it comes it'll make all your ventilating shafts and string hammocks look pretty silly. You can have grand pianos and electric cookers and potted palms, for all I care," Bromwich went on, generously; "they still wouldn't be a patch on this thing that I'm going to have." He swallowed a great gulp of air and disappeared beneath the bath water in an attempt to lower the Form 3 breath-holding record.

Bromo was like that, Jennings thought: always wanting to be a lone wolf and having a secret which no one else must know. And then, in the end, it always turned out to be such a feeble sort of secret that no one wanted to know, anyway. Still, you never knew. Perhaps he had thought of something rare, for a change; perhaps … Jennings' mind rambled on while his fingers sculptured the soap into a round ball. Then, with a sudden faint plop, the soap shot out of his slippery hands and landed on Darbishire, who was scrambling into his pyjamas.

"Who did that?" demanded Darbishire. He peered round vaguely, but he had left his spectacles in the dormitory, and without them the room was just a blurred mass of steamy figures.

"Sorry, Darbi," called Jennings. "I was just inventing a jet-propelled soap-rocket and it got out of control. Chuck it back, please; I want to see if I can …"

His words were drowned by convulsive blowings and heavings as Bromwich major broke the surface of the water, like a short-winded whale coming up for air. "Phew!" he gasped. "I bet *that's* a breath-holding record. I counted thirty-seven, quite slowly. Bet you haven't guessed it, yet!"

"Guessed what?"

"This secret thing my mother's bringing down for my hut." He smiled mysteriously. "You'd like to know what it is, wouldn't you?"

"No," said Jennings, bursting with curiosity. "I wouldn't listen if you told me."

"That's all right, then," said Bromwich, "because I'm not going to."

It was not until the following week that the top-priority secret was revealed, for the next day was Sunday, and the pond was out of bounds.

Immediately after preparation on Monday evening, Jennings and Darbishire hurried across to their hut and set about thatching the balder sections of the roof. Jennings had forgotten about Bromwich and his secret, and he was rather surprised when a thick black head of hair popped up from behind the hut and a triumphant voice said: "I've got it!"

"Got what?"

"Come and see!"

The two boys followed Bromwich major to his hut. The only way to enter was to lie down and slide through a hole in the reeds, for the lone wolf favoured a subterranean style of architecture. There was a straw landing-mat to break the fall of those who came in more quickly than they meant to, and then the visitor found himself in a natural hollow of the ground which had been roughly

roofed in. Faint beams of light trickled through the slats of the roof, but for a moment, the guests stood blinking in the dim-lit interior, unable to see anything at all. Then Jennings saw it.

"Gosh!" he murmured. "How super-cracking-sonic! You are lucky, Bromo: I wish I'd got one!"

"Got one *what*?" demanded Darbishire, peering short-sightedly through the gloom.

"There," said Jennings. "Look!"

Balanced on a broken cake-stand in the middle of the floor, was a tank of water. And in the tank was a goldfish.

"An aquarium—golly, how wizard!" Darbishire stood on one foot and flipped his fingers with delight. "Wherever did you get that from?"

"My mother brought it down by car yesterday," Browmwich explained. "It took her years to get here. She could only drive at about four miles a fortnight, in case she spilt the water. Not bad is he?"

There was no doubt that Bromwich major was devoted to his pet. He gazed lovingly into the tank and smiled at the goldfish like a fond parent at a school concert. The goldfish champed its jaws and goggled back unwinkingly. "I wanted one of these more than anything else," the owner went on. "He's the perfect ornament for a hut like this. You can keep your air-cushions and your hammocks ..."

"We haven't got any hammocks."

"Well, you can keep your prefabricated ventilating shafts."

"Thank you," said Darbishire. "We were going to."

"You can keep the whole lot," cried Bromwich with fierce pride. "All I want is my fish. Elmer and I are going to settle down together and ..."

"Who?" queried Darbishire.

"Elmer. That's my fish's name."

"Why?"

"*Why?* Well, why not? Why are you called Darbishire?"

"Oh, that's quite easy to explain. My father says that years ago our family used to be known as ..."

"All right, all right," Jennings broke in. "We don't want your family history right back to William the Conq." He turned to the proud owner.

"Thanks for showing us, Bromo. I think Elmer's super, and you'll never feel lonely now: you'll be able to sit and look at each other during the long summer evenings."

They left Bromwich to his fish and scrambled up through the doorway. As they walked back to their own hut, Jennings said: "You know, Darbi, a pet like that is just the right sort of thing for a boarding school. He can't escape, like guinea-pigs; you don't have to take him for walks and he doesn't eat much. Gosh, you can't go wrong with a goldfish, can you?"

"I bet *you* could," his friend answered. "If you were in charge of a high-spirited pet like that, I bet you'd manage to make a bish of it, somehow!" Darbishire's tone was light and bantering. He little knew how near the truth he was.

CHAPTER 2

LAST WICKET STAND

IT WAS on the following Wednesday that three boys retired to the sanatorium with mumps. The illness first raised its swollen neck among the thirteen-year-olds in the top form; by the next day it had spread to lower forms of life, and Binns minor, the youngest boy in the school, joined the ranks of the stricken. He would have been delighted at the idea of missing three weeks' work, if only he had not been feeling too ill to enjoy it.

"It's a swizzle," said Jennings, as they left the hut that evening. "There should have been a match against Bracebridge on Saturday, and now they'll have to cancel it."

"Can't be helped," replied Darbishire. "Mr. Carter said this afternoon that we could have first and second XI house matches instead. You're bound to be picked, and with any luck they may put me down as scorer."

Darbishire was not a good cricketer; but with a score book in front of him he was perfectly happy to sit in the pavilion all afternoon, well away from the hurly-burly of fast bowling. More important still, the scorer had the right to tell boys bigger than himself to move out of the light if they were blocking his view of the pitch. Sometimes, Darbishire wondered what would happen if he tried this on when he was *not* scoring.

His hopes were fulfilled. Jennings was picked to captain the Drake second XI in its match against the rival house of Raleigh, and Darbishire's name appeared on the bottom of the list as scorer. They both looked forward to a pleasant Saturday afternoon.

Unfortunately, they had not allowed for an unpleasant Saturday morning. Boy after boy awoke with a headache and was removed to the sick room to await the doctor's verdict. Gaps appeared in the house cricket teams and the rival captains dived lower and lower into the pool of cricketing talent in their efforts to find substitutes.

Jennings stood by the notice board just before lunch watching Stoddington, his house captain, making last minute alterations to the teams in his charge.

Parslow had just gone upstairs to Matron to report a sudden tenderness below the ears, and there seemed no one left to replace him. In despair, Stoddington's pencil scratched through the word scorer, and Darbishire, for the first time in his life, was promoted to the ranks of the Drake house second XI.

"Gosh!" exclaimed Jennings in amazement.

"Greatest news since the landing of Julius Cæsar—Old Darbi's been picked at last! And in my team, too; I must go and tell him. Get off my runway, Venables—I'm a jet-propelled strato-cruiser taking off on a super important mission. Eee-ow-ow … Eee-ow-ow!" He strato-cruised along to the common room, where he found Darbishire hard at work with drawing book and paint brush.

"What do you think, Darbi?" he began, giving his friend a hearty pat on the back. "Great news!"

"You great crumbling ruin," protested the artist, recoiling from the hearty pat. "Now look what you've done! You've made me do a smudge on this painting I was doing to hang up in the hut."

Jennings looked down at the work of art. It was a tasteful landscape, with cows grazing in the middle distance and an express train hurtling over a flimsy wooden bridge in the foreground. And it was still very wet.

"Sorry," Jennings apologised. "It won't matter, will it?"

"It wizard well *will* matter! I was just painting the grass when you jogged me, and now I've got a cow with a green face."

"Never mind," Jennings consoled him. "You can pretend it isn't feeling very well—that'll explain why it's a bit off colour. Anyway, I've got an urgent message for you; You've been picked for the second XI house match."

Darbishire heard the news with mixed feelings. It was an honour such as he had never dreamed of, but he was a little uncertain whether he would be able to rise to the occasion.

"Oh, well," he said, "this is my big chance, I suppose. My father says that Fate knocks once at the door of every man." For a moment he lapsed into a daydream of late cuts and off drives; of a glorious six over the bowler's head and tumultuous cheers from the pavilion. Then, with an effort, he brought his mind back to the realms of probability. "And you mean to say my name's actually up on the board?"

"Yes. In block letters."

"And not just as scorer?"

"No. Square leg and number eleven in the batting order."

"Golly, I wonder if they'd give me the list afterwards, so's I could send it to my father. Let's go and have a look at it; this sort of thing doesn't happen every day, does it!"

Together they strato-cruised back along the corridor and touched down by the crowd round the notice board. Darbishire spoke with the authority that his place in the team demanded: "Shift out of my light, Atkinson," he said. "You're blocking my view of the team."

It was Darbishire's performance in the junior house match that made Jennings decide to give his friend some intensive coaching. Raleigh batted first, and as the Drake bowling tended towards long-hops on the leg side, Darbishire was kept busy. Not that he actually saved any boundaries, but it was useful to have a willing fielder on the spot to retrieve the ball from the hedge.

The bowling strength of both teams had been badly affected by the absentees in the sick bay. Jennings and Bromwich major had to bowl throughout the innings almost without relief, and after the first hour's play they were tired and unable to maintain their length.

"Oh, gosh, Bromo," bemoaned Silly Mid Off, "can't you do better than that? That's two wides this over!"

"Sorry," returned Bromwich. "It's that bump on the pitch. Whenever I do a leg-break it turns it into a wide on the off."

"Well, do off-breaks, then."

"That's no good either. The last off-break that pitched on the bump nearly brained the square leg umpire."

Mr. Hind, a tall thin man with a quiet voice, was in charge of the junior game. "If things go on like this," he observed sadly, "you'd better get a scarecrow with outstretched arms to umpire at the bowler's end. I'm a trifle weary of signalling wides."

He sat on his shooting-stick and looked enviously across at Mr. Carter who was umpiring the senior match on an adjoining pitch. There, at any rate, one could be sure of good length bowling and promising batting strokes.

Jennings tried a change of bowlers, but it was not a success and after a few overs he put himself on to bowl at Mr. Hind's end. The telegraph board showed 66 runs for seven wickets, and the captain encouraged his men for an all-out effort. "Only three more chaps to get out," he told them. "Let's see if we can get the whole side out for under seventy."

The word spread round the fielding side. "Special effort, chaps. Everyone on their toes!"

Jennings swung his arm round like a propeller before starting his run up to the wicket. It was his method of generating current for an extra-special delivery, and though it did not always succeed, he felt it was worth trying.

This time, it worked. The ball pitched on the little bump and shot forward to hit the stumps at grass-top level: and the Raleigh batsman retired to the pavilion complaining about balls which cut through the turf like plough-shares. Jennings' luck held. His next ball was wide of the off stump and the new batsman prodded at it vaguely. By chance he touched it and the wicket-keeper held an easy catch. Two wickets in two balls! The Drake fielders went wild with delight, smiting one another on the back and dancing ungainly ballet steps round the wicket.

"66 for nine," said Jennings happily. "If I can get Thompson minor out this ball, it'll be a hat trick and they won't get seventy after all. Gosh, I've never done the hat trick in a house match yet."

Thompson minor always played the same stroke to every ball he received; he took a step backwards and swung his bat as though scything a field of corn. As Jennings first ball hurtled down the pitch towards him, Thompson played his unvarying stroke and the ball rose from his bat and curved gently away towards the leg boundary.

Atkinson was umpiring at square leg. Unlike Mr. Hind, he had no shooting-stick, so he sat on a reversed cricket bat instead. He ducked, and the ball lobbed over his head, straight into the hands of the square leg fielder.

If it had been a difficult catch, Darbishire would not have felt so unhappy about missing it. But it wasn't. The ball sank gently into his hands and his spirits soared in triumph: then, the ball dropped and his spirits with it. He stared aghast, unable to believe his eyes. For a second he had actually felt the ball nestling in his palms, and now the beastly thing had slipped through his fingers like an eel. It was incredible …. It was the end of everything …. It was …!

"Darbishire!" yelled the wicket-keeper, dancing behind the stumps like a cat on hot bricks.

The fielder came to with a jerk and saw that the batsmen were running. Perhaps he could run them out. Perhaps, if he threw very straight he could …. He swung his arm back hard for the return throw and the ball flew out of his fingers and landed in the hedge behind him. Mr. Hind signalled a boundary and four more runs went up on the board.

"Gosh, Darbishire, you are a ruin!" grumbled the Drake fielders as they gathered in the pavilion after the Raleigh innings had closed for 84 runs.

"Sorry," said Darbishire humbly.

"You bished up Jennings' hat trick and just chucked runs away," said Cover Point. "Messing up that throw in, after missing the easiest catch I ever saw. Anyone could have held a soft one like that."

"Anyone except Darbishire," amended Second Slip. "He couldn't even catch mumps with a shrimping net."

"Shut up," said Jennings, coming to his friend's rescue. "We can't all be Test Match cricketers. You may be good at one thing and Darbishire may be good at another."

"Such as what?"

"Well, like, say, for instance, inventing things. He's smashing at that. And he can do a better imitation of a train going through a tunnel than anyone else in the school."

"Thanks, Jen," said Darbishire gratefully. "I'm sorry about bishing up that catch off your bowling, though."

"That's all right," Jennings replied generously. "He wouldn't have been out even if you *had* caught it. It was a 'no ball'."

The Drake innings opened disastrously, and three wickets fell for only a dozen runs. Then Jennings went in and stopped the rot. This was only to be expected, for he would have been picked for the senior game if his own team had not been so short of bowlers. Batsmen came and went, and when 50 runs appeared on the board, Jennings had made 20 of them. Drake took heart, and the tail of the team wagged strenuously as it added a few more runs for each wicket.

The score was 79 for eight when Darbishire realised, with a qualm of mis-giving, that he was the next man in. He found a pad and strapped it on; the buckle was missing at the bottom, but there was no time to do anything about it, and he was still searching for a second pad when a burst of cheering from the field announced that the ninth wicket had fallen.

Darbishire glanced at the scoreboard and noticed that the score had crept up to 83. Jennings was still at the wicket, playing a captain's innings.

"Buck up, Darbi—you're in," announced Fine Leg.

"I can't go yet—I've only got one pad."

"Never mind about that. You won't be there all that long. Just stick in and let Jennings get the runs. Unless, of course, you get an easy one—then you can have a crack at it."

The last man in swallowed hard; it was stupid to talk about his getting an easy one. Things like that never happened to him.

"Go on, Darbi—don't hang about," said Mid On. "My nerves won't stand this suspense much longer." Two runs to make! The atmosphere pulsed with excitement.

Darbishire grabbed a bat and a pair of gloves and strode boldly towards the wicket, his single, broken pad flapping uncomfortably about his ankle. It was not until he reached the crease that he remembered that he had not taken his blazer off.

"Just a mo, please," he said, and fumbled at the buttons with his padded fingers, while the fielders shifted about restlessly. When the buttons were undone, the blazer slipped off his shoulders easily enough, but it was rather tight at the wrist and try as he would, he could not force his sleeves over his batting-gloves.

"Sorry about this," he apologised, with his arms pinioned behind his back. "I'm afraid I'll have to take my gloves off first."

The Raleigh fielders seethed with impatience. They, too, could hardly wait to get on with the game.

"It's no good," said Darbishire, a few moments later, "I can't get my gloves off behind my back; I'll have to get my blazer on properly, first."

"Here, let me help!" Jennings marched down the pitch to lend a hand. "We can't possibly wait while you mess about putting your gloves on and off. Bend forward and hold your arms out and I'll strip it off, inside out." He seized the hem of the blazer and heaved it over his friend's head, but again they were baffled by the tight cuffs. The batsman's head and neck were shrouded in blazer, and soon calls for help came from within.

"Hey, whoa, stop! I'm stuck and I can't breathe." He floundered helplessly about like the back legs of a pantomime horse looking for its partner.

"What's the matter?" asked Jennings, popping his head into the flannelly tunnel from the open end.

"This is ghastly," said Darbishire. "My cap's got stuck in the armhole and my glasses have come off. I think they've slipped down inside my shirt."

"Keep still—I'll see if I can get them for you."

There were queer movements inside the blazer, as though two old-fashioned photographers were sharing one head-covering between them. Then one of the headless bodies backed out of the tunnel and stood breathing lungfuls of fresh air.

"Oh, for goodness' sake get a move on!" called Venables from the bowler's end, while the rest of the fielders hopped up and down and waved their arms in wild gestures of frustration.

At last Darbishire was ready to face the bowling. The fielders closed in, prepared to pounce like hawks if the batsman should spoon up an easy catch. They looked at one another and smiled craftily; they had met batsmen like Darbishire before.

Just as the bowler started his run, Darbishire realised that he had strapped his pad on to the wrong leg. But he could not change it now, unless he stopped the game and removed his gloves again, and he decided that this might not go down well with the other players.

He was pondering the problem when the ball came hurtling towards him. It was one of Venables' special deliveries, noted for pace rather than accuracy. The ball flashed past the batsman, past the stumps, past the wicket-keeper's clutching gloves and sped away with First Slip in pursuit.

Darbishire turned and watched it. "Gosh," he observed to the wicket-keeper. "That was a fast one, wasn't it! I didn't even see it coming. Look at old Bod legging after it like blinko. I bet he ..."

"Quick, run!" yelled a voice behind him and, turning, the batsman found that Jennings had arrived from the bowling end. For one agonised moment they both stood in the same crease, while Temple fielded the ball and threw it back towards the pitch.

"Get back!" cried Darbishire.

"I can't. I've got here, now. Run!"

Darbishire ran, but without much hope. Temple's throw had reached the middle of the pitch and the cover point seized it and hurled it with all his force at the bowler's wicket. It missed the stumps by half an inch and streaked away past mid on. Darbishire breathed again and didn't stop running until he reached Mr. Hind, five yards behind the wicket.

"Gosh, sir, did you see that?" he asked the umpire. "I thought I'd had it that time, sir. If only it had been half a ..."

"Darbishire!" yelled the Drake team from the pavilion. "Run up, you idiot, run up!" They clutched their heads and writhed in nervous despair.

"Wake up!" said Mr. Hind. "There's another run on the overthrow, if you're quick."

"Oh, gosh, yes, of course!"

Jennings had almost reached the crease again before his partner was off the mark on his second run, and this time Darbishire's luck was out. Three-quarters of the way along the pitch, he stepped on the end of his flapping pad and tripped himself up. The next second the bails were whipped off and the match was over.

Darbishire rose slowly to his feet, numb with misery. If only he had been more alert, this would never have happened. his big chance had come and he had not lasted long enough to face two balls. What would his father say? What were his team-mates thinking?

Judging from the noise his team-mates were making, they were taking it very well. They were waving pads and bats in the air and shouting themselves hoarse. Jennings ran up and slapped his partner on the back. "Well done," he said. "Jolly spivish effort!"

"Well done?" queried Darbishire. "But I didn't do anything except get run out first ball."

"What does that matter?" returned Jennings. "We won the match, didn't we? We'd crossed on that last run before you went *doyng* on your face, so that makes our score 85."

"Oh yes, of course, I'd forgotten about that. And it was our last-wicket stand that did the trick, wasn't it?"

"That's right. And you got the winning run without even touching the ball!"

Darbishire beamed with delight. "It sounds super when you put it like that," he said. "I bet my father will be ever so pleased when I write and tell him."

They entered the pavilion amidst a salvo of cheers. In point of fact, the applause was for Jennings who had saved the game with a determined 33 not out, but the number eleven batsman could not resist the temptation to bask in the reflected glory. He raised his cap and smiled modestly.

After all, he had been to a lot of trouble to score that bye.

CHAPTER 3

OPERATION 'EXERCISE'

THERE WAS no evening preparation on Saturdays, and after tea Jennings and Darbishire sped away to the hut.

Jennings had decided to make a broom out of twigs, but first it would be necessary to drain the floor so that it was dry enough to be swept. No sooner had he started work than he heard his name being called, and galloping footsteps approached from the suspension bridge. It was Atkinson, an excitable boy of ten, who occupied a hut near the water's edge.

"Oh, there you are, Jen," he cried, as he charged through the undergrowth. "Bromo major's got the mumps!"

"Bad luck!" said Jennings. "I thought his bowling was a bit off colour this afternoon."

"Yes, it's ozard, isn't it! He went up to Matron just after the house match, and he's sent you an urgent message via Matron, via me, to you. He wants you to look after his goldfish. He's as sick as mud at having to leave it behind, because he's so spivishly devoted to it."

"I've noticed that," chimed in Darbishire emerging from the hut. "He just *lives* for that fish. And so he should, really, because poor old Elmer's got no one else in the whole world, except Bromo. He's its next-of-kin, as you might say."

"Can't he take it up to the san. with him?" suggested Jennings.

"Gosh, no!" protested Atkinson. "It might catch mumps, and a goldfish with swollen gills would look ghastly. Of course, it may be mumpy already, as Bromo's been looking after it. Might be a good wheeze to stick a label on the tank—*Beware of Mumps. Do not touch.* Anyway, will you take the job on?"

Bromwich had a younger brother in the lowest form, but he was considered to be too young to bear such a heavy responsibility. As Atkinson pointed out: "You need a Form Three-er, at least, to take on a job like this. A Form One-er would be bound to make a bish of it, and besides you and Darbi have had mumps already, so you won't go teetering off to the san. before Bromo gets back."

Jennings pondered for a moment. Taking care of a fish who boasted a next-of-kin was a serious business and not to be undertaken lightly. At the same time, it was gratifying to think that he had been chosen for this position of trust. Clearly, it was his duty to shoulder this burden so that Bromwich could enjoy his mumps with an easy mind.

"All right," he said, "but I don't know much about goldfish. What do they eat?"

"That's easy; they eat eggs."

"Don't be such a prehistoric remains, Atkinson," said Jennings curtly. "They'd never be able to crack the shells."

"Not hens' eggs, you ruin—ants' eggs. They love them."

"Oh, yes, of course," said Jennings, and wondered how Elmer would like his eggs prepared. Boiled? Scrambled? Perhaps if he was sickening for mumps a little raw egg would be just the thing. In that case, all they would have to do would be to find an ant and persuade it to lay an egg.

But there was no need for this. When they slithered into Bromwich's semi-basement to take charge of Elmer, they found a tin of ready-made fish food and a flower pot containing a culture of small white worms: this, obviously, was Elmer's meat ration.

"I wonder if we ought to feed him right away," queried Jennings. "He looks pretty hungry to me. Look how's he champing his jaws."

"All goldfish do that," replied Darbishire. "It's the same as chewing the cud. They're rather like cows in that way."

Very carefully, they carried the tank and the food back to their own hut. Elmer would be happier, they decided, in an up-to-date, air-conditioned apartment than he would be in the dim-lit gloom of the Bromwich elephant trap.

For some days, Jennings and Darbishire tended Elmer as though he were one of the family. They became acutely fish conscious; they put the tank outside the hut door on pleasant evenings so that Elmer might enjoy the waning sunshine; on dull evenings, they kept him indoors. They spent hours in preparing him tasty snacks and watching him eat them; and Elmer, from his tank, would see blurred faces beyond the glass with mouths which opened and shut in time with his own.

"We ought to send Bromo a news bulletin," Jennings decided at the end of a week. "He may be getting a bit anxious."

"Good wheeze," Darbishire agreed. "You write it while I put him out for his airing. Or do you think he ought to stay in tonight? There's no sun to speak of and it might rain."

"Don't be such a crumbling ruin, Darbi. Considering he's swimming about in cold water all the time, a few drops of rain aren't going to make him much wetter."

"Maybe not," Darbishire demurred, "but the wind's a bit fresh, and we don't want him to get in a draught."

"That's all right: the cold water will keep the wind off. Don't fuss so, Darbi—you're like an old hen with a chicken. Elmer knows how to look after himself; he's a jolly clever little fish."

"So he should be," said Darbishire, as he carried the tank through the doorway. "They say fish is good for the brain, so if you're fish all over, like Elmer, you ought to be fairly bursting with intelligence."

They finished the news bulletin before they went to bed and despatched it to the sanatorium, via Matron.

"Elmer is keeping fit and not fretting," it read. "Has hearty appetite and drinks like a fish. Spends all day doing the breast stroke backwards. Have told him you will be back soon, so don't worry."

Bromwich major was extremely pleased with the news bulletin, and pinned it on the wall above his bed.

There was always plenty to do at the little hut, and a few evenings later, when Darbishire was on the roof, thatching a recent leak, he was troubled to hear waves of song wafting out through the front door, while occasional snatches filtered through the thin patches in the western wall. The tune was *John Brown's Body*, but the words were Jennings' own:

> "If triangles are equal, they are said to be congruent,
> If triangles are equal, they are said to be congruent,
> If triangles are equal, they are said to be congruent,
> And the angles at the base of an isosceles triangle are equal."

The last line required a great deal of practice and the soloist started again. "If triangles are equal ..."

When Darbishire could stand the song no longer, he crawled to where the ventilating shaft stretched its stately neck into the air and shouted down it: "Pack it up, Jen, for heaven's sake! What's the idea of kicking up that ghastly hoo-hah?"

The drainpipe had been in use as a speaking tube for some days, and Jennings had fitted a home-made two-way ear-trumpet at a convenient height from the ground. "Don't get rattled, Darbi," his voice boomed back up the tube. "It's my new way of learning geometry. It's easier if you put it to music."

"Yes, but—good gracious, why do geom in your spare time?" Darbishire's feelings were outraged.

"Don't you remember what Mr. Wilkins told us when he gave us that test last week? He said the whole form had made a frightful bish and he was going to test us again, tomorrow."

"Yes, but all the same ..."

"Mind you, I'm not going to make a habit of working too much in my spare time, but I haven't been getting on too well with Old Wilkie lately, so I thought if I composed a special geom song, he'd see how keen I was."

Darbishire considered this. Mr. Wilkins had a temperament like a volcano. He could be pleasant enough when he chose, but at other times his mood was uncertain. Some unguarded remark would lead to earth tremors and rumblings deep down inside the crater, and the next moment the volcano would erupt, pouring its angry lava in all directions and leaving a trail of desolation and detentions in its wake.

"M'yes," Darbishire said thoughtfully. "Not a bad idea. He might let us all sing it in class. How does it go?"

They held a rehearsal—Darbishire kneeling on the roof and bawling the words down the drainpipe, while Jennings sang into the shaft from below and accompanied the duet with drum music on the water-supply-cum-fire-extinguisher.

As they were practising the difficult last line for the tenth time, Jennings broke off and called out: "Hey, that's enough, Darbi; we're frightening Elmer. He's carrying on like a submarine out of control."

"What's he doing?"

"I don't quite know. He keeps going to action stations and submerging all in one breath. Come down and see for yourself—I don't like the look of this at all."

Elmer was certainly in a lively mood. He darted to one end of his tank and then, with a sudden flip of his tail that rippled the surface and disturbed the pond-weed, he shot away to the other end and started the performance all over again. He seemed so far removed from his usual placid self, that the boys became worried.

"It can't be because he's hungry," said Jennings, "and if our famous duet upset him, there's no need for him to go on hoofing about now that we've stopped."

Darbishire consulted Bromwich major's little book on the care of goldfish. He read through the symptoms of every ailment that could possibly attack the scaly inhabitant of a glass tank, but nothing seemed to fit the facts. And it couldn't be that he had caught mumps from his owner, he decided as he put the book down, for none of Matron's patients had carried on in that extraordinary way before departing for the sanatorium.

"I don't think he's ill at all," said Jennings. "He's just feeling restless and wants a spot of exercise. After all, if you had to live in a titchy little tank, that there wasn't room to swing a cat in, you'd get a bit browned-off."

"I should be a wizard sight more browned-off if someone *did* start swinging cats," retorted Darbishire. "Still, perhaps it is a bit cruel keeping him cooped up. It's a pity he isn't a dog—then we could take him for walks on the lead."

"Gosh, yes," Jennings exclaimed. "Why not!"

"Don't be such a bogus ruin, Jen. You can't take a fish for a walk."

"No, but we could let him have a decent swim. Not in the pond, of course—it's too muddy and he might get bitten by a moorhen. But we could let him do a couple of lengths in the swimming bath—he'd love that!"

"We-ell," said Darbishire doubtfully, for the suggestion bristled with snags, "if we did that, how would we get him out again? This needs thinking out carefully."

Seldom has the welfare of a goldfish been discussed in such loving detail. Elmer's health and happiness, his imagined likes and dislikes were all carefully considered as the plan to give him a worthwhile treat gradually took shape. Finally, it was decided that he should be placed in Darbishire's butterfly-net and lowered into the swimming bath. Jennings could then walk slowly along the edge, while Elmer swam beside him in the net. He would be free to revel in his change of surroundings, yet unable to escape or take a wrong turning. As Darbishire pointed out, it would be rather like catching shrimps.

"But when can we do it?" he queried. "It wouldn't be safe to give him his exercise while everyone else is splashing about, and we're not allowed to go to the bath at any other time."

"I vote we do it immediately after prep tomorrow," said Jennings. "There won't be anyone there because swimming is in the morning on Tuesdays. And I know where the key's kept; it's on a hook outside the staff room door."

"There'll be an awful hoo-hah if anyone finds out. You know the rule about not going in the bath without permish," objected Darbishire.

"But we're not going *in* the bath, you ancient remains! It's Elmer who's going to do that. We're going to stay nice and dry and walk along like barge horses on the towpath."

The whistle sounded in the distance and the boys wended their way back to the school buildings. "Now, don't forget," said Jennings, as they queued up for the suspension bridge. "Directly after prep tomorrow evening; we'll have masses of time before the dorm bell. I'll collect Elmer and you get your butterfly net, and we'll get cracking on Exercise Goldfish."

"Not *Exercise* Goldfish," corrected Darbishire. "You mean, *Operation* Goldfish. You only call it Exercise when it's a practice, and this is the real thing."

"Well, in this case, the real thing is to give Elmer some exercise, so we'll call it 'Operation Exercise.' Buck up, Darbi, it's your turn for the bridge."

Form 3 sat a little uneasily in their desks the following afternoon, waiting for Mr. Wilkins to arrive. In front of them were their geometry exercise books, marked with impatient squiggles of red ink, and bearing terse comments in the margin. Last week's test had not been a success.

Venables said enviously: "I wish I'd got mumps; I don't know this stuff any better now than I did last week and I only got six marks out of ten. How many did you get, Darbi?"

"Well, as a matter of fact," Darbishire apologised. "I had rather an off day last Tuesday and I only got four."

"Only *four!*" echoed Jennings incredulously from the row behind. "I should have thought you could have done better than that, Darbi. Four out of ten—gosh, that's ozard!" He leaned forward and flicked over the pages of his friend's book. "And look, Old Wilkie's written *Gross carelessness* in the margin. Golly, Darbi, that's pretty feeble. I bet your father would have something to say about that!"

Darbishire pinkened. It was admittedly a lapse, for he usually managed to hold his own in Mr. Wilkins' class; and the Rev. Percival Darbishire would certainly not be at a loss for words if he heard that his son, Charles Edwin Jeremy, had failed to make the grade. Annoyed, he picked up Jennings' book to see how much better his friend had fared. Then his eyes opened wide in indignation.

"Well, I like that!" he cried. "You've only got *two*, Jennings! Trying to make out that yours was better than mine!"

"I didn't," Jennings defended himself. "I only said four out of ten was pretty feeble. Especially when you've got *Gross Carelessness* in the margin."

"Well, you've got *Carelessness* on yours, too."

"Ah, but yours is *Gross*. That's much worse! I bet you a million pounds it is."

"And I bet you a million pounds it isn't."

"Right-o," said Jennings. "I'll ask Old Wilkie when he comes in."

He had not long to wait.

Along the corridor and into the classroom strode Mr. Wilkins, and his footsteps could not have echoed more loudly if he had been wearing divers' boots. He was a large man, quite young and full of an energy which overflowed in a torrent of restless activity.

"Right," he boomed, as he swung the door to behind him with a crash. "All ready for the test? Question one: What are congruent triangles? Question two: What are alternate angles? Question three: ..."

"Oh, sir!" protested the class, searching feverishly for pens and rulers. "Not so fast, sir!"

"Can't wait all day," Mr. Wilkins rattled on. "There's work to be done. Ten questions: anyone not getting more than seven right stays in tomorrow afternoon. Question three: ..."

Jennings put up his hand. "Please sir, shall we number them, 'one to ten' sir?"

"Of course. How else could you do it? Question three: ..." Mr. Wilkins paused and looked hard at Jennings. "Oh, yes, Jennings—that reminds me. If you don't do very much better this time, there's going to be trouble. Your answers last week were deplorable; I've never seen such an appalling example of rank sloth and indolence."

"That's what I wanted to ask you, sir." After all, there was a million pound wager at stake. "Is rank worse than gross, sir? I mean, wasn't Darbishire's equally rank, sir?"

"I think he means don't they both rank equally, sir," suggested Darbishire, helpfully.

"They were both bad," said Mr. Wilkins. "Nothing to choose between them."

"But sir," Jennings persisted, "Darbishire's must have been worse than mine, because a gross is a hundred and forty-four, isn't it, sir?"

"I—I—what on earth's that got to do with it?"

"Well, sir, gross carelessness must be a hundred and forty-four times worse than ordinary carelessness, surely sir."

"I—I—Corwumph!" barked Mr. Wilkins. "I haven't come here to listen to a lot of nonsense. I've come here to find out how much you know about congruent triangles."

"Oh, I know quite a lot, sir. I made up a song about them. It goes to the tune of …"

"I don't want to hear a song; I want to get on with the test. Question three …"

The test proceeded briskly. Too briskly for some of them, and Mr. Wilkins grew extremely impatient with boys who asked him to repeat question six when he was about to announce question ten. At last it was finished and the books were collected and laid upon the master's desk.

For the second half of the lesson, Mr. Wilkins went further into the question of triangles which were similar to one another in all respects. He invented a problem about a man who lived in a village with the unlikely name of *A*, and who wanted to cross a river to another village which rejoiced in the improbable name of *B*. It seemed that, by walking a measured distance to the west and taking two bearings from a church dedicated to Saint *C*, the traveller was constructing two invisible triangles which enabled him to work out the breadth of the river *D*.

All this Mr. Wilkins demonstrated on the blackboard, while Darbishire came to the conclusion that the only thing wrong with his pontoon-suspension bridge was its lack of congruent triangles.

Jennings' mind, however, was not wholly concentrated on the problem on hand. Dimly, he wondered why this traveller was drawing dotted lines all over the countryside, and not merely on the bends of main roads; but in the main his thoughts were of Elmer and Operation Exercise. Bromo would be ever so pleased when he heard of the care and devotion which was being lavished on his next-of-kin. He might even … Jennings came to with a start, for Mr. Wilkins was speaking to him.

"What have I just been saying, Jennings?"

"You said that if you knew all about similar triangles, it helped you to cross a river, sir."

"Quite right!" For a moment Mr. Wilkins had thought that the boy had not been paying attention, but it seemed that he was mistaken. "And how exactly would you go about it?" he inquired.

Jennings thought desperately. "Well, sir, I suppose you'd make big wooden ones, so that you could sit on one triangle and paddle across with the other."

"I—I—Corwumph! Are you trying to be funny?" "No, sir, honestly, sir." And honestly, he wasn't.

"But you—you *silly* little boy, how could you ...? You haven't been following the problem at all. Very well, we'll see how much you knew in the test." He took Jennings' book from the pile and glanced through the answers. "H'm; seven out of ten. I'll set you an exercise to do tomorrow afternoon."

"Oh, but sir, you said I'd be all right, if I got seven."

"I said if you got *more* than seven," returned Mr. Wilkins. "And I might even have let you off with seven, if I thought you'd been trying for the rest of the lesson. But your conduct all afternoon has been verging on the insolent. As soon as I came in the door, you started twittering about gross carelessness being something to do with the multiplication table, and your answer about the traveller crossing the river was nothing short of impertinence. Come to me after the lesson and I'll give you something to keep you busy tomorrow afternoon; and if I get one more facetious reply to a question of mine, I'll—I'll—well, you'd better look out."

Darbishire did his best to comfort his friend after the lesson. "Never mind, Jen. Old Wilkie will soon get over it. My father says that it's always darkest just before the dawn and ..."

"Yes, but it's a jolly swizzle," Jennings declared. "I wasn't trying to be funny. I daren't open my mouth now, in case he thinks I'm being insolent; and that'll lead to another row, so that's a swizzle multiplied by a swizzle—it's a double swizzle."

"No, it's a swizzle squared—not a double swizz," Darbishire pointed out. "For instance, double twelve is only twenty-four, but twelve squared is a gross."

"Well, that proves what I said in class," Jennings answered warmly. "If it works with swizzles, it's the same with carelessness, so you owe me a million pounds."

But very soon his mood became more cheerful; the punishment would not have to be done until the following afternoon, so it would not interfere with Elmer's swim which was scheduled to take place that evening.

CHAPTER 4

ELMER FINDS A LOOPHOLE

OPERATION 'EXERCISE' did not work out quite as they had planned it. Shortly after evening preparation, when there was still a clear half-hour before bedtime, Jennings staggered round the corner to the indoor swimming bath with the goldfish tank in his arms. Darbishire was waiting for him with his butterfly net and the key, and furtively they let themselves in.

Elmer was no longer showing signs of restlessness. He remained quite still near the bottom of his tank, and only the occasional flapping of a fin told them that he was awake.

Darbishire was rather worried now that the time for action had arrived and he would have been more than willing to call the whole thing off. But Jennings would not hear of it; apart from the pleasure which Elmer would certainly derive from swimming a couple of brisk lengths, Jennings was intensely curious to know whether the experiment would be a success.

"After all," he argued, "Elmer's been putting on a lot of weight lately with all that food we've been giving him, and Bromo wouldn't like it if he got too fat. So I vote we give him a quick dip and let him do a length or two just to get his weight down."

"All right, then," Darbishire agreed, and held his net at the ready. "Hadn't we better start off in the shallow end?"

"Why? You don't think he'll feel nervous if he's out of his depth, do you?"

"Maybe *he* won't, but *I* shall."

Carefully, the fish was transferred to the butterfly net and lowered into the water. Jennings held the handle and moved slowly along the edge of the bath. It was a great success to start with and, as Jennings pointed out, everything was going swimmingly and Elmer would have taken the situation in his stride, if he had had anything to stride with.

Darbishire lowered his voice to a respectful whisper: "I expect he's wondering where he's got to, don't you? He had a sort of puzzled look on his face when I popped him in the net."

"I bet he's enjoying the exercise," Jennings replied. "And Bromo will be ever so pleased because he won't be nearly so fat when he comes down."

"Oh, he will," protested Darbishire. "He's bound to be fatter after lying in bed for three weeks."

"No, you ancient ruin; I meant the fish, not Bromo!" Jennings laughed aloud at the absurdity of such a misunderstanding. "Ha-ha-ha! You are a bazooka, Darbi. You thought I meant Bromo: ha-ha-ha!"

"And you really meant Elmer!" Darbishire joined in, and waves of hearty laughter echoed hollowly from the high roof of the building.

"Gosh, that was funny," laughed Jennings. "I must remember to tell Venables. You thought I meant—ha-ha-ha—and all the time I really meant—ha-ha-h ... Glumph!" The hearty laughter stalled in mid-burst and was followed by a cry of anguish. "Oh, gosh, quick, Darbi! The fish—it's gone!"

"What! It can't have."

Jennings jerked the net clear of the water. It was empty. For some seconds they stood staring in horrified amazement while little driblets of water trickled down the mesh and dripped back into the bath. Then, when the first impact of the shock was over and the boys inspected the net at close quarters, they found a medium-sized hole in the bottom.

"Oh, heavens, Bromo will never forgive us if anything happens to Elmer," moaned Darbishire.

"He can't have swum far yet; let's see if we can see him," said Jennings. "The water's a bit dirty, though. We *would* wait till it's nearly time to have it changed— I can't see the bottom at all!"

The water was certainly cloudy. The bath was a small one, and Robinson, the odd-job man, changed the water every three weeks: and judging by the state of it on that fateful Tuesday evening, the bath was more than ready for its three-weekly renewal.

Jennings and Darbishire knelt down and peered into the murky depths. Once, Jennings caught a glimpse of a golden streak near the surface, but the fish was more than an arm's length from the side. Jennings grabbed the net, and leant over the side while Darbishire grabbed his friend's ankles, but by that time, Elmer was out of range and out of sight.

"I wonder whether we could lure him to the side with bait," Jennings pondered. "Go and fetch the fish-food and that flowerpot with the worms in, Darbi, while I stop here on guard."

His friend returned some minutes later with the bait. He had also brought an armful of pond-weed in the hope that Elmer would be attracted by the foliage he knew so well. It was rather muddy, for Darbishire had gathered it fresh from the pond, but he dropped it into the bath and hoped for the best. Jennings sprinkled half a tin of fish-food on the water and submerged the flowerpot beneath the surface in the butterfly net.

It was all in vain. No fin rippled the water, no jaws rose to take the bait.

"Oh gosh, this is ozard!" cried Darbishire in despair. "Why do these frantic hoo-hahs always have to pick on us to happen to? My father knows a proverb which says you should never meddle ..."

"All right, all right," retorted Jennings sharply, for he, too, was feeling anything but happy. "I've heard quite enough about what your father always says about everything. It'd be a wizard sight more to the point if he knew a proverb about how to get a goldfish out of a swimming bath."

"Well, he does know one about there being as many good fish in the sea as ever came out."

"Honestly, Darbi! If you can't think of anything better to say than ..."

The shrilling of a distant bell cut into his words, and miserably he said: "Oh, gosh! There's the dorm bell. We'll have to go."

"But we can't go," objected Darbishire. "Bromo would have a relapse if anything happened to Elmer. And we can't ask Mr. Carter or anyone to help because of being in here without permish. Oh, goodness, why did we have to go and lose him?"

"It was your fault for having a net with a hole in it," Jennings answered. "Anyway, we haven't lost him because we know where he is. He won't drown and he can't get out, so we'll leave him in the bath tonight and come down before breakfast tomorrow and have another go. We're bound to catch him then."

"All right, then," Darbishire agreed, "but we shall have to think of a better method. What we really need is a tennis net or something we could drag along the bath like a deep sea trawler."

They hid the empty tank in one of the cubicles, and Darbishire took his net with him so that he could repair the hole. In case Elmer should feel hungry Jennings emptied the rest of the fish food on to the floating bait, and while he was doing so, he accidentally knocked the flowerpot into the bath. As it sank to the bottom, it added its earthy mixture to the already discoloured water.

They were replacing the key outside the staff room when Atkinson came hurrying along. "Oh, there you are, Jen," he said. "I've just had another message from Bromo via Matron, via me, to you. He wants to know if Elmer's still enjoying himself, and he hopes he isn't being any trouble."

"I should say he's enjoying himself like a house on fire," said Darbishire mournfully. "He's probably laughing himself black in the gills at this very moment."

"And he's not being any trouble?"

"Oh, no," replied Jennings in a faint, far-away sort of voice. "He's not being any trouble at all, thanks very much."

Jennings trudged slowly up the stairs, and from a landing window he caught sight of Mr. Carter and Mr. Wilkins on the tennis court, battling for the last point of a keenly-fought game. He stopped for a moment, and, as he watched, Mr. Wilkins slammed the ball hard into the net, and the game was over.

Masters had all the luck, Jennings decided. No troubles or worries, and nothing to do all evening except to enjoy themselves how and when they pleased. He sighed and passed on up the stairs.

Outside, on the tennis court, Mr. Carter replaced his racket in its press while Mr. Wilkins slackened the net.

"Phew!" Mr. Wilkins mopped his brow. "That last set was pretty strenuous. What about coming for a swim?"

"I'd rather cool off a bit first," replied Mr. Carter.

"It'll be dark before we finish if we don't go now; the dormitory bell went five minutes ago. Hind has just been whistling the boys back from the pond." Mr. Wilkins laughed. "Poor old Hind! I'll bet he'd rather come in for a nice cool dip with us, than traipse about on dormitory duty."

Mr. Carter was not quite sure that he wanted a nice cool dip, but he accompanied his colleague to the swimming bath all the same. When he saw the state of the water he *was* quite sure!

"No," he said firmly. "I'm not swimming in that. I'll wait until Robinson's changed the water."

"You shouldn't bother about a little grime on the surface," replied Mr. Wilkins genially, as he disappeared into a cubicle to change. "It does you good to have a swim every day. Takes your mind off Form 3."

"My mind doesn't need taking off Form 3."

"Well mine does," came through the cubicle door. "That boy, Jennings, for instance. He was deliberately trying to give me facetious answers all through the geometry lesson this afternoon."

Mr. Carter sat on a bench and filled his pipe. "I wouldn't be too sure they were *meant* to be facetious, Wilkins," he said. "They may have sounded funny to you, but that's because, at the age of ten, Jennings' mind doesn't work in quite the same way that yours does."

"Nonsense; you're making excuses for him," replied his colleague. "If I had my way I'd ... I say, Carter, there's a glass tank in this cubicle. Where on earth has that come from?" But there seemed to be little point in pursuing the matter, while the swimming bath lay cool and tempting before him.

Mr. Wilkins was a strong swimmer, but an uncertain diver. He stood poised for a moment on the springboard and then launched himself into the air. There was a sharp smack as he hit the water, and Mr. Carter hastily moved back as the wash billowed over and drenched the matting round the edge of the pool. Mr. Wilkins swam under water for a few strokes and then spluttered his way to the surface.

"Ah, that's better!" he called. "You should have come in, Carter; it's lovely in here."

"I'll take your word for it," replied Mr. Carter, eyeing the water with distaste. Vaguely he wondered how a film of biscuit crumbs—or was it sawdust?—came to be floating on the bath at all. In point of fact, it was powdered fish-food, but he had no means of knowing that.

"Well, as I was saying," Mr. Wilkins went on, rolling over on his back and churning the water noisily with both feet, "I warned Jennings that if I had any more funny answers from him, I should go off the deep end about it."

"What did you say?" Mr. Carter found it difficult to hear above the splash of his colleague's vigorous back-stroke.

"I said I'd go off the deep end."

"You've just done that," said Mr. Carter. "I felt the splash."

"No, what I meant was ..." Mr. Wilkins broke off and roared with laughter. "Ha-ha-ha— That was jolly good! I could make up a funny story out of that— Form 3 would love it. I'll tell them I was just going to dive and I thought about Jennings, so I went off the deep end. Ha-ha-ha ..." The mirth ended in a sudden gurgle as the swimmer's face disappeared beneath the surface. A second later, when he came to the top, his jocular mood had gone, for few people can indulge in hearty laughter under the water without serious discomfort.

"Ach! ... Gll! ... Pff! ... Corwumph!" gasped Mr. Wilkins. "I say, Carter, this water's filthy."

"I can see that. We can't let the boys use it again until it's been properly cleaned out. I'll tell Robinson to start draining it, right away."

"And look at the muck in it," protested the swimmer. "Dash it, I got an earful of pondweed when I went under just now. That sort of stuff shouldn't be growing in an indoor swimming bath. And besides that .... Good heavens!"

"What's the matter?"

A look of amazement passed across Mr. Wilkin's damp features. "I say, Carter," he gasped, "I'm seeing things. I—I've just seen a fish!"

"Nonsense," replied Mr. Carter. "This isn't an aquarium."

"No, but, dash it, I did see it; it shot right past me. Some sort of carp, it looked like. I've had enough of this—I'm coming out." And with swift strokes, Mr. Wilkins swam to the side and climbed from the water. He was gravely perturbed. Things had come to a pretty pass, he thought, when the school swimming bath sprouted pond-weed and teemed with marine life.

"Impossible," Mr. Carter told him. "You imagined it."

"I tell you, I *did* see a fish," his colleague insisted. "It swam right past me snapping its jaws. It was as big as that, easily." He held out his hands to demonstrate the size; then, noting Mr. Carter's smile of disbelief, he reduced the dimensions to about a handsbreadth. "It must have been that big, anyway," he maintained.

"What a pity it got away! A specimen that size would look most imposing if it were stuffed and put in a glass case," replied Mr. Carter, still wearing his amused smile.

Mr. Wilkins gave him a look. "You don't believe me, do you? You think I'm trying to be funny."

"No funnier than Jennings tries to be when he gives you an answer you didn't expect."

There was a puzzled frown on Mr. Wilkins' face all the time he was dressing. He couldn't have been mistaken about a thing like that; and yet ... He gave it up. That sort of thing didn't happen in well-regulated preparatory schools!

As the masters were leaving the bath, they met Robinson, the odd-job man, on the door-step. He was known to the boys as Old Pyjams, for no better reason than that his opposite number, the night-watchman, was known as Old Nightie. It was no news to Robinson that the water needed renewing, and indeed he had arrived for that very purpose. He always opened the sluice valve in the evening, he explained, so that the water would have all night in which to drain away, and the bath would be ready to be cleaned the following morning before it was re-filled.

"Does it take all night to empty?" asked Mr. Wilkins.

"Oh yes, sir; very slow to drain it is because of the filter. We had that fitted two years ago on account of the boys dropping things into the bath, accidental like, and losing them for good and all."

He was a young man, was "Old" Pyjams and always ready for a chat. "You'd be surprised at the things I find washed up against the filter sometimes when I clean the bath out," he went on. "Gym shoes, cricket balls, towels—all manner. Why, I found a wristwatch on the bottom last summer; been there the best part of three weeks. Wasn't going, though," he finished sorrowfully.

When the masters had gone, Robinson opened the sluice valve and "tut-tutted" at the colour of the water, now draining slowly away. It was less than three weeks since he had re-filled the bath and he could hardly believe that seventy-nine boys could make so much water so dirty, in so short a time. But then, he was not allowing for a tin full of fish food, an armful of pond-weed and a flowerpot full of earth.

At the first note of the rising bell, Jennings leapt out of bed and roused the sleeping Darbishire with an impatient jerk of the sheet. As a rule they rose in a leisurely manner and spent some time practising clove-hitches with their dressing gown cords, but today urgent work lay ahead.

Venables, Atkinson and Temple, with whom they shared Dormitory 4, had only arrived at the yawning and head-scratching stage when Jennings and Darbishire hurried from the room.

Jennings went for the key while Darbishire fetched his butterfly net from the games room.

"I've botched the hole up a bit," he said as they met outside the swimming bath, "but it's rather like locking the stable door after the horse has bolted."

Jennings inspected the repair work. "I should think the horse could still get through this net, the way you've mended it."

"Which horse?"

"The one you were talking about."

"Oh, but there isn't a horse, really!"

"You said there was."

No, it's just a saying. I didn't mean it literally. We don't really want to catch a horse, do we?"

"Well, stop nattering about stable doors, then," said Jennings, as he fumbled with the lock and stepped over the threshold. "It ought to be pretty easy to catch him now the ground bait's had time to work, so all we've got to do is to lure him to the side, and I'll lean over and …. Oh, gosh! … Oh, crumbs! … Darbishire, look!"

Darbishire *was* looking. Together they stood and stared at the empty swimming bath in dismay. Little pools lay in hollows all along the bottom and the flowerpot was floating against the strainer at the far end. But of Elmer there was no sign.

They climbed down to the floor of the bath and inspected each puddle with care, for some of the hollows were deep enough to afford temporary shelter for a three-inch fish. It was all to no purpose, and even a minute inspection of the filter failed to reveal any fish-like trace.

"This is ozard," moaned Darbishire. "He must have gone down the drain with the water. Gosh, what a frantic bish! Whatever will Bromo say?"

"Quite a lot, I expect," Jennings answered unhappily. "He may even have a relapse. After all, how would you feel if someone told you that your next-of-kin had gone down the plughole in the bath?"

"He wouldn't," Darbishire objected. "My father says that our bath at home is too small for him to lie down in properly, so he couldn't …"

"Well, you know what I mean. Now we must keep calm, Darbi, and think things out. If we can find where the water goes when it runs away, there's just a chance we might be able to find him. It's a million to one, I admit, but he may still be alive."

"Do you think so?" breathed Darbishire. "My father says that while there's life there's hope."

"Well, provided Elmer's got enough water, we can still go on hoping."

"That's right," Darbishire agreed. "All he needs is plenty of hope and water." He brightened a little and the numbed look faded from behind his spectacles. "Hope and water," he repeated. "Gosh, Jen, I could make up a creasingly funny pun about hope and water, if I set my mind to it."

Jennings turned to his friend and his expression was a mixture of anger and despair. "Dash it all, Darbi!" he protested. "This is no time to be making ridiculous Form 1 jokes. This is a matter of life and death!"

"Sorry, Jen," said Darbishire humbly, and followed his friend out of the swimming bath.

CHAPTER 5

THE KETTLE OF FISH

DURING BREAKFAST, Jennings thought hard. He was more than willing to confess to his presence in the swimming-bath, if such a course would help to restore Elmer to his tank. But he felt that the staff would show little sympathy towards the fate of one small fish, and they would certainly forbid rescue operations if this meant interfering with school routine.

The best course, he decided, would be to find out what happened to the water when it flowed away. Until he had done so, it would be wiser to say nothing, for Bromwich major was only just recovering from an attack of mumps, and one must never alarm an invalid in a delicate state of health.

After breakfast and during break, Jennings made a few guarded inquiries, and one of the gardeners told him all he needed to know. After passing through the filter, the water was carried underground by pipes until it emerged in a ditch near the pond. Then it flowed across a meadow which the boys seldom used, for this part of the school grounds was rented by a neighbouring farmer.

Wednesday was a half-holiday, and immediately after lunch, Jennings and Darbishire set out on their errand of mercy. Operation Rescue had replaced Operation Exercise and, as Jennings pointed out, this applied to Operation Geometry Exercise as well, for Elmer's recapture must certainly be attended to without delay.

They passed the pond and followed the ditch across the meadow, examining every foot of water as they went.

"This seems pretty hopeless to me," Jennings observed after nearly an hour's fruitless search. "We've come about a hundred miles already, and we haven't seen a whisker of him."

"Of course we haven't—they don't have whiskers," Darbishire corrected. "Now, if we were looking for a cat, you *could* say we hadn't seen a whisker."

"But we're not looking for a cat, you prehistoric remains!"

"No, but *supposing* we were."

Jennings, mudsplashed and miserable, turned on his companion with some heat. "What's the point of *supposing* we're looking for a cat, when you know wizard well we're looking for a fish? Come on, Darbi, we've got to follow this ditch till we get to the end of it—wherever that is."

"That'll be about another hundred miles, I expect," said Darbishire. He removed his spectacles and polished them with his tie. "Oh, gosh, isn't this a ghastly hoo-hah! There's just about everything else you can think of in this ditch—frogs and toads and newts and stinging nettles and old boots—everything except a goldfish."

They both knew in their heart of hearts that the quest was a failure, but neither of them would admit it. Darbishire replaced his glasses and his gaze wandered listlessly round the meadow. "Where have we got to?" he demanded. "I've never been here before. Aren't we out of bounds?"

"We're still on school property," Jennings told him, "only we don't come here because Farmer Arrowsmith uses it to graze his old cow in."

"Oh, I see," Darbishire replied. "That explains why ... Oh! I say, Jen, I believe I can see it, now I've cleaned my glasses."

"Oh, wizzo!" shouted Jennings, his hopes rising like an express lift. "Quick, Darbi—where?"

"Over there, look!"

Jennings followed the line of the pointing finger to where a middle-aged cow seemed to be playing some form of basketball with a turnip. Patiently he explained the difference between a cow and goldfish.

"Oh, I didn't mean Elmer," Darbishire pointed out. "I meant I could see Farmer Arrowsmith's old cow. What do you think we ought to do? She's coming over here."

"Do? We needn't do anything. Cows don't hurt you."

"They do if they're bulls," said Darbishire uneasily. "And, anyway, I'm not very fond of cows, even if you're sure that's what it is. I've got a sort of feeling about them."

"You must be like my Aunt Angela. She has the same sort of feeling about cats. She hates them; she can always tell when there's a cat in the room."

"Well, I could always tell if there was a cow in the room," retorted Darbishire logically; and he sidled towards a tree whose branches offered shelter in case of attack.

"Don't be such a great funk, Darbi!" snorted Jennings contemptuously. "You don't want to be afraid of a harmless old ..." He broke off and glanced at the cow with sudden misgiving. She had abandoned her basketball and was charging towards the boys as fast as her horny hoofs would permit.

Jennings stared: this cow was not friendly, perhaps she held strong views on the laws of trespass; perhaps she felt as strongly about boys as Darbishire felt about cows; perhaps … He ceased his speculations and joined his friend in the lower branches of the tree.

The cow arrived at the tree and moo'ed at them from below. Then, as nothing happened, she thudded away to resume her game on the far side of the meadow.

The boys were tired of the ditch, so they sat for a while in the tree, discussing what to do next. It was clear that they were wasting their time, to say nothing of incurring further trouble; for Jennings should have been hard at work on his geometry exercise, and Darbishire should have been playing cricket. Finally, they decided that the music would have to be faced, and the news of his sad loss must be broken to Bromwich major without delay. They would buy him another fish—two fishes, if he liked, plus any other form of compensation that he might demand. With the best of intentions, they had done Bromwich a great wrong, and they were prepared to stand with bowed heads while his wrath cascaded about their ears.

They felt a little better after this decision and were about to climb down from the tree, when they observed Mr. Wilkins crossing the meadow. "Oh, golly, we've had it now!" said Jennings. And he was right—they had!

"What on earth are you two boys doing up there?" Mr. Wilkins had the sort of voice that would be highly commended in any competition for town criers, and though he was still forty yards from the tree, there was no need for him to raise his voice above its normal volume. "You've no business to be in this part of the grounds at all," he went on, as the boys climbed down and stood guiltily before him. "You haven't finished that exercise yet, have you, Jennings?"

"No, sir, I haven't *quite* got to the end of it yet, sir."

"Why not?"

"Because—well, because I haven't quite got to the beginning part yet, sir."

"Exactly," boomed Mr. Wilkins. "Just as I thought. And you climbed up that tree hoping that I shouldn't see you!"

"Oh, no sir, really," Darbishire assured him. "We thought we were going to be attacked by a fierce cow, but it was a mistake, and you turned up instead, sir." Even as he said it he knew that, as an excuse, it sounded rather feeble—especially as the cow was now out of sight.

Mr. Wilkins thought so, too. "Nonsense!" he said. "You were making a deliberate attempt to keep out of my way."

"Oh, but we weren't, sir, honestly. We never even saw you until you saw us," Jennings protested.

"No? Then do you mind telling me"—and Mr. Wilkins dropped his voice to a quiet, confident undertone— "do you mind telling me just what you *were* doing?"

"We—we were looking for a fish, sir."

"What! *Up a tree?*"

"Well, yes and no, sir. I mean ..."

"I—I—Corwumph! I've had quite enough of this insolence," barked Mr. Wilkins, turning three shades pinker. "I warned you only yesterday what would happen if I had any more funny answers from you. You'll go straight back to school immediately, and report to me in the staff room."

"Yes, sir."

Mr. Wilkins strode away, furious at what he considered to be a facetious and impertinent answer to his question, and the two boys turned their footsteps towards home. It was not a cheerful journey and after they had walked a hundred yards in silence, Darbishire said: "You are a fool, Jen!"

"Well, it wasn't my fault," his friend defended himself. "We really *were* looking for a fish."

"Yes, but you put it badly. Even Old Wilkie knows fish don't live in trees, unless you're speaking alley—er, alley-something."

"Alibi?"

"No, allegorically, that's it: it means saying something that sounds quite crazy, but it's all right really, because everyone knows what you mean."

"Do they? That's more than *I* do!"

"Well, it's like that chunk of English we had to learn for Mr. Carter, about sermons in stones, and books in the running brooks."

"You're bats!" Jennings retorted. "There wouldn't be any books in the brook unless someone had put them there."

"That's exactly what I mean. There wouldn't be any fish up a tree either because they can't climb. At least," he went on, "if one *did* climb a tree it'd be all over the newspapers. Big headlines: *Goldfish's Amazing Feat!*"

"Yes, it would be, if it had any, wouldn't it?"

"Wouldn't it *what?*"

"It'd be amazing if a goldfish had got any feet."

Darbishire began to realise that they were talking at cross-purposes. Curtly he said: "No, you ancient relic, I didn't mean that sort of feet."

"For heaven's sake stop talking nonsense," Jennings answered. "There's no point in arguing about what sort of feet it's got, if it hasn't got any."

They were too tired of the subject to talk any more, and they finished the journey in gloomy silence. They met Atkinson as they were crossing the quad; he came bounding towards them with another message he had received from Bromwich, via Matron, via him, to Jennings. Elmer's next-of-kin, it seemed, was thirsting for the latest bulletin about his pet's welfare.

"Well, actually, we've made a bit of a bish over Elmer, and we've lost him," Jennings admitted.

"Lost him!" Atkinson sounded incredulous. "Gosh, you must be spivish absent-minded! Have you looked carefully all round his tank?"

"It's worse than that," said Jennings. "He's gone for good. Darbi's going up to Matron to ask her to see Bromo and break it to him gently."

They had no time to satisfy Atkinson's curiosity, for Jennings had an appointment with Mr. Wilkins which it would be unwise to overlook. But his main worry was about Bromwich major: how on earth could he soften the blow? There seemed no answer to this problem and his heart was heavy as he knocked on the staff room door.

Mr. Carter was alone when Jennings opened the door and asked: "Sir, is Mr. Wilkins here, please sir?"

It seemed rather a pointless question to Mr. Carter, for the staff room was sparsely furnished and the chances that his colleague was hiding behind the bookcase were remote. He pointed this out.

"Yes, I see, sir. We must have raced him back, then," said Jennings. "I'd better go and look for him, because I've got to report at once." He was about to close the door behind him, when Mr. Carter called him back.

"By the way, Jennings: when you find Mr. Wilkins will you tell him from me that swimming will have to be cancelled this afternoon. Robinson hasn't finished cleaning the bath out yet."

"Yes, sir." And in a burst of confidence the boy added: "It was rotten luck that the bath was emptied last night, sir."

"I don't agree," said Mr. Carter. "It was high time that water was changed.

You probably won't believe it, but Robinson tells me that when he went there at half-past six this morning to see if, the bath was empty, he found ... I'll give you three guesses."

Jennings got it in one. "I know, sir: a goldfish!"

"Well, well," said Mr. Carter. "I might have known you'd had something to do with it. You'd better tell me what happened."

Jennings was thankful for the opportunity; his troubles had been preying heavily on his mind, and Mr. Carter was a very understanding sort of man. There was a punishment, of course—no swimming for a week for going to the bath without permission. But Jennings was glad about this, for if Bromwich was to suffer, it was only right that the culprits, too, should pay some penalty for their folly. Then he realised that Mr. Carter was still speaking, and what he was saying meant that Bromwich would not have to suffer after all.

"... and if it hadn't been for the strainer, you'd have lost him altogether," Mr. Carter finished up.

"Do you mean the fish is all right then, sir?" Jennings gasped in wonder.

"Perfectly. It's as lively a fish as I ever saw. Robinson found it flapping about in a puddle near the strainer, and the only thing he could find to put it in was a kettle that the night watchman uses for his tea."

"Oh, sir—how supersonic, sir! Thanks awfully, sir! Gosh, this is the best news I've ever heard, sir! May I go and get him and put him back in his tank, please sir?"

"The sooner the better," replied Mr. Carter. "Robinson's put the kettle in the woodshed for the time being. I said I'd let him know what to do with it, later on."

Outside in the corridor Darbishire was waiting. He had delivered the doleful news to Matron who had agreed to pass it on after tea, when her patient might be feeling strong enough to withstand the shock. After that, Darbishire went downstairs to wait for Jennings, and he was more than a little surprised when his friend shot out of the staff room wearing the sort of expression on his face that was not usually worn after unpleasant interviews with Mr. Wilkins.

"Did you find him, Jen?" he inquired.

"No, but I know where he is," Jennings called back gaily. "He's in a kettle in the woodshed."

"Who—Mr. Wilkins?"

"No—Elmer. Mr. Carter said they found him when they let the water out and he got stopped by the strainer."

"Who—Mr. Carter?"

"No, you ancient monument, I'm still talking about the fish."

"Oh, good!" cried Darbishire, as light dawned. "I thought your hoo-hah with Old Wilkie had been so ghastly that you'd gone stark raving bats and I should have to humour you."

The woodshed was on the far side of the kitchen yard at the rear of the main school buildings: the two boys dashed madly along the corridors and across the quad and never slackened pace until their goal was in sight. Speed was essential; not only because they were eager to see Elmer again, but also in case the night watchman should decide to make himself a cup of tea without first inspecting the kettle. Panting and breathless, the rescuers reached the woodshed and hastened inside.

Mr. Wilkins was a little late in arriving back at school, for he had met Farmer Arrowsmith and had been obliged to stop and listen to a short lecture on the state of British farming; but now he was anxious to deal with Jennings without further delay, so he took a shortcut across the kitchen garden in order to save time. As he picked his way across the cabbage patch, he caught sight of two figures disappearing through the door of the woodshed; one had dark brown hair, and the other was fair and curly. They were some distance away, but Mr. Wilkins had no difficulty in recognising them. After all, it was less than half an hour since he had seen them up a tree.

"I—I—Corwumph!" he muttered. He turned three shades pinker and his mood was volcanic as he altered his course and strode towards the woodshed door.

It was dark inside the shed, and for a moment the boys could see nothing. There was a window, but it was covered with cobwebs; and so, too, was Darbishire by the time he had groped his way past the bundles of firewood piled high upon the floor. Jennings found the kettle in the darkest corner and hurried with it to the window.

"I've got it, Darbi. Hurray, Elmer's saved!" he cried in triumph.

"Wizzo!" shouted Darbishire through his cobwebs.

Jennings brushed the dirt from one of the panes with his fingers, and a little light streamed in and lit up the occupant of the kettle. "He's all right, too," Jennings went on. "He's swimming about like blinko. Come over here and have a look."

"I can't look," complained Darbishire. "I'm covered in cobweb. I walked straight into the blackest one I ever saw. Or rather, I didn't actually see it, or I shouldn't have walked into it; and now it's all over my face, I can't see anything at all."

"I can," said Jennings. "I can see ..." He was going to say: "I can see Elmer doing his famous backwards breast-stroke," but a shadow passed across the window and the boy looked out to see who it was. "I can see Mr. Wilkins and I think he's coming in," he finished up, and his tone had lost much of its gaiety.

The door screeched open on its rusty hinges, and Mr. Wilkins burst in like the advance guard of an armoured column.

"Come here at once, you two boys," he boomed, and in the confines of the tiny shed his voice sounded as though the armoured column was making the most of its heavy artillery. "I told you to report to me in the staff room, Jennings."

"Yes, sir, I did, sir, but you weren't there, sir. I was going to come and look for you, sir, but ..."

"You didn't think you'd find me in the woodshed, did you?"

"Oh no, sir, but ..."

"But you thought it would be a good place to hide in," Mr. Wilkins broke in. "Trying to evade me, eh? So what's in the woodpile then?"

"That's Darbishire, Sir," Jennings explained. "He only looks like that because he's got a bit cobwebby, and we weren't hiding from you, honestly, sir."

"Then what on earth *are* you doing in here?"

"We're—we were looking for a kettle of fish, sir."

It was an unfortunate way to describe it and, as Darbishire remarked afterwards, talking about kettles of fish put the lid on it.

"I—I—Corwumph! I've had enough of these insolent answers. Gross impudence and rank impertinence! You'll come along with me to the Headmaster's study immediately."

Mr. Wilkins led the way out into the sunlight and the boys followed him. Darbishire made an attempt to tidy himself, but he merely succeeded in smearing the cobwebs over the cleaner parts of his neck and ears. He removed his spectacles and wiped the dust from the lenses with his even dustier fingers.

"We'll see what the Head has to say about deliberate attempts to be funny," said Mr. Wilkins. "And what's more, I gave you fair warning about ..." He stopped abruptly, for he had just noticed that Jennings was carrying an unusual object. "What have you got there?" the master demanded.

"It's the kettle of fish, sir," Jennings replied. "I told you there was one and you wouldn't believe me. Look, sir, you can see the fish swimming about inside."

Mr. Wilkins stared. "I—I—well, I—Corwumph!" he said. It was not a very profound remark, but for the moment he could think of nothing else to say.

They did not go to the Headmaster's study. They went, instead, to the staff room, where Mr. Carter filled in the gaps in the story for the benefit of his colleague. Mr. Wilkins was still very annoyed, but he was a fair-minded man, and when he realised that Jennings' answers had been made in good faith, and that the boys had had permission to visit the woodshed, he took a more tolerant view of their activities. They had already been punished for misusing the swimming bath, so apart from a few curt comments about geometry exercises, there was little more to be said.

"You can go now," said Mr. Wilkins when he had exhausted his stock of curt comments. "Go and start that geometry exercise at once."

"Yes, sir. Thank you, sir. Will it be all right if I put the fish back in his tank first, sir, and then tell Matron that she needn't break it gently after all, sir?"

"What on earth should Matron want to break it for? Look here, if you're starting ..."

"Oh, no, sir," Jennings explained hastily. "I don't mean break the tank—I meant the news. She won't have to tell Bromwich major that his next-of-kin has slipped down the plughole after all, sir."

As the door shut behind the two boys, Mr. Wilkins turned to his colleague with a puzzled frown.

"Next-of-kin?" he echoed. "What on earth's the silly little boy drivelling about, Carter? The trouble with Jennings is that he lets his imagination run away with him. Fish nesting in trees and lurking in kettles—he needs bringing down to earth. I've a good mind to make him write out 'I must not let my imagination run away with me' a hundred times."

Mr. Carter rose from his chair and knocked his pipe out in the fireplace. "I don't think I should do that, Wilkins," he said. "We all do the same thing at times, even though we're not ten-year-olds."

"Nonsense," replied Mr. Wilkins. "I've got my imagination under control all right!"

"I wonder! You remember that fish that frightened you out of the swimming bath, yesterday evening? A large carp, I believe, that snapped its jaws at you."

Mr. Wilkins could see where the conversation was leading. "I—I—well, what of it?" he demanded.

"I was only thinking," Mr. Carter went on, "that as it's the same one that you saw just now in that little kettle, it's either shrunk during the night, or you let your imagination run away with you yesterday, when you told me how big it was."

"I—er, h'm," said Mr. Wilkins thoughtfully.

"So I don't think that a hundred lines for Jennings would be quite fair in this case, do you?"

Mr. Wilkins frowned hard at the wastepaper basket for some moments. Then he said slowly: "Perhaps you're right, Carter .... Perhaps you're right."

CHAPTER 6

MAIDEN VOYAGE

THE LITTLE HUT was finished. The bulrush curtains flapped gaily over the unglazed window; the painting of the green-faced cow stared moodily from its picture-frame; on the threshold, the doormat welcomed visitors to *Ye Oldë Worldë Huttë* in letters of coloured bottle-top.

Some of the more ambitious ideas had been reluctantly abandoned. The Headmaster had refused to allow camp cookery on open fires even though the patent fire-extinguisher stood ready to hand; the refrigerator was not a success either, and the ageing pork pie had long since been thrown into the pond; but as the living room was becoming rather full of gadgets, the extra space was more than welcome.

There was nothing else to do now, except to enjoy the fruits of their labour, so Jennings invited Temple and Venables to a hut-warming party. They squatted on the floor—no longer wet, thanks to the special dehydrating canal—and ate walnut cake and sardines, which they washed down with a tin of condensed milk.

"Now it's all finished," Jennings told his guests, "we're going to take up some interesting hobbies with the hut as our headquarters. We can't just sit inside all the time, like a couple of spare dinners, and look at the furniture."

"We *were* going to collect tadpoles," added Darbishire, hacking two holes in the condensed milk tin with his penknife, "but after that hoo-hah about Elmer we both felt a little 'off' fish." His penknife penetrated the lid with a sudden gurgle, forcing little bubbles of milk through the outlet hole on the other side.

"Aerial bombardment would be a super-cracking hobby," suggested Venables. "We could climb up trees and try and score direct hits on other chaps' huts with hunks of turf."

"No fear," said Jennings firmly. "We've been to a lot of trouble to build decent shacks, so what's the point of knocking them down? Besides, our hut is a supersonic sight too near a tree—we'd be the first one to suffer the bomb damage."

Darbishire nodded in agreement and said: "That's quite right. It's like what my father says about people who live in glass houses not throwing stones, or rather, people who live in reed huts shouldn't bung turf—it's the same thing, really."

"It's not the same thing at all," objected Temple with his mouth full of cake and sardine. "If you can't tell the diff. between a glass house and an igloo ..."

"You don't understand. It's just a saying," Darbishire pointed out. "There are no such things as glass houses, really."

"There wizard well are!" Temple maintained. "We've got one at home. We grow tomatoes in it, so that proves it."

"Yes, I know, but I meant the other sort."

"What other sort?"

"The sort that if you live in them, you shouldn't throw stones."

"But a moment ago, you said there *was* no other sort. You told us there was no such thing."

"Yes, but I meant ... Oh, never mind. Have a drink!" And Darbishire licked his sticky fingers, and thrust the condensed milk at his guest.

Venables was forced to admit that aerial bombardment sounded rather feeble when compared with the idea which suddenly sprang up in Jennings' mind. "Let's make a model yacht," he suggested.

They seized upon his idea eagerly. The setting was perfect—a reed-fringed pond was just the place for hobbies with a nautical flavour. In a flash their minds leapt into the future, foreseeing squadrons of model yachts in full sail, skimming gracefully across the little muddy pond. They felt the thrill of the neck-and-neck finish in the famous four-lengths handicap race; they saw the annual regatta attended by craft which ranged from *J* class models down to odd bits of cigar-box with penholder masts. The possibilities of a yacht club were endless; they could build a club house with *Members Only* inscribed on the door; officers would be elected—presidents, secretaries, commodores and admirals who would be entitled to strut about wearing yachting caps.

In a few minutes they had formed a committee and were hard at work drafting the rules. Darbishire was appointed secretary and filled three pages of his notebook with the Minutes of the meeting. Then he read them out.

"*Rule One*. Any character wanting to join the club must have a boat that actually floats. *Rule Two ...*"

"Hang on a sec," objected Temple. "We're putting the cart before the horse.

We haven't got a boat between us yet, so we can't even be members, let alone commodores and things."

It was, without doubt, a serious drawback, and Jennings descended to brass tacks right away. "We'll have to get cracking and make one then," he said. "We can't have a model yacht club until we've got a model yacht."

They cancelled the committee meeting and set to work. Temple and Venables scavenged for suitable pieces of wood while Jennings went off to borrow a chisel from the carpenter's shop. Darbishire retired to his small back room, armed with his notebook, to design the stately lines on which the boat was to be built. If only he had brought his geometry box with him, he could have constructed his blue-print with more accuracy; but no one takes geometrical instruments to a hut-warming party, so he did the best he could with a stub of pencil, using a damp forefinger as a rubber.

The yacht was not built that day. It took two days to collect the materials, and a further three evenings' hard work was necessary before the craft could be described as remotely ship-shape. When at last it was finished, the four boys stood round in wide-eyed admiration!

"Isn't she rare," breathed Venables. "And she'll be sailing in uncharted waters too, because no one knows how deep the pond is in the middle."

"We'll soon find that out if she capsizes on her maiden voyage. If the mast's still showing above water when she's on the bottom, it can't be more than a foot deep," Temple argued.

The design of the boat had little in common with the usual type of yacht, for it was shaped rather like a flat-bottomed barge. It was three feet long: the hull was weighted with a small brick so that it would not ride too high in the water and, as a precaution, Darbishire's sponge had been built into the fo'c's'l, in case the vessel should not ride high enough. The sail had caused some trouble, for the school sewing room had turned out to be a disappointing marine store when Jennings went there in search of sail-cloth. In the end he decided to rig his handkerchief into a single square sail, as favoured by the Vikings. Experts would have been critical of the craft's ungainly lines, but the boys had made the whole thing themselves and they prized it above any factory-built model.

"Not bad is she!" cooed Darbishire. "Your handkerchief makes a supersonic sail, Jen."

And Venables added: "Quite out of the ordinary, too. You don't often see a pale black sail with blotches of red ink on it."

"My handkerchief is *not* pale black," Jennings defended himself. "It's just a rather dark white."

"Let's go and launch her now. I can hardly wait to see her skimming across the pond." Darbishire skipped up and down excitedly until he bumped his head on the hut's low ceiling and skipped no more.

"I vote we have a proper launching ceremony and crack a bottle of ginger pop against the bows," suggested Temple.

"We haven't got any ginger pop," said Venables.

"Well, a tin of condensed milk, then."

"Gosh, no!" Jennings was horrified. "The bows might bust before the tin, and then she'd founder in six fathoms of pond-weed and I shouldn't get my handkerchief back. It's a bit chronic, having to sniff all the time as it is."

They carried the boat to the water's edge, but unfortunately the whistle blew before they had time to begin the launching ceremony. They "tut-tutted" with exasperation.

"That means waiting till tomorrow evening. I'll never be able to hold out all that long," complained Temple.

"Tomorrow's Sunday," Darbishire reminded him, "and we're not allowed over here in our best suits, so we'll have to wait now till next week."

They could not bring themselves to face a forty-eight hours' delay. It was too disappointing after so many days of patient toil.

"There's only one thing for it," said Jennings: "we'll have to fox over here tomorrow afternoon and have a go then."

The little group glanced at one another doubtfully. Sunday afternoon spelt Walk during term time, and there was no way of avoiding it. Unless of course … Four minds reached the same answer and the expression on four faces plainly said they were all agreed.

"Right-o, we'll do that, then," said Jennings.

The Sunday walk at Linbury was not, except for the youngest boys, the dismal crocodile procession which wanders forth from so many school gates on Sunday afternoons. Linbury Court was on the South Downs, not far from the sea. There was a village half a mile away, and the small town of Dunhambury lay some five miles to the west. It was ideal country for walks for there was little traffic except on the main road which ran past the school gates.

The usual practice was for boys to give their names to the master on duty and then set off in small groups to walk as far as the sea and back. They could vary this if they wished and follow the footpaths across the open downland, but always they had to inform the duty master of their route and report to him when they returned at four o'clock.

If, however, some pressing engagement awaited their return to school—the launching of a model yacht, for example—then it was possible for the walk to be shortened. Not officially, of course, and never when Mr. Carter was on duty, but the thing *could* be done if one was prepared to take the risk.

Mr. Wilkins was the master on duty that Sunday: he sat in the staff room after lunch and jotted down the names of the boys as they reported to him. Presently four third-formers approached in a body. "Please, sir, will you put us down, sir."

Mr. Wilkins did so. 'Jennings—Darbishire—Venables—Temple,' he wrote, and looking up he inquired: "Are you going down to the sea?"

"Well, sir, *towards* the sea, sir," said Jennings, and left it at that.

And towards the sea they went. But after covering three hundred yards they swung round in a circle and arrived back at the far end of the school grounds near the pond. Cautiously they crept to the hut and carried the yacht down to the water's edge, but soon they stopped bothering about caution. No one was about, no one would disturb them: provided that they reported to Mr. Wilkins at four o'clock, all would be well. Or so they thought!

"We ought to name this ship," Darbishire said. "What about the H.M.S. *J. C. T. Jennings the First?* That's only fair, really, because it was all Jen's super-cracking wheeze in the first place."

"That's too many initials," replied the inventor of the super-cracking wheeze modestly. "I vote we call it the *Revenge* after Sir Richard Grenville."

"Coo, yes, that's wizzo: and this bunch of bulrushes can be Florés in the Azores where Sir Richard Grenville lay," cried Darbishire with enthusiasm.

They had recently studied Tennyson's *Revenge* in class with Mr. Carter and the poem had made a deep impression on Darbishire. He stood on the bank and declaimed dramatically:

"'At Florés in the Azores, Sir Richard Grenville lay,
And a pinnace, like a fluttered bird, came flying from far away:
Spanish ships of war at sea,
We have sighted fifty-three ...'"

Those two old moorhens over there can be the fifty-three ...

"'Then sware Lord Thomas Howard ...'"

The other members of the yacht club grew restive, for they were anxious to get on with the launching ceremony. "We can't wait for you to finish the whole poem, Darbi," they reminded him, and gathered round to watch the *Revenge* set sail on her maiden voyage.

"There she goes .... Pheew-doyng!" said Jennings as the craft slid down the muddy slipway and hit the water with a splash.

For a moment they panicked as the boat rocked from side to side, but a moment later she righted herself, and they breathed again and gave three cheers. Whispered cheers, though, for they had no wish to draw undue attention to themselves.

There was a slight breeze which caught the "pale black" sail and the *Revenge* veered out to the middle of the pond while the boat-builders danced hornpipes of delight. Two moorhens were enjoying a peaceful Sunday afternoon swim, but when they saw the strange craft bearing down upon them they made for the bank at top speed.

"Look!" cried Darbishire. "The Spanish galleons are in retreat at full steam ahead. The *Revenge* will go *slap-bang-doyng* into them, if they don't look out!"

"She won't," replied Venables. "She'll go *doyng* into those reeds on the far side. Then what are we going to do?"

"I'll hoof round to the other side and head her off." Jennings was in charge and gave the orders.

"Stand by for Operation Salvage!" he cried, and ran as fast as he could round the rim of the pond.

Darbishire climbed up a small tree where he could obtain a better view. "It's a wonderful sight from here," he announced. "Just like Sir Richard Grenville." Odd snatches of the poem raced through his mind in a tangled disorder of lines.

"'The little *Revenge* ran on sheer into the heart of the foe,
With her hundred fighters on deck, and her ninety sick below,'"

he recited.

"'Shall we fight or shall we fly?
Good Sir Richard tell us now,
For to fight is but to die!
There'll be little of us left by the time ...'"

"Yes, and there'll be little of our yacht left if she gets caught in those reeds," Temple pointed out. "She's heading straight for them at forty knots!" And a moment later his warning proved true and the *Revenge* stuck fast in the bulrushes.

By this time Jennings had reached the spot, but he was unable to reach out far enough to free the boat from its entanglements, for the reeds grew outwards from the bank and across the pond. There was only one thing to be done; a willow-tree grew on the bank and drooped its slender branches into the water. Jennings looked at it thoughtfully. If the branch would hold, he could crawl along until he was immediately above the *Revenge* and poke it back into clear water with a stick. The branch seemed fairly strong: he decided to try it.

On the far bank, Temple and Venables watched the salvage work with some anxiety.

"Looks massive perilous, doesn't it, Bod? I bet it won't hold him."

"It might, if he doesn't go too far, but he'll have to get nearly to the end before he can hoik it with that stick."

"Wow, it's quivering like an aspirin! Hadn't we better stand by with that inner tube in case he falls in?"

"He won't, if he's careful; and anyway, it's aspens that quiver, not aspirins."

"I bet you it's not. Besides, if that tree's a willow, it can't quiver like an aspen, so that proves it!"

"That's got nothing to do with it. It could be a Christmas tree for that matter—he'll still fall in if it won't hold him."

Darbishire looked down upon the discussion group with an air of detachment and wondered why they were making such a fuss. After all, *his* tree was quite safe and well away from the edge, and in his imagination he was sailing the Spanish Main with the more daring of the Elizabethan seamen. Would Sir Richard Grenville bother about getting his best suit wet? Would Sir Francis Drake turn back because the water was muddy? Darbishire stood up in his tree and encouraged the salvage work with lines of stirring poetry:

"'We have won great glory, my men!
And a day less or more
At sea or ashore
We die—does it matter when?
Sink me the ship, Master Gunner—sink her, split her in twain!
Fall into the ...'"

"Look out, Jen!" yelled Venables and Temple in unison, but the warning was too late. On the far side of the pond, Jennings felt the pliable branch sagging beneath his weight; it did not break, but, like the willow trees on *Linden Lea*, it bowed down low and gently tipped its burden head-over-heels into the water.

"Gosh, he *has* fallen in, too," Darbishire gasped in horror. "I didn't mean fall into the pond, I meant fall into the ..."

"Phew! There'll be a hoo-hah about this," breathed Venables, as Jennings rose to his feet, grabbed the *Revenge* and splashed damply up the bank.

Darbishire jumped down from his tree and rushed round to help his friend to safety. "Golly, Jen, you *are* in a mess! Are you all right?"

"Yes, *I* am," Jennings replied, "but my best suit isn't. I'm soaked to the skin."

They looked at the suit with horrified eyes. A black, fertile silt traced a pattern from shoulder to knees; little rivulets of muddy water trickled into the pockets, and pond-weed peeped shyly through the buttonholes.

"What a frantic bish! Why do these hoo-hahs always pick on *us* to happen to?" Darbishire wanted to know. "What are we going to do? You can't go back to school looking like Old Father Thames—Matron would be livid! That suit's nearly new, isn't it?"

Jennings nodded unhappily and wiped his face with the sail of the *Revenge*; it was the only portion of his clothing which was still dry. "This is ozard!" he lamented. "It's just trickling down me like the Niagara Falls!" He was worried, not merely on his own account, but because the disaster threatened the welfare of the whole colony of hut dwellers. Mr. Carter had warned them to avoid spoiling their clothes, and if this breach of rules ever became "front-page news" their activities in the area of the pond would come to an end.

There was only one way for the tragedy to be kept secret, and Jennings gave his orders as clearly as he could through teeth which were now beginning to chatter with cold. Venables and Temple were to hurry back to school and slip unnoticed into the dormitory; there they would find Jennings' weekday clothes which they were to bring back to the hut without delay.

"I shall want everything except a handkerchief," he told them. "You'll find them in my locker. Oh, yes, and bring a towel, too. Then, when I've changed, I'll fox down to the boiler-room and dry these wet things on the pipes. Go on, get cracking—I'm shivering like a brace of jellies already!"

"Come on, Bod," said Venables. "We'll have to be spivish careful we don't meet Old Wilkie on the way; and we'd better be pretty stealthy smuggling the stuff past Matron's room—she's got ears like a hawk."

"What about Darbi; isn't he coming with us?" asked Temple.

"No, he can stay and help keep the wind off me." And Jennings gave Temple an encouraging push to start him on his way. "Go on, get moving; I don't want to hang about here all day."

The relief party set off on its errand and Jennings squelched muddily back to the little hut. Darbishire followed carrying the *Revenge*. "Try not to leave dirty footmarks on the *Welcome* mat," he advised, but Jennings was past caring. The afternoon which had promised so well was petering out into a damp and chilly anti-climax. He sat back against the ventilating shaft and shivered.

"Golly, you *are* in a bad way," Darbishire sympathised. "Can't you stop your teeth chattering?"

Jennings turned on him angrily. "Of course, I can't! You have a bash at stopping them if you're so clever."

"All right, keep cool!"

"I *am* keeping cool. An ozard sight too cool for my liking."

"Never mind, Jen! The *Revenge* put the fifty-three Spanish galleons to flight, anyway. You ought to have seen those moorhens wobbling back to base!" Darbishire prattled on in an attempt to make his friend more cheerful. "It's all rather like the poem, in a way—us two being left all alone after the others have gone. Remember that bit where it says:

'And the sun went down, and the stars came out ...'?"

"If you think I'm going to stay here shivering till the sun goes down ..."

"No, but we can pretend you're one of the sick men down in the hold, who were most of them stark and cold."

"Huh!" Jennings' tone was crushing. "I don't have to do much pretending about that. I can feel frostbite setting in already."

Darbishire sighed as he carried the boat into the small back room. Until that wretched accident he had been quite carried away by the thrill of watching the *Revenge* riding the ripples on her maiden voyage; but now, all the poetry and glamour of the high seas seemed, somehow, to have faded, and nothing was left but a flat-bottomed barge, with a piece of sponge rammed into the fo'c's'l.

CHAPTER 7

THE BEST LAID PLANS ...

THERE IS something unusual about the stillness which descends upon preparatory schools on fine Sunday afternoons. Rooms which resound all day with shrill chatter, and corridors which throb with noisy feet become strange, unreal places when the building is deserted. By contrast, the silence seems twice as deep, and sounds which are seldom heard catch the ear with twice the expected volume. The ticking of a classroom clock, the rustling papers on the notice board beside an open window, the fly buzzing on the changing-room ceiling; these are the noises which go on all day long—the little lost murmurs which are swallowed up by the main stream of sound so that no one is ever aware of them.

Temple and Venables sensed something of this quietness as they crept through a side door into the empty hall. They had met no one on their journey from the pond, though they had taken special care when passing the Headmaster's garden and again as they crossed the quad. So far, all was well; none of the other boys had yet returned from his afternoon walk and there was no sign of the master on duty.

They pattered up the stairs, passing Matron's room on tip-toe; then on, and up the next flight to Dormitory 4.

"This is working out more easily than I thought," remarked Venables as he opened the locker marked *J. C. T. Jennings.* "There's nothing to go wrong now. All we've got to do is to grab this little lot and beetle back to the hut."

Everything was neatly laid out; suit, clean shirt, underwear, braces and socks. There was a pullover too, and though these were not worn during July, Venables added it to his collection in case of need. He bundled the garments together and shut the locker. "I'll carry these," he said. "You nip out on to the landing, Bod, and see if the coast's still clear."

"Right-o!" The whole thing had been so easy that Temple wore a smile on his lips and hummed gaily as he sauntered on to the landing. The next moment he was back; the humming had ceased and a worried frown had replaced the smile.

"It's no go, Ven," he whispered. "We're caught like rats in a trap!"

"Uh? What's happened?"

"Matron and Mr. Carter. They've just come out of Matron's sitting room and they're nattering away like blinko on the landing outside her door. We should never be able to walk past them carrying all this clutter—they'd spot it in a flash."

"Oh, gosh, this *has* bished it up!" Venables sat on his bed, and his gaze roamed round the room in search of inspiration. What on earth could they do? Could they smuggle the clothes downstairs in that laundry basket, he wondered? But Temple poured cold water on the scheme when his friend suggested it. People who spot things in a flash could spot them in anything, he pointed out. "Dash it all, Venables, they know wizard well we aren't the dormitory maids, and if we go staggering down the stairs with a massive great wickerwork hamper in tow, they're bound to think it funny. We'll just have to wait till they hoof off."

They waited five minutes and again Temple crept out on to the landing. He returned shaking his head glumly. "They're still there. Can't think what they can find to go on talking about, hour after hour like that. You'd think grown-ups would have something better to do, wouldn't you?"

It was Venables who made the first practical suggestion. He suddenly smote himself on the brow as befitted a genius in the throes of a brainwave and said: "I've got it! We'll drop them out of the window and they'll go *doyng* down on to the quad. Then we can stroll downstairs past Matron and Mr. Carter, beef round to the quad and pick them up."

Nothing could have sounded simpler. They performed a short dance to show how pleased they were with the idea and then Temple skipped over to the window, flung it open and looked out.

"Stand out of the daylight, Bod; I'm going to bung," announced Venables. "One ... two ... three ..." But with a sudden gasp of alarm, Temple withdrew his head and laid a restraining hand on his friend's arm. "Whoa, halt, stop! For Pete's sake, don't bung. Gosh, we nearly made a bish that time!" As he shut the window, he wiped imaginary beads of perspiration from his brow and his knees sagged with feigned weakness.

"What's wrong now?" demanded Venables, whose view was blocked by the bundle of clothes.

"Old Wilkie and the Head are standing just below the window. Phew, that was a chronic near squeeze! You'd have scored a direct hit on the Archbeako if I hadn't slammed the bomb doors in the nick of time."

They stood and looked at each other in blank despair. There was no way out; barriers sprang up at every turn. Surely no smuggler had ever had to face such difficulties.

"We've got to do something," said Venables five minutes later, after a furtive reconnaissance had shown that both the escape routes were still guarded. "We can't leave poor old Jen shivering his timbers and dripping like a tap, much longer."

"All taps don't drip; it's only when they need a new washer or something," Temple murmured vaguely.

"Don't quibble, Bod. We're not arguing about whether Jennings needs a new washer. What he *does* need are these dry clothes and somehow we've got to get them downstairs past Matron's observation turret. Why don't you try and think of something, instead of just sitting there and being feeble!"

"Well, I suppose we could, er—um …" Temple's mind was a blank and he spoke for the sake of speaking, but even as he fumbled with the problem the answer flashed into his mind. "I know!" he finished up brightly. "You could put Jennings' clothes on underneath your own. Matron will never notice. She'll just think you've been putting on a bit of weight lately."

Venables stared at his friend in open-mouthed admiration. Here was a plan as ingenious as it was simple. This time, nothing *could* go wrong. Venables wasted no time; his own suit was off in a matter of seconds and he was scrambling into Jennings' underwear, shirt and socks. He dressed hurriedly; two pairs of shorts; one pullover and two jackets, and Venables stood ready to descend the stairs.

"Wizzo!" said Temple delightedly. "No one'll ever spot it. Don't leave those spare braces dangling—they'll give the show away. How does it feel?"

"It's a bit warm," Venables admitted, "and a bit cluttered up round the shoulders; I'll have to walk without swinging my arms or I shall bust out at the seams. How do I look?" One hand on hip, he minced along the dormitory in imitation of a mannequin at a dress parade.

"You look super," Temple encouraged him. "I should never have known you were wearing two lots; old Jen's suit fits you down to the ground."

"It hasn't got to do that. Down to the knees is quite far enough for short trousers. Now, what else is there? Oh, yes, shoes and a towel."

The towel was wrapped round Venables' chest between the outer layer of shirt and the pullover. The jacket buttons strained at their threads but he dared not leave them unfastened in case anyone should see what lay beneath.

"We'd better go downstairs one at a time," suggested Temple.

"Well, of course, you crumbling ruin. If I start leaping the stairs three at a time, it's just asking for Matron to sit up and take notice."

"No, I didn't mean that. I meant I'll go on ahead and get Jen's shoes from the bootlockers and wait for you by the side door. Don't forget to speed up a bit going past Mr. Carter." Casually, Temple strolled out of the dormitory and sauntered down the stairs.

Matron and Mr. Carter were still on the lower landing discussing ways of improving the weekly shoe inspection. It was Matron's first term at Linbury; she was young and friendly and had a deep understanding of a boy's needs. They all liked Matron for she was a welcome change after her brisk and businesslike predecessor who had had little sympathy with junk-filled pockets and hair which would not stay parted. All the same, no Matron could be expected to take a tolerant view of best suits covered in fertile silt from the bottom of a pond.

Mr. Carter looked up as Temple came down the stairs. "You're back early, Temple. Did you go down to the sea?"

"We went part of the way, sir, and then we came back because—well, because we thought we'd come back," Temple finished lamely and hurried down to the bootlockers.

A minute later, footsteps sounded again on the landing above and Venables, portly and self-conscious, walked down the stairs. He moved stiffly and his eyes stared straight ahead. He was just disappearing down the lower flight when Matron called him back.

"Oh, Venables, you're just the boy I want. I've got your new blazer; they sent it along from the tailor's yesterday and I want to see if it fits. Come into my sitting room and try it on."

Venables rocked on his heels and clutched the banisters for support: "What—now, Matron?" he gulped.

"Yes, it won't take a minute."

"Oh, but Matron, I ..." He sought desperately for some excuse. "Couldn't I try it on after tea?"

"I shan't have time, then," Matron replied. "Come along, there's a good boy."

Numbly, he followed her into the sitting room, while Mr. Carter, who was seldom deceived by anything, came in after him and closed the door.

"Here we are," said Matron, taking a magenta-and-white blazer from its box. "Slip your jacket off."

"My jacket! Oh, but Matron, I ... I can't!" He clutched the garment tightly about his chest and a lost and helpless look glazed his eyes. But he could not stand like that for ever and at last, very unwillingly, he unbuttoned his jacket, revealing a similar one underneath.

"Good gracious, what's the idea; you're not cold, are you?" Matron asked.

"He shouldn't be," said Mr. Carter, making a closer inspection. "He's got a pullover, a towel and two shirts on as well." He investigated further. "H'm! Two pairs of trousers, with a tangled assortment of braces ... two pairs of socks .... Are you going on an expedition to the South Pole by any chance, Venables?"

"No, sir. Not the South Pole, sir."

"But you're going on an expedition somewhere, aren't you?"

"Yes, sir. You see, what happened, sir ..."

"I think I can guess." Mr. Carter glanced at the name-tape on the under-jacket. "Jennings has fallen into the pond. Right?"

"Yes, sir. Right in, sir."

"Oh, poor boy!" said Matron in a tone of such understanding that Venables gained a new respect for school matrons. "He'll catch his death of cold, hanging about in wet things. He'll have to have a hot bath at once."

"I'll go and fetch him. Take his clothes off, Venables, and wait here till I come back." At the door, Mr. Carter turned and said: "You know, Venables, you really are the *stupidest* little boy. Why on earth you couldn't say what had happened at the start instead of playing these ridiculous dressing-up games ...!" He heaved a deep sigh and strode on to the landing and down the stairs.

It was some time before Jennings realised that the relief party must have met with an accident of some sort. The sun had gone in and his clothes were sticking to him in damp, uncomfortable patches.

"Come on, Darbi, let's go back," he suggested. "We've been here simply hours and hours—well, twenty minutes anyway and still nothing's happened. They've had time to make me a suit and knit me two pairs of socks by now."

"But you can't go back like that!"

"It'll be all right if I'm careful. We'll fox up to the dorm and I'll change into my everyday clothes while you take my wet ones down to the boiler-room."

"It's a bit risky," Darbishire demurred, but he knew that action of some sort was essential. He glanced at his watch; it was later than he thought and at four o'clock everyone had to report to the master on duty. This was a strict rule and there could be no evasion.

He rose to his feet. "If only Venables and Bod hadn't failed us in our hour of need! I suppose they've just beetled off with a light laugh and left us to it. My father says that a friend in need is a ..."

"Come on, let's go!" Jennings crawled out of the hut and the two boys set off for the school buildings. Darbishire edged his way gingerly across the suspension bridge, but Jennings had no need for such refinements. He could not get any wetter, so he strode through the quagmire, mumbling threats.

"Wait till I see those two again! Leaving me to catch frostbite and chilblains and things—it's an ozard caddish trick!"

"Yes, I know. Sir Richard Grenville didn't just abandon his casualties like that," Darbishire replied as he rejoined his friend on dry land. "The *Revenge* ran sheer into the heart of the foe with ninety sick below, so that proves ..."

"It must be nearly that now; it's cold enough," said Jennings through chattering teeth.

"It must be nearly *what*?"

"Ninety-six below freezing."

"I didn't say ninety-six *degrees*, you ancient relic; I said, 'Ninety comma, sick men'."

"You mean *coma*, not comma," Jennings retorted. "It's a sort of thing you go off into, if you're feeling as sick as I am. And Old Wilkie will be going off into one, if we don't report to him by four o'clock."

They left the wood and ran towards the cricket pitches; luck was on their side to start with for the grounds seemed deserted, but as they were passing the hedge which bordered the Headmaster's garden, Jennings clutched his companion by the sleeve and dragged him into cover. "Ssh! There's someone coming!"

"Who?"

"I don't know, but I think it's a master. Quick, let's get through here."

Jennings knelt down and crawled through a gap in the hedge; Darbishire followed, considerably shaken. "But we're not allowed in here," he protested. "It's the Archbeako's garden. He attacks at zero feet with all his ammo blazing, if he finds anyone in here."

"We'll have to risk it, that's all."

They advanced a short distance into the garden and crouched behind a cucumber frame, while the footsteps drew near and passed by on the other side of the hedge. It was Mr. Carter, and he was heading for the pond.

When the master had gone, they crawled back on to the path and Darbishire breathed a sigh of relief. "Phew, that was a bit close! He didn't see us, though … I wonder where he's going?"

"Oh, nowhere special; he often beetles about. Good job we left the hut when we did, or he might have found us there and I shouldn't like him to know I'd got into this mess."

The boarders were returning from their walks when Jennings and Darbishire rounded the corner by the swimming bath, and Mr. Wilkins was on the quadrangle checking the names on his list as the boys reported to him. Clearly, it was impossible to gain the dormitory from this direction, so the two boys turned back and approached the building from the other side. They crossed the kitchen garden, skirted the woodshed and slipped into the basement through the window of the tuck-box room.

They avoided the main staircase and crept up the back stairs which brought them to the top landing at the rear of the building.

"Ssh! We're in open country now," Jennings whispered. "Can't you stop your shoes squeaking, Darbi?"

"Of course I can't—it's even more difficult than stopping your teeth from chattering," his friend replied. "And anyway, what about *your* shoes! They're going squelch-squelch every time you take a step and you're leaving wet footprints all along the passage. The sooner you get your feet dehydrated, the better."

They reached the dormitory without being seen and Darbishire's voice sounded confident again as he said: "Well, we've got here all right. It ought to be plain sailing from now on."

"Don't talk to me about sailing—plain or coloured. I've had enough for one day. You get my dry things out while I take this wet clutter off." Jennings walked into the dormitory and started to undress; his jacket dropped to the floor with the "plop" of a wet dishcloth.

"Bod and Ven need their brains seeing to," Darbishire remarked as he made for his friend's locker. "If they can't see your cupboard when it's bang in the middle of the room with your name on it, they must be bats."

"D'you mean crazy, or as blind as bats?"

"Both. I'll chuck your dry things …" For a moment there was silence, and then Darbishire's cry of amazement rang round the room. "Oh, gosh! Jennings! Oh, golly—they're not here!"

"What!" Jennings came rushing over and looked aghast at the empty locker. Not quite empty, however, for on the bottom shelf was a pair of pyjamas and six clean handkerchiefs; but his everyday suit, his shirt, his underwear—everything needed for a change of clothes was missing.

"So they must have taken them, after all," he said bitterly. "But where to? We know they haven't gone to the hut again, or we'd have met them coming back."

"No, we'd have met them *going*. They couldn't be coming back because they ..." Darbishire broke off; someone was approaching the dormitory door.

Jennings grabbed his wet jacket and crouched between the beds. If this was the master on duty making a surprise inspection of the dormitories, there was just a chance that he would not look ...

The door opened and Temple walked in.

"Oh, there you are!" he said as Jennings raised his head. "I wondered whether you'd come back."

"I should wizard well think I *have* come back," exclaimed Jennings angrily. "You and Venables are ozard cads, leaving me to suffer like that. If I'd stayed out there any longer, I should have fossilised into an icicle."

"Yes, well, sorry about that, but something went wrong." Briefly, Temple explained the plan that had been forced upon them; explained, that is, until he reached the point in the story where he had hurried downstairs to await Venables' arrival by the bootlockers.

What had happened after that, Temple did not know; he had waited and waited and Venables had not come. Then he had searched for him—still without result. In Temple's mind, the extraordinary disappearance of his friend ranked high amongst the great unsolved mysteries of the age, and until this problem was solved, Jennings' dry clothes would have to be regarded as lost in transit.

It was a dismal story, but worse was to come. "And Old Wilkie wants to know why you two and Venables haven't reported that you're back from your walk," Temple went on. "Everyone else got themselves ticked off hours ago, and Wilkie's charging round like a bull going *doyng* in a china shop, looking for you."

Darbishire looked at the sodden figure of his friend with sympathy and said: "We'll have to go and report, Jen. When Mr. Wilkins gets into one of his famous bates, he's worse than fifty-three Spanish men-o'-war with their battle thunder and flame."

"But I can't go like this! Do you think I could get into one of your suits?"

"Gosh, no!" replied Temple. "I'm fatter than you, and Darbi's too small. You'd look like a pumpkin in a peanut shell. Wilkie would spot it at once."

Their luck was no better when they searched Venables' and Atkinsons' lockers, for the owners' weekday suits had been taken to the sewing room for minor repairs.

The situation seemed hopeless, and as the three boys stood debating what was to be done, a heavy tread was heard on the landing below and the loud tones of the master on duty floated up the stairs and through the open door. "Who's that up there in Dormitory 4?" called Mr. Wilkins.

Jennings flashed a glance at Darbishire. "Try and head him off," the glance said, and Darbishire walked out on to the landing.

"It's me, sir! Darbishire, sir! I've just come back from the walk. Will you tick me off, please sir?" he said.

Mr. Wilkins ticked him off in no uncertain terms. "You're nearly ten minutes late reporting," he said, amongst other things. "And where are Venables and Jennings?"

"Jennings is in here, sir. Will you tick him off too, please sir?"

Mr. Wilkins bristled: the rules of the school concerning Sunday walks were quite plain—each boy had to report personally to the master on duty. "If Jennings is there," he barked, "you can tell him that I'll give him just one minute to report to me in my room. And if he's not there then, I'll—I'll—well, he'd better look out!"

Mr. Wilkins strode off along the landing and a moment later the door of his room banged noisily behind him.

410

CHAPTER 8

THE SMALL BACK ROOM

As the last seconds of the minute of grace ticked away, there was a knock on Mr. Wilkin's door. "Come in!" he called.

"It's only me, sir; Jennings, sir," came a reluctant voice from without. "I won't trouble you by coming in, sir. I just wanted to report that I've come back."

Mr. Wilkins frowned at the door panels. It was something new in his experience that Jennings did not wish to put the master on duty to any trouble. "Open the door and come in properly," he boomed. "Don't stand outside gibbering at me through the keyhole. I've been searching the building for the last ..."

The door opened and a familiar figure walked in, with a self-conscious look on his face. Although it was just after four o'clock in the afternoon, the new arrival was wearing a dressing gown and pyjamas.

"I ... I ... Corwumph! What on earth's the meaning of this?" demanded Mr. Wilkins.

"You told me to report to you, sir. You see, I've just got back, sir."

"You didn't go for a walk in your pyjamas, did you?"

"No, sir; I had to change. That's why I'm a little late in reporting. You see, sir, my best suit got a few spots of damp on it, sir."

"Spots of damp! Why should it? It's not raining."

Jennings looked out of the window; unfortunately the sun was shining again now. Would Mr. Wilkins *never* stop asking questions to which there were no answers—unless the whole colony of squatters was to suffer for the misfortunes of a single member?

"No, it's not actually raining, sir," Jennings admitted, "but the weather looked a bit unsettled, so I thought it might be better to change first and be on the safe side."

It was not a very convincing answer and Mr. Wilkins' eyebrows shot up and he turned three shades pinker. "But you—you *silly* little boy," he expostulated, "you—you uncouth youth. Why put your pyjamas on before the rain starts? I—I mean, why put them on at all? It's perfectly dry outside, and even if it wasn't, you could have changed into your weekday suit."

"I couldn't do that, sir; Venables is wearing it."

"What! Whatever for? Hasn't he got one of his own?"

"Yes, sir, and he's wearing that too—his own Sunday suit, that is, and a few of my other clothes as well."

"I—I—Corwumph! Don't talk such ridiculous nonsense!"

Mr. Wilkins rose from his chair and paced the room with his hand to his head. Why couldn't small boys say what they meant without dragging in so many things which had nothing to do with the topic under discussion? This didn't make sense, whichever way he looked at it; he was still searching his mind for some reason why Jennings should put his pyjamas on because the weather was unsettled, and now the issue was being clouded by Venables taking his afternoon stroll, clad in layer upon layer of grey flannel suiting!

Mr. Wilkins decided that he could solve this problem only if he kept very calm and took everything in its right order.

"Now, look here, Jennings!" he said reasonably. "How on earth can anyone be wearing your weekday suit on a Sunday, as well as his own Sunday suit on a week day? I mean, er—well, you heard what I said. What I want to know is, why is Venables wearing your suit?"

"Because we're both about the same size, sir."

Mr. Wilkins shut his eyes and gritted his teeth. He was not a patient man by nature, but no one could say that he was not doing his best in difficult circumstances. "Where is Venables?" he asked weakly.

"He's disappeared, sir."

"Oh, he has, has he! Well, listen to me. I don't know what all this dressing-up in dressing gown nonsense is all about, but I'm not going to have it. You'll go and find this vanishing Venables at once; get your Sunday suit from him and report back to me wearing it."

"But Venables hasn't got my Sunday suit, sir."

All Mr. Wilkins' resolutions about patience and forbearance vanished in an explosion of exasperation. "But you—you *silly* little boy—you just told me that he *had*!"

"No, sir. He's got my weekday one, sir. P'r'aps I'd better explain from the beginning."

He had not proceeded far with his explanation before there was a knock at the door, and Matron and Mr. Carter joined them. Matron was carrying the missing clothes over her arm and in the interval before the door closed, Jennings caught a glimpse of Venables signalling sorrowfully to him from the corridor. His smile of apology was wan and he twisted his fingers with embarrassment and remorse.

Matron's concern was all for Jennings' welfare, but Mr. Carter had had a fruitless journey to the hut and he was not looking very pleased. He did, however, have the advantage over his colleague of knowing what the trouble was all about.

"Thank goodness you've come!" Mr. Wilkins greeted them. "I can't make head or tail of this trumpery moonshine about Tennyson's *Revenge* and a yachting club. All I know is that this boy reported to me wearing his dressing gown. What do you make of that?"

"I think it's very intelligent of him," Matron answered unexpectedly. "It's not every boy who would have thought of getting ready for a bath without being told."

"Bath? At this time of day!" queried Mr. Wilkins. "Whatever for? Hasn't he had one lately?"

"I've had one, sir," Jennings admitted. "Sort of accidentally in the pond, sir."

Sternly, Mr. Carter said: "We'll talk about the cold bath after you've had your hot one, Jennings. Matron's orders are that you have it at once and make sure the water's hot."

"Yes, sir." Jennings took his clothes and departed thankfully for the bathroom. When the door had closed behind him, Mr. Wilkins sighed deeply and said: "Well, I don't understand what it's all about, but it strikes me that's a rather unnecessary sort of order, Matron."

Matron looked puzzled. "Why?" she inquired.

"Well, you don't have to tell a boy like Jennings to get into hot water. I mean, dash it, he's in hot water all the time!"

It cannot truthfully be said that the four members of the yachting club enjoyed that Sunday evening. After chapel, Mr. Carter sent for them and although he could sympathise with good intentions, he could not shut his eyes to breaches of school rules. Thus it was not Jennings' accidental plunge which worried Mr. Carter; it was the fact that they had not observed the rule about going for a walk.

For the rest of the term, he decreed, they would not be allowed out by themselves, and on Sundays they would have to accompany Binns minor and his cronies on the Form I walk—a shrill-voiced crocodile which set forth in charge of a master.

This was punishment indeed, for the indignity of being shepherded about with eight-year-olds would be heightened by the mocking comments of their own colleagues in Form 3. Even the shallowest bonehead would be able to think of some apt and unkind remarks to add to their discomfort.

In addition to this, Jennings was to pay with his own pocket-money for the cleaning of his best suit. Mr. Carter made an entry in his cash book and the account of J. C. T. Jennings was reduced by five shillings and sixpence.

"With regard to the huts," Mr. Carter finished up, "I shall leave the decision to the Headmaster, and until you hear what he intends to do about them, you may carry on as usual."

The Headmaster made no reference to the huts when he gave out the orders for the day at breakfast the following morning. Jennings and Darbishire listened with their fingers crossed and breathed a sigh of relief when the period of danger was over. Was it possible, they wondered, that the Headmaster considered that they had been punished enough already and was not going to take further action?

That evening, after preparation, they went across to the little hut as usual. Jennings took with him two pieces of broken mirror which he had found in the wastepaper basket and which, if skilfully handled, would convert the ventilating shaft into a periscope. They worked on it for some time without success and finally they had to dismantle the shaft altogether.

"It's this bent bit in the middle that's the trouble," Darbishire decided. "When you bunged your famous two-way ear-trumpet into it you must have bashed it up a bit, and any fool knows you can't see round corners."

"Well, what are we wasting our time making a periscope for, then?" demanded Jennings.

"So's we can see round corners."

"You just said we couldn't!"

"Ah, but what I meant was—well, never mind. I vote we take the shaft outside and straighten it before we start the heavy construction work. There's a good chance the roof won't fall down, if we bung a stick or something in its place for the time being."

The periscope very nearly worked when it was finished. One piece of mirror was wedged in the top of the shaft at an acute angle, and the second piece was placed in the ear-trumpet, half-way down. Those with keen eyesight were almost sure that they could see objects moving at a distance.

Darbishire's eyesight was not keen, but his imagination was good. "I can see someone coming across the suspension bridge," he exclaimed as he peered into the lower mirror. "It looks like Binns minor to me."

It was not Binns minor. It was M. W. B. Pemberton-Oakes, Esq., M.A.(Oxon.), Headmaster, and he was coming to make a personal inspection of the activities by the pond.

His first thought, when he had heard of the yachting fiasco, had been to place the whole area out of bounds, but he had postponed his decision when Mr. Carter had spoken strongly on the hut-dwellers behalf. Indeed, the boys would have been surprised if they could have heard how persuasively Mr. Carter had argued as he sat in the Headmaster's study that morning. He had pointed out that hut building was an admirable outlet for the surplus energy which bubbles up in boys like water in a pressure-cooker; he had touched upon the advantages of healthy exercise and upon the joy of home-made possessions—a joy which was out of all proportion to the value of the objects possessed. Mr. Carter had not stressed the educational value of the enterprise, for he doubted whether there was much to be learned from squatting in wattle igloos and eating walnut cake and sardines; but for a harmless relaxation there seemed no better way of spending the odd hour before bedtime.

"Harmless?" queried the Headmaster. "You seem to forget, Carter, that we're discussing this subject mainly because one boy has soiled a perfectly good suit."

"I don't think that will happen again, sir," Mr. Carter replied. "Admittedly, they were extremely foolish, but I feel it would be a pity to come down too heavily on them merely because of one lapse."

"H'm!" The Headmaster paced his study thoughtfully. "I shall go and see for myself exactly what *is* happening over there. Until I have done so, I shall keep an open mind on the subject. Whether I allow the activities to continue after my visit will depend upon whether I form a favourable impression of what I see."

Unfortunately, the first thing the Headmaster saw on his way to the huts was the suspension bridge, and the first impression he formed was that it would bear his weight.

He had reached the middle of the bridge when it started to sink slowly into the quagmire beneath. For a moment he hesitated; then with a leap such as he had not attempted since his undergraduate days, he cleared the remaining distance in a bound. The bridge, relieved of his weight, rose slowly from the mud to its normal height.

It was then that Darbishire made the discovery with the periscope and spun round to see who the visitor really was. "Golly, it's the Archbeako!" he exclaimed. "I wonder what he's come beetling over here for!"

"I can guess," Jennings answered. "And the less yachting equipment he sees lying about, the better. Where's the *Revenge?*"

"It's in the small back room."

"Well, cover it up with the door-mat then, and try and look as though you're engaged on important research work on the life cycle of tadpoles."

"But I don't know anything about tadpoles. I didn't even know they had cycles," Darbishire pointed out.

"They don't have cycles—they go in them."

"Don't you mean they go *on* them?"

"Oh, don't be such a bogus bazooka, Darbi! Buck up, he's coming!" Jennings thrust the *Welcome* mat into his friend's hands and pushed him into the small back room. He returned the ventilating shaft to its usual work of propping up the roof, and then he glanced quickly round the hut. Everything was in order; provided that the conversation was kept away from sailing and model yachts, there was nothing to prevent the Headmaster's visit from being enjoyed by all parties.

The word had passed from hut to hut: "Archbeako on the prowl!" and everywhere a frantic tidying-up was in progress; Brown major cleaned his muddy shoes on a tuft of grass; Binns minor, who was up a tree piloting a jet-fighter, parachuted to the ground without even waiting for the signal from his control tower to land on the runway; Rumbelow grabbed a school text book which he had been using to block up a hole in the roof of his hut, and sought a safe hiding place for it beneath his jacket. No effort was spared to give the unexpected visitor a favourable impression.

Mr. Pemberton-Oakes walked slowly across from the bridge, his keen eye taking in every detail of the scene. His first real surprise was when a bodiless head suddenly appeared in the long grass at his feet. It smiled politely and said: "Good evening, sir," before it disappeared into the ground like a fox going to earth.

The Headmaster's surprise was natural, for it was the first time he had seen

Bromwich major looking out from the front door of his semi-basement elephant trap. Bromwich, now happily restored to health, returned to his living room and told Elmer to behave himself because a distinguished visitor was in the offing.

The distinguished visitor moved on and glanced into each hut as he passed. The squatters gave him smiles of welcome; they had ceased all active and noisy pursuits and were trying to look as though their greatest pleasure was to stand in respectful silence and listen to the croaking of the frogs in the pond. When Mr. Pemberton-Oakes reached Jennings' little hut, he stopped.

"Good evening, sir!" said Jennings and Darbishire in restrained tones.

"Good evening! So these are the huts of which Mr. Carter speaks so highly! H'm! I cannot think why you should choose the muddiest corner of the school grounds for the erection of these—ah—sorry-looking shanties of twig and bulrush. I am further at a loss to understand, Jennings, why you should be standing in a puddle with only one shoe on."

"I'm sorry, sir! I didn't notice the puddle; and I've been using my other shoe to hammer our periscope into shape, sir."

"Really! And where is your tie, Darbishire?"

"It's—er, I know it's about somewhere, sir." It was difficult to explain, without going into technical details, that his tie was an important part of a patent window-opening device; and somehow Darbishire did not think that the Headmaster was in the mood for technical details.

"I have come over here to satisfy myself that these huts are a suitable feature of our out-of-school activities," the Headmaster went on. "So far, I have seen little evidence to support such a belief. This, I gather, is your hut, Jennings?"

"Mine and Darbishire's, sir."

"*Mine and Darbishire's!*" repeated the Headmaster in a shocked voice. "I should have thought, Jennings, that the elementary knowledge of English grammar which even you possess, would have prompted you to say, 'Darbishire's and mine'."

"Yes, sir."

No one could say that Mr. Pemberton-Oakes was not thorough. At the expense of a ruffled dignity and damp patches on both knees, he crawled inside the little hut to make a closer inspection. Jennings and Darbishire stood outside anxiously, listening to the muffled sounds which came from within.

"This is ozard egg, isn't it?" whispered Jennings. "He seems in a bit of a bate, too. I hope he doesn't stop us coming here."

"We needn't despair yet," Darbishire muttered from the corner of his mouth. "My father says that you should never meet trouble half-way, and there's just a chance that ... Gosh, *whatever* is he doing?"

They strained their ears, trying to follow their visitor's progress from the sounds that filtered out through the door, but as they could see nothing, they could only guess at what was really happening inside.

In point of fact, very little was happening. The Headmaster found nothing to which he could take exception and he had decided that perhaps Mr. Carter was right and there was, after all, no reason why these innocent pleasures should not be followed in moderation. A closer supervision by the master on duty would be advisable, but that could easily be arranged.

If the Headmaster had left the hut then and there while his mind was still full of favourable impressions, all might have been well; but it was not to be. He was on the point of leaving when he noticed the hole leading to the small back room. Now, what could that be? Perhaps he had better investigate; a quick glance would be sufficient, for he was ruining the knees of his trousers, and the sooner he could stand upright, the better.

Mr. Pemberton-Oakes was half-way through the entrance to the small back room when he realised that he was stuck. After all, the hole was designed for small inventors only, and for a fully-grown adult to try to force his way through was asking for trouble The Headmaster tried to move forwards and a shower of reeds and brambles fell upon him from the roof; he tried to move backwards, and the movement loosened the ventilating shaft which Jennings had not had time to replace securely.

There was no doubt about it—Mr. Pemberton-Oakes was securely wedged on all sides. Distinctly annoyed, he tried to struggle to his feet and force his way out by sheer strength. As he rose, the walls rose with him, the roof caved in and the ventilating shaft toppled forward, pinning him to the ground in a welter of branches, bulrushes and home-made furniture.

A sack-like object dropped from above and landed a short distance in front of him. The Headmaster could not move, but he could see: and what he saw on the sack-like object did nothing to improve his feelings: *Welcome to Ye Oldë Worldë Huttë*, it said.

Jennings and Darbishire watched with mounting horror. Earthquakes and landslides seemed to be happening before their eyes; the little hut was heaving like a thing possessed, and they were powerless to do anything about it.

"Oh, golly!" breathed Jennings in dismay. "He's smashing the place up like a bulldozer. I knew the roof wasn't safe—I hadn't got time to bung the shaft back properly."

"He seems to have got stuck in the back room boys' department," said Darbishire, and timorously he called: "Er, are you quite all right, sir?"

Their visitor was not quite all right, and Jennings decided to take action. "Come on, Darbi, we'll have to rescue him before he does any more demolition work!" But it was difficult to know where to start.

The rescue party was soon joined by a score of volunteers from neighbouring huts. They arrived demanding to know what was going on, and their crisp comments on the situation had to be quickly and sternly silenced; for though the Headmaster was not in sight, he was only too plainly within earshot.

"We'll have to take the roof off," Jennings announced, and in a lower tone, he added: "Buck up, you chaps, for goodness' sake. He's done as much damage as three atom bombs already, and if he puts his foot through the ventilating shaft, we'll never be able to use it as a periscope."

The willing hands went to work and soon the snapping of branches told that the work of rescue was getting under way.

"This is ozard," groaned Darbishire, as he helped to lift the roof. "He's bound to be in the most frantic bate when he gets out. My father says that one woe doth tread upon another's heels, so fast they ..."

"Well, stop treading on *my* heels and help me get this branch out of the light," suggested Atkinson. He was red in the face with the exertion and he was enjoying every minute of it. But after all, he could afford to—it was not *his* hut.

A minute later, Mr. Pemberton-Oakes arose from the ruins and shook stray twigs and brambles from his clothing. His feet were damp, for the emergency drinking supply had been overturned when the walls collapsed; his tie was awry and his hair was untidy, but his face showed no sign of emotion. The rescuers noted this and fell silent, for everyone knew that the more deeply the Headmaster felt upon a subject, the less he showed his feelings in his expression.

Finally, he spoke. "This area of the grounds will be placed out of bounds for the entire school forthwith," he began. "From what I have seen, I consider that the building of huts is not a suitable occupation for boys of your age. Your clothes are untidy, your boots are dirty and if you are permitted to continue in this way, unchecked, it will undermine the pride which you should be taking in your personal appearance. You will all return to school and set to work with clothes-brush and boot polish to make yourselves presentable." He paused, and a far-away look appeared for a second in his eyes before he went on: "Of what has happened since I arrived, I shall, for the moment, say nothing."

With heavy hearts the squatters turned and made for the school buildings. So that was the end of the huts! And all thanks to Jennings!

"It *would* be Jennings who had to go and bish it up for everybody," grumbled Thompson minor.

"Huh! Just like Jennings to make a hut that falls down *doyng* as soon as the Archbeako beetles inside!" moaned Rumbelow.

"Gosh, Jennings, you *are* a ruin!" The evening air was heavy with reproaches—low-toned criticism which was not supposed to reach the Headmaster's ear.

Mr. Pemberton-Oakes waited by the huts until all the boys had disappeared in the direction of the school buildings. Somehow or other he had got to get back across the pontoon-suspension bridge, and he had no intention of doing *that* in front of an audience!

CHAPTER 9

ENGLAND WINS THE ASHES

IN THE dormitories that evening, Jennings found himself the centre of a swirling cyclone of resentment. Oddly enough, his critics did not blame him for short-circuiting the Sunday walk or for spoiling his best suit in the pond—they could sympathise with things like that. But what really infuriated them was the fact that his hut should have collapsed on the Headmaster; this, they maintained, was the cause of the ban, and the blame for it must be laid at Jennings' door.

"I'm just about fed up with you, Jennings," said Temple, as he undressed. "All that guff we had to put up with about your famous two-roomed hut standing in its own grounds—and then it goes and sits down in them while the Archbeako's paying you a friendly visit."

Venables added an unfriendly glance and said: "You're an ozard swizzler, Jennings. To think Bod and I actually sat inside that tottering ruin of yours, eating walnut cake and sardines! We might have been buried alive any moment." He shivered at the thought of his narrow escape.

"I couldn't help it," Jennings protested. "That small back room wasn't built for grown-ups of riper years. And, anyway, if he'd kept still and not shoved like the back row of a rugger scrum, we'd have had him out without any hoo-hah."

Atkinson looked up from the wash basin: "Don't make feeble excuses! You've made a frantic bish of the whole issue. I bet no one else's hut would have pan-caked if the old man had gone inside."

Loyally Darbishire came to his friend's assistance. "Don't you be so sure," he said. "If he'd walked two inches more to the left when he was coming across, he'd have gone *slap-bang-doyng* through Bromo major's roof and perhaps even landed up in the goldfish tank."

As junior partner in the little hut Darbishire came in for a certain amount of reproach, and it seemed unfair to him that Venables and Temple, who had been as keen as anyone on the yachting expedition, should now put all the blame on the owners of the unfortunate shanty. Surely they could see that no building of reeds and branches could withstand the bulldozing tactics of a fully-grown headmaster.

Mr. Carter was on dormitory duty that evening, and he was quick to sense that the usual, friendly atmosphere of bedtime was missing. There was little he could do about it, though he was very short with anyone who had more to say about the subject than was necessary.

When the boys were in bed, Mr. Carter called for silence and then made his way to the Headmaster's study. He often went there in the evenings to discuss the events of the day and the plans for the morrow.

"Come in and sit down, Carter," the Headmaster greeted him. "I'm just finishing off a notice."

The school secretary was away that day and Mr. Pemberton-Oakes was trying his hand at typing. It was the first time he had done so, and he was making less progress than he had hoped.

Mr. Carter sat in an armchair and glanced at the evening paper while the Headmaster turned again to his typewriter. It was slow work, but he persevered, and at five-second intervals the silence was broken as one more letter was tapped on to the sheet of paper in the machine.

"Tut-tut-tut! I'd no idea that typing was so difficult," observed Mr. Pemberton-Oakes. "My secretary dashes these things off without even looking at the keyboard. Now where on earth is the comma—I'm sure I saw one somewhere! … Ah, yes, here it is …. Oh dear, how unfortunate—it's turned itself into a question mark!"

"Can I help?" volunteered Mr. Carter, laying down the newspaper.

"Oh, no, thank you! I'm just typing a memorandum to pin up on the notice board." And three minutes later he added: "On second thoughts it would be considerably quicker to write it out by hand. Somehow, I don't think that this quite conveys my meaning." He rolled the paper from the machine and passed it to his assistant.

"NOTICE," it read. "In fiyutre no buys will be preMnitted to bluild nuts ub the neiHghbourhoof uf the pond? & the a£5rea will be plAvced ou98t of hounds ½%."

"You're quite right, sir," Mr. Carter agreed. "I think I know what you mean, but it's a little obscure in parts."

The Headmaster tore it up, and as he dropped the pieces in the wastepaper basket he said: "It must be very useful to know how to type. However, perhaps you would pass it round amongst the staff, that in future no boys will be permitted to build huts. I'm placing the whole area of the pond out of bounds from now on, because I'm unable to agree that this particular form of recreation serves any useful purpose." He pursed his lips and shook his head slowly. "Any visitor going round the school, Carter, and seeing the boys in the untidy and dishevelled state they were in this evening would be certain to form the most unfavourable impressions."

Mr. Carter agreed about the visitors, but he pointed out that he always insisted upon the boys making themselves presentable as soon as they arrived back in the school buildings.

The Headmaster was not satisfied. "I've no doubt you do, Carter, but it still isn't good enough. It is essential that the boys should pursue their outdoor hobbies in a neat and orderly manner. This morning, for instance, I had a letter from General Merridew; he's bringing his daughter-in-law and his grandson down to see the school next Friday. Frankly, I shudder to think of the General's remarks if he found that the boys were not looking as smart as they did when he was a boy at school, here."

"Is the grandson coming to us as a boarder?" inquired Mr. Carter.

"I hope so. He will be entered as a new boy for next term, provided that his mother is satisfied with what we have to show her. The choice of school rests with her because the boy's father is stationed abroad in the Navy. I should like young Roger to come here; his father was an Old Linburian and so, of course, was his grandfather."

Mr. Carter had met the grandfather on several occasions. Lieut.-General Sir Melville Merridew, Bart., D.S.O., M.C. was one of the most distinguished of all the Old Boys who had spent their early years at Linbury, and as the donor of the *Merridew Inter-House Sports Cup*, he was a notable figure at every Speech Day gathering.

The Headmaster picked up the General's letter from his desk and quoted: "My grandson, Roger, is nearly eight years old and I am keen to carry on the family tradition and send him to Linbury. In my view it is high time that the lad went to his preparatory school and had a few of the rough corners knocked off him. However, his mother must make the decision, not me, so I shall bring her and the boy along next Friday if this is convenient."

Mr. Pemberton-Oakes laid down the letter and turned to his assistant. "I am determined that General Merridew shall not be disappointed," he said. "He is a man of high standards and he expects the best, so we must ensure that everything he sees affords him and Mrs. Merridew the utmost satisfaction. I gather, from what the General told me last term, that Roger is—ah—how shall I put it? Well, he is a high-spirited child and his mother has always allowed him to do very much as he pleases."

Mr. Carter nodded; he had met that sort of boy before and he knew that after a very short space of time, the newcomer would find his feet and appear little different from his fellows. It was surprising how easily the spoiled, the highly-strung and the "difficult" boy forgot his temperamental moods when once he found himself part of the little world of boarding-school life.

"I shall show the General's party all over the school and all over the grounds so that they may see things for themselves," the Headmaster went on. "Now, perhaps, you understand why it would be inadvisable to allow the boys to continue their games by the pond. Can you imagine a man like General Merridew entering his grandson for a preparatory school where the boys are plastered in mud from ankle to eyebrow?"

"Perhaps not," Mr. Carter agreed. "But if they see the school running normally, they'll be able to judge our methods for themselves and they'll be bound to agree that the boys are very happy here."

The Headmaster strolled over to the window, where he stood enjoying the cool night air. At length, he said: "I rather think, Carter, that something more than that is called for. Knowing General Merridew as well as I do, I feel that next Friday will be an occasion that demands something more than the normal effort. The building must be tidied from top to bottom and the grounds swept from end to end; the boys will wear their best suits and I shall ask Matron to see that no boy needs his hair cut or wears shoes which are in need of repair."

"M'yes, but ..." Mr. Carter began doubtfully, but the Headmaster was in full spate and was in no mood to be interrupted. "I will see the housekeeper in the morning," he went on. "Luncheon next Friday must be prepared with particular care. Tablecloths, of course, and clean napkins for the boys; now what do you think, Carter, about a vase of flowers on all the dining-hall tables?"

"I think it would be a mistake. I think your visitors would be able to form a better opinion of the school if they see us as we usually are."

"In this case, I think not," replied Mr. Pemberton-Oakes. "The General has a right to expect the best from his old school and we should be failing in our duty if we did not provide it. Yes, Carter, I'm determined to see that no effort is spared in making a favourable impression on General Merridew and his party."

Jennings and Darbishire were the last to reach the cricket field after preparation on Wednesday evening. As they were crossing the quad, Jennings said: "I'll give you some coaching as we can't go to the hut, Darbi. Heaven knows you need it badly enough—you bowl like a flat-footed newt!"

Darbishire clutched his cricket bat and made no answer. There *was* no answer as far as his bowling was concerned, and he knew it.

All the cricket nets were occupied when they arrived and Jennings made for one at the far end where the other members of Dormitory 4 were disputing an l.b.w. decision. The argument revolved round the point of whether Atkinson could be "out" if the ball had struck him above the shoulder. Temple maintained that he could.

"But it can't be l.b.w. Bod—you got me on the nose," Atkinson protested.

"Well, you shouldn't stick your nose in front of the wicket," came the reasoned reply.

"It was your fault for bowling a sneak. I had to get down low to it and then it jumped up and bashed me on the bonce."

"It's time you were out, anyway, Atki," Venables chimed in; as next man in, he was not in favour of giving the batsman the benefit of any doubt. "After all, you'd have been caught at cover point off the ball before if we'd had a fielder and the net hadn't stopped it."

"You're bats! I hit it to leg, and cover point's on the off."

"Ah, but if you'd been left-handed, cover point would have been fielding on the other side."

The argument seemed as though it might last forever, so Jennings called out loudly: "I say, you chaps, can Darbi and I play in your net?"

The players ceased arguing and joined forces against the new enemy.

"No, you can't," said Temple curtly. His attitude plainly indicated that people who put other people to great inconvenience by building huts which folded up like opera hats at awkward moments could expect no favours. Venables and Atkinson nodded in agreement.

"But there's nowhere else we can play. All the other nets are full up," Jennings pointed out.

"That's your bad luck," retorted Atkinson. "Anyway, it's hopeless letting Darbishire play—he's such a rotten bat."

"You mean he's *got* a rotten bat, not he *is* one," Venables corrected.

"No, I don't. It's an expression like, say, for instance ..."

"My bat isn't a rotten one," Darbishire defended himself. "My father made 17 not out with it, last year when he was playing for our village, so that'll show you!"

Temple, Venables and Atkinson hooted with laughter. "Gosh, Darbi, that's an ozard feeble sort of score. Couldn't he do better than that?" asked Venables.

"Oh, yes, he made 236 all in boundaries once."

"Phew! Not bad!" Atkinson was impressed. "Who was he playing against?"

"Well, that time he was playing on the beach and my mother was bowling with a tennis ball, but it proves my bat isn't so feeble as you make out."

"Well, anyway, you can't play here," said Temple. "We got here first and bagged this net just for us three."

Jennings and Darbishire did not argue, for it was plain that they were not wanted. The week had not been going well for them; Sunday had seen the sailing disaster, on Monday the huts were banned and the next morning a long-expected tuck parcel had arrived from Jennings' mother. Normally this would have been regarded as a red-letter day, but the food had been specially ear-marked for a feast in the little hut and it had arrived too late.

Sorrowfully they trudged away from the nets, towards the hedge which surrounded the Headmaster's garden. "What about this coaching, Darbi—shall we have a bash at it here?" Jennings asked.

"It's a bit near the Beako's garden," Darbishire demurred. "What if I walloped a ball over the hedge?"

Jennings laughed. "I can just see you doing that! Dash it all, Darbi, you couldn't even hit the side of a house with a bulldozer. I know," he went on. "Let's have a Test Match. You be Australia and I'll be England."

"That's not fair," Darbishire protested. "I'm *always* Australia. I'm never allowed to be England."

"Of course not. You're not good enough to play for England. Besides, the Australians are better really—they nearly always win the Ashes."

Darbishire frowned hard at his cricket bat while he sought for the flaw in this argument. Then he said: "Yes, but if I'm not good enough to play for England, why am I good enough to play for Australia, if they're better?"

"Because, if you're playing for Australia, England will be able to win the Ashes, so if you're patriotic you ought to be proud to help your country like that."

They had not brought any stumps with them, so they piled up their jackets to make a wicket, and Darbishire stripped for the match, still complaining that he had been chosen for the wrong side. Jennings' appeal to his patriotism had made things more difficult, for it seemed to suggest that he should play for one team while hoping that his opponents would win.

"I'll tell you what let's do, then," the England captain said graciously, but ungrammatically. "Australia can bat first and if they're out first ball, England will put them in again. That's fair enough, isn't it?"

He paced out the pitch while the Australian opening batsman took his stance at the wicket and made a few graceful practice strokes in the air. To fit himself for his part, he hummed a few bars of *Waltzing Matilda* and raised his imaginary cap to an imaginary crowd who were clapping till their imaginary palms ached.

At the other end of the pitch, Jennings was swinging his arm round and round to generate the current for his first ball, when Bromwich minor sped across from the nets.

"Message from Mr. Carter," he announced. "He says you characters are playing too near the Archbeako's garden, and he's going to take off on a roof-level attack if you don't budge farther off."

"Mr. Carter said that?"

"Well, he used different words, but that's what he meant. He says the Head's threatened to stop us playing here after prep if we go too near his hedge. Can't stop—I'm in next and Mr. Carter's in our net, bowling supersonic leg-spinners." And the messenger hurried off.

Jennings glanced round the cricket field, but he could see no other suitable place where an important Test Match could be held, for seventy-nine boys divided up into nearly twenty separate groups took up all the available space. What should he do? Perhaps if he moved his pitch, say, two or three yards to the left, he would be complying with instructions.

He knew, of course, that this was not quite what Mr. Carter had meant, but it was a move in the right direction and, anyway, the master seemed too busily engaged with his leg-spinners to notice how his orders were being carried out.

Jennings trotted down the pitch to where the Australian opening batsman was now entertaining the imaginary crowd by balancing his bat on his chin.

"We've got to hoof farther off, Darbi," Jennings said. "Shift the wicket a couple of yards farther away from the hedge."

"All right. By the way, I vote you don't bowl your fastest, because I haven't got any pads."

"But this is a Test Match!" Jennings sounded shocked. "What would people think if Australia asked England to bowl easy ones at Lords in case they got a crack on the shin? Come on, let's get started!" He ran back to the bowling end. "Pla-ay!" he called, and the fight for the Ashes began in earnest.

The first ball was straight and slow; Darbishire missed it completely and looked round to see it nestling in the grey flannel wicket behind him.

"How's that? Out! Middle stump, first ball!" Jennings danced with delight. "Australia all out for nought—hurray!"

"You said first ball didn't count," the Australian team objected as it fielded the ball and threw it back.

"All right, then—we'll put you in again. Pla-ay!"

The Australian side fared no better in the second innings, which again lasted for only one ball. England was scornful. "Really, Darbi, you are feeble! What's the point of coming all the way from the other side of the world just to run away from the first ball you get! You'll never get a knighthood for your contribution to Sport if you don't do better than that!"

"It's all very well to talk," replied Darbishire, "but chaps at Lords who get knighted for their cricket don't have to play without pads, and my father says that ..."

"All right, all right! Let's get on with the game! We'll see if your bowling's any better than your batting."

As a leg-spin bowler, Darbishire had modelled himself on Mr. Carter, and he never tired of trotting along the corridors copying the master's bowling action as he went. Twelve short steps, a shuffle, a little jump and over came the arm with a flexible twist of wrist and fingers. Darbishire could imitate the movements perfectly but, somehow, whenever he tried it with a ball in his hand, something went wrong.

He paced out the twelve steps and turned to face the batsman. "Pla-ay!" he sang out. As usual, his run up to the bowling crease was faultless, the shuffle and the little jump were faithfully carried out, but as soon as the ball left his hand it developed a will of its own and sailed off towards square leg.

"Wide!" said Jennings disgustedly. "You are a prehistoric remains, Darbi; you only do sneaks or wides."

The bowler's pride was hurt. "All right then, I won't bowl any more. We'll say the match is over and you've won."

"But it can't be over—I haven't hit the ball yet."

"Yes, but I didn't score any runs and now I've bowled a wide, so that's a run to you and England have won the Ashes."

This seemed a little hard on England, who was stamping his feet with impatience to have a good crack at the bowling, and finally Australia agreed to carry on.

The reason why the Old Country scored no runs in the first over was because the ball never came near the batsman. Sometimes it rolled three-quarters of the way along the pitch, but by the time Jennings had rushed out to meet it, it was as lifeless as a bed-knob.

"This is ozard," he complained, after five minutes thwarted batting. "How do you expect me to make super-spivish strokes off double wides and balls that never get here! Try and pitch them up a bit more!"

It was then that Darbishire bowled a good-length ball. He ran the twelve steps, remembered the shuffle and jump and swung his arm over, quite convinced that this ball would fare no better than its fellows. And no one was more surprised than the bowler when it pitched well down the wicket and in a straight line with the makeshift stumps.

"Oh, good ball!" cried Jennings, and stepped forward and smote it with all his strength. It rose from his bat high into the air and curved away towards the hedge.

"Oh, good shot, Jen—wizard stroke," yelled Darbishire generously. "It's a six! It's going right over the ..." He stopped, for a crash of glass from behind the hedge told where the ball had landed.

For a few seconds they stared at each other in bemused silence. Then Jennings said: "I say, Darbi, did you—did you hear anything, just then?"

"I—er, I fancy I *did* hear a sort of tinkle, yes," Darbishire admitted in a strained, unnatural voice.

Jennings forced himself to make an unpleasant decision. "Come on!" he said. "We'll have to fox into the Head's garden and see what it is."

For a moment, Darbishire held back, his mind seeking faint hopes to cling to as a drowning man clutches at straws: perhaps the crash had nothing to do with Jennings' beautiful leg-drive; perhaps a cat had upset a nest of flowerpots at the very moment that the ball had disappeared over the hedge; perhaps .... Darbishire sighed. No amount of wishful thinking could alter the real cause of that crash. The horrible sound still rang in his ears.

"There's no point in going to see what it is," he reminded his friend. "I know

already; it's the Head's cucumber frame—the one we hid behind last Sunday."

"Yes, but we can't leave the ball there. You are a ruin, Darbi, sending down a straight one like that—I couldn't help swiping it."

"Well, I like that! A moment ago you were moaning because they *weren't* straight."

A quick look round the cricket field showed that no one else had heard the crash of glass. The little groups were still bowling at one another, and the thwack of the batsmen came distantly from the nets. It seemed strange to Jennings that no one should have noticed what, to him, had sounded like a whole colony of glass house dwellers disregarding the proverb about throwing stones; but no one was so much as glancing in their direction, so the two boys crept towards the gap in the hedge which they had found the previous Sunday. Jennings crawled through while Darbishire stayed outside and kept watch.

It was quiet in the garden, for the sounds of the cricket field were muffled by the thick branches of yew; quiet, but dangerous, for the Headmaster's garden was out of bounds. There, ahead of him, Jennings could see the cucumber frame, and as he hurried along the path towards it he knew what he would find. And he was right!

Of the three panes of glass which protected the cucumbers only two were intact. The middle pane was smashed to fragments, and lying amongst the cucumbers at the bottom was his cricket ball.

When Jennings emerged on the lawful side of the hedge a few moments later, Darbishire said: "Buck up, Mr. Carter's just blown the 'all-in'!"

"Okay, I'm coming!" Jennings slipped the cricket ball into his pocket. "The whistle's late tonight. It should have gone five minutes ago, by my watch."

Darbishire clicked his teeth with annoyance. "Doesn't that just prove how everything's against us?" he said bitterly. "If he'd blown it on time, this wouldn't have happened; we should have been indoors by now, instead of wondering what on earth we're going to do about that busted hunk of glass."

CHAPTER 10

ABSENT-MINDED AUNT

It was not until break the next morning that Jennings and Darbishire were able to discuss the new disaster in detail. Then, as soon as they were released from Mr. Wilkins' geography class, they made for the tuck-box room to talk the matter over. Fate, they agreed, was not even *trying* to be fair, for the last few days had brought far more than any average spell of bad luck.

They sat on Jennings' tuck-box, eating the remains of his parcel while Darbishire recalled all the wise words of his father about troubles and sorrows which followed thick and fast upon one another's heels. Normally, they would have had no hesitation in reporting the broken pane to Mr. Carter and offering to pay for the damage out of their pocket-money. But things were not normal that week; the disasters of Sunday and Monday had reduced their reputation to its lowest ebb—and if this new misfortune were to come to light, anything might happen.

"It's not only busting the glass, you see, Darbi," Jennings pointed out, "but we went on playing after Mr. Carter had told us to beetle off. If that gets into the headlines they'll stop the whole school from having cricket practice after prep." He sighed. "And it was such a super leg-drive, too!"

"And it was the first decent ball I've bowled this term," added Darbishire. "What an ozard swizz! Never mind, you got the Ashes—or the splinters, rather." He polished an apple on his sleeve and fell silent, for his friend was deep in thought.

For some moments Jennings sat turning over in his mind what was best to be done. The Headmaster had little time for gardening during the term, and as the frame was in a far corner there was a chance that the damage would not be discovered for some days. But it was bound to be noticed sooner or later, and then the trouble would start. Who broke this? Why were you playing so near the garden? Why didn't you move away when you were ordered to do so? And then the verdict—No boy is to practise cricket after evening preparation.

Jennings could imagine it all and hear the hostile comments of his colleagues. And, after all, he would deserve them, for twice in one week is rather too often for a third-former to bring a loss of privileges upon the whole school. Surely there must be some way out of the difficulty! If only the glass could be replaced before the damage was discovered; if only the Headmaster could find an undamaged pane the next time he strolled round inspecting his vegetables. An idea took shape in Jennings' mind and he broke the silence by saying: "Do you happen to know of any decent glass shops in these parts, Darbi?"

Darbishire looked puzzled. "Do you mean ones that sell glass or ones with masses of windows?" he inquired.

"I was just wondering whether we could buy a hunk without saying a lot about it."

"Gosh, yes!" cried Darbishire; his eyes shone with enthusiasm. "What about the Linbury Stores in the village? They sell everything—saucepans, postcards, paraffin, sticking-plaster ..."

"We don't want any saucepans, and sticking-plaster wouldn't be any good, anyway—that pane's in about five million small fragments."

"No, I didn't mean let's mend it. I meant a shop like that is sure to sell ordinary stuff like glass, isn't it?"

"Bound to," Jennings agreed. "Darbi, I think we're saved!"

They shook hands heartily and celebrated their salvation with a pineapple chunk apiece, from Jennings' parcel.

"All we've got to do," Jennings declared, "is to get some dosh out of the school bank, ask permish to beetle down to the village and buy a nice new slab of the right size."

"Bags you do it, then," replied Darbishire, wiping his sticky fingers on his tie. "I wouldn't know what to ask for."

"Don't be so bats—you just ask for glass."

"Yes, but they might have different sorts—frosted, or powdered—or stained-glass, even; and besides, do they sell it by weight or so many panes for six-pence?"

"Leave it to me!" said Jennings. "I'll nip back into the garden after lunch and measure it up; and after school this afternoon we'll go and ask Mr. Carter for some pocket-money."

Mr. Carter was marking exercise books when the knock sounded on his study door. He had already guessed who his visitors were from the whispered conversation which had been going on outside his room for the previous five minutes. The words were inaudible, but the high-pitched tone of the whisperers was unmistakable. "A secret and important plan is going to be carried out," the urgent undertones informed him.

Very few things happened at Linbury which escaped Mr. Carter's attention, and when his visitors entered he had no difficulty in seeing through the masks of innocence which veiled their faces. Either something had happened, or something was going to happen, Mr. Carter decided, and filed the observation away in his mind until it should be needed.

"Oh, yes, I want to see you, Jennings," the master said. "I sent a message to you yesterday evening to move your pitch away from the Head's garden. Did you do so?"

"We moved a little bit, sir," Jennings replied, "but there wasn't room to go far. We were having a private Test Match, you see, sir."

"I was Australia, sir," Darbishire added, "and England won by an innings and ten wickets. Australia made nought in both innings and England got one wide, sir."

"Really! Quite a phenomenal score," smiled Mr. Carter.

"Of course, they do better at Lords, sir, but that's probably because they don't have to bat without pads." Darbishire suddenly wondered why he was telling his housemaster all these details; could it be that he was prattling about nothing in particular merely to postpone the serious business for which they had come? He forced himself back to the matter in hand and gave his friend an encouraging nudge. "Go on, Jennings!" he muttered.

"Well, sir," Jennings began, "what we really came to see you about was to ask for some of our pocket-money, sir."

Mr. Carter looked interested. "I opened the bank after lunch, yesterday," he replied. "Why didn't you ask me then?"

"I didn't need it, then, sir. You see—well, actually, sir, it's a bit urgent, if you see what I mean, sir. I think I need about five shillings."

Mr. Carter did not ask why. Instead, he opened the cash book in which he kept records of the boys' bank balances. "Sorry! You've only got fourpence left," he said.

"Only fourpence, sir! But I had five and tenpence the other day!"

"Quite right! But I deducted five and six to pay for your suit to go to the cleaners. Perhaps you'd forgotten."

Jennings had, and a wave of gloom splashed over him. Where on earth was the money to come from? His friend could not help either, for when Mr. Carter turned to the account, the balance in favour of C. E. J. Darbishire was exactly one penny.

"Oh, well, it can't be helped then, sir; sorry to trouble you, sir," said Jennings; but as he made for the door, Mr. Carter called him back and said: "If this matter is really urgent, Jennings, and you'd care to tell me about it, perhaps I could help."

Jennings wanted to tell him; desperately he wanted to shed the load of this new trouble which was making life so difficult.

"Well, sir," he said, and then stopped. It would be most unfair on the rest of the school if evening cricket was to be stopped; was it right that seventy-nine boys should suffer for the misfortunes of two of their number? "No thank you, sir," he finished up. "It's quite all right, really."

Mr. Carter sat and thought for some while after the boys had gone. Why were ten-year-olds so obstinate? Why wouldn't they say outright what the matter was, instead of putting themselves and everyone else to unnecessary trouble. One thing, however, seemed certain; this plan of theirs, whatever it was, had depended on their being able to withdraw some money from the bank. That had failed, so now, perhaps, their scheme would be abandoned.

So thought Mr. Carter. But, for once, he thought wrong!

Downstairs in the tuck-box room, Jennings and Darbishire sat and stared at each other in moody silence. At last, Darbishire said: "We've just *got* to do something! We can't buy any glass if we haven't got any dosh, so I vote we go back to Mr. Carter and tell him what's happened."

"That won't help," answered Jennings glumly. "We still can't pay for the damage and there'll be a hoo-hah for everyone on top of that."

"There'll be a hoo-hah, anyhow!" Darbishire's tone was gloomily confident. "As soon as the Archbeako ankles round his garden, he's going to say, 'Now, who's been bashing a ball over my hedge?' And then ..."

Jennings jumped to his feet and suddenly the wide-awake look was back in his eyes. "I know!" he cried triumphantly. "My Aunt Angela!"

Darbishire looked doubtful. "Why, does she play cricket?"

"No, she plays croquet—at least she used to, about twenty years ago. Listen, Darbi, I think I've ..."

"Don't be such a bogus bazooka!" his friend interrupted. "Why should the Head think the glass was smashed twenty years ago by your aunt playing cro-quet?"

"I didn't say that. I meant there's a decent chance that the letter will come tomorrow."

"What letter?"

"Aunt Angela's. You remember my Aunt Angela, don't you?"

"The old geezer who doesn't like cats?"

"Yes, that's right. Gosh, why didn't I think about her before?"

"Think *what* about her?"

Jennings explained. Every month, Aunt Angela wrote her nephew a letter, and once a term she enclosed a postal order for ten shillings. She was rather forgetful and had to be reminded, at times, and on the last occasion that Jennings had written to her, he had pointed out, politely and tactfully, that this term's postal order was overdue. If all went well, her monthly letter would be arriving that week and, if it did, the postal order was sure to be enclosed.

They seized upon this ray of hope eagerly. Today was Thursday and they knew that the Headmaster was unlikely to visit the garden before the weekend. They plotted his probable movements in their minds; he would watch the cricket in the afternoons and work in his study in the evenings. Sunday afternoon was the only regular occasion on which Mr. Pemberton-Oakes was known to enjoy a stroll in his garden, and even if he did visit it before then, it was unlikely that he would include a thorough tour of the vegetable plot in his programme.

If, therefore, Aunt Angela's letter arrived on Friday or Saturday, they would have ample time to cash the postal order and restore the cucumber frame to its normal condition.

"It looks as though everything's going to be all right after all, then!" Darbishire exclaimed happily, when they had summed up their chances.

"M'yes," said Jennings, who realised the drawbacks better than his friend did. "The real trouble, of course, is that Aunt Angela's so spivish absent-minded."

"You mean, like a professor?"

"No, she's not like a professor at all. She's ..."

"I meant absent-minded. All profs are like that," replied Darbishire knowingly. "They do things like, say, for instance, they strike matches to see if they've blown the candle out and things like that. In fact, I heard a creasingly funny story about an absent-minded old professor who came home one stormy night and put his wet umbrella into bed and stood himself in the sink to drain." He laughed gaily at the absurdity of it; it was clear that Darbishire was already beginning to feel better.

"But Aunt Angela's nothing like that," Jennings objected. "She hasn't even

436

got an umbrella—she left it on a bus last Christmas, by mistake."

"Well that proves what I said," cried Darbishire logically. "She must be absent-minded!"

"Of course she is, you ancient ruin—I told you that to start with! You don't have to prove it! The only snag is that she's so cracking absent-minded she may forget to post the letter."

"Oh, surely not—not if she likes you! My father says that the heart that is truly fond, never forgets."

"You tell your father, from me, that he's got it all wrong," said Jennings. "It's the elephant who never forgets. Gosh, I *do* wish Aunt Angela was an elephant!"

Loud footsteps approached along the corridor and the door of the tuck-box room shot open as though a small charge of dynamite had been applied to the door-knob. When Mr. Wilkins was on duty, he made no secret of the fact, and his progress round the building could be heard and followed from attic to basement. The school found this useful, for it gave them time to switch to some lawful occupation before the master on duty arrived at any particular spot, and Mr. Wilkins seldom caught an offender red-handed. This time, however, his luck was in.

"What are you two boys doing down here in the tuck-box room?" he demanded.

"We're just having a chat, sir. And then we were going to get ready for cricket," Jennings replied.

"Well, you've no business to be chatting—you're supposed to be helping to tidy the school up. There's no cricket this afternoon; everyone's got to make the place look ship-shape for tomorrow. The Headmaster has some important visitors coming."

"Yes, sir. Where shall we start ship-shaping, then, sir?" asked Darbishire.

"Classrooms and common room first," ordered Mr. Wilkins. "Desks, lockers and shelves have all got to be turned out and all rubbish thrown away."

"Yes, sir."

The boys made for their classrooms and Mr. Wilkins' powerful voice followed them up the stairs: "And no slacking! I shall inspect the rubbish you've collected before tea, and if you haven't got plenty, I shall—I shall—well, you'd better look out."

As the boys trotted upstairs, they found everyone hard at work tidying up. The maids were washing the picture-rails, the housemen were polishing the door-knobs; Robinson was cleaning the windows, and Old Nightie had been roused from sleep at half-past four in the afternoon to dredge pellets of sodden blotting-paper from seventy-nine inkwells.

The air was heavy with the smell of floor polish, and on every landing, vacuum cleaners whirred, brooms swept, dusters flapped and mops splashed. The Headmaster was sparing no effort to impress General Merridew's party with the spick-and-span appearance of Linbury Court School.

The classroom was a hive of activity when Jennings and Darbishire arrived. Form 3 were carrying out their orders with a will, and their efforts at spring cleaning were raising so much dust that it was difficult to see across the room.

Bromwich major had prised up a loose floorboard and had collected a paper bag full of fluff and chalk dust; he wandered round the room looking for somewhere to put it, but as the wastepaper baskets were all full he had to replace his rubbish under the floorboards again. Then he went and had a few quiet words with Elmer; he apologised to him for having to tidy his tank away in the bottom of a cupboard, and promised that this state of affairs would be remedied as soon as the visitors had gone and things were back to normal. He muttered his apologies furtively, for people might think it odd if they saw him engaged in animated conversation with a goldfish.

"Come and do some work for your living!" Venables sang out as Jennings and Darbishire came through the door. "Bod and Atki and I are having a competition to see who can collect the most junk. I've got a smashing lot already and I'm keeping it in the wastepaper basket until I've got a whole heap more."

Atkinson walked by with his arms full of old newspapers and broken cardboard boxes and Venables eyed him with sudden suspicion. "Hey, Atki," he demanded, "where did you get all that?"

"I found it in the wastepaper basket," smiled Atkinson delightedly.

"But you can't have that! That's mine—I put it there," Venables protested.

"Well, if you put in the wastepaper basket, that proves you didn't want it."

"Of course it doesn't—I put it there for safety! You ozard oik, Atki, you've been pinching my litter. Put it back, at once!"

"Well, fancy making such a fuss about rubbish. Here you are—take it, if you want it!" And Atkinson scattered the junk pile in a wide circle at Venables' feet and skipped quickly out of range to the far end of the room.

Jennings entered the litter contest with gusto, but Darbishire preferred to scavenge alone. He made his way up and down the room on his hands and knees, spearing minute fragments of paper with a pen-nib. He was, in his imagination, a park keeper clearing up Hampstead Heath after a bank holiday.

Soon Mr. Wilkins looked in to see how the great tidying-up scheme was progressing. He had difficulty in seeing anything at all, for a choking pall of dust hung round the door, where Thompson minor had trodden on some small pieces of chalk and was now trying to fan the powdery remains towards the fireplace.

"That's enough!" called Mr. Wilkins loudly. "We'll leave this room till the dust's settled. All you boys go outside and start tidying up the quad. There's half an apple-core and a toffee paper in the far corner. Go and pick them up—the Headmaster doesn't want his visitors to wade knee-deep in litter!"

Outside on the quad, Jennings asked: "What's all this hoo-hah in aid of, anyway? Who's coming?"

"Sir Melville Merridew," replied Temple. "The old boy who gave the Sports Cup and makes all those speeches about his schooldays being the happiest time of his life."

"Oh," said Jennings, "I thought it was royalty, at least, judging by all this flapdoodle."

"The General's a very important character," Brown major explained. "He's been in the army since about the time of the Wars of the Roses, and he's been a military attaché as well. Mr. Carter says he'll probably come round and talk to us, so we'll have to be spivish careful how we behave."

"I shouldn't know what to call him if he talks to me," said Temple. "Do I say, 'Your Worship,' or 'My Grace' or what?"

They had tidied the quad by this time and stood about wondering what to do. Darbishire, more conscientious than the others, was dusting the gymnasium bootscraper with his handkerchief. He looked up importantly as Temple's query caught his ear.

"My father's got a little book about how to address important geezers and all that sort of thing," he announced. "F'rinstance, if, say, you want to write a letter to a high dignitary of the Church, you'd start off 'My Lord Bishop ...'"

"Yes, but he's not a bishop—he's a military attaché, whatever that is."

"I didn't think a chap could actually *be* a military attaché until Mr. Carter told me," Brown major put in. "I thought they were sort of despatch case things that you carry military secrets about in."

Darbishire rose from his bootscraper and peered at his companions through spectacles thick with dust. "Oh, no," he said, "a military attaché to a foreign country is something like an ambassador and my father's book says that if you want to write to a chap like that, you end up by saying: 'I beg to remain your Excellency's most obedient servant!'"

"I should jolly well think we are," said Brown major. "Look at all the orange peel and junk we've collected for him. It's enough to fill fifty military attaché cases!"

Darbishire was unwilling to let the conversation veer away from the interesting store of knowledge which he had acquired from his father.

"My father's book's got a lot more wizard information about other things, too," he went on, spearing a small leaf with his nib and placing the refuse tidily in his coat pocket. "Statistics, and things like that. F'rinstance, did you know that the population of China is so big that if you put them all in a long, unbroken line and made them march day and night without stopping, it'd take twenty years for them all to go past you? It's true!" He smiled knowingly.

"How do they know?" asked Brown major. "Have they tried it?"

Darbishire hadn't thought of that; it seemed unlikely, yet his father's book could not be wrong. Doubtfully he said: "Well, I suppose somebody must have done it, or they wouldn't know, would they?"

"You're bats!" said Temple. "What would happen when their shoes wore out? There wouldn't be anyone to mend them, because they'd all be marching. And they'd get a bit drowsy going all that time without sleep, wouldn't they?"

Darbishire began to have grave doubts, now that his imagination was forced to picture the marching column in action. "They'd have to sleep sometimes, of course," he agreed.

"But they *couldn't*," persisted Brown major earnestly, "because you said they had to march without stopping, and if they dropped out for a snooze or a snack every so often, there'd be a gap in the line."

"All right, then, perhaps there *would* be a gap."

Temple and Brown major whooped with triumph. "That proves you're wrong!" they chanted. "You said the line was unbroken! Darbishire's mad! Darbishire's crazy! Darbishire's as bats as two coots!" They danced round the student of statistics, plucking imaginary straws from their hair with gestures of feigned madness.

"Ah, but what I meant was ..." Darbishire broke off and turned to Jennings

440

for support, but his friend was unable to give it; indeed, Jennings seemed to be in need of support himself. He stood staring before him as though in a trance, and absently tugging at a button on his jacket.

"What's up?" Darbishire inquired anxiously, and he had to repeat his query three times before his friend came to with a jerk which pulled the jacket button right off.

He led Darbishire out of earshot of the prancing madmen and said: "Listen, I've just been thinking! We haven't got till Sunday to get a new hunk of glass. If that old general's going round the school tomorrow, the Head's bound to take him into the garden—he always does with visitors."

"Oh, golly, yes, of course!" Darbishire bit his lip thoughtfully. "And there just *couldn't* be a worse time to find it all smashed than when the whole place is supposed to be looking like Buckingham Palace and he's got baronets and things in tow. Oh, gosh, why do these things always happen to us!"

"Keep calm! We've got to put our faith in Aunt Angela," Jennings reassured him. "The Archbeak probably won't have got as far as the garden till the afternoon, and if that letter comes first post tomorrow morning, I'll fox down to the village shop in break and get the beastly stuff."

"Yes, but supposing anything goes wrong?"

"It won't. Things are ozard desperate, of course, but as your father says, 'While there's life, there's hope'."

But the odds were against them, and they knew it. Supposing the village shop had no glass in stock! Supposing Mr. Wilkins kept the form in during break! Supposing the Head showed his visitors round the garden before lunch, instead of afterwards! Supposing—and this was the greatest gamble of all—supposing that Aunt Angela forgot to post that letter!

Jennings swallowed hard. "Oh, gosh," he said, "I wish I hadn't said I wished Aunt Angela was an elephant. I didn't really mean it—honestly!"

CHAPTER 11

THE VISITORS ARRIVE

THERE ARE certain days which stand out in the memory long after they have been torn from the calendar: days when hope rides high and days when disappointment lurks round every corner. To Jennings, the second Friday in July was one of these days; it was a day when the needle of Fate's barometer swung from storm to sunshine and back again with baffling swiftness. It was a red-letter day.

It was a black-letter day.

It was Friday, the thirteenth!

Jennings woke early, and as soon as the rising bell sounded, he jumped out of bed and started to dress.

"What's the big rush—building on fire?" inquired Venables.

"Postman. I'm expecting a spivish important letter," replied Jennings, scrambling into his trousers. His movements were so hurried that he became entangled with his braces and had to start all over again.

Not that speed at this stage was really helpful, for even if the postman brought the expected letter, it could not be opened until Mr. Carter gave out the mail at the breakfast table; but anyone who happened to be on the spot when the postman arrived would be able to scan the envelopes—and Aunt Angela's handwriting was unmistakable.

Jennings washed and dressed and was about to leave the dormitory when Matron came into the room: "Good morning, Matron," came from five voices.

"Good morning! Best suits and clean clothes for everyone, today," she announced, "and an extra special wash behind the ears. You've all got to look smart for the visitors."

"My best suit's being cleaned, Matron," Jennings reminded her. "I haven't got to get undressed again, have I?"

"Yes, of course. Clean vest, shirt and socks. You'll find them all in your locker."

Jennings tore his clothes off as fast as he could, for the postman was due any minute now. Darbishire had only reached the stage of rummaging in his locker for a missing garter when his friend again dashed to the door, weaving his arms into his jacket as he ran.

Matron called him back. "More haste, less speed," she said. "You've forgotten to put your vest on. There it is, on your chair, look."

When Jennings had dressed for the third time, he hurried down to the hall, and was just in time to see the postman cycling away down the drive and a maid disappearing into the staff room with the letters. He told himself that it didn't really matter; he would know soon enough!

Mr. Carter sat at one end of the long dining-table glancing casually through the pile of envelopes which rested beside his plate of cereal. His movements were leisurely for he had the whole meal before him in which to attend to the post and he had every intention of finishing his breakfast first.

Half-way down the table Jennings and Darbishire sat side by side and seethed with impatience.

"Why on earth doesn't he give them out? I shall go off pop, if I don't know soon," fumed Jennings.

"I know—the suspense is unbearable," said Darbishire. "It's putting me off my breakfast. I can hardly manage this fifth hunk of bread and marmalade. It makes me go hot and cold to sit here watching him eating without a care in the world, and all the time we're waiting to know whether your Aunt Angela's memory has gone to seed, or not."

Mr. Carter finished his breakfast and strolled slowly round the dining hall, giving out the letters. Once he stopped just behind Jennings and the boy's heart leapt with joy; but the letter was for Darbishire and Jennings clicked his teeth with exasperation.

"There's not many left now," he muttered as Mr. Carter moved away: "If he doesn't come to it soon, we've had it!"

His eyes followed the master round the room; why was he being so slow about it? Why did he keep stopping for social chats? Why ...? He caught his breath in excitement for Mr. Carter was approaching once again, and a moment later the precious envelope was laid on the table beside Jennings' plate.

"Oh, thank you, sir! Super-wizzo-sonic thanks!" he beamed. His eyes were shining as he clutched Darbishire by the elbow and whispered: "We're saved, Darbi! It's good old Aunt Angela all right. That's her writing as plain as the nose on your face. Yippee!"

He turned the envelope over and over, as though it were some magic formula; he was so pleased that he could not bear to let it out of his grasp. He smiled at it, and fanned himself with relief and jogged his head from side to side in sheer high spirits. "Oh boy, oh boy, oh boy! Tiddle-um-tum-tum, tiddly-pom!" he crooned.

"Hadn't you better open it?" suggested Darbishire.

"Yes, of course, but the important thing is that it's actually come. Dear old Aunt Angela—she's got a memory like an elephant, after all, bless her!"

He tore open the envelope and took out a sheet of notepaper, and the next second, his eyes opened wide in horrified bewilderment.

"Dear Mr. Tomlinson," the letter said,
 "I shall be obliged if you will send me your catalogue of flowering shrubs as I have unfortunately mislaid the list which you sent me last month.
 Yours faithfully,
 Angela Birkinshaw (Miss)."

Jennings groaned; in a daze he passed the letter to Darbishire who read it and scratched his head in puzzled wonder. "Your aunt's bats!" he decided. "Why does she call you 'Mr. Tomlinson'? Have you changed your name by deed poll or something?"

"No, that's not me—that's somebody else," Jennings explained. "I see what's happened, though. She's written two letters and got her envelopes mixed up; I've got this Tomlinson bird's letter, and he's got mine. Oh, gosh, I take back all I said about Aunt Angela not being as absent-minded as a professor."

"What a ghastly bish!" said Darbishire, as the facts became clear. "And whatever must this Mr. Tomlinson be thinking?"

Jennings snorted. "Huh! It's what *I'm* thinking that matters. Never mind about Mr. Tomlinson—*he's* all right! At least he wizard well ought to be; dash it all, Darbi, he's got my ten bob!"

The deduction was correct. At the very moment that Jennings was bemoaning his fate, Mr. A. Tomlinson, *Nurseryman & Seedsman*, was standing in his suburban shop, pondering over a letter which had arrived by the morning post.

"Dear John," it began,

"I am sending you a postal order for ten shillings, which I expect will come in useful at the tuck-shop."

There followed three pages of good advice and news of Cousin Wilfred's white rabbits, and the letter was signed, "Your affectionate Aunt, Angela."

Mr. Tomlinson was surprised. He had not known that he had an Aunt Angela, and in any case his name was Albert, not John. However, ten shillings was ten shillings, so he slipped the postal order into his waistcoat pocket and whistled gaily as he opened the shop.

During morning break, a grey Rolls Royce purred quietly up the drive and came to rest outside the front door. From the car jumped a small boy wearing a green pullover and corduroy trousers, and he was followed a moment later by an attractive young woman, with blue eyes and fair hair.

Then, from the driver's seat stepped Lieut.-General Sir Melville Merridew, Bart., D.S.O., M.C.

"This is the old place, Diana," he said to his daughter-in-law. "Changed quite a bit from my time, of course, but if it was good enough for me and good enough for his father, it ought to be good enough for Roger, eh!"

General Merridew was tall, thin and very upright, with snowy hair and bushy eyebrows; the points of his handlebar moustache were just visible to anyone standing directly behind him.

The Headmaster received his guests in the drawing room. The General, he knew well, but he had not met the seven-year-old Roger and his mother before.

"So this is the young man, is it?" He smiled down at the General's grandson and extended his hand, but the boy quickly slipped his hands behind his back and stepped away out of range. He had not met any headmasters before, and he was taking no chances.

"Shake hands, Roger," urged his mother. "This is the Headmaster."

"Huh!" grunted Roger, not impressed. In point of fact he was bitterly disappointed. From all he had heard of these high-ranking humans, he had imagined that a headmaster must be about eight feet tall and dressed like a commissionaire outside a luxury cinema. Mr. Pemberton-Oakes was tall, but he was not eight feet; his suit was well-cut, but it was not a crimson uniform with gold buttons. Why, the man hadn't even a row of medals across his chest!

"I can whistle through the gap in my front teeth," Roger told him proudly. "I bet you can't!"

The Headmaster smiled and changed the topic of conversation. It was clear that the child had never been subjected to boarding-school discipline. Never mind—he would learn!

Mr. Pemberton-Oakes was proud of his school as he showed his visitors round that morning. The linoleum glistened and the brass door-knobs shone. Whenever they entered a classroom, a dozen boys with gleaming pink faces and well-brushed hair stood up smartly; no button was missing from any jacket, no sock hung limply round any ankle.

Even in Form 1 classroom, all ties were neatly knotted under the chin and not beneath the left ear as was their usual custom. Binns minor had spent twenty-five minutes polishing his shoes with his bath towel, and he edged his feet forward hoping that the visitors would notice the result. But he kept his hands behind his back, because his fingernails had absorbed nearly as much polish as his shoes.

Form 3 classroom was exceptionally tidy, for the havoc of the boys' spring cleaning had been put right later by the domestic staff. Jennings had disciplined a zig-zag parting into his hair, and although Friday was not his usual polishing day, Darbishire had cleaned his spectacles specially in honour of the occasion.

Both boys stood politely at ease when the party entered, and no one could have dreamed of the despair that filled their minds at the thought that a visit to the garden was high up on the list of the visitors' engagements.

"This is our third form," announced the Headmaster in so genial a voice that Venables had to look twice to see who was speaking.

"Splendid, splendid—fine body of lads, Headmaster; they do you credit!" said the General, who was deeply impressed by everything he saw. An orderly routine of obeying orders and jumping to it smartly was just the thing his grandson needed to knock the rough corners off him. "Well, Roger, how would you like to come to school here, eh?" he demanded.

"Huh!" said Roger and scowled at the bright shining faces of Form 3 with distaste.

Mrs. Merridew did not say, "Huh!" but she shared her son's doubts to some extent. Her own childhood had been spent in a boarding school where freedom was almost unknown, and it was this memory that made her keen to find a school for Roger where he would be able to enjoy himself in happy surroundings, free from the repressive atmosphere which had cast such a pall of gloom over her own schooldays. So far, all she had seen had confirmed her worst suspicions; Roger would never be happy in this formal, parade-ground of a place, where hair was so smartly brushed and shoes shone like mirrors. If she could have seen the boys under normal conditions, she would have known that things were not always like this but, as it was, Diana Merridew could not imagine these straight rows of tailors' dummies throwing off the shackles of dignified behaviour and enjoying themselves in a rousing rough-and-tumble.

She was wrong, of course—hopelessly wrong; and the pity of it was that Mr. Pemberton-Oakes had arranged this unnatural exhibition of highly-polished cherubs specially to please her!

The conducted tour of the building went without a hitch; the visitors were shown the oak-panelled library, the system of overhead ventilation in the dormitories, the patent, self-closing boot lockers, the thermostatically-controlled dishwasher in the kitchen and the up-to-date, tiled bathrooms with heated towel rails. They heard about the proud record of scholarships and the health-giving properties of the sandy sub-soil on which the school was built.

General Merridew was delighted with everything, but, as the tour proceeded his daughter-in-law became more and more convinced that Linbury Court was not the place for Roger. To judge from Mr. Pemberton-Oakes' remarks, his boys seemed to spend their free time in admiring the scenery and meditating deeply. This, his mother knew, would not suit Roger, who would be far happier making mud-pies out of the sandy sub-soil than in strolling quietly about on it without getting his shoes dirty.

It was a pity, too, that in the process of tidying up, all the things which Mrs. Merridew was looking for had been put away. One glance at the hobbies' room on a normal day would have shown her that the boys' out-of-school interests were well catered for; too well, perhaps, for floor and shelves would have been stacked high with model aircraft, puppet theatres, wireless sets, stamp albums, photographic equipment and shapeless pieces of leather and clay waiting to be coaxed into the likeness of home-made wallets and teapot stands. But now, these objects had all been locked out of sight in the cupboards, and the hobbies' room looked as bare and uninviting as a bus shelter.

The school was remarkably quiet during luncheon. The boys knew they had to be on their best behaviour and although the strain was severe, they kept their voices down to a polite hum and only occasionally spoke with their mouths full. The Headmaster was proud of them; the General was pleased with them;

but Mrs. Merridew was secretly appalled that seventy-nine boys could be so lacking in spirit.

"The old General looks spivish pleased about something," said Atkinson as he tucked into his pudding. "Hope he asks for a half-holiday!"

Venables cast a furtive glance at the top table where the guests were sitting.

"I expect he will, if he's in a decent mood," he replied. "When I'm a famous Old Boy in about a hundred years time I shall come back here three times a week and kick up a hoo-hah if they don't give a half-holiday every time I ask for one."

"You won't!" said Darbishire, from across the table. "You may *think* you will when you're young, but when you get past a certain age, you go bats. All grown-ups do; it's called, er—something like sea lion."

"Sea lion?" echoed Atkinson. "Gosh, I never knew that before. I suppose it's because they grow those walrus moustaches."

"No, it's not sea lion, it's ..." Darbishire struggled to remember the word. "Senile, that's it! It means that when you're about thirty-five or so your brain starts to pack up and you go as bats as two coots. I've often noticed it!"

Venables stole another glance at General Merridew who was beaming with pleasure at some story that the Headmaster was telling him. "I reckon you're right," he said. "After all, you wouldn't sit next to the Archbeako and still go on looking as pleased as a dog with two tails unless there was something the matter with you. I expect the poor old codger's been sea lion for years!" He shook his head sadly and took another mouthful of prunes and custard.

"I can't imagine an old geezer like that ever being a boy at school," pondered Atkinson. "He must have been here round about Queen Boadicea's time, I should think."

"He must have been young once," Darbishire pointed out. "Like all the chaps in those ancient school photos they've got in the attic. My father's in one of those—he was at school here years ago and I laughed like a drain when I saw his photo. He's wearing an Eton collar and one of those suits with a waistcoat and ..."

Darbishire found his left arm clutched in a vice-like grip. Jennings, who had scarcely spoken since the meal started was clutching his friend's sleeve, while his eyes flashed with the inspiration of genius. Darbishire stared in alarm; this sort of behaviour was likely to attract attention from the top table.

"What's the matter, Jen?" he asked. "Swallowed a prune?"

"Listen, Darbi, I've got a supersonic idea," his friend answered in a breathless whisper. "It's about the cucumber frame. I can't tell you now, because it's a top priority secret, but directly after lunch, we'll nip up to the attic and you'll see what I mean."

Luncheon took rather longer than usual that day, and it was further drawn out by the Headmaster's suggestion that the school would be deeply honoured if its most distinguished Old Boy would care to say a few words. General Merridew enjoyed making speeches and for twenty-five minutes he stood up and repeated, almost word for word, the same speech he had made on Sports Day the previous term. The boys listened patiently, for they knew the speech almost as well as the General did and they knew, too, that if it ran true to form, it would end up with a request for a half-holiday.

Their hopes were fulfilled, the half-holiday was granted and at two o'clock, seventy-seven boys filed quietly out of the dining hall and prepared for a long afternoon of cricket, photography and similar summer term pastimes.

The seventy-eighth and seventy-ninth boys, however, made straight for the attic. Jennings' plan was simple and he explained it to Darbishire as they pounded up the stairs.

"It was you talking about the old school photos that gave me the wheeze," he said. "Nobody ever looks at them now and the glass on one of those frames would just about fit over the cucumbers."

"Gosh, yes, massive idea! Saved at the eleventh hour!" Darbishire slapped his friend on the back and danced merrily up the stairs behind him.

Every year since 1875 the school had assembled for the annual photograph to be taken. The more recent ones were ranged in rows round the walls of the common room, but there was no space for the accumulation of three-quarters of a century, and each year as the new photograph was hung up, an old one was taken down and stored in the attic.

There was no one about when Jennings and Darbishire reached the top landing, but caution was necessary if they were to carry out their plan undetected. They would have to hurry, too, for the Headmaster's party had headed for the cricket field after lunch and in twenty minutes or so they would probably be making their way towards the garden.

Darbishire pressed the latch and the attic door opened with a piercing squeak.

"'Ssh!" said Jennings sternly.

"It's no good saying "Ssh!"" complained Darbishire. "It's the door that needs oiling, not me."

He led the way inside and stood blinking in the dusty gloom. There was a small skylight in the sloping roof and it allowed enough daylight to pass through for Darbishire to take in his surroundings.

The attic was full; there were broken beds and old desks and scenery from long-forgotten school plays. There was a magic lantern with tarnished brass fittings and a case of butterflies standing on a stack of out-of-date wall maps. There were surprising things too; useless, broken junk which it was difficult to imagine ever having been used in a boys' school—a perambulator, a parrot cage and a pair of ballet shoes.

The old photographs were in a far corner; some were hanging on the wall and others were stacked in heaps on the floor. Darbishire picked his way towards them. "It's pretty ghostly in here, isn't it?" he prattled. "I bet there's lots of mice about!"

Jennings had not heard for he was still on the landing, making sure that no one was about. He came in and the door closed squeakily behind him. "All clear! Let's get on with the job quickly," he said.

Darbishire sniffed and strained his ears; he was sure the place was overrun with mice for there was a strong mousey smell in the air. Perhaps they could catch one and keep it as a pet. "Listen," he whispered. "I thought I heard one, then, didn't you?"

"Didn't I what?"

"Didn't you hear it squeaking?"

"Of course I did," returned Jennings impatiently. "I'm not deaf, but we can't do anything about it if we haven't got an oilcan."

His friend stared at him in surprise. "You're bats! You can't stop mice squeaking with an oilcan!"

"Who said anything about mice? I'm talking about that wretched door. It'll give us away, if we're not careful."

"Well, I was talking about the mice and you said ..." Darbishire lapsed into sudden silence at the sight of Jennings' warning gestures.

"'Ssh!" he breathed. "We've got to keep quiet; Mr. Hind's room's just underneath here, don't forget. Now, let's get on with the job!"

Soon they found a frame which looked about the right size. Jennings lifted it from the wall, whipped out his penknife and slit the brown paper pasted round the edge of the frame. Then he removed the cardboard backing and eased the glass away from the photograph.

"There you are," he said triumphantly. "Hang on to the glass while I put my knife away."

He glanced at the yellowing picture in his hands and smiled. There were about sixty boys in the photograph and, to Jennings, their old-fashioned school uniform looked as odd as fancy dress. The smaller boys had long black stockings over their knees, while the seniors wore cycling knickerbockers, black bow ties and waistcoats which buttoned high over their chests.

The staff looked even more peculiar; a matron and a master's wife had skirts reaching to the ground and huge hats which blotted out the faces of the boys in the row behind them. The masters wore mortar boards and high stiff collars; beards and side whiskers grew in profusion.

Linbury Court School, Summer Term, 1895 was printed underneath the photograph in faded ink letters.

"Come and have a look at this, Darbi," said Jennings. "This is what you'd have looked like if you'd been here in your grandfather's time. Don't they look rare! Look at this funny old geezer in a white waistcoat and a watch-chain!"

For a moment they forgot the urgency of their errand and giggled quietly at the absurdity of school uniform in the nineteenth century. Then, Jennings said suddenly: "Here, what are we laughing at! We've got no time to hang about. I'll carry the glass and you go ahead and see if the coast's clear."

Darbishire tiptoed to the door and paused with his finger on the latch. "This dust's getting into my eyes and nose and everywhere," he whispered thickly. "I think I'm going to sneeze."

"You can't sneeze now; Mr. Hind might hear," Jennings protested in an undertone.

"I can't help it. I've got a tickle." Darbishire wrinkled his nose and blinked his eyes in a desperate effort to stave off the impending explosion. "Ah ... ah ... ah ...!" he panted.

"Shush!" urged Jennings.

"Yes, I will in a minute, but first of all I've got to ah ... ah ... ah-shoosh!"

It was a loud sneeze, as sneezes go, and the noise rang round the attic like a trumpet blast. A broken vase on the magic lantern vibrated in sympathy with the high-pitched note and echoed the sound like a distant air raid siren.

The two boys stood stock still and listened. Had Mr. Hind heard? Apparently not, for everything was quiet on the landing below and after a few seconds Darbishire ventured down the stairs to survey the route.

He stopped on the landing and beckoned to his friend to join him. Then he did the same thing on the next flight of stairs and in this fashion the boys descended to the main hall. The going was more difficult on the ground floor for there were blind corners to hamper them, but they managed well enough. Jennings crouched in doorways with the precious glass while Darbishire scouted ahead and looked cautiously round each bend.

"Come on; no one about," he called back over his shoulder and Jennings left cover and started on the next stretch of corridor past the library. He had gone half the distance when Darbishire, who was peering round the next corner, suddenly waved his arms in a desperate signal to retreat.

"Get back!" he breathed hoarsely. "Someone's coming! ... It's ... it's ... Oh, golly!"

CHAPTER 12

SHORTAGE OF GLASS

JENNINGS LOOKED round for somewhere to hide, but even as he did so he knew that it was hopeless. He was in open country and there was no time to go back.

As he stood undecided, Mr. Carter's voice sounded from round the bend of the corridor. "Well, Darbishire! Are you practising semaphore or merely waving a fond farewell?" And the next moment the master had turned the corner and his eye was on Jennings.

It is difficult to appear calm and collected when one is carrying a suspicious-looking object, but Jennings did his best. He smiled and said: "Good afternoon, sir. Jolly decent of the General to ask for a half-holiday wasn't it, sir?"

Mr. Carter was looking at the pane of glass and his mind was seeking some explanation. "What have you got there," he asked, "a portable windscreen?"

"No, sir. Just a piece of glass, sir."

"I can see that. Rather a dusty piece, too."

"Yes, sir." Jennings found the conversation difficult to maintain. He looked down at the glass as though surprised to find that he was carrying it. "Yes, it is rather dusty, sir, when you come to look at it. It might be a good idea if I cleaned it, don't you think, sir?"

"Why, Jennings?"

"Well, sir ..." *Why?* What on earth could he say? "Well, sir, then you'd be able to see through it better, sir."

Mr. Carter waited for further explanation and Jennings floundered on: "You see, it's just a piece of glass which wasn't doing much good where it was, so Darbishire and I thought we'd go and try and find somewhere where it'd be more use, if you see what I mean, sir."

Then, surprisingly, Mr. Carter said: "Run along, then, Jennings. Er—no don't run or you'll drop it. Walk along very carefully."

He watched the boys till they were out of sight. This must be part of the plan which they had been so busy discussing the other day, he decided. Now,

what on earth could they be up to? Clearly, they were on their way to carry out some urgent repair work, but—and here, Mr. Carter furrowed his brow in deep concentration—wherever had they found that pane of glass? He could have asked them outright, of course, but he had a fancy for letting things work themselves out to their logical conclusion. He could afford to wait. He knew, from experience, that he would find out the details sooner or later.

As they slipped out through the side door, Darbishire turned to his companion with a little, nervous laugh.

"Phew, what a bish!" he said. "Fancy running *slap-bang-doyng* into Mr. Carter like that. You don't think he suspected anything, do you?"

"No, of course not. He probably thought we were just, er—" Jennings searched his mind for some good reason to excuse their odd behaviour. "Well, there's no actual school rule that says you can't walk along the corridor carrying a hunk of glass, is there?"

"Perhaps not, but he must have thought it funny."

"I didn't hear him laughing."

"I mean the whole thing must have looked fishy. My father says that you should never ..."

"Don't natter, Darbi. We're engaged on a super-important secret mission and we don't want to get cluttered up with your father's famous proverbs."

Away to their left the cricket field was dotted with magenta-and-white blazers as the school settled down to enjoy the half-holiday, and in the distance Jennings caught sight of the Headmaster's visitors emerging from the cricket pavilion. So far, so good; masters and boys were well out of the way, but there was no time to lose, for the conducted tour would be almost certain to make for the garden as soon as their inspection of the pavilion was over.

The boys hurried to the gap in the hedge and crawled through. The pane hindered their progress to some extent and Jennings breathed a sigh of relief as he stood safely inside the garden with the glass still intact. Everything seemed very quiet now, and the afternoon sunshine bathed the garden in an atmosphere of peace and stillness.

Jennings found himself speaking in a whisper: "I say, isn't it lovely in here—so peaceful and picture-skew!"

"Esque," Darbishire corrected in a low voice.

"What did you say?"

"I said you mean pictur*esque*, not picture-*skew*."

"Have it your own way," Jennings answered. "There's no point in arguing about what sort of picture it is. After all, it's picture *frame* that we've got to worry about." He led the way along the path to where the cucumbers were ripening in the warm July sun.

First of all they picked up the broken fragments of the middle pane and laid them on the path. Then Jennings laid the new piece in position. It fitted well enough; if anything it was rather on the large side, but a small overlap on to the neighbouring panes was not likely to be noticed at a casual glance. He surveyed his handiwork proudly. "Looks fine, doesn't it, Darbi!"

"Smashing," his friend agreed. "It almost fits like a glove!"

"I'm not trying to make it fit like a glove," Jennings reminded him. "All I want to do is to give it a nice new pane."

"Tell it to eat green apples, then—that'll give it a nice pain," Darbishire replied facetiously. He was feeling so relieved at the successful outcome of their plan that a wave of lightheartedness swept over him and he shook with subdued laughter at his little pun.

Jennings looked at him in shocked surprise. "What are you laughing at?"

"I'm laughing at me," gasped Darbishire through cackles of delight. "I made a joke. You said: 'Give it a pane' and I said ..."

His friend snorted in disgust. "Oh, *that*! That's not funny. That's the feeble sort of joke that Binns minor and all that crush in Form 1 would make. Pull yourself together, man; we've got to clear up the broken bits and get out of here wizard pronto."

"Sorry, Jen," replied the humorist humbly and started gathering the fragments into his handkerchief.

There was a potting shed near at hand, so they carried the remnants of the broken glass inside and hid them behind a row of flowerpots. That was that! There would be just time to escape through the hedge if they went at once. Jennings dusted his fingers on his handkerchief and stepped outside.

The next second he was back in the shed again and pulling Darbishire down into the cover afforded by a large wheelbarrow. One glance along the path had told him that escape was out of the question; the General and the Headmaster were approaching. Already they had passed the rose garden, and they were heading straight towards the cucumbers.

Jennings groaned inwardly; if only he had been out in the open he would have seen them coming while there was still time to slip back to the hedge; but they had spent nearly two minutes in the potting shed and now their escape route had been cut off.

"What's the matter?" asked Darbishire.

"Archbeako and party—heading this way at forty knots. They won't come in here, though; we'll just have to lie doggo till they beetle off."

The situation was awkward, though not dangerous. At all events the main part of their scheme had been carried through, and a cucumber frame complete in every detail awaited the party's inspection.

A few moments later the sound of voices drifted into the potting shed and footsteps came to rest a short distance along the path.

"... now if only you could have seen the garden in April, General—the daffodils were a picture." The voice was the Headmaster's and it sounded uncomfortably close. "If you'll stand over here, you'll be able to see the laburnum trees to better advantage."

Jennings fixed his eye to a chink in the wall; General Merridew and his host were standing together beside the cucumber frame. Mrs. Merridew and her son were at the far end of the garden looking at the lily-pond and were making no effort to catch up with the others. Jennings took cover again as the General's deep tones boomed out in reply.

"Yes, very fine display, Pemberton-Oakes! This garden was always a picture in July, you know. I can remember the school photo being taken on this very spot, the first summer term I was here. Must be well over fifty years ago—round about 1896. Let me see, it was before Queen Victoria's Diamond Jubilee, so it must have been, er—um ..." There was a short pause while the Old Boy searched his memory; then he went on: "No, I'm wrong! It must have been 1895."

"Really! Well before my time, I'm afraid," replied the Headmaster.

The General heaved a sigh. He had enjoyed an excellent lunch, and now these familiar scenes of his childhood were giving him a feeling of homesickness for the vanished days of the 1890's. How it all came back to him! He could remember that photograph being taken as though it had happened yesterday; he had been wearing his first Eton suit and he had sat in the front row between old "Tubby" Tickner and "Tadpole" FitzArchway. What had become of them? He had hardly given them a thought since leaving school, but now they came flooding back into his mind with such freshness and vigour that it seemed as though Time had rolled back half a century in the space of a moment.

His eye was moist as he turned to his host and said: "I suppose that old photo was thrown on the rubbish heap years ago. Pity! I'd give a lot to be able to see that old group once again!"

"I can help you there," said the Headmaster, eager to please his guest. "We've got every photograph right back to the very first one. Very quaint, some of them. Ha-ha-ha! When we've finished our little tour of the garden we'll join Mrs. Merridew and Roger and then I can take you up to the attic and show you. 1895 you said, didn't you?"

"Oh, I hardly like to trouble you all that much, merely to satisfy an old man's passing whim."

"Not at all, not at all! I shall be only too pleased!"

Inside the potting shed Jennings and Darbishire stared at each other in dismay. This new development was going to lead to more trouble if something were not done about it very quickly. It was bitterly disappointing, for until this moment everything had gone surprisingly well. Jennings opened his mouth to speak and then shut it quickly as the conversation outside started again.

"What wonderful gladioli, Headmaster! ... And what's in this frame—cucumbers?"

"Yes, they're coming along nicely, aren't they! H'm, that's funny!" Mr. Pemberton-Oakes leant forward and examined the middle pane closely; there was dust on the glass and the marks of small fingers. Now, what did that mean? Surely no boy could have ...! The half-formed suspicion slipped from his mind as he turned his attention to what his guest was saying.

"Bit near the cricket field for a cucumber frame, isn't it? Wouldn't do to have any balls sailing over the hedge, eh what!"

"Oh, no! The boys don't play cricket near my garden," the Headmaster assured him. Then he took another look at the cucumber frame and he wasn't so sure!

"I suppose there'd be a terrible row if they did, eh! Ha-ha-ha—!" The General threw back his head and laughed heartily. "I remember once in 1896 I was knocking a cricket ball about with old 'Pongo' Bannerdale—he became an archdeacon, you know—and he sent down a long-hop and I hit it clean through the window of the headmaster's study. Ha-ha-ha! What about that, eh! Clean through! Ha-ha-ha!"

Mr. Pemberton-Oakes joined in the hilarity. "Dear me, how diverting!" he laughed. "Ah, well, boys will be boys! It must have made a deep impression on you, General, if you still remember it after all these years."

"It made even an deeper impression on the window pane, eh, what! Ha-ha-ha!" The General was in an excellent mood and his deep laugh pealed merrily through the still afternoon air.

Then the laughter faded and the footsteps died away as the two men strolled on to a distant part of the garden.

Jennings looked at Darbishire and shook his head in perplexity. He was surprised at Mr. Pemberton-Oakes joining in his guest's laughter. But his shock at this flippancy was nothing compared with his horror at the thought of what was going to happen next. Within a matter of minutes, the party would be heading towards the attic to inspect the 1895 school group. Every photograph from the school's foundation until recent times would be there, with one glaring exception. They would find a gap on the wall, the picture frame balancing on top of the magic lantern, the cardboard backing tossed untidily on to the perambulator and the very photograph which they had come to see resting between the bars of the parrot cage like toast in a toast rack. The human brain reeled at the thought of what would follow when this unhappy state of affairs was investigated at a later date.

"Come on, Darbi, quick. If we hurry we may just have time," said Jennings in an urgent, whisper.

"What are we going to do?"

"There's only one thing we *can* do. If they make a bee-line for the attic, they've wizard well got to find that photo in one piece when they get there. We shall have to take the glass off the cucumbers and beetle back with it. We may just do it, if we run."

The visitors had passed out of sight and the coast was clear as far as the gap in the hedge. Stealthily the boys crept out of the potting shed and started to put the emergency plan into operation.

"Oh, gosh, what a hoo-hah!" lamented Darbishire. "Supposing they decide to have another look at the cucumbers afterwards—we can't keep running backwards and forwards all afternoon with the same hunk of glass."

"We'll have to risk that. Anyway, there'll be an ozard sight worse hoo-hah if we don't get this glass back on the photo before they get there." He lifted the pane carefully and together they made their way back through the hedge.

Darbishire opened the side door leading to the hall. "Talk about a bish!" he observed bitterly. "D'you think the Head will get into a bate if he finds out?"

"Well, of course he will—he's bound to!"

"But he went off laughing like a drain about the old boy busting a window in the 1890's."

"Maybe he did, but if anyone busts one in the 1950's, he doesn't think it funny at all. It just goes to prove what you said about grown-ups going sea lion—they don't seem to understand things clearly after a certain age."

Darbishire scouted ahead and returned to say that the way past the library was clear of spectators. "I think I know why grown-ups carry on like that," he remarked as they started the next lap of the journey. "My father says 'Time heals all wounds' and as it's about sixty years ago since the old boy ..."

"Huh!" snorted Jennings. "If your father thinks I'm going to cart this slab of glass backwards and forwards for sixty years till the wound's healed ..."

The library door opened and Mr. Carter walked out.

"Hallo!" he said, "still taking pieces of glass for an airing?"

"I—er, well, sir ..." Jennings stopped. After all, what was there to say?

Mr. Carter looked at him curiously and observed: "You certainly think up some queer hobbies to occupy your free time. You'll have to come and take my french window for a breather when you've nothing better to do!"

By this time he had a shrewd idea of what was afoot. Later in the day, when the guests had departed, he would go into the matter in detail, but for the moment he decided to say no more. He turned and walked off down the corridor, leaving the boys guessing as to how much he knew; his back was towards them so they could not see the quiet smile which played round the corners of his mouth.

"Come on," said Jennings as the master turned the corner. "Ozard bad luck meeting him a second time, but I still don't think he suspected anything."

They mounted the stairs and hurried into the attic. Jennings said: "Ssh!" as the door squeaked open, but now it was a race against time and speed was even more important than secrecy.

Darbishire retrieved the photograph from the parrot cage while Jennings slipped the glass back into the frame. The backing was the difficult part for there were little nails set into the wooden frame at intervals, and these had to be bent forward to hold the cardboard in place. The nails were rusty and kept breaking off and they wasted precious minutes trying to bend them into position. They even took down some of the other pictures and tried to borrow some nails from them; but nothing would work properly, and the only result was that three unframed photographs were now spread out over the floor instead of one.

"This is ghastly!" said Darbishire as the last nail snapped off and failure became inevitable. "What are we going to do? They'll be here in a minute. I wish we hadn't done this! My father says that ..."

He broke off and listened. Footsteps were ascending the stairs and a voice was speaking.

"Only a few more stairs, General—we're nearly there," said the voice and a moment later the latch clicked, the attic door opened with an ear-splitting screech, and M. W. B. Pemberton-Oakes, Esq., M.A.(Oxon.), ushered his distinguished guests into the room.

CHAPTER 13

THE DIFFICULT GUEST

FOR A MOMENT the Headmaster was too surprised to speak; then, icily he demanded: "What are you two boys doing in here?"

And though there was a perfectly good answer to this question, Jennings did not know where to begin. Should he start with the absent-mindedness of Aunt Angela, the sentimental yearnings of General Merridew or with Darbishire's only straight ball in the England v. Australia Test Match?

"We—er, well you see, sir, what actually happened was ..." he began, but Mr. Pemberton-Oakes was not prepared to spend the entire afternoon in the attic and he broke in sharply.

"Don't prevaricate, Jennings. I demand a straightforward answer to a simple question. What were you doing when I came in?"

"I was putting a piece of glass in this picture-frame, sir."

The Headmaster glanced at the repair work spread out over the floor and jumped to the only conclusion which seemed to fit the facts. It was the wrong conclusion, but it was some days before he found *that* out.

"I see," he said slowly. "Yes, I consider that is a very creditable way of spending your leisure." And turning to his guests he went on: "These boys, instead of wasting their half-holiday in idle pursuits, have elected to repair the old school photographs as their good deed for the day."

The General smiled approvingly: Roger said "Huh!" and Mrs. Merridew thought what a pity it was that the boys were encouraged to grope about in dim-lit attics instead of enjoying themselves in the glorious sunshine.

"Very good of them," nodded the General. "I'm glad to think there's somebody who doesn't consider it too much trouble to keep the Old Boys' photos in a decent state of repair." He gave the Headmaster a reproachful look, for he felt rather hurt that these historic photographs should be stored in a junk-filled garret, while the more recent ones occupied places of honour on the common room walls.

Jennings' conscience woke up and prodded him into a second attempt to confess, but the Headmaster cut him short. "Of course, General, I always encourage the boys to spend their half-holidays in some useful and instructive manner," he said. "The odd-job man keeps a supply of glass handy for repairs of this kind but"—and a note of genuine surprise crept into his voice— "I must say, I hardly expected a couple of third form boys to think of asking him for some, specially for this purpose."

The two picture-repairers looked down at their shoes with becoming modesty. They would have to own up afterwards, of course, but it would hardly be fair to spoil the Headmaster's pride in their handiwork while his guests were still present.

Mrs. Merridew looked at the boys with sympathy. "Poor little fellows," she thought. "They're so repressed that they can't help looking guilty even when they're caught doing good deeds by stealth. This sort of place would never suit Roger!"

The Headmaster turned to the wall behind him. "Now, let me see, General, which was the photograph you particularly wanted to see?"

Darbishire picked it up from the floor and said: "Here it is, sir. This is the 1895 photo that we've been putting the glass on."

The Headmaster wheeled round and his eyebrows rose in astonishment. "And however did you know, Darbishire, which one it is that the General wishes to see?"

Darbishire shifted nervously from one foot to the other; he opened his mouth, but no words came. Fortunately, the General opened *his* mouth at the same time and a torrent of "Well, well, well's" and "Bless my soul's" rang round the room as the Old Boy seized the photograph and gazed at it fondly. "There I am, in the front row in my very first Eton suit—just as I thought!"

He held the picture under the skylight and looked at it for a long time without speaking. It was a sacred moment for General Merridew and no one liked to disturb his wistful memories of a by-gone age. After a full minute had passed he turned away from the skylight and his voice was unsteady with emotion as he said: "Well, well, well! How this old photo takes me back!" Then he blew his nose very loudly.

"Let me see, grandad," demanded Roger and climbed up on an old wash-stand and peered over the Old Boy's shoulder. "Golly, grandad, you do look funny—you haven't even got a moustache!"

The General was smiling again now and excitedly picking out his colleagues from the group. "By jove, here's Old 'Pie-face' Pottinger in the second row," he exclaimed. "He's doddering about in a bath chair, now. And bless me, if this isn't Old 'Bonehead' Blatterweather! I wonder what became of him?"

"You'd better run along, now," the Headmaster told Jennings and Darbishire, for he feared that the General's reminiscences might last some time. Mrs. Merridew thought the same, for she asked: "Do you think they might take Roger with them? He's getting rather bored, trailing round with us."

"Yes, yes, of course!" the Headmaster agreed. "You'd like to meet some of the boys, wouldn't you, Roger?"

"No," said Roger.

"But you'll have to get to know them if you come to school here, won't you?"

"I don't want to come to school here. I don't like this place. I think it's horrid!"

"Now, now, Roger," said his mother.

"Well, so it is! They've all got clean knees and I bet they're not allowed to climb trees and get in a mess. That's what *I* like doing!" he finished up proudly.

"Oh, but I'm sure you'll like *these* boys," persisted the Headmaster, favouring Jennings and Darbishire with a smile. They smirked back, secretly amazed that the Headmaster was capable of such affectionate feelings. They had never suspected this before, and even now they ascribed most of it to his efforts to humour a difficult child.

"I'd better introduce you, hadn't I?" the Headmaster went on. "This is Jennings, Roger; and this is Darbishire."

"How d'you do!" said Jennings and Darbishire.

"Huh!" said Roger.

Then they were introduced to Mrs. Merridew and the General; and Darbishire, who remembered what his father's book had said about ceremonial forms of address, replied to the Old Boy's greeting by saying that he begged to remain his lordship's most obedient servant.

"Take Roger round the school and show him the things that will be of interest to him," said Mr. Pemberton-Oakes. "Show him the books in the library, the scholarship honours boards, the collection of sports trophies and, ah, perhaps the tuck-shop, eh! Ha-ha!"

As the three boys left the attic, they could hear the General starting on what promised to be a long anecdote of his schooldays.

"Seeing old 'Bonehead' Blatterweather in this photo reminds me of the time in '97 when the bishop came to tea and left his hat in the hall." His deep, resonant voice followed them down the stairs. "Well, old Blatterweather put the bishop's hat on, just for a joke; and danced around in it. Suddenly, he looked up and there was the bishop and the Headmaster watching him from the top of the stairs ..."

The boys were out of earshot by now, and though Jennings would dearly have liked to know what had happened to Blatterweather, he thought it wiser not to loiter. Roger followed them, rather unwillingly, and as he did not seem disposed to talk, Darbishire turned to Jennings and said: "Phew! That was a bit of luck, wasn't it? I thought there was going to be the most hectic rumpus, and he was actually pleased with us!"

"Yes, but what fools we were not thinking of it before," Jennings replied.

"What! Mending all those old photo frames in our free time? No, wizard thanks!"

"No, you prehistoric ruin! Why didn't we think of the odd-job man? If we'd gone to Old Pyjams and asked him for a chunk of glass it would have saved all that wear and tear on our nerves."

"Well, we still need some, don't we?"

"Yes, and the sooner the better. Look, Darbi, you take Roger and show him the tuck-shop and everything and I'll go and find Old Pyjams, and if he's feeling decent and gives me a bit, I'll fox into the garden and fix it right away."

"Right-o," his friend agreed. "See you later, then. Come on, Roger—I expect you'd like to see the scholarship honours board first, wouldn't you?"

"No," said Roger decisively.

Jennings found Robinson in the boiler-room. Yes, he *had* got some glass, he admitted, but that didn't mean to say that he was willing to give away panes as freely as handbills. "Glass costs money, glass does," he said. "Those panes don't grow on trees, you know!"

"No, I didn't think they did," replied Jennings and wondered what a glass-leaved tree would look like. "But it's super urgent, Py—er, Robinson, really it is, and I could pay for it later on when I get some more money."

Grudgingly, Robinson agreed and led the way to the cupboard in the carpenter's shop where the glass was stored. Jennings selected a suitable piece and took his leave, murmuring voluble thanks as he went.

He clutched the new pane to his chest and hummed gaily as he started off along the corridor. Considering the narrow escapes they had had, it was amazing how well things were turning out, he thought. It would be the work of a moment to slip into the garden unobserved and …. His humming broke off in the middle of a note as Mr. Carter walked round the corner.

"You know, Jennings, this is getting monotonous," the master observed. "Every time I walk past the library, I meet you carrying a pane of glass."

Jennings agreed that it was a remarkable coincidence.

"This is the third piece in half an hour," Mr. Carter went on. "You haven't smashed three cucumber frames, have you?"

Cucumber frames! So Mr. Carter knew about it!

Jennings looked uncomfortable and said: "Oh, no, sir. We only broke one, really, but we've had to do a sort of shuttle service because of the shortage of glass, sir. Er—how did you find out, sir?"

"I put two and two together," replied Mr. Carter, "and they added up to Jennings and Darbishire continuing to play cricket near the Head's garden after they'd been told to move farther away."

"Oh! … Yes, sir. I'm very sorry, sir. I suppose there'll be an awful row, now you know, sir."

Mr. Carter thought for a moment before replying. "You know, Jennings, I should have been less inclined to take drastic action if you'd told me about it when it happened."

"I wish I had, sir! The trouble we've been to—you wouldn't believe it, sir! It's been more hair-raising than any punishment."

"Why didn't you own up in the first place, then?"

"Because of getting evening cricket stopped for the whole school, sir. P'r'aps if it'd been anyone else, the Head might have let them off, sir, but I've been in a lot of trouble lately, sir, and I didn't want everyone to be punished again, just because of me."

Mr. Carter took a less serious view of the matter when he realised what had prompted Jennings' unusual conduct. The damage would have to be paid for, naturally, but the boy had had so many punishments lately that Mr. Carter saw no point in giving him any more unless it was going to teach him the error of his ways. Good conduct, after all, was an attitude of mind, rather than blind obedience to a list of rules, and as punishment did not seem to work very well in Jennings' case, perhaps a reward for virtue would have more effect.

"Well, Jennings," he said slowly, "all I can suggest is that you make a determined effort to behave like a civilised human being. I shall put you on probation until this time tomorrow when I shall see the Headmaster and discuss the matter with him. That means you've got just twenty-four hours in which to pull your socks up …. No, no, you silly boy—I didn't mean it literally. Leave your socks alone when I'm talking to you. You've got until this time tomorrow in which to convince me and all the other masters that you are really trying. Understand?"

"Yes, sir. Thanks very much, sir. I'll try all right, sir. Honestly I will."

"Good. Now you'd better put that glass on the cucumber frame and then go out to the cricket field."

"Oh, but I can't sir. The Head's just told me and Darbishire—er Darbishire and I …"

"Darbishire and *me*," corrected Mr. Carter.

"Yes, sir; he's told us to take this new boy round and show him everything."

"He told *you* and *Darbishire* to do that?"

"Yes, sir."

Mr. Carter blinked in surprise. What on earth was Mr. Pemberton-Oakes thinking about? He had seventy-nine boys in his school and he had to pick Jennings and Darbishire, of all people, for a task which required skilful handling. Roger Merridew was a "difficult" child and quite unused to doing what he was told—so much Mr. Carter remembered from the Headmaster's remarks earlier in the week. Surely, then, it would have been better for him to be shown round by some reliable prefect!

Doubtfully, he said: "I see. Well, now you've got a chance to do something useful, Jennings, so mind you do it properly. When you're on probation for your conduct, we take a keen interest in how you carry out little jobs of this sort."

"Yes, sir. Thank you, sir."

Jennings walked on, his mind brooding on what his housemaster had said. "On probation" meant that he was being given another chance, and by a stroke of good fortune he had just been given a task in which he could prove his worth. He would look after this Roger Merridew as a mother hen tends her favourite chick; he would spare no effort to interest and entertain him. No one should say that J. C. T. Jennings had been entrusted with an important mission and had failed to make the grade.

He felt happier and just a little proud as he placed the glass on the cucumber frame—quite openly this time, for he had Mr. Carter's permission. Then he returned to the building to look for Darbishire and Roger Merridew.

He found them in the library. First of all he saw Darbishire standing help-lessly in the middle of the room and gazing into space with a look of glassy despair.

"Where's this Roger chap you're supposed to be looking after?" Jennings asked.

Darbishire pointed to the top of a bookcase and Jennings caught his breath in surprise. Roger Merridew was crawling along some ten feet above the ground and eyeing the space between one bookcase and the next in an expert manner. "He's going round the room without touching the floor," Darbishire explained.

"But he can't do that here—not in the *library*!"

"I've told him, but he won't take any notice of me. He says he can go round his bedroom like that in thirty seconds and he thinks this room's easier because he'll be able to swing on the curtain rod when he gets to the bay window."

"Gosh!" Jennings was appalled. Given the right time and place, he was as keen as anyone on this particular feat of gymnastics, and indeed, he held the Dormitory 4 record for the anti-clockwise "off the floor" circuit. But here in the library, where the furniture was polished oak and treasured silver cups gleamed on the mantelpiece, such a thing was out of the question. Besides, someone might come in at any moment and catch them!

"Hey, Roger, come down at once! You're not allowed up there!" Jennings called.

"Huh!" replied the shrill voice from somewhere near the ceiling. "I'm not afraid, even if you are! D'you want to make something of it?"

"Do I want to make something of *what*?"

"I don't know. It's a thing I heard a chap say on the pictures. Sounds good, doesn't it!" He narrowed his eyes and repeated the phrase from the side of his mouth. "Want to make something of it—huh?"

"I think it's a sort of challenge," said Darbishire. "He's insulted you and he wants to know whether you're going to fight him about it."

"He's crackers! I'm supposed to be looking after him—not bashing him up," snorted Jennings. "Come down here, at once, Roger, or I'll ..."

"You'll bash me up?" inquired Roger hopefully.

"No, I'll ..."

But at that moment Roger missed his footing in trying to leap from one bookcase to the next; he landed softly on a leather couch, but the shock had unnerved him and he opened his mouth and screamed at the top of his voice.

"'Ssh! For goodness' sake—'ssh!" Jennings urged. "You'll have everyone beetling in to see what the row's about." And sure enough, the library door opened a few seconds later and an anxious inquirer popped his head into the room.

It was Atkinson. "What's up? Place on fire, or ship sinking?" he asked.

"Neither."

"What's the air-raid siren for, then?"

"It's all right," Jennings explained. "We're just showing this chap round. The Head told us to look after him."

"Well, he didn't tell you to start torturing the poor little thing the moment his back was turned, did he? Dash it all, Jen. he's only half your size!"

"We never even touched him! We couldn't have got near enough even if we'd wanted to," protested Darbishire.

"No? Sounded as though you were killing a pig. Still, it's not my business." And Atkinson wandered off to fetch his batting-gloves from the tuck-box room.

Roger was quiet again now and Jennings decided to take a firm stand. "Now you've got to come round with us and look at everything we tell you to," he said. "We'll start here. This is the library ..."

"I've told him that," said Darbishire.

"... and these are all the books on the shelves."

"I can see that," said Roger. "You might as well say, this is the floor we're walking on, and up there's the ceiling."

Jennings ignored the tone of the small boy's remarks. It was clear that he had never been to school or he would not have been so outspoken to his seniors. Ah, well, he would learn! Jennings held him firmly by the elbow and propelled him through the door.

"Now, out here in the corridor, we keep the honours boards," the guide explained. "Now, if say, supposing you won a scholarship we'd bung your name up there on the wall. That'd be nice, wouldn't it?"

"Huh! You can keep your old boards," said Roger. "I'm not going to look at them and you can't make me." He shut his eyes tight. "Want to make something of that?"

Jennings shrugged his shoulders. "This is hopeless, Darbi! Still, we'll have to go through with it, because the Head's sure to ask us if we've shown him important things, like this."

"I can't see it! I've got my eyes shut!" squeaked Roger triumphantly.

"Well, you can wizard well listen while I read it all out. It'll serve you right, for not trying to be decent." Jennings' patience was wearing thin, but he set about his task with quiet determination and read aloud:

"1875 R. K. Blenkinsop, scholarship to Repton ...

1877 G. H. Johnson, scholarship to Marlborough ...

1878 C. L. N. Herbert-Jones, scholarship to Winchester ...

1880 ..."

Roger's loud yawn drowned the next name on the list. "How much more is there?" he asked.

"Just over seventy years! ... 1881 B. A. Dadds, scholarship to Harrow ..."

"I can't wait all that time—I shall be older than Grandad."

"Well, if you open your eyes and look for yourself I shan't have to read them all out."

"Huh!" said Roger, but he opened his eyes all the same. Then he said: "It's a waste of time showing me all these old things, because I can't read long words like that."

"Haven't you ever been to school?" asked Darbishire.

"No, but Mummy's teaching me, and I've got a reading book. I've got up to page seven. *Dan is a man*," he quoted by heart. "*Dan ran with a pan. The fat nag has a rag in a bag. Dan has a nap in the gap. A bad lad had ...*"

"All right, all right," said Jennings hastily. "I can see you're a jolly fine reader when you like, but we haven't got time for any more."

"What are we going to do, then—something nice?" asked Roger eagerly.

"Yes, of course. We'll go and look at the boot-lockers. That'll be super, won't it?"

"Huh! Is that all you can think of to do? This rotten old place is a washout, if you want to know what I think!"

There was nothing really wrong with Roger: nothing that a few weeks amongst boys of his own age would not put right; but as an only child, brought up without playmates, he expected to have his own way without the slightest regard for anyone else's feelings. School was a disappointment to him, and trudging round behind his elders had become a bore.

Jennings and Darbishire did their best to entertain him. They told him about Mr. Wilkins' geometry lessons, and the Headmaster's Latin class; they explained how many bad conduct stripes were needed for an afternoon's detention; they told him he must not run in the corridors or walk about with his hands in his pockets; they told him that he would have three baths a week and that his fingernails would be inspected before every meal; they told him when he must be silent and when he would be allowed to talk. In short, they did their best to prepare him for a normal school life, but the more they said, the more rebellious their guest became.

As they left the main building and wandered together towards the cricket field, Roger asked: "Don't you *ever* do anything nice at school? As far as I can see you spend all day reading dreary old books and washing your hands."

Darbishire hastened to correct this impression. "Well, we *did* have a super smashing thing we used to do, but it got stopped last Monday," he said. "We used to build huts near that pond over there." And he pointed towards the wood, past the cricket field.

"It was supersonic," Jennings added. "Our hut was easily the best, because Darbishire's a famous inventor, you know. You should have seen all the gadgets he made. You'd be surprised!"

"What's a gadget?" demanded Roger, showing some interest at last.

"Well, like, say, for instance, pieces of string so's you can open the front door without bothering to stand up, and an ear-trumpet so you can chat with anyone who happens to be on the roof." And Jennings painted an exciting word-picture of a squatter's life in the hut-colony before the ban was imposed. He spoke fondly of the ventilating shaft-cum-periscope; he dwelt on the joys of having an emergency drinking supply which could also be used as a patent fire-extinguisher; he added a few words in support of yacht clubs and pontoon-suspension bridges and touched on the delights of hut-warming parties when sardine and walnut cake were on the menu.

As the tale was unfolded, Roger gradually lost his sullen look and became more and more excited. Open-mouthed and round-eyed, he listened to the things that could be done in a community of squatters, and for the first time that day he felt that here was something worth looking into!

"You say you have feeds in these huts?" he gasped with delight. "Oh, goody, goody, goody! Come on, let's go over there and have one now!"

"We can't; they're out of bounds," Darbishire pointed out, and as this phrase was obviously new to Roger, he translated: "We're not allowed to go there, and in any case our hut's just a busted ruin, because the Head got jammed in the back room boys' department, and started lashing out."

"We'll go and mend it, then," suggested Roger, to whom school rules meant less than nothing. "And if no one's allowed over there, that's all the better 'cos there won't be anyone there to see us. Come on!" And he danced impatiently along the footpath.

"No, we're not going," said Jennings firmly, though he would very much have liked to fall in with Roger's suggestion; after all, they had been told to show their guest everything. On the other hand, it was also their duty to see that he behaved himself, and as he was the type of child who caused havoc in libraries, what on earth would he get up to if he were let loose in the untamed jungle beyond the suspension bridge?

"Come along; we're going back," decided Jennings and he and Darbishire turned and led the way towards the quad. They had gone some distance before they realised that their guest was not following hard behind them. Jennings glanced over his shoulder and then wheeled round and faced along the way they had come. "Hey, stop! Come back here!" he shouted.

But Roger Merridew had a clear start of fifty yards and was streaking towards the wood as fast as his short legs would carry him. If those huts were anything like as good as they sounded, they would be well worth a visit, he thought.

CHAPTER 14

HUE AND CRY

Scientists tell us that the human brain is like a commander-in-chief's headquarters during the course of a battle. From reports which reach his control-room, he builds up a picture of what is happening, weighs up the chances of this plan and that, and sends his orders to the battle-front.

So it was in the control room of Jennings' mind as he watched Roger Merridew running full tilt towards the pond. Eyes flashed a message to brain: *Enemy heading nor'-nor'-west at 6 m.p.h.* it ran. *Am keeping him under observation. Over!*

Quick as thought, the order was transmitted from brain to legs: *Take up action stations for pursuit of enemy, identified as R. Merridew. Proceed with caution: combat area known to be dangerous territory.*

Translated into human action this meant that Jennings took a quick glance round and then started to run. Reinforcements arrived—consisting of Darbishire—and the task force pounded forward after its quarry.

"We've no business to be going after him—there'll be a frantic blitz if we're copped out of bounds," panted Darbishire as he ran.

"Well, we can't just do nothing! Suppose he gets lost or something—what then? You are a bazooka, Darbi, telling him about the huts and calmly pointing out where they were."

"How was I to know he'd do a bunk? Anyway, we were told to tell him everything and we'd be failing in our duty as his lordship's most obedient servants if we hadn't. My father says ... Phew! Not so fast!" and the Rev. Percival Darbishire's gem of wisdom dissolved into gaspings and blowings as his son struggled to keep up the pace.

When they reached the wood, they caught a brief glimpse of Roger leaping across the wobbling struts of the suspension bridge, but by the time the boys had reached the spot, their quarry had disappeared amongst the huts.

Jennings called as loudly as he dared: "Roger, come out! We're not allowed over here!"

There was no answer and Jennings called again, but his plea fell upon deaf ears. Roger Merridew had gone to earth in Venables' low-built tunnel of a hut and he was looking forward to the most exciting game of hide-and-seek which he had had for some time.

"It's no good, Darbi. We'll have to go over the bridge and rout him out," said Jennings.

"But it's out of bounds! The Head said so; no one's allowed over the bridge because it's out of bounds! He put it out of bounds last ..."

"All right, all right, I *know*! You don't have to go on saying it's out of bounds a hundred and fifty thousand times an hour! Anyway, if we can catch him fairly quickly we'll be able to get back before anyone finds out. It should be all right," Jennings went on, "because at least we know the Head won't be coming over here .... At least, I shouldn't think so .... At least, I hope not!"

All the same, Jennings was worried. Mr. Carter had given him twenty-four hours in which to prove himself a reliable member of the community. Not more than thirty minutes of this time had passed and already he was breaking bounds and had lost a new boy entrusted to his care. And if he didn't find the wretched child very soon ...! He swallowed hard. Imagination boggled at what Mr. Carter and the Head would have to say about it!

Jennings led the way across the suspension bridge and the hunt started in earnest. Darbishire scoured the district round the edge of the pond, while his companion moved slowly forward searching the undergrowth on the higher ground.

But it was ideal country for a fugitive and Roger had the time of his life. He crept from hut to hut, taking cover behind the thick clumps of bulrushes, always on the move, always ready to double back on his tracks if his pursuers should draw near.

There were false alarms, too. Darbishire heard a rustling in the reeds and plunged after the sound only to find two moorhens enjoying the afternoon sunshine. He scowled at them, for the ground was soft and his legs were now muddy from knee to ankle. "Silly little birds!" he said crossly, but the moorhens took the scolding very well. It was almost as though the fifty-three Spanish galleons were getting their own back for the indignities of the previous Sunday!

So far, the pursuers had made no effort to go about their task warily. Indeed, they kept announcing their whereabouts with frequent appeals to Roger to come out of hiding—appeals which grew more desperate as time went on.

Finally, Jennings approached his partner with a new plan of campaign.

"We're just wasting our time, calling to him," he said. "And until we know roughly where he is, it's like looking for a needle in a haystack. I vote we lie doggo and wait till he gives himself away."

"Okay," Darbishire agreed. They were standing by Atkinson's tall, thin hut, so they slipped inside and stood quiet and alert.

Roger was disappointed when the sounds of the chase were suddenly hushed. It had been great fun, wriggling on his stomach through the long grass and crawling in and out of the huts. Once Darbishire had passed so near that Roger could have touched him, but a thicket of reeds had screened him from view and Darbishire had wandered by with his eyes straining straight ahead.

There had been few playmates in Roger Merridew's life and he was determined to make the most of a first-class game of hide-and-seek while he had the chance. There was no malice in his heart, no spite in his thoughts. It never entered his head that this exciting game could result in endless trouble for his guides.

He could hear nothing now. Had they gone away and left him to play alone? He rose to his knees and peered round; still no sound, still no one in sight. He stood up and skipped lightheartedly towards the pond.

Jennings saw him first; through a spyhole he had made in Atkinson's hut, he caught a glimpse of a green pullover and grey corduroy shorts making for the water's edge. He waited until the figure came nearer; then with a shout of "Come on, Darbi, quick!" he dashed out of the hut and raced away in pursuit.

Roger squealed with joy. So they *were* still playing after all! He took to his heels and dashed helter-skelter through a soggy swamp on the bank of the pond, splashing mud freely in all directions. On he ran without troubling to look where he was going, and a moment later, he tripped and fell headlong into a thicket of briars and brambles. Frantically, he struggled to his feet and dragged himself clear, leaving a portion of grey shirt and strands of green pullover behind him. As he pelted away, a six-inch gash showed in the seat of his corduroy trousers.

Jennings was gaining on him and Roger leapt at the first spot of cover he could see. It was the entrance to Bromwich major's semi-basement elephant trap, and he slithered blindly down the slope and rolled over and over on the earthy floor at the bottom.

The chase was over. Kindly, but firmly, Jennings helped the captive to his feet and escorted him up to ground level as Darbishire came dashing up to join the fray.

"Have you got him? Oh, wizzo!" he shouted, and then stopped and stared at the small boy in wide-eyed dismay. "Oh, golly, just look at him!"

Roger Merridew was not a pretty sight. He was mud-splashed from head to foot and thin red scratches ran down his arms and appeared again above the socks drooping about his ankles. The least observant spectator could tell that the child's clothes had lost something of their newness; shirt, shorts, pullover, socks, shoes—all carried evidence of his headlong flight through swamp and bramble.

Darbishire looked away. The sight was too much for him. Roger, on the other hand, was not interested in his appearance; he was beginning to take a fancy to these two boys who were doing so much to entertain him.

"Jolly decent game, isn't it!" he squeaked happily. "I was pretending I was an aeroplane."

"But look at your shoes!" lamented Darbishire. "They're wringing wet!"

Roger glanced down at his feet. "Well, let's pretend I was a seaplane, then, and I had to pancake on the water."

"Oh, golly, whatever are we going to do?" Darbishire wailed on. "I've never seen anyone in such a mess—except you last Sunday, Jen."

"Never mind about me," returned Jennings. "We've got to get this chap spruced up a bit before the Head starts looking for him." He pondered for a moment and then said: "Look, Darbi, if we smuggle him up to the bathroom, and bung him under the shower, I could take his clothes outside and give them a good brush."

"Yes, but they're torn! We can't sew them up without thimbles and bodkins and things, and if we go to the sewing room, there's bound to be a hoo-hah!"

"Well, let's get away from here, for a start. We don't want to be copped out of bounds."

In gloomy silence they made for the suspension bridge; only Roger was unconcerned. "It's all right," he told them. "I often get as dirty as this at home. Mummy won't mind a bit."

"Maybe your mummy won't, but our Headmaster *will*," Jennings replied. "Look at that great tear in your trousers!"

"That doesn't matter, either. I've got lots more pairs at home. I've got a blue pair and a green pair and a brown pair and a grey pair with white checks and ..."

"I don't care if you've got fifty million pairs at home! I don't care if they've got yellow spots and red, white and blue stripes! What I want to know is, whatever's the Head going to say when he sees you looking like a second-hand scarecrow?"

Darbishire touched his friend lightly on the arm. "You'll soon know, Jennings," he said in a flat, resigned voice. "He's zooming down on us for a roof-level attack!"

Jennings glanced across the bridge. Sure enough, three people were approaching from the direction of the cricket field. They were—reading from left to right—Lieut.-General Sir Melville Merridew, Mrs. Diana Merridew and M. W. B. Pemberton-Oakes, Esq.

Several things had happened during the previous hour which caused the Headmaster to wear a grim and forbidding expression as he led his guests towards the pond. The first one had been Atkinson's fault, and there was no excuse for it whatever.

Atkinson had not gone straight back to the cricket field after collecting his batting-gloves. The ear-splitting shrieks which had attracted his eager footsteps to the library had not been repeated, but he had hung around for fear of missing any further excitement.

He was disappointed, for the next time he had passed along the corridor he had found Jennings patiently reading the scholarship honours board aloud, while Roger listened with his eyes tight shut. Then they had moved off and Atkinson could think of nothing better to do than to resume his interrupted game of cricket.

He was crossing the main hall on his way out when he noticed a black homburg hat, and suddenly he felt an overwhelming desire to try it on. He knew that it belonged to the General and this added zest to his craving. The urge grew stronger, so, after a furtive look round, he tiptoed to the hall table, picked up the hat and placed it on his head.

It was a pity, he thought, that none of his friends was there to witness this daring act of bravado, but at any rate he would be able to boast for weeks to come that he had actually done something which no one else—except, of course, the General—had ever had the nerve to do.

The hat was too large for Atkinson; it came well down over his eyes and made his ears stick out like small pink wings. Greatly daring, he skipped across the hall to admire his reflection in a mirror, and while he was in the very act

of making faces at himself in the glass, he heard a sound which made his heart leap and his blood run cold.

It was a loud bellow, and it came from the top of the stairs behind him. Scarlet with embarrassment, Atkinson wheeled round and snatched the hat from his head. He was, of course, too late, for there, staring down at him were the Headmaster and General Merridew.

The bellow was repeated and, to his amazement, Atkinson realised that the General, far from being angry, was roaring with laughter.

"Ha-ha-ha!" he laughed as he came down the stairs. "Old 'Bonehead' Blatterweather to the life! Caught in the act, just like old 'Bonehead' and the bishop, eh, what!"

"Precisely," agreed the Headmaster. His feelings were mixed. Politeness to an honoured guest urged him to indulge the General's sense of humour, but on the other hand, he was extremely annoyed with Atkinson for taking such an inexcusible liberty. The Headmaster did his best; with his right eye he tried to freeze Atkinson with an icy stare, while his left eye lit up in lively appreciation of the General's joke. The strain on his facial muscles was considerable.

"Well, well, well!" the General went on genially. "What a coincidence! Takes me right back to 1897. The bishop's hat was a black one, too. Rather like mine except that it had strings on it."

He dabbed his mirth-damped eyes on his handkerchief while Atkinson stood first on one foot and then on the other, his mind reeling with bewilderment. He had done something frightful, and he could not understand what the joke was. Why did the General think his name was Blatterweather? Who was 'Bonehead'? What had 1897 got to do with it? Where did the string-hatted bishop come in?

Atkinson gave it up and, mumbling profuse apologies, he replaced the hat on the hall table and was allowed to escape.

Diana Merridew had watched the little comedy and had said nothing. She was mildly amused at Atkinson, and a little worried at the Headmaster's disapproval. Knowing Roger as well as she did, she could foresee that Mr. Pemberton-Oakes was going to have quite a busy time registering disapproval if ever her son became a boarder. Her depression deepened as they made their way to the study where tea awaited them.

"Now, I think you've seen everything," said Mr. Pemberton-Oakes, "so it only remains for me to tell you something of our methods here at Linbury. By means of small classes, we maintain a very high standard of academic work and promising boys are always coached for scholarships." He felt that he was talking rather like the school prospectus, so he went on in less formal tones: "Tell me, Mrs. Merridew, would you say that Roger is a studious boy, by nature?"

Mrs. Merridew thought of Roger's reading lessons and shook her head. *Dan is a man* could hardly be described as a high standard of scholarship.

"Work isn't everything," said the General. "I always came bottom of the form when I was here. What young Roger needs is firm discipline with no nonsense, to learn to play the game and to take a pride in his appearance. I remember a poem I learnt years ago—I forget how it goes, but it sums it all up neatly. I expect you know the one I mean."

"You need have no fear on that score," the Headmaster answered. "Our discipline here is based upon mutual respect and we are most particular about personal tidiness." He waved his hand towards the window through which a group of boys could be seen playing cricket. "Take any one of those boys," he invited generously, "and you'll find him smartly turned out with a spick-and-span neatness which will stand comparison with any school in the country."

"Yes, I'm sure it would!" said Mrs. Merridew.

The General rose to his feet. "There's a breathless hush in the—er, there's a breathless hush, *somewhere*," he declaimed, waving his teacup in the air.

"I beg your pardon?" queried the Headmaster, out of his depth.

"I think my father-in-law means it's very quiet in here," interpreted Mrs. Merridew.

"No, no, I don't, Diana," said the General. "I was trying to remember that poem:

'There's a breathless hush in the close, tonight,
Ten to make and the match to win,
A bumping pitch and a ...'

something or other, and then it goes on to say, 'Play up, play up! and play the game!' That's what I was trying to think of; and the second verse starts off ..."

Mrs. Merridew knew that the General would be prepared to recite ill-remembered verses of poetry until dark unless something were done about it, so she rose and said: "Thank you so much for showing us round, Mr. Pemberton-

Oakes. It's very kind of you to have taken all this trouble."

"Not at all," smiled the Headmaster, "and if you could let me know fairly soon whether Roger is to come here in the autumn, I shall be happy to make all the necessary arrangements."

"I can tell you that now," she answered.

"Splendid! You'd like me to enter him for next term?"

"No, I'm afraid not."

General Merridew nearly dropped his teacup. "Eh, what's that, Diana?" he barked. "You ... you're not going to send him?"

Mrs. Merridew shook her head.

"But, dash it all, Diana—why ever not? Very fine prep school—Linbury. And as smart a body of lads as you could hope to meet in a month of Sundays. Bless my soul, I don't understand this at all! If it was good enough for me it ought to be good enough for a young scamp like Roger."

"It's not that," Mrs. Merridew replied quietly. "If anything, it's the other way about; Roger isn't good enough for Linbury, if goodness means changing him into a highly-polished little boy with smartly-knotted bootlaces."

"Oh, but really, I hardly think ..." the Headmaster began, and then fell silent, uncertain what his guest really meant.

"Please don't be offended," she went on. "But, you see, I went through all this business of being polished till I shone when I was a girl. Where I went to school, we were never allowed to behave naturally, and we loathed it. And I decided that any son of mine should have a chance to grow up in happy surroundings where he could enjoy a certain amount of freedom. I admit everything here is organised most efficiently, but from what I've seen, the boys aren't given much chance to be themselves." She hated saying it, and she felt worse when she saw that Mr. Pemberton-Oakes was hurt by her remarks, but after all, she must be free to decide important things like this for herself.

The Headmaster was not so much hurt, as stunned! Surely one did not have to look far to see signs of freedom and self-expression: the hobbies room, for instance, containing every device from puppetry to percussion bands: or the hut colony, where the boys had, until lately, been encouraged to express themselves in a dozen different forms of art and craft.

But there was no point in listing these activities, for Mrs. Merridew had seen no sign of them. Too late, the Headmaster decided that he had stressed the wrong things and shown his guests a school which was too good to be true. The best suits, the close haircuts, the unbelievable tidiness of everything had been a mistake. Perhaps Mr. Carter had been right after all; perhaps it would have been better if the school had been wearing its normal "lived-in" appearance.

General Merridew was as disappointed as the Headmaster, but he could not persuade his daughter-in-law to change her mind. "Pity!" he murmured. "A great pity. I'd set my heart on the boy coming here. That would have made three generations of Merridews who were proud to have spent their earliest schooldays in the old place. However, it's up to you, Diana, and if you feel like that about it, there's no more to be said. We'd better go and find Roger and get back to town."

They all strove hard to make casual conversation as they left the study, but the polite chat sounded rather forced. The Headmaster was distressed to think that his school was not considered suitable for the grandson of its most distinguished Old Boy; and Mrs. Merridew felt uncomfortable in her mind, for she knew what a blow her decision was to the two men.

When they reached the quad, the Headmaster beckoned to Bromwich major who was coming in from the cricket field. Bromwich wondered what was coming. Had Elmer been discovered in the classroom cupboard? Apparently all was well for the Headmaster said: "I want you to find Jennings and Darbishire for me. Tell them to bring Roger Merridew to the hall."

"Yes, sir." And Bromwich made off again towards the cricket field.

"Bromwich!" The Headmaster called him back. "You are not likely to find them out of doors. I imagine that they will be somewhere in the building."

"Oh, but sir, I know where they are! I saw them about twenty minutes ago and they were running ..." He stopped abruptly, conscious that he had said too much.

"Well, go on, Bromwich! In which direction were they going?"

Bromwich bit his lip in an agony of indecision. He had thought it odd at the time that Jennings and Darbishire should be heading for the prohibited area as fast as they could run; and if he now blurted out this information, the Headmaster might think it odd, too. But one cannot stand mute for ever and finally he was obliged to say: "Well, sir, I thought I saw them going towards the pond, sir."

"The pond! But surely, I made it quite clear that ...! All right, Bromwich—you may go. I will attend to this." And turning to his guests the Headmaster explained: "There seems to have been a slight—ah—misunderstanding. If you would care to walk over with me, we shall probably meet the boys returning."

Thus it was that, glancing across the suspension bridge, Jennings caught sight of the three persons whom he least wanted to see at that particular moment. The Headmaster, for his part, did not seem particularly pleased when he saw Jennings; but when he caught sight of Roger Merridew, he was speechless.

"Well—I ... Good gracious! ... Bless my—! Words fail me!" he said, when speech returned. "Jennings and Darbishire, come here at once!"

They came. Slowly and hopelessly they crossed the suspension bridge and ranged themselves before the Headmaster, while Roger danced behind them waving happily to his mother.

Mr. Pemberton-Oakes looked at them with that expressionless face which always denoted trouble of the worst possible kind. Then he said: "I have never, in the course of my professional career, known anything to equal this flagrant act of disobedience. I entrusted this boy to your care. Why, therefore, you have taken him out of bounds and allowed him to get into this dishevelled condition, I am at a loss to understand." He paused for an explanation.

"We were just trying to be his lordship's most obedient servants, sir," Darbishire began, but Jennings interrupted: "We're very sorry, but we couldn't really help it, sir. Roger wanted to come over here, and we said he couldn't, and he said ..."

"That's quite enough, Jennings," replied the Headmaster. "I really cannot believe that two boys of your age could be forced to come here against your will by a small boy some three years your junior and scarcely more than half your size."

"Oh, but sir, you don't understand ..." But the Headmaster had turned away and was apologising to Mrs. Merridew in a dozen different positions. "I'm most terribly sorry this has happened," he assured her. "An occurrence of this sort is very rare here, believe me, and I shall see to it that the culprits are severely dealt with."

"Please don't apologise," Mrs. Merridew answered. "Roger doesn't look any the worse for it; in fact he's beginning to look more like his usual self."

"I'm all right, Mummy," Roger broke in. "I like this school now, 'cos these boys have been playing hide-and-seek with me. It was ever so exciting and we've all had a lovely time!"

The remark was made in all innocence but to the Headmaster it could mean only one thing. Sternly he ordered Jennings and Darbishire back to school with instructions to report to his study after breakfast the next morning.

As they walked across the cricket field, the high-pitched squeak of Roger's merry prattle faded behind them. "Listen to him!" groaned Darbishire. "It's all very well for him—he's enjoying it! He hasn't got a hectic blitz coming to him after breakfast tomorrow! I don't know what the young people of today are coming to! I'm sure we never carried on like that when we were young—well, younger than we are now, anyway!"

"You're quite right," Jennings agreed. "You see things differently when you get old. Take this afternoon, for instance; all that rushing about has put years on me." He sighed deeply. "Any more hoo-hahs like that and I'll be as sea lion as two coots by the time I'm grown up!"

CHAPTER 15

MR. WILKINS HITS A SIX

IT WAS a perfect summer morning. The dew sparkled on the close-mown turf of the cricket square and the sun, still low in the east, shone from a cloudless blue sky. It was early, and the dormitories were still draped in a pall of sleep as Old Nightie, the nightwatchman, emerged from the gloomy depths of the stoke-hold and plodded flat-footedly on to the quad to sniff the soft morning air.

It smelt good to him after the choking fumes which hung, thick as fog, around the boiler. He took a heavy silver watch from his waistcoat pocket, saw that it was one minute to seven and trundled off to the electric bellpress to rouse the sleeping school to the glories of another day.

There were five sleepers in Dormitory 4, and three-fifths of them awoke to the summons of the rising bell with joy in their hearts and a song on their lips. The song was tersely criticised by the remaining two-fifths who were feeling neither joyous nor musical.

"Put a sock in it, for Pete's sake!" complained Jennings, as the top notes of Venables' piercing soprano invited all nymphs and shepherds within earshot to come away. "It's all very well for you to lie there singing the top of your head off. You wouldn't feel so wizard pleased with yourself if you'd got to stop one of the Archbeako's rockets after breakfast."

Dormitory 4 had heard the sad story of Roger Merridew's visit to the pond, and they sympathised.

"After all, it wasn't your fault, Jen," Temple pointed out. He threw back the bedclothes and tried to pick his shirt up from the floor with the toes of his left foot. "Just tell the Head that the chap did a bunk and you had to follow him."

"I told him that yesterday and he didn't believe it because he said Darbi and I were twice the size of that chap, put together."

"He didn't mean if Roger was put together—he meant if *we* were," Darbishire explained. "Or rather as we were both twice his size, we ought to have stopped him because we'd have been four times as big, if we were put together, if you see what I mean."

Nobody did, and Venables said: "You're bats! If you and Jen were put together you'd hardly be able to move, let alone run four times as fast. But I still don't see why this chap wanted to run away from you, anyway. He must have been crazy!"

"Oh, yes, he is!" Atkinson sounded quite definite on this point. "I happen to know it runs in his family. I expect he's caught it from his grandfather, because he's as crackers as two cuckoos."

"What—old General Merridew! How do you know?" asked Temple.

Atkinson lowered his voice to a confidential undertone. "Well, yesterday afternoon, he thought I was a chap called Blatterweather and he said he hadn't got any strings on his hat."

"Who hadn't—Blatterweather?"

"No, the General. He got the date wrong, too. He kept thinking it was 1897. I couldn't understand all he was talking about, but the poor chap was raving like a coot."

Dormitory 4 sounded interested in this odd behaviour and pressed for details.

"Well, I happened to be in the hall ..." Atkinson paused; on second thoughts it would be embarrassing to confess that he had been caught red-handed wearing the distinguished visitor's hat. "And—and, well, that's all, really. He just came downstairs and started having these delusions."

His roommates nodded in understanding. The man was obviously senile.

The conversation rambled on, but Jennings was too much upset to listen. It was not the thought of punishment that worried him, but something far more serious. He had failed the Headmaster and had let the school down badly in the presence of visitors. Obviously, he reasoned, Roger Merridew was to have come to Linbury as a new boy, but now, thanks to that wretched business by the pond, his mother was bound to have changed her mind.

He put this aspect of the matter to Darbishire as they stood cleaning their teeth by the wash basins. "Now, supposing you were this chap's mother, Darbi, and ..."

"I'm not," Darbishire objected, foaming at the mouth with pink toothpaste, "and what's more, I never shall be!"

"Maybe not, but look at it from her point of view. If Roger was your son, what would you do?"

"I'd keep very quiet about it, and try and pretend he wasn't," Darbishire decided. "And if that didn't work, I'd never let him out of my sight, unless I went with him."

"Don't be so feeble, Darbi! What I mean is, supposing you were going to send him to school here, because you'd heard Linbury was a pretty decent sort of a joint, as schools go, and then, when you got here, something happened like—well, you know!"

His friend nodded. There was no avoiding the fact that if Roger was sent to some other seat of learning, the blame would be placed at their door.

"Why does it always have to be *us* that these things happen to?" complained Darbishire. "There are seventy-nine chaps in this school, and they have to go and choose us to take charge of that slippery little Roger, just because we happened to be in the attic."

"It goes farther back than that," said Jennings. "It goes right back to when we had that hut-warming party with Ven and Bod and they agreed what a good wheeze it'd be to make a home-made yacht."

"That's right! If they hadn't been so keen to sail it at once, you'd never have fallen in and then the huts wouldn't have been out of bounds yesterday."

"Yes, and on top of that, they wouldn't let us play cricket in their net, so we just *had* to play our Test Match bang slap next to the Head's garden; so if anyone was to blame for that direct hit on the cuke frame, it was Bod and Ven!"

Darbishire was shocked at such villainy. "Gosh, what rotters they are. Doing all that and then expecting us to take the blame for it! Let's go and tell them what spivish cads they are, shall we?"

"Yes, all right." But even as they wheeled round from the basins they realised the uselessness of such wild reproaches, and changed their minds. In their heart of hearts they knew that no amount of righteous indignation would shift the blame from where it really lay.

Jennings and Darbishire were very quiet during breakfast and though their friends tried hard to cheer them up, the shadow of the Headmaster's study seemed to lie across every mouthful of fried bread and tomatoes.

It would be of little use for them to protest their sorrow, for the damage was already done and the Headmaster, not knowing Roger as well as they did, would dismiss their explanation as an unworthy evasion of responsibility.

At five minutes to nine, the two boys set off for the study. They were accompanied part of the way by a small crowd of well-wishers and sympathisers who trooped behind like a funeral procession, uttering words of doubtful comfort.

"D'you think they'll get a swishing?" asked Atkinson.

"Oh, they're bound to," said Bromwich major. "What a pity it's the summer term. If it was winter they'd be wearing thicker underpants."

Binns minor on the fringe of the group provided realistic sound-effects of the Headmaster's cane in action. "Pheew-doyng! ... Pheew-doyng!" he squeaked, but the others silenced him abruptly.

"Buzz off, Binns," they said, and Binns buzzed.

The procession halted at a safe distance from the study and Jennings and Darbishire walked on alone. When they reached the door, Jennings said: "Go on, Darbi—bags you knock!"

"No, bags *you*!"

"One of us has got to."

"Well, you do it then. I'm not much cop at knocking on doors. I might make a bish of it."

"All right, then. Let's get it over!" Jennings tapped the panel softly and then held his breath until the summons to enter came from within.

The Headmaster's face was devoid of expression as he looked up from his desk. A bad sign, they told themselves as they waited for the storm to break; and indeed, Mr. Pemberton-Oakes had no intention of disappointing them for he was feeling particularly angry. Admittedly, the boys' actions had not influenced Mrs. Merridew, for she had made her decision before the unfortunate incident had been discovered: but on the other hand, their deliberate breaking of bounds had caused a very embarrassing situation.

The Headmaster cleared his throat. He had decided to talk for some thirty-five minutes on the error of foolish behaviour and then to drive home his argument with the cane which he kept in the corner cupboard. He stared at them in silence for some moments; then he said: "I have given some thought to your extraordinary behaviour yesterday afternoon and, frankly, I am at a loss to understand it."

"It wasn't really our fault, sir. You see ..."

"That will do, Jennings. Actions speak louder than words and no amount of explanation will convince me that what I saw yesterday with my own eyes ..."

At that moment the telephone rang and the Headmaster lifted the receiver. "Hallo! Linbury Court School," he said icily, annoyed at the interruption. "Yes, it's the Headmaster speaking .... Who is that ... Oh! hold on a moment, will you!"

He nodded an order to Jennings and Darbishire to wait outside in the corridor, and as the door closed behind them he spoke again into the telephone.

"Good morning, Mrs. Merridew," he said. "Roger has suffered no ill-effects, I trust?"

"Oh, no, he's perfectly well, thank you!" Diana Merridew had a pleasant voice, but even if she had croaked like a frog her next words would still have sounded as music in the Headmaster's ears. "I've been thinking things over," she said, "and I should like to send Roger to Linbury next term, if it's convenient for you to have him."

Convenient to have him! No news could have been more welcome, for now there would be no rift between the school and its most distinguished Old. Boy.

"Yes, yes, of course, I should be delighted," replied the Headmaster, "but I thought—ah—from what you said yesterday I was led to suppose ..."

"I've changed my mind," said Mrs. Merridew. "As a matter of fact it was that little scene by the pond that decided me."

"By the pond! But surely ...!" For the life of him the Headmaster could not make sense of it.

"Yes; you see, I'd been judging the school by the parade-ground inspection you'd prepared for us. The General was frightfully pleased by it, of course, but it made me think that if school life was going to be like that all the time, it wouldn't suit a boy like Roger."

"Oh ... H'm ... Well, of course we *did* make a rather special effort for your visit," the Headmaster conceded. "I must confess that normally we tend to become—ah—somewhat less formal than our tour of the school seemed to indicate."

"So I gather from what Roger has been telling me. He says the boys build the most wonderful huts and have feasts in them and sail model yachts on the pond. It sounds splendid fun; and Roger can hardly wait to come to school and start building one himself."

The Headmaster's brow puckered in a frown of indecision. To explain that the huts were now a thing of the past and the pond was out of bounds would mean that the youngest Merridew would not be sent to follow in the footsteps of his distinguished grandfather. Perhaps he *had* been rather harsh in banning this innocent activity merely because Jennings' hut had collapsed at an inconvenient moment.

"I think you can rest assured, Mrs. Merridew," he replied, "that Roger will be given ample scope to indulge in suitable forms of outdoor recreation."

"That's fine, then. Oh, yes; and those two boys who organised that wonderful game of hide-and-seek for him—you won't be annoyed with them, will you? Roger says it wasn't their fault that his clothes got in that state."

Again the Headmaster pondered: then, he said: "Quite frankly, Mrs. Merridew, I had intended to punish them severely."

"Punish them! Oh, but surely they deserve a reward more than a punishment; I was going to ask you to thank them for me, because I should never have decided to send Roger to Linbury if they hadn't shown me the more human side of school life."

For some minutes after he had replaced the receiver, Mr. Pemberton-Oakes sat and stared out of the window, deep in thought. He sat so long that Jennings and Darbishire, on the other side of the door, began to wonder whether they had been forgotten.

"I wish he'd get a move on. I want to get it over as quickly as poss," whispered Jennings. "I can't think what he's doing. I heard him put the phone down five minutes ago."

"I expect all this waiting's part of the punishment," Darbishire whispered back. "You know, like the Spanish Inquisition where they keep you hanging about in suspense, and give you plenty of time to get the wind up before they get cracking with the instruments of torture. I read a story once about a chap who'd been captured by cannibals, and when they got him in the pot they were such a long time rubbing two sticks together to get the fire started that this chap would have lent them a box of matches, if he hadn't been tied up so's he couldn't move." He shook his head sadly. "Of course, he escaped in the end, though. They always do in books. It's only in real life that there's no getting out of it."

The only consolation they could think of was that it was ten minutes past nine and they were missing the first part of Mr. Wilkins' algebra lesson; but this was cold comfort compared with what would be awaiting them when the Headmaster once more bade them enter.

At that moment, he did: and when the boys had ranged themselves before his desk once more, he said: "Well, and what have you two got to say for yourselves?"

Jennings caught his breath in surprise. The voice sounded so warm and friendly. Could it be a trap to lull them into a feeling of false security? Was it another method of building up the suspense like that endless waiting in the corridor? Still, the Headmaster was waiting for an answer of some sort, so Jennings said: "Please, sir, we're very sorry we made such a mess of Roger, sir."

"Ah, well, it was just an accident, I suppose," replied the Headmaster, unexpectedly. "And it's had its compensations. You'll be pleased to hear that he'll be coming to school here next term." He paused as though in doubt about what to say next.

"Yes, sir," they said, blankly. This interview was not going according to plan. They had come prepared to stop a rocket and the Headmaster was taking a very long time about igniting the fuse. Darbishire was put in mind of his story about the cannibals rubbing pieces of wood together. Should he offer to help? Anything would be better than this uncertainty!

He was just piecing a sentence together in his mind when the Headmaster went on: "I have been thinking over the whole question of these huts, and I have come to the conclusion that there is, after all, something to be said in their favour. Properly organised, they could provide excellent opportunities to develop a knowledge of woodcraft, nature study, bird-watching and—ah, perhaps an occasional picnic might not come amiss, eh?"

"Yes, sir, of course, sir, but I thought ..." Jennings stopped, unable to make head or tail of this sudden change of opinion. But then, he knew nothing of what had been said over the telephone!

"I propose, therefore, to remove the ban which I imposed last Monday," the Headmaster continued. "Let me see, there is no cricket match this afternoon so it might be a good idea for you two boys to go over there during net practice and repair the damage to your hut which took place on the occasion of my visit."

"*Thank* you, sir .... Thank you very *much*, sir .... Thank you very much *indeed*, sir."

"Mrs. Merridew has asked me to express her thanks to you for the—ah—services which you rendered yesterday afternoon. Your assistance as guides had more successful results than I had at first supposed and I am cancelling my rule about the huts as I feel that your efforts deserve some recognition. Run along, now, both of you. I'm sure you don't want to miss any more of Mr. Wilkins' algebra lesson than is necessary."

Jennings and Darbishire left the study in a daze of happy bewilderment. When fortune smiled unexpectedly, it was better to accept it as a pleasant surprise than to inquire into the reasons behind it.

They walked along the empty corridor in silence, but when they were approaching Form 3 classroom, Jennings said: "You know, Darbi, I think all grown-ups are crazy. One minute they're in a supersonic bate and there's a hoo-hah going on, and then, before you know where you are, they're actually saying thank you for being decent and talking about picnics and things."

"It proves what I've always said," Darbishire returned gravely. "After a certain age, they get odd. Just because they look normal, it doesn't nesser-celery mean they're not sea lion—er, I should say it doesn't necessarily mean they're not senile," he corrected himself. He was still feeling rather confused.

"I should think the Head's definitely senile by now. He must be well over thirty—more than that perhaps, even. Say, seventy-five or eighty!"

"Never mind, we can go and build our hut again this afternoon. Isn't it wizzo!"

Form 3 looked surprised when Jennings and Darbishire came into class wearing broad smiles of satisfaction on their faces; they were even more surprised, when, at the end of the lesson they crowded round Jennings' desk and asked him what had happened.

"I bet it hurt!" said Venables. "I bet he'd been sharpening that old cane till he'd got an edge on it like a razor. How many did you get?"

"We didn't get any. He was in rather a decent mood and he seemed quite pleased to see us," Jennings answered.

Form 3 were incredulous. "D'you mean to say you didn't get six of the best?"

"No. He thanked us for all the help we'd been."

"Rot!" said Temple. "Don't you believe him! He's just trying to be funny."

"No, I'm not. It's quite true, isn't it, Darbi?"

"Yes, and that's not all," Darbishire confirmed. "He said we could go and play in the huts again and have picnics."

Form 3 laughed merrily at this innocent leg-pull. Ah, well, they thought, Darbishire *will* have his little joke!

"I can just imagine what would happen if we believed them," laughed Atkinson. "Supposing we all ankled over to the huts, and when Old Wilkie pranced up breathing fire, we calmly told him that Jennings and the Archbeako had got together and decided to put the pond in bounds again!"

Temple said: "I dare you to try it, Atki. After all, Darbishire *did* say it was all right, so it wouldn't be your fault if there was a hoo-hah."

"No wizard fear! Let Jen and Darbi do it first."

"Yes, we're going to," said Jennings unexpectedly. "We're going over there after lunch instead of playing in the nets."

Cricket practice for the whole school was the programme that afternoon. Had things been normal, the first XI would have been playing a return match against Bracebridge School, but the mumps epidemic had disorganised the fixture list, and though all the convalescents were now back in school the period of quarantine had several days to run.

Mr. Wilkins strode round the field noting with approval that everything was under control. In one corner, Mr. Carter was coaching the first XI in fielding practice and, nearby, Mr. Hind was bowling in one of the nets.

All the boys were busily occupied and the thwack of ball against bat rang out on all sides. Mr. Wilkins' satisfied glance circled the field. Then he gave a sudden start, shaded his eyes from the strong sunlight and stared unbelievingly.

Scampering and skipping happily along the path which led to the pond were two boys. The master's vast voice boomed out across the cricket field: "Jennings and Darbishire, come here!"

The happy scamperers stopped in mid-skip; then they turned and made their way back to Mr. Wilkins.

"Yes, sir?"

"Where are you two boys off to?"

"We're going over to our hut, sir."

"But, you silly little boys, the huts are out of bounds!"

"No, they're not, sir. They were, sir, but they're not now, any longer, sir," Jennings explained. "The Head gave us permission to go there this morning, or rather, he gave us permission to go there this afternoon—not this morning. Well, what I mean is, he gave us permission this morning to go there this afternoon, sir."

"Nonsense! You've been getting things round your neck, again. The Head's said nothing to me about altering the rule. Go and join that net over there and I'll give you some coaching."

"Oh, but, sir, the Head really did say we could—honestly, sir!"

"Don't argue, Jennings. I'm on duty and I've heard nothing about it, so that's that."

It was useless to protest, so the two boys followed Mr. Wilkins to a net where Temple, Atkinson and Venables were lobbing easy long-hops at Bromwich major.

"Come along, Bromwich, you've been in quite long enough! Let someone else have an innings," ordered Mr. Wilkins. "Now, who shall it be?"

It was agreed that Darbishire was more in need of batting practice than anyone else and soon, padded and gloved, he was at the wicket, prodding halfheartedly at the balls which flew at him thick and fast from the queue of bowlers at the far end of the pitch.

Mr. Wilkins watched for a few minutes with mounting exasperation. Then he marched into the net and delivered a spate of good advice from behind the stumps. "No, no, no, Darbishire—that's no way to play a forward stroke. You've got about as much idea as a sack of potatoes! Hold your bat straight, you silly little boy, and don't step away to the leg every time."

"Yes, sir—er, no, sir." The batsman tried hard to cope with the good advice in the right order.

"Now, let me see you do it properly!"

"Yes, sir."

A medium-paced ball arrived and Darbishire stepped back to leg and swung his bat as though wielding a scythe. The ball passed underneath and uprooted his off-stump.

"Tut-tut-tut!" clicked the coach and clasped his brow in anguish. Then he decided to give a personal demonstration. "Come away from the wicket and give me the bat," he said. "Now, send down a good length ball, Jennings, and all you others watch closely!"

"Yes, sir," they chorused, and Darbishire retired to the bowler's end, unpadding and ungloving himself as he went.

"Now, watch carefully. I shall come right forward to it and open my shoulders and drive it over mid-on's head to the boundary," prophesied the batsman, "so all you fielders had better move out a bit deeper." He took guard, patted the pitch, glanced round and then took up a purposeful stance.

Jennings swung his arm round and round to generate the current. He was hoping to bowl what he called one of his extra special super-cracking-sonic snorters. Much to his surprise, he did! And the batsman's middle stump shot out of the ground with a sharp click and landed at the back of the net.

Mr. Wilkins was even more surprised than Jennings. "Oh! ... H'm ... Very good ball, Jennings," he said, while the fielders danced up and down with wild gestures of congratulation.

Atkinson rushed into the net and retrieved the stump. "It was a good ball, wasn't it, sir! Why did you let it get you out, sir, instead of clouting it to the boundary as you said, sir?"

"I—er, it took me off my guard."

"But it couldn't have done, sir. You'd just taken guard."

"H'm, yes, well now, that was a demonstration of how *not* to play a good-length ball. Just as well to show you the wrong method so that you can compare it with my next stroke which will be the *right* way."

He took up his stance again, hoping that the next delivery would be easier to cope with; and when a glance at the bowler's end showed him that Darbishire proposed bowling the next ball, Mr. Wilkins stopped worrying. At any rate, his wicket would be quite safe!

"Coming down, sir. Pla-ay!" called Darbishire, and pranced along to the crease in close imitation of Mr. Carter's bowling run. He swung his arm and gave the ball a little twist as it left his hand.

Temple was standing some ten yards outside the net in the direction of cover point. The next moment he yelled aloud as Darbishire's famous leg-spinner swung round in a semi-circle and caught the fielder on his right ear. "Ow! ... Coo! ... Gosh, you are a great clumsy hippopotamus, Darbi!"

"Sorry, Bod—it slipped! Did it hurt you?" inquired the bowler, unnecessarily.

"I should think it wizard well did!" He tossed the ball back and moved away in the direction of the pavilion. "I'm going to take cover before the next one," he announced in aggrieved tones. "You need a crash helmet and armour plating if you're going to stay out in the open when Darbishire starts bowling. Let me know when the 'all-clear' goes, Bromo!"

Darbishire looked downcast as he picked up the ball. "May I have another go, please, sir?" he asked.

"Yes, Darbishire, I think you'd better," the master replied. "Just a *leetle* straighter this time, if you can manage it. Try and get it in the net, if that's not asking too much!"

"Yes, sir. Ready, sir? ... Pla-ay!" Again Darbishire ran up to the wicket. Twelve short steps, a little jump and then, to his great delight, the ball sailed straight down the pitch.

"Oh, smashing ball, Darbi!" cried Jennings generously.

"Good ball!" called the batsman at the same moment, and stepped forward and hit it with all his strength.

Mr. Wilkins' forceful character was as evident in his cricket as it was in everything else he did. One glorious over of hard-hit boundaries was worth a whole afternoon of snail-paced scoring, in his estimation. Thus, when Mr. Wilkins hit a cricket ball, he hit it hard and true, with all the weight of his thirteen-stone-six behind it; and as he smote Darbishire's second ball he felt the exhilaration known only to a hard-hitting batsman who sees the ball soaring into the blue, far beyond the boundary.

"Oh, jolly good shot, sir!" cried all the fielders in ecstasy. "Talk about a beefy swipe!"

"Wizard drive, sir! Gosh, what an outsize clout!" came from Temple, still taking cover by the pavilion steps.

"It's still rising! Golly, I've never seen such a smasher," breathed Jennings.

Up and on soared the ball, past the other cricket nets and over the tennis courts; then, as its speed slackened and it began to lose height, they saw it disappear over the hedge of the Headmaster's garden.

Mr. Wilkins was smiling broadly. "Well, now, that's the correct method of playing a ..." He stopped abruptly; far away, beyond the hedge came the unmistakable tinkle of a pane of glass shattered into a thousand fragments.

"Good gracious!" exclaimed Mr. Wilkins.

CHAPTER 16

HAPPY ENDING

JENNINGS TURNED to Darbishire and his voice was hushed with awe and wonder. "I say, Darbi, did you hear that crash just then?"

"I fancy I *did* hear a sort of musical tinkle, yes," his friend agreed.

Only too well he knew what had happened. How could he be mistaken about a sound which had rung in his ears and haunted his dreams for two whole days and nights? This time, however, it was somebody else's fault and that made all the difference in the world.

"You know, Jen, there must be something rather special about my bowling," he observed. "P'r'aps it's got some sort of magnetic attraction that only operates on cucumber frames. I've only bowled two really decent balls this term and both of them have landed up in the same place. Funny, isn't it!"

"It'll be a supersonic sight funnier in a minute," said Jennings. "The Archbeako's beetling out of his garden gate like a torpedo. I can't see his face from here, but I should say he's going to action stations for a point blank broadside!"

"Golly, poor Mr. Wilkins!" murmured Darbishire sympathetically. "He'll have to stop the rocket this time, won't he? D'you think the Head will be in much of a bate?"

"Of course he will, you prehistoric remains! If he *wasn't*, we needn't have gone to all that trouble when *we* did it. He's bound to look on it as a ghastly catastroscope—or whatever you call it, and there'll be the most frantic hoo-hah—you see if I'm not right! Good job it's Old Wilkie and not us! Come on, let's go and see what he says!"

Mr. Pemberton-Oakes seldom visited his garden on Saturday afternoons, but a thought which had lain hidden in his memory since the previous day had suddenly occurred to him after lunch. He remembered that the middle pane of the cucumber frame had borne traces of dust and small fingermarks when he had been showing the General round the garden.

Now, that was unusual and called for investigation, so he went to his garden

497

while the thought was still fresh in his mind. Odd, he thought, as he bent down and peered at the glass. Very odd! For the dust had disappeared and the fingermarks with it. It was not until much later that he learned from Mr. Carter that the pane had been changed since last he had seen it.

This pane, also, was destined to be short-lived, for even as the Headmaster stood and pondered, a cricket ball shot over the hedge and crashed through the glass not two yards from where he was standing. Fortunately, he was not hurt, but the suddenness of the crash startled him, and he was distinctly annoyed as he retrieved the ball from the bottom of the frame and set forth across the cricket field to seek the cause of this untimely occurrence.

He soon found it. Mr. Wilkins, surrounded by a small cluster of boys, was approaching from the nets. Mr. Wilkins was a big man and the size 4 bat which dangled from his fingers looked absurdly inadequate for a cricketer of such muscular proportions.

"What happened, Mr. Wilkins?" the Headmaster inquired.

At the rear of the group Jennings nudged Darbishire as though to say: "Now for it! This is where we sit back and have a hearty laugh!"

"I'm afraid I knocked the ball over your hedge, sir," Mr. Wilkins replied.

"Really!" The Headmaster measured the distance with his eye. A truly remarkable stroke! His annoyance vanished now that he knew the accident was not the result of stupid little boys playing too near his hedge. "My word, Mr. Wilkins, it must have been an excellent drive," he said in tones of deep admiration. "I wish I'd seen it!"

"It was a wonderful shot, sir," said Atkinson.

"I've never seen such a good hit in my life, sir," said Bromwich major.

"I can quite believe it," replied Mr. Pemberton-Oakes. "I congratulate you, Mr. Wilkins. I hope all you boys were watching closely so that you could appreciate the finer points of the stroke." His gaze roamed round the group. "Perhaps, one of these days, Jennings, you will be able to make a hit like that, eh—ha-ha-ha!"

Jennings gave a sickly grin and said nothing.

The Headmaster turned to Atkinson: "Go and find Robinson. Tell him what has happened and ask him to fit a new piece of glass to my cucumber frame as soon as he can."

"Yes, sir."

Atkinson sped away on his errand and the Headmaster and his assistant strolled back towards the net. "You'll be playing against the Australians,

Wilkins, if you go on like this, eh! Ha-ha-ha!" And Mr. Wilkins joined in the Headmaster's hearty laughter.

For some moments Jennings was too overcome to say a word. He stood staring after the retreating backs of the masters, shocked beyond measure at the rank injustice of what he had just heard. At length he said: "Well! Did you hear *that*, Darbi? Did you ever hear anything like it? Gosh, that's the most unfair thing I've ever heard of in the whole of my life!"

"I should jolly well think it is," Darbishire agreed warmly. "It gives me a heart attack when I think of all the things we had to put up with when *we* bust it."

The long list of their misfortunes flashed through their minds; the uncertainty of Aunt Angela's crumbling memory, the shock of meeting Mr. Carter at nearly every corner, the frenzied hide-and-seek in the potting shed and the nerve-racking repair work in the attic with footsteps approaching the door.

"Yes, and now Mr. Wilkins does exactly the same thing, and instead of getting in a bate, the Head laughs like a drain." Jennings' face was flushed with resentment. "Gosh, Darbi, it must be wonderful to be grown-up—you can get away with *anything*!"

The Headmaster and Mr. Wilkins were joined by Mr. Carter when they reached the nets, and for some minutes the masters stood chatting of routine affairs while the thwack of bat against ball sounded in the background.

"I wanted to have a word with you, sir, about Jennings," said Mr. Carter. "I put him on probation yesterday and I should like to know whether the rest of the staff are reasonably satisfied with his behaviour."

"I can tell you what *I* think," Mr. Wilkins chimed in. "I think his conduct is most unsatisfactory and shows no sign of improving. Don't you agree?"

"No," said the Headmaster, unexpectedly. "I don't agree at all, Wilkins. Both Jennings and Darbishire were extremely useful and co-operative in entertaining young Merridew yesterday."

Mr. Wilkins stared in surprise. Never before had he known the Headmaster to contradict an unfavourable opinion about those particular boys. But then, Mr. Wilkins knew nothing of the part they had played in influencing Mrs. Merridew.

"Incidentally, I told them they might go over to their hut this afternoon. I wonder why they haven't done so," pondered the Headmaster.

"That was my fault," the duty master admitted. "They did say something about it, but I thought it was some trumpery cock-and-bull story they'd made up."

"Not a bit of it! I am removing the ban on hut-building. Mrs. Merridew was most impressed when she heard that organised picnics in the huts are such a popular feature of our—ah—less formal activities."

Mr. Wilkins began to wonder whether his superior was suffering from an attack of sunstroke. "But we haven't *had* any organised picnics in the huts!" he protested.

"Exactly! But that can soon be remedied." And the Headmaster strode away to the kitchen to ask the housekeeper whether she could prepare seventy-nine packets of sandwiches at short notice.

Jennings was moodily uprooting a dandelion with the toe of his shoe when Bromwich major bore down upon him. "Message from Old Wilkie," he announced. "He says you can hoof over to your hut if you want to. The man's mad, of course, because everyone knows they're out of bounds."

"No, they're not! I told you this morning what the Head said." Jennings' depression vanished and the wide-awake look came back into his eyes. "Come on, Darbi, let's go and get cracking on the building programme."

The little hut was not so seriously damaged as they had at first supposed. The roof was off, of course, and parts of the walls were as pitted with holes as a colander; but most of the remnants were lying close at hand and it would not be difficult to make a workmanlike job of putting them together again.

They rooted about in the remains, salvaging what they could of their home-made furniture. A few pieces were missing and Darbishire said: "I think we ought to make an inventory first, so's we can see what we've got."

"No fear! An inventory's the one thing we can do without to start with," Jennings answered. "If we hadn't had one last time, the Head wouldn't have got stuck trying to get into it."

Darbishire made pitying noises, as though humouring a dull-witted imbecile. "Don't be such an ignorant bazooka—you can't get stuck in an inventory. It's a sort of list!"

"No, it's not. It's a place where people go and invent things. How could our small back room be a sort of list?"

"I don't know how it could *be* one, but it's *got* a sort of list all right. It's listing about forty-five degrees to starboard and if we don't get cracking and prop it up, we shan't have the place shipshape before dark."

They worked busily for more than an hour, by which time the hut was beginning to look more like its usual self. Darbishire's watch had stopped, but keen pangs of hunger told them that it must be nearly tea-time, so Jennings trotted across to the bridge to see whether anyone was still about on the cricket field. What he saw when he arrived was so unexpected that he opened his mouth and scratched his head in bewilderment. Urgently, he called: "Darbi— quick, come here!"

"I can't—I'm busy," came the muffled answer from inside the small back room.

"But, it's urgent!"

"Yes, and so's this job I'm doing. The emergency drinking supply must have had a nest of tadpoles in it when it got knocked over; there's a plague of young frogs hopping about on the *Welcome* mat."

"Never mind that now! Come over here at once. It's important!"

Grumbling at the interruption, Darbishire made his way over to the bridge. Then he, too, stared in surprise and pushed his spectacles up on to his forehead so that his vision was not clouded by the dusty lenses. "Gosh," he gasped, "what is it—an invasion?"

Stampeding through the wood towards them came seventy-seven boys clutching paper bags and plastic beakers, while the staff followed behind at a more dignified pace. The Headmaster was making good his promise to Mrs. Merridew, and the first of the picnic teas was getting off to a good start.

Over the bridge swarmed the advance party of squatters, waving their paper bags in the air in joyous lightheartedness of spirit. Binns minor waved his too wildly and dropped it into the quagmire below, but Matron was bringing up the rear with reinforcements of cake and sandwiches, and Binns was spared the gruesome fate of death from starvation.

The boys crossed the bridge in single file, but when the masters arrived at the quagmire they stopped, and Mr. Carter said: "We shall have to do something about this bridge. It'll never stand your thirteen-stone-six, Wilkins."

"Leave it to me! I wasn't in the Scouts for nothing," replied his colleague, and the two masters set to work with stout branches and quickly constructed a craftsmanlike bridge which was guaranteed to bear any weight up to three hundredweight.

The staff came across then, and wandered round from hut to hut, accepting an unwanted sandwich at one and half a slice of cake at another, so as not to hurt the feelings of their hosts.

"Sir, Mr. Carter, sir, come and have tea in our hut, please, sir," begged Venables and Temple.

"No, sir, come to mine, sir," pleaded Atkinson. "Mine's miles better! You can stand up in it, and if you go to tea with Venables, you'll have to lie flat all the time, and you'll probably get indigestion, sir."

"Oh, but, sir, ours is tons better than Atkinson's, sir!" urged a dozen voices.

"I've got an air-cushion in mine, sir—come and try it!" invited Martin-Jones.

"Don't you risk it, sir," counselled Darbishire. "I know that air-cushion. It's got a slow puncture and you'll be in a draught all the time you're sitting on it, sir!"

Robinson, the odd-job man was kept busy running a shuttle service of lemonade jugs between the kitchen and the new bridge. It was exhausting work and the Headmaster decided that a few responsible boys could do the job equally well. He called for volunteers and was rather surprised when every one of his seventy-nine boys rushed forward to apply for a post as jug-bearer. But he was not to know that each volunteer had already made up his mind to be attacked by an uncontrollable thirst as soon as he was out of sight.

Bromwich major was one of the five boys selected, and when he returned to the huts on his first trip it was noticed that, instead of a jug of lemonade, he was carrying a tank of water in which a small goldfish seemed to be practising the breast-stroke backwards. If there was a picnic going on, Bromwich decided, Elmer was not going to miss any of the fun.

When the last sandwich had been eaten and the last beaker of lemonade had been drained, the squatters returned to their pond-side occupations at the point where they had left off nearly a week before. Mr. Carter helped Jennings and Darbishire to fix the ventilating shaft so that it would never again collapse at an awkward moment; Mr. Wilkins helped Martin-Jones and Paterson to make a rope ladder, and the Headmaster strolled round the pond, pleased at the sight and sound of so much enjoyable activity.

Outside a very small hut nestling in a clump of brambles, he came upon a sign which read *No Hawkers*, and beneath this Binns minor was adding a post-script in red crayon—*Privet, Keep Off*. He stopped writing when he looked up and saw the Headmaster standing behind him, and his tongue, which had been copying each letter in the air as he wrote, now returned to its normal duties.

"Please, sir, would you like to see inside my hut, sir?" he asked in his shrill, Form 1 treble.

"I think it might be better if I didn't, Binns," replied Mr. Pemberton-Oakes. "I shouldn't like to damage your hedge—though frankly I see no sign of it."

"Which hedge, sir?"

"The privet hedge to which you allude, rather discourteously, in your notice."

The youngest boy in the school looked blank for a moment and then squeaked out: "Oh, but sir, that spells *Private*, not privet."

"Does it, really! They must have changed it without letting me know," smiled the Headmaster. He strolled on, feeling rather surprised at himself, for he did not often make little jokes at the Form 1 level of humour.

Inside the little hut everything was in its place, thanks to the help that Mr. Carter had given with the ventilating shaft. Darbishire spread the *Welcome* mat outside the front door and Jennings built a special shelf for the *Revenge* to stand on until they were ready to sail it again. Brand new bulrush curtains hung over the glassless windows, and Darbishire's painting of the green-faced cow watching the train cross the flimsy bridge hung in its usual place. They were proud of that picture; somehow it lent an air of culture to the homely living room.

Jennings was feeling happier than he had done for weeks, especially now that Mr. Carter had told him that his probation was over. He glanced across to where Darbishire was shooing the last stray frog through the front door and said: "I bet you a million pounds, Darbi—well I haven't got a million pounds, but I bet you a penny—I bet you no one would have thought that we'd be sitting here enjoying ourselves, this time yesterday."

"Well, of course they wouldn't—we *weren't* sitting here this time yesterday," his friend objected.

"No, I mean this time yesterday, nobody would have thought we'd be sitting here enjoying ourselves, this time today. Everything was in such an ozard hoo-hah then, and whatever we tried to do turned out to be a bish." He scratched his nose thoughtfully. "And now look at us—sitting in the little hut, full to bursting, with Old Wilkie and the Archbeako popping in every so often to see if we're getting on all right. It's crazy, isn't it!"

Darbishire said, gravely: "That just shows you how things happen. My father says that every cloud has a silver lining, and it's always darkest just before the dawn."

"Your father thought all that out by himself?" asked Jennings, impressed.

"Yes, of course. He's always saying things like that, only you won't let me finish telling you, as a rule."

"Well, you can, this time. I'm feeling in a generous mood."

"Thanks very much. Well, what my father means is that sometimes, like, say, for instance, in our case, everything looks as black as—as black as your handkerchief"—Jennings let the insult pass— "and it's so dark you can't see your hand in front of your face ..."

"What do you want to see your hand for?"

"You don't *really* want to see your hand."

"You just said you did!"

"Ah, but what I meant was—well, anyway, what it all boils down to is that everything comes out all right in the end."

"Yes, I know what you mean," said Jennings. "It's what they call a red-letter day. The huts are put in bounds again, we have a supersonic picnic, there's no prep and the masters are in such a cracking good mood you can hardly tell they're human beings, at all!" He heaved a sigh of deep satisfaction.

It was growing late and soon the whistle would blow and the squatters would be streaming back to school and up to the dormitory; and tomorrow a new day would start, bringing new problems to face and new crises to cope with. But why worry about tomorrow? It was today that mattered and nothing could spoil that now.

Jennings glowed with quiet happiness and suddenly, for no reason that he could think of, he laughed aloud.

"What's the matter?" asked Darbishire.

"Oh, nothing! I just felt like it. You know, Darbi, when things are going well like this, I can almost believe those old geezers who come down on Speech Day and tell us that being at school is the happiest time of your life."

"Well, that's going a bit far," his friend demurred. "Let's say it's the second happiest. The *first* happiest is all the time you're *not* at school."

They fell silent then. Darbishire lay on his stomach, his elbows on the ground and his chin cupped in his hands. He was full of lettuce and tomato sandwich and he was feeling blissfully content.

Jennings squatted on his heels in the low doorway of the little hut, listening to the busy sounds of the neighbouring squatters. Darbishire was a good sort, he reflected, but he couldn't agree with that last remark of his. Surely there was a lot to be said for being young and being at school. Why, at times like this he could almost believe that those old Speech Day geezers really *did* know a thing or two after all!

JENNINGS AND
DARBISHIRE

CHAPTER 1

HAPPY RETURNS

FOR one fleeting moment after he awoke, Jennings lay still, puzzling over the urgent message that was hammering at his sleepy brain and demanding to be let in. Something important had made him wake early: what on earth could it be? Then he remembered. It was his birthday!

His first impulse was to leap out of bed with a joyful "Wacko!" and broadcast the news at full volume to the sleeping dormitory; but second thoughts warned him to wait until the mounds under the neighbouring bedclothes had yawned and stretched themselves into human shape. After all, he reasoned, eleventh birthdays only happen once in a lifetime, and it would be a waste of important news to make the announcement to an audience still drowsy with sleep.

Jennings sat up and glanced at the next bed along the line where Darbishire lay sleeping. Of course, Darbishire was his best friend, and best friends are different. It would hardly be fair, he decided, to let a decent chap like old Darbi snooze away the precious minutes of a red-letter day like this. He must be roused at once!

There was a comfortable, care-free feeling about the friendship between Jennings and Darbishire. It had started when they had met as new boys at Linbury Court Preparatory School, and had deepened its roots as they had weathered a year of school life together. Yet in appearance and character the two boys were as different as chalk from cheese. Jennings was a lively, impulsive boy with a wide-awake look in his eyes and a briskness about his movements. He had a flair for being in the swim—and sometimes out of his depth—when any unexpected splash ruffled the smooth waters of boarding-school life.

Darbishire's was a less adventurous spirit. Although Nature had never intended him for a man of action, loyalty to Jennings demanded that he should try his best to become one. And try he did, in his own vague and unpractical way.

Very little of Darbishire was visible as he lay asleep that morning. Just a tangle of fair curly hair and the tip of a nose that twitched like a rabbit's, at the ticklish touch of the blanket. From the bed-rail above the pillow, a pair of spectacles hung perilously by one earpiece.

"Wake up, Darbishire, wake up!" A hand shook the hunched shoulders and Darbishire opened one eye.

"What's the matter—fire practice?" he demanded sleepily.

"No, you coot. Today's the day! My birthday!"

"Uh? Oh, yes, of course. Wacko! Many happies." And Darbishire closed his eye and turned over to enjoy a few more minutes of refreshing sleep.

He might have known better!

"Oh, wake up, Darbi!" Jennings persisted. "If we get dressed in top gear we can get downstairs before the postman comes. It's nearly time for the rising-bell."

"It always *is* time for something before you're ready for it," came in sleepy tones from beneath the blankets. "I reckon they must be making the nights a lot shorter these days. It seems only yesterday that I went to bed."

"Well, so it was! You wouldn't say cootish things like that if you were awake. Buck up and get weaving! I'll race you getting dressed, if you like." As Jennings danced away to the wash basins, his mind's eye conjured up a vision of perspiring postmen pedalling up the drive with parcels of intriguing shape balanced on their handlebars.

He smiled his congratulations at his reflection in the mirror, and a moment later noisy splashings announced that he was celebrating the occasion with a special birthday wash. Two minutes of energetic flannelling and thirty seconds of foaming at the mouth with pink toothpaste, and the ceremony was over.

He turned away from the basin to see Darbishire, still in his pyjamas, practising clove-hitches round the bed-rail with his dressing gown cord.

"Oh, for goodness' sake," Jennings protested, "how can we have a race if you go on sitting there?"

"Just coming," Darbishire apologised. "I was only practising my knots."

"What knots?"

"You mean which knots—not what knots. Whatnots are something quite different."

"Different from what?" Jennings demanded.

Darbishire yawned: he was still very sleepy, and this was a difficult question. "I don't know," he confessed. "Different from whichnots, I suppose. Mind you, they're all jolly useful, whichever sort you do. People often tie knots in things to remind them not to forget things—like, say, for instance, your birthday."

"But you know that already," Jennings argued as he waved his arms into his shirt, "and there's nothing else you've specially got to remember, is there?"

"Oh, yes," Darbishire replied earnestly. "Tying a knot in my dressing gown cord reminds me that I've got to get up as soon as I've done it."

The rising-bell sounded as he spoke, and all along the dormitory heads stirred on pillows and jaws yawned their greeting to the new day. In the beds beyond the wash basins, Venables, Temple and Atkinson came to life and started a lively debate about whether they had had kippers or sausages for breakfast the previous Friday week.

Venables, an untidy boy and tall for his twelve years, was certain it had been kippers, and sought to prove his argument by shouting twice as loudly as the supporters of sausage.

Jennings bore down upon the discussion group.

"I say, I bet you characters don't know what day it is," he began.

"It's Friday," replied Venables. "Just a fortnight since we had kippers for breakfast."

"Ah, yes—but what else?"

"What else? Porridge and bread and marmalade and ..."

"No; I mean there's something special about today."

"Sausages for breakfast?" queried Temple hopefully.

"No, you clodpoll. It's my birthday!" And Jennings jumped upon Atkinson and punched him lightly in the ribs, to show that all was well with the world.

"Oh, wacko! Hope you get a decent cake," said Venables.

"Bags I have Atkinson's hunk, if it's marzipan, because he doesn't like it," Temple put in quickly.

"Don't worry. There'll be massive chunks for everybody," Jennings assured them. "My mother's sending me a super-cracking-sonic cake. I'm just hoofing down to the hall now to see if the postman's come."

Gargling strange engine noises from the back of his throat, Jennings raced down the dormitory. As it was a special occasion he decided to be a jet-propelled fighter: he wheeled in and out between the beds, banking steeply and varying the roar of his engine with each sharp turn. He was just going into a power dive to avoid a chest of drawers, when the dormitory door was flung open and the master on duty appeared, without so much as a gale warning to forecast his stormy approach.

"Jennings! Come here!"

The jet-fighter switched off its engine and made a forced landing on the runway between two beds. But the damage was already done; for the master on duty was Mr. Wilkins and he was eyeing the unhappy aircraft with displeasure.

Mr. Wilkins was large and energetic, with a voice and footstep to match his muscular frame. He could be pleasant enough when he chose, but he was not, by nature, a patient man and he could never quite fathom why boys of eleven would neither reason nor behave in the intelligent manner of their elders.

"What on earth were you making that ghastly noise for, Jennings?" he demanded, slamming the door behind him with a crash that made Jennings' engine-gargling sound like the soft whisperings of the wind in the willows. "And why are you dressed already? You know perfectly well you're not allowed out of bed before the rising-bell goes."

"Yes, sir: I was in a rather special sort of hurry, with reasons, sir."

Mr. Wilkins was not interested in reasons. Curtly he said: "The rule says, no getting up before the bell. Very well, then, you can stay in during football this afternoon and do some work for me. Now get undressed again and wash properly."

"Yes, sir," said Jennings, and the thrill of the birthday morning seemed suddenly blurred. Why did things like that always have to happen on a day like this? Chaps who had birthdays in the holidays just didn't know how lucky they were.

As he turned sorrowfully away, a sockless Darbishire came slithering along the dormitory and skidded to a halt before the duty master.

"Please, sir! Mr. Wilkins, sir!"

"Well, what is it, Darbishire? Hurry up, I'm busy."

"It's his birthday today, sir."

"Oh!" A sudden, almost magical change came over Mr. Wilkins; in a moment his impatient frown was gone; his eyebrows, arched in exasperation, dropped to their normal level and the ghost of a smile did its best to haunt the corners of his mouth. Darbishire had found the chink in his armour!

"Oh! Well, if it's his birthday, I suppose we'd better give him another chance. All right then, Jennings, we won't say any more about it this time."

Mr. Wilkins stalked down the dormitory, trying hard to make up for his burst of generosity by barking more brusquely than usual at everybody who was *not* celebrating a birthday that morning. The fact was that his violent manner concealed a kind heart; its beat was sometimes a little weak, but it was there and, at odd moments, ready to persuade its owner against his better judgment.

Jennings flashed Darbishire a look of gratitude and murmured: "I thought I'd had it that time. Decent of you to barge in like that."

"That's all right," smiled the benefactor modestly. "You can call it my birthday present to you, if you like. I was a bit worried about not having anything to give you, but now I've dished out this special birthday treat, that let's me out nicely."

"But you haven't given me a treat!"

"I wizard well have! If you don't think stopping Old Wilkie from kicking up a supersonic hoo-hah isn't a decent birthday present, then all I can say is ..."

"All right: we won't argue. Buck up and put your socks on and we'll go down and see if the post has come."

Together they left the dormitory and hurried down to the main hall where they found the morning mail stacked on a table.

"Wacko! There's a whole pile of letters for me," Jennings cried excitedly, hopping from one foot to the other. "And three parcels. The big one's my cake and the square fat one's probably Aunt Angela."

Darbishire peered at the parcel through dusty spectacles. "Don't be crazy; she couldn't be that shape unless she'd been cremated."

"No, you prehistoric ruin! I mean that's good old Aunt Angela's present. And this is my father's writing on the oblong one."

The third parcel was marked *Fragile—with care*. Jennings strained his eyes at the oblong package as though the keenness of his gaze might penetrate the thick brown paper. "What sort of things would be labelled *Fragile*?"

"Teapots, electric light bulbs, cut-glass vases," hazarded Darbishire helpfully.

"You're bats! What would *I* do with a cut-glass vase?"

"Keep flowers in it."

"But why should my father think I wanted one?"

"I never said he did! You asked me what was fragile and I said ..."

"All right; don't let's go through it all over again." Jennings prodded the fragile parcel thoughtfully. "I shall go off pop if I don't find out what it is soon. All I can feel is a wedge of packing."

"Shake it and see if it rattles."

"No wizard fear—it's fragile already. I don't want my parcel going off pop as well as me."

So, in order to avoid the risk of an untimely explosion, they took the parcels along to the tuck-box room and opened them at once.

The large one contained his birthday cake, as he had expected, and it looked so inviting that Darbishire's nail scissors were brought into play and snippets of icing were hacked off and sampled. *J. C. T. J.*—*Many happy returns* was written on the top in sprawling chocolate letters.

Next came the parcel marked fragile. It was big enough at the start, but as layer upon layer of shavings was removed to litter the floor, it seemed to Jennings that whatever lay within must be shrinking in the most alarming fashion. Frenziedly he hurled out handfuls of tissue paper, as though speed at reaching the middle was the only way to save the contents from disappearing altogether.

At last he got there; and a warmth of happiness spread over him as he lifted his father's present from its nest of wrappings.

"A camera! Gosh, how super-wacko-sonic! It's the one thing I was hoping he wouldn't give me anything else except!" he crowed delightedly, and turned the small object over and over in his hands. "We can do all sorts of things with a camera, can't we, Darbi!"

"We'll bust it, if we do," his friend warned him solemnly. "Much better just to use it for taking photos with."

"That's what I meant. I can take one of you standing up, for instance, and you can take one of me, say, sitting down, and then I can take one of you sitting down and you can take ..."

"There's another parcel to open yet."

"Oh yes, of course. Good old Aunt Angela!"

As Jennings tore the wrappings from the last package his eye lighted on a square cardboard box. *The Ideal Junior Printing Outfit* was inscribed on the lid, and below this was pasted an illustrated label showing two boys engaged in printing a highly-coloured magazine on an up-to-date printing machine seldom seen outside Fleet Street. Considering the amount of printer's ink they were using, their fingers were remarkably clean.

The contents of the box, however, were more modest than the label suggested. Raised letters made from small pieces of rubber were neatly arranged in a slotted wooden frame, and a pair of tweezers was provided for removing the type and setting it up in the printing block. The whole thing looked absurdly simple; a quick choice of letters, a slick jab at the ink pad, and the thought behind the printed word was inscribed for ever in a vivid mauve hue.

"Golly, how socko!" breathed Darbishire. "We can print our names on all our private possessions, and stick up notices like, say, *Keep Out*, or *Venables is a clodpoll!*"

But Jennings' ideas were more ambitious. "The first thing I'm going to use it for is to answer all these birthday letters," he announced. "It'll save masses of time because I always write the same thing to every one, anyway."

With extreme care, Darbishire removed a row of letters from the box and held them with the tweezers. He peered at them closely, for his spectacles still bore the previous day's film of dust and gave a blurred, frosted-glass appearance to everything in sight.

"I can't make out whether these are *e*'s or *a*'s," he said doubtfully. "My father says that in the olden days they used to ..."

But at that moment he squeezed too hard with the tweezers; the little rubber pellets shot from between the prongs and catapulted through the air to the four corners of the room.

"You clumsy bazooka!" Jennings said heatedly. "We'll have a frantic job to find them with all these shavings about."

"Super sorrow; they were a bit slippery."

On hands and knees they began the search among the piles of shavings and the yawning cracks between the floorboards, but the breakfast bell sounded before so much as a single rubber pellet had come to light.

"Oh, fish-hooks, what are we going to do?" lamented Darbishire. "All those letters I lost were the same sort. We'll be up a gum tree if we don't find them."

A quick glance in the box showed that Darbishire was right. The letters were arranged alphabetically—a batch of *a*'s, the same number of *b*'s, then *c*'s and *d*'s ... and then came the gap. There wasn't an *e* in the box!

"We'll come back and have another squint after breakfast," Jennings decided, as he put his presents in his tuck-box. "We're bound to find them then."

But after breakfast was too late. When the boys returned, they found that Robinson, the odd-job man, had been busy. The room had been tidied, the shavings removed: dust, rubbish and stray rubber pellets had all been swallowed up by the vacuum cleaner.

For some moments they stood staring at the orderly rows of tuck-boxes.

Then Jennings turned and led the way upstairs to the common room.

"Well, this *has* bished things up," he complained bitterly. "How am I going to write my birthday 'thank-you' letters now?"

"Perhaps you could think of something to say that doesn't need any *e*'s," suggested Darbishire.

"Huh! You try, if you're so clever. Besides I had a supersonic idea during breakfast about something we could do during hobbies' hour next week. I've finished my clay modelling and Mr. Wilkins gets in a frantic bate if you just swing about on the desks and say you haven't got anything to do."

"You mean we could stick up our *Keep Out* notices and things?"

Jennings looked scornful. "No, something a wizard sight better. I vote, why not let's start a Form Three specially printed magazine. I could be chief editor and you could be the office boy or a journalist or something. We could get hold of all the latest news, print it on my outfit and then stick it up on the notice board."

"Gosh, yes: super-wacko wheeze!" In a sudden flash of imagination Darbishire saw himself as the bustling, eagle-eyed crime reporter, pounding along on the trail of sensational scoops. "Who's that?" people were saying, as he raced along vague, unspecified streets. "Why, don't you know! That's C. E. J. Darbishire, ace news-sleuth of the Form Three newspaper. He's quite a legend in stop-press circles."

Then the little dream faded, and more seriously he turned to Jennings and said: "Yes, but it's going to be jolly awkward if we can't print any news that's got an *e* in it."

"That's all right. I'll ask Aunt Angela for some spares. And while we're waiting for them we can plan out what sort of things we're going to print."

Jennings was so pleased with his idea that he went on thinking about it for the rest of the morning. In fact, it was in the middle of Mr. Wilkins' algebra class after break that he conceived the brilliant idea of appointing himself chief press-photographer. He wondered why he hadn't thought of it before. After all, every decent magazine illustrated its columns with photographs, and here was he with a brand new camera just asking to be made use of! He made a note on his algebra book to raise this topic at the editorial conference called for the following week, and then set about the important business of enjoying his birthday to the full.

It was a good birthday, too, considering that it came during term time; and the kind Fate that looks after people on these occasions rallied round and did what it could to help. It provided his favourite pudding at lunch time, and saw to it that there was enough for a second helping; it allowed him to find his best form during football that afternoon, so that he scored two goals and walked off the field feeling right up on top of the world. And finally, the kind Fate persuaded Venables and Atkinson to borrow eleven torch bulbs and a supply of batteries, and spend the half-hour before tea wiring them to Jennings' birthday cake to compensate for its lack of candles.

The illuminations were a great success, and actually stayed alight for short periods when no one happened to be jogging the table.

After tea that evening, Jennings settled down in the common room to answer his birthday letters. He was anxious to try out his printing set on something fairly simple to start with, so that he might master any unexpected snags before starting on the more difficult task of coping with a magazine.

Patiently he set up the type; the missing *e*'s were rather a problem and he had to substitute *x*'s in their place, which gave the correspondence a secret, code-like appearance. His first attempts were a failure because so many of the letters seemed to turn themselves upside-down, or decided to face the wrong way, in spite of the compositor's most careful attention. But he persevered, and when Darbishire burst into the common room half an hour later, Jennings was able to show him the results of his labours.

"It works wizardly, Darbi," he greeted him. "Come and have a look. All I've got to do now is ..."

"Yes, but hang on a minute; I've got something to tell you," Darbishire began.

"Never mind other things now. What do you think about this?"

"I was only going to say ..."

Jennings thrust the top sheet of paper into Darbishire's hands, and was too wrapped up in his own triumph to notice that the hands were dirtier than they should have been, and that his friend's whole appearance suggested that he had just finished a hard day's work in a corporation rubbish dump.

"Not bad, is it!" Jennings said proudly. "Of course, we'll have to wait for those *e*'s before we get cracking on the mag."

Darbishire postponed his explanations and read the sheet of paper held before his nose.

"Dxar ..." the circular began.

"I hopx you arx quitx wxll. I likxd thx birthday prxsxnts I had vxry

515

much indxxd. Dad sxnt mx a camxra and Darbishirx gavx mx a spxcial trxat ..."

Darbishire broke off his reading and said: "Well, I know what you mean, of course, but if you listen to what ..."

"If you're worrying about the *x*'s, you needn't, because I've put a special PS. on Aunt Angela's letter. It's a bit tricky asking for something when you haven't got any to explain with, but I expect she'll understand."

Aunt Angela's postscript read:

"Plxasx sxnd mx somx morx of thx lxttxrs that comx bxtwxxn *d* and *f*."

As he finished reading it, Darbishire fished in his pocket and produced a small handful of rubber pellets.

"Here you are," he said as he put them on the desk. "These are the *e*'s I lost this morning."

"What!"

"Yes, I've just spent the last half-hour scrounging through the dustbag on the vacuum cleaner. You can do all your birthday thank you letters again properly, now."

"No wizard fear!" returned Jennings firmly. "We've got to get on with our magazine, and there's a lot more in that than just setting up the type and sitting back and twiddling your thumbs. We've got to get hold of the latest news and take photos of it and ... and, well, that may sound easy to you, but all sorts of things can happen, and perhaps even one or two things might go wrong before we get the hang of a super important job like this."

Jennings never spoke a truer word! But even so, he had no idea of just *what* could happen, or *how* wrong things could go.

CHAPTER 2

THE UNWELCOME GIFT

IT was generally agreed that the hobbies' hour was the most popular item on the timetable. It was held on Mondays during the Christmas term, and an added delight was that it took the place of evening preparation.

The Headmaster, Mr. Pemberton-Oakes, had decreed that the hour should be used for creative activities and, accordingly, he expected a quiet and restrained atmosphere to prevail.

In this, he was unlucky; for few boys can create quietly when their tools are hammer and saw, and there is something about paint and glue, strip metal and balsa wood, which plays havoc with a restrained atmosphere.

There was, therefore, a purposeful bustle in the hobbies' room after tea on the following Monday. Venables and Temple were modelling an African landscape on a sheet of corrugated iron: large lumps of coke, tinted with poster paint, formed rocky mountain slopes where plasticine elephants stalked amongst an undergrowth of twigs and shavings. It was a convincing jungle scene—apart from a miniature telephone kiosk and three polar bears in the north-west corner.

Atkinson was constructing a patchwork Red Indian wigwam from snippets of grey flannel and darning wool which he had borrowed from the sewing room. Bromwich major was hard at work on a rabbit hutch; he had no rabbit and no hope of ever possessing one, but as a hutch was the next best thing he was determined to make a good one.

It was in this hive of creative activity that Jennings and Darbishire settled down, with notebook and pencil, to their editorial conference. They sat at a table between Thompson, who was making a puppet, and Binns minor, who was making a great deal of noise.

"Now, first of all, Darbi, we've got to think of a name for our magazine," Jennings began. "So I vote, what about calling it the *Form Three Times?*"

"Not long enough," objected Darbishire. "Most decent papers always have a whole chunk more, like, say, for instance, '*with which is incorporated the Lower Hockleton and District Illustrated Mercury and Weekly Advertiser.*'"

"Huh! They wouldn't say all that if they only had a titchy little rubber printing outfit to do it with. The less we start incorporating the better, until we've got the hang of things." Jennings glanced at the agenda in his notebook. "Now, by rights, I ought to be chief editor because it's my printing outfit, but I don't mind putting it to the vote, just to be fair."

Darbishire's eyes brightened behind his spectacles: he would dearly have liked to be chief editor.

"Wacko!" he agreed. "But I vote we're not allowed to vote for ourselves because my father says it's swanking to blow your own trumpet."

"All right, then. I'll blow your trumpet, if you blow mine. Here's a bit of paper to write your vote on."

The ballot resulted in a tie, each candidate polling one vote, and the deadlock was finally solved by the toss of a coin. Jennings was appointed editor with Darbishire as his chief assistant. There were other vacancies to be filled, and the editor lost no time in filling them. "You can be chief Special Correspondent and Gardening Expert as well, Darbi, and I'll be chief Sports Reporter and Press-Photographer."

"Couldn't we swop? I'd much rather be the Sports Reporter."

The editor looked reprovingly at his staff. "You're crackers!" he said. "You know wizard well you play football like a left-footed sparrow. Who on earth would want to read what *you* wrote?"

The chief Special Correspondent sighed. He knew this was only too true. "Well, couldn't I write under a *nom de plume*? Then no one would know it was me."

"Write under a *what*?"

"A *nom de plume*. It means a pen name. I could call myself Half-time Henry or Touchline Timothy or something."

"You can't possibly have a pen name, because we shan't be using pens. Of course, you could have a *nom de printing outfit* if you're all that keen on it."

The discussion went forward at a brisk pace. Soon they had decided that the first number of the *Form Three Times* should appear towards the end of the following week. It was to be printed on single sheets of paper, and limited to one copy, posted on the common room notice board.

Their voices grew louder as their plans progressed; and as the news of their venture spread across the room, the space round the editor's table became thronged with elbow-jogging helpers anxious to contribute news items for publication.

Binns minor had the shrillest voice in the room and trumpeted his announcement into the editor's ear in a series of nerve-racking shrieks.

"If you bods want a basinful of really smashing news, you can come to me for it. Honestly, Jennings, I'm not pulling your leg. There's been a Mysterious Disappearance!"

"Who's vanished—Mr. Wilkins?" inquired Darbishire hopefully.

"No: my left football boot's been stolen out of my locker. And if you want to know what I think, I shouldn't be surprised if there's been an organised gangster on the job, because I've worked out how he could have done it. He could have left his car on the quad while we were all in class and ..."

"Don't be so bats, Binns! Why should any one want to pinch just one boot?"

"He might have been a chap with only one leg."

"He'd have a bit of a job playing football, then, wouldn't he?"

Binns minor hadn't thought of that, and by the time he had worked out a convincing answer, the editor's ear was busy with an exclusive news scoop from Temple about a threatened detention class.

There was no shortage of news, but it was not *new* news, and when the throng of elbow-joggers and shoulder-tappers had thinned, Jennings faced the fact squarely.

"What we've got to do, Darbi, is to get going with the camera," he decided. "If we can get some decent action photos it may liven things up a bit."

"Righto! We could start tomorrow, if the sun's out. You can take a photo of me, sitting down, and I can take one of you standing up and ..."

"Gosh, no; that's no earthly use. Who wants to see your face plastered all over the wall? What we want is something like the winning goal in the Cup Final, or jet fighters zooming into a power dive."

"Or the semi-final of the Form Four chess championship."

"Yes, that's the idea—plenty of action. We might go down to the harbour and get a photo of a battleship or ..."

"You're crazy," interposed his assistant. "You couldn't get a battleship into Linbury Cove. There's only a titchy little wooden jetty, and anything bigger than something quite small would get stuck in the entrance."

"All the better if it *did* get stuck—it'd make a smashing photo. I vote we ask permish to go next Sunday, when we're out for our walks. Then we can develop it in time for the first edition."

The more Jennings thought about the photographic expedition, the better he liked it: it would bring a breath of the outside world into the narrow limits of boarding school life and stamp the *Form Three Times* as an up-to-date paper whose roving press-photographer kept a finger on the pulse of the world's affairs. But it would be some days before the boys could obtain permission to leave the grounds, so they spent the intervening time searching for items of news.

They unearthed the sensational story of how Atkinson had found a caterpillar in his cabbage; but as it had happened the term before last, they felt that this could hardly be headlined as late news. As chief crime reporter, Jennings compiled a list of the defaulters in Mr. Wilkins' detention class, with details of their misdeeds and a brief note about their previous convictions. And Darbishire, to his great delight, secured a scoop by being on the scene when Bromwich major broke the Dormitory 6 breath-holding record by staying under the bath water for a count of thirty-eight.

Sunday seemed a long time coming round that week, and when at last it did arrive, it was a wet one; but after lunch the weather cleared slightly and the boys lost no time in handing their names to Mr. Carter, the senior master. Then, armed with the camera and shrouded in raincoats, they hurried along the downland paths which led through Linbury village to the sea.

"This is super, isn't it!" said Jennings, as the harbour came in sight. "If we can get a decent photo for the front page …" He broke off and hopped up and down in triumph. "Oh, wacko, Darbi, we *can*! I can see the mast of a ship tied up to the jetty."

"Battleship?" inquired Darbishire, but without much hope. He removed his drizzle-spotted glasses and wiped them on the sleeve of his raincoat.

"No; it's a fishing boat. Let's go and have a squint at zero feet."

The rain had stopped now, and a watery sun was doing its best to pierce the grey clouds as the two boys slithered and skidded down the wet chalky path to the shore.

It would be stretching the facts to say that Linbury Cove was a harbour, although a wooden jetty stretched out from the shingly beach, and here yachts and small craft were occasionally moored and fishing boats took shelter when the Channel was rough. There was only one boat at its moorings that afternoon—a fishing vessel with its port of origin painted on the stern in yellow letters.

"Golly, it's French," exclaimed Jennings in surprise. "It's got Boulogne on the back."

Darbishire looked slightly shocked. "You are an ignorant bazooka, Jen; you ought to know ships don't have backs. You mean it's got it's name abaft."

"Well, it's French, anyway."

"Abaft isn't French. It's English for the wide end of the boat. But what I can't understand is what it's doing here at all."

Darbishire's surprise was natural, for it was not often that anything but local craft put into Linbury Cove: but the Channel had been squally on the previous night and the *Sainte Marie*, fishing far from home, had been only too ready to seek refuge in the bay. Soon the weather would be calm enough to put to sea again, but for the moment the five members of the crew were content to sit about on the deck, mending their nets and peeling potatoes.

Jennings took two snaps of the stern; one with his finger over the lens, and one without. Then he said: "I wonder if they'd let us go aboard and take them in a group?"

"We could ask them; they might even pose for us. I say, won't everyone at school get a shock when they see the French fishing fleet all over page one!"

"It'll be a bit of a shock for the camera, too," said Jennings. "I've never seen such a plug-ugly bunch of characters in my life."

There was some truth in this remark, for the crew of the *Sainte Marie*, in their working clothes, would have won no prizes at a fashion show. All five wore greasy blue overalls, faded and stained to such an extent that it was impossible to distinguish the patches of oil from the patches of blue cloth which seemed to be all that held the garments together. Their seamen's caps were shapeless with age and their ancient sea-boots flapped in folds about their ankles. They were tough, wiry men with weather-beaten features, stubbly chins and—as it turned out—hearts of gold.

"Well, it's no good just standing and looking at them," Darbishire observed. "My father says you should strike while the iron is hot, and faint heart never won fair lady."

"I'm not striking any one with hot irons, whatever your father says; and I don't want a fair lady—I want a photo of a fisherman."

"Go on, then; ask them. I dare you to."

Jennings favoured his assistant with a superior smile. Little things like this were all in the day's work for a keen press-photographer. Politely, he called:

"Er—excuse me; just a moment, I say!"

There was no answer from the boat, where five pairs of hands toiled amongst tarred netting and potato peel. Jennings tried again—louder this time. "Ahoy there! Attention all shipping!"

The hands stopped work; five oily peaked caps swivelled round and five whiskery chins were tilted upwards towards the jetty.

"Excuse me," Jennings repeated, "but my friend and I were wondering whether you'd mind frightfully if we came on board and took a snap of you for our mag."

No answer. Puzzled stares greeted the polite inquiry, and after ten seconds of embarrassing silence Jennings felt that more explanation was called for. "What I mean is, we thought you'd make a supersonic picture just sitting there and messing about with those nets."

"*Comment?*" It was the smallest of the Frenchmen who spoke; a thin, dark-haired man with beetling brows and a chin like emery paper.

"What did he say?" whispered Darbishire.

"I'm not sure. It sounded like 'come on!'"

"I know it did, but I think he really said *comment*. That means how many, or what, or something in French. At least, I think it does."

"I only want to take one photo. I'd better tell him." And raising his voice Jennings called: "One will be enough, thank you."

The little fisherman looked helplessly at his equally bewildered colleagues. "*Comment?*" he inquired again.

But things were no clearer up on the jetty. "It can't mean *how many* because I've just told him that, and now he's asked again. Perhaps he does mean *come on*. Let's go, anyway."

An iron ladder stretched from the jetty to the craft below. Jennings led the way and a few moments later the boys had scrambled over the gunwale on to the deck.

Seen at close quarters, the *Sainte Marie* was picturesque, but untidy; tangled coils of rope lay ready to trip the unwary foot; loaves of bread and tins of engine oil lay side by side on the deck, and everywhere there was a strong pervasive smell of raw fish.

The fishermen smiled and nodded at their visitors; but they said nothing, for the very good reason that they spoke English no better than the boys spoke French. Jennings felt that it was up to him to establish friendly relations. "Good afternoon; it's jolly decent of you to invite us on board," he began.

"*Comment?*" This time the speaker was a twinkling-eyed man with tiny gold earrings.

"We can't *come on* any more—we're abaft already," Darbishire explained. But the expressions on his hosts' faces remained blank and he turned to Jennings in despair. "This is hopeless, Jen. They just don't understand English."

"Perhaps they would if I spoke a bit louder." And this time he shouted at the top of his voice: "Please—can—I—take—your—photos?"

For one second the fishermen stared blankly and then, all together, they burst into a torrent of rapid idiomatic French, with wavings of oily fingers and shruggings of eloquent shoulders. Jennings and Darbishire stood and listened and understood not one word of the stream of sound that was cascading about their ears. Suddenly it stopped.

"*Comment?*" queried Jennings brightly. He knew he was safe in saying that.

The twinkling-eyed man laid a hand on his shoulder. "*Nous ne comprenons pas: sommes français. Nous ne parlons pas anglais du tout.*"

"He says they don't speak English," interpreted Darbishire. "You'll have to talk to them in French if you want that photo."

"Who, me? No wizard fear," replied Jennings. "You're tons better at it than I am. You were fifth in French last term and I was only two from bottom."

"Yes, but that doesn't mean to say …

"Oh, go on, Darbi; don't be feeble. I tell you what—I'll appoint you Special Foreign Correspondent to the *Form Three Times*."

Darbishire was delighted with his new appointment, but appalled at the responsibility that went with it. How on earth should he begin? The only French sentence he could call to mind was a passage which had caused him some trouble in class the previous day. So far as he had been able to judge, the translation was: *The gentleman who wears one green hat approaches himself all of a sudden.* Somehow this did not seem a promising way of starting a conversation about photography.

"Just ask if we can take their photos," Jennings urged.

"I couldn't; it'd mean using irregular verbs. They only come at the end of the book, and if these chaps haven't had a very good education they might not have got up to them yet. Give me a bit longer; I'll think of something."

While Darbishire was thinking, Jennings tried mime. He pointed the camera at the fishermen and smiled; but instead of posing, the crew clustered round under the impression that they were being invited to make an inspection at close quarters.

The small dark man poked a finger at the lens. "*Qu'est-ce-que c'est?*" he inquired with interest.

Jennings looked appealingly at the interpreter. "What did he say, Darbi?"

"Well, actually, *qu'est-ce-que c'est* means 'what is this that this is,' if you follow me, but what I think he's trying to ask ..."

"Oh, this is hopeless! Surely you can tell them that we want a fisherman to pose for a photo!"

"I'll have a bash," the Foreign Correspondent agreed. In his mind he ran through the present tense of the appropriate verb. Then he cleared his throat and announced: "*Attention mes braves! Nous voulons du poisson* ... er, no, hang on a sec—that's not quite right. What I mean is ..."

But a sudden wave of understanding had spread over the faces of the crew now that their visitors' purpose was clear.

"*Ah! Vous voulez du poisson. Attendez!*" And with one accord they turned and hurried down into the hold of the boat.

Jennings watched them in surprise. "Where are they all beetling off to?" he demanded.

The interpreter avoided his friend's eye. "Well, I'm afraid I made a bit of a bish," he confessed. "I couldn't think of the word for 'fisherman' and in the heat of the moment I said *poisson*, which means fish."

"You mean you called them a bunch of fish and they've got insulted and ankled off?"

"No. I think I said we *want* some fish."

Jennings clicked his tongue reproachfully. "Well you're a smashing Foreign Correspondent, I must say! Fifth in French last term and you can't even chat to a few old geezers who probably haven't even looked at a French grammar book since they left school."

Darbishire sighed: being an interpreter was not as easy as it sounded.

"Never mind," Jennings consoled him. "I've got a supersonic photo for the front page. They don't know I took it because they were all listening to you telling them they were a bunch of fish, but it should be pretty decent if it comes out."

Darbishire's spirits rose again. "Goodo! We'd better beetle off home then. I'm glad it's over; the strain of talking in a foreign tongue was beginning to tell on me."

They turned to go, but before they had reached the ladder they were stopped by hoarse cries from the open hatchway. Then, one after another, the five members of the crew emerged on deck bearing gifts of plaice, mackerel and cod.

Smiles shone through the grime on the fishermen's faces; for had they not triumphed over the barrier of language to fulfil the wishes of their guests? They advanced upon the boys with hands outstretched, and each hand held a scaly gift.

Jennings backed away in alarm. "Oh, golly, they're not for us, are they—I hope!" But from the encouraging smiles of the donors, it was only too obvious that they *were*.

"Thanks very much; er—*merci beaucoup* and all that, but we couldn't possibly ..."

"*C'est pour votre maman—vous comprenez?*" explained the man with the beetling brows. And then, with great mental effort he sought to make his meaning clear in English. "You geef ze feesh at your mozzer for ze soup."

Jennings looked blank. "I don't think I've got a mozzer to give it at," he faltered.

"*Comment?*"

"What he means is, we've got to take the fish home to our mothers," Darbishire interpreted.

"Tell him you don't have mothers at boarding school; say we're super grateful for the offer, but the deal's off."

"I couldn't possibly. There's too many irregular verbs. Let's take the fish and get weaving—it's the easiest way out."

"But we don't want the wretched stuff. What could we do with them?"

"That's not the point," Darbishire insisted. "They're a present. They think we came on board specially to ask for them and they'll be as upset as two coots if we don't take them with us."

There was nothing for it but to follow Darbishire's advice. Gingerly, Jennings held out his hand and took the unwelcome gift. Then the rest of the fishermen hurried forward with their offerings, which the boys accepted with strained smiles.

To climb the ladder with their slippery burdens was out of the question, and for a moment Jennings hoped that this might prove an excuse for leaving their presents behind. But no! The beetle-browed fisherman unearthed a sheet of newspaper from under a pile of netting and made up a clumsy parcel.

A salvo of friendly farewells followed the boys up the ladder and along the jetty. And this was only natural, for the crew of the *Sainte Marie* were warm-hearted men who took pleasure in performing little acts of kindness.

CHAPTER 3

CONTINENTAL BREAKFAST

As soon as the boys were well away from the *Sainte Marie*, Jennings lost no time in criticising the crew's little act of kindness. And most of the blame fell upon the Special Foreign Correspondent.

"You great, prehistoric clodpoll, Darbi," he complained, as he led the way up the cliff path. "What did you want to go and make a frantic bish like that for? It's all very well not wanting to offend them, but we can't cart this parcel back to school with us."

"Why not? There's no rule about it, is there?"

"There's bound to be. Raw fish probably counts as tuck, and Matron would get into a ghastly bate if we marched into tea with them. And even if there isn't a rule, they'd soon make one up. Rule number nine million and forty-seven: 'Any boy beetling into class with twelve slippery raw fish shall hereby be liable to be detained during Mr. Wilkins' pleasure.'"

It was clear that difficulties lay ahead and it seemed to Jennings that their best course would be to dispose of the parcel before they reached the school gates. But this was not so easy as it sounded. There was little cover on the open downland, and to make matters worse a middle-aged woman with a fox terrier was walking along the track a few yards behind them. Surely she would think it odd if finny gifts were strewn in her path; and no attempt at concealment would deceive the terrier, who was even now sniffing round Jennings' heels with an inquisitive air.

"We can't dump them now, or she'll probably report us for wasting food, or cruelty to dumb friends or something," Jennings decided. "They would have to wait until the woman was out of sight and then ... But why should they? A foolproof idea flashed into Jennings' mind; an idea so simple, yet so attractive that it was worth taking a few risks in the carrying out.

"I tell you what, Darbi," he went on, "we'll fox them back to school with us and smuggle them down to my tuck-box."

"Righto, then! And we can take them home to our mothers at the end of term as the man told us to."

Jennings gave his friend a pitying look. "You may think yourself a supersonic interpreter, Darbi, but you've got about as much brains as this fish. Can you imagine what they'd be *like* in about eight weeks' time?"

"I see what you mean," replied Darbishire thoughtfully, "but in that case what's the point of smuggling them back with us?"

"To eat, of course."

"What—raw! Dash it all, Jen, I'm not a sea lion."

As they followed the footpath back to Linbury, Jennings explained his plan. They would rise early the following morning and develop his film in the school darkroom, as camera-owners were encouraged to do. Then, safely behind the bolted darkroom door, they could fry a tasty fish breakfast over the gas-bracket on the wall. Kitchenware could be improvised from developing dishes, and the problem of finding a substitute for cooking fat could be solved with a little serious thought.

Darbishire's eyes lit up with excitement. Here was a scheme with no snags attached to it, and the mark of genius lay in the fact that, once inside the dark-room no one, not even a master, would think of demanding admission for fear of spoiling the film.

"Oh, wacko, Jennings; jolly good idea—*bon idée!*" Darbishire stopped short, surprised at his ready command of the French language. "Gosh, did you hear what I said then? *Bon idée!* There you are, you see! My French is masses better already, just from having a little informal chat with a few natives."

"Those chaps weren't natives—they were Frenchmen," Jennings returned curtly. "Natives don't speak French; they say things like *wallah-wallah* and *m'bongo-m'bongo*."

"No; you're thinking of Africans. Our fishermen-geezers were natives of France, so of course they spoke French. Every one's a native really—even us."

"I'm not; I don't speak French."

"But you don't *have* to. Don't you see …"

The pointless argument rambled on until the boys were within sight of the school gates. Then Jennings became alert; the utmost caution was necessary if his plan was to succeed.

He sent Darbishire ahead to make sure that there was no one about on the drive; then, as his arms were cramped from carrying the parcel, he laid it on the ground. It would have to be re-wrapped before it could be carried indoors, he decided, for it had never been a tidy parcel, and now the newspaper was sodden and clammy.

He had just started on this task when Darbishire came hurrying out of the school gates. Alarm and despondency were written all over his features.

"Mr. Carter!" he gasped in a voiceless whisper. "He's coming down the drive!"

Hastily Jennings gathered up the parcel. His intention was to conceal it beneath his raincoat, but as he lifted it from the ground the sheet of newspaper dissolved in pulp and the scaly contents cascaded on to the road with a soft, depressing slither.

For a moment Jennings stared at the burst parcel in dismay. Then, quickly, he stooped and began stuffing the tell-tale evidence into his raincoat pockets.

Darbishire's expression registered distaste.

"They'll make a super-chronic mess," he observed.

"Can't help that! If Mr. Carter sees them, bang goes my famous wheeze. Come on, don't just stand there, like the back of a bus queue; he'll be round the corner in half a mo."

Unwillingly, Darbishire helped in the task and in a matter of seconds the boys' pockets were bulging to bursting point, and Jennings was looking round desperately for some place to conceal the last fish for which neither of them could find room.

At that moment the scrunch of Mr. Carter's footsteps was heard turning the corner of the drive. Jennings took the only course which remained open; snatching off his cap, he laid the last small mackerel inside and then replaced his headgear with feverish haste.

The cap had never been a good fit, and now it perched high up on top of his head like a carnival novelty. It was a makeshift move, but it would have to suffice, for the master was approaching now.

Mr. Carter was a friendly-looking man who had reached the comfortable years between youth and middle age. He was quiet and unexcitable—a man whom all the boys liked and turned to in their troubles. He had only one serious failing, so far as the boys were concerned, and this was that however skilfully a wrong-doer might conceal his misdeeds, Mr. Carter always found out!

"Good afternoon, sir," said Darbishire politely and raised his cap with a courtly flourish: Jennings dared do no more than tweak the peak and pray that Mr. Carter would stop staring in that marked manner.

"Good afternoon. You're back early. Did you have a successful expedition?" Mr. Carter inquired.

"Yes thank, you, sir. We went to the harbour." Jennings hoped that his voice did not betray his anxiety. Perhaps if he chatted quite naturally the master would not notice anything was amiss. "I took a jolly good photo of the abaft end of a boat, sir, and another one of a group of natives. At least, that's what Darbishire says they were, but they were practically white, really sir."

If only Mr. Carter would not continue to stare like that! Surely he did not suspect anything! Darbishire took up the tale in an effort to divert attention from the bulging cap.

"They weren't really natives, sir—they were aliens, but I found I knew their lingo fairly well, so I was able to have quite a little chat with them, sir."

This was too much for Jennings. Even at the risk of inviting Mr. Carter's stare again, he could not let the Special Correspondent claim his miserable failure as a triumph.

"Darbishire's just swanking, sir," he interposed. "They were Frenchmen, and he told them they were a bunch of fish."

"That must have been very comforting for them," said Mr. Carter. "There's nothing like a friendly word to make a foreigner feel at home in a strange land."

"Oh, sir, I *didn't* call them that, sir! Jennings' French was so mouldy that he couldn't follow what I was talking about."

"And could the Frenchmen?" inquired Mr. Carter.

"Well, yes and no, sir. They said a lot of things very fast that weren't in the grammar book, but I don't think their French was very good really. They hardly used the list of pronoun objects and things at all, sir."

Mr. Carter took a deep breath and said: "The first thing you two boys can do, is to go and empty your pockets. Fish may be good for the brain, Jennings, but it should never be applied externally."

So Mr. Carter *did* know! It just didn't seem possible to keep anything from him.

"I'm sorry, sir," Jennings apologised. "They were a present, you see. We didn't really want them but we didn't know enough French to explain properly."

"I see. Well, I suggest you dispose of it, and the sooner the better, considering that it's been mixed with whatever rubbish you normally carry in your raincoat

530

pockets. After that, Jennings, you can hang your coats out to air and then wash your hair."

"Yes, sir."

Deflated in spirit, the members of the photographic expedition wended their way up the drive. But by the time they had reached the quad Jennings was feeling more cheerful. After all, they still had the photographs, and matters would have been much worse if Mr. Carter had decided to punish them.

Darbishire, however, was still wrapped in gloom. He had been looking forward to that early breakfast.

"What ghastly feeble luck," he lamented. "It's always the same whenever we get a really first class idea."

"I don't see that we've got much to moan about," Jennings replied, as they turned into the main building. "We've still got to develop the photos and then— well, Mr. Carter didn't say we *weren't* to eat them, did he?"

"The photos?"

"No, you clodpoll. Why don't you listen properly!"

"But Mr. Carter said ..."

"He didn't say anything of the sort. He just told us to *dispose* of them; and the best way to do that is fried, with pepper and salt, if you can get some. We can empty our pockets, as he told us to, and put the fish in my tuck-box. After all, I'm sure he didn't really mean we were to waste it."

Jennings and Darbishire spent the rest of the time before tea in making preparations for the morrow. First it was necessary to obtain permission to use the darkroom. They decided that it would be wiser not to ask Mr. Carter, so they sought out Mr. Hind, a studious man with a tired voice, who taught History in the lower forms. Mr. Hind gave his permission freely; he was a keen photographer and only too pleased to encourage the boys in their hobby.

The next requirement was a supply of cooking fat. Jennings unearthed a bottle of cricket bat oil, left over from the summer term, but after some argument they decided that this might be lacking in vitamins, so they ate dry bread at tea-time and smuggled their pats of butter out of the dining hall in an envelope. So far, so good; whichever way they looked at it, the scheme seemed flawless.

It was nearly seven o'clock when Jennings slipped out of bed the next morning and shook the sleeping Darbishire into wakefulness. There was a risk, of course, in rising before the bell, but risks have to be faced when important issues are at stake.

Darbishire, however, thought otherwise. The weather was bleak and uninviting; his bed was warm and comfortable, and the idea of filleting raw plaice in a cold darkroom did not seem nearly so attractive as it had done the night before.

"Couldn't we do it some other time? One day next week, say," he suggested.

"No, we jolly well couldn't; the fish won't keep. It's highly fragile, don't forget."

"You mean perishable; it was your camera that was fragile and my father says that you should never ..."

"Never mind what your father says. I shall be perishable if you keep me hanging about on this cold lino much longer. I'm pretty well perished already."

It was useless to argue and Darbishire knew it. Still bleary with sleep, he crawled out of bed and felt vaguely about for his socks.

As soon as the boys were dressed they tiptoed out of the dormitory, to the accompaniment of a piercing squeak from Jennings' house shoes. They called at the tuck-box room for the fish, now re-wrapped in a strong brown paper bag, and then made for the darkroom with as much speed and as little noise as they could.

Darbishire heaved a sigh of relief as he bolted the door. "Phew! Thank goodness we didn't meet any one in the corridor. Which shall we do first—cook or develop?"

"I've done the developing," Jennings answered, to his friend's surprise. "I came in last night just before the dorm bell went, so's we could have more time to get cracking with our famous breakfast."

"Oh, wizzo! Have they come out all right?" "Not too mouldy! The fishing ones are super, but I kept forgetting to wind the film on when I took the earlier ones and I've got a snap of Venables saving a goal all mixed up with the back view of Mr. Wilkins' head taken through the library window."

This was not the time, however, to examine the photographs, for more immediate tasks were waiting to be done. Jennings picked up a celluloid developing dish and rinsed it out at the little sink in the corner. It would never do for the well-cooked breakfast to taste of hypo! Then he produced the butter from his pocket and four plaice of medium size from the parcel.

Darbishire watched spell-bound. Now that things were going smoothly he was beginning to enjoy himself. And what added to his pleasure was the thought that as the fare had been provided by Frenchmen, they could boast to their friends of enjoying a genuine continental breakfast.

This cookery stunt of yours was a massive brainwave, Jen," he said admiringly. "We should have been up a gum-tree otherwise, because if we couldn't have eaten it, it'd just be what my father calls a white elephant, wouldn't it?"

Jennings looked up from his preparations. "What'd be a white elephant?"

"This fish would."

"Listen, Darbi, I've got quite enough trouble cooking fish without starting on white elephants as well."

"I wasn't asking you to; you couldn't cook a white elephant really, because there's no such thing."

"You said there was. You said our fish was one."

"Ah, but what I meant was ..."

"If you want to be useful, Darbishire, you can wizard well stop nattering about elephants and shut the window. Any one about on the quad will know we're not developing a film if we haven't got the black-out up."

The windowpanes were coated with black paint to exclude the light. Darbishire closed the window and at once the little room grew dark. Jennings groped his way round the table and found the box of matches which was used for lighting the stub of candle in the red darkroom lamp. He had, by this time, placed the butter in the developing dish, so all that remained to be done was to light the gas jet and hold the dish over the flame until the butter melted.

He lit the gas. He held the dish over the flame. And then it happened!

There was a sudden flash and tongues of flame were licking the sides of the dish and leaping towards the ceiling.

Jennings said: "Oh, gosh!" and dropped the dish on the floor.

"Help! What's up?" gasped Darbishire in alarm. "Look out, Jen, or you'll set the place on fire." It was a pointless remark, for the fact was only too obvious.

Feverishly Jennings sought some fire-fighting weapon; and as the nearest thing to hand was the parcel of fish he grabbed it from the table and dropped it on the flames billowing up from the floor. There was a dull thud, a spurt of smoke and the fire was out.

"Whew! Talk about a ghastly bish!" Jennings wiped imaginary beads of perspiration from his brow.

"What happened?"

"The developing dish was a celluloid one—that's what! I ought to have used an enamel one, really."

"I should think you jolly well ought!" returned Darbishire indignantly. "You are a dangerous maniac, Jen. Every one knows celluloid burns like blinko."

"Don't get in a flap. It's all over now."

But it wasn't all over. Acrid fumes of burnt celluloid were spreading over the room like a dense fog. Jennings coughed; politely at first, but as the fumes thickened he was unable to control the tickle in his nose and throat. Then the gaseous fog reached Darbishire by the window and paroxysms of coughing echoed round the darkened room.

"Open the window, quick," gasped Jennings.

Darbishire fumbled with the catch, threw up the lower sash and poked his head out into the cool morning air. "Phew, that's better! You've no idea how decent fresh air smells when you've just had a shortage of it."

He removed his spectacles and dabbed his streaming eyes. Then he replaced his glasses and looked through them; and what he saw caused him to shoot back into the darkroom and slam the window shut.

"What's up?" Jennings' voice came out of the darkness.

"Mr. Wilkins! He's outside on the quad. He saw my head pop out."

"Oh, golly!"

"Yes, and that's not all! He saw it pop back again, too, and he must have wondered ..."

"Ssh!"

Both boys stood still and listened; the room was not yet clear of fumes and it was all they could do to stifle their coughs.

They had not long to wait. Footsteps sounded on the gravel outside and a purposeful knuckle tapped on the glass.

"Open this window at once!" Mr. Wilkins' tone indicated that he meant to investigate the mystery of the popping head without delay. But he could not see through a coat of black paint and the inhabitants of the darkroom were overcome by a sudden deafness.

Mr. Wilkins rapped again. No answer. What on earth could those silly little boys be playing at, he wondered? Had they hurried out of the room at his approach? He decided to find out.

The footsteps scrunched again and died away as he turned the corner of the building and entered the front door.

"Oh, golly, he's coming round," moaned Darbishire. "Whatever shall we do? He knows we weren't developing because of having the window open."

"We'd better open it again, now he's gone and let another basinful of this smoke out," Jennings suggested. "He'll be bashing on the door in half a sec and we'll have to let him in. Buck up, we've no time to hang about!"

With one accord they threw themselves into a frenzied scurry of tidying-up. Darbishire flung wide the window, and then took off his jacket and fanned the air. Jennings gathered up the charred remains of the developing dish and dropped them in the sink. The roll of negative and a bottle of hypo were displayed on the table to show how busily they were absorbed in photography, and in a few moments the darkroom had almost assumed its normal appearance.

Only one thing seemed oddly out of place: behind the door was a medium-sized parcel of plaice, mackerel and cod.

CHAPTER 4

CONJURING TRICK

L. P. WILKINS, Esq., M.A. (Cantab.), was a man of vigorous action. He made no secret of his outflanking movement, but strode heavily along the corridor and rattled the handle of the darkroom door.

"Open this door, immediately!"

Mr. Wilkins had a voice which would have been audible above the clatter and roar of a brass foundry. It was useless, then, to plead inattention or hardness of hearing. What was to be done? Darbishire stood on one leg and gaped in dismay at the parcel behind the door.

"Oh, golly, we shouldn't have done this! He'll see it when he comes in, and there's just nowhere to hide the beastly stuff. My father says that ... Gosh, Jen, what*ever* are you doing?"

Jennings was doing the only thing he *could* do. He was tucking the parcel of fish under the tail of his jacket; then he took up an unnatural stance with his hands clasped firmly behind his back.

"How many more times have I got to tell you to open the door?" Mr. Wilkins was growing impatient and the panels quivered and heaved as though a small bulldozer were at work on a demolition site.

Darbishire hastily drew back the bolt and the door flew open.

"Now what on earth's going on in here?" But Mr. Wilkins' nose answered this question for him as he inhaled the atmosphere. "I—I—Corwumph! Something's been burning!"

"Yes, sir. A developing dish caught fire by accident, but it's all right now, sir," Jennings assured him.

"We'll soon see about that." Mr. Wilkins strode across the threshold and stood sniffing like a bloodhound. He was determined to be thorough: he examined the charred remains in the sink, knocked the roll of negative off the table and upset the hypo bottle in his efforts to leave no stone unturned. As he moved about the room, Jennings moved too and took care never to turn his back.

Finally the master spoke: "I don't know much about photography, but if it's necessary to set the place on fire and befoul the atmosphere for miles around, it's not the hobby I took it for. Have you boys got leave to be in here?"

"Well, sir, last night Mr. Hind said I could develop my film, but I don't actually think he knows we're in here at the moment, if you see what I mean," Jennings replied.

"So you're here without permission?"

"Well, in a manner of speaking, I suppose we are, sir."

"Never mind the manner of speaking, Jennings, or I shall do some speaking in a manner you won't appreciate. And what's more you're up before the rising-bell again! Go up to my room and wait for me."

"Yes, sir."

Jennings backed out of the doorway like a medieval courtier in the presence of royalty. The clasped hands and the forward thrust of the shoulders gave him an air of studious detachment which he was far from feeling: but he could not relax his attitude without dropping the parcel.

Darbishire did his best to cover his friend's retreat and as they went along the corridor he whispered: "What are we going to do? We can't take it up to Old Wilkie's room?"

He bitterly regretted, now, that he had ever taken a hand in the venture. Everything had gone wrong. And if, in addition to their other troubles, the fish was to be discovered after Mr. Carter's instructions of the previous day, it would shed a new and sinister light upon their early-morning activities.

"If only we could dump the beastly stuff somewhere!" Jennings said as they climbed the stairs. But it would have been asking for trouble to stray from their route, with Mr. Wilkins so hard upon their heels. For a moment Jennings considered slipping the parcel inside an empty laundry basket on the first landing, but Matron made an untimely appearance just as he was about to lift the lid, and the attempt had to be abandoned.

Along the landing and up the next flight of stairs they dragged their unwilling footsteps, while their hopes of finding a hiding place faded with every yard. At last they reached Mr. Wilkins' door.

"Surely there's *somewhere*," groaned Darbishire, looking, despairingly along the top landing. "He'll be here in a second; he's talking to Matron just below."

Jennings wasted no time. "Open his door quick!" he ordered.

Darbishire stared aghast. "Have you gone stark raving bats! We can't hide it in there!"

"There's nowhere else, is there? Anyway it's only for now. We'll get it back afterwards."

With some misgiving Darbishire pushed open the master's door and the boys scuttled inside; but luck was against them. Mr. Wilkins' study was furnished with a table, three chairs, a locked cupboard and a glass-fronted bookcase. There wasn't enough cover to hide a shrimp, let alone a medium-sized parcel of fish. And heavy footsteps were sounding on the stairs.

"Nip out on the landing and keep him talking," urged Jennings.

"What about?"

"Anything you like. Just chat naturally."

"I can never think of anything to say when I'm trying to be natural," Darbishire objected, "and it seems crazy to start talking about the weather ..."

"Oh, go *on*, Darbi. Do as I tell you!"

Unwillingly, Darbishire left his friend and hurried through the door. The master was at the top of the stairs now and his expression suggested that he was in no mood to be delayed with polite remarks about the weather.

"What were you doing in my room, Darbishire?" he demanded.

"Er—just coming out, sir."

"I can see that, you silly little boy. I distinctly told you to wait outside my room, not to go blundering in. You and Jennings cause enough chaos when you get loose in a darkroom; heaven knows what you'd get up to in a civilised sitting room. Blow the place up, I expect!"

In two strides Mr. Wilkins was through the door and inside his study. Darbishire followed, feeling empty inside and trying to keep his mind off what was going to happen next. It could be only amatter of seconds before ... Darbishire blinked through his spectacles and then opened his eyes in astonishment.

Jennings was standing on the hearthrug; his hands hung freely at his sides and there was no bulge beneath his jacket. Darbishire cast quick, anxious glances about the room; the furniture was exactly as it had been when he had left ten seconds before.

Then where on earth—and Darbishire searched his mind in vain for an answer to the riddle—where on earth had Jennings hidden the parcel?

From his earliest years Darbishire had always been fascinated by conjuring tricks. At Christmas parties he would watch spellbound as some talented friend of the family produced a string of knotted handkerchiefs from a top hat or caused the ace of spades to vanish into thin air and come to light in a flower pot. But never had he seen a trick to equal the *Mystery of the Disappearing Fish-bag!*

The thing just wasn't possible! Less than a minute before, Jennings had been wandering distractedly round the room clutching the parcel beneath his jacket. Now, by some uncanny sleight of hand, the unwanted bulge had dissolved into the atmosphere.

Darbishire peered round the room seeking the solution to this paragon of parlour tricks. Was there an unsuspected trapdoor beneath the carpet? Had the bookcase a false bottom or a sliding panel? Perhaps the trick was done by mass-hypnotism or the use of mirrors. Perhaps, even ...

"What on earth is the matter with you, Darbishire? Have you lost something?" Mr. Wilkins' voice cut into the boy's speculations and brought him back to reality with a start.

"Er—no, sir. Or rather, yes, thank you, sir, but it doesn't matter really."

"Then stop gaping at the furniture like a village idiot, and listen to me. It's quite obvious that neither of you are fit to develop your own photographs— quite apart from the fact that you were doing so without permission and before the rising-bell."

Mr. Wilkins was justifiably annoyed. Every morning before breakfast he liked to take a brisk walk, swinging his arms vigorously and inhaling deep lungfuls of fresh air. This morning, however, he had been obliged to cut short his health-giving exercise and grope about a dingy darkroom, breathing the pungent fumes of what he wrongly imagined to be photographic chemicals.

"I've just about had enough of this stupid nonsense," he continued. "You will both do an hour's work for me on Saturday afternoon and take a black stripe for your conduct books. And I warn you that if there's any more of this—this juvenile delinquency—I'll ... Well, you'd better look out!"

"Yes, sir."

Outside on the landing, Jennings heaved a sigh of relief and said: "Well, that wasn't so bad, was it? Or rather, it'd have been a wizard sight worse if he'd known what had *really* been cooking in the darkroom, because ..."

"Yes, but where is it?" Darbishire broke in urgently.

"The darkroom? You know that as well as I do. Downstairs through the basement."

Darbishire danced with impatience. "No, you prehistoric clodpoll! Where's the parcel of fish?"

"Oh, that! Well, as a matter of fact I had a rare brainstroke after you'd beetled out. You see, I knew I'd got to do something, quick."

"And what did you do, quick?"

"I bunged the whole caboodle up Old Wilkie's chimney."

"What! ... Oh, gosh!" Darbishire stared at his friend in wide-eyed dismay. Of all the places to put it ...!

"What else could I do?" Jennings defended himself. "It's all very fine for you to stand there 'Oh, goshing,' but I bet you couldn't have thought of anything better on the spur of the moment."

Now that the *Mystery of the Disappearing Fish-bag* was solved, Darbishire began to think that perhaps it wasn't such a good trick after all.

"But we can't leave it there for ever and ever," he protested. "Mr. Wilkins would have to wear a respirator and summon the insanitary spectre."

"Summon the *what*?" Into Jennings' mind floated the picture of an unhygienic ghost haunting the master's study.

"I mean the sanitary inspector," Darbishire corrected himself. He was still feeling rather confused.

"Don't get in a flap, Darbi; I'll think of something. It's goodbye to our early breakfast, though; by the time we get it back, it'll be hardly worth eating."

As though to compensate them for their loss, the breakfast bell rang at that moment, and Jennings and Darbishire joined the stream of boys which flowed from the dormitories and cascaded down the stairs like a human waterfall.

"Where have you two been?" Venables demanded from across the table, as they sat down to breakfast. "Atkinson and I have been searching the dorm for you. We wanted to demonstrate our famous patent invention of putting our pullovers on before taking our pyjama jackets off."

"Why?" inquired Darbishire without enthusiasm. He felt he had seen enough tricks for one morning.

"Well, why not? It's a socko idea," said Atkinson. "We get dressed first and then work our pyjama-tops down our shirt sleeves and out at the wrist. Pity you missed it."

Jennings hastened to explain their absence. "Mr. Hind said I could do my film in the darkroom last night, and just because a developing dish went swoosh when we were using it as a frying pan, Old Wilkie came charging in like an armoured column and kicked up a hoo-hah."

"What did you want to fry it for?" demanded Venables. It seemed an odd thing to do with a roll of film.

"Oh, I don't mean the photos; we were frying the fish."

"What fish?"

"The ones in Mr. Wilkins' chimney."

This was too difficult for Venables, and it was some time before he had sorted the jumbled explanation into some semblance of order. Then he said: "Well, you've got nothing to worry about. It should be pretty easy to nip in and hoik it down when Mr. Wilkins isn't there. I bet I could do it without being copped."

"All very well for you to talk! I'd like to see what sort of a bish you'd make of it," said Jennings.

It was, of course, the only solution and he had already made up his mind to try it when conditions were favourable. All the same, he was not going to let Venables or any one else suggest that the task would be easy.

Darbishire made a poor breakfast that morning. As he toyed with his baked beans—a poor substitute for fried fish, he thought—the question of retrieving the parcel was uppermost in his mind. Jennings had bungled things badly; perhaps the keen brain of C. E. J. Darbishire could save the situation. He would go to Mr. Wilkins' room and knock boldly on the door; if there was no answer, it would mean the coast was clear. If there *was* an answer—well, that would have to be faced when the time came. In any case the sooner this miserable business was cleared up the better, for today was Monday, and that evening he and Jennings hoped to start printing the first number of the *Form Three Times*.

Mr. Wilkins was enjoying his after-breakfast pipe when the first knock sounded on his door. He called: "Come in!" and was surprised to hear a pattering scurry outside, as though some heavy-footed rabbit were making for cover on tiptoe. He hurled open the door and caught sight of a curly-headed figure disappearing down the corridor.

"Darbishire!" he shouted.

The figure skidded to a stop, and bent down to retrieve a house-shoe which had been travelling too fast to obey the halt summons.

"Sir?"

"What on earth are you doing?"

"Putting my shoe on, sir."

"I can see that, you silly little boy. That doesn't explain why you knocked at my door and then skated off down the corridor. Do you want to see me?"

"No, sir. Not specially, thank you, sir."

"Then what *do* you want?"

Darbishire considered. What he had *really* wanted was to find the room empty, but that was not the sort of answer that would be well received; and as the owner of a tender conscience he could not bring himself to say anything which was not strictly true. What else did he want? There must be *something* if only he could think what it was. At last he said: "Well, sir, I *could* do with a stamp, sir; then I could write to my grandmother."

"Then why not ask for one in a civilised manner?" simmered Mr. Wilkins. He led the way into his study and took down the folder in which he kept stamps for the boys' letters.

Darbishire stood in the doorway and cast furtive glances at the fireplace. It looked all right, but ... Was it his imagination, or was there a faint tang in the air? He sniffed, and was still not sure; so he inhaled a series of long, deep breaths—and was suddenly aware that Mr. Wilkins was looking at him in a puzzled manner.

"What are you snuffling for? Playing at bloodhounds?" the master inquired.

Darbishire's lungs were so full of air that he could not reply without risking a minor explosion. Instead he held his breath, hoping that Mr. Wilkins would turn his attention to other matters. He hoped in vain, and five seconds ticked by while the master grew more bewildered and Darbishire became pinker and pinker in the face. Then, with a sound like a punctured bicycle tyre, he gave up the unequal struggle.

"I was just holding my breath, sir," he explained, somewhat unnecessarily.

"Well, don't do it here," said Mr. Wilkins. "My study's not the place for breath-holding contests or any other sort of nonsensical buffoonery. Here, take your stamp and go and pretend you're a vacuum brake somewhere where I can't hear you."

"Yes, sir."

Darbishire was a frequent visitor to Mr. Wilkins' study that day; but on every occasion he found the room occupied and had to improvise some reason for his visit. At break, he bought another stamp. Just before lunch he called to ask Mr. Wilkins for his autograph. After lunch, he looked in to ask whether "Sir" could tell him what the time was.

By five o'clock, Mr. Wilkins was tiring of his visitor: he had sold him four stamps, lent him an india-rubber, undone an almost inextricable knot in the laces of his football boots and admired a snapshot of the Rev. and Mrs. Darbishire on the beach at Bournemouth. It seemed that the only way to secure a few minutes' peace would be to go for a walk. So Mr. Wilkins went.

"If that problem child comes knocking at my door again, he's going to be unlucky," he said to himself, as he strode down the drive swinging his arms vigorously.

As it happened, Darbishire *was* unlucky, for he missed his chance while the coast was clear. He, also, had grown tired of his visits to the study, and could think of no further excuses to offer. So he denied himself the doubtful pleasure of a ninth trip and went to look for Jennings instead.

He found him in the tuck-box room, gathering together the news items for the first edition of the *Form Three Times*.

"Where have you been, Darbi?" his friend demanded. "Every break today you've beetled off somewhere just when I wanted you to help me with the photos for our magazine."

"I've been doing a special priority secret service job, getting that bag back," Darbishire explained.

"Goodo! What have you done with it?"

"Well, I haven't exactly quite got it, yet. But I've kept Old Wilkie under pretty close observation all day, and, honestly, Jen, I don't know how we're ever going to get in there. He sticks in that room like a hermit in his cell."

"He won't feel like staying there much longer, if we don't get that parcel out. Another few days and he'll begin to wonder what's gone wrong with the ventilation."

"Oh, golly, I wish we'd never done it!" lamented Darbishire. "We must just keep very calm and think out what to do. My father knows a quotation from *Horace* about keeping a balanced mind in adversity."

Jennings snorted. "It'd be more to the point if *Horace* had told him one about how to get things out of chimneys. I can't think why you have to clutter the place up with your father's famous wise sayings; we've got enough trouble on our plates already."

Darbishire sank wearily on to a tuck-box and said nothing. It was at times like this that what his father said seemed truer than ever.

CHAPTER 5

THE "FORM THREE TIMES"

THERE seemed little point in visiting Mr. Wilkins' room again that evening, and Jennings decided that an expedition would have more chance of success if the attempt was postponed until later in the week.

So during tea that evening he thought out a workable plan: Wednesday was a half-holiday, when Mr. Wilkins would be in charge of their football game. As soon as the final whistle sounded, Jennings could hurry indoors and retrieve the evidence, while Darbishire delayed the referee on the football pitch with abstruse questions about the off-side rule.

It was a simple scheme which gave every promise of running smoothly; even the short delay in its execution would not matter because there was little risk of the well-wrapped parcel proclaiming its presence in a cool chimney before Wednesday. The planners charged their beakers and drank to the success of their scheme in weak tea, for now they could devote the evening to the important task of printing the *Form Three Times*.

There was a clear hour before bedtime when the editors settled down in the hobbies room, armed with their notebooks, the *Ideal* printing outfit and the photographs of the *Sainte Marie*.

The remaining photographs on the film were not altogether successful, for Jennings' failure to wind the spool between each snapshot had produced some odd results. A picture of Darbishire posing by the garden roller was disfigured by the ghostly apparition of Bromwich major floating in mid-air in the background; while a more freakish double exposure, taken from the football pitch, gave the impression that the goalkeeper was trying to save Mr. Wilkins' head from going through the library window.

Regretfully, the editors dropped the useless prints into the wastepaper basket and started to set up the headlines for the front page. For a while they worked happily, fitting the little pellets into the wooden slots with infinite patience, and producing a line of print which, though unevenly spaced, was certainly legible.

But when three-quarters of an hour had ticked away and the first paragraph was still unfinished, they began to realise that their enthusiasm had blinded them to a serious drawback: the *Ideal Junior Printing Outfit* was all very well for dashing off brief notes of thanks, but a full-sized magazine was a different matter altogether. Some words were taking more than a minute to piece together, and every now and then progress came to a standstill as the printers searched feverishly through their stock for some letter which had strayed from its place in the queue of alphabetical order.

"This is hopeless! We'll never get finished at this rate," complained the chief editor; his patience had been wearing thin ever since his assistant had dropped a question mark into the inkwell. "There's twelve pages to do yet, and we're still up at the top of page one. It'll take us about ..." There was a pause while he sought the answer in mental arithmetic ... "it'll take about ninety-six weeks if we don't step up our output a bit, and all the news will be as stale as buns, years before it gets printed."

The assistant editor rose from examining the cracks between the floorboards where he had been carrying on a search for straying letters. "I don't want to say anything against your Aunt Angela's generous present," he remarked, "but if she'd only given you a proper typewriter, we might be getting somewhere— if only we knew how to type."

"Gosh, yes, that's not a bad idea! Let's type it," Jennings replied. "We can still use the printing outfit for headlines and stop-press and stuff like that."

"That's all very well, but we haven't got a typewriter."

"No, but Mr. Carter has," said Jennings promptly. "And he's always on at us to get cracking on highbrow stuff like magazines and wallpapers."

"The *Form Three Times* isn't wallpaper. It's a wall newspaper, and that's quite different. Besides, would Mr. Carter let us borrow the machine?"

"I'm pretty sure he wouldn't. But if we ask and he says No, he may feel a bit uncomfortable, after all he's said, and offer to type it for us."

Mr. Carter was marking essays in his study when the polite rap on the door announced that he was about to receive visitors. He guessed from the sound of the knock that they had come to ask a favour; for it was neither the timid tap of one who reports for punishment, nor the urgent panel-beating of the bearer of important news.

"Well, Jennings, what can I do for you?" the master asked as the two boys ranged themselves before the writing table.

"Well, sir, Darbishire and me hoped you'd do us a favour, sir."

Mr. Carter winced. He had a tidy, grammatical mind. "No; Darbishire and *I* hoped you would do us a favour, Jennings," he corrected.

Jennings looked surprised. "Did you, sir? Darbishire never told me."

"I mean, Jennings, that you should say Darbishire and *I*, not Darbishire and *me*."

"I see, sir. Well, would you do Darbishire and I a favour, please sir?"

Mr. Carter closed his eyes. Very patiently he said: "This time, Jennings, it's correct to say Darbishire and *me*."

Jennings felt that the object of their visit was being obscured by grammatical argument. "Well, anyway, sir, the point is that Darbishire and I or me, are writing a magazine and we wondered if we could borrow your typewriter to biff out parts of it on, sir."

"I'm afraid not. It's not a toy, you know."

"I know, sir. That's what we thought you'd say. I hope you didn't mind our asking, sir." He made no move to go, but stood silent and hopeful.

Mr. Carter guessed what the silent hope was about and said: "Of course there's just a slight chance that I might be willing to type it for you. Let me see first if it's worth doing."

He glanced through the items in the notebooks. From time to time he groaned at the literary style and tut-tutted over the handwriting; but then, those were matters which could be remedied when the magazine appeared in its finished form. Finally he laid down the notebooks and said: "Very well: I'll type it for you. Is this all there is?"

"There's just a bit more, but we can do that on our printing outfit, sir," Jennings answered. "We thought of putting in a couple of competitions to help fill up space a bit, but we haven't decided what they're to be yet."

Mr. Carter narrowed his eyes as he glanced once more at the pencilled scrawl before him. "Why not have a handwriting competition?" he suggested. "Anything that would improve the writing in this school would be worth trying."

"Good idea, sir. That'll do wizardly for one," Darbishire agreed. "And for the second one we could have ... what?"

Again Mr. Carter sought inspiration from the rough copy in his hands. "What this magazine needs is a higher literary standard. I think you might persuade your readers to try their hand at writing an original poem or something of that sort."

"Rather, sir. Super idea!" said Jennings. "And we could offer really decent valuable prizes such as—er, well, double-decker sponge cakes, for instance."

"But we haven't *got* any super double-decker sponge cakes," the assistant editor pointed out.

"No, I know, but *if we* had! Think what decent prizes they'd make! Why, any one with any sense would have a bash at writing a chunk of poetry if there was a sponge cake going for a prize." Jennings' eyes shone with enthusiasm as he warmed to his theme. "And what's more, I'm pretty sure my Aunt Angela would send me a couple if I told her they were to encourage poetry and stuff. She's ever so keen on culture."

The first number of the *Form Three Times* appeared on the notice board the following morning, and created a considerable stir throughout the school. Here and there an item of news was printed in the vivid mauve hue of the *Ideal Junior Printing Outfit*, but the main part of the journal was neatly typed, and—thanks to Mr. Carter—correctly spelled.

Atkinson was thrilled with the account of his year-old discovery of the caterpillar in the cabbage, and stood for minutes at a time, staring at his name in typed capitals. Binns minor was secretly disappointed that the riddle of the missing football boot had not been included. He had found his boot by this time, but he would have been more than willing to hide it again in order to make his story sound more probable.

By break time, every one had heard about the magazine: every one except Bromwich major, who was a lone wolf and a law unto himself. Jennings came across him in the tuck-box room, working on an air-conditioning plant for his rabbit hutch.

"I say, Bromo, have you seen my magazine?" Jennings began excitedly.

"No, I haven't," answered Bromwich curtly. "You're always losing things and expecting every one to know where they are."

"No, you clodpoll, I haven't lost it! I mean have you seen it up on the wall?"

Bromwich major looked interested. "Golly! However did it get up there?" he wanted to know. Patiently Jennings explained, and Bromwich decided to go and see for himself.

When they arrived in the common room they had difficulty in getting near the notice board for the throng of readers who were absorbing once again the news which they had known about for some time. However, the front page photograph of the crew of the *Sainte Marie* was new to them all and caused a certain amount of speculation. Jennings had forgotten to write a caption for it and opinions differed as to whether they were Chinese bandits or miners queueing up for pit-head baths.

But it was the two competitions which attracted the greatest interest. After all, here were double-decker sponge cakes being freely offered, and what more could any one want than that?

"I could do with one of those sponge cakes," said Bromwich major.

"So could I. I've a jolly good mind to have a shot at writing a home-made poem," said Atkinson thoughtfully. He turned to Venables, who stood beside him in the queue. "You ought to walk away with the other comp, Venables. Your writing's super!"

"Oh, I don't know," replied Venables modestly. "I haven't decided which one to go in for yet." He edged his way forward to the board and read out the rules which Darbishire had hastily added in pencil after the magazine had been typed.

"*All competition entries must be in by Friday week. Do not write on one side of the paper ...*" He broke off, puzzled, and then shouted: "Hey, Darbishire, come over here. Your rules are stark raving crackers!

If we can't write on one side of the paper, what *can* we do?"

The assistant editor was standing, proud and important, on the fringe of the group. "You can write on the other side, can't you?" he asked reasonably.

"How are we to know which the other side is?"

"It doesn't really matter. It's just that it's easier for the editors to correct if you only write on one side at a time; or rather ..."

"You mean, we mustn't write on more than both sides altogether?" asked Atkinson.

"Yes—er, no, you coot. It's obvious what it means if you've got any sense."

Venables turned again to the rules. "*Take your made-up poem or about twenty lines of your best handwriting to the Competition Editor's Office, Tuck Box Room, and don't forget to write 'Comp' in the top left-hand corner.*"

"I can't reach the top left-hand corner of the tuck-box room unless I stand on the table," Atkinson objected.

"It doesn't mean that, you ancient ruin! You're just not *trying* to understand." Darbishire clutched his forehead in exasperation, and the action knocked his glasses askew so that they sat across his nose at the angle of a percentage sign. He had spent some time in compiling the rules and had gone to the trouble of adding: *The Editor's indecision is final.* It was, therefore, understandable that he resented these flippant remarks.

"Come on, Venables; Darbi's getting batey," said Atkinson. "Let's go and have a shot at making up a few wads of poetry."

When Jennings awoke next morning the thought of food was uppermost in his mind. There was nothing unusual about this, for it was one of his favourite waking thoughts; but on this occasion it brought no feeling of joy. Fish and sponge cakes: both were items on the day's programme which called for skilful handling.

He knew he could rely on Darbishire to help him in the first project, but the second depended upon the co-operation of his Aunt Angela and this was a cause for anxiety. His aunt was kindhearted, but she had an uncertain, sieve-like memory; vague promises to make sponge cakes would be of no use if the goods failed to arrive in time for the prize-giving. Already the more legible writers had begun uncrossing their nibs and searching for clean blotting paper, while the poets were scratching their heads and looking thoughtful.

Aunt Angela's help must be enlisted without delay, Jennings decided. He would write to her at once and underline his requirements twice in red ink: *two double-decker jam sponge cakes, not less than approx. nine inches across, please*. That should do the trick!

He started the letter during morning break and finished it in Mr. Hind's history lesson. The next problem was the clearance of Mr. Wilkins' chimney, and the two boys put the finishing touches to their plan as they changed for football that afternoon.

"Now, don't forget, Darbi, we've got to get cracking on this wheeze just as though it was an important military operation," Jennings explained. "I shall be the commandos doing the dangerous part, while you're the supporting troops engaging the enemy to give me cover. Zero hour's directly after football, and we beetle off to action stations as soon as Old Wilkie blows for time."

"Hadn't we better synchronise our watches?" inquired the supporting troops.

"How can we? We shan't be wearing them during the game. It's all quite simple, really. You just have to keep him nattering on the pitch till you see me wave from the quad. That means I've liberated the parcel and dumped it out of sight somewhere."

The scheme, though flawless in theory, did not work out so smoothly as they had hoped.

The weather was blustery that afternoon; the game was scrappy and Mr. Wilkins was not sorry when the time came for him to blow the final whistle.

As the echoes of the shrill blast died away, Darbishire approached the referee with a look of earnest inquiry on his features.

"Sir, please sir, would you explain something, please sir?"

"Well, what is it? Hurry up, I don't want to hang about out here all day."

"Well, sir, if, say, supposing I was centre forward for the white shirts and I kicked the ball to Temple, who was on the right wing with nobody in front of him, and he missed it and, say, Binns, who was left-half for the colours, got it and headed it to Martin-Jones, only it was intercepted by Atkinson, who was a white, and he hoofed it down to Bromwich major at left back, and Thompson was coming up behind him in a coloured shirt with no one in front of him—would it be off-side, sir?"

Mr. Wilkins was out of his depth. "Would *who* be off-side?"

"Well, say, Thompson, for instance, sir. Or if not him, then one of the others—if say supposing, just before that, somebody else, like Brown or Paterson or someone had beetled up from nowhere into the other side's penalty area, sir?"

Mr. Wilkins was unwilling to give a decision on such tangled data. "It depends on who played the ball last, and anyway, I can't follow what you're talking about. Come up to my room with me and I'll lend you a copy of the laws of the game; then you can work it out for yourself." He turned and made for the touchline.

Darbishire hopped from one foot to the other in frustration and grief. Jennings would not have had nearly enough time to carry out his part of the programme. "Oh, sir, wait! Don't go, sir, yet, sir, please sir! Do you think I played well, this afternoon, sir?"

"Frankly, no."

"Oh, well, if I go in goal now, will you give me a few practice shots to save, sir?"

"Not in these shoes, thank you. Besides, it's too cold to stay outside. I'm going indoors to put a match to my fire. I'm expecting the Headmaster at four o'clock and he won't want to ..."

Mr. Wilkins broke off and looked more closely at the small figure hopping round him in agitated circles. There was something unusual about the boy's appearance, and for a moment he couldn't think what it was. Then he said: "Where are your spectacles, Darbishire?"

"My spectacles!" Darbishire bit his lip and his hand rose to his face in alarm. "Oh, goodness, sir! I must have lost them on the pitch. I know I had them when the game started."

Mr. Wilkins tut-tutted at the everlasting carelessness of small boys. Then he improvised a search party of every one who had not already disappeared indoors, and for ten minutes they picked their way gingerly up and down the field. It was Temple who found the missing glasses hanging perilously from the goal-net by one ear-piece.

"Coo, thanks ever so much, Temple. I was getting worried about them," beamed Darbishire. He remembered now; he had hung them on the net for safety when he had been sent to keep goal during the second half: oddly enough, it made little difference to his performance as a goalkeeper whether he could see the ball clearly or not.

Darbishire replaced his glasses and thanked the unwilling searchers a dozen times. As he followed them off the field he couldn't help thinking how strange it was that his carefully planned delaying tactics had failed, yet his object had been achieved by genuine means. It was safe now for Mr. Wilkins to go indoors, and light fifty fires if he wanted to. Jennings would have had plenty of time.

But Jennings was finding things more difficult than he had bargained for. He had hurried off the field at the scheduled time and reached Mr. Wilkins' room safely. No one was about, so he opened the door and went in. A fire was laid in the grate, but fortunately it had not been lighted. That was a bit of luck, he decided. If any one had put a match to it while the chimney was still blocked it would have ... But nobody had, so why waste time thinking about it!

In two strides he was at the fireplace; then, kneeling he reached up the chimney—and his clutching fingers closed on empty air!

For a moment panic seized him. Mr. Wilkins must have found it! Then reason returned and told him that this was not possible. Mr. Wilkins was not the sort of person to keep such a discovery secret. There would have been an immediate outcry, with alarms and excursions to all parts of the building in an effort to find the culprit.

Jennings groped again and poked his head into the fireplace, but he could see nothing. He must have pushed it farther up than he had thought; perhaps the chimney had a ledge; perhaps it had ...

Jennings froze! Footsteps were approaching along the corridor—heavy, adult-sounding footsteps. Would they pass by or would they come in?

He was not kept long in suspense, for it was barely three seconds later that the door swung open and M. W. B. Pemberton-Oakes, Esq., Headmaster, stood on the threshold.

CHAPTER 6

THE INCOMPLETE ANGLERS

ACUTELY embarrassed, Jennings scrambled to his feet while the Headmaster stood silently noting the grimy hands and the freckles of soot.

"May I inquire what you're doing, Jennings?"

It was impossible to tell from the Headmaster's tone whether he was surprised or angry, for he was a man who seldom betrayed his feelings.

"I was—er, I was just putting my head up the chimney, sir."

"So I observe; and I am somewhat at a loss to understand why."

Jennings shifted his feet uncomfortably. "I just wanted to see if I could see up, sir."

"I see." Mr. Pemberton-Oakes had been dealing with inquiring minds for so long that the explanation seemed reasonable. Thirty-five years of schoolmastering had taught him that eleven-year-old boys would perform the most extraordinary actions for reasons which no adult could hope to understand. They would stand on their heads without apparent cause and paint walrus moustaches on their faces with watercolours; they would smear their fingers with marmalade and plasticine and then set about some task requiring delicacy of touch—such as dealing a pack of cards or practising the violin. Thus it came as no surprise to Mr. Pemberton-Oakes to hear that Jennings should feel an urge to poke his head up the chimney to see how much blackness met his gaze. Such actions were only to be expected. His eye travelled down from the soot-streaked face to the muddy boots.

"I assume, Jennings, that Mr. Wilkins has sent you here to await his arrival," said the Headmaster. "But that is no reason why you should have come upstairs in your football boots. Go down and change them at once."

"Yes, sir."

As Jennings left the room he noticed that Mr. Pemberton-Oakes made no movement to follow. Obviously he had come to see Mr. Wilkins and intended to wait in the study until the master arrived. What on earth was to be done?

Jennings descended to the book-lockers in a daze of indecision and he was still staring at his football boots with unseeing eyes when Darbishire slapped him between the shoulder blades a few minutes later.

"All fixed up nicely?" Darbishire inquired brightly. "I kept Old Wilkie out of the way, but you never came and gave me the all-clear. Just as well you snaffled that parcel when you did, because he's just gone upstairs to light his fire."

"What!" Jennings spun round like a weathercock.

"Yes; he's making it cosy because the Archbeako's coming to see him." And then something in his friend's glassy expression spread a horrible doubt through his mind. "You—you don't mean you've made a bish of it?"

Jennings nodded. "The Archbeako ankled in in the middle and ticked me off for sticking my head up the chimney with my football boots on."

"Oh, fish-hooks! Why didn't you take your boots off first?"

"I wouldn't have been able to see any better if I had—I haven't got luminous toe-nails."

"No, what I meant was … oh, never mind!" Darbishire sounded badly rattled. "The damage is done now, and there'll be the most frantic hoo-hah when it all comes out."

"When *what* comes out? The news or the parcel?"

"Both, I suppose. First we didn't get rid of the beastly stuff when Mr. Carter told us to; second, we opened up a fried fish shop in the darkroom; third, Mr. Wilkins will get asphyxiated when he lights his fire, and fourth—well, anything might happen. My father says that when sorrows come, they …"

But Jennings was not listening. He was frowning into space and racking his brains for a way to meet this new crisis. Suddenly, he smote his brow and said: "I've got it, Darbi! We'll go fishing."

Darbishire stared at his friend in horror-struck amazement. "We wizard well *won't*!" he said decisively. "I've had enough of that sort of caper to last me for a long time. Any one arranging fishing trips, or even serving it up with chips, can include me out of the party, thanks very much."

"No, listen; we can't get at it from below, so we'll have a bash from above. All we need is a hook and a long piece of string, and there we are."

The essence of Jennings' plan lay in the fact that Mr. Wilkins' chimney emerged on to a flat roof, surrounded by a stone balustrade. Very properly, the roof was out of bounds, but it could be reached from an attic window which opened directly on to it. If the parcel was not too tightly wedged, might it not be possible to retrieve it by lowering a hook down the chimney?

"H'm! It *might*! And it might *not*!" objected Darbishire, when the details of the scheme became clear.

"It's our only chance," Jennings urged. "Let's get changed quickly; then I'll go and bag a hook from somewhere while you scavenge for a bit of string."

They changed out of their football clothes in record time, and as he was bundling his sweater on to his peg, Jennings' eye lighted upon a small brass hook screwed into the wall beside it. Its real purpose was to accommodate the overflow of football garments, but it would serve equally well for a roof-angling expedition. He was unscrewing it when Darbishire returned from a scavenge hunt round the boot lockers, clutching a tangled mass of knotted string.

"How long would you say Wilkie's chimney is?" the scavenger asked.

Jennings considered. "About as long as a fairly medium-sized piece of string, I should think."

"Yes, that's what I thought. This ought to do the trick, if I can get the knots out; and I'll join my football boot lace on the end just to be on the safe side."

After that they found a broken door-knob in the wastepaper basket and tied it on as a weight, to ensure that the hook would go right down the chimney.

Then, armed with hook, line and sinker, they tiptoed up to the attic, climbed out on to the roof and hurried towards their action station.

For the second time in twenty minutes zero hour had arrived!

Mr. Wilkins sat on a hard, upright chair beside his unlighted fire and hoped that the Headmaster would not stay too long. It was not that Mr. Wilkins was unsociable, but rather that his visitor was occupying the only comfortable chair in the room, and he had been looking forward to sitting there himself.

However, Mr. Pemberton-Oakes seemed in no hurry to cut short the discussion on the mathematics syllabus which was the reason for his visit. Already he had expounded his views for over quarter of an hour, while his assistant said: "Yes, I quite agree," at regular intervals.

"Now this question of a weekly algebra test for all forms," the Headmaster was saying. "I consider it a matter of the greatest importance that boys should be made to check their answers in order to avoid absurd and incongruous results."

"Yes, sir, I quite agree," said Mr. Wilkins.

"Furthermore, we must impress upon them the practical value of alge-

braical problems by showing them that x's and y's are merely symbols repre-
senting ..."

But this time, Mr. Wilkins wasn't listening. He had just caught sight of
something even more absurd and incongruous than an unchecked algebra result,
and he was staring at the fireplace, his eyes bulging with bewilderment. Surely,
he must be mistaken! It must be some trick of the fading light. He sat bolt
upright and blinked; but when he looked again at the fireplace, the *thing* was
still there.

"... because, unless we succeed in stimulating the boys' interest and holding
their attention, all our work will be so much ..."

The Headmaster stopped, suddenly aware that his assistant's interest was no
longer being stimulated, nor his interest held by the question of the weekly
algebra test. "Really, Wilkins, considering how important the matter is, I think
you might show a little more ... Good gracious!"

Mr. Pemberton-Oakes had seen it now, and in silence the two men stared at
the fireplace where a small brass hook, weighted with a broken doorknob, was
swinging gently to and fro like a noiseless pendulum.

For some seconds they watched, their eyes swivelling from left to right, like
spectators at a tennis tournament. Then Mr. Wilkins spoke.

"I ... I ... *Corwumph*!" he said.

"But what on earth is it?" queried the Headmaster.

"It's a small brass hook, weighted with a broken ..."

"Yes, yes, yes, I can see that, Wilkins. But what's it doing in your fireplace?
Is it some contraption you use for boiling kettles?"

"No, no, I assure you! I don't boil kettles. When I want a cup of tea I usually
go next door to Matron's sitting room. She often makes a pot of tea about ..."

"Wilkins, this is hardly the moment to discuss your domestic arrangements,"
the Headmaster broke in. "Someone is up above on the flat roof. I suggest that
you go and investigate forthwith."

"Yes, yes, of course." And Mr. Wilkins charged away on his errand like a
forward breaking loose from a rugger scrum. The door banged behind him
with a force that dislodged a picture from above the mantelpiece and sent a
current of air swirling about the Headmaster's ankles.

When the tumult had died away, Mr. Pemberton-Oakes had another look at
the fireplace, but the hook had disappeared. "Now, I wonder exactly what is
happening up above," he asked himself.

Things had not been going well on the roof, and Jennings and Darbishire had been beset by difficulties from the moment of their arrival.

To begin with, not *one*, but a whole forest of chimneys stretched their necks into the fading light, and it was impossible to tell which one of them belonged to Mr. Wilkins' study.

"It's hopeless," said Jennings. "We can't go dropping hooks down all of them. We'd better say, *eena meena mina mo* and hope for the best."

Darbishire had a better idea. "Mr. Wilkins is bound to have lit his fire by now," he reported incorrectly. "So it must be one of those with smoke coming out."

Jennings clicked his tongue with impatience. "Don't be such a bogus coot, Darbi! If he *has* lit it, the smoke won't be coming up this way—it'll be back-firing all over his room. I vote we listen at all the ones without smoke and see if we can hear any coughing and spluttering coming up the spout."

They wasted precious minutes with their ears glued to the cowls, but no distress signals came from below. Finally, Jennings selected a chimney at random and dropped the weighted hook down inside.

"It's either this one or the next," he prophesied as the hook disappeared from view, "because Old Wilkie's room looks out over the quad and I ... oh, gosh, Darbi! I've got a bite. There's something on the hook."

"Oh, wacko! First shot, too! Can you hoik it up?"

"I don't know. I'll have a try."

Jennings manoeuvred the hook round and round in the confined space, and presently his efforts were rewarded. He gave a gentle pull and felt the hook rising with its prize embedded on the end.

"I've got it! Wacko!" he cried, his eyes gleaming with triumph.

Darbishire danced happily amongst the chimney pots. Success at the first attempt seemed too good to be true.

It was! And the dancer stopped in the middle of a wild cavort as the hook came to the surface dragging half a disused starling's nest with it.

"Oh, fish-hooks! It's only a bird's nest," Jennings snorted and the gleam of triumph went out of his eyes. "I ought to have guessed, really, because it was quite near the top and I couldn't have shoved the parcel all that way up."

He tried again, and this time the hook sank right down the well of the chimney as the line was paid out from above. Soon the string was stretched to its full length, but the weight had met no obstruction.

Disappointed, Jennings grunted: "Wrong chimney! It must be down to the fireplace by now. I can swing the hook from side to side quite easily, look."

"No good telling me to look," returned Darbishire. "I can't see what's going on down below."

But though Darbishire couldn't, Mr. Wilkins *could*! For it was at that moment that he caught sight of the small brass hook floating gently into the fireplace, and lost the drift of the Headmaster's studied remarks.

Neither Jennings nor Darbishire had any idea of the keen interest with which their salvage operations were being followed on the floor below, and after half a minute of random twiddling, Jennings heaved on the line and the hook rose to chimneypot level.

"We'll try the next one," he said. "We've probably been fishing down Matron's sitting room chimney, by mistake. Golly, wouldn't it have been awful if she'd seen the hook coming down!" He gave a little embarrassed laugh at the absurdity of such a happening.

As they moved to the neighbouring stack, it occurred to Jennings that he might be able to locate the right chimney by straining his eyes into the tunnel of darkness. If there was nothing in the way he should be able to see a pinpoint of light from the fireplace below. He pressed his face on to the rim of the next chimney and opened his eyes wide.

"Whatever are you doing now?" demanded Darbishire, impatiently.

"I'm peering into the darkness in the hope of seeing a light." The answer was not audible to Darbishire for it went straight down the chimney, which amplified the words like a megaphone and sent them booming out of the fire-place in the room below.

It was Matron's room; and she was pouring out a cup of tea when the voice of doom echoed hollowly down her chimney. Fortunately, her nerves were strong, but even so the sudden shock made her leap like a ballerina; the teapot danced in her unsteady grasp like a fire-hose out of control, sending a jet of hot tea into a potted plant on the sideboard.

When she recovered, she sat pondering over the message she had received from outer space! *Peering into the darkness in the hope of seeing a light!* It was as though some minor prophet were warning her of the shape of things to come.

Unaware of the havoc he had created below, Jennings raised his face from the chimneypot. "Can't see a thing," he announced.

"I can," Darbishire jerked out nervously. "I can see Mr. Wilkins coming through the attic window, and he looks as though he's going into the attack at roof-top level."

Darbishire's fears were justified. Mr. Wilkins swept over the flat roof like a ridge of high pressure approaching from Iceland. "I ... I ... Corwumph! What the ... Why the ... What are you two boys doing up here? You've no business to be on the roof. You know perfectly well it's out of bounds."

"Yes, sir."

They stood unhappily before him; Darbishire shock-headed as a dandelion, and Jennings with a thick black circle running right round his face, where Matron's chimneypot had left its mark.

"It strikes me you're going off your heads," stormed Mr. Wilkins. "Of all the nonsensical buffoonery and thick-skulled balderdash, I've ever come across, I've never seen anything to equal the stupidity of dangling guided missiles down fluepipes, without rhyme or reason!" He paused for breath.

"I'm sorry, sir, but we weren't sure it *was* your chimney, sir," Jennings apologised. "We only—er, we only thought it *might* be."

"But you—you *silly* little boy, what do you want to put things down *any one's* chimney for? You're not Father Christmas, are you!"

Mr. Wilkins' voice rose to an exasperated squeak, and his hands seemed to be conducting an invisible orchestra as he groped for some shred of reason behind the fantastic absurdity of such behaviour.

"Well, sir, it was like this," Jennings explained. "We wanted to make sure that your chimney wasn't blocked, in case you decided to light your fire, sir."

"And why should you think that my chimney might be blocked?"

"They are sometimes, sir. And we were quite right as it happened, because we found this thing stuck in yours, sir." Jennings picked up the crumbling bird's nest and held it out for the master's inspection.

Mr. Wilkins looked at the bird's nest with distaste. It was an unpleasant object to have blocking up one's chimney and certain to have caused great inconvenience if it had not been removed before his fire was lighted.

"H'm!" said Mr. Wilkins. The temperature of his indignation dropped a few degrees and he scratched his ear thoughtfully. Perhaps the silly little boys had meant well in their muddle-headed way; though why any one in their senses should choose to play at chimney sweeps on draughty rooftops was more than he could imagine. Moreover, school rules could not be lightly broken for the sake of doing good turns, however praiseworthy the intentions were.

"Go downstairs at once," Mr. Wilkins ordered. "And when you've washed your face, Jennings, I'll set you both some work to keep you out of mischief for the rest of the day."

In gloomy silence the boys climbed back through the attic window and went downstairs to the washroom, where Jennings soaped his face and transferred part of the sooty circle to the rim of the basin; the rest, he wiped off on the roller towel.

"I still don't see what's happened, Darbi," he said. "If that hook really went all the way down Wilkie's chimney, why didn't it collide with the fish-bag?"

"Search me," said Darbishire. "It's just one of those mysterious things no one can explain, like flying saucers and how they built Stonehenge."

The washroom had been empty when they had arrived, but now Venables sauntered in to remove the inkstains from his fingers before tea.

"I've been looking for you two characters," he began. "I've done you a supersonic favour."

"Thanks very much; that was decent of you," said Darbishire. "What was it?"

"Well, Matron wouldn't let me play football this afternoon because of my cold, so I thought it would be a good wheeze to snaffle that fish out of Old Wilkie's chimney while every one was outside on the pitch."

"What!" Jennings spun round so violently that the towel came away from the wall and the roller thudded to the floor with a bang. "You mean to stand there and say it was *you* who took it?"

"Of course it was! I said at breakfast the other day that it shouldn't be too difficult. I'd have told you before only I couldn't find you. Where have you been?"

"Oh, nowhere special," said Darbishire in a flat, resigned voice. "We've only been up on the roof fishing for the beastly thing, with Old Wilkie going berserk and running amok round the chimneypots."

"Super sorrow; I thought you'd be jolly grateful."

"Oh, we are! Please don't apologise. Next to having a picnic in a crocodile swamp, I can't think of a better way of spending a half holiday."

The parcel awaited them in Venables' tuck-box.

"I'm going to bury it directly after tea," Jennings decided. "I've just about had enough trouble over fish and I never want to look another one in the face again."

The tea bell rang and Venables smiled broadly as he turned to leave the room. "That's just where you're going to come unstuck, Jennings. I happen to know we're having kippers for tea this afternoon!"

CHAPTER 7

SPONGE CAKE SUBSTITUTE

The main purpose of the tuck-box room was, naturally enough, to provide storage space for tuck-boxes. It had not been designed as an editorial office, and Jennings and Darbishire had to carry out extensive alterations before they could set about marking the entries for the *Form Three Times* competitions.

First they piled up tuck-boxes to form a flat-topped desk, and then they pinned notices about the room. *Keep Out—Strictly No Admission* was inscribed beneath the window; and in case this should seem rather forbidding, *Visitors Welcomed* hung from the lampshade and struck a kindlier note.

The magazine now boasted two suites of offices. The news department still had its headquarters in the hobbies room, but as this was neither quiet nor private, the editors had set up an annexe amongst the tuck-boxes, where competition entries could be studied without the competitors breathing down the judges' necks and trying to sway their decision.

By the following Friday week the entries had arrived, but the sponge cakes had not. This was serious, for the editor had publicly announced that he would present the prizes before tea on the following day.

"I can't think what's come over Aunt Angela," Jennings said, as he and Darbishire made for their private office after evening preparation. "It's over a week since I wrote and asked for those double-deckers. Mind you, I know she's as absent-minded as two coots, but you would think she'd try to remember, especially as I went to the trouble of underlining it in red ink."

Darbishire nodded. Aunt Angela's forgetfulness had caused chaos the previous term, when she had sent her nephew's postal order to the wrong address.

"People who are like that ought to do something about it," he said. "Like, say, for instance, tying knots in bits of string, so it reminds them to remember not to forget things."

"You'd need something better than a bit of string for Aunt Angela," Jennings retorted. "She's so chronic she'd have to go around with a fifty-foot tow-rope

561

full of clove hitches and bowlines before she'd remember everything." He shook his head sorrowfully. Absent-minded aunts ranked high amongst the problems of modern times to which there was no real answer.

There was still half an hour before bedtime as Jennings settled down at his editorial desk. He took a bundle of envelopes from his jacket pocket and passed them to his assistant.

"You sort the home-made poems from the best handwriters, and I'll use my indecision to pick out the winners. And we'll disqualify any one who hasn't written *Comp* in the top left-hand corner."

Darbishire flicked through the little stack of envelopes, saying: "Comp, comp, comp," as he checked the observance of the rules. "Yes, they've all got it on … oh, wait a sec; here's one that hasn't." He peered in puzzled wonder at the writing on the envelope.

"Bung it in the wastepaper basket," was the editor's stern decision. "We can't have chaps forgetting simple instructions like that, or they'll grow up as scatterbrained as Aunt Angela."

"That's who this one's addressed to!" said Darbishire. "And, what's more, it's in your writing."

"What?"

"Look for yourself. *Miss Angela Birkinshaw*, as plain as a pikestaff."

He tore open the envelope and glanced at the contents: a passage underlined in red ink caught his eye: … *two double-decker jam sponge cakes, not less than approx. nine inches across, please.*

There was reproach in the assistant editor's pale blue eyes as he handed the letter to his chief. "You great, crumbling, addle-pated ruin, Jennings. You've forgotten to post it!"

Jennings stared at the letter in guilty dismay. "Oh, fish-hooks! If that isn't the rottenest bad luck," he complained. "I must have been carrying it round for days, and now it's got mixed up with the competition envelopes. I know I meant to post it because I can remember doing it."

"Don't be crazy! How could you have posted it, if here it is!"

"No, I mean I can remember *meaning* to post it. It's just ozard hard cheese that I forgot."

"It's nothing of the sort. It's chronic absent-mindedness."

It was not often that Darbishire could criticise his friend without having to shoulder part of the blame himself. Now, however, he had a clear case, and could afford to let himself go without restraint.

"Of all the prehistoric clodpolls I ever met, you get the bronze medal for beetle-headedness," he said warmly. "There you sit, calmly wondering whether your aunt's memory has gone to seed, while all the time the letter's still cluttering up your pocket. My father says that people who ..."

"Oh, shut up, Darbi! I may have made a bit of a bish, but you needn't go on tearing strips off about it all night. What we've got to think of now is what on earth we're going to do."

Jennings relapsed into a thoughtful silence, for the snags that lay ahead were only too obvious. The poets and the penmen had worked hard on the competitions, and if the advertised prizes were not forthcoming at the proper time there would be trouble. The reputation of the *Form Three Times* was at stake.

Presently Darbishire said: "I don't suppose the village shop would sell double-decker sponge cakes, but if we got permish. to go into Dunhambury, we might get them there."

"And what do we use for money? I've spent all my rhino on another film for the camera. How much have you got left?"

"About one-and-fourpence. It'd pay the fares all right, but there's not much point in going if we can't afford the cakes when we get there."

Jennings shrugged and said: "We'll think of something! Let's have a look at the comp entries first. If we're lucky they'll all be so ghastly that we shan't have to give any prizes at all. Wouldn't it be smashing if they were!"

It was an odd remark from one who had been hoping that the competition would reveal hidden talent, and it served to show how deeply the lack of prizes was preying on the editor's mind.

There were six envelopes marked *Comp.* The entry was smaller than they had been expecting, for many would-be competitors had dropped out of the running through lack of ideas or pressure of business. The editors were thankful now that the field had been narrowed. Even so, with no prizes to offer, six entries were still half a dozen too many.

Darbishire sorted out the sheets of paper and dropped the envelopes in the wastepaper basket. To his surprise, all six were poems. No one, it seemed, had entered for the handwriting prize after all.

"Well, that's a good thing," said Jennings. "If no one's gone in for it, that makes one sponge cake that we don't need."

"Yes, but who makes the other cake that we *do* need?" demanded the assistant editor.

"Let's not worry about that till we've seen whether the poems are mouldy or not. You read them out while I keep my fingers crossed and hope for the worst."

Darbishire glanced at the first manuscript. "This one's pretty ribby for a kick-off. It's Binns minor's famous effort." And he read aloud:

"'I am a pirate on the sea,
And I am most mel*ancholee*.'"

"You're most *what*?" queried the chief editor.

"It isn't really mel*ancholee*, but you have to say it like that to make it fit. It's—er—it's melancholy, I think. Yes, that's what it really is."

"Never mind what it really *is*. What is it *really*?"

"Melancholy? It means sad. Just like us if we can't think of a prize for ... Well, I'd better get on, hadn't I?

'The crew are in a gloomy mood
Through being rather short of food.
For quite by chance I dropped their suppers
Through the scuppers ...'

That's enough of that one! Isn't it ghastly!"

"Frantic," Jennings agreed. "We needn't give a prize for that, anyway."

Darbishire continued to shake his head sadly over Binns minor's poetic shortcomings. "Now, if I'd been writing that poem, I should have written that last line a lot better. How would it be if I touched it up a bit by altering it to ..."

"But, you radioactive clodpoll, Darbi, we don't *want* to make it better! The worse they are the less chance there is of having to give a prize that we haven't got."

"Sorry; I was forgetting." Darbishire picked up the next sheet and announced: "Cricket—by C. A. Temple.

'You have to have a wicket
Before you can play cricket.
One day, we made 63 for 9,

And the credit for this was all mine.
The bowling was fast, but in spite of that,
Not an eyelid did I bat.'"

The assistant editor stopped reading and giggled. "Golly, isn't it feeble!"

"It's worse than that. All that stuff about his eyelids not batting doesn't even make sense," Jennings replied. "If he hadn't had his innings they might have written, *Temple—Did not Bat* in the scorebook. But they wouldn't put it about his eyelids, would they?"

"I don't think you quite understand," Darbishire explained. "It's what they call odi-itic—er—idiomatic, I should say."

Jennings did not argue the point. With two poems already rejected, the chances of having to award a prize were growing more remote; his only fear was that as the remaining poems could hardly be worse than the first two, they must be better. He stopped worrying, however, after hearing Bromwich major's rhymed couplets on how to build a rabbit hutch. Atkinson's effort about a visit to the zoo was, if anything, worse; and Thompson's poetic inspiration had ceased to flow after the first three lines, and his entry was rejected out of hand.

"That only leaves one more," said Jennings, as contribution number five slithered into the wastepaper basket. "Gosh, I do hope it's mouldy."

Darbishire glanced at the writing on the last sheet of paper and said: "This one's by Venables. Listen!

'Break, break, break,
On thy cold grey stones, O Sea!
And I would that my tongue could utter
The thoughts that arise in me.

O well for the fisherman's boy,
That he shouts with his sister at play!
O well for the sailor lad,
That he sings in his boat on the bay!'"

Jennings was deeply impressed. "Phew! That's not bad, is it! Who did you say wrote it?"

"Venables."

"He never did!"

"He must have done. That's Venables' writing; I'd know it anywhere. Not a blot on the whole page. Hang on, there's a bit more yet.

'And the stately ships go on
To their haven under the hill;
But O for the touch of a vanish'd hand,
And the sound of a voice that is still!

Break, break, break,
At the foot of thy crags, O Sea!
But the tender grace of a day that is dead
Will never come back to me.'"

There was a short silence. Then, rather grudgingly, Jennings said: "H'm! Well, his poem's certainly a lot better than the others. Mind you, I don't suppose Wordsworth and Tennyson and all that lot would think much of it, but it's not bad for a chap of twelve."

"That's what I was thinking," Darbishire answered. "We'll wizard well *have* to give him a prize for a super decent effort like that. Unless, of course, we can find something wrong with it."

But though they pored over the verses for some time, they were unable to make any serious criticisms. "There must be *something* the matter with it," Jennings argued. "What about the way he keeps on repeating 'O well'? He says 'O well for the fisherman's boy' and 'O well for the sailor lad.' People wouldn't really say that, would they?"

"Perhaps he couldn't think of anything else to put, so he just thought, 'O well,' and let it go at that."

Jennings frowned thoughtfully at the sheet of paper. "We can't disqualify it just because of that; somebody'll kick up a hoo-hah if we do. I suppose we'll just have to think of something else for a prize, that's all. If only I hadn't forgotten to post that letter!" He shook his head in self-reproach. "Oh well, I suppose it can't be helped."

Darbishire looked up sharply. "There you are! You've just said it."

"Said what?"

"'O well.' You said people wouldn't really say that."

The editor thumped his desk in exasperation. "Look here, Darbishire, what's the good of my trying to find something wrong if you keep cracking everything up to the skies and saying how marvellous it is?"

"Sorry, Jen. If you think it's rotten, don't give a prize."

"I *don't* think it's rotten. It's supersonic, and I'd give him a sponge cake like a shot, if only I'd got one to give. Let's think what we could dish him out with instead."

No word was spoken for some minutes as the editors paced to and fro among the tuck-boxes, racking their brains until they ached. But neither of them could think of a prize which was not immediately vetoed by the other. Darbishire's proposal that Jennings should award his camera was met with an indignant refusal: and Jennings' suggestion of Darbishire's four-bladed penknife led to a bitter and fruitless argument.

The discussion was interrupted by the ringing of the dormitory bell and the boys went up to bed with the problem unsolved. As they undressed, they were surrounded by the unsuccessful competitors demanding to know how they had fared.

"Have you marked those poems yet?" shrilled Binns minor, twirling his socks before his face like contra-rotating propellers.

"Yes. There was only one decent one," Jennings replied.

"Mine?"

"No. Yours went into the wastepaper basket."

"Oh!" The propellers stopped whirling and Binns minor turned away, as gloomy as the melancholy pirate of his imagination. He had spent a lot of time on that poem.

"What about mine?" queried Temple.

"Yours was pretty feeble, too," said Jennings. "I shouldn't really tell you who's the winner, because it's still on the secret list, but if you promise not to spread it, I don't mind saying that Venables' effort was a smasher."

"Good old Ven!" cried Temple generously; and unmindful of official secrets, he shouted down the dormitory: "Hey, Venables, you've won first prize in the wallpaper comp."

Venables raised a partly-washed face from the basin. "Have I? Oh, wacko!" he exclaimed, and came hurrying along, showering a spray of soap bubbles over every one in his path. "When do I get the sponge cake?" he demanded.

The editor seemed not to hear, and the question was repeated. Then he said: "Well, there's been a bit of a bish over that. There aren't any going just at present."

"What! You mouldy swizzler, Jennings! I demand a prize! You promised it!" Venables' sense of fair play was outraged; and indeed the whole dormitory was stirred by such rank injustice.

"You can't get away with that, Jennings! You could be had up for fraudulent confidence tricks," said Atkinson.

"If I don't get my prize, there's going to be some bashing-up going on round these parts," threatened the angry winner: he was far too indignant to notice the uncomfortable trickles of water coursing down his chest.

"All right, all *right*. Don't get in a flap. You'll get your prize; don't you worry!"

"Double-decker sponge cake?"

"No; something better. Something ten times better! It's a secret till the prize-giving tomorrow, but I guarantee you'll like it."

These were wild statements, and Jennings knew it; but the reputation of the *Form Three Times* was at stake, and no other course was open to him.

Reassured, Venables returned to his washing and the crowd faded away from Jennings' bed. When they had gone, Darbishire said: "I'm jolly glad you've thought of something, Jen. What is it?"

"I don't know, yet."

"But you just said ... Oh, fish-hooks!" His friend's announcement had sounded so convincing that Darbishire was sure some bright idea must have occurred to him. Now, it seemed, the editors would be branded as unscrupulous confidence tricksters—to say nothing of the threatened violence which would have to be faced if Venables' demands were not met. Moreover, the prize must be something worth having. It would be asking for trouble to foist some worthless object on a winner who was looking forward to something ten times better than double-decker sponge cake.

"Couldn't we sell something, and buy something else with the money?" Darbishire spoke in low tones so that none but Jennings might hear.

"I'm not parting with my camera or my printing set, thanks very much."

"No, I mean some old relic that's worth a lot just because it's ancient. If only we'd got something like that! You'd be surprised how much antiques and things are worth. My father knows a man who's got a book written by some old geezer round about Julius Cæsar's time, and he says it's worth about a hundred pounds."

"Who says—Julius Cæsar?"

"No, you clodpoll! My father says. It's a rare first edition, you see."

"What's the good of telling me all this? I haven't got anything written about Julius Cæsar's time. Except, of course, my Latin book. They're always saying what sort of a time he had, in that."

"Oh no, that's no good at all. I'm talking about valuable first editions that collectors go in for when they're about a hundred years old—the books, I mean—not the collectors."

"I bet my Latin book's not far short of a hundred, anyway," Jennings maintained. "It's terribly dog-eared; and what's more, I'm pretty sure it's got 'first edition' printed inside. There are only about two like it in the whole school; apart from me and Venables, every one else has got much newer ones."

"Don't be a coot, Jennings! You're not going to tell me that your Latin book is really valuable!"

Jennings' voice rose in exasperation. "But you great bazooka, Darbi—it was you who just said it *was*! When I thought I hadn't got an ancient priceless book, you told me how rare they were. Now I find I *have* got one you tell me they're no good. Make your mind up, for goodness' sake! You can't have it both ways!"

Darbishire didn't want it both ways. Nothing would have pleased him more than to discover that Jennings' Latin book was as valuable as the mouldering tome belonging to his father's friend. He knew that *Grimshaw's Latin Grammar* was in short supply for there were not enough copies to go round the class; and if Jennings really *did* own a first edition …! "Go and fetch it, Jen. We might be able to find out, if we examine it closely."

It was nearly time for the dormitory light to be put out, but Jennings was willing to risk the master-on-duty's wrath when such an important issue was at stake. Quietly, he slipped out of the dormitory and down the stairs to his classroom.

A few moments ticked by while he rummaged in his untidy desk; somehow the larger books always seemed to rise to the top, and leave the smaller ones in a muddled heap below. But at last he found it. *A First Latin Grammar by Arnold Grimshaw, M.A., D. Litt. Late Lecturer in Classical Studies in the University of Oxbridge. First Edition MCMLII.*

Jennings furrowed his brow as he strove to translate the Roman numerals. *MCMLII*. That must be ... Er—um ... Yes, of course: 1852!

Holding the precious volume more carefully than usual, he slammed down his desk-lid and scampered back to his dormitory. As he ran, his mind was busy working out a plan of campaign. First he must find out, upon good authority, if the book was as valuable as the evidence suggested. If it was, he would sell it for—well, Darbishire had mentioned a hundred pounds as a likely figure; but even if it produced rather less—say about ten shillings, for instance—there would still be enough to buy Venables his sponge cake and leave some over for a modern edition of the book at the published price of four-and-sixpence. This part of the scheme was most important; for though the book was his to dispose of, his imagination boggled at what the Headmaster would say if he arrived in class without one. Why, if the Head ever got to hear of ...!

Jennings stopped dead in his tracks, for the object of his thoughts was standing at the top of the stairs, regarding him with the look which he reserved for boys who were discovered out of their dormitory after lights out.

"Come here, Jennings," said Mr. Pemberton-Oakes.

It was too late to conceal the Latin book; and with an empty feeling inside him, Jennings realised that Question Time was about to begin.

"Are you aware, Jennings, that your dormitory light was put out nearly five minutes ago?"

Jennings fumbled with his dressing gown cord and answered with a low buzzing noise which could have meant either "Yessir" or "Nosir."

"Then I am somewhat at a loss to understand, Jennings, why you are not in bed."

"I just slipped down to my classroom to get a book, sir."

Mr. Pemberton-Oakes raised one eyebrow. He held strong views about reading under the bedclothes by torchlight.

"And how, may I ask, do you propose to read in total darkness?" But at that moment he caught sight of the book which Jennings was holding, and his expression changed. "*Grimshaw's Latin Grammar*, eh! Well, well, Jennings, I must confess that I am surprised at your choice of bedtime reading. Does this indicate that you are at last proposing to take the subject seriously?"

Jennings smiled modestly. "Oh, I don't know, sir. I just thought I'd have a look through it before lights out if there was time. Or perhaps in the morning, before I get up, sir."

The Headmaster nodded approvingly. He had misjudged the boy. Admittedly, his work had not shown much promise so far, but if he was willing to pursue his studies in his free time, there was still hope of improvement.

"I congratulate you, Jennings. You have left it too late for this evening, but I can imagine no better way of starting tomorrow than by putting in ten minutes' concentrated revision of *Grimshaw's Grammar*. A most invaluable book."

"Thank you, sir." It seemed a good moment to obtain an expert opinion. "Would you say it was very rare, sir?"

"It's almost unobtainable, if that's what you mean. I've had copies on order for months," the Headmaster replied. "A very interesting man—Dr. Grimshaw. I used to attend his lectures at the university."

Jennings opened his eyes wide in astonishment. "You—you've actually seen him, sir?"

"Frequently."

Jennings continued to gape. At that rate, Dr. Grimshaw must be about a hundred and fifty years old. No wonder he was interesting!

"It says here, sir," he pointed out politely, "that he wrote this book in 1852."

Mr. Pemberton-Oakes glanced at the title page. "No, Jennings. *MCMLII* is—well, work it out for yourself. A mental revision of Roman numerals will do you no harm before you drop off to sleep. Good night!"

He hummed softly to himself as he strode off down the landing. It was most gratifying that his patient efforts to interest the boy in Latin were now beginning to bear fruit—most gratifying! Of course it was stupid of him to make a mistake of a hundred years in translating the Roman numerals, but a little concentrated revision would soon put that right.

Jennings hurried into his dormitory and groped his way to his bed, to find Darbishire anxiously awaiting his return.

"Have you got it, Jennings?" he breathed in the hissing, voiceless whisper he used after silence had been called.

"Yes. And you're quite right. The Archbeako says it's as priceless as coots' eggs."

"Golly! The Head actually said that?"

"He used different words, but that's what he meant. Here you are; see for yourself."

Darbishire stretched into the darkness and his hand closed upon the precious volume. Then he burrowed head-first down his bed and switched on his torch. From without, a pale, ghostly haze could be seen shimmering round the bed, as though the blankets were phosphorescent.

Very carefully Darbishire studied the pages. They were yellowed and musty: which was not to be wondered at, for Jennings had left the book out all night in a thunderstorm. But to Darbishire's unpractised eye the discoloured markings were proof of old age. He spent some time poring over the author's qualifications on the title page, and then he switched off his torch and crawled back to the surface where the air was fresher. His untucked bedclothes gave him some trouble for the rest of the night.

"It's a rare first edition, all right," he confided to Jennings in a whisper. "I don't suppose it's as valuable as my father's friend's antique geezer's book is, but it's bound to be worth something. All really old books are."

Jennings raised his head from his pillow. "We were wrong about that. The Archbeako seemed to think it was quite modern."

"He must be stark raving bats! Any one can see how old it is, and what's more the author's dead, so that proves it."

"How do you know he's dead?"

"It says so in the book. It calls him a *Late Lecturer.*"

"That's nothing to go by. It probably means he's never on time for his lectures."

"I bet you it doesn't!" Darbishire maintained. "I bet you a million pounds that 'late' means dead. I read in the paper once about a chap called the late Mr. Somebody-or-other and it turned out he'd been dead for years."

Jennings wasn't convinced. "But how can this book have been written by a dead man?"

"Well, perhaps he wasn't dead when he wrote it, but he is now," came the logical answer.

"Have it your own way; it isn't worth arguing about. The point is that whether he's alive or not, I've got the Head's word of honour that the book's invaluable. So first thing tomorrow, we'll decide how we can sell it for a lot of rhino."

They fell silent then, and in the few minutes before he dropped asleep, Jennings' mind was picturing wealthy collectors bidding frantically against one another for possession of the late lecturer's contribution to classical studies. It was kind of Fate, he thought, to point such a clear way out of their difficulties.

CHAPTER 8

THE BRILLIANT FORGERY

IDEAS which seem brilliant at bedtime often lose their appeal when reviewed in the clear light of morning: cracks appear in the structure of flawless plans, and damp patches seep through the joints of watertight schemes.

Thus it was that, as Jennings stirred his breakfast tea on the following morning, his high hopes of the night before dissolved as swiftly as the sugar in his cup.

To begin with, there was no second-hand bookshop nearer than the market town of Dunhambury, and Mr. Carter would never give them permission to make so long a journey. And even supposing they reached Dunhambury, would they be able to find a bookseller willing to pay anything from ten shillings to a hundred pounds for the works of A. Grimshaw, D.Litt? It seemed extremely unlikely.

He was about to confide his doubts to Darbishire, when Venables spoke from across the table.

"You'd better not forget my prize, Jennings. It's got to be something good, too, or else ..." And he narrowed his eyes and sliced off the top of his egg with gestures full of meaning.

"Yes, what's it going to be?" demanded Atkinson.

Jennings looked thoughtful. "I can't tell you yet, because"—he might as well admit it— "well, because I haven't got it yet." And as a storm of protest rose from across the table, he added quickly: "But it's all right. I'm going to sell my Latin book and buy something with the rhino."

"Sell your Latin book!" The table was aghast. Eyebrows shot up like window-blinds, and mouths which had opened to receive spoonfuls of egg remained ajar in sheer astonishment.

"Yes, as a matter of fact I happen to know it's worth quite a bit. It's a genuine first edition, you see."

"But what will you use in class?"

"Oh, that's all right. The Archbeako won't know, because I shall buy a later model of the same make."

The words were thrown out casually, and only Jennings knew the uncertainty that lay behind them. But there could be no going back now; there would be a dozen witnesses to speak against him if he failed in his quest.

There was no football fixture that Saturday, and village leave was granted after lunch. That meant that the boys might go as far as the village and buy sweets at the *Linbury Stores and Post Office* or doughnuts and ginger-pop at the little cottage with the notice in the window: *Chas Lumley—Home-made Cakes and Bicycles Repaired*. But Jennings and Darbishire had other plans.

After lunch, they gave in their names to Mr. Carter and set off down the drive; but before they had reached the gates there was a pounding of footsteps behind them, and Venables came rushing to catch them up. In his hand he carried a copy of *Grimshaw's Latin Grammar*.

"Hang on a sec," he panted, as he drew level. "Are you characters *really* going to Dunhambury?"

"Ssh! Don't broadcast it," hissed Jennings. "If Mr. Carter finds out we're going farther than Linbury village there'll be the most supersonic blitz."

Venables looked up and down the drive to make sure they were unobserved. Then he said: "It's about these Latin books. Mine's a first edition, too, so I wondered if you'd mind taking it along with yours."

"I wouldn't sell yours if I were you," Darbishire advised. "Jen's only sacrificing his because of the sponge-cake famine."

"Oh, go on; be decent!"

Jennings considered. It would be just as easy to dispose of two volumes as it would be to sell a single copy, if the Headmaster's word was to be trusted. "All right; bung it over," he agreed.

"Coo, super thanks," grinned Venables. "There's just one thing, though. Make sure you can buy a cheaper edition before you get rid of the rare one. The Archbeako will go berserk if I haven't got a book for his class on Monday."

Jennings and Darbishire hurried down the drive and turned out of the school gates. There was a Request Stop some fifty yards along the road, but it would be risky to board a bus so near the school premises, so they made for the fare stage round the corner.

Time was short, for Dunhambury lay some five miles to the west and they were due to report back to school by half-past four. For quarter of an hour they waited by the bus stop, flipping their fingers with impatience as the precious minutes ticked by. At last a single decker bus appeared round the bend and stopped in answer to their frenzied waving.

The journey to Dunhambury was uneventful. Darbishire bought the tickets and made a note in his diary to claim his expenses if the expedition should prove successful. Twenty minutes later they were picking their way through the Saturday afternoon shopping crowds and looking with a desperate urgency for a second-hand booksellers.

"Oh, fish-hooks, this is feeble," lamented Darbishire, after they had wandered the length of the main street without success. "It's all ironmongers and corn-chandlers along here."

"There must be one somewhere," Jennings urged. "Unless they're all too busy mongering iron and chandling corn to have any time over for books around these parts."

"Shall we ask?"

"Whether they're too busy to read?"

"No, you clodpoll! Shall we ask where a shop is?"

"Better not. This is a top priority secret mission, don't forget, and we don't want every one to ..." Jennings stopped and looked at his friend oddly. "You crazy maniac, Darbi, what have you still got your school cap on for? Do you want every one to know?"

"Oh, sorry." Darbishire snatched off the offending garment and stuffed it in his pocket.

They turned down a side street, past garages and greengrocers and little cafés; and they were beginning to despair of finding what they wanted, when Jennings came to a sudden halt and pointed hopefully at a small shop on the other side of the road.

"Look, Darbi. Over there! It's just the sort of place, isn't it!"

Darbishire looked. "Golly, yes! Masses of ancient, prehistoric books! I shouldn't be surprised if some of them go right back to William Caxton's time."

They hurried across the road for a closer inspection of the premises.

Thos. Barlow—Bookseller was inscribed in faded gilt letters above the shop front. Books were heaped untidily in the window, but it was so long since the glass had been cleaned that it was impossible to read their titles. Outside on the pavement, more volumes were stacked on an unsteady trestle table.

"Pretty risky, leaving these out in the street," Darbishire remarked. "They might be valuable first editions, like my father's friend's priceless old relic."

Jennings removed a well-thumbed copy of the *Complete Works of Alfred, Lord Tennyson* from the top of the pile and blew the dust off its covers.

"I should think this one must be pretty expensive—it's fat enough," he observed. "Half a mo—it's got the price inside."

"A hundred pounds?" queried Darbishire hopefully.

"No, ninepence. Perhaps it's only a second edition, though. Let's go in, shall we!"

It was a dark little shop, and just for a moment they thought it was empty: for Thomas Barlow, bookseller, was a man who matched his surroundings so closely that he might have been camouflaged to tone with his dingy background. Standing there behind the counter, he seemed as faded as the gilt lettering above his door; his clothes were as dusty and dog-eared as the books on his shelves, and he peered at his customers through spectacles no cleaner than his plate-glass window.

"Well?" he inquired, in a high-pitched croak.

Jennings handed him the two copies of the book he carried. "How much would these be worth, please?" he asked anxiously.

Mr. Barlow pushed his spectacles on to his forehead so that he could see more clearly.

"H'm. *Grimshaw's First Latin Grammar.* Ah, yes, a very good book, this. Worth its weight in gold."

He flicked through the pages and seemed not to notice the frequent ink and finger stains and the occasional missing page. "Very good condition, they are. Beautiful binding," he assured them.

"You really think so? Oh, wacko! D'you hear that, Darbi! We're in the money, this time." Jennings turned back to the counter. "How much, then, please?" he asked.

Mr. Barlow pursed his lips and looked up at the ceiling. "Let's say five shillings each, shall we?"

"Oh! Is that all?" Jennings could not keep the disappointment out of his voice. Five shillings seemed a far cry from a hundred pounds. Why, it was barely enough to buy copies of the cheaper edition and left practically nothing for Venables' prize.

"They're a bargain at the price," wheezed Mr. Barlow. "You wouldn't buy them cheaper than that, anywhere."

"*Buy* them! But I don't want to buy them—I want to *sell* them," Jennings insisted.

The bookseller's gaze came down from the ceiling and he looked at his customers sharply. "Let me get this straight," he said. "Didn't you get these books from that table outside my shop?"

"Heavens, no! We brought them with us. They're ours—really they are!"

"How do I know you're speaking the truth?" came the unexpected reply. "I've been caught that way before. People bring me in a book and I give them a good price for it, and all the time it's my own property they've picked up outside the door. I fetched a policeman to the last one I caught playing that game."

"Oh, but honestly, we're not playing any game. You must believe us!" Jennings' tone was urgent. The situation was delicate enough as it was; if the police were called in, there was no knowing where the whole miserable fiasco would end. He began to wish they had never embarked on the scheme. Ever since breakfast that morning his enthusiasm had been cooling: now, it had become ice-bound.

But apparently the bookseller was satisfied with his customer's answer, for he picked up the volumes again and grunted: "These books aren't much good to me. Been knocked about too much. Pages missing and what-all."

"But you just said what good condition they were in," Darbishire pointed out.

"M'yes, but that was before I knew you wanted to *sell* them. Tell you what— I'll give you threepence each for them."

"Threepence! Gosh, that's a swindle!" Jennings felt suddenly angry. "They were worth five shillings each a minute ago when you thought we wanted to buy them."

Mr. Barlow arched his eyebrows and the movement sent his glasses slithering down on to his nose again.

"That's business, sonny," he explained in his husky croak. "These old copies aren't worth … Hey, just a moment! I had someone in asking for *Grimshaw's Grammar* not so long ago. If I've got a customer waiting, I might see my way to …." His voice trailed off as he searched beneath the counter for his order book. Soon his head came into view once more and a parched smile was spread thinly across his face.

"Yes, I thought so! The Headmaster of Linbury Court Preparatory School asked me to send him any copies I came across."

He seized the two volumes and planked three sixpences down on the counter. "Ninepence each, I'm giving you. That's three times the proper price. You can't want fairer than that, eh!"

Jennings and Darbishire stared at Mr. Barlow in horrified dismay. Their minds reeled at the thought of Mr. Pemberton-Oakes paying five shillings for a book which he fondly believed to be in Jennings' desk. Why, they couldn't even have accepted a hundred pounds a volume in circumstances like that!

"I—I don't want to sell them. I want them back," Jennings jerked out.

But Mr. Barlow now seemed reluctant to part with them. "You won't get a better price anywhere else. Robbing myself, that's what I'm doing. Tell you what, I'll make it one-and-nine for the two of them."

"No, really, thanks. They're not for sale."

"Not for sale! What d'you mean, not for sale? You just said that's what you'd come in here for."

"Yes, I know, but I've decided to change my mind, quite suddenly."

With very bad grace the bookseller pushed the books across the counter and pocketed his coins.

"Strikes me you need your heads seeing to; coming in here, wasting my time and not knowing whether you want to buy books, or sell them. Go on, get out of my shop, and take your books with you!"

They were only too glad to go!

Once outside the door, Darbishire said: "Phew! That was a near-miss, wasn't it! I can just imagine the Archbeako buying those books and finding your name inside." The very thought of it was so shattering that he leaned heavily on Mr. Barlow's trestle-table while he recovered from the shock.

Unfortunately, the table made a poor shock-absorber. There was a sudden movement from beneath as the trestles collapsed and the stack of books thudded to the pavement.

"You clumsy clodpoll! Now look what you've done!" barked Jennings.

"Sorry, Jen! It was that stupid table. I only touched it ever so …"

"Quick; pick them up before the old codger comes out of his shop! I've had enough of him to be going on with."

Hurriedly they replaced the fallen trestles and stooped to gather up the books. Luckily, Mr. Barlow had not heard the crash and remained in his shop unaware of what had happened.

"Put them back tidily," said Jennings, as he retrieved the *Complete Works of Alfred, Lord Tennyson* from a puddle in the gutter. The volume was streaked with mud and had to be dry-cleaned with a handkerchief.

Carefully, Jennings inspected the pages for signs of damage. "There! I think it's all right now, so we'll just put it ..." He broke off and stared in surprise at the printed page before him.

"What's the matter?" asked Darbishire anxiously.

"Gosh, Darbi! Golly! What do you think I've found?"

"A priceless prehistoric book-mark?"

"No, nothing like that. Listen to this on page 134 of Tennyson's poems:

'Break, break, break,
On thy cold grey stones, O Sea!
And I would that my tongue could utter
The thoughts that arise in me.'"

"Yes, it *is* rather lovely, isn't it!" said Darbishire with deep appreciation. "You know, Jen, I think I've heard that poem before, somewhere."

"I should wizard well think you *have,*" cried Jennings. "The next verse goes on: 'O well for the fisherman's boy.'"

Darbishire had placed it by this time. "That's right! Of course! It's Venables' famous prize poem."

"It jolly well isn't! It's Tennyson's. It's in his book, so that proves it!" His voice rose excitedly. "You see what this means, Darbi? We've been made the victims of a brilliant forgery. Venables never wrote this poem—he stole it from Lord Alfred Tennyson!"

Darbishire's expression was thoughtful. "I think it's the other way about," he observed.

"What! You mean Lord Alfred pinched it from Venables?"

"No, I mean you've got the name the wrong way round. You should say Alfred, Lord—not Lord Alfred. My father says that if a chap inherits a title ..."

Jennings turned on his friend impatiently. "Don't quibble, Darbishire! We've been swizzled! We've got proof here of the dirty works of Venables in the complete works of Tennyson. Gosh, what a mouldy cad Venables is, pinching Alfred Lord's poem like that. Why, it's enough to make him turn in his grave."

They replaced the book tidily and hurried off to catch the bus. Jennings was smouldering with indignation. It was as though the mud he had wiped from the second-hand volume now besmirched the fair name of Venables. Let him talk his way out of *that*, if he could!

The only consolation was that as the winning poem was now disqualified, the editors would not have to present a prize after all: which was just as well, as they had no prize to present.

"What a ghastly bish it all is," lamented Darbishire, as they stood by the bus stop. "And it was such a lovely poem too." Dreamily, he recited:

> "'And I would that my tongue could utter
>   The thoughts that arise in me.'"

Jennings snorted angrily. It was clear that *his* tongue would have no difficulty in uttering the thoughts that arose in him the next time he met Venables.

CHAPTER 9

JENNINGS PRESENTS THE PRIZE

AT the moment when Jennings and Darbishire were boarding the four-o'clock bus for their return journey, Venables was trotting light-heartedly across the quad, unaware of the serious charge he would be called upon to answer. He hummed gaily as he made his way into the building and upstairs to Mr. Carter's room.

"Please, sir, I'm back from the village, sir. Will you tick me off on the list, please."

Mr. Carter did so and said: "If you're going along to the common room, Venables, you can pin this notice on the board for me."

"Certainly, sir." Venables took the sheet of paper and glanced at it. *There will be an inspection of all textbooks at 5 p.m. this afternoon*, it said.

Suddenly, he felt uneasy. Why this sudden interest in textbooks, he wondered? Supposing Jennings had let him down! Supposing he did not return in time! Worst of all, supposing he had sold the valuable first editions and had then been unable to buy any cheaper copies!

Anxiously, he asked: "Why are we having an inspection, sir?"

"It's time we made a check," Mr. Carter replied. "There's a shortage of Latin grammars and the Head wants to find out how many are missing."

A shortage of Latin grammars! Venables shuffled his feet nervously. If Jennings had bungled things, the shortage was going to be uncomfortably acute!

"Are they difficult to get, sir? The cheaper editions I mean."

"Practically impossible," said Mr. Carter. "I think they must be out of print at the moment."

Venables went downstairs seriously perturbed. He was a boy who believed in steering clear of trouble, and he bitterly regretted his rashness in having had anything to do with the scheme at all. Why, oh why, had he entrusted his book to Jennings? No longer could he look forward to receiving his prize with an easy mind. In fact, he no longer cared about the prize at all: but he *did* care about his Latin book!

JENNINGS PRESENTS THE PRIZE

In the common room he found Temple and Atkinson glancing through the *Form Three Times*.

"It's about time they got cracking on the next copy," Temple was saying. "This ancient old ruin will be growing whiskers if it stays up much longer."

"Give them a chance! There's a lot of work in printing a magazine, don't forget. I expect Jennings is just waiting for some more news to happen."

They made way for Venables to pin up the notice, which they read without much interest. Book inspections were nothing to get excited about—provided that the books were there to be inspected.

Worried and anxious, Venables told them what had happened.

"... and he was going to sell it and buy me a cheaper one, and now this mouldy inspection's coming off to bish up the whole issue," he finished miserably.

"I shouldn't worry. You'll get your second edition one as soon as Jennings gets back," said Temple.

"But I shan't! Mr. Carter says you can't buy them any more, and Jennings is bound to have sold the old ones before he finds out. It's just the sort of thing he *would* do."

"It's your own crazy fault for giving it to him," was Atkinson's verdict. "I've told you fifty million times that Jennings' mighty famous wheezes always come unstuck." He shook his head sadly. "It's no good giving you good advice, Venables; it just goes in one ear and out of the other like water off a duck's back."

"Oh, don't talk such antiseptic eyewash, Atki," said Venables, testily. "What's my Latin grammar got to do with a duck's back, anyway?"

"It's just a saying. Every one knows that if you pour water on a duck's back, it runs off."

"I don't blame it," said Temple. "So would any one if you did that to them."

"I don't mean the duck runs off—I mean the water does," Atkinson explained impatiently. "Anyway, let this be a lesson to you, Venables. I reckon it'll be curtains for you at five o'clock."

"Huh! *And* for Jennings—I'll tell him a thing or two," threatened Venables. "Just you wait till he gets back, that's all. Just you wait!"

They waited for twenty minutes. Then the common room door burst open and Jennings and Darbishire stood panting on the threshold. They had run all the way up the drive, but Jennings still had enough breath left to deliver himself of a few well-chosen words.

"So there you are, Venables, you miserable specimen! You'll be pleased to know you're a mouldy swizzler and a rotten bogus cheat. We've caught you red-handed in the act, and don't try to deny it, or you'll get your chips!"

The threats were wasted on Venables. "Thank goodness you've come back, Jen. Quick, have you got my Latin book?"

"Never mind about Latin books. You're a thief! You've stolen Lord Alfred's works."

The little crowd which had been gathering in the common room pricked up its ears.

"Stolen Alfred's works!" echoed Temple blankly. Who on earth was Alfred? he wondered. It sounded like a grandfather clock or an engine of some sort.

Darbishire pushed his way through the crowd, waving a sheet of paper which he had retrieved from the tuck-box room, on his way upstairs.

"Proof! Proof!" he shouted dramatically, and held the vital evidence two inches from the defendant's nose. "You see this, Venables, with *Break, Break, Break*, on it?"

Venables nodded. He could hardly avoid seeing it at such close range.

"You don't deny it's your writing, do you?"

"No, of course I don't," replied Venables. "It's the one I sent in for the competition."

"Well, it *isn't* your writing! It's Alfred, Lord Tennyson's," Jennings announced in firm tones.

Venables looked at him in amazement. "You're cuckoo! D'you think I don't know my own writing?"

The interested spectators were well out of their depth by this time, and Darbishire did his best to make matters plain.

"No, listen; we know it's Venables' writing, but we've found out that he didn't make the poem up and Tennyson did—which proves he's a fraudulent forger. What have you got to say about that, Venables, old boy?"

The common room buzzed with excitement. Fraudulent forgeries were not discovered every day of the week! All eyes were on Venables, and the excited buzz died away as he opened his mouth to speak.

"But I didn't send it in for the *home-made poetry* section," he said. "I sent it in for the *best handwriting* comp. The rules said you'd got to write about twenty lines, so I copied this poem out of a book. I never pretended I'd made it up myself."

Jennings' jaw dropped slightly. This, then, was the explanation. He could have kicked himself for not having thought of it. Avoiding his co-editor's eye, he mumbled: "Oh! H'm! Yes, I see." And to bolster up his tottering prestige, he added: "Yes, but how were we to know which one you meant it for? You should have said which one it was on the back."

"I couldn't do that. The rules said write on one side only," Venables explained. "If you don't believe me, take a squint at the envelope. That'll tell you plainly enough!"

The editors, accompanied by the prize-winner and the entire crowd of interested spectators, descended to the tuck-box room where, from the depths of the wastepaper basket, Darbishire produced the missing envelope. In addition to the name of the sender, it bore the words *Handwriting Comp.* in the top left-hand corner.

"Sorry, Jen," said Darbishire humbly. "I must have overlooked it in the heat of the moment."

"Yes, and what about his prize?" demanded Temple. "You promised it before tea, don't forget, so you'd better get weaving and hand it over."

The prize! In the light of this fresh evidence something would have to be done. For there could be no denying that Venables' handwriting was neat and legible, and as the only entrant in that section he was entitled to have his labours rewarded.

But with *what*? Jennings gave it up in despair. He had solved a whole series of difficult problems only to find himself back where he started. He took a deep breath and said: "Well, it's like this; we *were* going to get you a double-decker sponge cake with the rhino we got for the Latin books, but ..."

"Oh, golly!" Venables exclaimed, with a start. He had forgotten all about his Latin book in the hectic argument of the last ten minutes. That wretched book inspection would be starting at any moment, and there was Jennings calmly talking about the money he had obtained for the precious volume.

"You're an ozard rotter, Jennings!" he burst out angrily. "You can keep your mouldy double-deckers, I don't want them! All I want is my Latin book back."

A tiny ray of hope was switched on in Jennings' heart. "More than anything else?" he asked.

"Yes. It's the only thing I *do* want; but if you've sold it, what's the good of arguing?"

Jennings climbed up on a tuck-box and beckoned to the interested spectators. "Gather round, everybody!" he called loudly. "The *Form Three Times* famous handwriting prize is now going to be publicly presented to the lucky winner."

"I don't *want* a prize. I want my Latin book back," complained the lucky winner. But his protests were lost in the volume of applause which greeted the announcement. When it had ceased, Jennings began his speech.

"Ladies and Gentlemen—er, no, cut out the ladies—Gentlemen and others! I am very proud at being asked to come here this afternoon to tell you—er, that I am very proud to come here."

"Hear, hear!" said Darbishire, trying his hardest to sound equally full of pride.

"Get a shift on; it'll be five o'clock soon," said Bromwich major.

"All right; don't get impatient." The speaker cleared his throat. "Instead of a supersonic double-decker jam sponge cake, as advertised, the first and only prize will be this—er, this valuable prize, which I bet the winning character will like ten times better."

Venables had been listening without much interest; but now his heart missed a beat, for Jennings had taken two copies of *Grimshaw's Grammar* from his pocket and was solemnly holding one of them out towards its rightful owner.

"Oh, wacko!" yelled the prize-winner, as he grabbed the book and danced round the tuck-boxes with heartfelt relief. "So you didn't sell it, after all!"

After that there were solemn hand shakings, for Jennings felt that he should conclude the ceremony in the formal manner of the distinguished visitors who presented the school prizes on Speech Day. On those occasions the speaker always wound up his remarks with some apt quotation from the classics. Perhaps he could do the same.

Assuming a pompous, speech-day manner, he said: "Finally, then, gentlemen, I would ask you to remember the valuable words of the late Dr. Grimshaw which he has expressed so well in his priceless book, '*Amo, amas, amat, amamus, amatis, amant!*'"

But the prize-winner was not listening to the sound advice. He was hurrying through the door, hoping to be first in the queue for the five o'clock book inspection.

The wise sayings of Darbishire's father were well-known—and equally well ignored—throughout the school. At times of crisis, *My father says ...* was sure to be followed by some gem of wisdom advising patience, courage, caution or hope to suit the occasion. And now that the prize-giving ceremony had been such a success, Darbishire lost no time in hammering home the need to press on with the next number of their magazine.

His father's stock of action proverbs came in useful for this, and during the next few days Jennings was continually urged to take bulls by the horns and strike irons while hot. Time and Tide, it appeared, were positively churlish about being kept waiting.

"That's all very well," said Jennings during hobbies' hour the following Monday, "but we're a bit up a gum-tree for news at the moment. That's the trouble with boarding school—you never get anything decent happening, like revolutions and earthquakes and crime waves and things. It seems a bit feeble to have big headlines about Bromwich minor winning the Form Three ping-pong championship, but we'll have to make do with it, if we can't find anything else."

"And I vote we don't have any competitions this time," Darbishire advised. "They're too much strain on the nerves. Besides, we can't go *on* giving chaps their own property back as prizes or they'll think it a bit odd."

It was Jennings who suggested making a special feature of the 2nd XI "away" match against Bracebridge School. The game was fixed for the following Saturday, and as it involved a journey by bus and train, he decided that the occasion should be well worth writing about.

The first step was to appoint Darbishire chief press photographer, for Jennings was certain to be selected for the team. He was a promising player and had once had a trial for the 1st XI, but he was considered too young to hold a regular place among the thirteen-year-olds. Now, he had found his feet to some purpose as a keen and useful member of the 2nd XI. He was rather unwilling to allow Darbishire full control of the camera, but he was forced to admit that he could not possibly play centre-half and take snapshots at the same time.

Darbishire was delighted. He had always wanted to be in charge of the camera and as he had no hope of being chosen for the 2nd XI, he was the obvious choice.

The next move was not so simple. School teams had never been known to take press-photographers with them, and there was the gravest doubt whether the Headmaster would grant the necessary permission. Better by far to apply for the job of linesman and hope that the duties would allow for a little amateur photography to be carried on during the course of the game.

To their surprise, the plan succeeded. Mr. Carter, when approached, was quite willing to appoint Darbishire linesman, and Jennings spent the next few days coaching him for his two duties.

Darbishire was an apt learner. Soon he could take photographs without including his forefinger in the picture, and every night at bedtime he practised his linesmanship by charging up and down the dormitory waving his vest above his head, in place of a flag. Venables and Atkinson lent a hand by heading rolled-up socks over imaginary touchlines, so that he could give his decision about the throw-in. By the time Saturday arrived, he felt confident of coping with any problems of photography or flag-waving.

Mr. Carter and Mr. Wilkins took the team to Bracebridge School; they caught the bus to Dunhambury station and made the rest of the journey by train. The team was excited and eager, for not only were Bracebridge certain to give them a good game—they were also certain to give them a good tea afterwards.

When they reached their destination shortly after two o'clock, the Linbury team were taken upstairs to a dormitory to change: the linesman, having nothing to change, was shown into an empty classroom to await his colleagues.

It seemed odd to Darbishire to be in a school and yet form no part of it. It was not merely that the surroundings were different, for indeed the classroom was very similar to his own. There was the same smell of ink and chalk dust, the same over-full desks with lids which wouldn't quite shut: the lost rubbers hiding beneath the radiator and the badly-aimed balls of old blotting paper which had fallen short of the wastepaper basket, all seemed familiar. And yet, somehow, he did not feel quite at home. He sat down in a back row desk and read the history notes still chalked up on the blackboard.

Presently the door opened and a long crocodile of Bracebridge boys came winding in. They were about his own age, and in their grey suits and regulation school socks they might almost have been his Linbury colleagues. Only their faces were different.

The faces looked at Darbishire, mildly surprised to see a stranger in their midst.

"I've been told to wait here," he explained to a round-faced boy with large pink ears, who came and sat in the desk beside him.

"Why, what have you done wrong?" inquired the pink-eared one.

"Nothing. I'm the Linbury linesman and special press-photographer."

"Oh! Well if I were you, I'd beat it before old Foxy Type gets his gun-sights on you."

"Who's Foxy Type?"

"Huh! You'll soon find out if you stick around these parts," came the cryptic answer.

By this time, the Bracebridge crocodile had occupied all the desks and over-flowed on to the benches at the back of the room. There must have been about thirty of them, Darbishire reckoned. He felt suddenly aware that he was intruding; he would beat a retreat, as advised, and find his own way to the football pitch. He picked up his camera and his flag and rose to make his way out of the room.

"Sit down, that boy!" rasped a crisp, metallic voice; and looking up, he saw that the master's desk was occupied by a hatchet-faced man with thinning hair and bushy eyebrows.

This, presumably, was Foxy Type! His gaze was directed downwards at a book on his desk and he had only caught the movement of a grey suit from the corner of his eye. Darbishire felt the time had come to explain.

"Excuse me, sir ..." he began; but he got no further for the master, still with averted gaze, called out: "Quiet, that boy! One more word from any one, and I'll have you all back here this evening, as well."

"But, sir ..."

"Right! The whole lot of you will come back after tea!"

Darbishire sat down again, conscious of the hostile atmosphere. He would obviously have to secure his release more tactfully. He raised his hand.

"Put that hand down!" said the master without raising his eyes to see whom the hand belonged to.

Outside on the football pitch, a whistle blew. Darbishire grew tense with anxiety; the match had started, and nobody had come to fetch him. Instead of running up and down with his flag at the ready, here he was, a prisoner in a detention class, guarded by this curiously named F. Type, Esq. It was a little hard, he told himself, that he who spent so much time trying to avoid being kept in at his own school should run *slap-bang-whomp* into this packet of trouble as soon as he set foot in Bracebridge. A nice way to treat an invited guest! Why, he didn't even know what he was being detained for!

Minutes ticked by, and still Darbishire sat and seethed with baffled fury. He felt as out of place as a chess champion in a rugger scrum. Would no one come to his rescue? He nudged his pink-eared neighbour, but the boy merely shrugged helplessly. It was clear that they had a healthy respect for this Mr. Type, or whatever his name was.

"Stop fidgeting in the back row," came from the master's desk. "You're all going to sit still in perfect silence until I ..."

The words trailed away, as the bushy eyebrows narrowed in a frown and a pair of steely blue eyes were focused on the back row desk. Mr. Fox, alias Foxy Type, had spotted what was amiss.

"We appear to have caught an unusual—ah—specimen in our net," he said, with rather less edge on his voice. "I don't recollect having seen that face about the premises before; the loss, of course, is mine. But tell me, dear boy, to what are we indebted for the honour of this most delightful visit?"

"Please, sir, I got in by mistake," said Darbishire.

"Tut-tut! Too bad, too bad! And very careless of you," mused Mr. Fox with heavy humour. "It is a well-known fact here at Bracebridge that my detention classes, like the humble spider's web, are easy to enter but extremely difficult to leave. Are you sure you wouldn't prefer to stay and keep us company?"

"Quite sure, thank you, sir."

"Pity! However, we won't press you, as you seem anxious to be on your way. But don't hesitate to come and pay us a visit, any time you're passing. We'll keep a desk aired for you."

Darbishire scuttled from the room and didn't stop scuttling till he had found his way to the football pitch. Things were not going too well, he thought.

But worse was to follow before the day was over.

CHAPTER 10

DESTINATION UNKNOWN

If only Darbishire had made his escape a little earlier, he could have taken a photograph of the winning goal, which was scored by Temple in the opening minutes of the game. But by the time the linesman had arrived panting at his action station, the play had settled down to a level struggle between two well-matched sides, and no more goals were scored.

It was a good, fast game; too fast for Darbishire to make much use of the camera, for when the play was near his touchline he was too busy with his linesmanship, and when the ball veered across the pitch the players were too far away to be photographed.

Jennings did not discover this till they were in the railway carriage on their return journey.

"Smashing game, wasn't it, Darbi!" he said. "Did you get a photo of the winning goal?"

The cameraman had to confess that the only photograph he could be sure of was a snap of Bromwich major sucking a lemon at half-time.

"Well, you're a bright sort of character, I must say!" Jennings complained. "For all the help you've been, you might just as well have been back at school sitting in the classroom."

Hastily, Darbishire changed the subject. "Supersonic tea, they gave us, wasn't it? That shepherd's pie was the wizardest garbage I've tasted for months. I had three refills."

In the corner seat, Mr. Carter raised a pained eyebrow. "You had *what*, Darbishire?"

"Oh, sorry, sir. I mean I had three helpings of that delicious dish, sir."

A mumble of protest arose all round the carriage. "Coo, that's not fair, Darbishire wolfing three helpings. I only got one," complained Venables bitterly.

"Same here," grumbled Temple. "They told me they'd run out of shepherds

591

by the time I'd got enough space for refuelling; and no wonder with old Darbishire belting into it like nobody's business."

"I don't think the linesmen deserve any tea at all," added Atkinson. "After all, any one can prance up and down the touchline like a lobster in elastic-sided boots, and wag a flag till he's black in the face."

"Hear, hear!" said all the players who had had less than three helpings.

It was clear that linesmen as a class were unpopular, so Darbishire turned to admire the scenery through the open carriage window. But his critics would allow him no peace.

"There you go—bishing up all the regulations," bristled Atkinson. "There's a warning about people like you over the door. Can't you read?"

Darbishire glanced upwards. *It is Dangerous for Passengers to put their Heads out of the Window*, he read.

"I didn't put my *heads* out," he defended himself. "I've only got one head to put. That notice is bats. It ought to say—*No Passenger must put his own head out.*"

"Fair enough! That means we can put somebody else's head out," said Bromwich major. "Whose shall we put?"

"Darbishire's, of course—he's only the linesman," was the unanimous verdict of the critics.

Jennings rallied to his friend's assistance. "It's jolly well not fair, all setting on one chap. The trouble is the railway people aren't very good at bashing out notices. What they should say is *All passengers must not put his, her or its head out, respectively.*"

"You couldn't put your head out respectively," Atkinson objected. "What you mean is, *reflectively*. Because if you did, and another train came along with a supersonic *whoosh-doyng*, it wouldn't half give you something to reflect about."

Mr. Carter groaned quietly. One of the disadvantages of being a schoolmaster, he maintained, was that one had to listen to idiotic nonsense for long periods. However, the train was approaching Dunhambury station by this time, so his ordeal would not last much longer.

"Start getting your cases down, and don't leave anything on the rack," he ordered. "Have you got your gloves, Jennings?"

"I think so, sir. Here's one in my pocket, and the other's about somewhere, sir."

"Where are your football boots, Venables?"

"In my case, sir. I wrapped them in my clean towel because they were a bit muddy, sir."

The train slowed and stopped, and Mr. Carter led the way on to the platform, while from the next carriage stepped Mr. Wilkins and the rest of the team.

They had no time to waste, for the bus back to Linbury was due to leave in less than two minutes; so Mr. Carter hurried ahead to detain it at the bus stop, leaving his colleague to marshal the boys on the platform and bring them along as quickly as possible.

"Come along, you boys, come *along*," commanded Mr. Wilkins in a voice which could be heard clearly above the explosive wheezings of a goods engine standing at an adjoining platform. "Get into line, Rumbelow, you silly little boy. This is no time to go loco-spotting."

He turned and marched rapidly towards the barrier, with the team trotting obediently at his heels. Jennings and Darbishire hurried along at the tail of the procession, but after they had gone a few yards, Jennings suddenly stopped. He dropped his suitcase and started beating his raincoat pockets as though coping with an outbreak of fire.

"What's the matter?" asked Darbishire.

"It's my glove. I've lost it! I must have left it in the train."

"Oh, fish-hooks! Are you sure?"

"Yes. I've got this one in my pocket, look, but there's not a sausage of the other one anywhere. Let's beetle back to the carriage and see if we can find it. We'll soon catch the others up, if we run."

Hastily they retraced their steps along the platform, as Mr. Wilkins and the rest of the team disappeared through the barrier and out of the station with never a backward glance.

It took the glove-hunters some seconds to find their compartment. "Here we are," cried Darbishire, tugging at a door. "This must be the one, because it's got that notice about not sticking heads out of windows."

"They *all* say that, you crumbling clodpoll! Ours was much farther down."

Very soon they identified their carriage by a toffee-paper sticking to the window. In they jumped and searched frantically on the racks and beneath the seats. They found a newspaper, a bag of peanut shells and an empty teacup, but there was no sign of a fleecy-lined glove.

"It must be somewhere. Look harder!" Jennings urged.

"I *am* looking harder. My eyes are popping like balloons, but it just isn't

here. I think we'd better get out now. The train will be starting in a ..."

It was at that moment that a porter slammed the door behind them and waved a "right away" signal down the platform. The electric engine which, until then, had been mumbling "*jigger-jigger-jigger*," suddenly became silent and pulled smoothly away from the platform.

"Oh, gosh, it *is* starting!" yelled Darbishire in wild alarm. He made a dive for the carriage door, but was thwarted by the raised window from reaching the handle on the outside.

Jennings had leapt, too, and for a few feverish seconds all was confusion as he pulled downwards on the strap while Darbishire pushed upwards to lift the window-frame in its socket. By the time they realised they were working against one another, it was too late. The window came down with a bang as the end of the platform streaked past their horror-struck faces.

"Oh, golly, whatever shall we do?" moaned Darbishire, while Jennings leaned out of the window uttering vain cries for help.

"It's no earthly good doing that, Jen. No one'll hear you. Besides, it's dangerous to put your head out: the notice says so."

Jennings withdrew his head from the danger zone. "I'll pull the communication cord," he cried in reckless despair. "That's not dangerous, at any rate."

"It wizard well *is!* Unless, of course, you happen to have four pounds nineteen and tenpence ha'penny on you. Go ahead and pull it, if you have, because I've got the other three ha'pence to make up the five pounds fine."

A moment's reflection showed that Darbishire's advice was sound; pulling communication cords would only lead to more trouble. But something would have to be done, for although the situation was desperate already, it would become even worse when Mr. Wilkins discovered what had happened. To miss the bus by accident was bad enough, but to catch the train by accident was nothing less than a catastrophe.

Now that the first shock was over, Jennings felt cold and empty inside, but he refused to allow his feelings to get the better of him. He must keep calm and plan out the next move.

"Don't worry, Darbi," he said with forced assurance. "We'll just have to stay where we are till we get to the next station, and then we'll walk back and hope we haven't been missed."

Darbishire flapped his fingers and hopped from foot to foot in agitation. "But how do we know the train's going to *stop* at the next station? It might be an express—next stop Land's End or John o' Groat's, or somewhere."

"It couldn't be both—not unless it went different ways at the same time," Jennings pointed out. "The real trouble is that Mr. Carter's got our tickets, so it may be a bit tricky getting off the platform."

"Oh, fish-hooks! I hadn't thought of that. Why do these frantic hoo-hahs always have to pick on us to happen to? My father says that ..."

"Never mind what your father says! And stop jigging about like a cow on an escalator—you're giving me the fidgets. We'll manage all right."

Darbishire slumped into a corner seat and watched the rolling downland speeding past the carriage window. In his mind he compiled a gloomy catalogue of their troubles: (*a*) Prosecution by railway company for travelling without ticket; (*b*) Persecution by Mr. Wilkins for disobeying orders and being absent without leave; (*c*) Listed at local police station as Missing Persons with no visible means of support. And all because that prize bazooka, Jennings, had achieved new heights of clodpollery by losing his ... Darbishire abandoned his catalogue and sat bolt upright, his eyes staring in amazement.

"I say, Jennings: there's your other glove, look—on your hand!"

Jennings shook his head. "No, it isn't. This is the one I *haven't* lost."

"But it can't be. You said you'd got the other one in your pocket."

Jennings' hand shot up to his mouth in guilty realisation. Then he felt in his pocket and produced the missing glove.

"Oh, heavens! Yes, you're right, Darbi. I was so busy searching my pockets for the second one I didn't spot I'd got it on all the time. What a decent bit of luck you noticed it!"

Darbishire thumped the carriage cushions with exasperation. "Luck! Gosh, I like the cheek of that! You land us *slap-bang-wallop* into the most supersonic bish since the Battle of Hastings and then sit there calmly talking about decent chunks of luck! Dash it all, Jen, here we are tearing off towards Land's End or somewhere at a hundred miles an hour, and before we know where we are, we'll find ourselves—goodness knows where!"

"No, it's *after* we know where we are that we'll find out where we've got to, because ..."

Just then the train slowed down and both boys swivelled round to the window. A platform came into view, then a station sign-board marked Pottlewhistle Halt.

There was no doubt about it—they were stopping, and Jennings felt his spirits rising with renewed hope.

"Well, it's not Land's End, anyway, or we'd be able to see the Scilly Isles," he observed with an attempt at heartiness.

"Don't talk to me about the Scilly Isles. I *could* make a frightfully witty remark about a silly something else I can see, but I don't think this is the moment for jokes, somehow. My father says there's a time and place for everything."

"He's right for once, too," Jennings replied, as the train stopped and he opened the carriage door.

"This is the time and place for getting out of the train."

It was a very small station. From the wooden shanty which served as booking office and waiting room an elderly porter came out and shouted what sounded like "*Pollwillall! ...Pollwillall!*"

But nobody else left the train in spite of this invitation, and Jennings seized Darbishire's arm and drew him into the shelter afforded by a stack of milk churns. The porter was looking towards the front of the train and had not noticed them, but with no other passengers to cover their retreat, caution was necessary.

They crouched behind the milk churns hardly daring to breathe, and a moment later they heard the scrunch of heavy boots as the porter marched flat-footedly down the platform to the guard's van.

There was a thud as a sack of fertilizer was dropped on to the platform, and an even louder one as a crate of eggs was heaved into the van. Then the train moved on, the footsteps approached the milk churns, passed by and died away as the porter lumbered back into the booking office.

Jennings heaved a sigh of relief. "Phew! He never spotted us, thank goodness! Come on, we'd better beat it while the coast's clear. It'll be dark in two shakes of a lamb's tail."

Behind them a low wooden fence ran the length of the platform, and the boys had no difficulty in climbing over and on to the country lane beyond. Jennings was beginning to enjoy himself. It was, he felt, something of an adventure.

Not so, Darbishire. The camera slung round his neck might have been a millstone and his linesman's flag hung limp and drooping as though in surrender. In addition to his other troubles his conscience had started to worry him about travelling the extra distance without a ticket: he made a mental note to send the railway company sixpence in stamps at the earliest opportunity.

"I've had enough of this," he complained, peering shortsightedly into the gathering gloom. "Strikes me it's more dangerous than sticking your head out of the window. Still, it's your fault we're here, so you'd better start leading the way back."

It was a reasonable suggestion: the only snag about it was that Jennings had not the slightest idea which way to go, and could see no signpost to guide him.

Pottlewhistle Halt was a station which seemed to have been built with no clear purpose in mind, for it was situated in open country, some distance from the nearest village. No bus route served it, few passengers used it, and only the slowest of trains ever stopped there. It did, however, possess an old-world charm, and the view from the platform was delightful.

The South Downs lay on either side and a country lane wound its way past the station, up the hill, and through a little wood. After that it climbed the steep slope of the Downs and branched out into a network of footpaths.

"I vote we follow this lane. We're bound to strike the Linbury road after a few miles," Jennings decided.

"A few miles—phew! You seem to forget I've been hoofing up and down the touchline all afternoon, wagging my flag. I think we ought to ask someone if it's the right way first."

"How can we? There's no one about to ask."

"Ask the old porter—he's about."

Jennings shook his head. "Don't be such a prehistoric remains, Darbi! We've got to keep out of his way in case he finds out about the tickets. Why, it'd be a wizard sight more dangerous asking him than putting your head out of the window."

It was growing dark as they set off up the hill and there was a peaceful still-ness in the evening air which did much to comfort Darbishire's anxiety.

"It's supersonic scenery round these parts; rather like Gray's *Elegy* that Mr. Carter was reading to us last week," he observed. "I can just imagine the lowing herd winding slowly o'er the lea and the ploughman homeward plodding his weary way; can't you?"

"Better wait till we've actually plodded home before you start nattering about weary ways," Jennings advised. "If we don't get weaving a bit faster than this the curfew will have tolled the knell of parting day before you can say 'Fossilised fish-hooks.'"

CHAPTER 11

THE SEARCH PARTY

As the five o'clock bus from Dunhambury left the town and sped along the Linbury road, Mr. Carter turned to his colleague in the seat behind him.

"It's as well I ran ahead and stopped the bus. There isn't another one for two hours," he said.

Mr. Wilkins nodded. He was still breathing heavily from the exertion of shepherding his flock along the road to the bus stop at a brisk eight miles an hour. Now, at last, he could relax.

"I suppose you counted to make sure that all the team were with you?" Mr. Carter asked.

"Well, actually, no, I didn't," Mr. Wilkins admitted. "What with you holding the bus back for us, and the conductor waving to us to get a move on, I didn't have time. But you needn't worry, Carter; they're all here, right enough. I'll count them now, if it'll make you feel any happier."

The magenta-and-white caps of Linbury Court School were easily distinguishable in the crowded vehicle, and Mr. Wilkins could see them all from where he sat—Venables and Atkinson in the front seats, with Temple and Bromwich major just behind: across the gangway he noted Rumbelow,

Martin-Jones, Binns major and Nuttall, and in the back row were Parslow and Thompson.

"That's queer! I can only see ten," muttered Mr. Wilkins. "There must be one I haven't counted."

"There should be *two* more," corrected Mr. Carter. "Eleven in the team, plus a linesman makes ... Linesman! Yes, of course; where are Jennings and Darbishire?"

Mr. Wilkins looked baffled for a moment. Then he said: "They *must* be on the bus, somewhere. Perhaps they've gone upstairs."

"Upstairs!" Mr. Carter's voice rose in shocked surprise. "This, Wilkins, is a *single-decker* bus!"

"Eh, what's that! I ... I ... Corwumph! Good heavens, so it is. I never noticed!"

"Well, really, Wilkins! You were responsible for seeing every one off the platform. Surely I can leave a simple job like that to ..."

"All right, all right, all *right*!" Mr. Wilkins was inclined to grow excitable at times of crisis. He leapt to his feet for a rapid recount, calling loudly: "Hands up, everybody! Put your hands up; I want to see who's here."

The Linbury boys obeyed, and a middle-aged lady with a shopping basket shot both hands towards the ceiling, under the impression that an armed hold-up was in progress.

"Quickly, now. Hands up all the boys who aren't here—er, I mean, has any one seen Jennings and Darbishire?"

Again he counted, but the total remained obstinately at ten.

"Are you sure they're not here, sir?" queried Thompson.

"Of course I'm sure, you silly little boy. They wouldn't have put their hands up if they were; or rather, they would have put them up if they ... oh, be quiet!" Mr. Wilkins was feeling rather confused. Action, prompt and immediate, was called for, and he pushed his way along to the door at the back. "I say, conductor, stop the bus! You're going the wrong way—I mean, I want to get off!"

By now, the team was agog with excitement and the other passengers were seething with curiosity.

"Just like old Jennings to go and make a bish of things!"

"Perhaps they were in a hurry, so they've run on ahead."

The bus buzzed with wild speculation, and the lady with the shopping basket crouched low in her seat, expecting any second to hear the sharp crack of revolver shots. She had spent the afternoon watching a gangster film at the Dunhambury *Empire*, and the memory was still vivid.

It was Mr. Carter who restored order and persuaded his colleague to return to his seat. He pointed out that no useful purpose would be served by alighting on a deserted country road two miles from the town. By the time they had walked back, it would be dark and they would probably miss the boys in the maze of streets near the station. Far better, he reasoned, to return to school first and telephone the station to see if they were still there.

"They may even have got back on the train to retrieve their belongings and been carried on to the next stop," he pointed out with brilliant guess-work.

"And where's the next stop—Brighton?" snorted Mr. Wilkins.

"Oh, no. It's only a local train. The next station is a little place called Pottlewhistle Halt."

"I'll *Pottlewhistle Halt* them if they have! I tell you, Carter, when I get hold of Jennings and Darbishire I'll ... I'll ... well, they'd better look out!"

"Quite. But if *you'd* looked out at the bus stop it would have saved a lot of trouble," Mr. Carter reminded him.

Soon the bus drew up at the school gates, and when the remaining five-sixths of the team had been hustled indoors, the two masters made for the telephone in Mr. Carter's study and put through a call to Dunhambury station. Unfortunately, no one there could throw any light on the whereabouts of the two boys and the senior master wore a worried frown as he replaced the receiver.

"I'll go along and tell the Head at once," he said. At the door, he turned and added: "If you want to be useful, Wilkins, you can phone the next station down the line and see if they got off there."

"Yes, of course; I'll do it right away." And Mr. Wilkins strode over to the telephone as the door closed behind his colleague.

The next station down the line! That would be ... Mr. Wilkins paused in the act of picking up the receiver. What *was* the name that Carter had mentioned in the bus? Whistlepottle Halt? ... Pottlewhistle Halt? ... Or was it Haltpottle Whistle? Mr. Wilkins could not be sure.

"It's either Whistlehalt Pottle or Pottlehalt Whistle," he muttered to himself as he sat with the receiver to his ear, waiting for *Enquiries* to come to his aid.

When it did, he said: "Oh, hullo, *Enquiries!* Can you put me through to a station called Whistlepott Hortle, please? ... What's that? There's no such place? Well, try Haltpottle Whistle, then."

The operator regretted that she couldn't find that place either, but after Mr. Wilkins had suggested Haltwhistle Pottle and Pittlewhostle Halt, she said she thought she knew where the caller meant.

"Oh, good—that's more than *I* do," said the caller thankfully; and a few moments later the voice of the elderly porter sounded on the line.

"Hullo, are you Whistlehalt Pott? I want to speak to the stationmaster, please," said Mr. Wilkins.

A burring Sussex accent replied that the stationmaster had gone home to his tea.

"Well, never mind, you'll do just as well if you're the Whistlehalt Pott porter.

Can you tell me whether the last train from Dunhambury halted at Pottlewhistle Stop? Er, stopped at Pottlewhistle Halt? ... Oh, good. Well did you notice if two boys in school caps alighted at the station?"

The voice replied that there wasn't much at Pollwillall for *any one* to feel pleased about.

"No, no, no. I said alighted, not delighted. I asked you whether they got off."

There was a pause at the other end of the line, and then the voice declared that it was a funny thing that he should be asked that question: for bless his soul if he hadn't seen two boys walking away from the station towards Cowpatch Wood just after the train had left. He had thought to himself that such a thing was queer—distinctly queer, seeing as how he hadn't seen them get off the train—but there it was!

"Thank you very much. Goodbye!" Mr. Wilkins replaced the receiver, and heaved a sigh of relief.

Now, at least, they knew roughly where the boys had got to. All that was needed was for some responsible person to walk over the Downs towards Pottle-whatever-it-was, and meet them.

He hurried from the room and along to the Headmaster's study where he found Mr. Pemberton-Oakes frowning over Mr. Carter's news.

"But this is ridiculous, Carter," the Headmaster was saying. "Surely we can win a football match without losing part of the team in the process! I shall telephone the police station immediately."

"It's all right—I've found them," Mr. Wilkins burst out. "Or rather, I know where they are."

"Oh, good! You got through to Pottlewhistle Halt then?" asked Mr. Carter.

"So that's what it's called, is it! You might have told me," replied his colleague. "Yes, I've been through, and the Pottleport Halt whistler—er, the Whistlehalt Pott porter—er—the man in charge of the station saw them making for some woods."

The Headmaster continued to frown thoughtfully. It was quite dark now and the boys might easily lose their way—if, indeed, they ever knew it in the first place—among the criss-crossing footpaths which led over the Downs to Linbury. Now, what would be the best course to pursue, he wondered? ... Ah! He had it! A search party of some half-dozen or more persons equipped with torches and whistles would be the best way of contacting the missing boys in the darkness.

The rest of the school were having tea, and time would be lost in selecting and briefing suitable boys for their task; but the 2nd XI, still in their outdoor shoes and raincoats, could set off at once. They were the obvious choice, for they had had their tea at Bracebridge and already knew the purpose of the search.

Five minutes later, the ten remaining members of the team were standing in a group on the quad, listening to their instructions.

"We're going over the Downs towards Pottlewhistle," Mr. Carter told them. "Jennings and Darbishire are bound to be approaching from that direction, so we'll all keep together until you're given the order to spread out and search. Then you'll keep in touch by listening for whistle signals. Three long blasts will mean that you're to report back to Mr. Wilkins or to me at once. Now, have you all got torches?"

"I told them to go and collect them," said Mr. Wilkins. "We shall need them too, because ... Oh, I say, Carter, I haven't got one myself! In the heat of the moment I quite forgot to go and fetch it."

Mr. Carter sighed. He felt that the search party would get on much better if only Mr. Wilkins would agree to stay at home; for with his colleague playing a major part in the expedition, there was always the chance that they would lose the rest of the team instead of finding the two who were missing.

But Mr. Carter didn't say so. Instead, he asked: "Has any boy got a torch to lend Mr. Wilkins?"

"Yes, I have, sir. Here you are, sir; you can have this one," said Temple generously.

"Thank you," said Mr. Wilkins. "Are you sure you won't need it yourself?"

"Oh, no, sir, that's all right. It's no good to me, sir—it hasn't got a battery."

"I ... I ... Corwumph! But, you silly little boy, what's the good of ..."

"I think we'd better be going," said Mr. Carter hastily. "Just stand still while I count you all."

He switched on his torch and checked carefully; ten boys, plus two masters. Satisfied, he gave the order. "Right: lead on down the drive, Venables!"

The search party was on its way!

The network of lanes and footpaths between Pottlewhistle and Linbury offer a choice of picturesque walks on fine summer afternoons. On dark November evenings, however, they lose much of their charm, and by the time Jennings and Darbishire had covered three miles they were beginning to tire of the Sussex countryside.

If only they had followed the road, they might—with luck—have found their way back to school unaided; but unfortunately Jennings trusted to his sense of direction to guide them safely through what he hoped was a short-cut.

It wasn't; and very soon they had to admit that they were hopelessly lost. For twenty minutes they followed a footpath which led them to the summit of a grassy hill. Then, for no apparent reason, the path stopped short like an escalator disappearing below ground level.

"Oh, fish-hooks, this is feeble!" lamented Darbishire. "We must have walked about a thousand miles, and I'm so hungry I'm beginning to rattle. What couldn't I do with some more re-fills of that shepherd's pie!"

"If only we could be sure we were going the right way," said Jennings in a worried voice. "We may be walking round and round in circles like chaps in a fog."

"Or in the desert," Darbishire added gloomily. "They walk for miles through never-ending sand and then, when they're just about dead from hunger, they see supersonic oasis-*es* with masses of stuff to eat like boxes of dried dates and palm trees."

"If I saw a mirage I'd rather it was bulging with shepherd's pie."

"M'yes, but you wouldn't be able to eat it, because you can only see mirages properly when they aren't there," Darbishire explained. "Or rather, when they *are* there, you can't see them quite plainly, if you see what I mean. That's why they call them mirages, and my father says ..."

"Oh, don't talk such aerated eyewash, Darbi," said Jennings, coming to a halt. "The only thing I can see quite plainly is that it's too dark to see anything at all. Why, I can hardly see my hand in front of my face."

Darbishire sank down on the damp grass for a rest. "I shouldn't strain your eyes trying to. It's only ..."

"Oh, goodness!" Jennings abandoned his hand-raising experiment and turned towards his reclining friend in dismay. "I say, Darbi—what do you think?"

"I don't know. Whatever I think it's bound to be wrong—it always is," came in complaining tones from ground level. "Go on, you tell me what I think, if you're so clever."

"I've lost my glove again!"

"You can't have lost it *again*, because you never really lost it properly the first time. I expect you've got it on. Have a look and see."

Curtly Jennings pointed out that if it was too dark to see his hand in front of his face, there was little chance of seeing his glove there, either. He turned back along the way they had come and followed the path down the hill for a few yards. He knew his glove couldn't be far away, for he remembered twirling both of them round and round like propellers, less than five minutes before.

Wearily, Darbishire rose to his feet and followed his friend down the path. He was cold and hungry and very unhappy; but as he was lost anyway, it mattered little to him whether they went forward or retraced their steps.

For a hundred yards they wended their way, feeling with their feet and stopping now and again to investigate some black shape which turned out, on closer inspection, to be a mole-hill or a tussock of grass.

"I'm just about fed up to the eardrums with all this mooching about," Darbishire complained. "I wish there was someone about we could ask; if only there was a ploughman homeward plodding his weary way, or even a double-decker bus winding slowly o'er the lea that we could catch."

"You've got a hope!" Jennings retorted. "We're more likely to catch frostbite from being marooned all night with only one glove. I bet there isn't another person about for miles."

It was then that they heard the whistle—three long, low blasts sounding distantly from the bottom of the hill. Jennings gripped his friend's arm and his voice throbbed with excitement.

"I say, Darbi, did you hear a whistle just then?"

"That wasn't a whistle: that was a moping owl," Darbishire decided.

"But there were three of them!"

"All right then, three moping owls; or the same owl moping three times. Besides, owls don't whistle; they go *tu-whit tu-whoo* and to the moon complain, of such as wandering near ..."

"Oh, shut up! I wish you'd leave Gray's *Elegy* out of this. Listen, there it is again!"

There was no doubt about it. The blasts were nearer now, and with a sudden start of joy, Jennings recognised them. "Oh, wacko! It's Mr. Carter's referee whistle."

Darbishire was sceptical. "You're bats! How could it be? You must be hearing things."

"Of course I'm hearing things. I just heard Mr. Carter's whistle."

"No, I mean you're hearing things that aren't there. It's probably a mirage, only as it's too dark to see, it's affecting your ears instead of your eyes."

But a few moments later the 'mirage' grew more distinct and the whistles were followed by distant shouts and the flashing of torches. Then the shouts sounded closer, and the boys recognised Venables' high-pitched voice and heard Atkinson call in reply. Shortly after that a beam of torchlight fell upon Temple and Martin-Jones coming up the grass slope at right-angles to the footpath. Another torch flashed away to the left, and Mr. Wilkins' stentorian bellow could be heard telling Bromwich major to look where he was walking.

"The whole team's there," Jennings gasped in surprise. "Fancy meeting them wandering about miles from anywhere. They seem to be looking for something too. I wonder what on earth it can be!"

Oddly enough, it never occurred to either Jennings or Darbishire that they might be the object of the search. To them, the most likely explanation was that the team had missed the bus at Dunhambury and were walking back to school over the Downs. Perhaps they, too, had tried to take a short-cut with unfortunate results.

"Wacko! We're rescued! Let's beetle down the hill in top gear and join them," cried Darbishire.

But Jennings advised caution. It was just possible, he reasoned, that in the scurry of missing the bus and hampered by the approach of darkness, no one had noticed their absence. After all, who could tell, without a careful check, whether there were ten boys or twelve in the party? If, then, he and Darbishire announced their return to the fold with joyful wacko's and hearty back-slappings, Mr. Wilkins would realise that they had not been amongst those present during the past hour. He would probe into the matter; unpleasant facts about accidental train rides would emerge and a whole chapter of misfortunes would come to light which would be better forgotten.

"Yes, there's something in that," Darbishire agreed. "What had we better do, then?"

"We'll just join up with them quietly, one at a time, and not say much, for a kick-off. They won't notice in the dark; and when they've found the way, we'll all get back to school without any one knowing we haven't been with them all the time. Go on, you hoof off and join them, and I'll follow in a minute."

Darbishire set off down the path, taking care to keep out of the beams of the torches sweeping over the hillside. Jennings watched until his friend was swallowed up in the darkness: then he strolled slowly after him.

CHAPTER 12

THE SHADES OF NIGHT

HALFWAY up the hill, Mr. Wilkins paused to rally his forces.

"Keep together, you boys. Don't straggle, or you'll get lost. And if any one thinks he hears a ... be quiet, Venables, when I'm talking!"

"I *was* being quiet, sir."

"Well, don't be quiet so loudly! It's difficult enough to keep track of you in the dark without ... Now, where's Mr. Carter got to?"

"He's still over by that barn, sir. I heard his whistle a moment ago," said a voice in the darkness.

"Good! I'll give an answering whistle so he can join us, and then we'll press on." Mr. Wilkins searched through his pockets in vain. "Tut-tut-tut! I seem to have left my whistle behind at school."

"I can lend you one, sir," said another disembodied voice. "It isn't much of a thing, though. I got it out of a cracker last Christmas, sir."

"Never mind where you got it, so long as it works." Mr. Wilkins groped in the gloom and found himself holding a thin wooden reed, barely an inch long.

In the distance, three long, low blasts boomed out like a lightship's siren as Mr. Carter sought to make contact with the main party. Immediately, Mr. Wilkins put the toy whistle to his lips and blew with all the strength of a north-easterly gale. A thin, high-pitched *pheep-pheep*, like the chirrup of a newly-hatched chick, was audible at a distance of three yards, and the boys around the whistler collapsed with laughter.

"Oh, sir! What a feeble whistle, sir!"

"Golly, sir! Is that your famous jet-propelled, short-wave radar transmitter, sir?"

"I... I ... *Corwumph!* Be quiet and listen to me. When we get to the top of this hill, half of you will go with Mr. Carter towards Haltpottle and the rest will come with me towards ... Who's that boy straying about? I said no one was to go wandering off."

"I think it's Atkinson, sir," guessed Temple: though, in point of fact, it was Darbishire making a roundabout approach.

"No, it's not me; I'm here, sir," Atkinson's voice piped up from the outer darkness.

Mr. Wilkins strained his eyes trying to identify the shapes milling around him. "I can't see who's there and who isn't. Stand still, everybody—I'm going to count you."

He marched round the little group, prodding each boy in the chest and calling his number aloud. A note of bewilderment crept into his voice as he reached the end of his census. "... eight, nine, ten, *eleven*!"

Eleven! It couldn't possibly be eleven: they had only ten to start with!

Mr. Carter arrived at that moment. He was followed at a discreet distance by Jennings, who passed unseen into the midst of the group, as Mr. Wilkins turned to his colleague in despair.

"This is hopeless, Carter! I'm trying to count these boys and they keep moving about in the dark."

"Is any one missing—apart from the two we're looking for?"

"I don't think so. The last time I counted it came to one more than it should have done." The master's voice sounded strained as he started his check all over again. "One, two, three, four, five ... tut-tut, I don't know whether I've counted that boy over there. Is it you, Bromwich?"

"I don't know, sir; I can't see."

"You don't *have* to see, Bromo. You know if it's you, don't you?" said Venables.

"Oh yes, this is me all right, but I don't know whether I've been counted," Bromwich major explained.

The note of strain in Mr. Wilkins' voice grew more marked as he grappled with his counting.

"... six, seven, eight, nine, ten, eleven, *TWELVE!*"

The last word was uttered in a strangled squeak, as though the speaker's vocal chords were strung to the tension of a violin's E string.

Twelve! The thing was fantastic! Somebody must have moved twice; or perhaps two people had moved once; perhaps ... Mr. Wilkins gave it up. At any rate, their numbers were not short, so now they could press on with the business in hand.

The party moved slowly up the hill, straining their eyes and ears for any sign of the missing boys. But they did not look behind them or they might have observed that the objects of their search had attached themselves to the fringe of the group. As they wandered on, Jennings peered about as keenly as the official searchers, for he was still hoping to find his fleecy-lined glove.

At the top of the hill they all stopped to pick up their bearings and the two masters held a short conference.

"This seems to be the end of the path, Carter," said Mr. Wilkins doubtfully. "Now I wonder what lies over there to the north?"

"I think it's the way back to Pottlewhistle Halt, sir," said Jennings helpfully.

"Don't interrupt, boy, when I'm talking to Mr. Carter. I've had enough of Whistlehalt Pott for one evening, and besides ..."

Mr. Wilkins stopped abruptly. The voice from the darkness had had a familiar ring. For a moment he could have sworn it was ... But how could it be? "Which boy spoke just then?" he demanded loudly.

"I did, sir," replied seven boys who were enjoying a lively discussion about how far cats could see in the dark.

"No, no, no—not you people! Somebody else; I was almost sure ..." He turned again to his colleague. "I say, Carter, I'm hearing things. Somebody spoke just then, and it sounded like Jennings."

"That's just wishful thinking, I'm afraid."

"Yes, I suppose it must have been. This business is getting me down. I tell you, Carter, I'll be thankful when this wild-goose chase is over. I wouldn't be surprised if those two silly little boys have turned up at school by this time, and here we are traipsing about all over the countryside, and ..."

A loud shout came from a patch of shadow a few yards to the right.

"Ooh, sir! Quick, sir! Come over here, sir—I've found something."

"Who's that?"

"It's me, sir—Temple. I've just found a glove by this rabbit hole, sir."

Instantly, torches clicked on and beams of light were focused on the speaker. Temple was kneeling on the turf a few paces down the hill, and in his hand was a fleecy-lined glove. He screwed up his eyes as he held the name-tab up towards the torch-light.

J. C. T. Jennings. I've found Jennings' glove," he shouted in triumph.

"Wacko!" cried the owner, but his exclamation was lost in the stampede to investigate the find at close quarters.

The discovery put new heart into the searchers.

Here was a clue which proved that they were on the right track after all.

Why, with any luck the absentees might even be within earshot, and Mr. Wilkins lost no time in giving his instructions.

"We'll all shout together at the top of our voices," he commanded. "Take a deep breath, every one. Now! One, two, three ..."

"*JEN-NINGS*!" A vast wave of sound rolled over the quiet downland, scaring the wild creatures of the night and setting the farm dogs barking in the valley below. Faintly, the echo returned from the surrounding hills ... "*JEN-NINGS*!"

"Yes, sir?" said Jennings briskly.

He was standing just behind Mr. Wilkins, and he had to sidestep smartly as the master recoiled from the shock and swung round like a rotating gun-turret.

"I ... I ... I ... *Corwumph!* Who spoke then? Who said 'Yes, sir'?"

"Me, sir—Jennings. I thought I heard you calling me, sir."

"But ... but ... you're standing right here in the middle of us!"

"Yes, sir. I wondered why you were shouting so loudly, sir."

It was perhaps as well that Mr. Wilkins' features were obscured by the shades of night, and that the emotions searing through him were not visible to the naked eye. His jaw dropped through thirty degrees and his lips moved as though he would speak. But, for the moment, the fount of speech was dry.

The rest of the party were equally surprised by Jennings' unexpected appearance. They surged round him, voicing exclamations of disbelief.

"I say, it's not *really* you, is it, Jen?"

"Of course it's me. And old Darbi's about somewhere, too. We've been here some time."

"Why didn't you say so before?"

"Well, nobody asked me before."

"If you want to know what *I* think, you've no business to be here at all. You're supposed to be lost," grumbled Martin-Jones. He felt, somehow, that he was being cheated.

Mr. Carter rescued Jennings and Darbishire from the jostling crowd around them. He listened to a brief outline of their misfortunes, and wisely decided to leave the details until they had returned to school.

"Well, I'm glad we've found you at last," he said. "We've been searching high and low."

"Yes, sir; so have I," Jennings answered.

"You've been searching? Whatever for?"

"For my glove, sir. Wasn't it a good job Temple found it! Matron would have been awfully fed up if I'd gone back without it, sir."

"*Doh*!" An anguished gasp of exasperation rang out loud and clear as Mr. Wilkins found his voice again. "I ... I ... Really, Carter, it's too much! Any one would think we'd got nothing better to do all night than grope our way round the rural parish of Whistlepottle like a pack of moles."

"Never mind, Wilkins; we can start making for home now."

"Yes, yes, yes, I know, but the whole thing's too ridiculous, Carter! Here have we been traipsing round looking for two wretched little boys, who have been traipsing round with us looking for a wretched little glove!"

As they descended the hill, Darbishire sought out Jennings and fell into step beside him.

"I say, did you hear what Mr. Wilkins said just then, Jennings?" he asked. "If we're still somewhere near Pottlewhistle we must have been walking round in circles like chaps in a mirage."

"Huh! A mirage is nothing to get excited about," his friend answered as he pulled on his newly-found glove. "Just look at Old Wilkie—*he's* walking round in circles like a chap in a trance!"

It was late when the search party reached Linbury Court and later still before the boys had finished their supper. But despite the lateness of the hour, Jennings and Darbishire were summoned to the Headmaster's study before they were allowed to go upstairs to their dormitory.

They spent an uncomfortable twenty minutes listening to Mr. Pemberton-Oakes' reproving words, and wondering what action he was going to take when he came to the end of them. Many of his observations they had heard before, and it was no news to them that he was "somewhat at a loss to understand" their motives, or that he "asked himself why they should fail to observe the rules of civilised behaviour."

But behind the Headmaster's ponderous words was a feeling of relief that the boys had come to no harm. He was a fair-minded man and he realised that the escapade was due more to muddle-headed reasoning than to disobedience. However, as the culprits had caused a great deal of trouble, neither of them would be allowed to accompany a school team to an "away" match for the rest of the term. Jennings and Darbishire went upstairs to their dormitory in a subdued frame of mind.

"Talk about mouldy luck!" Jennings complained. "It's not so bad for you because you're not in the team, but there are at least four more 'away' matches I shall have to miss; and some of those schools dish out a supersonic tea after the game."

"Never mind, you'll be able to spend more time on our mag," Darbishire consoled him. "We ought to be getting the next number out pretty soon, now."

"With a nice front-page picture of the winning goal in the Bracebridge match, I suppose!"

Jennings wasn't going to let his assistant forget his shortcomings as a press-photographer. "Honestly, Darbi, you're about as handy with a camera as a carthorse on stilts. You turn up when the game's half over and load yourself up with three refills of shepherd's pie before any one else can even get their forks on the job. If you want to know what *I* think, you've bished up the whole day. I should never have left my glove in the train if I hadn't been worrying myself bald-headed about what you were going to get up to next."

"But you *didn't* leave it in the train. And besides ..." Darbishire stopped. The criticism was grossly unfair, but perhaps it might be better not to argue about the photographs of the Bracebridge match while the little matter of shepherd's pie still rankled in the minds of the team. They would have to think of something else for the front page—the story of their accidental train ride, for instance: that should make good reading!

In his mind's eye he pictured the banner headlines: *Jennings and Darbishire Discover Search Party* ... And underneath, in smaller type: *Search Party Discover Fleecy-Lined Glove.*

The story sounded so promising that he reached for his diary and began writing a rough draft as he sat up in bed.

An enthusiastic gathering took place near Pottlewhistle Halt last Saturday evening, when the mysterious disappearance of a missing glove led to an interesting episode, he wrote. *Asked by our Special Correspondent to comment on the proceedings, Mr. L. P. Wilkins, the well-known schoolmaster, said ...*

But at that moment, Mr. Carter put out the dormitory light and the observations of Mr. L. P. Wilkins were, fortunately, lost in the darkness.

In the next bed, Jennings, too, was pondering on the comments of the "well-known schoolmaster." Mr. Wilkins, it seemed, had taken the events of the evening badly. On the way home he had announced firmly that never again would he make a journey by land, sea or air, if either Jennings or Darbishire were included in the party.

This was quite the wrong attitude, Jennings thought. A little more friendly give and take was needed, and less of this gunning for innocent victims like trigger-happy outlaws of the middle west. However, masters always had everything their own way, so if Mr. Wilkins felt aggrieved, Jennings felt it was up to him to put matters right. He would show his willingness by working his hardest in class, and by laughing the loudest whenever Mr. Wilkins made a joke. He would make cheerful conversation and be on the spot to open doors: he would ... Yes, why not? A vague thought which had been ambling aimlessly round his mind for some days now leapt to attention and proclaimed itself a Bright Idea.

Jennings leaned out of bed and reached towards Darbishire. His fingers made contact with a lock of curly hair: he tugged gently.

"Oh, shut up! I was just going off to sleep," came in muffled tones from the next bed.

"Yes, but listen: I've got a massive wheeze. You know we were wondering what we could put in the *Form Three Times* instead of a competition?"

"A fine time to wake me up with wheezes!"

"Ah, but this is urgent. I've just thought how would it be if I wrote some life stories of famous characters like, say, for instance, Julius Cæsar and Oliver Cromwell and all those bods?"

"Sounds a bit feeble to me."

"Yes, but that's not all. Old Wilkie's got his gun-sights on us, so I thought it might put him in a decent mood."

"Why should *he* want to read about Oliver Cromwell?"

Jennings clicked his tongue impatiently. "No, you clodpoll! We'd include Old Wilkie in our *Famous Lives*, and perhaps some of the other masters too."

"We'd better call them *in*famous lives then and bung in a few chronic characters like Nero and Macbeth to keep him company," mumbled Darbishire sleepily.

"Oh, no; we've got to be really decent to Wilkie for a bit," Jennings decided as he smoothed his pillow. "After all, we owe him something for all the trouble he went to tonight."

CHAPTER 13

THE INITIAL DIFFICULTY

UNFORTUNATELY, the *let's-be-decent-to-Wilkie* campaign was not an immediate success. During the next few days Jennings and Darbishire performed many acts of kindness designed to brighten Mr. Wilkins' life and smooth his troubled path.

They almost mended his fountain pen for him after Jennings had accidentally knocked it off the desk; they woke him from an after-lunch snooze to ask whether he would care to see a watercolour of a strato-cruiser which Darbishire had just painted; and they helped him to blow up the footballs—until, by some mischance, Jennings punctured a new bladder with the football lacer.

But their efforts to lend a helping hand struck no answering chord in Mr. Wilkins' heart.

"It's almost as though he doesn't want to be done good to," Jennings observed, as they waited for the master to arrive for an algebra lesson, a week after the campaign had started.

"Perhaps he'll be a bit more friendly when he sees what a decent write-up we give him in our magazine," Darbishire replied. "How are you getting on with those famous life stories, by the way?"

"Fairly well. I've done Julius Cæsar, but there wasn't much to say about Oliver Cromwell, so I'm going to do one of Mr. Carter to help fill up the space. Mr. Wilkins' is the most awkward one, though: I can't find out how old he is or what his initials stand for, or anything. It's jolly difficult writing a chap's biography when his past is just a closed book."

They spoke in whispers, as though fearful of disturbing the scholarly atmosphere which the Headmaster had told them should prevail before the start of a lesson: but though the room was quiet, the atmosphere was not so scholarly as it might have been.

Temple was twanging soft notes on a guitar made from elastic bands stretched across his pencil box; Atkinson was dredging pellets of blotting paper from

614

his inkwell and using them to block up the cracks between the floorboards. Bromwich major was making a watch chain with paper clips and Venables was contorting his facial muscles in an effort to look like a rabbit. It was, in short, an ordinary class waiting for the lesson to begin.

Nor had they long to wait. Heavy footsteps sounded in the corridor, the door swung back, shivering on its hinges, and Mr. Wilkins made his usual brisk entrance.

"Good morning, sir," said Form Three politely.

"'Morning. I'm going to show you a new sort of sum this lesson, so sit up straight and keep your wits about you."

Form Three sat up, but the keeping of wits about them was a different matter, for Mr. Wilkins' explanation of the new sums was not easy to follow. There was, for example, the problem of the man who walked at the odd speed of x miles an hour for the unusual time of y hours.

Jennings was unwilling to believe that such a thing was possible; he had never seen a signpost or a speedometer marked in x's, nor yet a clock with y's on its dial. He thought Mr. Wilkins might be interested to know this, and told him so. Other boys raised questions which the master considered equally fatuous, and he was out of patience with the whole form by the time he had finished his explanation.

"We'll see how much you've taken in," he said: "You can work out the next one for yourselves." And he wrote a similar problem on the blackboard and sat down at the master's desk.

The problem again concerned a journey from one milestone to the next, and once more the data consisted of x's, with a few y's thrown in for good measure.

"Do we have to work it out in our books, sir?" inquired Martin-Jones.

"Of course. You don't imagine I want it embroidered on the lampshade, do you!" came the curt reply.

Temple put up his hand. "Please, sir, that sum's impossible to answer, sir. You haven't told us how far it *is* from one milestone to the next. We can't work it out until we know that, can we, sir?"

Mr. Wilkins took a deep breath to cool the impatience rising inside him. "There would be little point, Temple, in having milestones that were not exactly one mile apart," he said, and left his desk to see how the back row was progressing. "Well, Bromwich, have you worked out how long it would take?"

"Yes, sir: three days, sir."

"Three days to go a mile! Don't be ridiculous, you silly little boy. Why, a snail could do it in that time!"

"I was pretending it *was* a snail, sir. The sum didn't say it had got to be a man, so I thought, now supposing this snail ..."

"I ... I ... *Corwumph!* ... Well, Darbishire! I suppose *you're* going to tell me you've worked it out in earwigs!"

"No, I used a proper man, sir, and it makes the sum come out much faster. According to my figures he must have finished the journey shortly after half-past *z*, sir."

Mr. Wilkins drew in his breath like a vacuum cleaner coping with an obstinate fluff-ball. Then he clasped his hand over his eyes and tottered blindly back to the master's desk. He stopped abruptly when he bumped into it, but the exercise must have made him feel better, for his tone was back to normal when next he spoke.

"Hands up all boys who have put down 'twenty minutes' for the answer."

No hands went up and Mr. Wilkins began to simmer again. "This form needs waking up! Not one right answer to a perfectly straightforward sum. Very well. I'll have the whole lot of you in here at quarter-past four on Saturday and we'll go through the examples again."

Form Three received the news without enthusiasm. The 1st XI would be playing a "home" match on Saturday, which everybody would be required to watch; but when the game ended at half-past three, village leave would be granted. Mr. Wilkins had purposely chosen an awkward hour for his detention class, for the journey to the village took ten minutes each way, and with so little time to spend when they got there, it would not be worth their while to go at all.

Jennings was not worried about missing village leave, for he had no money to spend, and anyway, he had planned to devote the time to finishing his life stories for the magazine. Publication date had now been fixed for the following Tuesday and there was much work to be done.

The algebra lesson ended when the bell rang for break, and Mr. Wilkins went along to the staff room for a well-earned cup of coffee.

"I've just about had enough of that Form Three," he confided to Mr. Carter. "I gave them a simple problem this morning and the whole lot behaved like half-wits—if that! Still, they're not going to get away with it. I shall make them sit up on Saturday afternoon, believe me!"

The second post had just arrived, and on the mantelpiece was a letter addressed to L. P. Wilkins, Esq., in his sister's writing. Most unexpected, he thought, as he tore open the envelope: for his younger sister, Margaret, was usually too busy nursing at a London hospital to spare much time for correspondence with her brother. He was very fond of his sister, which was not surprising, for she was a very likeable person. He unfolded the sheet of notepaper and read:

> DEAR LANCELOT,
>   I shall be spending next weekend with some friends near Brighton, so I thought it would be a good opportunity to break my journey and look in to see you for an hour or so about tea-time on Saturday. I gather I can catch a bus from Dunhambury to Linbury, but don't bother to meet me; I expect I shall be able to find my own way.
>   Love,
>   MARGARET.

He folded the letter and put it back in the envelope, as one of the other masters drew near. It would never do for his colleagues to find out that his first name was Lancelot. Naturally the Headmaster knew, and so did Mr. Carter, for few facts escaped *his* attention: but so far as the school in general was concerned, L. P. Wilkins preferred to be known by his initials.

Not that there was anything *wrong* with Lancelot: it was a splendid name for the right sort of person, but somehow Mr. Wilkins felt that the right person was not him. Had his name been Bill or Jack or Tom, he would have made no secret of it. But Lancelot … oh, no!

On the staff room notice board was a list of the masters' duties, from which he learned that Mr. Carter would be in charge of the school on Saturday afternoon and evening. That fitted in excellently: the detention class would be over by quarter-past five and he would then be free to entertain his sister and show her round the building.

Most of the masters drifted out of the staff room when they had drunk their coffee, and only Mr. Wilkins and Mr. Carter were left, when a knock sounded on the door a few minutes before the end of break.

The visitor was Jennings—feeling a little uncertain of the reception that awaited him.

"It's about our magazine, sir," he explained. "I'm writing the lives of famous characters like Oliver Cromwell and people, sir, but we thought chaps might get a bit bored reading them, so we're going to put in a few *in*famous characters as well—like you and Mr. Wilkins, sir. Or rather," he amended hastily as a loud "Corwumph!" came from the direction of the mantelpiece, "I should say, characters who are not quite so famous as Oliver Cromwell, but are more interesting to read about."

"Go on," said Mr. Carter in the resigned voice of one who sees difficulties ahead.

"Well, sir, masters never tell people what they were like when they were at school, or whether they had any exciting adventures before they grew old; and those are just the sort of things that'd go down ever so well in a wall-newspaper, sir."

Mr. Wilkins grunted his disapproval. "I'm not having anecdotes of my nursery days stuck up all over the common room, thanks very much."

"I see, sir." Jennings braced himself and took a deep breath because he knew that his next question might not be well received. "Well, sir, perhaps we could manage to write a chatty paragraph if we just knew what your initials stood for, sir."

A deeper shade of pink suffused Mr. Wilkins' cheek. "My name, little boy, is L. P. Wilkins. And what L. P. stands for is not your business."

Jennings shuffled uncomfortably at the rebuke. "No, sir, of course not. Sorry, sir."

He had not meant the question to sound impudent, but it seemed that he was skating on thin ice so far as Mr. Wilkins was concerned. Perhaps Mr. Carter would be more helpful: there was no secret about *his* first name because he signed himself Michael Carter quite openly in autograph books. His age, of course, was another matter and it would be futile, as well as bad manners, to ask what it was, considering that grown-ups always gave some impossible answer such as a hundred and six last birthday. On the other hand, some vague clue would be useful to a biographer and, with some diffidence, Jennings suggested this.

"What sort of a clue?" asked Mr. Carter, puzzled. "Well, like, say, for instance, sir, whether you can remember the first motor car, or if you were alive before they invented ration books."

Unlike his colleague, Mr. Carter was more amused than annoyed. He thought for a few moments and said: "Well, Jennings, Mr. Wilkins has been telling me that Form Three maths needs more practice, so try working this out. Five years ago, I was twice as old as you will be in four years' time, and in ten years' time I shall be five times older than you were two years ago."

He said it so rapidly that Jennings blinked and said: "Oh, golly, sir. I'll have an awful job scrubbing round that one. It's worse than the sums about the chap charging along at x miles an hour, sir."

Another grunt of disapproval came from the region of the mantelpiece. "I suggest, Jennings, that you stop being inquisitive. If you've nothing better to do than waste our time asking a lot of silly questions, you'd better run along."

As Jennings left the room he couldn't help thinking that the campaign to make Mr. Wilkins happier was not making much progress. Why, the man was growing even more surly, if that were possible!

The bell for the next lesson sounded and he hurried back to his classroom to find Darbishire impatiently awaiting the result of the interview.

"Did you get anything out of them, Jen?"

"Not a thing! Tight as limpets, both of them. I'll just have to put something like *Mr. Michael Carter is a gentleman of riper years whose age is a problem for mathematicians.*"

"And what about Old Wilkie?"

"He's worse. His past is obscure and he doesn't want it talked about."

They sat down at their desks and opened their books for the Headmaster's Latin lesson. While they were waiting, Jennings scanned his list of the famous and not so famous. It bore the names:

J. Cæsar.

Sir F. Drake.

Mr. M. Carter.

Messrs. O. Cromwell and L. P. Wilkins, Esq.

The late Dr. A. Grimshaw (deceased?).

Presently he said: "I wish I knew what L.P. stood for."

"Lowest prices—loose pages—lost property," hazarded Darbishire, looking up from his reading of the late doctor's *Latin Grammar.*

"Oh, don't talk such antiseptic eyewash, Darbi! How could he have a name like Lost Property?"

"Who?"

"Mr. Wilkins, of course."

"Oh, sorry, I didn't know you meant him. You just asked what it stood for."

But there seemed no way of finding out, and by tea-time Jennings had almost decided to scrap his life stories of the less famous and stick to people like O. Cromwell, Esq.

At least, he knew what the O stood for!

CHAPTER 14

VENABLES STANDS TREAT

It was just after lunch on Friday that Venables sprang his pleasant surprise. The idea came to him quite suddenly as he was on his way up to the common room. He was pretending to be an articulated lorry at the time, and the first sign that Jennings and Darbishire had of his approach was the roar of internal combustion rattling through his vocal chords as he manoeuvred the imaginary vehicle through the narrow doorway and parked it in a one-way street behind the ping-pong table.

"You're just the characters I'm looking for," he began, as soon as he had switched off his engine with a nerve-shattering clearance of his throat. "I've decided to do you a supersonic favour because you've been pretty decent to me lately."

The pretty decent ones exchanged surprised glances. "Have we?" asked Jennings.

"Oh, yes! I haven't forgotten how you presented me with my Latin book the other week, and on top of that, Darbi let me scrape out his empty jam pot at tea, last Tuesday."

"Oh, forget it," replied Darbishire generously. "Any time I've got a pot going begging with nothing in it, you're quite welcome to the scrapings."

It was then that Venables outlined his plans for the big treat. By the morning's post he had received a ten-shilling note from his uncle, with instructions to spend it sensibly and not squander it on selfish pleasure. And what, Venables had asked himself, could be more sensible than investing part of it in a few shillingsworth of well-chosen doughnuts? Surely, no one could accuse him of indulging in selfish pleasure if he invited two friends, renowned for their decency, to join him!

"So I thought, how would it be if we all three beetled down to old Mrs. Lumley's home-made cake and bicycle shop during village leave tomorrow afternoon," he went on. "She's got fizzy drinks in all colours and her supersonic home-made doughnuts are quite famous in cake-eating circles."

"Coo, thanks very much, Venables—that'd be smashing!"

The guests shook their host's hand like a pump handle and thumped him on the back as though spring-cleaning a carpet. And Jennings added: "I've always liked you, Venables. Haven't I always said so, Darbi? Haven't you often heard me say that old Venables is a ..."

Suddenly he stopped and the carpet cleaning ceased in mid-beat. "Wait a sec. though; we're all being kept in for old Wilkie at quarter-past four tomorrow."

The announcement came as a jet of water on the leaping flames of their joy. "Oh, fish-hooks, I'd forgotten about that! We'll have to call the whole thing off, then," said the host gloomily.

"Oh, no! Don't be such a mouldy cad, Venables," cried Darbishire in dismay. "Couldn't we go next week instead?"

Venables was willing to postpone the feast, but Jennings vetoed the suggestion with some vigour. It occurred to him that if their host's enthusiasm was given a breathing-space, the invitation might not be repeated. A week was a long time: long enough for warm feelings of generosity to congeal into a jelly of indifference; long enough for the money to be spent on other things. Why, there was no knowing *what* might happen if the treat was postponed for a week.

"I vote we go tomorrow," he said firmly. "We'll have masses of time if we beetle off as soon as the match is over. Old Wilkie ought to be pleased, really, because we'll have more strength to cope with all that x and y caper if we've just done a spot of refuelling on ginger-pop and stuff."

They went into the matter in some detail. Allowing ten minutes each way for travelling, they would still have a clear twenty for the feast. That, surely, would be ample time for spending a few shillings in a sensible manner!

"All right, then; we'll do that," Venables agreed. "But we mustn't hang about and waste time. We'll have to keep up a steady x plus y miles an hour all the way down to the village."

On Saturday morning the weather was cold and damp, but it cleared slightly by lunch time and the 1st XI match was played with a pale sun shining overhead.

Jennings, Darbishire and Venables stood on the touchline with sixty-five of their colleagues and cheered the remaining eleven on to victory. The game ended on the stroke of half-past three, and ten minutes later Venables was leading his panting guests along the village street to where a notice in a cottage window said: *Chas. Lumley—Home-made Cakes and Bicycles Repaired.*

"Here we are," said Venables, pushing open the garden gate. "Of course, it's only a little place. If it was a smart restaurant they wouldn't bother about repairing home-made cakes."

The Lumley catering and engineering organisation was conducted on a modest scale, and the firm's chief business consisted of old Mrs. Lumley serving cakes and minerals in the front parlour, while Chas. repaired punctures in the garden shed.

There was not much room in the parlour and on the rare occasions when customers called for refreshment, they would sit round the little table in the window, after carefully shoo-ing a cat from each chair and removing Mr. Lumley's spare waistcoats from the chair-backs.

The three boys hurried into the cottage and threaded their way to the table through the gaps in the furniture.

"Make yourselves comfortable," Venables invited generously as he sat down. "It's my ten bob and you've got my permish to go ahead and order anything you like—except a home-made bicycle."

"Coo, thanks," beamed Darbishire, edging his way on to a chair which was already occupied by a large black cat. "Good puss, good puss!" he said: which was not strictly true, for the cat stuck out its claws and hissed at him. As it was unwilling to move, he had to balance himself on the rim of the chair and remember not to lean back.

Mrs. Lumley plodded heavily out of the kitchen to welcome her first customers of the day.

"Yerse?" she inquired.

"A plate of home-made cakes and doughnuts and three bottles of fizzy ginger-pop, please," Venables ordered importantly after conferring with his guests.

Darbishire followed Mrs. Lumley's slow plod back to the kitchen with anxious eyes. "I hope she steps on it," he observed.

"There won't be much left of the doughnuts if she does. She's got shoes like violin cases," Jennings pointed out.

"No, I mean I hope she steps on the gas and gets a move on; it's about a quarter to four already."

Mrs. Lumley had not hurried for forty years and had no intention of doing so now. She pottered slowly around the kitchen gathering up doughnuts, washing out glasses and breaking off from time to time to see if the cats' supper was simmering nicely on the kitchen range. At last she returned to the front room and set plates and bottles on the table with an appetising clatter.

"Thanks awfully," said the customers, and wasted no time in setting about their meal. The doughnuts were delicious, for there was no doubt that Mrs. Lumley was a good cook.

"It doesn't come to more than ten shillings, does it?" asked Darbishire, with his mouth full of doughnut and his mind full of earnest resolutions not to put his host to too much expense.

"Oh, no! Three shillings, that'll be," said Mrs. Lumley. "But you needn't pay now, ducks. You get on and enjoy it. I'll be through in the kitchen if you want any more."

For three minutes the champing of jaws was the only sound in the room. Then Jennings said: "Aren't these cakes supersonic! I haven't tasted anything like them since I was young—well, younger than I am now, anyway."

"Yes, and it's smashing pop, too. It's jolly generous of you to treat us like this, Venables. My father says that a generous impulse is ..."

Darbishire's voice trailed away and he stared at his host in alarm. "I say, Ven, what's the matter? Are you feeling all right?"

"Mm? What's that? Oh, yes, I'm all right, thanks," came from Venables in a faint, far-away sort of voice.

Jennings looked up from his plate and he, too, frowned in puzzled wonder. For their host's doughnut lay untasted on his plate and the pop level had not ebbed from the rim of his glass.

"What's up, Venables? Indigestion or something?" "No, I'm all right, thanks. I just had a sudden thought—that's all."

"You needn't worry about the detention, if that's what's biting you. If we start back in about five minutes we shall have bags of time."

"It's not the detention," replied Venables. "It was when you asked the old girl how much the bill came to. I suddenly thought to myself: 'Gosh!' I thought."

He broke off, overcome by some emotion, and stared with unseeing eyes at a china dog on the mantelpiece.

"Well, go on," Jennings prompted. "What happened after you thought 'Gosh'?"

With an effort Venables pulled himself together. "Well, after I'd thought 'Gosh,' I thought a bit more and then I thought 'Golly!' I thought—I changed my jacket after lunch because Matron wanted to sew a button on."

"What about it?"

"Well, don't get in a flap; everything will come out all right in the end—I hope, but ..." Venables ran his tongue over his dry lips. It was clear that he was approaching the climax of his story. It came with a rush: "... you see it was then I remembered I'd left my ten-shilling note in my other jacket that Matron's got."

"What!"

"Super sorrow and all that. It was just an accidental bish."

"Oh, fish-hooks, this is frightful!" wailed Darbishire. "We're half-way through these cakes and drinks now. Why do these hoo-hahs always have to pick on us to happen to? I'm not old enough to cope with these catastro-scopes."

For some seconds they sat and stared at one another while their minds grappled with the problem. Four doughnuts and two bottles of pop had already been consumed, and they hadn't a penny between the three of them to pay the bill. What was to be done? Explain their plight to Mrs. Lumley and ask to pay at a later date? Impossible! She looked the sort of woman who wouldn't have trusted her own grandmother, let alone strangers with hearty appetites and empty pockets.

"There's only one thing to be done," Jennings decided, and turned to his host. "You'll have to hoof back to school at something a wizard sight faster than x miles an hour, Ven, and get that ten-shilling note from your other jacket; Darbi and I will sit here and go on eating as though nothing had happened until you get back. Whatever we do, we mustn't let Mrs. Lumley smell a rat."

Then came the second difficulty. Venables' double journey and the final return of all three to school would normally take thirty minutes of brisk travelling. Darbishire looked at his watch: it was one minute to four.

"Sixteen minutes to zero hour. We'll never do it in the time!"

"Yes, we will if Ven runs like blinko. Fifteen minutes all told for hoofing and one minute to pay the bill. Go on, Venables, get weaving, for Pete's sake; we've already wasted nearly half our spare minute in talking about it."

The host zigzagged his way out past the clutter of furniture, and a moment later they saw him sprinting down the village street in his race against the clock. He ran with a long loping stride which put new heart into the watchers at the window. Why, if he could keep up that pace for a mile, he would be there and back almost before they had finished their sixth doughnut ... *If* he could keep it up!

Darbishire turned away from the window. "Eat up, Jennings; we mustn't let the old girl suspect anything. If she knew we were calmly putting ourselves outside three shillingsworth of doughnuts without a pennyworth of rhino to pay for it, she'd go off pop."

Jennings nodded absently. He was wondering whether Venables would be able to get back with the money before they had finished the cakes on the plate. If not, they would have to order more—or be faced with the bill!

"We've got to keep up appearances, that's what we've got to do," Darbishire prattled on nervously. "My father says that appearances are deceptive, but ..." He stopped as the kitchen door opened and Mrs. Lumley appeared.

"Thought as how I heard the front door slam," she said.

"Yes, it was our friend. He's just gone outside for a little while to—er, to take some exercise. He'll be back soon," Jennings explained.

Mrs. Lumley's eye fell upon the now empty cake plate. "Made short work of me doughnuts and no mistake. Are you going to settle up now, ducks, or do you want some more?"

Faced with an embarrassing alternative, Jennings made the only choice he could. "Well, yes, I suppose we'd better have a few more, I'm afraid—I mean, we'd like some very much."

"Right you are, ducks!" Mrs. Lumley returned to the kitchen, and Darbishire turned to his friend with alarm in his eyes.

"You ancient historic monument, Jennings; what did you want to order more for?"

"I had to! You heard her ask if we were ready to pay. If we don't go on eating and drinking and pretending everything's all right, she'll smell a rat as sure as eggs."

"Yes, I know, but all the same ..."

It was a rash move, and the thought of the risks involved destroyed the last traces of Darbishire's hearty appetite. "I shan't be able to enjoy the next lot at all. I shall be wondering about Venables all the time. Supposing he sprains his ankle? ... Supposing something goes wrong? ... Oh, golly, what a gum-tree we shouldn't half be up!"

"Don't be such a gloomy specimen, Darbi! He'll be back with the money in less than ten minutes, so nothing *can* go wrong. You see if I'm not right!"

While Venables was pounding along Linbury Lane, Mr. Wilkins was rounding up Form Three for the detention class, for he was anxious to make a prompt start or, better still, to begin a few minutes early.

His sister's letter had not said what time she was coming, but he was assuming that she would arrive at about five o'clock. In that case he would have to dismiss his class before the full hour was up, so it was most important that no time should be wasted in getting down to work.

Form Three were more than willing to fall in with Mr. Wilkins' wishes. They took the view that the sooner they started, the sooner the miserable business would be over and done with.

They sat down at their desks, and Mr. Wilkins called the roll. It gave him no pleasure to find that their were three absentees.

"Tut-tut-tut! Why on earth can't everybody be ready, when I'm in a hurry," he complained.

"They've gone to the village, sir," Temple informed him. "But they said they would be back by quarter-past."

"Well, I'm not waiting all afternoon for them. If they're not here in a couple of minutes, I'll—I'll—well, they'd better look out!"

"Wouldn't it be better if *we* all looked out, sir?" Atkinson suggested. "Then we might be able to see them coming."

"No, it would not. Open your textbooks at page fourteen and read through the examples it gives." And Mr. Wilkins strode from the room and made for the landing window to see if the missing boys were even now panting up the drive, eager to get to grips with algebraical problems.

They were not; but Mr. Carter was coming up the stairs and had to stop and listen to an account of his colleague's difficulties.

"You see, the point is, Carter, that my sister's coming this afternoon, and I want to get this class off my hands before she arrives. If she turns up before I'm free, would you mind seeing that someone takes her up to my room? She's not been here before and she doesn't know her way about."

"Certainly," Mr. Carter replied. "Would you like me to look after your class for you, in case she arrives early?"

"No, no. I shall have finished with them by five o'clock, if only I can get started. Trouble is, I'm three boys short, but as soon as ..."

He broke off and listened, as a curious noise was wafted up the stairs from the hall below. It was a sound that might have been made by a tank engine puffing up a steep gradient, a pressure cooker announcing that lunch was ready, or even a two-handled saw churning its way through a tree-trunk.

In point of fact, it was none of these things. It was Venables gasping for breath, as he started on the last lap of his marathon run to Matron's room to retrieve his ten-shilling note.

"Ah, here's one of them coming now. Lucky for him! He's just in time." And Mr. Wilkins called loudly: "Come along, Venables! Hurry up, boy, I've been waiting five minutes for you already."

The runner wheezed up the stairs and sagged exhausted against the banisters. His face was a brilliant scarlet; his hair and forehead were bathed in perspiration; his collar clung damply to his neck and his socks lay in folds about his ankles. His shoulders heaved: he could not speak.

"Glad to see you've been hurrying," said Mr. Wilkins briskly. "Run along to the classroom and get your books out. I'm starting right away."

By the time his heart had stopped pounding and his breathing was again under control, Venables found himself sitting at his desk, while Mr. Wilkins paced the classroom explaining the importance of x and the advantages of y. He was not pleased when a hand rose, and Venables said: "Please, sir, I can't come in to class just yet, sir."

"What do you mean—you *can't* come in? You *have* come in. And only just in time, too."

"I've got to go down to the village again, sir. It's urgent!"

"You'll do nothing of the sort."

"But, sir, I *must*, sir. I've left Jennings and Darbishire down there."

Mr. Wilkins bristled. *He'd* have something to say to those two gentlemen when they condescended to turn up!

"Can't I go and fetch them, sir? They'll never get back without me."

"I ... I ... *Corwumph!*. Are you trying to be funny, boy? They know their way back; they're not half-wits—well, they are, *practically*, but that's neither here nor there."

"But, sir, you must listen, sir. You see what happened was ..."

"Be quiet, Venables! I don't want to hear another word. We've wasted enough time as it is."

Mr. Wilkins glared angrily and turned three shades pinker. He was standing no nonsense from Venables—or from Jennings and Darbishire, either! Obviously the three of them had put their heads together and hatched a plot; all this nonsense about one of them going off to fetch the others was merely an excuse to waste time and miss half the detention class. When the conspirators realised that their scheme had misfired, they'd come back, quickly enough! Mr. Wilkins smiled grimly. *He* was not the sort of man to be taken in by childish pranks!

"But, sir, it's urgent, sir! You don't understand."

"Silence, boy!" roared Mr. Wilkins in a voice of thunder. "Don't you dare argue with me. You'll do as you're told, or it'll be the worse for the three of you!"

Venables shrugged helplessly. He had done his best in the teeth of fierce opposition. He felt sorry for Jennings and Darbishire but, after all, what more could *he* do about it?

CHAPTER 15

THE PAYING GUEST

THERE are times when an unkind Fate will swoop down upon its prey like a goshawk; at others, it will play a cat-and-mouse game with its victims' dwindling hopes. Upon Jennings and Darbishire awaiting the hour of liberation in Mrs. Lumley's cottage, Fate used its delayed action technique and withheld until too late the sad news that Venables was not coming back.

For the first ten minutes after his departure they kept their fingers crossed and went on eating doughnuts. For a further five, they tapped their feet and fidgeted—to the annoyance of the cat population who were trying to sleep.

By quarter-past four they knew that their host had failed them and that trouble lay ahead in the stern shape of Mr. Wilkins. But it was not until twenty-eight minutes past the hour that they realised what deeper troubles were even now at their door in the portly shape of Mrs. Lumley. For stacked upon the table were the plates and bottles which they had felt obliged to order in their attempt to keep up appearances and stave off the evil moment when the bill would have to be paid.

"Why doesn't Venables *come*!" moaned Darbishire for the fifth time in three minutes.

"If you ask me, he's a treacherous traitor," Jennings retorted angrily. "Wait till I see him again! I'll make him live to regret it!"

"When *I* get hold of him, he'll regret it, but he may not live—not more than long enough to regret it, anyway."

It was not often that Darbishire bore ill-will towards his fellow creatures, but now he was shocked beyond measure by what he imagined to be Venables' heartless conduct. A nice sort of treat this was turning out to be! He looked at the table with a jaundiced eye.

"Have another doughnut, Jen? There's just one left."

"Golly, no, I couldn't. I should burst; I've had about seven already and four bottles of ginger-pop."

"It's time we got cracking and asked for some more, all the same. We haven't

631

had a fresh lot for ages and ages and she's beginning to give us those funny looks again. If she smells a rat, we're sunk, don't forget!"

Jennings groaned quietly. "I know, I know! But it's got past smelling a rat by this time. She'll be sending for the Pied Piper of Hamelin or the corporation rodent inspector if we don't do something about it soon."

There was no denying that Mrs. Lumley had been looking at them curiously for some little time, but this was due to sheer surprise. Never had she seen so few boys eat so many doughnuts; and little did she know that each mouthful nearly choked them!

"Oh, fish-hooks! She's coming back again. Try and look hungry, Darbi!" Jennings whispered, as the kitchen door opened with a squeak.

"You can't look hungry when you've just had to loosen your belt," Darbishire complained. He shook his head sadly, for he was very fond of home-made cakes and would often lie awake at night wondering what it must be like to eat so many that he just couldn't eat any more. Now, he knew!

"Tut-tut! Well, I never!" exclaimed Mrs. Lumley, eyeing the cluttered table. "You lads have got an appetite, that I *will* say. I don't think you'd better 'ave no more, or you'll be queer. Let's see now, that's fourteen cakes and doughnuts you've had altogether, and seven bottles of fizz—er, that'll be, er—um, nine-and-sixpence, please."

Jennings shifted uncomfortably in his chair. The time had come to explain and it was not going to be easy.

"I'm afraid there's been a bit of a bish," he began.

"There's been a *what*, ducks?"

"There's been a sort of accidental mistake—quite by accident, of course. You see ..."

Mrs. Lumley checked the bill. "No, ducks; there's no mistake. Nine-and-six it'll cost you, though where you've found room to put it all is more than ..."

Darbishire had been staring out of the window with glassy eyes. Suddenly he gave a convulsive start and crowed, "Wacko!" For he had heard the click of the garden gate and had caught a glimpse of a human shape behind the holly bush.

His heart leapt with joy. Venables was coming back! Good old Venables! He had not failed them after all! Mindless of Mrs. Lumley's bewildered expression, he leaned across the table and whispered the glad tidings in Jennings' ear.

"Oh, goodo!" cried Jennings. "We're saved, then! And we're still sixpence inside the limit."

Good old Venables! The chap must be hungry after his long journey: it was only fair that he should be allowed to enjoy the last sixpennyworth of his uncle's present. Jennings turned to Mrs. Lumley.

"If you don't mind, we'll just have a last plate of doughnuts for our friend, please."

"But I thought as how he'd gone."

"Yes, but he's come back. Just a last sixpenny-worth for the road, and then we'll be off."

As Mrs. Lumley returned to the kitchen, the front door opened and the two boys leapt to their feet to greet their long-lost host.

"I say, Venables, you have been a ..."

Jenning's voice clicked off suddenly like an unpopular radio programme. For the door had opened to admit a complete stranger.

The newcomer was an attractive young lady in her early twenties. She was slim and fair, with a gay sparkle in her eyes and a friendly smile about her lips. She was smiling now as she set down her suitcase and said: "Do you mind if I join you at your table? There doesn't seem to be anywhere else to sit."

"Um? Oh, yes, please do; that'll be all right; delighted," mumbled Jennings in a daze; and he made a movement to clear the crockery from the place where Venables had sat.

Darbishire, too, had risen to greet his host and now leaned weakly against the mantelpiece muttering to himself: "*Not* Venables! Oh, my goodness, it isn't Venables! All that hoping we were saved and now it isn't Venables after all!"

"Be quiet, and pull yourself together, you coot! You're chuntering like a village idiot," Jennings told him in a warning whisper. "You needn't go on and *on* saying who it isn't. We know by now, and anyway, it's not polite." He turned back to the young lady and gallantly removed a struggling ginger cat from her chair.

All the same, he could sympathise with his friend's shocked reaction, for this new development was enough to numb the nerves of the strongest. And to make matters worse, they had just ordered a further sixpenny worth of doughnuts in celebration!

"You seem to have been doing yourselves well," said the young lady, waving a hand towards the empty plates and bottles.

Jennings nodded. "We—well, we sort of had no choice, if you see what I mean."

The newcomer looked at the boys with a new interest. She had often heard her brother speak of the amount of food which schoolboys were reputed to eat, but she had never really believed him.

The boys, for their part, looked at the newcomer with no interest at all; she seemed a poor substitute for Venables and his ten-shilling note. They noticed, of course, that she was young and attractive. They even noticed the initials *M. W.* on her suitcase, but this rang no bell in their minds; and, indeed there was no reason why it should have done, because there was little family resemblance between Margaret Wilkins and her elder brother, Lancelot.

She was slim and he was burly; she was soft of speech and light on her feet, whereas her brother had a voice like a loud-hailer and footsteps which echoed like a deep-sea diver marking time with his boots on. In character, the two differed just as widely, and Margaret regarded her brother's turbulent manner with quiet amusement. In spite of this, however, they managed to remain on the friendliest of terms.

Although Jennings and Darbishire noticed nothing unusual about Miss Wilkins, she could see at a glance that something was very much the matter with *them*; and when the new consignment of cakes had arrived and she had ordered a cup of tea for herself, she said: "You don't look very cheerful. Aren't you going to eat these cakes she's just brought?"

"No thanks," Jennings answered weakly. "If I looked another doughnut in the face, I should explode."

"Something's gone wrong, hasn't it?" she asked. They nodded miserably.

"Won't you tell me what the matter is? I might be able to help."

Jennings shook his head. "It's very decent of you, but I don't think you could. There's only one person who could help us, and he's not here. He invited us out to a special feast, and just as we were half-way through the first plateful he had to go and think 'Gosh!'"

Miss Wilkins looked puzzled. "He had to go and do *what?*"

"Oh, he didn't really have to *go* anywhere to think it. He just sat there where you're sitting now and thought it. And after he'd thought 'Gosh!' once or twice, he calmly turned round and told us he'd left his rhino behind."

"His rhino? Does he work in a zoo?"

"Oh, no: Jennings means his money," Darbishire explained. "And he didn't actually turn *round* and tell us, because he was facing us all the time."

"Well, you know what I mean," said Jennings.

"Oh, yes, *I* do, but perhaps this lady doesn't. She might think he hadn't got the face to tell us so he swooshed round and looked out of the window."

"I think I understand—so far," said Margaret. "Won't you go on?"

And by degrees she coaxed more of the story from them and learned who they were and which school they came from.

"... and of course, it may not really be all Venables' fault." Jennings finished up. "Because there's a mouldy detention class we're supposed to have gone to, and if he's been nabbed for that we shall have to go on eating for simply hours and hours yet—perhaps all night even!"

Miss Wilkins sympathised. The prospect of continual doughnut-eating to allay Mrs. Lumley's suspicions was too horrible to think about. She suggested a remedy: "If you can't leave till the bill's paid, perhaps you'll let me pay it for you."

"Good gracious, no; we couldn't possibly!" Jennings protested. "We wouldn't dream of taking money from you. After all, you're practically our guest; we invited you to sit at our table."

Margaret changed her line of approach. "We could call it a loan. Then you'll be able to go back to school and repay me when you've found your friend."

A loan from a guest! Jennings didn't like the idea at first, but there seemed no other solution.

"Well, all right, then; thank you very much," he said. "You could be a sort of *paying* guest, couldn't you? And we'll let you have it back the minute we've seen Venables—if he's still alive after Old Wilkie's finished with him."

"Who?" she inquired.

"Old Wilkie—Mr. Wilkins by rights; he's one of our masters and he goes berserk and charges about like a fire-breathing dragon when he's in a bate."

"Really!" Margaret raised an interested eyebrow. It was obvious from the way he spoke that the boy had no idea that he was addressing the fire-breathing dragon's sister. She was about to enlighten him when he hurried on:

"Yes, honestly! You'd never believe the chronic hoo-hahs Old Wilkie kicks up unless you'd sat through one of his mouldy algebra lessons. And it's no good trying to be decent to him—he just goes into the attack like an armoured column and won't listen. I've met some frantic types in my time, but Old Wilkie— phew!"

It was not, Miss Wilkins decided, a good moment to claim kinship to an armoured column. After all, a guest—even though only a paying one—should not embarrass her hosts when they had troubles enough already. All the same, she could not help feeling rather surprised at Jennings' description. She knew her brother was inclined to be explosive when things went wrong at home, but she had never given much thought to the way in which he dealt with his boys at school.

So, wisely, she changed the subject, and as the boys seemed in some hurry to be gone, she drank up her tea and asked whether she might walk back to school with them.

"Righto! Then we can give you the money," said Darbishire. "Of course, it's probably taking you out of your way. I hope you won't mind."

"Oh, no, I'm going to Linbury Court in any case. I'm calling to see someone. In fact, I should have been there by now, but I wasn't sure of the way and I got off the bus in the village, by mistake."

Darbishire looked at her in some surprise. Was she a parent?

"If you don't mind my saying so, you look a bit young to be some chap's mother," he said politely.

"No, I'm not that. I'm—er, I'm some chap's sister."

She called to Mrs. Lumley for the bill and suggested that they should take the remaining doughnuts back to school for Venables. They agreed with some reluctance, for Venables was not a very popular character with either of them just then.

"Ten-and-tuppence all told, ducks," said Mrs. Lumley. "Tuppence for the tea and ten shillings for the rest. And if these here lads gets the collywobbles after all that lot, don't say as I never warned you."

They set off along the village street, Jennings carrying Margaret's suitcase and Darbishire carrying the spare doughnuts in a paper bag. They were deeply grateful to their paying guest and thanked her a dozen times for coming to their rescue. But behind their gratitude lurked the thought of what was going to happen when they got back to school.

It was nearly five o'clock by now and they would have missed most of the detention class—perhaps all of it! What on earth would Mr. Wilkins say!

Margaret sensed their worry and asked them questions about the more pleasant side of school life to keep their minds off their immediate future. They told her about the *Form Three Times* and the trouble they were having with the forthcoming number: which brought the conversation back to the delicate topic of Mr. Wilkins.

"I'm sure he's not really such a monster as you make out," said Margaret, after listening to a catalogue of her brother's shortcomings.

"Oh, but he is—he's worse!" Darbishire confirmed. "He's not like the other

masters at all. Now, Mr. Carter's jolly decent; so's Mr. Hind, and even the Archbeako—he's the Head, you know—even *he's* more or less human when he's in the mood. But Old Wilkie—well, I ask you!"

Margaret felt that the discussion had gone so far that it might as well be thrashed out properly. Perhaps, from her deeper knowledge of Mr. Wilkins, she might be able to put matters right.

"But what exactly is it that you don't like about him?" she asked.

"Well, we don't mind him barking at us when we've done something wrong— we do, sometimes," Darbishire admitted. "But it's just the same when we're trying to be decent. Take the other day, for instance: Jennings wanted to have a bash at writing the life stories of famous and unfamous characters, like, say, Mr. Carter and Mr. Wilkins for this magazine we told you about. You know— what they were like when they were young, and what their full names were."

"We know Mr. Wilkins' initials are L. P., but what *that* stands for is a mystery," Jennings added. "I doubt if any one knows really."

Margaret smiled. So Lancelot was secretive about his romantic Christian name! That was another thing she hadn't known before.

"Of course, we didn't dare ask him how old he was," Jennings went on. "He's not the sort of chap you can ask questions like that."

"And did Mr. Carter tell you his age?"

"Well, no, actually, he didn't, but we could find out if we wanted to, because he's got to the sort of age you can only work out by algebra," Jennings explained.

"Good gracious! That sounds terribly ancient."

"Well, you know, you need x's and y's like the old geologist geezers use for finding out how old fossils and things are. Mind you, I don't mean Mr. Carter's as old as all that, but I bet he's at least thirty."

He prattled on about the responsibilities of editing a high-class magazine and touched lightly upon the trials of press-photography and the imperfections of the *Ideal Junior Printing Outfit*.

"Your magazine sounds splendid to me," said Miss Wilkins. "We must have a chat about it before I go. Perhaps I could help you with a few ideas."

The boys thought the suggestion extremely unlikely—coming as it did from one who was merely "some chap's sister"—but they were too polite to say so.

They had reached the school gates by this time and their uneasiness increased as they went up the drive.

"We'd better say goodbye now," said Jennings. "I'll get Venables to bring that money to you, because I don't suppose we'll see you again before you go."

Margaret was sorry to hear it. "But aren't we going to have a chat about your magazine?" she asked.

Jennings shook his head. "I don't see how we can. You see, being stranded in the village means we've missed the detention class."

"Is that serious?"

"*Is* that serious! Is *that* serious! Old Wilkie will be in such a bate he'll—well, if you hear a super-sonic explosion in about five minutes' time, you'll know we've just reported to him."

"You ought to hear Jennings' famous imitation of Mr. Wilkins' getting in a bate and going off pop," said Darbishire. "Do it, Jen! It's good enough for television, really it is!"

"I wouldn't say that," replied Jennings modestly. "It's just a little thing I worked out. It goes like this." He held his breath until he was red in the face and then, with arms flailing like a windmill, he burst out: "I ... I ... *Corwumph!* I've had enough of this trumpery moonshine, you uncouth youth, you ... you *silly* little boy!"

"I should never have believed it," said Margaret solemnly.

"Oh yes you would, if you'd ever seen Mr. Wilkins—it's just like him," Darbishire assured her. "It's taken Jen months of practice to get it right." He smiled his congratulations to the impersonator and then turned again to the paying guest. "By the way, who is it you've come to see? We could round him up for you if you like."

"Don't bother. I'll find my way about."

"Well, don't go wandering into Mr. Wilkins' room by mistake, if you want to get off the premises in one piece," Jennings advised. "He'll be hopping mad by this time and just ripe for the big explosion."

At that moment, Mr. Carter came out of the front door and made his way down the steps and across the quad towards them.

"Good afternoon; my name's Carter," he said. "You must be Miss Wilkins, I imagine."

Margaret admitted her identity with a smile.

"I'm glad you found your way safely," said Mr. Carter. "If you'll come along with me, I'll take you up to your brother's room. I promised to look out for you, because he's been busy with a detention class, but he'll be free in a moment."

From the corner of his eye Mr. Carter noticed a strangeness in the manner of Jennings and Darbishire. They stood rigid as though in a trance, pink of face with open mouths and staring eyes. Jennings dropped the visitor's suitcase as though the handle was red-hot, while Darbishire's fingers made little twitching movements on the small paper bag he held in his palsied grasp.

Mr. Carter turned hurriedly away from the unnerving sight. Why must boys always choose a moment when guests were present to look as though they were suffering from sunstroke and delayed concussion, he wondered? He picked up the suitcase and led the way up the steps.

"It must be some time since you've seen your brother," he said. "I expect you'll have plenty to talk about."

Her reply sounded clear and distinct in the ears of the spellbound audience at the foot of the steps.

"Yes, rather! There's quite a lot I'm just dying to tell him," she said.

CHAPTER 16

VISITOR FOR MR. WILKINS

ANY one who has stepped under an ice-cold shower-bath under the impression that it was a hot one, will know something of the shock that Jennings and Darbishire felt when they realised that their paying guest was a close relative of Mr. Wilkins.

For a few seconds after Mr. Carter had closed the front door, the two boys stood riveted to the ground with horrified surprise. Then, in a strained, unnatural voice, Darbishire said: "I just can't believe it! I simply *cannot* believe it! I feel faint; I should collapse if it wasn't for all these doughnuts inside me. Old Wilkie's sister, of all people! And we've gone and put both feet *slap-bang-plonk* into the stickiest bish in history."

It is doubtful whether Jennings heard him, for his mind was reeling at the thought of the terrible thing he had done: all those pointed remarks about fire-breathing dragons; and, worse still, the famous imitation of L. P. Wilkins, Esq., in a bate! What must she have thought!

"Why *ever* couldn't she have told us she was his sister in the first place!" he demanded. "It was a mouldy trick keeping quiet about it and letting us go on talking."

"M'yes, but I *do* see her point," Darbishire replied reasonably. "If Old Wilkie was my brother I shouldn't be so proud of it that I'd want to go round telling every stranger I met. What worries me is how we're going to face him, now she's gone and told him everything."

Steeped in gloom they made their way indoors and hung their caps and coats in the changing room. The detention class had just been dismissed and the corridors were alive with third-formers, their heads still swimming with algebraic problems.

"You two are going to get your chips all right," Temple prophesied as he met them on the stairs. "Old Wilkie was as livid as mud when you didn't turn up. He nearly went off pop."

"Don't talk to me about going off pop—I've just had seven doughnuts."

Darbishire thrust the paper bag into Temple's hands. "Here you are—eat these! We *were* going to give them to Venables, but I don't feel like being decent to him just at present."

It was growing dark now, but through the window, Jennings could just make out the form of their late host, hurrying over the quad towards the drive at the same record-breaking pace he had shown an hour earlier. He must be stopped at once, Jennings decided: and calling to Darbishire, he dashed out of the building in pursuit.

Venables had nearly reached the end of the drive when he heard the shouts behind him and came to a halt. He seemed surprised when he saw who his pursuers were.

"Oh, there you are! How did you get back? I was just hoofing down to Old Mother Lumley's to liberate you. I've got my ten-shilling note, now, look."

"You're a mouldy cad, Venables—leaving us stranded in the middle of all those doughnuts," Jennings cried as he bounded up to the would-be rescuer. "We had to eat the whole ten shillings' worth and you can jolly well fork out the rhino."

Venables looked alarmed. "Oh heavens, no! I only meant to spend half that, even when I was with you. And now I haven't had any and you've got out anyway, it's not fair to expect me to fork out at all."

In vain they reasoned with him as they retraced their steps up the drive; but Venables was not interested in their private debts and maintained that they had had no right to spend on such a lavish scale.

"Well, you shouldn't have pushed off and left us," Jennings argued. "We've been exposed to the most frantic dangers, what with Old Wilkie gunning for us because we weren't there, and Old Mrs. Lumley after us because we still *were*. And what's more we've got indigestion, and on top of that our paying guest's turned out to be a wolf in the grass."

"You mean a snake in the grass," corrected Darbishire, who liked to have things right, even at times of crisis. "My father says it's wolves who go about in sheep's clothing."

"What do they want to do that for?"

"Oh, they don't really!"

"You said they *did*."

"Ah, but that was just a saying. You don't actually find wolves wearing sheepskin waistcoats and things, any more than you really have snakes in the grass."

"But you *do* have snakes in the grass. Where else would you expect to find grass snakes?"

"Well, I wouldn't expect to find them in Mrs. Lumley's tea-shop pretending to be angels in disguise, and being Mr. Wilkins' sister all the time."

The conversation seemed to be drifting away from the point, which was that their next move must be in the direction of Mr. Wilkins' study. Their hearts quailed at the prospect—not because of the punishment which they might well expect for missing the detention class, but because *she* would be there.

She would have told him all by this time. Why, she might even make them repeat their rash words or ... But, no ... Never again, Jennings felt, could he bring himself to utter the words of his famous impersonation.

They left Venables in the hall and slowly, very slowly, mounted the stairs. At the top, they sat down on a laundry basket; they felt they needed a five-minute break to gather strength for the ordeal which lay before them.

"Bags you knock and go in first when we get there," Darbishire urged. "I shouldn't have the strength. My mind's wobbling too much at the thought of her actually sitting there, at this very moment, and telling Mr. Wilkins everything we said about him."

The boys would have been surprised if they could have seen Miss Margaret Wilkins at that very moment. Admittedly, she was sitting in the armchair in her brother's study, but if she intended to pour forth outraged complaints she was taking a long time to set about it. Instead, she sipped a cup of tea and ate the crumpets which he had prepared specially in her honour.

"It's quite a change to see you in these surroundings," she said. "But you shouldn't have gone to all this trouble, Lancelot. I had a cup of tea before I arrived."

He looked up sharply at the mention of his Christian name.

"If you don't mind, Margaret, we'll leave the *Lancelot* out of it; I don't want it broadcast."

"But why not? You've always been Lancelot at home."

That, Mr. Wilkins explained, was different. At home, his name sounded perfectly natural, but if it was to be bandied about the school he would never know a moment's peace. One might as well be called Donald Duck or Muffin the Mule!

"What shall I call you then—Old Wilkie?"

"I—er, well, it's better than Lancelot, anyway. It's what the boys call me, when I'm not supposed to be listening. You can leave out the 'Old' though; it's just a sort of courtesy title."

He jabbed the toasting fork into a crumpet and held it in front of the fire. Margaret watched him with interest. Was he really as heartless as the boys made out? She had always thought of him as a simple soul beneath his bluff exterior. A little forthright, perhaps, but ...

"Have another cup of tea!" invited the simple soul.

"No, thanks, Lance—er, Wilkie. I had some in the village with two of your boys. Jennings and Darbishire they said their names were. I thought they were rather nice."

"What!"

The toasting fork quivered like a harp-string and the crumpet fell into the fire with a sizzle, as Mr. Wilkins leapt to his feet and stared at his sister in surprise.

"You ... you mean to tell me—well, dash it all, Margaret, this is a fine thing! They were supposed to be in my detention class—not guzzling food with my own sister. So that's where they were! They're going to find themselves in so much trouble they'll begin to wish ..."

"But it wasn't their fault! They were frightfully upset about missing your class, but they were stranded without any money."

Mr. Wilkins was not impressed. He stopped staring and turned to cope with the flaming crumpet which was filling the room with a pungent smell of roasted dough. He tried to spear it with the toasting fork, but only succeeded in knocking it farther into the fire; which did nothing to improve the state of his feelings. Curtly, he told his sister that in matters of school discipline he was not prepared to listen to excuses from an outsider. Jennings and Darbishire would be severely punished—and that was that!

He was rather surprised, therefore, when she asked whether she could see them again before she left. "What on earth do you want to do that for?" he demanded.

"I promised to give them some suggestions for their magazine," she explained. "I gather you weren't very helpful when they wanted to write your life story."

"I should think not, indeed. My life story! Never heard such trumpery moonshine. Anyway, they've had to think again because I didn't tell them anything."

"That's why I want to see them. I could tell them all sorts of interesting things."

There was a hint of mischief in Margaret's voice which made him look at her with sudden misgiving as she went on: "Do you remember that time when you were very small and you had six helpings of Christmas pudding? I remember father saying, 'Lancelot, my boy, let this be a lesson to you never to ...'"

"For heaven's sake!" Mr. Wilkins' voice rose in wild alarm. "You'd never tell them a thing like that; don't be such a rotter, Margaret!"

She smiled and repeated his words: "'Don't be such a rotter, Margaret!' I remember your saying that, years ago, when you fell out of the apple tree on to the compost heap and got your best suit dirty. Now I come to think of it, that wouldn't make a bad story, either."

"I ... I ... but dash it all, Margaret, you know perfectly well that wasn't my fault. The branch was rotten—it let me down."

"It wasn't the boys' fault that they didn't turn up for your class. Their friend let *them* down."

Mr. Wilkins blinked in amazement. He had been looking forward to entertaining his sister to tea and crumpets, and chatting pleasantly of family matters. Well, they were chatting of family matters right enough, he told himself, but hardly in the way he had been expecting. Besides, it was sheer nonsensical tomfoolery to compare his unfortunate mishap in the apple tree all those years ago with Jennings and Darbishire missing his detention class.

It wasn't the same thing at all, and the sooner Margaret realised it, the better.

But she *wouldn't* realise it! "It's exactly the same sort of thing," she argued. "They were both the silly kind of accident that boys are always getting involved in. And if you can't see it now, try reading about it in the life story of Lancelot Phineas Wilkins, Esq., when it comes out in the next number of the *Form Three Times*!"

Mr. Wilkins rocked top-heavily on his heels and clutched at the bookcase for support. "I ... I ... *Corwumph*! But Margaret, you couldn't ... You *wouldn't* ..."

She nodded. She could ... She *would*!

The crumpet had burnt itself to a cinder and mechanically Mr. Wilkins opened the window to let in a breath of fresh air. He felt he needed air; preferably a cool current playing round his temples to keep his emotions from flaring up as surely as the ill-fated crumpet.

He leaned against the windowsill, deep in thought, and gradually the evening breeze calmed his feelings and set his mind upon a track it had not travelled for a long time. It took him back seventeen years to the days when his voice was shriller, his hair thicker and his knees dirtier than they were now. Now he came to think of it, he must have been a rowdy little specimen himself in those days, and quite capable of behaving in the same idiotic way as Jennings and Darbishire .... H'm! Perhaps he *had* been a bit hasty. After all, Margaret was a very good judge of these matters, and if she was so sure that the boys were the victims of an unfortunate accident, he was prepared to take her word for it. Especially as the alternative was the probability of seeing chatty childhood anecdotes about Lancelot Wilkins, Esq., in the *Form Three Times*!

He turned back from the window and said: "I don't want to be unfair, Margaret, so I'll tell you what I suggest: I'll just make them do the sums they missed this afternoon, without giving them a further punishment for missing them."

"That sounds fair enough," she replied, with all the reasonableness of a younger sister who has got her own way.

"And—er, you won't—er—" How should he put it? Mr. Wilkins fumbled for the right words as he brought the conversation back to a delicate subject. "What I mean is, you won't say anything about Lancelot Phineas and all that apple-tree nonsense, will you?"

"No," said Margaret, "provided you agree to be perfectly sweet to them when they come to explain their absence."

"*Perfectly sweet!*" echoed her brother in tones of outraged horror. "I ... I ... Corwumph! ... Perfectly sweet, I ask you!" He sank into a chair, *corwumphing* softly and muttering "Perfectly sweet!" through clenched teeth. He groped feebly for the teapot on the table. He felt he badly needed a cup of strong tea.

It was not long before the patter of feet was heard on the landing and a whispered argument broke out beyond the door. The words were not clear, but the tones had the breathless tension of a debate that has reached a critical stage.

"Wss wss wss I vote wss wss Mr. Wilkins wss wss wss," said the first whisperer.

"Bzz bzz bzz my father says bzz bzz bzz," answered the second.

After that came a shuffling of feet as though a drill squad was falling in and picking up its dressing from the right. Then, the knock at the door and the drill squad marched in—a sad faced column, one abreast and two deep.

"Please, sir, we've come to report to you, sir."

"Ah, yes, of course! Come in, Jennings and Darbishire." Mr. Wilkins greeted them with the heartiness of a man determined to be perfectly sweet even though it killed him. "Well, well! I thought you might drop in to see me. You—er, you've met my sister, I believe."

He smiled and waved a hand in her direction, but neither of the boys felt equal to meeting her eye; so they mumbled polite throat noises and stared down at their shoes.

"I suppose you've called about the—the little informal class I arranged for this afternoon," Mr. Wilkins went on with a sidelong glance to make sure that his sister was paying attention to his charm of manner. He was taking no chances where she was concerned!

Jennings found his voice. "We're most terribly sorry we were absent, sir, and for everything we said, too, sir."

"Ah, well, accidents will happen! Pity you missed it, though. We learned quite a lot."

The two boys couldn't believe their ears. What on earth was the matter with Mr. Wilkins? They had arrived with nerves braced to withstand the shattering thunderbolts of his wrath, and lo and behold! they were being welcomed like film stars at a gathering of their fans! The thing just didn't make sense. Surely, by now, he must have heard a repeat programme of their ill-chosen comments! Why, then, they wondered, was he not towering with rage and tearing off strips left, right and centre?

"I think the best thing will be if you come and see me before you go to bed and we'll work through some of those examples together, shall we?"

"Yes, sir: willingly, sir. Thank you very much, sir." Darbishire wriggled his toes in embarrassed gratitude. And Jennings asked, with wonder in his voice: "But ... is that *all*, sir?"

"Yes, that's all. Unless—oh, yes, have something to eat before you go."

Mr. Wilkins was thorough: if he'd *got* to be perfectly sweet, he'd do the job so well that no criticism could be levelled at his perfect sweetness. He thrust the crumpet plate towards Jennings, who recoiled at the sight of food at such close quarters.

"Oh, no, really—thanks very much all the same, sir."

"Go on, boy—have a crumpet when I tell you to!"

"But, sir, I couldn't, sir I"

"Nonsense!" said Mr. Wilkins heartily. "Boys can always eat crumpets. Why

I remember when I was your age—er, well, never mind—have a crumpet!"

They were saved by Margaret coming to their aid. "I shouldn't press them if I were you, *Mister* Wilkins," she advised. "I think they've had enough for one afternoon."

Mr. Wilkins put the plate back on the table, and then stiffened suddenly as his sister went on: "By the way, Jennings, I was going to give you some suggestions for your magazine, wasn't I?"

"Well, yes, you *were*, Miss Wilkins. But after what I said, I thought—I mean—I didn't think ..." His voice trailed off in guilty silence.

"But I should be only too pleased to help! Now let me see! What can I tell you about my brother that would make interesting reading!"

Mr. Wilkins gripped the tablecloth in alarm. Surely she wasn't going back on her word after he had fulfilled his part of the bargain!

"Now, look here, Margaret, be fair! You distinctly promised ..."

"Don't interrupt, dear, I'm trying to think ... Oh, yes! Some years ago my brother ..."

Pink with indignation, Mr. Wilkins swung round and faced his sister. "Margaret ... I ... I ... Corwumph! I won't have it; I forbid you to ..."

But what was the use of protesting? Nothing short of physical violence could stem the flow of her harmful chatter. He stared at the speaker with unbelieving eyes. That his own sister, of whom he was so fond, should let him down after promising faithfully ... He listened, numb with embarrassment, as she continued.

"Don't be so modest, Mr. Wilkins! I'm sure you wouldn't mind their knowing this; some years ago, Jennings, when my brother was at the University, he rowed in the Cambridge crew that won the Boat Race three years running."

The words acted like magic. Jennings and Darbishire skipped up and down, flapping their fingers with delight.

"Golly, did he really! How supersonic; I say, congratulations, sir!"

"Wacko! What super-cracking, jet-propelled news! May I shake hands with you, sir?"

The magic spell worked more slowly on Mr. Wilkins; but when he had recovered from the shock, he stood pleased and beaming, and uncertain what to say.

"Oh, sir, this is wonderful news, sir. Fancy you being a famous oarsman, sir! Why didn't you ever tell us before, sir?"

"Well—I—er ... Doesn't do to blow your own trumpet," said Mr. Wilkins, and blew his nose instead to cover his embarrassment.

There was no reason, of course, why his distinguished athletic record should not be known, but it was hardly the sort of thing that a modest man could have revealed himself. Now that his sister had done it for him, he glowed with a quiet pride and felt absurdly shy.

"You shouldn't have told them, Margaret," he said, with good-humoured reproof which suggested that he would have been disappointed if she *hadn't*.

"You're not so unfamous as we thought, sir," said Darbishire, his eyes shining triumphantly behind his spectacles. "Why, you'll be the hero of the school when the *Form Three Times* comes out."

"I'm quite sure you don't want to fill up your paper with unimportant things like that," said Mr. Wilkins modestly.

"Oh, but we *do*, sir! It's just the sort of thing we need. We may print it, mayn't we, sir?" Jennings begged. "And I'd like to take a photo of you and put that in. It'd look ever so smashing on the front page: *Mr. L. P. Wilkins, the famous rowing Blue.*" And then, carried away by the excitement of the moment, he asked: "What does *L. P.* stand for, sir? We really ought to put your full name in to round it off nicely, don't you think, sir?"

It was an unfortunate question, and for a second it seemed that the joyful atmosphere might dissolve in a sudden squall of disapproval.

Tactfully, Margaret saved the situation. "In athletic circles, Jennings, my brother was always known by his initials, so it will be quite correct to describe him as L. P. Wilkins, Esq."

Satisfied, the boys took their leave and bounded out through the door in happy contrast to their recent dismal entrance. But a moment later, Jennings was back.

"Please, Miss Wilkins, I quite forgot to tell you about that ten shillings we owe," he said. "Venables won't agree to pay, because he says we went over the limit, but if you wouldn't mind waiting, Darbishire and I could send you sixpence a week for twenty weeks."

"That's all right, Jennings; you can forget about it. In any case, you agreed I was to be a *paying* guest," she said.

"Oh, but really, we couldn't possibly let you ..."

Miss Margaret Wilkins rose from her chair and stood with shoulders squared, the light of battle gleaming in her eye. For the first time, Jennings noticed a faint family resemblance to her brother, which became more marked as she announced in firm tones:

"You may or may not know, Jennings, that the Wilkins family can be very severe when they like. If you argue with them they become fire-breathing dragons of the most frantic type. So if you don't stop talking nonsense about that ten shillings, I shall—" She sought in her mind for the right expression— "I shall get in a supersonic bate and explode!"

"Yes, Miss Wilkins ... Thank you, Miss Wilkins," said Jennings meekly, and tiptoed out and closed the door.

CHAPTER 17

HERE IS THE NEWS!

AT a table in a corner of the hobbies' room sat the editors of the *Form Three Times.* Their brows were furrowed in thought and their teeth bit deeply into the pencils rooted between their jaws; for it was Monday evening and zero hour was almost upon them, when Mr. Carter would be ready to tap their pencilled paragraphs into neat typescript.

They had been careful to allow no leakage of the news about Mr. Wilkins' fame as an oarsman, which they were planning to spring upon their readers as a sensational surprise. It had not been easy to keep the topic to themselves, when all over the weekend they had been bursting to tell every one they met. But they had kept their secret even in the face of direct questions.

"What happened when you reported to Old Wilkie?" Venables had asked at breakfast on Sunday morning.

"Nothing much. He went through the sums with us before the dorm. bell last night," Jennings had answered.

"Yes, but before that—what sort of punishment did he dole out?"

"Well, he *was* going to make us eat a crumpet, but he let us off." It was a mystifying reply, but Jennings refused to enlarge upon it.

Now, however, the time had come to put the finishing touches to their exclusive story and the editors were determined to make a success of it.

"We ought to do a big mauve headline on the printing outfit," said Jennings. "*L. P. Wilkins, Esq., is an old ...*"

"Gosh, be careful, Jen! We called him enough names to be going on with on Saturday afternoon," Darbishire cautioned.

"No, I was going to say *L. P. Wilkins, Esq., is an old Cambridge Blue.* That's quite a decent thing to say about any one. In fact I'd never have said all those others if I'd known before. It sort of puts a chap in a different light if you know he's rowed in the Boat Race, doesn't it!"

Darbishire nodded his agreement. "He was quite human when I had a chat with him about it after chapel yesterday. He says you have to be as keen as a beaver if you want to get picked for the crew. He and another chap used to get up early and practise every morning."

"Perhaps that'd be a good way to start off our chatty paragraph, then. Something like: *When Mr. Wilkins was young he always used to have a row with someone before breakfast.*"

Jennings wrote it down, and then grinned as the double meaning dawned on him. "Goodness, we can't say *that*, Darbi! There's two ways of pronouncing *r-o-w* and it sounds as though he was always kicking up a hoo-hah."

"That wouldn't surprise me, either—knowing Old Wilkie," said Darbishire. "Still, it might be better to say that when he went *rowing* he always used a boat, so chaps won't jump to the wrong conclusion."

"But that's stark, raving crackers! Of *course* you'd go rowing in a boat— where else?"

It was these stumbling blocks in the path of English composition which delayed their work and accounted for the furrows on their foreheads. They tried many ways of making their meaning clear: they put Mr. Wilkins in a boat, in brackets; they added a footnote that the words *row, rowing, rowed*, must be rhymed with *flow, flowing, flowed*, and not with *vow, vowing, vowed*. They even tried to avoid using the word altogether and wrote that L. P. Wilkins, Esq., was famed for his Oxford and Cambridge boat-racemanship.

And finally, they crossed most of it out and took their notebook to Mr. Carter, whose brow also became furrowed as he struggled to read the manuscript. But after careful revision he was able to tap the paragraphs into some semblance of order on his typewriter.

Jennings and Darbishire went upstairs to bed in a state of pent-up excitement. Soon their closely-guarded secret would be common property; Mr. Wilkins would be acclaimed a hero and the editors of the *Form Three Times* could bask in the reflected glory of the light which he had hidden for so long under a bushel.

"I can't get over Old Wilkie being a famous sportsman," mused Darbishire, absently stretching his garter on to his head like a tight-fitting halo. "It's a good job we found out, because his life story needed livening up a bit. We're like these old historian geezers discovering new facts about the life of Oliver Cromwell."

"Except that it didn't happen as long ago as all that," Jennings reminded him. "It's Mr. Carter who's so old you have to work it out by algebra. I got him to tell me that sum again, but I couldn't work it out with x's and y's so I used a's and b's instead."

"And what's the answer?"

"Well, it's just possible I made a bish somewhere, because according to my figures he must have been a hundred-and-six last birthday. It just shows you can't believe everything grown-ups say."

"It's the way their minds work when they get old," Darbishire assured him. "You just can't tell what they're going to do next. Look at Old Wilkie last Saturday: there we were quaking and shivering with nerves at the thought of him going off like a depth-charge, and ten seconds later our nerves were shaking and quivering with surprise because he never exploded at all!"

"Never mind; there'll be an explosion all right, tomorrow, when the chaps find out that our jet-propelled fire-breathing dragon is really a famous sporting character in disguise. Just as well we can prove it, because no one would ever think he was a sheep in wolf's clothing, to look at him—would they!"

Jennings prophecy proved correct. The *Form Three Times* appeared on the common room notice board at break the next morning, and everybody was so busy discussing the sensational news on page one, that they had no time to spare for reading the rest of the paper.

This was a pity, for there were some interesting items for the student of current affairs: page two offered an account of the 2nd XI match against Bracebridge and a thrilling story of how two members of the visiting party had stumbled upon the remainder, whom they found benighted on the treacherous grassy slopes of Pottlewhistle. On page three were Gardening Notes by *Our Horticultural Correspondent* and some hints on *How to Play Football*, written— but wisely not signed—by C. E. J. Darbishire.

The winner of the handwriting competition could have seen his name in block capitals on page four; and here, also, the unsuccessful poets were highly commended in smaller type. A new *Life of O. Cromwell* on page five might have proved useful to any serious student of history; and those who favoured hobbies of a practical sort could have enjoyed an article on *Cooking and Photography*, by J. C. T. Jennings, in which the author stressed the importance of doing only one of these things at a time.

But in spite of this rich offering, the eyes of the readers remained fixed on page one, where their minds were stirred by the story of three historic Boat

Races in which L. P. Wilkins, Esq., had been a prominent member of the Cambridge crew.

And after they had read it, a change of heart came upon them and they went about telling every one they met what a decent chap Old Wilkie was, and how they had always liked him really, only they'd never thought of saying so before.

Mr. Wilkins signed two dozen autograph books that morning, and then shut himself in his room and refused to answer the door. He avoided looking at the notice board for three days, but on the evening of the fourth, after the boys were safely in bed, Mr. Carter met him tiptoeing furtively away from the common room door.

Casually he inquired: "Well, Wilkins, what do you think of your biography?"

"Silly little boys!" replied Mr. Wilkins. "If only they'd show as much interest in their algebra as they do in the Boat Race we might be getting somewhere. *Silly* little boys!"

But it was clear from his tone that he was really rather pleased.

Next day, the Headmaster honoured the common room with one of his rare visits. The editors were there and watched from a polite distance as he stood and read the magazine from end to end.

"I wonder what he thinks of it!" whispered Darbishire.

"You can never tell with the Archbeako," Jennings whispered back. "He's got one of those faces that don't light up very much."

Something, however, must have registered, because Mr. Pemberton-Oakes strolled over and had a word with Mr. Carter, who was supervising the common room's activities; and from their glances at the notice board it was obvious what the two men were talking about. As soon as the Head had gone, Jennings and Darbishire made a bee-line for the duty master.

"Sir, please sir, what did he say, sir?"

"Yes, sir; did he like it, sir?"

"I think so," Mr. Carter replied. "He told me he approves of creative hobbies of this kind, because as well as being valuable in themselves, they keep you out of mischief."

"Oh, wacko! That's jolly high praise, isn't it, sir! We thought he'd be pleased with all the culture and stuff, because Darbishire says that his father says ..."

Jennings stopped, puzzled by the quiet smile which had appeared at the corners of Mr. Carter's mouth, as though he was deep in the enjoyment of some private joke.

"What's the matter, sir? Have I said something funny?"

"No, no," said Mr. Carter hastily. "I was just smiling at the idea of the *Form Three Times* keeping you out of mischief."

"Why, what do you mean, sir?" asked Darbishire.

Mr. Carter thought for a moment; then he said: "Well, during the last few weeks, some odd things have come to my notice. I remember hearing of queer developments in the darkroom and an unexpected obstruction in a chimney, which occurred after you had returned from a journalistic expedition bearing a parcel of fish. I put two and two together—and decided not to inquire into the matter too deeply!"

The faces of his audience showed that they agreed with the wisdom of this decision.

"I remember, also, a sudden interest in Latin books that the Headmaster happened to mention," Mr. Carter went on. "I'm not quite sure what was behind it all, but I *do* know that when we arranged to hold a textbook inspection at short notice it caused quite a stir throughout Form Three."

"Yes, sir … Sorry, sir. I didn't know you knew all that, sir," Jennings mumbled. The conversation was taking an awkward turn; was Mr. Carter preparing for action?

Jennings needn't have worried. Mr. Carter's private detective service was efficient, but he seldom interfered unless matters threatened to get out of hand. The master was still wearing his quiet smile as he turned to leave the room: at the door he paused.

"Don't look so baffled, Jennings," he said. "I think the *Form Three Times* is an excellent paper and well worth doing. And, what's more, I've every reason to be grateful to this—er, creative hobby of yours for keeping you out of even *worse* mischief!"

The editors exchanged glances as the door closed, and Darbishire heaved a sigh of relief.

"Well, fossilised fish-hooks! Fancy him guessing all that!" he murmured. "I've always said that's the one snag about Mr. Carter—he finds out simply *everything*."

"You don't have to tell *me* that," the chief editor answered. "But he's pretty decent the way he never gets in a bate about it and kicks up hoo-hahs: not like *some* people I could mention, even if they *did* row in the Boat Race!"

Jennings grinned as his mind travelled back over the misfortunes of the past few weeks. He looked up and saw that Darbishire was grinning too, and a moment later both grins broke into peals of laughter.

They felt pleased and proud and light-hearted; the *Form Three Times* had been well worth every bit of their trouble. Admittedly, it had given them some anxious moments, but now that these were safely behind them, they could see the funny side of things. And, after all, what more could any one want than that!